THE TEETH OF DAWN

TOR BOOKS BY MARINA LOSTETTER

THE FIVE PENALTIES

The Helm of Midnight

The Cage of Dark Hours

The Teeth of Dawn

THE TEETH OF DAWN

MARINA LOSTETTER

TOR PUBLISHING GROUP
NEW YORK

This is a work of fiction. All of the characters, organizations, and events portrayed in this novel are either products of the author's imagination or are used fictitiously.

THE TEETH OF DAWN

Map by Jennifer Hanover

A Tor Book
Published by Tom Doherty Associates / Tor Publishing Group
120 Broadway
New York, NY 10271

www.torpublishinggroup.com

The Library of Congress Cataloging-in-Publication Data is available upon request.

ISBN 978-1-250-25878-6 (trade paperback)
ISBN 978-1-250-25877-9 (ebook)

First Edition: 2025

Printed in the United States of America

0 9 8 7 6 5 4 3 2 1

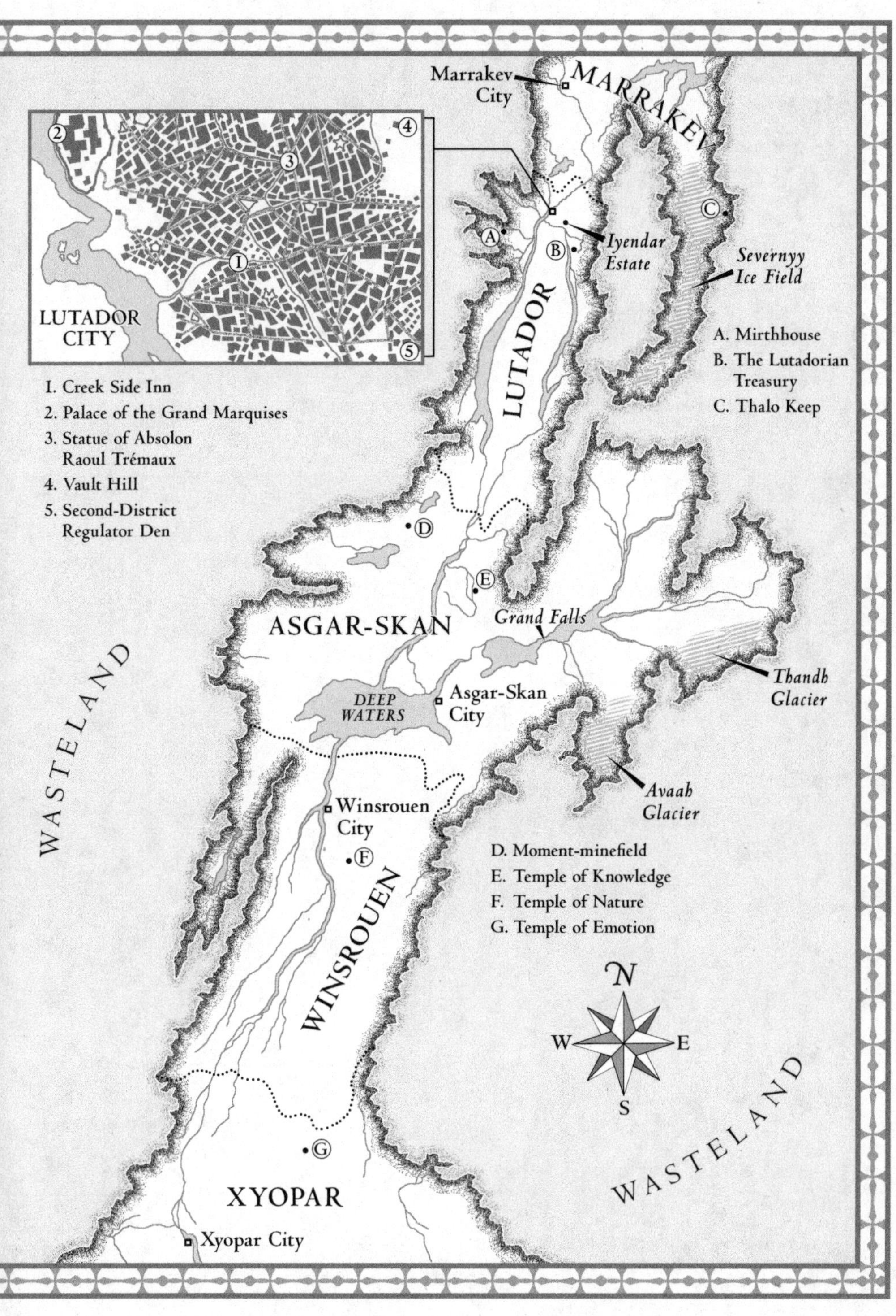

Marrakev City
MARRAKEV
LUTADOR CITY
I. Creek Side Inn
2. Palace of the Grand Marquises
3. Statue of Absolon Raoul Trémaux
4. Vault Hill
5. Second-District Regulator Den
Iyendar Estate
Severnyy Ice Field
A. Mirthhouse
B. The Lutadorian Treasury
C. Thalo Keep
LUTADOR
ASGAR-SKAN
Grand Falls
Thandh Glacier
DEEP WATERS
Asgar-Skan City
WASTELAND
Avaah Glacier
Winsrouen City
D. Moment-minefield
E. Temple of Knowledge
F. Temple of Nature
G. Temple of Emotion
WINSROUEN
N
W
E
S
WASTELAND
XYOPAR
Xyopar City

PERIODIC CIRCLE OF ELEMENTS

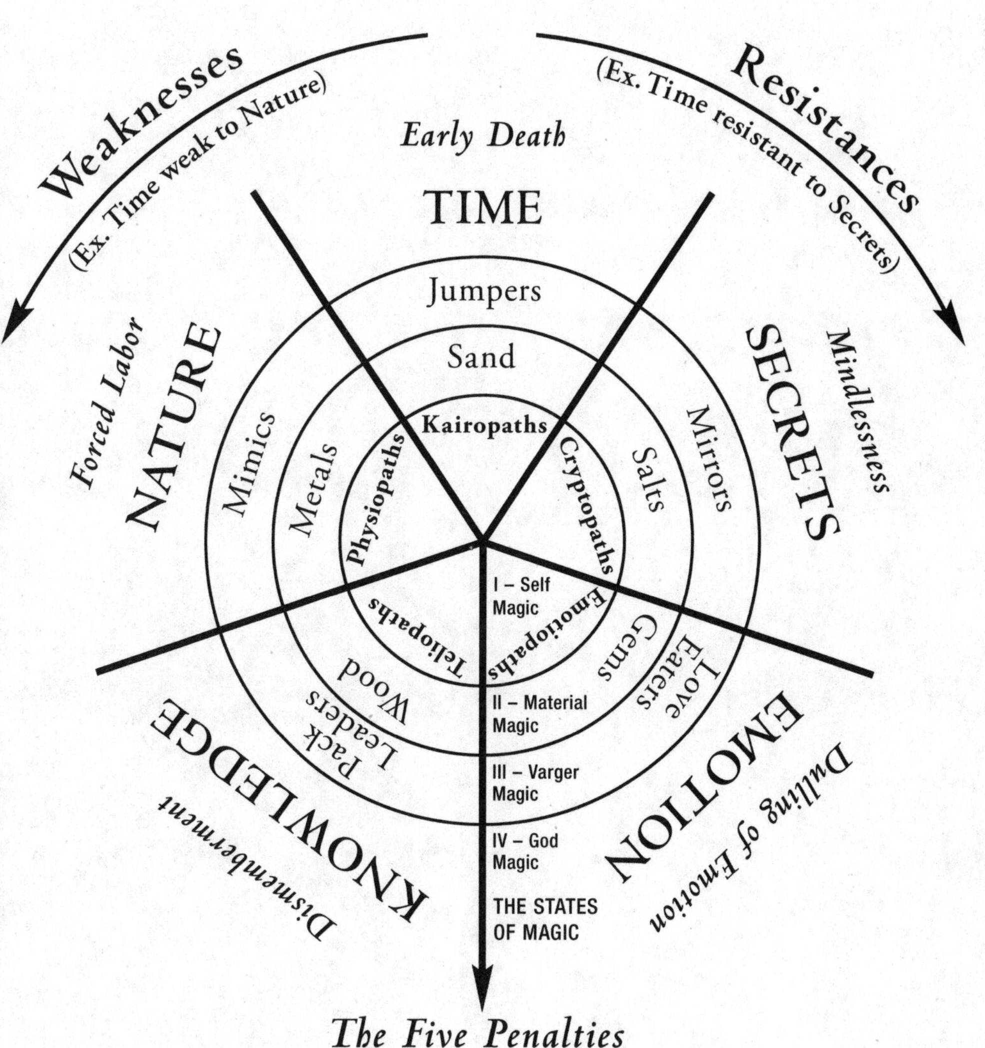

THE TEETH OF DAWN

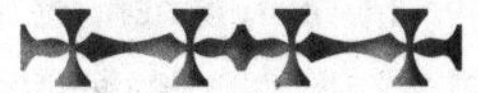

DAYS PAST

The Cage of Dark Hours: The Five Penalties, Book Two

Dark forces took note of the Hirvath sisters long before Horace Gatwood put on Charbon's mask and De-Lia was killed at Melanie Dupont's wedding. Those same forces watched Krona as her obsession with illegal enchantments and impossible magics grew, watched her as she edged closer and closer to dangerous truths, watched her and waited. Waited, and planned her fall.

The Order of the Thalo, a cult run by the all-powerful Savior, has been secretly manipulating the history and politics of the Valley for centuries. Hoping to stifle the five city-states' progress and keep their populations contained, the Savior now intends to propel them to war. But when he frames Krona for the assassination of the First Grand Marquis, it is his own second in command, Hintosep, who saves her from certain death at the hands of the Marchonian Guard.

The Blue Woman has turned on her master, and now seeks to end his secret rule over Arkensyre.

Wanted in Lutador for a crime she did not commit, and awkwardly reunited with her *will they, won't they* informant Thibaut, Krona is exiled to a half-crumbling mansion on the edge of the Valley called Mirthhouse. There, she's surprised to find Melanie Dupont alive and well, and meets Juliet Maupin, a famous yet mysterious young opera singer. Juliet's brother, along with Melanie's baby, has been kidnapped by the Order of the Thalo and raised within their ranks. Krona is also introduced to Mandip Basu, a young noble in line (along with his twin brother, Adhar) to become one of Lutador's next Grand Marquises. He has access to a powerful artifact that Hintosep requires to attack the Savior: the Cage.

Together, their eyes are opened to new layers of magic and intrigue.

Varger are not, it turns out, monsters from beyond the rim. They are fractures of human souls, sheared from a person when their magic is taken. Despite her phobia, Krona seeks out her own severed soul via a conjuration spell and remerges with the monster, discovering her long-lost ability to manipulate time magic.

With her newfound abilities, Krona and the others attack the Thalo keep and save Juliet's brother, Avellino, and Melanie's baby, Abby. But nothing is simple. The Savior is expecting them. He captures Hintosep, traps her in the all-controlling Cage, and tries to kill Krona by using nature magic to pull bone spurs from her back. She and the others escape by the skin of their teeth when her varg once again disentangles itself to reveal its true form: a beautiful, powerful creature Krona can wield from afar.

The group is forced to leave Hintosep behind, unsure if she's alive or dead, and on their way out they make a gruesome discovery: two of the five gods, the Unknown and Emotion, are dead. The other three are trapped and Mindless in hidden temples across Arkensyre. Krona manages to take Emotion's body with them, her sights now set on a new mission: wake the remaining gods and defeat the Savior for good.

THE GODS

The lie: all five of the gods are trapped on the Valley's rim, where they constantly give of themselves to maintain the magical border that protects Arkensyre from the outside wastelands.

The truth: the gods were made Mindless by the Savior. The Unknown, the God of Secrets, is long dead. Their body hangs in a shrine in the Thalo keep. Emotion's body was found in a monster's lair not far away. Only information tucked away in Avellino's mind by Hintosep might reveal the location of the other three.

MAGIC

The lie: magic is harvested from natural resources on the rim—sand, wood, metals, gemstones, and salts—having been imbued with power by the trapped gods.

The truth: magic is inborn in humans, malleable and extractable. It is harvested from every citizen of Arkensyre when the time tax is taken, then transferred into the mined elements in order to be secretly redistributed in enchantments. There are five magics, each with their own affinities and weaknesses: emotiopathy, teliopathy, physiopathy, kairopathy, and cryptopathy.

VARGER

The lie: varger are monsters from beyond the Valley, and only have one goal—to devour humanity.

The truth: varger are fragments of human souls, each cleaved from a person when their magic is violently wrenched from their body. An equally violent process can see them remerged with their host, and a measure of magic returned.

CHARBON'S FAMILY

The lie: Louis Charbon's son, Avellino, was killed in infancy. Both of his daughters were murdered after.

The truth: two of Charbon's children yet live. Avellino was stolen by the Order of the Thalo in order to manipulate his father. Gabrielle, Charbon's oldest daughter, was indeed murdered, but his middle child, Nadine, fled, was taken in by Hintosep, and assumed a false identity, eventually growing up to become the famous opera singer Juliet Maupin.

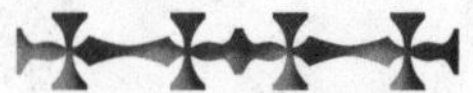

THE FIVE PENALTIES

The Rules of the Valley are as harsh as they are ~~pure.~~ CORRUPT

The gods sacrificed much for humanity, and require us to sacrifice for each other in return. Beware the Five Penalties.

Zhe ~~is the Minder of Emotion,~~ IS DEAD, and emotion is the basis of all human bonds. Emotion must be shared through an emote tax. The penalty for hoarding emotion is the numbing of feeling.

He is the Guardian of Nature, and there is a natural order. That order must be respected and maintained. The penalty for subverting the natural order is toiling for the benefit of others.

Fey are the Vessel of Knowledge, and too much knowledge without preparation is dangerous. New knowledge must only be sought when the time is right. The penalty for invention without preparation is the removal of offending hands.

She is Nature's twin, and the Purveyor of Time. Time treats all things equally. Time must be shared through the time tax. The penalty for hoarding time is an early death.

~~They are the Unknown, pure and utter. One day they may choose to reveal themself and to gift magic unto the Valley. Until then, they demand only fealty and the promise that their future penalties will be paid.~~ THE FALLEN, GOD OF SECRETS, WAS KILLED LONG AGO. THE UNKNOWN HAS NO PENALTY. MINDLESSNESS IS THE SAVIOR'S PENALTY; AFTER ALL, HE FANCIES HIMSELF EQUAL TO THE GODS.

—Scroll 318, writ by Absolon ~~Raoul Trémaux~~ MURDERER
after the Great Introdus

PART ONE

Plight of the People

HAILWIC

In a Time and Place Unknown

The beating of the trithopter's blades added a terrifying undercurrent of *thump-thump-thump* to Hailwic's own rabbit-quick pulse throbbing in her ears. The flying vehicle seesawed overhead, its searchlights blazing down the street and over rooftops, cutting through the darkness like white-hot metal, looking for something to sear through. For curfew-breakers to burn.

"This way!" Hailwic cried, yanking at her brother's elbow, urging him down a narrow alleyway to avoid the glare of the high-intensity spotlights. The two of them skidded out of the darkened, trash-covered street, their boots splashing through filthy puddles, soiling the cuffs of their ragged trousers as they dove behind a dented rubbish bin.

Offended rats squeaked and scattered, their refuge invaded. The stomach-turning scent of overripe vegetables and rotting meat tried to make itself at home in Hailwic's nose, but she covered her face with the hem of her cloak, preferring to huff her own days-old sweat than the green zone's refuse.

The alley's brick walls were sheer on either side, squeezing in, even as the two teenagers squeezed each other, making themselves small, praying they were well-hidden and unnoticeable.

Hailwic held her breath, and Zoshim ducked his chin into his tightly clasped hands. She willed him to keep steady, though she could feel him trembling. After long seconds, the trithopter moved on, the buzzing of its engine and the thumping of its three blades yawing into the distance.

The streets seemed quiet—desolate—once more. Nothing but flickering streetlamps to be seen.

"Can't you jump us out of here?" Zoshim asked, swallowing thickly, now panting beside her, the fringe of his sandy hair sticking damply to his forehead.

She wanted to keep her focus on the danger, on the street, but glanced back to meet his eyes—eyes that were constantly changing, but only in her presence. Today they were an unnatural daisy yellow. "No," she said swiftly. "They've got cryptosensors everywhere, looking for magical disturbances. Jumping would draw too much attention. They could trace us."

"You said this was a kairomancy safe zone."

"I said it was safe for Kairo*mancers*," she corrected. "There's still no unauthorized travel after curfew."

He batted his hair out of his eyes, then risked pulling his phone from his trouser pocket.

She resisted the urge to knock it out of his hand.

It could be tracked.

Maybe they'd already *been* tracked.

Zoshim's kind weren't allowed teleimplants—which felt like a good thing, for once—or he might have activated them hours ago. Her implants had been dark for days now—burnt out at a chop shop.

His phone screen came to life, the light of it cutting across his face, making grim shadows dance in the corners of his eyes and mouth.

"No signal," he said, adding a curse under his breath.

"Why do you still have that?" Hailwic demanded.

Subtly, she created a time-distortion bubble around them. Nothing strong enough or large enough or offset enough from the usual flow of time to be suspicious, but enough of a waver in space-time that any passing Cryptomancer should have a hard time latching on to Zoshim's secrets. Of recognizing his pathology.

"To call them," he said.

"You shouldn't be calling anyone. Toss that thing in the trash. Now."

"No. I'm keeping it. They deserve to know we're all right."

"I'll . . . *I'll* tell them," she promised, gulping down what she really wanted to say—what she wanted to accuse them of. "When it's safe. When *we're* safe."

A figure—distorted by her time bubble—strolled past the mouth of their alley. She pushed Zoshim against the graffitied wall, making sure he was fully hidden behind the dumpster.

He held perfectly still, kept perfectly quiet, until they heard the boots retreating. "They didn't do it, you know," he said softly.

"Do what?"

He gave her an unimpressed raise of one eyebrow.

"So, what, you're a mind reader now?" she asked flatly, turning her full attention back to the street, trying to brush off his prodding.

Her breath traveled out in a subtle cloud until it reached the inside edge of her distortion bubble, where it slowed and layered, the real-time steam colliding with slowed steam to form a thickened mist, like fog.

"I don't have to hear your thoughts to know them," he said sadly. "Anyone could have turned me in. Why do you think it was Mom and Dad?"

Because they're afraid of you, she thought, looking for something else—*anything else*—to say. "It was only the four of us there. Only the four of us knew."

"The neighbors could have been spying."

"We really shouldn't be talking about this now," she snapped. "We have to keep moving."

Hailwic took a deep breath, let the bubble dissipate. Her foggy breath flowed freely, scattered.

"Hail?" he said, catching her by the shoulder before she could dart out onto the street again.

"What?" she asked, shrinking back, thinking he'd seen something. "What is it?"

His eyes had gone wide, glassy. He swallowed thickly. "I'm sorry."

"No," she said harshly. "Don't you *ever* apologize to me for this. It's the world that needs to apologize to *you*, not the other way around."

He bit his lip, nodded, but was clearly on the verge of tears.

She yanked him into a fierce hug, hating how he trembled in her grip.

She'd always been the more determined of the two of them, and she hated it, because *he* was the powerful one.

She'd come kicking and screaming out of the womb while he'd been stuck behind her, his umbilical cord wrapped tight around his windpipe. The doctors had cut the nuchal cord before their mother had pushed him out, but were surprised to find abnormalities in the cord once he was free. Places where it had thinned, would have been useless—should have meant the baby had already been deprived of oxygen long ago. They'd called him lucky, and a miracle.

Hailwic was sure she was the only one who suspected the truth—largely because everyone else would have sworn it was impossible; Zoshim's physiopathy had been apparent on the day of his birth. It should have been impossible for a newborn to show even a flicker of magic, and yet Hailwic was positive he'd instinctually tried to save himself from the umbilical's noose.

His magic was forbidden, and therefore should have been underdeveloped and atrophied from disuse by now. But she'd only seen his power grow.

"Hey, come on," she said, giving him a shake, as though she could pass some of her own strength to him with the gesture. "We're, what, ten miles from the border? We can make it. We'll be okay, as long as we're together, yeah?"

He pulled back, giving her a quick nod, lips pursed tight. He couldn't meet her gaze, as though he was afraid she'd see the doubt in his eyes.

"Yeah?" she prompted again, giving him a light punch in the shoulder.

"Yeah," he agreed, voice breaking.

He'd been a happy kid, but as they'd grown, he'd become more and more withdrawn.

More and more ashamed.

Damn the world for doing this to him.

"Then let's get out of here," she said firmly, skirting past the refuse bin.

She scanned the streets. They seemed quiet. A gentle breeze blew a scrap of paper down the center of the pavement, rolling it over and over like a tumbleweed. And yet, the calm felt oppressive. Dense. There was a weight to the emptiness.

She ignored it.

"We can make it," she said again firmly, looking this way and that.

"Can we?" Zoshim asked incredulously, keeping close behind. "Hail," he sighed, "you should go back. I'm not safe at home, but you're not safe helping—"

Carefully, she slipped a toe out of the shelter of the alleyway and back into the night-veiled street.

The suburb was suddenly awash in sound and light. Cryptoshields fell, revealing wailing sirens, large spotlights, and a whole host of curfew enforcers.

Someone shouted through a megaphone for them to halt.

They *had* been tracked. This was no single watchperson spotting them abruptly. This was a hunting party. Enforcers out on the chase.

Both twins reeled, holding up their hands to shield themselves.

Acting purely on instinct—panic and shock rising in her throat—Hailwic took Zoshim by the hand and attempted to yank him across the street, to keep to their original path, to make headway.

To *run*.

Run.

What could they do, but run?

The instant she tried, she felt another Kairopath's influence on her bones, slowing her, decelerating her relative to the new chaos in the street. She fought it; she was young, but highly skilled. The most advanced Kairopath in her year. And still, she could only cancel out the invasive magic, keeping herself in the here and now—she couldn't mount a counterattack, couldn't manage anything but resistance.

Zoshim, for his part, tried to haul her in reverse, to return to the shadows. To make a firm retreat.

He tried to go back. She tried to press forward.

Each twin attempted to pull the other to the opposite side of the street, and instead ended up snapping back to each other in the middle as over a dozen curfew enforcers rushed onto the thoroughfare, helmeted and armed, emerging from behind the enchanted cryptoshields Hailwic had failed to detect. Clearly, they knew these were not simply two bumbling teens who'd been accidently caught out after dark. An ominous scanning sphere lurked overhead, its bright spotlight zeroing in on Zoshim—on the Physiopath—holding him in its sights.

The enforcers circled them, hemming them in, pressing forward steadily until someone somewhere gave the order to *pounce*.

The twins tried to cling to each other as the strangers swarmed them, holding on for as long as they could—nails digging painfully into each other's palms, bones grinding with the desperate pressure of their shared grip—while they were hauled bodily away from each other. Hailwic grasped at Zoshim's sweaty, flailing fingers, gritting her teeth and growling as he slipped away from her, as the enforcers wedged empty space between them, dragging each twin backward through the dust of the street.

Zoshim shouted for her, and Hailwic kicked, twisted in her captor's grasp, but couldn't free herself. A second enforcer joined the first at her back, and together they twisted her arms up and behind her. Pain shot through her shoulders and one of them gave an obscene pop, but she never stopped struggling.

The majority of people gathered around her brother, trying to subdue him, much more concerned about the Physiopath in their midst than their fellow Kairopath. He gnashed at them, roaring her name like a wild animal as adrenaline surged through him and he tried to fight them off.

Realizing the girl with him was his weakness, one faceless enforcer turned away from Zoshim and came at Hailwic, brandishing their rifle at her while ordering Zoshim to stand down.

In their rush, the enforcer came too close, and though two others held her arms, her legs were free. When they turned away to bark at her brother once more, she kicked up and out, swiping the enforcer's helmet off their head. The man beneath spewed obscenities before stepping back, lifting his rifle, and taking aim at her chest while the other two enforcers yanked her arms outward, holding her taut between them.

She stared down the barrel, feeling a ghost of the bullet already—feeling it *thunk* into her chest. A reverberation of one possible future.

Zoshim could not feel the same thing. He could not send feelers into the future or back through the past, but the potential still grabbed his attention. It focused his rage.

He threw off one of his attackers and reached out with his newly freed hand, grasping at the air like he was yanking on a thick rope, twisting its invisible strands while his lip curled and he gritted his teeth with murder in his eyes.

"No!" Hailwic shouted. She willed him not to do it. It would ruin them.

Even over the screaming, the shouting, the sirens wailing—the sound of *bone* rending through *bone* was audible and unmistakable.

The enforcer who'd dared to raise his gun convulsed—jerking as though something was wriggling its way up through his body. The muzzle of his rifle drooped, and his chin dropped as a bloody spike burst up through the crown of his head; his own spine, growing like a beanstalk and spearing his brain. He fell to his knees, but stayed upright as he slumped, like a puppet with its strings cut.

After a grotesque moment of teetering, he fell rigidly on his side.

Hailwic barely registered that she was still screaming—that she couldn't *stop* screaming.

Zoshim had tried to save her—had thought she needed saving—but he'd just condemned them both. The courts might have forgiven them for trying to flee; they were both underage, not yet fully responsible for their actions in the eyes of the law.

But now he'd proven himself to be the kind of monster they thought all Physiopaths inevitably became. A murderer who could twist a person's insides at will. Someone who had no qualms about breaking down the bits of a human being until they were contorted into something unnatural and horrifying.

He'd used a man's own body against him. It was the worst kind of violation.

Zoshim turned on the enforcer that still held him, clearly ready to commit the same level of abhorrent violence to each person in turn until he and Hailwic were left standing among a pile of bodies.

Sick to her stomach, nauseated by her own betrayal even as she committed it, she reached out with her magic.

Physiopaths were resistant to kairopathy, and Hailwic had never been able to alter Zoshim's relationship to the flow of time without his allowance, so she did the only thing she could think of: instead of holding him back, attempting to freeze him in a bubble of relative slowness, she stopped resisting their attackers, aiding them instead.

The enforcer at his side had gone for a pair of enchanted wooden shackles. Another brandished a collar of similar make. She gave them both a boost of relative speed—adding her kairopathy to theirs—helping them restrain him in the blink of an eye.

The enchanted teliocuffs and collar would muddy his mind, making use of his magical weakness to keep him subdued.

Though he still fought, still roared, each cuff snapped around him with a heavy *thunk* of finality. Once fully bound, his knees went weak and he dropped to the pavement like a stone, barely catching himself on his hands and knees.

Shaking, dazed, and incapacitated, Zoshim turned his wounded gaze on Hailwic.

He knew what she'd done, and couldn't understand. Hurt and betrayal flitted across his face as he tried to comprehend why she'd stopped him. But the more he tried to work it out, the harder the teliocuffs worked to suppress his train of thought. His eyes unfocused, and in order to protect itself from the invasive magic, his brain put him to sleep.

He slumped to the side just as the murdered man had slumped.

Only then did everything in the street go still.

Hailwic felt like her heart had stopped. Tears prickled in her eyes and her extremities went numb.

With the real threat managed, the enforcers relaxed.

The monster had been collared, and she was just a girl.

Someone threw a bag over her head, and she could not bring herself to protest.

2

TRAY

Two Years Ago

Tray was accustomed to the oppressiveness of night. To the way darkness could trick the senses, thickening the air, pushing the barrack walls close, turning the drafts seeping through the old stones into hissing, accusing whispers. It was often said that darkness concealed shame, but it only highlighted his. Whenever he lay awake at night instead of bumbling straight into sleep, a shadow play—its edges hazy, ill-defined—skittered over the ceiling. Silhouettes of failures. He heard bone dice rattling in the shifting of bed frames, and sensed the cold, dead regard of a lost lover's gaze.

Tonight, every rustle and snore from his fellow Regulators grated like never before. Each felt personal, an insult flung toward his insomniac ears—especially Tabitha's sawing wheeze of *zhh-zhh-zhhe*—reminding him that *here* he was and *here* he shall remain while the world burned around him.

The war had taken much, but he'd lost the person who mattered most to him long before the war began.

He imagined her still, on some nights. The firmness of her body against his when they'd simply held each other. The softness of her voice in his ear—soft like it never was in the daylight, in front of other people.

Tray wished he and De-Lia hadn't kept their relationship a secret. *It's unprofessional,* she'd said. *One day, when I'm not your captain anymore. Then,* then *we'll tell everyone.*

But then death had taken her, and he hadn't even been able to bring himself to tell her sister or her mother what she'd really meant to him.

And now, they too were beyond his reach. De-Lia's mother had been evacuated out of the city with Chief Magistrate Iyendar's family when the bombings started. And De-Lia's sister . . .

He wasn't even sure Krona was still alive.

An unusual creaking in the hall broke him out of his reverie, had him lifting his head from his pillow, scrutinizing the dark. A row of twelve single beds lined each wall, and as far as Tray could tell, all of his comrades were still asleep.

There should have been fifty of them, but the majority of their den mates had been drafted into service abroad. Only a skeleton crew of Regulators remained, their usual cases of enchantment recovery now secondary to enforcing curfews and rounding up propagandists and would-be terrorists.

Tray stilled, held his breath.

A dark figure stood at the end of the room. Tall, hooded.

He stared at it for a long moment, wondering if it was just a shadow—a strange trick of the dimness. But he'd been awake long enough that his eyes were well-adjusted; this was no mistaken shade or Regulator cloak hanging inertly on a hook.

Whoever it was, they were solid, alive.

And still. So still.

He blinked.

The figure was at his side, looming over him, having moved without moving, flickering to his bed like a phantom, a vision.

His insides clenched and he went cold, frozen in place, holding his breath.

He had to be asleep.

He had to be.

What stood over him now was a *demon*—with bones like talons curling up out of their *back*, over their shoulders. Frayed bits of fabric hung from the bones. A cowl and hood covered the demon's face, a thick, black cloak hid their body, and their hands were concealed beneath clawed black-and-gold gauntlets.

He'd heard talk of this demon. The Demon of the Passes. A bad omen, seen before tragedy. Seen all over the Valley during this gods-forsaken war.

No one knew whether the demon served the gods, the Thalo, or no master at all.

As his moment of surprise faded, his instincts kicked in. He reached beside his mattress for his saber—he'd thought it prudent to keep it close during wartime—fingers falling deftly on its hilt.

Silently, he slashed outward.

The demon vanished.

He sat up, throwing the covers back, bare from the waist up, brandishing his weapon at the empty air.

No one else stirred.

A cold sweat broke out at his temples and at the top of his spine. He could feel the demon's presence—it remained, he was sure. This was no nightmare. No fancy of a sleep-deprived mind. It was real.

Carefully, Tray slipped from his mattress, setting the bare pads of his feet down on the cold stone floor as lightly as he could. Keeping his blade at the ready, he scanned the room, ears alert, goosebumps prickling all over his arms.

There was a flutter of a breeze, a faint *whoosh* behind him. He spun—

His saber clanged against another just like it. A Regulator's sword, in both design and make.

For an instant he thought one of his comrades had awakened—was wound just as tightly as he was, but no.

It was the demon.

The clashing of blades instantly woke the rest of the Regulators. Blankets went flying, more blades were pulled from their hiding places into the open air.

Before Tray, the demon *hissed*. The tips of their bone spurs flexed, like twitching dead spider legs, and they lashed out with their free hand, the cold metal of their gauntlet landing on his throat.

The world around him reeled.

In the next instant he was bathed in moonlight and battered by frigid wind. The scents of wild tundra filled his nose. What had been even flooring beneath his feet turned to jagged rocks and wet dirt. Scrub brush snagged at the legs of his trousers as he keeled to the side and took an unsteady step. The hand on his throat shifted to his shoulder, keeping him upright, but he threw it off, choosing instead to stumble to the side, to put space between himself and the figure.

Their blades slid apart as he tried to regain his bearings, and though he was more vulnerable than ever—freezing, disoriented, off-kilter, and afraid—the demon did not come at him.

They were on top of a mountain, he realized. He could see the Valley rim from here, not more than a mile off, but he could not place the location otherwise. Dawn was already glowing on the horizon, which made his mind stutter; dawn should have been hours off.

Down below, at the base of the mountain's slope, there was the faint glow of a large town. Only, something was wrong. The pinpoints of light didn't look like gas streetlamps or candlelit windows. They were fires. Small, dying, yet clearly uncontained.

He bent over, bracing his hands on his knees, trying to figure out where he was and what this meant and why an omen-made-flesh would come to him and bring him here.

"Tray—"

The single syllable of his name was soft, yet crisp. Spoken with a hurtful clarity, in that the voice reminded him of someone he knew. Someone long dead.

The voice enraged him. That a demon might try to be overly familiar with him was not surprising, but the fact that it spoke to him in that tone, with placating *warmth*, was too much.

Growling, he spun, raising his saber once more.

"Tray, we need—"

He lunged.

And they disappeared.

Just as he thrust forward, anticipating plunging his weapon into their side, the demon vanished. Not in a cloud of smoke or flash of light, and not like the Thalo puppets of legend. More like . . .

More like a varg. Like a jumper.

Suddenly there were palms against his back, shoving.

His bare feet skid painfully as he overbalanced. His arms flailed outward and his saber was plucked from his grasp. He tumbled forward, catching himself on his exposed forearms, landing hard on his knees.

The demon kicked him over—onto his back—before he could heave another breath.

Above him, both blades glinted dully in the growing light. The demon had disarmed him—had claimed a second Regulator's saber.

Whose had been the first?

Tray curled his fingertips into the dirt, determined to spring back to his feet.

But in the next instant the figure dropped down, straddled him with two crossed blades at his throat. "Are you ready to listen now?" they asked, tone weary and put-upon.

Tray realized the voice wasn't simply reminiscent of someone he knew. It *was* someone he knew.

She was *alive*.

Or maybe this was a dream after all.

The tension left his body.

"Krona?"

Apparently satisfied with the shift in his demeanor, she pulled the blades from his throat and thrust both sword tips into the ground on either side of him. With a quick flick of her wrist, she threw back her hood and shimmied her cowl down below her chin. "Took you long enough."

She still wore her hair in many fine braids, still had that same determined set to her jaw, lift to her chin. But there was hardness in her eyes that he'd rarely seen—and never directed at *him* before.

He blinked at her, baffled. "Took me . . . ? Krona, what—? *How?*" He couldn't put his questions into words. The last time he'd seen her was the night of the First Grand Marquis's assassination—of which she'd later been accused. She'd contacted him only once in the ensuing days and then, nothing.

"How?" he asked again, gesturing, generally, at all of her. At her existence, her attire, and those gods-awful *bones*.

She stood and offered him a hand up. "It's a long story."

Once on his feet, he wrapped his arms around himself. "Then tell it to me while you build us a fire. Did you have to kidnap me in the middle of the night?"

"I wouldn't have kidnapped you at all, except you drew your saber and woke up the entire barrack." Despite her chiding tone, she disentangled her cloak from about her shoulders and unclasped it from around the bones—two slits had been cut in the back of the cape, allowing the strange growths to poke through.

He tried not to stare, sure they were part of her oncoming tale. "Thank you," he said quietly as she passed him the covering. Beneath, she wore a bright blue leather brigandine with a lamella of diamond-shaped steel plates, each one decorated with a different etched hunting scene highlighted with gold. It looked old—not of this era—and expensive.

Wrapping the cloak about himself, he looked down again at the huge swath of smoldering land that lay before them. The buildings and trees and soil looked like they'd all been churned and then charred.

"Where are we? Is that—?"

"Clavaburn," she said. "Wiped off the map."

She'd carried him to the southern border of Asgar-Skan. Nearly all the way to Winsrouen.

By the five—*how*?

A strong northerly gust nearly ripped the cloak from him, and he clutched it all the tighter, putting his back to the wind. "Why are we in Clavaburn?" He hated how high his voice was, how it squeaked on the upturn of the question.

"Winsrouen is advancing—marching more troops northward. They declared Clavaburn reclaimed for the empire, but the townsfolk resisted. This was the army's answer. And you can still see them, marching on, just there."

A mass of people—little more than a bulk of black in the low light—slouched northward, ever steady.

In the village below, a lone bull bellowed forlornly.

"They're expanding their borders," she went on, "looking for more territory—but their ultimate quarrel is with Lutador proper, and Xyopar is willing to join that fight now that Asgar-Skan has halted all trade southward. It's only a matter of time before Marrakev either has to close itself off to the rest of the Valley or ally with its neighbor. This"—she pointed sharply—"is what awaits hundreds of villages just like it.

"I wanted you to see it, so you can better understand what I've been doing since I was framed for the First Grand Marquis's assassination. Hearing about the war is different from moving through it. This peak used to be a favorite sanctuary for me. Lonely, out of the way. A place I could rest for a moment, where I could bring Thibaut, or whoever, to just share a moment."

Tray pulled his nightclothes closer as the crackling of timbers collapsing cut sharp and high through the night. A renewed swirl of sparks danced below.

"Settle in," Krona said. "I'll get you warm."

Tray found a boulder to perch upon, glad there was an outcropping to shield them from the wind, while Krona went to a nearby fissure in the rock, popping the seal on a secret stash of supplies wedged inside. She brought him a chemise, some hardtack, and began building a small fire.

He watched her carefully, gaze still drifting to those *bones*—to the organic way the top knuckles on them flexed unconsciously, subtly. Like a jaw clenching or a finger twitching. Unlike the horns on their Regulator helms—false and inert, meant to intimidate—these were a part of her. Alive.

Impossible.

"Just tell me," he said carefully, running his fingers over the cloak's fabric, at a loss for what to do while she worked. "Are you . . . are you alive? Or is this . . . are you . . . are you still human, or . . . ?"

Maybe she was a spirit. Or a vision.

Maybe Tray wasn't really on this mountaintop.

Maybe something—safe or sinister, who could say?—had wormed its way into his mind.

"I'm alive," she reassured him, pulling off her gauntlets to better wield her flint. "I'm still me."

He had no means to test that assertion. If this was a dream, she knew what he knew. If she was something else in Krona's form, well . . . what did it matter if he proved it? Any being that could take him instantly from one side of the city-state to the other could do with him as it liked, whether he accused it of tricking him or not.

Sparks flew.

Some of them took.

Krona blew gently on the small flames before finding her own stone seat, though not across from him. Next to him. Like she would have in the old days.

Because they were colleagues.

Friends.

As good as family.

Would have been family, truly, in the eyes of everyone, had De-Lia lived.

As the sun crested the Valley's rim, she regaled him with a story that he would have taken as pure fancy had he not just been privy to her power. A tale of varger and Thalo and death and life and gods.

Gods.

Krona had discovered the Thalo stronghold, and at its center, a man more influential than any king or marquis or eze. The Savior, whose agents whispered in the ears of the powerful and pitiful alike, guiding the forward trudge of history with an invisible hand, ensuring prosperity one minute and devastation the next.

He'd orchestrated the assassination of Lutador's First Grand Marquis, and the failure of the pan-Valley rail project, and the war—ensuring the city-states would be at one another's throats.

And Krona had been building an army to end him.

She explained the painful process of merging with a varg, of becoming one with it; a piece of herself, separated from her by a grotesque ritual during the time tax that nearly everyone had been subjected to since time immemorial.

He tried to imagine joining with a varg, having magic at his fingertips. The power of an enchantment, but inside himself, and he found it stirred a strange ache in his chest.

Krona told him she'd located two of Charbon's children, and met a woman named Hintosep who'd built rebel cells all over Arkensyre.

She told him the tale of fleeing the Savior's keep, and liberating a god's corpse. "You're sure?" he asked after her lovingly detailed description of the massive body she'd found—one with eggplant-purple skin, crystal casing, amethyst eyes, and a bird skull where a face should be. "You're sure the body you have is Emotion's and not some . . . some . . . ?"

He couldn't complete the thought. What else could it be?

And still, *how do you kill a god?*

How was such a thing possible?

"I didn't want to believe it either. But yes, I'm sure. Emotion is dead. The Unknown is dead. Time and Nature and Knowledge are all trapped, their wills removed, minds secreted away by the Savior. We have to free them and we have to kill him, to take back the Valley. To take back our lives."

Tray dipped his head into his hands. It was a lot to accept. He might have truly doubted had it been anyone else telling him. With a sigh, he forced his chin up. "Why now? You've been missing for a year. Why come for me now? Why tell me all this now?"

"Is it not enough that I missed you?" she asked, her expression going slightly cold, hurt.

They'd been friends since childhood; which meant he knew her better than that. "There's a reason you stayed away. And there's a reason that's changed."

She nodded, holding her hands out to the flames to warm them. "Because I'm ready now. I didn't want to get your hopes up unless I was sure. But she'll need you."

"Who?"

"De-Lia."

Every time Tray grew sure he was awake, she flung something else at him that felt like a dream. "*Krona*," he said slowly, tone long-suffering. "She's dead."

"I didn't say she wasn't." Her gaze was earnest, reflecting the morning light as she looked at him. "I know what she was to you. Her echo showed me."

He glanced away, flung his gaze far over the cliff. "You shouldn't be able to remember that."

"Except she was my sister."

They both knew sometimes the enchantment worked differently if you knew the person in life; if you had your own memories to pin theirs upon.

"I don't know everything about the two of you," she assured him. "But I've gathered enough. And when we bring her back, she'll need you."

His hands trembled as his heart rate picked up. He clenched his jaw, and couldn't force himself to look at her again, because he didn't want to hope. He wasn't over De-Lia—doubted he ever would be—but he'd reached acceptance. He was at peace with her absence. Or, he thought he was.

But the certainty in Krona's voice made that peace crack. Gave it sharp edges.

Krona was new again—she'd always been strong, determined, but now . . . now she projected dominance and assuredness, enough to evoke terror. Enough to evoke *awe*.

Perhaps she really could command life and death.

He swallowed harshly, throat gone tight, tongue gone thick. "These new powers of yours, they're enough that you can—?"

She swiftly put a hand on his shoulder, made him look at her. She shook her head, and his stomach dropped. "No. But you can't tell me the gods can create the Valley, create all of humanity, but can't reverse one little death. I have pieces of her—building blocks. Her echo, her journal, her sand, her varg. I still need to retrieve the blood pen, and I hope you'll help me with that. Then we'll have it all: body, mind, magic. The gods won't even have to start from scratch. And they'll owe us."

"*Owe* us?" he scoffed.

"For freeing them," she said practically. "Hintosep knew; they're the only ones who can defeat the Savior. We need them, and they need us."

"But they're—they're *gods*. You think you can demand favors from—?"

She pinned him with a harsh stare. "You think the gods have no sense of justice? Of gratitude?"

He said nothing. Nibbled a bit of hardtack instead.

Tray had never considered himself overly virtuous—his gambling habit was proof enough of that. And he certainly wasn't particularly pious, but he'd always had faith in the gods—in their gifts. And there was something *comforting* about them sacrificing themselves to seal Arkensyre away from the world. They were protective, ever-present, yet distant. Docile.

The idea of them *awake* and *ready* and roaming *free* . . .

It's one thing to believe in gods. It is quite another to meet them.

"I need to know," she said. "Are you with me? Can I add you to our number?"

He knew she'd been watching him closely as she spoke frankly of the plan to wake the gods, subvert the Savior, and free the Valley, unable to sugarcoat her intentions for him, even if she'd wanted to.

She was looking for a reason to send him back, he realized. He knew a *no* would see him instantly in his bed again, but even a simple *yes* wouldn't be enough. She didn't mind if he showed signs of doubt, or hesitancy. Those were expected. She knew he had a fighting spirit, though, and any spark of outright hostility toward her goals would give her cause to doubt—not doubt *him*, but whether or not his loyalties could be remolded.

His breath ghosted into the air, despite the morning sun's bright glow and the nearby fire. He gazed steadily into the flames, considering. "This means abandoning my post," he said flatly.

"Yes," she offered without argument.

He rubbed his hands together absently, considering.

Since the assassination, Lutador was not the Lutador he'd pledged himself to.

"Three weeks ago," he said, "we had a concern in your old neighborhood. An ink chemist was drawing up antiwar pamphlets."

Krona frowned. "Why were you called in?"

"That's the thing," he said gruffly, "it had nothing to do with enchantments. Lampblack ink, rag paper. No enchanted supplies, no enchantments stolen, no enchantment misuse, no extortion, no bribery, no . . . no nothing." Swallowing thickly, he looked up at Krona. "All she did was criticize the Second Grand Marquis for turning his grief into everyone else's grief.

"He's become paranoid—brutally so. His brother was killed in the man's own bed during a night of celebration. Well, nights of celebration are no more. Curfews are stricter, and people dare not say a harsh word against the nobility for fear of reprisal.

"We were ordered in to the chemist's, told to detain her. And to . . ." His jaw tightened, stopping him from spitting out the rest.

"And to what?" she prompted—gentle, but insistent.

The memory still made acid rise in his throat. "And to burn her shop."

He felt more than heard her draw a breath, ready to say something, but in the end she held fast, remained quiet.

"Our detail has been cut in half," he said, instead of answering her unspoken question. "Just me, Royu, and Tabitha. But everywhere we go, whenever we're called in these days to something . . . *political* . . . there's a Marchonian there. Someone who was tied to the First, who has yet to be tied to another First because the fucking Second keeps convincing the council to hold off the elections. So it was us, and a Marchonian, and a couple of the Watch from the jailhouse down the way. And when one of the watchmen spoke up first—immediately objected to burning the place—the Marchonian ordered him to take off his boots."

Tray tilted his head when Krona's brow furrowed. "I know, the rest of us made that same face. But we weren't going to argue with a Marchonian over boots. So, the watchman does it. He stands there in his hole-riddled socks while the Marchonian circles him."

Like a gods-damned vulture, Tray realized now. Like a vulture looking for a tender spot on a carcass.

"The Marchonian goes around once, then twice, just appraising him, silent as all get-out, until he gets behind him again and draws his sword. Quick as anything, the Marchonian bends down, slashing the man's tendons from his calf to his heel. On both legs."

Darkness flooded over Krona's features. A darkness Tray shared.

"Tabitha and Royu carried that man and his newly useless feet out into the street while I and the rest of the Watch . . ." His head drooped; he caught his forehead in his hands. The weight of it, *fuck,* he hadn't fully felt it until now—until this impromptu confession. It felt like purging his soul. "I lit the fire. Gods help me, I lit it."

She grasped his shoulder in a show of comradery, but still remained silent. No patronizing *there, there now,* no reassurances or words of absolution. But no condemnations, either.

She didn't need to condemn his actions when he fully condemned them himself.

"I think they hanged the ink chemist," he blurted. "This is *not* what Regulation is supposed to be. My job was never about protecting the egos of powerful men by destroying the lives of others. This is not my purpose, and this is not the Lutador I swore to serve."

"Even the Lutador we swore to serve wasn't—" She cut herself off.

"What?"

Her gaze went distant as she clearly relived her own haunting memory. "We chopped off a man's hand for wanting to look too closely at the stars."

That frank assessment shouldn't have been the punch to the gut that it was.

"We are told all our lives that the penalties are just, so we simply believe them just. But look at me," she said, opening her arms, inviting his stare. "If there was ever a person who deserved to pay all five penalties at once, it's me. According to the scrolls, I'm a walking blasphemy. But the scrolls aren't everything. They leave so much out, and that has to be on purpose. As for the law . . . people make laws. There's nothing holy about them. People are fallible, and so are our rules.

"The assassination, its aftermath, has just brought that fact to the fore, put it on display."

She shook her head, pulled her arms in again to hug herself. "I don't know if I'm . . . if I'm making my point. If Hintosep were here, she'd have said it sharp as a razor. She'd have cut to the quick of it."

"I don't know her," he said swiftly. "I know *you*. I understand."

"Then help us. Help *me*. Come work by my side. Regulation is no longer worthy of you as its agent, but Lutador still needs you."

If Tray was honest with himself, he'd been waiting for something like this. Not for Krona to materialize out of thin air, but for a call to *let go*. A reason to move on. Honor and loyalty had him clinging to his post, pretending he was still serving ends he agreed with by means he might not. But that hadn't been the case for a long while now, and he just needed an opportunity to break away.

"Yes," he said firmly. "Yes, I'm with you."

"Excellent," she said, clapping him on the back with a smile—a smile that reminded him so much of De-Lia it hurt.

Krona stood, clearly making to snuff out the fire.

Ah. Time to move on already, then. Decision now made, she was preparing to send him back to the barracks. "How long do I have to gather my things?" he asked.

"We'll see to your affairs later," she said. "Now I'm taking you to your new home."

Waving her hands over the fire, she molded the time around it, made the fire burn itself out in a matter of seconds while creating a funnel around its heat output, letting the sudden flare of thermal energy burst skyward instead of outward, dispersing it safely.

"Take up your sword, Master Amador," she said. "Welcome to the rebellion."

3

AVELLINO

Now

Avellino never broke stride as he was whisked from the interior of Mirthhouse on the fringe of Lutador's rim to the bottom of the Valley basin in Asgar-Skan. The change in altitude popped his ears, the transition from dry cold to damp heat instantly making sweat break out around the neckline of his robes.

Fragrant jungle pressed in on all sides, nearly obscuring the thin, well-trod path where the three of them alighted. The canopy overhead sliced up the bright sunlight, but the shade provided no reprieve from the soaring temperatures. Frogs and birds immediately protested their sudden appearance, squawking and chirping as they bounded away, and several somethings in the ferns and vines of the underbrush scurried off with a leaf-shaking vengeance.

Avellino took a deep breath, scenting the damp, mildewy balm of fungus and moss beneath the sharpness of something blooming nearby.

Krona held his hand tightly as they touched down, clutching Juliet's hand with equal security in her other. "All right?" she asked them both.

They nodded.

"Good. Check the usual communication points and I'll meet you at the camp tomorrow. Then we can forge ahead, see if we can finally find the temple."

Hopefully they'd find themselves in the presence of a god soon.

Knowledge, to be exact.

Hintosep had utilized Avellino's mind as a living lockbox for centuries' worth of gathered mysteries, enigmas, and arcane understanding, leaving him with a treasure trove of secrets to sift through.

Each tidbit of understanding required careful deciphering in order to translate it into actual knowledge he could utilize. He had to pick apart her puzzles, weave together tapestries from loose threads, and slot together each wayward piece until the picture clarified.

And he'd nearly resolved this one.

The Savior had removed the gods' minds and hidden their bodies away in sacred Thalo temples all over Arkensyre. Avellino *knew* where those temples were, he did. Hintosep had buried their locations deep in his mind. He just needed to recognize the clues for what they were.

The Savior's dread was written into the aura of each hint she'd given him. The man might not fear much, but Hintosep had known he feared the gods. The Savior and his Order had controlled—suppressed, stagnated—the arc of human history, and the gods would put an end to it. See him punished for it.

After making sure the pair of them were set to start out on their trek, Krona jumped away again, leaving the siblings to their work.

Once they were alone, the first thing his older sister did was *fuss*. She took him by the chin, tilting his face this way and that, examining her handiwork.

Though the humidity made him want to dab his forehead, he knew better than to rub at his throat or touch his face—the blue lines and swirls painted there were impeccable, but would smear under too much attention. Juliet had applied them perfectly, cheerfully singing through the duty the entire time, doing herself up just the same right after, painting her face like she was about to take the stage or take the town, rather than take a dangerous leap disguised as a Thalo.

She was always like that: merry in the face of danger. Her confidence was contagious, her brazenness enviable. To her, every mission was an adventure, and every companion a great foil for her wit.

Every companion save him, it seemed, since she could not stop *babying* him. Especially when no one else was around.

He tried not to be irritated by it, as his irritation felt unfair to her. He'd grown up oblivious to her very existence, whereas she'd spent much of her life trying to get to him—to *free* him. And even though she respected his abilities as a full Cryptopath, she could not leave off worrying.

She gave him and his paint an affirming nod before taking up her pack. "Come along."

He bit his tongue, though he wanted to point out that *he* should lead. They were on Thalo trails, after all.

She was dressed just the same as he was, in the guise of a full member of the Order of the Thalo, with false tattoos that covered not just her face, but the exposed portions of her arms as well. She wore the robes Avellino had worn when he'd escaped from the keep; he'd grown several inches in the past three years, and the robes' hems now hit him (unbecomingly) mid-shin.

He'd taught her the style of the keep, helped her braid her blond hair and weave it just so. And yet, no matter how perfectly she looked the part, she could not quite manage the hollowness he'd come to expect in a Thalo expression. He hadn't realized that's what it was—hollowness—until he'd escaped. The Savior cultivated oppression, squashed the concept of personal wants, personal goals. Everything, even one's thoughts, were supposed to be in service to Him. An inner life was no life at all if it was not given to service of the Savior.

Juliet, fundamentally, could not hide the light in her eyes, no matter how stiff her posture or dower her expression.

So far that light had not given them away.

Furrowing his brow with determination, he followed her, clutching at the front of his robes, anchoring himself with the weight of the alexandrite pendant that dangled, hidden, against his breastbone.

It was a gift from Abby—who'd been given to him as a baby to look after by Hintosep, back when Avellino had still been simply Thalo Child. Zhe was once his charge, but these days, in many ways, Abby felt like his sibling. Perhaps even more so than Juliet.

The pendant hadn't always been alexandrite. Originally it had been a chicken bone. A thigh bone, meant for the rubbish heap. Abby had taken a liking to the shape of it, and, using zhur budding physiopathy, had transformed it.

Zhe'd given it to Avellino on his last birthday.

He hadn't even known when his birthday was—let alone that was something one celebrated—until Juliet had mentioned it.

There were so many differences between the rest of Arkensyre and the Thalo keep, he was sure it was impossible to catalog them all.

The pair aimed for a cluster of over-tall tualang trees that sat near the edge of a narrow river, marking a well-worn Thalo path. Hiking upstream, they followed the trail the water cut until they arrived at a boulder with hidden Thalo markings before veering into the dense jungle once more.

The day passed slowly as they trod in relative silence, not wanting to give their presence away to any nearby Thalo, but also not wanting any attention from some of the toothier species native to Asgar-Skan. Unlike the bears in Marrakev—who ran from voices, who could be easily avoided if one were inclined to keep up a loud trail song—the great cats of the jungle preyed on the boisterous.

They checked a few hidden caches to see if any Thalo communiques had been planted, but came up empty.

Avellino had hoped for one more sign that he was on the right track, but was nevertheless confident he knew where he was going.

Flashes of images in his mind gave him clues to each temple's location. A desert oasis surrounded Emotion's. A metal mountain held Nature's. A beautiful waterfall marked Knowledge's, and Time . . . Time was someplace dark and hot.

And, of course, he knew exactly where the body of the Unknown—the Fallen—was, suspended out in the open in the Savior's keep.

Five gods, five locations. With information Avellino had been able to glean from Thalo operatives throughout the Valley, they'd managed to track down Emotion's temple in Xyopar and Nature's high on a cliff in Winsrouen, though both temples had proved impenetrable thus far. Hopefully they'd have better luck with Knowledge's.

But Time—Time still eluded them entirely. Logically she was somewhere in Lutador, and yet no one had yet been able to suggest a place that even remotely resembled the flashes in his mind. They'd tried the hot shops of the most esteemed glassmakers, and the darkened tunnels surrounding the gas pipes that kept the palace furnaces alight. Nothing had looked right. Nothing had *felt* right. He was at a loss.

Knowledge's temple had proved only slightly less troublesome. For someone not from the region, much of the Asgar-Skanian jungle looked like any other part. It had taken years of dedicated research and reconnaissance to bring them here, now.

As he and Juliet approached the enchanted border buried in the ground around their intended campsite, Avellino set a hand on Juliet's shoulder to slow her. They both softened their steps and perked their ears, looking for any sign the camp was already inhabited by members of the Thalo Order.

They'd run afoul of lesser Orchestrators and the like before.

Today, the camp was empty.

"Well, then that's bedding sorted for the night," Juliet said. "Proper this time. Why don't you settle in, dear brother, and I'll go a-hunting for a bite of bird?"

"We shouldn't separate. And we shouldn't get too comfortable. I want to be able to move quickly if Thalo stumble onto us," he said.

She sighed. "All right, hardtack it is. *Again*. But we're not forgoing a fire. Can't have you freezing to death in the middle of the night."

"I'm already sweating as it is. Would you have me burn up instead?"

"Oh, tosh. Sit down while I make camp."

"We can *both* make camp."

"I'm not putting you in harm's way. You know very well these stash boxes can be booby-trapped."

"And I'm the one who can detect the traps, not you!"

"You'll be sure to point them out, then." She put her hands on her ample hips and frowned at him. He wasn't sure why it struck him in the moment, but he was caught by the absurd realization that he was thin and lanky and she was short and round. Together, they were an encapsulation of their parents, from what she'd told him.

Perhaps the unimpressed expression she wore at this very moment was a reflection of their mother's.

Or their father's.

He tried not to think about that. He often tried not to think about Louis Charbon at all. "You'd wrap me in twelve layers of linen and feather pillows so as not to be threatened by the nefarious corners of Mirthhouse's walls if you could," he said instead, shoving his intrusive family thoughts aside.

"And would that really be so bad?" she quipped back. "I'm sorry you have an adoring older sister who can't stand the thought of you succumbing to the least bit of harm—"

"An errant bruise does not require the amount of fussing you seem to think—"

"But as I was robbed of *my* older sister, I think you'll forgive me for leaning into the part."

They both fell silent. Juliet's eyes went wide and she clamped her mouth shut.

During their minor squabble, they'd been keeping their tone light. Avellino was irritated with her mother-henning, but hadn't actually been out to make her feel bad about it. By the same token, clearly Juliet had been treating the moment as a bit of fussy banter. She hadn't meant it to take a turn for the serious, to reveal the wellspring from which all her worry bubbled.

Their eldest sister, Gabrielle, had been murdered by Fiona Gatwood and Eric Matisse, long after Avellino had been stolen from his family, but before Juliet had learned of the Thalo and their meddling.

After an awkward few beats, where neither of them seemed prepared to address the sorry fact of Gabrielle's gruesome departure from this world, Juliet cleared her throat. "Well, let's get to work, shall we?"

She immediately went about making the campsite just a little more comfortable, a little more bearable, as Avellino stood there, stuck in his head.

She might dither over him, but she'd also never judged him. She'd never dismissed him or pushed him or done anything but be there for him. She fussed over him the way he fussed over Abby. And though he was far too old for it, perhaps he could let her have it, for now.

He went to build a small fire, and she gave him a grateful smile. She was crouched down, digging out their paper-wrapped dinner when he suddenly blurted, "Will you tell me about her?"

Juliet had told him little stories about her childhood before, but those had only seemed to contain Gabrielle in passing. Incidentally. He hadn't pushed. She dodged painful topics like one dodged rain puddles in the street, skillfully sidestepping and spinning off in a new direction.

Now, she stilled, looked up into the darkening forest, but did not look at him.

"It's . . . it's been a long time," she said, her voice wavering ever so slightly. Clearly that time had not dulled the memories.

Instantly, he felt guilty for asking. She'd *been there* when Gabrielle had been brutally killed. When Una, their mother, had been forced to make a terrible decision and whisk young Juliet—then called Nadine—away while her eldest daughter's murderers were still in the house, on the prowl.

Una had fled with her one remaining child and never looked back. When she herself had grown sick and died only a few years later, Hintosep had finally revealed herself. Had taken Juliet on, having accepted her part in making the young girl an orphan.

Juliet had found the strength to tell him all that before, in bits and pieces. But she never talked about who Gabrielle and Una—and, yes, even Louis—were as *people*. Perhaps because it was easier to explain the gruesome facts if she could separate them from the individuals she'd loved.

"She was prim and proper in a way I never could be," she said with a watery half laugh, as though there were tears already in her throat that had yet to make an appearance in her eyes. "Very *yes, Mommy, yes, Daddy.* I think maybe because she was the oldest. She *loved* rules." At that, Juliet rolled her eyes and stuck her tongue out. "Her room was always so clean. The maids never had to pick up after her."

"Maids?"

She waved her hand absently at him before realizing the question was earnest. He had no idea what she was talking about.

"People one can pay to clean up your messes for you."

"Oh. Thalo don't use time vials, but you mean like the Mindless in the keep?" he asked smoothly.

She openly balked, pulling a pained face. "Well, they keep their autonomy, but . . . more like the Mindful, I suppose?"

He nodded his understanding. He was still trying to get a handle on the ways of the world outside the keep. He was still separated from much of the Valley's cultures—tethered as he was to the resistance and Mirthhouse, which was full of people who'd thrown off their city-states much as he'd thrown off the Order.

"We bickered," Juliet admitted with a sigh, referring back to Gabrielle once again. "But we did love each other. I love her still. I've loved you all, still," she said, finally turning to him with a sad smile. "No matter how long gone from my sight."

He knelt down next to her, then slid his arms hesitantly, but firmly, around her shoulders. Gently, she brought one hand up to clasp at his arm.

They hadn't hugged often. Avellino wasn't much for physical touch—he'd been trained to stay distant, and found too much nearness to anyone but Abby made him uncomfortable. But Juliet was just the opposite. Touch was how she showed attentiveness and love. He understood that, wanted to give her that.

Together, they sat in silence for a time, until a sudden shock of light from between the fanned leaves in the distance made them both stiffen.

They scrambled to make ready—for what, they weren't sure. Juliet's hand went to the dagger hidden in her robes and Avellino prepared to hide their presence; he found maintaining invisibility difficult, having been under-trained, and could only sustain it for short bursts.

The both of them held their breath, waiting.

If it was simply hunters, the camp's barrier should keep them hidden and protected. If it was Thalo, then they'd have to do some quick thinking.

No matter how much he tried, Avellino had never been able to shake his constant vigilance. Even in Mirthhouse, in a warm bed with a locked door and the safe house surrounded by budding Kairopaths, he woke at the slightest provocation. Thalo could be anywhere, lurking around any corner. They could still conceal themselves from an untrained time wielder's eye, and some could shield themselves even from him.

Gerome could be anywhere. Could be everywhere.

He was constantly in Avellino's dreams, both as tormentor and protector. As counselor and coercer. And here, in a camp built by Thalo, meant for Thalo, even though he logically knew he was prepared to meet the challenge, he still felt the same oppression he had in the keep. Like punishment was waiting just around the corner, no matter how well he performed his task.

Suddenly, Krona burst through the tree line, holding up a light vial.

"Oh, thank the gods," Juliet said, letting out a breath. Immediately she was bounding away, toward the light. She was her chipper self again. "We weren't expecting you until tomorrow."

"Malek's conjuration was another dud," Krona said with a shrug, "so no new varg hunt to plan."

Conjurations were a crude form of magic, something between the enchantments created from stolen magics and the free-flowing abilities that could be directly wielded by a skilled hand.

Hintosep had developed a conjuration to track an individual's varg, but the results seemed inconsistent.

"The light appeared in that same spot?" Juliet asked. "The empty field?"

"You mean the one cleared for the pan-Valley railway that we've gone to a dozen times and found absolutely no varger, despite following all the signs?" Krona said with an edge of sarcasm. "Yeah. Only, it's not an empty field any more. The war's taken over. Place is crawling with soldiers now. They've even subsumed some of the surrounding farms."

"That's, what, twenty failed conjurations?"

Krona let out a heavy sigh. "If Hintosep were here, maybe she could tell us why some of them just don't work right, but I don't understand it. For now, I suppose we should just be grateful when they do."

"We still don't know if the trail is safe," Avellino whispered tensely. "We should keep quiet."

"Come to the fire, my dear," Juliet bade Krona.

The former Regulator pocketed her enchantment and sat herself on a downed log. "Any new intel?"

"Nothing," Avellino said. "But I'm still sure I know where I'm going. The last messages we intercepted were fairly clear. We're on the right trail. I'm positive we'll find Knowledge tomorrow."

The next day, a glorious waterfall greeted them at the end of a long hike, and Avellino's heart swelled. This was it, the exact waterfall imbedded in his mind. The one Hintosep had gifted him.

It wasn't nearly as large as the Grand Falls, whose magnificent sheet of water plunged four thousand feet into the burial pool below. This was humble in comparison, but no less awe-inspiring for it. Its curtain of water fell perhaps only a few hundred feet, and it was nearly as broad as it was tall. The basin below was deep, with emerald-green foliage growing over its edges and down under the water, bleeding toward a dark center that turned midnight blue, hinting at harrowing depth. All around, the air smelled alive, and the midday sun overhead sent rainbows slicing through the water spray.

On another day, Avellino would have liked to bask in its beauty for a time. Here, there was no hint of war. This place felt untouched by human conflict. But today it wasn't just a spot of gentle reprieve. It was the herald of discovery. They were one step closer to obtaining the ultimate weapons against the Savior: the gods themselves.

They stashed their packs in a stand of rocks, where Avellino covered them with a cryptopathic concealment just to be safe.

"Wait here," he told the others, knowing that there would be traps and safeguards, just as there'd been on the cliff top and at the oasis. Measures to keep out the uninitiated and let the Thalo through.

Carefully, he mounted the slick, growth-covered stones around the basin's edge, inching his way to the waterfall itself, hoping the spray wouldn't make the dye on his face run. The outer layer of Avellino's robes, usually wispy and light, soon grew clingy with dampness.

Behind the roaring of the water came the slightest tinkling sound—impossible to hear unless one was pushing toward the fall itself. Bone chimes—the femurs and jaws and ribs of animals all strung together, dangling in their own curtain behind the falls. The water's rushing created a gust that rattled through them in warning.

The chimes formed a web over what looked like nothing more significant than a divot in the cliff, but Avellino knew better; Hintosep had poured nearly a lifetime's worth of Thalo learning into him. He wasn't arrogant enough to think she'd given him *all* her secrets, but she'd used him as a vessel for her knowledge. She'd made him her unwitting apprentice in case something should happen to her.

He'd still had to hone his skills—knowing how to do something and actually doing it remained two distinctly separate things—but he was improving all the time.

And now, he used one of her forcibly imbued lessons to look *further*. To use his magic to see the secret imbedded in the stone.

A doorway of salt, disguised to look like granite, sat recessed into the side of the cliff, waiting. It pulsed as though alive—as though humors ran through it. It was magic that vibrated the crystal, undoubtedly directly from the Savior's own hand.

He hesitated, as he always did in these moments, confronted by remnants of his old life. The lessons imbued in him as Thalo Child, deep in the Savior's keep, surrounded by mystery and mystique, were not so easily shaken. The scales had been lifted from his eyes, yes, but the shimmering, plated armor of majesty that came from living as one of the Order still informed who he was, no matter if he wished to fight it or embrace it.

Breaching this sanctum was both rebellious and blasphemous, not to his brain but to his body. It protested even as he pushed forward. He had to force himself through it—swallow down the dread and continue.

There were things about his past he knew he could never escape, only accept.

Just like he'd had to accept that he'd been stolen from his parents as a baby.

Just like he'd had to accept that he'd had a whole family who'd loved him, missed him, and was now . . . gone. All but Juliet.

Just like he'd had to accept that that same emotion, *love*, had driven his father to commit grisly murder after grisly murder.

For someone else, it might be easy to look at all that had passed and blame themself. If his father had not grieved him as dead, then none of those horrors would have happened. But at least Avellino was far enough removed from the reality to understand that his role in that story had been as an object. He was no more to blame than the scalpel itself. He understood how adults objectified children, turned them into tools—that was what the entire Order was built on. How Gerome had treated Avellino, and how Hintosep had treated Gerome before that.

Understanding he had his own agency, outside the keep's walls, had perhaps been the most difficult thing to accept of all.

Which was why he now clung to it so covetously. Why he demanded Juliet slacken his leash, why he asserted his lead role even if something inside of him craved to let someone else go first.

Forcing himself past the bones, letting them clink a ghostly melody in his ear, Avellino put the water spray at his back and held his fingertips against the hidden door, sending out tendrils of Secret magic, searching for traps.

Effortlessly, he unthreaded the bits of power meant to keep the average folk at bay—little bombs of cryptomancy that would muddle the mind and turn any jungle explorers around, marching them back from whence they'd come while erasing the memory path that had led to this font. Simply woven, easily discoverable by a Thalo his age, even if he hadn't had centuries of Hintosep's knowledge at his command.

And yet, he was wholly aware of how much he *didn't* know, whether because it had failed Hintosep's own understanding, because she'd failed to give it to him, or because he'd failed to interpret all she'd planted in his mind properly.

Thus, he was still cautious when he opened the door—when the salt melted and fell like the water behind him—leaving nothing but a gaping hole into the cliffside beyond. The yawing darkness immediately echoed the sounds of the jungle falls back to him, illustrating the cavern's size and depth as efficiently as any torchlight.

Avellino moved into the darkness, pushing through it like a thing of substance, as though it were a physical curtain blocking the light instead of the absence thereof.

This too was an illusion.

Secret magic fundamentally worked three ways: through misdirection, obfuscation, and removal. Misdirection forced a mind to look at something besides the secret, obfuscation muddled what was there—confused the straightforward—and removal made a secret of things that should have been known.

A sacred place like this was heavily inundated by all three.

He didn't have the power to dispel the false void, but Hintosep had left him a pattern of steps. He knew where to tread. Where to place his feet, and where not to put his hands. The cavern walls pulled in close here near the entrance, and brushing them would set off alarms in the keep.

Escaping the dark was like exiting a haze—wisps of it curled away, dissipated, and all that was left was a cold, steady light. Too steady—like the light that had bathed the secret passage that had led to Emotion's body.

This glaring, unnatural shine illuminated a vast hollow in the rock—a grotto, its depth and height impossible to calculate as, to the eye, it seemed to change shape and size by the moment, yawing wide, then tall, then shrinking in on itself.

The rock hollow could have been twelve strides across or twelve hundred—twelve *thousand*, even. The structures in it could have been twelve inches tall or twelve hundred stories.

The effect was purely optical—an illusion created by secret magic to mask the realities of the cavern—but it was enough to turn the stomach and make the feet unsteady.

Somehow, he managed to make his eyes focus, to find one shape and size and hold it steady in his gaze—to demand, with his magic, that the room *still*, if nothing else. The pulsating illusion slowed, settled. Found a sensible shape and size—something close to twenty stories tall and three hundred feet across. Even if Avellino couldn't be sure it was the *truth*, it was manageable. He took a halting step forward—into the inch of water that covered the entire cavern floor, making it slick and perilous.

When his vision held, he allowed himself to analyze the structure at the cave's center: the temple they'd been searching for.

One might expect anything built inside a cave to be carved from stone, but the grotto's pillars and its central architecture were all wood. Everything was fashioned out of trees, both living and dead. How the artificial light was able to sustain them in place of the sun, Avellino couldn't say. But here, in the colossal cave and shallow water, they flourished. Roots coiled up like the backs of great serpents, breaking free of the floor only to burrow back into it. Massive leaves created a glittering canopy, the light catching them like emeralds. Every portion of the trees bore symbols, etchings, reliefs, and frescos. Even the living leaves flaunted designs—swirls not unlike a Thalo's tattoos, only in bright green.

And in the center of it all, a treehouse. Not the kind Juliet had described to him—those that wealthy children liked to play in. And not the kind dotting the Marrakevvian countryside. This was a strange, rickety-looking thing, in stark contrast to the intricacies and ornamentation all around it.

A central tree cradled the structure, which was built from the cave floor up and looked as though it would fall over and smash to pieces if not for each branch just barely suspending it. Each board was noticeable—rough-hewn and inexpertly nailed. The building was far too narrow for its height, and each floor sat unevenly upon the next, leaning heavily against the tree. Not a single right angle graced the structure, though every corner looked as though it was *intended* to be ninety degrees. Most of the windows and doorways were dark, open, lacking glass or curtain or shutter. The depths of the interior were dim, inscrutable.

The entire house gave the impression of a fainting person—someone who'd gone weak and boneless, just barely kept from the floor by someone else's arms. And it was stuffed in a space far too small, pressed up against the cavern ceiling, bent under the weight of it.

The sharply pitched roof had a single gable at the front, crowning the only bit of decoration on the entire sorry thing: a stained-glass window, depicting a decrepit individual, Knowledge femself. The withered god, old and hooded, skin dark, face hidden. Yellow and orange panes surrounded the figure like a spray of sunshine.

Hintosep's secrets told him that behind that window the sleeping god sat on a throne, waiting. Waiting to be reunited with feir mind.

Avellino fell to his knees in the shallow water—not just the effort of fighting the deceptive magic draining him, but the rapture of the moment sapping his strength.

Finally. They were so close. The gods, and the Valley's salvation, were almost within reach.

He let himself have a moment to gulp down the emotion rising in his throat—his gratefulness, his weariness, and his hope were all overwhelming. He wished Hintosep were here. To all the gods, he wished it.

But she was gone. Her sacrifice had given them this, and he needed to honor it.

When he'd composed himself, he returned to Juliet and Krona, guiding them inside. Krona's resistance to Thalo magic didn't prevent the unnatural darkness from clouding her vision, but it did help her steady the cavern's size in her mind. Poor Juliet whirled when the yawing became too much, falling into Krona, burying her face in the former Regulator's armor-clad chest.

"Stay close to me," Krona whispered, her eyes fluttering shut for a moment as she performed some form of kairopathy invisible to Avellino, but apparently effective. Juliet stood straight again, blinking rapidly as though she'd just come awake. "Better?"

"Better," Juliet agreed.

They tried to move slowly, silently through the grotto, clearly all feeling the weight of the place, the importance. A god slept here. Mindless, will-less, but a god nonetheless. Despite their best efforts, they could not keep the water under their feet from splashing and swirling, and Avellino's robes—now soggy—dragged.

The treehouse loomed like an ancient watcher, regarding their approach like a gargoyle—a vicious protector, a watchdog, rather than anything resembling a welcoming home.

When they drew close, it creaked and popped, groaning just as an ancient tree would under heavy wind.

A growl. A warning.

And yet, the front door swung inward.

Not an invitation.

A dare.

A dare Krona was clearly in no mood to entertain if she didn't have to. She looked up at the stained-glass window, her brow furrowing for an instant before she jumped, disappearing before Avellino's eyes, only to reappear a minute later, landing at great speed and skidding to a stop just feet away.

"Is it warded to keep you out, like the Savior's keep?" Juliet asked.

"No, but there's no way to pinpoint a landing spot. It's always risky for me to jump without being able to envision my destination first, and nothing is as it seems in there. I was just . . . *falling*."

The front door opened a little wider, creaking as it went.

A dare and a half, then.

"In that case, shall we?" Juliet asked, sweeping her arm in the door's direction. She was obviously trying to be her usual chipper self, though her words were little more than breathy, and she could not keep a tremor of doubt from creeping in.

Krona craned her neck back to look at the top of the building, hunched precariously, bent, like it was trying to support the roof of the cave and nearly failing. The stained-glass portrait of wizened Knowledge seemed to wink at them in the unnatural light, beckoning.

This was so very different from Nature's stoic, impenetrable prison.

"We keep together," Krona ordered. "We do not move forward until both Avellino and I are satisfied with a path's viability. Agreed?" She held up her right hand, calling a faint, swirling purple haze to her fingertips. It was her fen, at the ready. What had once been her varg—a snapping, mindless, pained enemy—was now both a part of her and an ally, ready to be summoned and parted from her if need be.

"Agreed," Avellino and Juliet chimed together.

None of them were under the impression the inside would behave as any ordinary house. And yet, they could not anticipate exactly what kinds of obstacles might lay within.

They swept the front porch for traps, and found none save the rickety nature of the wood itself. Krona took the first step, pausing as her wet boot touched down, waiting for something to happen—for the door to snap shut, for a beast to crawl out of the darkness, for the house to grow fangs and try to eat her itself. But nothing came.

She gestured for them to follow.

Every board protested their bootfalls, creaking and squeaking and occasionally threatening to break with the snapping of fibers, but all remained intact.

The darkness beyond the open door seemed to be that self-same sort that guarded the cave entrance, except when Krona stepped across the threshold it vanished. Gaslight flames sprang to life in sconces on the walls, illuminating a staircase that rose directly from the entry way up, up, up—zigzagging its way in a long spiral that looked wholly impossible for the house to contain.

A hand-woven rug sat at the staircase's base, and a hall stretched off into what looked like a cobweb-covered kitchen beyond. Peeling wallpaper that might have once been bright blue with little pink roses on it had mostly faded to an odd pale yellow where it clung to the walls.

"It's like it really was a house once," Juliet said, daring to raise a hand and touch a faded outline on the wall where a picture had once hung. "But someone twisted it."

"But a house from where?" Krona asked.

Most of the buildings Avellino had seen in Asgar-Skan were built to guard against rot, as the warmth and humidity meant the jungle was encroaching all the time—its variety of life taking hold wherever it could. Roofs and floors were all fired tiles, many outer rooms were open-air with only finely woven nets as walls to keep out the insects. Lizards and birds often came and went freely. Lumber was used for support beams, but it was well-sealed with pitch.

This was a house out of place, out of time, out of proportion.

Knotted tightly together, the three of them pushed inside. The door slammed shut of its own accord, surprising no one.

The rumble that followed set Avellino's teeth on edge. The snapping sound of collapsing timbers was unmistakable, as was the quivering of the house itself. "It's coming down," he shouted, turning toward the door again, only to have Juliet catch his wrist.

"It isn't," she insisted. "It's just trying to scare us."

"It's trying to do more than that," Krona said.

When Avellino looked back, the staircase was gone. Rickety doors now stood before them, uneven on their hinges. Heart sinking, Avellino pulled out of Juliet's grip and jerked the front door open, only to find more house on the other side instead of the cavern grotto.

"What are we dealing with?" Krona asked him.

Taking a deep breath, trying not to let the trap shake him, he felt for the cryptomancy at work. The truth of their surroundings peeked at him here and there, but only for an instant. He wasn't skilled enough to banish the magic entirely—all he could do was tug back the curtain to lay the machinations bare. "Illusion. Mostly. To hide the true path through the house."

Still holding the beginnings of her fen up on her fingertips, Krona slowly pulled open one of the doors before them, revealing that, while they were still in the entryway with the staircase beyond, it had all been tipped on its side. The flaming sconces were now at their feet, with the staircase crawling up the side of the wall like a great coiling centipede.

"This may take a while, loves," Juliet said.

On their guard, they ventured forward. The winding, sideways staircase was not impossible to climb as long as they balanced themselves on the rot-ridden banister, climbing across the newly created rungs like they were part of a particularly rickety ladder. Once they alighted on the wall of the next landing, the world moved again, and the trio clung to one another tightly, terrified of being crushed or flung back the way they'd come.

When the house settled again, they found themselves on the ceiling, with no easy way to access the stairs.

"Shall we try a door?" Juliet proposed.

"Yes," Avellino agreed. "The stairs . . . aren't really where they seem to be. That's not the way up. Not anymore."

They braved signs of shifting and collapse at every turn. All they had to do was look away for a moment—blink—and walls would become ceilings, ceilings would become floors. Seemingly flat surfaces tilted suddenly. Doors disappeared, not to be seen again unless one of them miraculously caught it out of the corner of their eye, as fleeting as a mote. Not only that, but the true way forward could only be seen from certain angles, and—as they discovered—all others eventually led to a sharp plummet through a gossamer-thin spider-webbing of a floor.

Avellino was the first to put his foot straight through an illusion, to nearly tumble down the three stories they'd already traversed.

His stomach dropped, swooped, feet catching on nothing as he strode forward confidently. One minute solid wood, the next nothing but air. And he knew in a flash there would be nothing but air between him and the stone floor of the grotto as he tumbled down.

Only Juliet's quick reflexes kept him in the house. She yanked him from the unseeable hole, pitching them both backward and to the floor.

"I'm sorry, I'm sorry," he said, grasping at his chest, breath coming quick.

"The traps here make the security mazes in Lutador look like child's play," she said, helping him up and dusting him off. "It'd be impossible to get off the first floor without a Thalo aide and a Kairopath. I suppose we should at least be happy knowing the gods are secure."

"Security is relative," Krona said stiffly, picking her away around a chandelier bursting out of the ceiling-turned-floor. When the crystals began to vibrate, she turned on it quickly, encasing it in a time bubble, halting whatever defensive mechanism she'd inadvertently activated.

They moved more slowly after that, inching their way upward. Hours upon hours passed, and Avellino lost track of how many floors they'd conquered—mostly because he wasn't sure they'd conquered them at all. A glance out any given window could not be trusted, and he was sure they'd inadvertently backtracked more than a few times.

Must and rot and, oddly, bergamot tea were the prevailing aromas as they moved through the house, strengthening whenever they came too close to a single corner and the entire building *leaned* in that direction, threatening to topple.

The fine hairs on the back of Avellino's neck prickled when they alighted at what seemed to be the very top of the stairs. Instead of feeling triumphant or relieved, unease settled over him. Before them stretched a long hall. A single glowing globe of light swayed on a long string in the center, subject to the whims of an earthquake only it could sense, throwing ghastly shadows about.

A few feet past it, imbedded in the ceiling, was a trapdoor. Below, a long, red carpet—red as blood, and shaggy like an animal—covered the floor and flowed up the sides of the walls, as though it were a living, growing thing.

"I don't like it," Juliet said.

"Don't think we're supposed to like it," Krona countered, inching ahead, toe tapping the shag.

Avellino held his breath, expecting something to happen.

Everything, save the light, was still.

Concentrating, he reached out with his cryptomancy, looking for the secrets that must guard this floor, and found nothing novel. Nothing they hadn't already encountered. The hall's proportions were stretched to obfuscate their concrete dimensions—a mild illusion, compared to the rest of the building's insides.

Krona too seemed similarly surprised by the calmness of what was surely the penultimate floor. The trapdoor had to lead to the attic, where Knowledge waited.

They all sensed a trap, but there was nothing they could do except move forward and hope they stumbled upon a tell before a trigger.

Juliet slid onto the carpet behind Krona, kneeling down to run her fingers through the loose weave, pinching the threads, trying to make sense of them as something other than what they seemed.

Behind her, Avellino kept his eyes on the staircase, even as he followed, taking careful steps backward along the questionably lit hall. It would be just like the Savior to lure them into a dead end and send a beast in after.

The trio was quiet, their breathing shallow. Avellino strained his ears, looking for some clue above the muted thuds of their footsteps and the awkward creaking of the house. The swinging, bulbous light provided the only counterpoint, its chain squeaking as it swayed.

Time stretched, but the hall did not. Each step took them closer to the attic door as it should. Instead of the floor, it was the light's chain that elongated, its squeaking increasing, becoming a sharp, ear-piercing crescendo as they approached.

When Krona reached it, the thing hung at chest height, still swaying wildly across her path.

Gently, she reached up to still it.

The shadows stopped dancing.

The hall became perfectly placid.

But only for the length of a breath.

The stench of wet decay increased.

And the carpet *came alive.*

A ripple ran along the entire length of it, bucking Krona upward, sending her off-balance before the far end of the carpet curled itself up like a giant tongue, swiftly winding up around her, smothering her before rolling on, slamming into Juliet and twisting her up just the same.

Avellino cried out, trying to dodge back the way they'd come, but too late. The red strands of the carpet grabbed him—no longer long shag but instead sticky fibers, slick and cold, like strong strands of fungus, their stink just as musty.

The carpet pinned his arms to his sides, covered his face, the fibers sticking and snagging, pulling at his robes.

All three of them were pressed together inside the molted thing, crushed up in the fabric-that-wasn't, squeezed in great coils—like those of a python.

Avellino heard a distant cracking, wood splintering, as he tried to free a hand, a leg—anything.

In the next instant the tongue unfurled, flinging him to the side—flinging them all away. He braced himself, expecting to slam into a wall, but instead found himself in the open air, free-falling.

The house had scooped them up and spat them out.

And the cave floor would not be welcoming.

Avellino held out his hands, bracing, anticipating his wrists shattering and his arms breaking and his jaw hitting the stones with a heavy *crack*.

But then something large and warm and living slid beneath him, slowing his descent. It was amorphous at first—solid, yet translucent—but swiftly took on the familiar flash of antlers, wings, and equine body of Krona's fen. Ninebark caught him expertly, sailing to scoop up Juliet and Krona in succession, easing them down to the cavern floor, dumping them on slick, wet stones with a spray of water rising up all around before unceremoniously disappearing as Krona's exhaustion peaked.

Avellino's entire body jolted, shocked by the firmness of what could have been a devastating impact—his bones seemed possessed of their own imagination, thinking they'd hit the rock at speed and with a great force. An echo of a broken ache filled him momentarily, flushing his body hot and cold before his senses caught up to reality. He was fine. They were all fine. They'd escaped.

Suddenly there were dripping blond strands of hair dangling in his face. "*Avellino,*" Juliet said, his name like a swear. For a moment he thought she was accusing him of something, but it was the opposite. She was dithering again, brushing back his fringe, looking him over frantically for injury.

This time, there was no annoyance. Warmth bloomed in his chest. She *cared. This* was family. Not the bastardized thing Gerome had swathed him in back at the keep, which had been blunt and edged in turn, snide and wounding. The Thalo version of family was demanding and slithering, it snapped and cracked at its members, calling shallow cuts *care* and insults *love*. This was an imperfect thing from Juliet—and from Krona and Thibaut and Mandip and all the rest—but it came from a different place. The same place his love for Abby came from.

"Ow," he mumbled, rubbing at his tailbone.

Juliet frowned sympathetically, then ruffled his hair. "Nothing but a bruised backside?"

"There wasn't exactly time for finesse," Krona said regretfully.

"Never apologize for saving our skins, dear one." Juliet gave her brother space, then flopped onto her back to stare at the ceiling, her yellow hair floating in the shallow pool along with other bits of jungle jetsam.

Krona was up again already, stretching her neck and rolling her shoulders, staring at the treehouse with new determination. "Take a minute," she said. "Then we go again."

"Must we?" Juliet whined, though it was no real protest.

"We must," Krona apologized.

The house was no less maze-like the second time through.

Or the third.

Or the fourth.

Every time they reached the penultimate floor, the house forcefully flung them from the premises, no matter how ready they made themselves.

Krona tried to fight the carpet-tongue and only made things worse. She sliced at it with her saber, thinking to cut clean through, but the red threads stuck to the blade, trying to snag it away, catching hold just like the sticky tendrils in a carnivorous plant snagged its prey.

The more she pulled at her saber, the longer the red threads grew, reaching for her and curling, taking hold instead of merely expelling. It tore at the bindings of her armor, stripping much of it away. It could take her leathers, but she refused to let go of the sword. Roaring with frustration, Krona was the one to spit them out of the house this time, creating a lens and forcing them through, cutting the threads off at the quick when she collapsed backward into the shallow water, the flat of her saber held tightly to her chest with a few red threads still clinging.

"I think we should step back and consider a different strategy," Juliet said, robes now thoroughly soiled.

Krona rubbed at her face, looked down at herself. At the very least, she'd been left her trousers and undergarments, but the blue-and-silver brigandine was gone.

"Blue was never your color anyway, darling," Juliet said, patting exhaustedly at Krona's arm, clearly trying to lighten the mood and soften the loss.

The armor had been Hintosep's once. It was another part of her, gone.

Avellino, fearing he'd lost his own treasure, fumbled for the alexandrite chicken bone on its cord. To his relief, it was still there.

"If she'd been here . . ." Krona said with a sigh.

"No, stop," Juliet chided. "I knew Hintosep far longer than you, and while she was a glorious woman—and a strategist nearly beyond reproach—you would have had to save our skins just the same. She might have been able to warn us about the shaggy trap, but I dare say her plan for getting by it still would have been *leave it to Krona*."

"And so we'd still end up here," Krona said, lightly flicking water in Juliet's direction.

Avellino didn't say anything. If Hintosep had been here, she would have taken them straight to the top, he was sure.

"Exactly." Juliet rose to her feet, a jump in her step, though she was soaking head to toe. "Now, dear, if you'd be so kind. It might be sweltering in the day, but the damp does indeed become chilly in the night." She held out her arms in a graceful, expectant gesture.

"I don't do parlor tricks," Krona said, standing herself, the irritation in her voice clearly a front for fondness.

"And I'd never ask you to," Juliet countered. "Any good member of the Borderswatch knows wet socks can be the death of you."

"Then I'll jump us back to Mirthhouse as soon as we leave this cursed cave."

"Oh, you will not," Juliet said quickly. "I have a reputation to uphold. I'd rather show up in nothing but a pair of knickers—dry ones, mind you—than a sloppy, slimy, droopy set of robes. I look like a pile of neglected washing. But, if you don't want to waste energy wicking away this puddle water, then perhaps we should take a cleansing dip in that picturesque pool outside."

Krona considered, then sighed. "How do you always make indulgences seem sensible?"

"Because they *are* sensible," Juliet countered with a wink. "What's not sensible is enduring miseries when you don't have to."

The trio gathered themselves up and took one last look at the treehouse. The stained glass still loomed above like a single giant eye, and Avellino felt a bit like the house was snickering at them, cajoling them to try again.

As they moved back toward the entrance, with Avellino once again leading them through the substantive darkness, he couldn't help but think of Hintosep. A woman who'd wielded sharp blades and sharp intellect alike. He'd feared her and revered her, hated her and loved her, and last he'd seen of her she'd been covered in blood and subsumed by Orchestrators.

These gifts she'd given him were both intrusive and precious. She'd ripped Abby from zhur parents, but had brought zhim and Avellino together.

A part of him hoped she was still alive, and another hoped she was gone and no longer had to trouble herself with the machinations of this world.

HINTOSEP

The steady *drip, drip, drip* from a leak in the ceiling—the water sluicing down to the dungeon from who-knows-where—had, at first, driven Hintosep closer to madness than even the Cage itself. But now, after three years, she'd become so accustomed to it the sound had long since faded in her ears. The sound *was,* and yet it *wasn't.* Like so much around her. She'd similarly grown numb to the scrabbling little rat feet that dug into her when one of the creatures occasionally clawed their way into her lap for warmth, and the spiders that would brave her body to weave their webs between the clawed arms of the Cage.

None of the rats had tried to bite her, miraculously. Perhaps that was somehow Absolon's doing; she knew he'd be none too pleased if he came for one of his monthly visits only to find her bones picked clean by vermin. He drew his pleasure from her continued torture, and she couldn't suffer properly for her betrayal if she was dead.

And by that same token, he had to keep her healthy.

Which was its own kind of torture.

Hintosep knew what it was to be alone. She'd spent years on the rim as a Guardian, watching over the Ascendant until they'd completed their transformations, keeping a weathered eye out for varger packs that the people of the Valley had missed or could not control. Years with nothing but the wind and the cries of carrion birds echoing in her ears. No voices—no whispers or murmurs or shouts. She'd never been lonely then. What she wouldn't give to be back there now.

She heard the footsteps coming every day, like clockwork. Their gait steady, even.

She heard them now. A fixed tempo as firm as that *drip, drip, drip* that used to steal her sanity.

The Cage's control kept her sitting upright, staring at her cell's barred door with a gruesome smile plastered to her face. She couldn't even glare defiantly when the door's rusted hinges squeaked. She couldn't spit at the sandaled feet that stepped over the threshold.

She couldn't bite at the pale throat that she'd already scarred with the tear of her teeth.

Gerome—wearing a simple headband with a fringe of onyx beads that dangled into his eyes just as surely as his black hair—paused in the doorway, as he always did, just staring.

Not at her.

At the Cage.

He salivated over the many golden legs that wrapped around her head like a possessive, bony hand, admired the way its pincered feet dug into the meat of her face, wounding her—scarring her—as it controlled her. Eventually his eyes strayed outward, taking in the relaxed line of her body—empty of will, and as inert as a puppet.

The envy in his gaze was always open, evident.

He wished their places were reversed.

In one hand he held a stone bowl of stew. In the other, a chamber pot.

Thank the sky it wasn't wash day. Enduring his careful, reverent bathing was always humiliating.

Eventually he shook himself from his reverie, setting the chamber pot in the corner before commanding lightly, "Stand."

Without any desire to heed him, she did.

Her muscles were stiff. Her entire body ached from sitting in one position for so long. Her knees protested, but she surged upward—not ignoring the pain, but in spite of it.

Gerome was the Cage's Possessor now. He controlled her body for her, just as she'd once done for him long ago.

"Come to me," he directed.

Three years ago, when she'd first been put into the Cage, she'd resisted, but it made no difference either way. Her stride was the same, lazy and relaxed, no matter if she mentally struggled or gave in. Her will made no difference.

That was the point.

Once she stood before him, he allowed himself to stare again—eyes tracing each hard line of metal, the longing in his eyes deep and fierce.

Gerome was a burdened soul who wished to relinquish his control. He saw relief in the Cage. Respite. A state of being free from decisions, free of responsibility, obligation, and concern.

As a child, he'd given himself over to the Cage thoroughly, and with pleasure.

But that kind of freedom in the Cage could only come with trust. When *she'd* been *his* Possessor, he'd had the utmost faith in her, in the Thalo, in the world in which he lived. His days in the Cage meant he had to do nothing but simply exist in order to please, in order for her to give her approval. Letting go of his willpower had been praiseworthy, and he'd known she would never make poor decisions for him in its place.

Now, she had none of that trust for him in return.

Tension flitted through the line of Gerome's body, and he raised a hand as though he meant to caress the metal legs with more than just his gaze. But the moment passed swiftly, and he returned his attention to the task at hand: feeding.

Every mealtime, she expected to be given rancid meat or moldy bread, but as always, the stew smelled spiced and rich and hearty. The care they showed for her health helped them believe they were treating her well. She was a tortured prisoner, but she was *their* tortured prisoner. Once beloved, once an authority, now looked after—for her own good.

She was supposed to be learning a lesson in the Cage—that's what the artifacts were for, of course. Correction. Indoctrination.

Instead of handing her the bowl, Gerome plucked the spoon up and held a bit of broth out for her. "Eat," he directed.

Unable to stop it, she let him feed her like a child, one spoonful at a time. It tasted as good as it smelled, but that was a consolation, nothing more.

She had no idea how long Absolon intended to keep her like this. Perhaps forever. At the very least, she knew he would not let up until he could probe her mind with his perverted, stolen powers of teliopathy and find her resolve shattered.

Which would not be today.

Or tomorrow.

She'd lived a life so long she wasn't even sure how many centuries old she was anymore. And she would hold on for twice that long still.

Her will was caged, but she refused to let it die.

After she'd gulped down half of her meal, a new set of footsteps echoed their way down the hall. Upon hearing them, Gerome paused, looked puzzled.

His confusion made Hintosep's stomach shrivel, and nausea bubbled up in her throat. He turned to look over his shoulder, swiftly moving out of the doorway when he saw who it was. Without a word, he lowered both the bowl and his head—averting his eyes out of respect.

Absolon swept into the cell, thick traveling cloak affixed to his shoulders, a black mask—smooth, but covered in abstract silver filigree—hiding all but his eyes. He held something blue in both his hands. Phthalo blue. Thalo blue.

Gerome clearly hadn't been expecting the Savior, which did not bode well for Hintosep.

Gently, and without acknowledging Gerome, Absolon approached her, reaching up to thumb at a small dribble of broth that had slipped down her chin. She wanted to flinch away from his touch. She wanted to bite his hand.

"Foolish child," he whispered to her, reading her thoughts, patronizing tone rife with paternal affection. He turned to Gerome. "I'm bringing her back into the Order today. Back into my service."

The Possessor looked up abruptly, surprised, but Hintosep herself harvested no hope from the pronouncement.

"She's useless down here," Absolon continued. "One of our strongest, holed up in a cell. *Wasted*. But no more." He held up the blue thing so she could see it better—so she could *recognize* it. It was one of her leather brigandines—her finest—the straps cut, the back split open in two places, clearly modified. Little flecks of red string clung to it. "Besides," Absolon went on, "it seems some of her *pets* have been poking around in sacred places." He tossed the armor into a corner of her cell like it was a useless scrap.

After a beat of silence, Gerome ventured to speak. "Shall I remove—?"

"Of course not," the Savior replied lightly. "Both of you, come."

With that he swirled back out of the cell, footsteps falling away just as swiftly as when he'd arrived.

Gerome hurriedly set the stew down on the stone floor, hands shaking. "You heard Him," he said, commanding the Cage. "Do not keep the Savior waiting."

Hintosep lurched forward.

For three years she'd imagined stepping beyond her cell, out of the confinement of these close, cold walls—but now she wanted to fall back, to stay in the safety and certainty of the dungeon.

Better to be Absolon's favorite prisoner than another one of his favorite weapons. She'd seen what happened to those.

Absolon marched her through the keep openly—without a physical or magical shroud—past priests and children and Mindless alike. She had no way of knowing if Absolon had told the entire order of her downfall, or if seeing her like this was new and shocking. She could not raise her chin to preserve her dignity, nor could she look the bystanders in the eye as she passed. Regardless of whether or not they'd known of her plight, all stopped and bowed in the Savior's presence, waiting for this small procession of three to sweep by before going about their daily business.

Her feet followed Absolon of their own accord, and she could just barely hear the soft pitter-patter of Gerome's sandals as he strode behind her.

The high levels of the keep were as cold as the dungeon, and she wondered why she'd never noticed before. True, she wore only the rags of her former robes, without the usual fur-lined cloak or blue leather armor she was so accustomed to. And yet, seeing her home like this, as a prisoner rather than a resident, seemed to emphasize the frigidness of the icebound castle far more than her lack of outer layering.

Though the keep's halls were winding and many, it didn't take her long to realize to what end the Savior was marching: to his secret stash of minds.

The stash that had been raided years ago, if everything had gone to plan.

Absolon seemed calm, if determined. His emotions even, content. Until they reached their destination, she had no way of knowing if it was because Avellino and Krona had ultimately failed to retrieve the gods' minds, or if it was because he did not yet know they were missing.

If he simply didn't know, that was a good sign. A mark in Hintosep's favor. It would only be further proof that his abilities were weakening, that his greed for powers beyond his own had indeed put a strain on his innate cryptopathy.

She still wasn't sure how he'd managed to imbue himself with all five magics. She'd had nothing to do but think these last few years and still she wasn't sure what kind of dark experiments he'd been running. She hadn't seen him apply his magical engineering skills in millennia.

They reached the thick wall that contained the marble prison for the minds, and the Savior paused only briefly to be sure the hall was empty—that there was no one there to observe his use of time magic. There was nothing to indicate this wall was any different from any other in the keep—that it contained the most precious trinkets in all of the Valley: halite crystals, filled with the minds of Absolon's enemies.

Between one blink and the next, he disappeared, jumping into the hidden, walled-in vault.

Hintosep wished she could see the expression on his face the moment he realized she'd outwitted him. She knew he would never show his surprise or despair or shock to her willingly. All she'd receive was his anger.

Within moments he jumped into the hall again, snarling, his robes swirling, twisting about his ankles as his fury drove him forward. "*You*," he growled, advancing on her with a terrifying heat in his gaze and a livid hunch to his shoulders.

She couldn't reel back in fear, she couldn't thrust herself forward in defiance. The Cage kept her neutral, her expression slack and uncaring, which seemed to work in her favor. Even if she felt intimidated by his display, she could not convey it, which wound him up further. She was blank as the nearby wall by his own doing, making his outburst impotent.

He pressed into her personal space and she held fast. He came closer still and she did not move—so close, she could hear him grinding his teeth in frustration behind his mask.

She could do nothing but stare straight forward, and so did not see the twitch of his fingers, could not anticipate his hands flying up to her face. It startled her, cold shock pouring down her spine like ice water as his fingertips shot in between the Cage's metal legs to dig into her skin.

In all the years he'd kept her in the Cage, no one had laid a hand on her in fury. The only touch she'd known was Gerome's maddening, caring caresses. It was both terrifying and exhilarating to feel his nails pressing half-moons into her cheeks. She'd nearly forgotten what it felt like to have adrenaline burst through her body, preparing her for a fight—a fight she could not engage in, to be sure, but still, it was a thrill.

And then there was magic in her mind, digging through both her conscious, open thoughts and her deeply held secrets.

He had yet to notice most of the walls he'd placed in her mind were gone. Had yet to realize she remembered the day of the Fallen's murder and who she really was.

"Of course," he said suddenly. "The Kairopath."

And then they were moving again, winding back through the keep, though this time their trajectory took them down, down, down into the castle's bowels.

The three of them alighted at the end of a spiral staircase and were presented with the gaping maw of the varger gallery. Hintosep, of course, hadn't stepped foot inside since the day she'd revealed her betrayal, and from the way Gerome swallowed harshly behind her, she was sure he hadn't either.

As they crossed the threshold and the bottle-barkers within stirred in their sculpted glass cases, Gerome swooped past her, falling into step directly behind Absolon. She assumed he didn't want to look at her. She hoped he felt the ghost of her teeth on his windpipe just as she felt an echo of his warm blood sliding down her throat. She might have been captured and Caged that day, but in her book it had been a triumph. Her only regret was that she hadn't sunk her incisors deep enough, that she hadn't been able to rend enough flesh from Gerome's throat to put him down for good.

Hintosep knew she wouldn't have been able to kill Absolon then. She hadn't intended to. His time was coming. Krona and her company would see to that.

The gallery was dim, as usual, and the Savior made no move to activate the lamps overhead. She was disappointed to see that every pedestal was occupied—the varger that Krona had released were bottled once again.

Each monster vibrated in its prison as they passed, and a slight ringing—high-pitched—reverberated through the room as the glass bottles began to sing.

Absolon ignored them, aiming for the rear of the gallery, to the Reliquary, where the seven artifacts were kept when not in use.

He brushed aside the black curtain that separated the two rooms, and the three of them alighted in a soft space filled with gauzy hangings. The delicate drapery of reds, pinks, and purples fluttered in the slightest of air currents, nearly aglow with the light streaming down from high above. The light was not natural, nor was it from enchantment.

It came from a different kind of engineering entirely.

They stepped through the fabrics—each brushing over Hintosep like a gentle hand in benediction—to reach the dais at the Reliquary's rear. There, a carved relief of tortured figures held the artifacts aloft, each on display in their own specially fashioned setting when not in use.

Each artifact was an enchantment of immense power, with aspects of the five magics uniquely woven together to create an object unrivaled in function. Though they were all different, the end goal of their usage was the same: control.

The Eye, the Song, the Wing, the Teeth, the Rage, the Fruit, and the Cage.

Absolon reached for the Teeth, as Hintosep expected he might.

They gleamed a sadistic silver on their cushion, a disembodied smile that looked ready to snap off any fingers that got too close. As Absolon reached for them, she found herself wishing they *would*.

The Teeth were made of three nested sets of not-quite-human-looking silver jaws, bound together on the end of a gauntlet. Inside the gauntlet's fist, different levers controlled which set of teeth could extend out on their long, snakelike proboscis. The internal set was tiny, the jaw smaller than an infant's. The middle set was the closest to a human adult's in both shape and size. The largest, outermost set looked the sharpest, the most pointed, and was accompanied by two long saber-teeth swooping downward from the top of the jaw.

When all three sets of the Teeth were used in tandem, they could tear through reality—similar to how she'd torn through Gerome's throat. She'd witnessed their joint usage once; the cataclysmic effect of all three sets clamping down together, seemingly on nothing, but then pulling, tearing, twisting space and time until Absolon had torn open a gaping wound.

A wound that had *bled*—its shimmering, mercuric purple-black drops evaporating as soon as they'd splattered against the ground.

On the other side of that wound had been a place purely of Absolon's imagination. A small pocket-reality born of his brain, unstable and unable to abide anything from their world burrowing inside it except the wielder of the Teeth himself. From that pocket, Absolon had pulled creatures—abominations that would be his guard dogs, monsters that could not be made living by even the most advanced Physiopaths, living things held together by will and magic rather than physics or biology.

The ground on which reality had bled was made unwalkable, and the wound in the world had remained open—a permanent scar with a constant howling beyond.

No one—not even Absolon, as far as she knew—had ever gone back to the place reality had been rent. He'd bricked it away, covered it over—turned it into another dead crag in the icefield.

Hintosep had no reason to believe he wished to create another wound like it.

For a moment, she wondered if the artifact could be used to tear around the bits of the Cage burrowed into her—if the Teeth could bite away just enough flesh to free her without killing her.

A useless thought. A silly whim.

Absolon slipped the gauntlet on, turned his hand palm up and pulled down harshly on the hidden levers. The outermost jaws sprang open, revealing the middle set stretching out on its long neck, then he pulled again and the smallest set slid forward between the already outstretched maw. Their full extension gave the impression of a silent-yet-echoing scream before Absolon made them all retract suddenly, as though the improbable creature was, nauseatingly, swallowing its own tongues.

She waited, then, to be gutted. She knew the smallest set of teeth could be used to rearrange her insides, to *implant* something there, if he so desired. This was how it was used by its Possessor to educate young Thalo; their small bodies turned into hideaways. Keys tucked next to lungs so that every breath would remind them of secrets, a blade carefully positioned next to a heart to teach them their Possessor held their life in their hands—even a worm slid into a gut to pointedly convey how life lives on life, that *parasitic* and *symbiotic* are really not all that divorced from each other.

Absolon could use Hintosep's body to conceal something, or he could bury a seed in her gut and watch a magically infused plant destroy her from the inside out as it grew. She could be made to incubate something against her will, or become just another box for his many enchanted tools, filled up to bursting.

He could even choose to hide a mind inside her, and the Teeth would ensure that her body did not reject it.

And yet he did not turn on her. Did not use the Teeth on her as they'd been used on so many initiates, to make them understand that their bodies belonged to the Order, not themselves.

"Come," he said once again, this time laying a hand on her shoulder and squeezing ever so slightly. Gerome grasped her just the same on the other side. She felt a strange rush, a disconcerting whirling, and then she was stumbling on the spot, kept upright only by their hands.

It took her a moment to realize they'd jumped. Not far. They were still in the keep. Into a high-ceilinged storage room not much bigger than her cell. It had been recently cleaned out, its interior dusted off. One lone, empty pedestal sat to the side, a replica of the Teeth's cushioned nesting atop.

Instead of turning toward the pedestal, Absolon moved to face an empty expanse of wall.

Ah, so it was the middle set he was after.

Extending the gauntlet once more, he released the second set of teeth and let them bite against the wall, opening and closing the jaws swiftly before dragging them across the stone—the metallic scrape echoing through the room, making Hintosep wish she could, at the very least, cover her ears and block out the obnoxious whine of it.

Though he clearly dragged metal across stone, in the gauntlet's wake a rift opened, the edge of it curling and buckling in the Teeth's grasp like a curtain drawn aside.

The strong, humid spice of the jungle wafted through the opening, along with birdsong, frog chirps, and the deep burring of some hoofed mammal, as though Absolon had simply opened a window into one of Asgar-Skan's rainforests.

This gateway had been created through similar magic as a Kairomancer's jumps, except the portal would remain open for as long as Absolon willed it, leaving a burrow, like one a worm could carve through an apple. Or through an initiate's insides.

Which meant that, unlike a Kairomancer's jumps, the magic wielder did not have to be present for someone else to use the doorway. She assumed he must have a reason to create such a tear. And a plan for protecting this room—the keep—from being breached.

Absolon turned back, gesturing the other two forward. "We will check on each god, fortify their bonds, and be ready."

Gerome used the Cage to prod Hintosep forward. Before she stepped through into the waiting trees beyond, Absolon pinned her with his gaze, then gently lowered his mask with his free hand.

Gerome gasped, turned away, shielding his eyes out of respect.

But Hintosep knew this face. She'd known this face since she was young, in a time that he'd thought he'd wiped from her mind. Now, even if she'd been able, she would not have shied away from it.

His was such an average face. One that could get lost in a crowd, especially in some place like Lutador or Winsrouen, where the native people were lighter of skin and paler of crown. Mousy brown hair that curled slightly, brown eyes, firm jaw with a weak chin. Not unpleasing to the eyes, nor overly attractive. He was what he was: simply a man. A man whose lifespan had stretched for centuries upon centuries, though he didn't look past forty.

She wanted to begrudge him that youthful look. So many others had withered and grown old while he remained constant. That was the point, of course. He wasn't simply a constant for his own sake, he insisted. He was a constant for Arkensyre's sake.

She herself had allowed excess age to touch her when she didn't have to. She could have taken the time injections he'd offered her earlier, retained her youth from the Introdus. But she hadn't wanted to *waste* the time then—having no concept of how much he'd take *and take and take* from the people in the years to come.

He was only doing this—revealing himself to her now—because he wanted to invoke familiarity. A sense of personal history that only they two shared.

They were all that was left from the beginning, after all.

Them and the gods.

"What you have attempted to ruin, I will make right," he promised. "Perhaps I put too much on you, expected too much. If you were angry with me, you should have taken it out on me. Instead, you chose to inflict your rage upon the Valley. Shameful. But I will fix it." He replaced his mask. "*I will fix it.*"

With that, he shoved her through, into Asgar-Skan.

5

KRONA

Krona's comings and goings from Mirthhouse in a swirl of nothingness were so frequent now as to be commonplace. She, Avellino, and Juliet alighted in the dining room, just in front of the rear doors that led out into the gardens. No one batted an eye, stepping around the magically appearing bodies as though stepping around a darting house cat—with only the slightest of hitches in their stride.

She never failed to wonder at that in and of itself—how quickly awe morphed into banality. How swiftly sensational power bled into the ordinary. She could still draw awe out of someone who'd only been with the rebellion a few months, but to those who'd known her from her kairopathy's start, her magic had lost its shock value.

There was comfort there—in knowing that perhaps one day everyone in the Valley would have such a reaction, that they themselves would have such capabilities at their fingertips.

The safe house was, per usual, bustling with activity. There was little time to rest these days, little time to pause.

The first floor of the mansion was massive, with two large wings of rooms framing the central gathering place, which was itself split in two by a massive stone hearth, with the kitchen and dining area on one side and a lounge on the other. A second-floor balcony lined the living space below, branching off into yet more second-floor bedrooms and offices.

Mounted animal trophies adorned the walls, and the sconces and chandeliers were made up of antlers, which gave the whole place the impression of a hunting lodge.

They were indeed on the hunt these days, but not for anything so pedestrian as deer or bear.

Tray stood over the dining table, the leaves of it flipped over to reveal the etched map they used for conjurations—the crude spells that allowed them to locate individual varger, whether they were running wild or trapped in glass in one of the city-states' vaults. Malek—one of their best varg hunters, a curly haired youth from Xyopar, the one whose conjuration had so recently failed—stood next to him, along with Nannette, an elderly Marrakevian woman whose merger with her own varg had left her worn-down and housebound.

Krona normally wouldn't have let someone of such advanced years and failing health partake in a hunt, but Nannette was the rare overlooked Cryptopath.

She'd remained with her family instead of being swept off to the Savior's keep. As such, she was the best at administering conjurations—at discovering such hidden truths.

It seemed the three of them were trying again, with Nannette trailing a potion-soaked cloth across the full expanse of the map while Tray assisted.

After sending Avellino and Juliet off to compile their reports, Krona drew closer to the map, only to spot the little fairy lights laid out as they were before, with the varger of Malek's immediate relations placed around the Valley, largely centering in Xyopar, while his own light hovered uselessly in the pocket of land just south of Lutador's border.

Malek's shoulders slumped, and Krona patted his back in comradery.

"We thought, maybe if we used my pa's line as the tracer instead of Ma's . . ." he said, disappointed. Then his face hardened. "I've helped hunt plenty of varger for other people. It's *my* turn."

Patience was not one of Malek's virtues.

In a foul mood, he stomped away, and Nannette scurried to comfort him as Tray wiped the map clean again. "Did you three fare any better?" he asked Krona.

"We found it. But don't get too excited, we couldn't breach the inner sanctum."

"Not *yet*," he said. "Nothing wrong with baby steps. Progress is progress. With the gods, with reuniting people and their varger, with—" He paused suddenly. "With De-Lia."

Not long ago, the two of them had completed their mission on Vault Hill—had finally been able to retrieve the blood pen with De-Lia's blood still encrusted along its insides.

Tray had integrated himself easily over the past two years, was now as much a member of the rebellion as any other—at ease, solid as a rock in his new role. When the time came, De-Lia would find him an easy touchstone for her newly re-founded life.

Krona knew she herself had changed too much since De-Lia was lost to provide any sort of grounding for her sister—both physically and spiritually. De-Lia would undoubtedly ask some of the same questions Tray had: *Are you a spirit? Are you alive?*

She'd need Tray.

Over the past year, Krona had thought about collecting their maman as well. Not just for De-Lia's sake, of course.

Krona had watched Acel take care of De-Lia's horse, Allium, from a distance for years now, spying on them from the edges of the Iyendar estate. And while her maman did seem sad at times, she also seemed . . . less *burdened*. Once, while strolling through the garden, Acel had smiled at Stellina—the Chief Magistrate's teenaged granddaughter—brightly, in a way she hadn't smiled at Krona in years.

It had cracked something in Krona's heart—made her *jealous*, of all things, of a child. And yet, Krona realized that Acel had grieved and *grown*. She hadn't been able to do that after their papa had died. She hadn't been able to after De-Lia had died. Krona wanted to resent the idea that *her* assumed death had finally closed the loop for her mother, allowing her to let go, but, ultimately, she wanted her maman, above all things, to be happy. Maybe she wasn't there yet, but she was healing in Krona's absence in a way she never could have in her presence.

Krona's family was fractured, scattered. But Tray was right, they were making progress on all fronts. Eventually they'd all be together again.

"Have you seen Thibaut?" she asked him.

Tray appeared strangely caught off guard by the question. "Not—not recently."

"Could you send him to the war room if you do?"

"Of course."

She raised an eyebrow at him, but he already had his head down again, cleaning up the messy remains of the crude spell, so she left him to it.

On the way to the war room, she noted Hintosep's katar was not in its proper place on the mantel. She tucked that away for inquiry later, after she'd written up her report on the mission's findings.

An ethereal tug on her bone spurs drew her attention up to the stairs. Abby—Sebastian and Melanie's five-year-old—peeked at her through the decorative slats of the railing. Krona curled a finger at zhim, then pointed toward the war room. Zhe nodded—a determined look on zhur plump little face. Hurrying down the stairs, zhe flung zhur arms around one of Krona's legs, hugging her close. Krona ruffled Abby's curls before making a show of striding forward while the child still clung, letting out an exaggerated grunt as though laboring to lift a great weight.

In truth, Abby was getting big for these games. Krona would miss them when zhe outgrew them.

The child giggled and let zhurself be hauled forward, toward the large room.

The suite used to be Hintosep's base of operation, her office. It was here she'd lain out their plan for sneaking into the keep to steal the children, and though Krona had fitted herself in between the remnants of Hintosep, she'd never been comfortable fully making it her own. The Thalo woman's presence was everywhere. The shelves and bookcases were heavy with her trinkets and tomes, the broad planning table was still laden with her scrolls, and the drawers in the stately desk still carried the essence of the various tonics and spices and perfumes she'd kept there.

The ghost of the former Orchestrator, the former Guardian, was everywhere in this house, and Krona had no desire to drive it off. Now, besides an office and war room—with a large, heavy desk on one side and the planning table on the other—it was also a shrine.

In more ways than one.

Emotion lay on a wooden platform constructed especially for zhim, under the far wall where the room's expansive windows lay. Hazy light filtered down between the midnight-blue curtains, the smoke from prayer candles still swirling though they'd been blown out not long before Krona's arrival. All around, excess candle stubs and remnants of offerings crowded the plinth, like one might leave at a shrine of the five: strands of dried berries and nuts, small bundles of herbs and flowers, glass coins and shiny stones. Few of their ranks came from noble families, and even fewer had brought any wealth with them, but every last gemstone they had had been placed alongside the crystalline body, whether loose or set.

The corpse was small by god standards. Or, at least, as Krona had always pictured the gods in her mind. Avellino said the Unknown was *stories* tall—a behemoth of vaguely human form.

In contrast, Emotion was no colossus. Zhe was perhaps twelve feet crown to toe. So . . . *manageable* as compared to the former image in her mind.

And yet, still a giant next to someone so fundamentally human as Krona.

She wondered what the others might look like. If the differences between the Unknown and Emotion were anything to go by, each would be unique and wonderous in their own right.

Emotion's body was encased in a thick layer of clear crystal, and zhur head was not so much a head as a bare bird skull; one with a sturdy horn that curled back in on itself atop the long, sharp beak. From the eye sockets grew clusters of amethyst crystals, and across the beak and its horn were deeply etched filigree designs. Zhur fingers were elongated—the nails themselves made of yet more amethyst, and zhur skin shifted hues from pale violet at zhur fingertips up into deep eggplant purple at the upper arm. That rich purple, echoing the most stunning amethyst, persisted across zhur shoulders and up zhur neck.

Amethyst. So much amethyst.

Enchanted amethyst held admiration.

As a Regulator, Krona had seen people wear enough of it to bend their emotions toward obsession, fixation.

People often wore rapturestones to religious services. But now, having stared down at Emotion countless times, she couldn't fathom why coterie-goers didn't drape themselves in admirationstones.

Both Krona and the little one paid homage to the dead god, cupping their hands in the sign of the Valley. A pang reverberated through Krona's chest, as it did every time she stood here. A knot of loss, of longing. She'd thought she would have gotten used to it by now—knowing that two of the Five were gone, dead. But it struck her afresh all the same.

Perhaps it was because it felt unnatural for Krona to visit a body instead of sand. But there was no burning a god, and that wasn't Emotion's tradition anyway; in Xyopar, bodies were left to the desert winds, hot sun, and frigid nights. They were mummified by the elements, and displayed on great precipices or clustered together inside caves. The living visited great necropolises—cities just for the dead.

When she glanced down at Abby, zhe looked far too solemn for such a young child. Serious, yet bright-eyed, Krona often found herself—sometimes in the small, sleepless hours of the morning—imagining not a different life for herself, but a different life for Abby. Zhe'd been through much, and carried such a weight. Zhe was like no one else alive—a full Physiopath, with all the development of zhur power still ahead—and because of that could not simply have a childhood like any other. Krona could not ignore Abby's significance to their cause—the freedom of the Valley—simply because she would have preferred to leave a child to their innocence.

Krona retrieved her log book from the desk before settling in for one of their ongoing sessions, sitting herself cross-legged on the floor in the middle of the tightly woven Asgar-Skanian rug. The position made it easier for Abby to reach her spurs. With practiced deftness, Krona removed her shirt, leaving her in just her chest bindings, and pulled the long strands of her braids forward over her dark shoulder, leaving the protruding bones unimpeded.

Abby took up zhur usual position behind Krona, gently tracing the spurs with zhur tiny fingers, humming to zhurself, sensing things about Krona's body she herself could not.

Zhe was the reason Krona could move any part of the spurs, was the reason they were jointed at all and the sharp ends of them not permanently pointed at her own throat. It had taken Abby nearly a year of focused work to figure out how to joint the top-most sections of the bone, and then how to create internal ligaments that would allow Krona's mind conscious access to their movement.

Abby wasn't their only Physiopath at the safe house. And of course, Krona could have made her way to any number of other safe houses in their network looking for the most skilled Physiopath to press into her personal service. But Krona wanted to give this task to Abby. Zhe was the only Physiopath they had who'd never been severed from magic at all. Abby had no varg to remerge with, nothing to reclaim. Zhur abilities could be nurtured and trained from their beginnings, and Krona thought it important to see to the child's magical education as best she could. After all, it was possible that Abby wasn't just the only living, unsevered Physiopath, but perhaps the first unharmed Physiopath in *millennia*.

They still had little knowledge of how the process that disconnected them from their magic might dilute their powers—take away something that could never be reclaimed. Abby deserved to reach zhur full potential—a potential perhaps out of reach for everyone else under the Savior's rule.

Krona tried to focus on her reports while Abby worked, keeping everything precise and factual, attempting to keep her thoughts from trailing into *guilt* and *want* and the anxieties that came with leadership—of being responsible for everyone under this roof, and many roofs beyond. Juliet and Avellino each returned in time with their own reports, and a few others came and went, asking questions or paying respect to Emotion. Krona successfully buried her stray thoughts beneath her work, and it wasn't until a warmth glided down her spine—as though Abby was pouring a soft trickling of bathwater onto her from above—that she allowed herself to think once again of herself.

Something *new* stirred in her back—new nerves lighting up, new ligaments growing and pulling taut. She gasped softly when she moved the muscles of her upper back and the spurs shifted in a new way. The entire structure on her left *flexed*, like the bones of a hand.

Krona's chest swelled with sudden excitement, sudden joy. Zhe'd done it—the little one had done it! She could feel the way the bones now twisted, folded back down, like a wing. She could finally—*finally*—tuck one of the structures away.

It was the one thing she'd longed for since the Savior had cursed her with these. She hadn't wished them away so much as she'd wished for control. The ability to regain her bodily autonomy by having the structures obey her. To have her flesh and blood belong to *her* and no one else.

It was such a simple thing, freedom of movement. Others had suggested she saw the bones off—even Melanie had said it was possible, and safe to do. That would have allowed her to sleep on her back, at least—a feat she'd been unable to achieve for years. But somehow removing them hadn't felt like the thing to do.

It wasn't what she needed.

Someone else might have been satisfied cutting them away, but for Krona, the only way to block out the memory of the Savior twisting her, using her own body against her, was to feel the bones *reclaimed*.

And Abby, *zhe'd done it*.

Abby clapped zhur hands, and Krona bit her tongue, not wanting to interrupt the child's focus, but internally Krona *soared*. Her lip trembled, her chest swelled, and her emotions suddenly felt too big for her body. She hadn't realized what this would mean to her if Abby could accomplish it, how much *relief* and *joy* and *triumph* would move through her in the moment.

When she felt the same sensations in her right spurs, the dam broke. Krona couldn't hold back anymore. Abby jumped for joy, and Krona dropped her face into her hands, letting out a light sob.

Confused, the child knelt by her side in an instant. "Does it hurt? Did I hurt you?"

Raising her head with happy tears in her eyes, Krona whirled and scooped Abby into a hug. "No, you did so well. You fixed me," she assured zhim.

Krona flexed and flapped what were now more akin to a small pair of bone wings than curved, gnarled spurs. She could raise them up and curl them forward like claws, or fold them down and stow them against her spine.

She had a renewed sense of freedom, and couldn't help the hope that flooded her chest.

Krona dried her eyes and sat, clinging to Abby, for a long few minutes. Her happy reverie was eventually interrupted by another hardy knock at the door.

She gave the child a pat on the back, took a steadying breath, then stood and ordered, "Come in."

Mandip swung himself through the open door, holding on to the jamb like it was the only thing keeping him upright. "They're back!" he announced with a grin. He was out of breath, brown skin bright, rosy-cheeked, his mop of black curls ruffled, like he'd just sprinted a mile.

"Who's back?" Krona demanded.

The grin slid from the would-have-been Grand Marquis's face. He composed himself, straightening his spine, automatically dredging up his noble formality in response to her tone. "The hunting party," he explained, voice laced with confusion, dark brows drawing together. "I thought—?"

Just like that, her floating sense of optimism deflated, and her stomach sank. "He *didn't*," she gasped.

The missing katar.

Of course.

She should have guessed.

"What? He said you knew." Mandip ran a nervous hand through his hair. "He said you—"

"We both know better than to take Thibaut at his word," she said sternly.

Hunting parties were never to leave without her. Never.

Suddenly Sebastian—Abby's father—was in the doorway as well, tall, dark, well pressed as always. She could feel him trying to calm her before she even said anything, the cool tendrils of his emotive magic pressing against her like the gentle currents of a stream.

"*Don't,*" she chided him, moving toward the door, her new wings all but forgotten.

Krona may have been the first, but Sebastian had been the second person to remerge with a varg. Knowing he was an Emotiopath, that his varg had to be a love-eater, had been key.

Steadily, they were building an army. An army of fen-wielding magic users to match the Savior's army of Thalo. But tracking down an individual's lost magic, healing their being by returning their varg, was still difficult and dangerous these three years on.

Morgane had dropped into a coma from the strain and physical trauma; it had been two years and she had yet to reawaken. Jorge had lost a foot—had it eaten by his own inner beast before the two of them could be locked together and become one.

Others had *died*. Friends had been lost on hunts to teeth and claws, and friends had been killed during attempted mergers with bottle-barkers who'd instead eaten them from the inside out. Not everyone wanted to risk death in exchange for power. People like Mandip and Juliet had little desire to track down their missing magic, and for good reason.

As dangerous as all varger were, most of those who'd died attempting to rejoin had been trying to rejoin with pack leaders and regain their teliopathy.

Pack leaders were the largest, most intelligent of all varger. The rarest only in the sense that they were smart enough to elude detection and capture while still eating their fill. They were the most dangerous to stalk on a hunt. The most likely to kill their own hosts.

Thibaut's varg was a pack leader.

She pushed past Mandip and Sebastian back into the great room, fighting off the fear that wanted to cut through her—sharp like a blade. The intensity of it was severe and anxiety-inducing in a way she hadn't experienced in a long while. Not since confronting the Savior.

A shiver racked her, and she had to brace herself against the nearest wall as her magic seeped from her veins, quickly coalescing beside her, manifesting.

The creature kept herself diminutive, the size of a dog, ceding to the space around her. She pushed her scaled, horselike head into Krona's palm, fluffing her wings.

"Yes, I know," Krona said, patting the fen's insistent snout.

Ninebark, Krona had named her. After a common flower, just as De-Lia had named hers. It was also a private joke, given that her fen had eight legs.

Unlike varger, which more or less all shared a similar shape, fenri manifested uniquely—a reflection of their host, of the one from which they'd been cleaved. Krona had seen two more with wings and horselike bodies, similar to Ninebark, though they only boasted four legs and one had a lion's head and one a bird's. She'd seen a fur-tuffed snake, and a fire-ringed fox, and a bulbous insect. Even a floating rainbow-scaled fish.

No two were exactly alike.

Ninebark only manifested uncalled when Krona needed extra comfort or emergency aid. It wasn't difficult to discern why she'd untangled herself from Krona now.

The hunting party burst through the main doors, bringing cold air and a light drift of snow with them. They chattered brightly as they began to take off their gloves and capes. Everyone was flush-faced and grinning, but their smiles fell and they all backed away as soon as they saw Krona and Ninebark approaching.

Before she could confront Thibaut, though—who was set low, hunched over his boots in the entryway—Melanie, her loose brown curls a wild mane around her head despite her attempt to pin them behind her ears, slid between Krona and her target, holding out a staying hand. "Krona, *Krona,* I know what you're going to—"

"I expect this kind of thing from *him,*" Krona bit out, punctuating the last word with a thrust of her chin in Thibaut's direction. He had yet to look at her. "But you? Agreeing to go off, to *let* him—"

"I'm a grown man," Thibaut grumbled from his knelt position.

"One who can't heed a simple order to save his life," Krona snapped back. "We *agreed.* We agreed you wouldn't try to remerge until we'd uncovered the gods. Juliet, Avellino, and—"

She stopped, realization forcing her tongue to stumble. She spun, looking for them. "Juliet!" she shouted.

Instead, Tray came running.

"Krona, we—"

"You all planned this," she hissed in incredulous disbelief. "We were nearly eaten by a treehouse and Juliet *still* stalled me so—"

"So he could choose for himself," the songstress said, sliding sidesaddle down the banister from the second floor, now changed into one of her fluffiest skirts, tulle and crinoline everywhere. Mandip met her at the bottom, offering his hand and helping her land lightly on her feet. "Believe me, darling, we didn't plan this particular subterfuge—"

"Betrayal," Krona grumbled.

"—lightly. You *can* be wildly overprotective."

Krona made to protest, but the truth of it snapped her mouth closed again. She sighed deeply, pinching the bridge of her nose. "At least you came back with all of your fingers and toes."

Everyone around her stiffened.

"Yeah . . . about that." Thibaut finally looked up, raising his pale right hand, revealing why he'd been fumbling with the laces of his boots for so long.

It was heavily bandaged. In a misshapen sort of way.

Beside her, Ninebark whimpered.

Krona could feel her face shift through a multitude of expressions.

Damn him. The idiot.

Clearly having seen Krona's irritation blossom into full worry, Melanie ducked out of the way as Krona rushed forward. "Be careful. His ribs," she warned lightly.

Krona's hands went to Thibaut's boots, working them free for him as he tried to reassure her it wasn't anything to get riled up about. But he hissed through his teeth when he sat up straight, and there was still blood seeping through the bandage on his hand—despite it being thoroughly attended to by their best healer, Melanie.

"It's just a pinkie," Thibaut said, trying to brush it off. "Who needs a pinkie anyway?"

Melanie cleared her throat.

"All right, and a few knuckles gone on my ring finger," he admitted. "I gave myself quite a mauling, but it's done now."

Krona tossed his boots aside. "You could have been killed," she said through clenched teeth, straightening his chemise, his jacket. Fussing, she knew she was fussing.

"And yet I still reside amongst the living."

"Not for lack of trying," someone in the party mumbled.

Thibaut pointed over Krona's shoulder. "You, Magnus, hush." He stilled Krona's fidgeting hands, grasping them against his chest. "I'm home now. If my ribs weren't in such a state, I'd demand you carry me bridal-style to our bed chambers."

"Oh, you come home in pieces and expect me to *attend to you*, do you?"

"You could play the doting wife, and me a soldier back from the war."

"Doting wife?"

"I said *play,* dearest."

His eyes were wide, earnest. Reassurance and love were clearly writ across his features. He understood her worry, her fear. They both knew she'd been unfairly coddling him—putting off the hunt for his varg, always delaying with another excuse.

When she'd first figured out that Thibaut's magic was Knowledge, she almost hadn't told him. She'd almost decided to hide it from him—to pretend she didn't have enough information to go on. She knew it was selfish, and unfair, and ultimately that was why she couldn't keep it a secret. But still, she'd put this off because she couldn't stand the thought of losing him.

Of course, that was exactly why the frustrating man had taken matters into his own hands when her back was turned.

Gently, she cupped his stubbled chin, pursing her lips in a stern frown as he gave her a soft smile.

She knew he didn't really begrudge her overprotectiveness. She loved him dearly—the idiot—and she tended to lose the people she loved.

Even so, she should probably be angrier with him—with *them*—for deceiving her. They'd betrayed the agreed-upon order of things, undermined her authority. And yet, it didn't feel that way. They'd done what they'd done not just out of love, but principle.

Thibaut's varg had been roaming close to Mirthhouse lately. They'd all seen the opportunity, and there was no reason to pass it by.

"The merger was a success, then?" she asked softly.

In answer, he brought their foreheads together, holding her close with his good hand, and for a moment the world disappeared around them. Krona's mind was filled with warmth and light.

"I can hear your thoughts, if you let me," Thibaut whispered.

And soon there was a distant call.

Not exactly Thibaut's *voice* in her head, but a sense of him. She wondered if he'd be able to speak inside her mind like Hintosep could, one day, or if that clandestine communication was the realm of Cryptopaths exclusively.

The sensations in her mind were similar to when Hintosep had invaded her thoughts, yet somehow distinctly different. That had always felt intrusive—oppressive. Like the more she struggled against it, the easier it was for Hintosep to use it. It was a thing her mind could be *made* to listen to. This felt more like a gentle give and take. Like someone asking for a door to be opened, rather than forcing it open. His abilities were the inverse of a Cryptopath's: she could hide secrets from him, but openly share knowledge.

The warmth and light grew.

He couldn't feed her feelings—that was the sole realm of an Emotiopath, someone like Sebastian. Instead, she could feel him offering sense memories, knowledge they shared about each other. He brought up reminiscences, experiences. Little intimacies. Touches. Tastes.

She let out a shaky breath when a particular memory sent a heady rush of lust straight to her core.

Smarmy bastard.

Quickly, she pulled back. "You don't get to sweet-talk your way out of this. I'm angry with you."

"I didn't say a *word,*" he replied softly, voice rich and gravel-filled.

Krona shook her head. "Fuck you." She laughed, trying to stay cross but failing miserably.

"Yes, please," he replied with a wink.

"At the very least I'm getting you somewhere where I can help heal that hand and get a look at your ribs," she said, standing, crossing her arms, not offering to help him up.

"Close enough for me," he proclaimed happily, hopping up with a wince, but doing his best to hide it.

She took him by the forearm and led him out of the foyer, through the milling people, and over to the staircase. Ninebark chased them, growing more ethereal with each galloping step until she became a blanket of faint light that snaked up Krona's spine, melding back into place.

Krona intended to get him to their room, behind closed doors, but found she couldn't wait. Upon the landing she grabbed his face and kissed him forcefully, backing him to the nearest wall.

In turn, he let out an undignified squeak, but that only elicited a giggle. She was angry and relieved and so in love all at once. "You stupid, stupid man," she chided, the heat in her voice laced with fondness.

He had the wind-worn bouquet of the forest all over him, with his usual bright spice beneath.

"I should put you in your place," she whispered against his lips, pressing up against him.

"Mmm," he agreed in a gravelly hum. "And that's in our bed, is it not?"

She shook her head affectionately at his cheekiness. "You're incorrigible. Show me more," she breathed, leaning her forehead against his again. "Share with me."

A sunset from atop one of Lutador's tallest buildings. His first taste of Marrakevian sticky rice. Juliet, Avellino, and Abby in the garden, all giggling as they shooed away wild rabbits. Mandip flushing at one of Thibaut's cruder jokes.

Then, music. In a dark place, a fast beat tapped out on something tin, with heavy shadows flickering across the walls and low ceiling as dancers twirled in a circle in front of a fire. It was cold and damp, smelled faintly of piss, and yet the sense of *knowing* she had about the place was deep and anything but repulsive. There was history here, family.

As she tried to descend further into the scene, it pulled away. Not fading gradually as the others had, but forcibly yanked, as if Thibaut had set the wrong thing in front of her—like it was a glass of moonshine when she'd ordered cherry cordial.

"Wait, what was that?"

He pulled back, twisting his lips as if he'd rather not say. Shooting his gaze to the floor, he admitted sheepishly, "The Dregs."

"Why did you take it away?"

"You don't want to see that."

"Where you came from?"

"It's not exactly glamorous."

"Are you under the impression I think you glamorous?" Krona tried to keep her tone teasing, but when his gaze flickered back up to hers, she realized this was no laughing matter. "Thibaut—"

"I know you're aware of my humble beginnings, but—"

"Humble doesn't equal shameful," she said quickly, firmly.

"Not all of my memories from there are happy."

"But that one was, wasn't it?"

"Yes."

She kissed him softly. "You don't have to hide such joys from me," she assured him, silently cursing every noble who'd ever said a cruel word about the Dregs in front of Thibaut.

A whole class of people delighted in pushing others to the fringes and then deriding them for being there. She could only imagine the number of times Thibaut had felt forced to laugh at a joke at his own expense, or to grit his teeth and nod along to protect his livelihood even as his people were disparaged.

She knew Thibaut had aspired to a life of luxury, had likely internalized much of the humiliation the rich anointed on the poor, and wished she could wash away that undeserved shame.

Perhaps it was best to change the subject.

She flexed her new wings as she pulled back, letting them fan out to their full extent, and his eyes went wide—big as saucers. "Your—your *bones*—"

"Abby did it," she said with a smile, and if her wings had feathers, she would have fluffed them. "Full range of motion." She let them twist and curl like fingers in demonstration.

Thibaut's eyes grew dark, lidded. He kissed her again. Slowly. *Thoroughly.* Deeply enough that she went weak in the knees.

"You are an amazing woman, you know that?" he said, voice low and rich.

"Trying to flatter yourself out of a punishment, are you?" she teased.

"Oh *no*," he declared, putting on an air of false scandalization. "I would *never* assume I could escape justice simply by appealing to your vanity, of course not. I expect to earn my pardon through carnal pleasures."

"You've bruised ribs and lost half your hand, will *nothing* cool your humors?"

"Not when it comes to you. Besides," he said, chipper, as they hurried on once again, finally reaching their door, "you'll help me close up the wounds and make those pesky bruises vanish. And then, since young Abby has tended so well to you, perhaps zhe can help restore a digit or two."

Their bedroom was a modest space—the two of them had little need for more. A narrow bed sat against one wall near the door, and not far from its foot stood a tall dresser. A changing screen, which had been ornate back in its day but had suffered much wear and tear in its life, blocked some of the direct light shining through their single window. The rug on the floor was filled with holes and made of cut-up old shifts. There was nothing ostentatious about the room, and, save for De-Lia's jaguar mask hanging on the wall, it was unadorned.

A small safe was hidden behind the changing screen, containing the bits of De-Lia's life-force that Krona had been able to snatch back over the years. The blood pen, along with the hourglass in which her sand was stored, and the enchanted journal with her writings.

Monkeyflower, her varg, was still contained in a life-sized glass jaguar jar, bricked into one of the shallow caverns beneath Mirthhouse.

Thoughts of De-Lia were never far from Krona's mind, but she batted them away like cobwebs now. Her days were so harried Krona felt like she barely had time to breathe—to pause—to stay perfectly present in any one moment before leaping to the next.

But Thibaut was good at getting her to *slow*, to simply exist with him for a time.

They gently undressed each other, Krona helping his wounds march forward through time as she uncovered them. A dark purple splotch low on his belly turned yellow then vanished beneath her sliding fingertips. An abrasion on his thigh was gone after a trail of her lips. She made him lie facedown on the bed and found all the tender spots along his spine before settling her palms around his sides, dragging them down his ribs to heal and titillate in turn.

She let his hand be, knowing Melanie would complain if she wasn't allowed to oversee the healing. Which was fine. She didn't need Thibaut's hands this evening.

Keeping him prone, she pinned his wrists above his head and straddled his hips, kissing across his neck and shoulders. He whined, halfheartedly trying to roll over so he could face her, but she simply smiled into his yellow hair, knowing he would ease into her command, allowing her to take her pleasure however she saw fit.

The sun sank below the horizon long before she allowed him out of bed again, and only because she'd taken her fill, satisfaction pouring through her like warm molasses. Sticky sweet.

They'd missed dinner. After throwing on their house coats, they trekked downstairs again, ignoring the single catcall leveled at them by Juliet.

"Subtlety never was her style," Thibaut said to Krona, while everyone else heartily ignored the singer's inappropriate outburst.

The two of them scrounged what they could from the large cauldron of soup cooling in the darkened hearth, Thibaut asking questions about *her* ill-advised afternoon adventures before wandering over to the dining room, where the leaflets of the etched map had once again been flipped and hidden.

Thibaut slid into a chair, wincing a little while Krona smirked. After she took up the seat next to him, they settled in to eat. After only a single bite, Thibaut suddenly went rigid, pausing with his spoon halfway to his mouth. His brows knitted together as he stared, shocked, into the middle distance.

"What?" Krona asked hurriedly, eyes darting in the direction of his dumbfounded stare like she might find a monster looming.

His spoon fell from his uninjured hand with a clang, splashing his soup and sending the scent of miso wafting into the air. Reaching out, he swept his palms across the table like he'd never touched polished wood before, disbelief coloring his features. "I—it's—" He couldn't force the words out.

"What is it?"

"It worked."

"What worked?"

He stood and slapped the middle of the table. "The conjurations. They *all* worked."

She furrowed her brow, her own soup forgotten. "What are you saying?"

"Those 'failed' conjurations weren't wrong. There—" He tapped a spot on the table firmly, on the backside of the etched map. "There is a varger nest beneath Arkensyre."

"How do you know?" she asked.

He looked at her pointedly. "Because I *Know,* with a capital *K*."

KRONA

Magic is like a brush in a painter's hand, Krona thought, *each artist wields it differently.*

Thibaut was not their first Teliopath, but he inferred information differently than both Rodrigo and Frasha. The two of them could read books with a touch, take in any written information wholesale by nothing more than simple proximity. Thibaut instead plucked information from the air—not from the writing on an object, but from the object itself.

"It's swirling all around us," he told Krona. "Knowledge seeps from the pores of everything. It's like a light haze in my mind, mostly. I can't get hold of it. But some of it thickens—some of it screams out for attention. It's like the residue of pneuma in the conjurations is calling to me."

Krona remained by his side while he stayed at the table with the map for the rest of the evening, even as Melanie came to check his wounds and summoned their most experienced Physiopath to see what could be done about his missing fingers.

Others periodically came and went, intrigued at the prospect of such a find. Occasionally, Thibaut demanded additional scrolls, other maps. They knew there was no way to access the nest in its immediate vicinity, so there had to be tunnels or caves. Some ingress they'd overlooked.

"How could there be a nest we don't know about?" Tray asked as he returned from the war room with a smattering of hand-bound notes.

"There's one varg for every person who's ever had their magic stolen by the Savior," Avellino said. "One for every person since *the beginning*."

"Millions, then."

"At *least*," Juliet said, flitting about with one of Hintosep's books in her hand (it didn't seem to have anything to do with geography or varger). "Think of how many people are born in Arkensyre every year, and then how long humans have been in the Valley. Though the early accountings are, to borrow an artist's term, *sketchy*, we've been here for thousands of years."

Krona considered. "The Borderswatch doesn't catch nearly enough every year to account for them, one to one," she said. "And the vaults would be overflowing even if they did. We should have realized." She sighed deeply, rubbed at her eyes. Though her tumble with Thibaut had eased her tense muscles, she still needed a proper rest to recover from the hazards of Knowledge's temple.

As the hours went on, the crowd in the dining room began to thin. Even as Krona's eyelids grew heavy, Thibaut remained fixated on solving the problem in a way she'd never seen before. He could be dogged and dedicated, of course—despite his usual air of flippancy—but above all he truly valued his beauty sleep. His access to magic had lit a fire in him. He behaved as though the secrets of the universe would be revealed to him any moment, if only he stared at the clues long enough.

Krona awoke with a start. She hadn't meant to fall asleep—couldn't remember falling asleep. She still sat at the table, slumped over, head cradled on her arms, which each now bore imprints of Arkensyre's rim from the etching. Most of the lights in the house had been doused. Only a single oil lamp sat flickering on the table itself.

But she was alone.

"Thibaut?"

He wouldn't have gone to bed and left her to develop a crick in her neck.

His chair was pulled out, various maps and books still strewn about, as though he'd left suddenly.

Taking up the lamp, she tiptoed into the kitchen, but it was empty. As was the living room. All the hallways were dark. The bustling of daylight hours had fit itself neatly into little rooms, leaving the main house as silent as the Lutadorian catacombs. She wondered if he'd gone out to speak with the guards on shift, but a small thump drew her attention to the war room.

Though she knew Mirthhouse intimately, there was still something unnerving about it in the night, and the sound she heard was not a beam popping or the walls settling. There was no reason for someone to be bumping around her office at this hour, and besides their fens, they had no pets to speak of.

The lantern light revealed the door ajar, and everything sat dark and still beyond. A swallowed sort of silence greeted her as she widened the gap, like the room itself was holding its breath. Behind the frosted glass of the globe, her single oil-born flame caught Emotion's crystal encasing immediately, the facets each stealing the light for their own purposes, bouncing it across the god's body, making it glow.

Standing between Krona and Emotion, cutting through the crystalline glare—swallowing up the light the way a thick cloud swallows up the moon—was a silhouetted figure. One she knew well.

But he was still. Too still.

"Thibaut?" she asked softly.

He didn't answer.

She strode farther in, raised the lantern, illuminating his pale face.

He stared straight through her, expression blank and haunting.

"*Thibaut!*" she demanded, spooked by his rigidity.

Thibaut flinched to the side, struck by her voice as surely as an open palm. He blinked, wide-eyed, and began to dither. "Wh-where—?"

Shaken, yet relieved, Krona took him by the uninjured hand. "Let's get you to bed."

Groggy as he was, Thibaut still latched on to Krona's unease. He held her close as they mounted the stairs and shut themselves in their room.

As he rid himself of his clothes, Krona stood by the door, leaning on it for support. "De-Lia was a sleepwalker," she reminded him. "It was worst at the end, when—"

"It's just the teliopathy," he said quickly, pulling his night shirt over his head. "Just my fen taking my feet places without me."

She nodded, pursing her lips.

"You're still discovering new things about your kairopathy every day," he reminded her. "You feel things sometimes that you can't explain. Things feel different sizes, you said. Like they're more or less than they seem. Fuller or thinner. I don't understand what that means, but I know it's just the magic working. Right? Same here."

It made sense—his body was simply adjusting to the reintegration.

The more they learned about magic, the more Krona realized they didn't understand. She used to think the rules surrounding it were clear-cut. Not *simple*, but easily digestible. Now she knew that enchantments themselves were just the fundamentals. Elementary creations. They were the equivalent of basic arithmetic, while this new, innate form was something beyond calculus—it was a brand-new area of mathematical study, one that would take years of pursuit in order to grasp.

And yet, the reminder of De-Lia's downward spiral left Krona on shaky ground. She took a deep breath, but her lungs hitched.

"Hey." He hurried to her side, cupped her cheek. "I'm all right."

She wanted to believe him.

But it happened again the next night.

And the next.

She found him in the same place every time, hovering near their dead god, his face devoid of expression, as though all thought had fled his body.

"You're going to have to chain me to the bed, I suppose, nothing else for it," he tried to tease after he'd awoken.

Truthfully, she was in no mood for jokes, but she attempted to lean into their well-worn bantering. "Maybe focusing so hard on finding an entrance to the nest is taxing what little brain power you had to begin with."

"Oh, har har," he said, mordant.

This time when they emerged from the war room, it was to a light from the kitchen and a tinkling bit of hushed laughter. Instead of heading straight to bed, they followed the sound, finding Juliet and Mandip sitting on the counter, having raided the icebox. They had their heads bent together and two spoons poised over one bowl, which could have held curd or jam or cream, it was difficult to tell from where Krona and Thibaut peeked at them from around the hearth.

It was a soft, quiet scene. Innocent and intimate. Full of affection.

The pair deserved their privacy. "Let's let them be," Krona whispered, and Thibaut nodded.

If they didn't protect moments of a little joy, a little peace, then what were they fighting for?

"There."

From high atop a Borderswatch blind just south of the Lutador–Asgar-Skan border, Krona and Thibaut turned their attention not outward at the mountain peaks that marked the edge of the Valley, but inward, to a desolated slip of land cradled by thick surrounding jungle. Along what used to be a corridor meant for the failed railway, trenches now scarred the land. Long pieces of iron, once meant to ferry travelers from one city-state to the other, now barred them as part of a makeshift wartime wall.

Copses of trees had been burnt or cut down, smudging the landside brown and black. The bodies of both people and horses were piled about—one heap roaring with fire. Luckily the winds took the smoke to the east, away from Krona and Thibaut's vantage point.

A vast field of moment-mines stretched from one end of the front line to the other, with soldiers from the Winsrouen incursion sniping at the joint Asgar-Skan and Lutadorian forces from the south, afraid to advance farther for fear of stepping on a mine and getting picked off as easily as targets at a practice range.

Through her spyglass, Krona saw one man—war-crazed—break rank and charge.

The guns that used to only be handled by the likes of superior guards, like those on Vault Hill, had heavily proliferated since the start of the war, and their range and accuracy had increased by violent measures. Bullets whizzed by the sprinting soldier, and mud and dirt from the upturned field splashed across his black-and-white uniform as he went.

He managed a hundred yards before his foot found a mine.

The soldier froze, locked in time.

A hailstorm of bullets followed.

He was already dead, time and space simply needed to catch up.

Shifting her focus away from the doomed man, Krona remained attentive to the mission at hand.

"There?" she asked, following Thibaut's outstretched finger to the Winsrouen side of the minefield.

"I can't pinpoint it any more precisely. But somewhere near the trenches, for certain."

"I'm not jumping us into a warzone without exact coordinates."

"Well, then we likely need a non-magical way of getting them," he countered.

A small groan emanated from behind them. Krona, unbothered, turned swiftly and snapped her fingers, putting the Borderswatch sentinel they'd "borrowed" the blind from back in another limited time bubble—much like the ones the mines created.

"Perhaps it's time we called in a favor with another displaced Basu," she said.

⁂

Mandip's brother, General Adhar Basu, struck a commanding figure in the field tent. Though the two of them were twins, their likeness was simply fraternal, and as Krona observed their clandestine meeting from the shadows, shielded temporarily by Avellino's growing cryptopathic skills, she was struck by how the brothers' time apart had emphasized their few similarities.

"I thought the Demon of the Passes would have sent you my way sooner," Adhar said, voice deep, his hair and beard both shorn in a close-cropped military styling.

"We try not to interfere with the city-state to city-state conflict," Mandip said after hugging his brother, stepping back to take a square-shouldered stance of formality. He'd let his dark curls grow out, and he usually presented as meeker at Mirthhouse. But here, with family, the old lessons of authority and noble command clearly came back to him—his posture seemed second nature.

Their noble mannerisms felt out of place on this newly regained ground. The tang of scorched earth and gunpowder filled the air—offensive and sharp. The tent itself was dirty, ragged, had survived deluges and molding and tears, but only the most necessary repairs had been made. Adhar's uniform was clean, but worn—threadbare at the knees and elbows. His unit had clearly gone without all but the essentials restocked for quite some time.

"Unfortunate," he said, taking a step in the tight space as though he longed to pace. This was no command center, simply a private place to sleep. His cot, a chamber pot, and a small washbasin were all that occupied the dirt floor. "Winsrouen might not have carved its way up Asgar-Skan's western expanse if we'd had your Demon on our side. We might not have an invading force nearly knocking at Lutador's gates."

"She—Krona—all of us—fight for Arkensyre as a whole. There's a bigger push driving this war, one beyond politics. If we don't stop this larger threat, the war will only worsen. Arkensyre will be set backward."

"So you've said before," Adhar acknowledged, tone leading. He was clearly wounded that his brother wouldn't tell him more, but at least he believed him. Krona had demonstrated her power more than once in his presence since Mandip had revealed to his brother that he was still alive.

Mandip did not offer extra explanation.

The pause between them drew out, and next to Krona, Avellino fidgeted.

Sweat was already breaking out across his brow as he struggled to keep himself and Krona hidden from Adhar's view.

Krona held out a hand, freezing Adhar for a brief moment as the man's lips finally parted to speak. Mandip shot her a look, and she noticed that the sharp glint in Adhar's eyes was the same.

"We need to keep this brief," she explained. "Avellino can only hold out so long."

"I'm fine," the boy countered, voice laced with tremors.

"I'll hurry," Mandip said, face softening as he gave her a slight nod.

She released Adhar.

"I'll help you any way I—" Adhar began.

But Mandip was already halfway to unfurling a map drawn by one of Mirthhouse's naturalists. "What can you tell me about this section of the front lines? We're looking for unusual geographic markers. Tunnels, caves. Strange outcroppings that stand alone."

"There's an abandoned mine here," Adhar said, pointing firmly. "Hard to tell there's even an entrance unless you know what you're looking for. Heard the Winsrouen army tried to stash supplies there, but they got swallowed up by a sinkhole."

"Why was it abandoned?"

"Frequent cave-ins, I think."

"What kind of mine is it?"

Adhar looked taken aback. "I—I don't know."

It was clear he thought he *should* know.

Krona and Avellino shared a look. She hadn't theorized as to how a varger nest could come to be underground, but until now she hadn't ruled out the possibility that the monsters had gathered there naturally. But missing information like this—something that should be simple and obvious but was disturbingly absent when looked for—often meant Thalo.

"What about the Winsrouen forces here? If my people were to make an expedition to the mine, what should we know about the army awaiting us?"

"Intel says they've got cannons on the way," Adhar said, tracing a line with his finger from the mine to an origin point in the south. "They're going to treat this like a fortress siege, trip all the mines and flood the battlefield. But we're going to destroy the supplies—hopefully the whole route—before they arrive. If we're lucky. I'd say, if you want in, I suggest going sooner than later. This dead-land standstill will be easier for you to navigate than a full-on barrage."

"I'd rather not risk excess lives," Krona said, her voice only masked, not hidden, in Adhar's ears. He looked around, unable to pinpoint its location. "Once we're in, I can pick safe jump points, but I have to have eyes on the entrance, a working knowledge of the area."

"So, sooner it is," Mandip said, calm in the face of his brother's bewilderment.

"She's here, then?" he asked.

"She's everywhere," Mandip said, feeding the myth, though it clearly disturbed him to twist the truth for his brother. "I must go."

"Be careful . . . bhaijan," Adhar said.

An echo of the strained reverence that had existed between Krona and De-Lia now permeated the air between the twins. There was love, but also distance. Distance even when in the same room. And it pained Mandip.

He pursed his lips, eyes watering suddenly. He hugged his brother once more, then fled the tent. Krona and Avellino followed. Without a word, she touched Mandip's shoulder and kept hold of the boy's hand, whisking them away in a jump.

Krona wasted no time organizing their incursion into the mine. Given its proximity to the war, accessing the nest was to be one of their most complex operations to date, putting Hintosep's network of resistance to the test. Krona gathered as many fen-powered Kairopaths as possible, as well as those rebels who'd trained using De-Lia's mask.

Krona hadn't donned her sister's jaguar mask in years. Her relationship with De-Lia's echo had proven just as complicated as her relationship with the woman herself. But that didn't mean her sister's echo went unused. De-Lia had willed it to her for a purpose—for her skill in quintbarrel marksmanship. Not everyone had the capacity to suppress an echo, but those who showed even the slightest promise had become Krona's priority. She'd trained them personally prior to bringing Tray aboard, and had made it his primary responsibility after. De-Lia's mask had become vital in their quest to reunite the resistance members with their varger.

The echo's knowledge only passed to a wearer while in use, but repeated training meant De-Lia's technique became muscle memory.

Now they had an expert unit of quintbarrel users. Varg hunters. As invaluable as those who'd regained their magic.

She couldn't imagine staging this incursion into Thibaut's hidden varger nest without such a company at her back.

Warm rain drenched the land when her two squads touched down, the Kairopaths ferrying the varg hunters in their jumps. Krona had Avellino in one hand and Thibaut in the other. The instant splatter of loose mud up her legs was little more than a distraction. Krona blinked water out of her eyes, taking only a moment to survey the trench they'd landed in before shouting her orders.

They'd taken the Winsrouen soldiers by surprise—most of those on duty were firmly focused on the minefield, their rifles in hand and at the ready, should the Lutadorian and Asgar-Skanian forces decide it was time to push them back. Those off-duty were trying their best not to sit in the gathering puddles, their originally black-and-white uniforms now black and gray or black and brown.

Two soldiers closest to Krona sat upon excavated stones, an upturned crate between them with a cheap version of Marquises and Marauders atop. Their game was not a relaxed one, not even a simple off-duty distraction. It was nothing but a way to occupy their harried minds until they were called to stand once again.

Both men were drooping. Their eyes sat deep in their skulls and heavy bags hung beneath their eyes, as though sleep had eluded them for many nights. The dirt and bitterness of war clung to them like the smoky remnants of a campfire.

Before they could so much as blink in her direction, Krona engulfed them in a time stop.

Up and down the trench—which stank of rot, the aroma of rainforest bastardized and all of its greenness turned ugly—the other Kairopaths did the same, creating bubbles of pause, freezing the soldiers before many of them had noticed the intruders.

None of the Winsrouen troops got so much as a shout off, but a few were more keen-eared than others. Several had begun to re-aim their weapons, and one poor soul—missing his leg, the tourniquet fresh and bloodied—drew a knife from his unfortunate hollow down in the mud.

When all was said and done, less than a minute had passed, and the entire unit was contained. But there were plenty of other soldiers up and down the trench lines, and the pause would not hold forever.

As easily as they'd neutralized sixty combatants in an instant, their incursion was still not without its dangers or constraints.

The majority of the Kairopaths remained in the trench, securing the area. As the dozen varg hunters boosted themselves up and over the mud banks into enemy-controlled territory, shots fired from the distance. Krona and the handful of Kairopaths following threw up time shields to slow any munitions that might reach their marks, protecting the hunters' backs as they raced across the short distance to their destination.

The mine entrance wasn't far beyond the enemy line, and was indeed unusual. Most mines in Arkensyre either burrowed into the mountains that built toward the rim, or were open pits. This instead was in an unusually placed bulk of stone. Larger than what one would call a boulder, but almost too insignificant to call an outcropping. A blister of stone sticking out of what used to be thick jungle on the edge of the open field. And the entrance was not a wide mouth waiting for a pushcart, but a seemingly natural crack in the rock, widened through the ages, but set at an inconvenient angle that forced Krona to either duck or lean awkwardly in order to make it inside.

A flash of memory hit her as she crossed the threshold. This crack that proved to be more was much like what De-Lia had described finding all those years ago when they were children. The place she'd discovered Monkeyflower shot through with golden needles—the *wrong* needles. And now again, Krona hoped to find varger.

She was the only Kairopath that ventured beyond. The others stayed behind to guard the entrance. After her came Avellino, then half the quintbarrel wielders, then Thibaut hemmed in by the rest of the hunters at his back.

Inside, Krona broke a light vial, illuminating the mouth of the mine. Its shine highlighted all the quintbarrels at the ready, and the chains of prepped ethereal-varg-trapping bottles dangling from everyone's belts. There was no way to know what kinds of monsters they'd encounter. The nest could be all vapors, or the varger could be well-fed.

Support beams kept the ceiling secured, and pickax strikes had left deep gouges across all the walls. Not far in, the mine sloped downward, the depths of it obscured by rock. Before the incline lay a sinkhole; a dark shaft with no bottom in sight, its edges spanning the entire floor of the manmade cave, blocking further exploration. Likely the very hole that had swallowed the soldiers' supplies.

The darkness in the sunken shaft felt unnatural, though. It ate up the light vial's glow rather than giving way. And the trappings of the rest of the dig area were, on closer inspection, superficial. It was like a storybook mine, with all the trimmings of real excavation, but none of the know-how or practical intent.

The air possessed the same sort of wrongness as Knowledge's temple. Thalo machinations were indeed afoot.

Avellino clearly felt it too. As he leaned over the sinkhole, a frigid blast of heaving wind twisted up from its depths, forcing him back in surprise—the sound of it hollow and raspy like a death rattle.

"Which way?" Krona asked Thibaut. "Into the hole, or across it to access the mine?"

Thibaut closed his eyes, trying to read their surroundings. "One is the true way and one is a trap," he warned.

"Wrong," said Avellino under his breath. "They're both traps."

"Into the mine proper," Thibaut said after a time.

"You're sure?" Krona asked.

"Not at all," he declared brightly. "But as we lack spelunking equipment and I doubt you want to jump blindly into a bottomless pit, I'm picking the more straightforward option."

"You're here because you're an environmental Teliopath," Krona said. "Not because you can flip a coin."

"Would you rather I wave my hands in the air, squint really hard, then announce I've had a magical epiphany when I have not?"

She glared at him.

"Didn't think so. All I've got to go on at the moment is practicality and vibrations."

"Avellino?"

"If the sinkhole only opened up when the Winsrouen army trespassed, it makes sense to assume it was meant to bar entry, not facilitate it."

"See, the boy's on my side."

Getting around the sinkhole may have been a major feat for someone needing to traverse it in the physical manner, but with a Kairopath, it was simply a matter of a few quick jumps to move their entire party from one side to the other. Hardly an obstacle at all—which made Krona all the more wary.

They ventured on, but Krona strode backward with her palm on the hilt of her sheathed saber, watching the pit with suspicion, sure that as soon as she lost sight of it behind the rocks the trap would spring. She imagined a great lift rising from the depths, delivering a menace ready to trap them or devour them. Varger or worse could bubble forth, and all she'd need to do was let her guard down. If the red tendrils of the attic carpet had taught her one thing, it was that even the most innocuous sights could be latent snares.

A shiver went up her spine when nothing pursued.

More light vials cracked open as they lost the sliver of sun provided by the mine's rift of a mouth. A dry, unnatural cold made those most thinly dressed clutch their damp clothes close. The varg hunters moved with precision, sweeping the length of tunnel ahead, checking every nook and recess for threats. The mineshaft was uneven, the ceiling low, and Krona's line of sight was short and narrow. Bends were many, and the darkness that lay just beyond their light vials' reach was oppressive. Engulfing. The blackness that swallowed up their trail from behind came swiftly and solidly, as though it wished to batter them if only it could get close enough.

Avellino dispelled the occasional illusion of a cave-in or solid wall, but Krona could tell, deep in her bones, that they were missing something. Her skin itched with it. She imagined hidden eyes watching them, hidden hands reaching for them.

That sense of foreboding only heightened when they reached a round, intricately carved door.

The tunnel widened here into something closer to a cavern. In the scattered light, Krona couldn't tell what the door was made of. At some angles it shone like polished wood, at others it seemed more like dull stone—though a darker, sandier stone than that of the mine around them. It spanned nearly floor to ceiling, taller than all of them, and had no apparent lock, handle, or hinge. Instead, long, thin spikes jutted out from its edge, seemingly holding the disk of it in place. The carving was largely abstract, and reminded Krona of a coin, of the imprints in glass time discs. But there were runes as well—the type of symbols she'd only ever encountered etched by the Thalo.

Thibaut approached carefully, reaching out his wounded hand. He didn't touch, but he read, plucking through the invisible air currents of environmental knowledge around him to find whatever information about the door his infant magic could sense.

"Physiopathy," he said.

Krona put a hand on his shoulder. "Lucky us, we have a Teliopath."

All magic came from people, and all types of magic were entwined—just as humanity was entwined in a constant state of push and pull. A circle of resistances and vulnerabilities.

Time plodded on, straight and true, but could never shake the transformative power of nature's evolutions. Nature could be overtaken by knowledge—the ingenuities of the hand and mind. Knowledge itself often meant little when faced with the searing intensity of emotions, but emotions were easily manipulated by secrets—secrets that crumbled with the passage of time.

Krona's kairopathy would have no effect on the door, however—

"Knowledge beats nature," Thibaut said, pushing up his shirt sleeves. First he studied the markings, caressing the door with his gaze and his magic and nothing else.

Everyone held steady while he worked, the silence stretching. The acoustics of the mine were such that every small scuffle of a boot or sniffle from a nose bounced off the walls, amplified and pointed.

"Needs a lover's touch," Thibaut whispered eventually, running his gloved hands over the grooves, digging into the fissures and tracing them with deft fingers. He hummed as he swiped at the runes—as intuitive in reading the mechanical needs of the door as he was at reading the sensual needs of Krona's body.

A faint trail of light followed his fingers when he settled upon the right pattern, quaking slightly—shimmering its approval.

"Shouldn't the password be secret?" Krona asked from over his shoulder.

"Oh, I'm sure it is," he said with a sly smile, "but the fingerprints themselves are clear as day."

He gave the door a gentle pat when he finished, as if to thank it for its service. A faint rumble followed. Krona tugged him back as the door began to move—not rolling away or swinging outward, but contracting until it hung perfectly in the center of a gap wide enough for a human to traverse.

Thibaut was far too smug. "Seems the Thalo aren't prepared for the likes of us," he said with a wink.

"Don't get cocky," Krona warned him, waiting for the other shoe to drop.

Avellino made to enter first, but Krona held him back, approaching herself, holding her light vial high. Inside, the walls were knitted over with the webbing of generations upon generations of spiders, and patted through with dust and rock, making it feel more like they were in a tunnel swathed in dirty wool than covered in cobwebs. The occasional remains of something crunched underfoot—bones, shells. Bits of things Krona could not identify as animal or human. But for the most part the tunnel was clear.

She braced for a beast. For a giant spider to make itself known, or for an abomination of the Savior's making to spring from the head of the narrow tunnel.

Nothing came.

Eventually, curtains of false darkness—like in Knowledge's temple—swallowed up their lights, but Avellino led them through. Krona felt the blackened illusions flutter past her, over her, around her, like thin gossamer sheets. On the other side, the mine did not become a simple cave like she'd anticipated. The crudeness of the shafts they'd passed through now seemed doubly unusual as they entered into tunnels with intricately carved pillars and archways, the gray-black rock giving way to a sandy-red stone Krona had never seen in Asgar-Skan.

The ceilings were not exceptionally high, but they were no longer uncomfortably low. The stone beneath their feet had been smoothed to that of a sidewalk, and the rounded edges of rooms appeared well constructed. Large columns, both decorative and supportive, spiraled up at even intervals—each one wider at the base and top, delicate and thin at the middle. It was no longer a space for rough excavation, but for comfortable inhabitation. Or, at least, it had been once.

The pillars reminded her of the ruins in Lutador's Dregs, only—

"These are different," Thibaut said, running one gloved hand down the grooves of the nearest support. "They're older."

"But the Dreg ruins are remnants of the first war after the Introdus."

"Thought to be," Thibaut corrected. "But there's . . ." He put both hands on the pillar, closed his eyes, then leaned his forehead against the rough stone when even that wasn't enough to read the rock. "There's a depth here that . . . Krona—" He reached for her, took her by the hand and laid it next to his own splayed palm. "Can't you feel it?"

"How would I—?"

"Trust me, just focus. How old?"

Oh. That strange sensation she'd been getting as she brushed by things—people, buildings, animals, mountains—perhaps *this* was what it was. Some were like small pebbles, they took up little space in a way, but other things felt bigger than they were. Trees seemed like towers, boulders like mountains. A simple ring had seemed to have the vastness of a treasure hoard all by itself.

Had she been sensing their time? Their state of being relative to one another? She usually thought of time as something to be drained away, as a commodity mostly lost, rarely gained. But simply *being* took up time. It was like each object and living thing warped reality around them, creating a wake in the fabric of the universe—a wake that became larger and larger the longer they endured. Some wakes were more like ripples. Those pebble people—children, small animals—left simple little blips in a pond. But this, these pillars whose wake had begun when they were carved, when they became—out of solid natural stone—what they were now, their wake was like a parting of the Deep Waters, from its surface all the way down to its silty bottom.

And she felt that parting the instant she understood what she was sensing. Felt it like a slice through reality all around her, stealing her breath with its vastness.

"These are older than anything else I've encountered in the Valley," she agreed, snatching her hand back, disquieted.

Maybe they were older than the Valley itself.

But that would mean . . . That would upturn the very foundations of Arkensyre. Krona's understanding of the world had already been tilted by Hintosep; she wasn't sure how to deal with such an implication without a mentor to guide her through.

"Where the hells are we?" someone whispered.

Secrets, Krona thought, *we're in the land of secrets.*

They kept going, and the incline kept them descending.

The initial chill of the cavern—like an ice house—waned as they went deeper. Not only that, the temperature continued to rise, taking them from bone-chilling cold to sweat-inducing hot.

Lights automatically flickered on, making everyone stumble and jolt. Quintbarrels rose to aim at nothing.

Heart beating fast, Krona shielded her eyes from the sudden glare, looking up to the cavern ceiling to pinpoint the source.

They were almost like the oil lamps in the vaults on Vault Hill—those triggered and reset by clever clockwork switches. Except these, like the lights in the strange place they'd found Emotion, did not flicker like flames. They were steady, and buzzed as though powered by gnats or flies. Krona did not see any switches or levers to activate them. As the party moved forward, a new light illuminated every time someone moved directly beneath it, creating a rolling wave of light that started at one end of the tunnel and illuminated a few feet at a time in turn, snapping on in front of them and dousing just as quickly behind.

"We're getting close," Krona said confidently.

These were the hallmarks of the Savior's works—strange incongruencies, forbidden knowledge, forbidden works of invention. She could almost taste his influence on the air, and while it frightened the others, it excited her.

At this point, she expected to *hear* a change before seeing one—assumed varger growls or rattling enchanted glass would herald their arrival at the nest—at the *hoard*—before they turned a corner to confront it. So, when a sharp downward slope in the floor spilled them out abruptly in a vast cavern of intricate containers and pipework, a sudden awe overtook her, along with everyone else.

While Krona hadn't grown up on a farm, her childhood home had been flanked by several. Tray's family had owned sheep, horses. Their most southernly neighbors had kept goats. Not far up the road had been an orchard—one of many—where the sweetest pears grew. One season, she'd seen the farmer coring out tree after tree, creating deep boreholes. They were looking for beetles, trying to figure out how far the infestation had spread. Those holes had been smooth-edged and deep, pulling out layers and layers of tree growth to examine. She'd looked at the coring samples with awe, surprised by how much of a tree's history—its time—could be traced by its bones.

The cavern they entered now was like one of those boreholes—deep and smooth-sided, though the size of it felt impossible. The perfect circle of the walls flung away from the entrance like arms opened wide. The ceiling lay so high above them that the unnatural lighting—mostly at their feet now, and illuminating everything from the walkways—left it in gloom.

Krona was sure the Palace of the Grand Marquises could fit inside.

She did not speak for fear of it echoing.

Greenish-blue glass vats boiled all around, each large enough to hold the party, their tops capped in the five major metals. While the others marveled at them, Krona stopped in her tracks, instantly recognizing the strange roiling within for what it was.

They'd found it. The hoard.

A vast storehouse of ethereal varger.

Fear rose in Krona's throat—the type of fear most deadly beasts could never inspire. Her vargerangaphobia would never fully leave her, she'd come to accept that, but she'd learned to cope with it. She closed her eyes, breathing deeply, pulling in air and releasing the chilling tension that wanted to take hold.

She *would* move among them. She *would* find out how to tap them. She *would* take advantage of this treasure trove they'd been given.

Thibaut squeezed her hand, she squeezed back then stepped from the entry shaft into the cavern proper.

The air moved here—but it was layered. Near the floor to the tops of the vats, it was hot and dry, devoid of the Asgar-Skan humidity that stuck in the nose and throat. Vents lined the walls just a hair's breadth above head-high, and a dry wind was forced through them, angled down somehow—controlled—while fans set above the vents drew all hints of moisture upward, creating a haze—not quite a fog, not quite a cloud, but a thickness that obscured and concealed, helping the dark heights of the ceiling stay hidden.

Metal walkways kept the party from striding on the cavern floor proper, and between a few of the grates she saw working bellows, like those in a hot shop. How they were powered, Krona couldn't say.

There was no magic or device she knew of that could create such a place, with its clean slices though rock, strange devices, and sheer size. But, she supposed, the power of the gods *could* be great enough.

She refused to entertain the idea that the Savior was powerful enough all on his own.

Lan, one of the hunters, approached a vat, holding out a hand in fingerless gloves to entice a bottle-barker forward. A dozen of the creatures congregated near them, drawn like magnets to the nearest human—and that was only a fraction of one vat's inhabitants. When Lan let their hand touch the glass, they yelped, yanking it back, sucking at their fingertips. "It's *searing*."

Krona wondered if the vats' size required additional energy input beyond the normal, stable enchantment of the glass in order to keep the sheer number of varger contained. Thick glass pipes—all roped in metal threads—rose up and away from the vats' lids. Tracing them with her gaze, she realized all the connections snaked toward the center of the borehole, coiling and twisting over one another on their way there.

They'd come here to steal varger. They could only do that by understanding the Thalo containment system.

Ignoring—to the best of her ability—the many eyes and jaws and eager tongues manifesting in the vats all around, Krona headed for the bull's-eye of the cavern. Her boots clanged unnaturally on the corrugated walkway, sending unnerving jolts through her as she traversed the maze of giant bottles. The farther inward she drew, the older the vats looked. The glass had dirtied, a flaky whitish substance—salt—clung to the brims, like the crystals had grown over time, untended. It created long fingers down the sides of the innermost bottles, and the light made it look drippy and gauzy. It was a different kind of webbing—a casing as tight as anything spiders could have spun, and in many ways just as fragile. It sealed over the tops of everything like candle wax.

The tangles of piping eventually dove into a large central pit, each creeping down the side of the nearest encrusted vats to line the floor before curling over the pit's edge to disappear below.

Runes and abstract patterns circled the edge of the hole, giving it a sense of grandeur and giving Krona pause. Whatever was down there held great significance to the hoard, to the Thalo.

Avellino hurried past Krona. "I know this place," he said, wonder thick in his throat. He nearly stumbled over his own feet in his hurry to get to the brim, eagerness tipping him forward too quickly. At the edge, he fell to his hands and knees between two thick-bodied pipes, staring with the wide eyes of a child who's caught his own reflection in a pond for the first time.

Anticipation made Krona's palms tingle as she inched up behind him.

She'd expected another deep hollow—one to mirror the borehole that was the cavern. But the pit was no more than six feet deep, though at least triple that in diameter. Imbedded in its bottom, a giant hourglass on its side—only half of each bulb arcing above the circle of uneven piping winding around them. The sand inside lay evenly distributed between both bulbs—grainy and white.

Rising out of the sand in one bulb was a glimpse of a smooth, pale hip—human, though giant—and the grains in its sister had parted to reveal the crest of a feathered wing—iridescent black.

Krona's breath caught.

They'd found a bounty. Not just a vast store of bottle-barkers, not just the key to their "failed" conjurations.

They'd stumbled onto Time's temple, her resting place.

They now had the location of all five gods.

The Valley's salvation was close at hand.

7

HAILWIC

In a Time and Place Unknown

"Three years for aiding and abetting was a harsh punishment for a minor, though I think the judge would have thrown the book at you if not for your actions during the arrest itself."

"You mean when I betrayed my brother and ensured he'd be locked away for the rest of his life."

Hailwic sat across from the arbiter, a massive mahogany desk between them. He reclined in a tall-backed leather chair with lumbar support while she hunched forward in a plastic seat meant for a child, rather than a twenty-year-old woman. Her wrists were cuffed in enchanted metal, stifling her magic. Which was a shame, because if she could do anything to make this meeting go any faster . . .

"I mean when you prevented a massacre," he clarified, adjusting his glasses on his nose. "As is, Zoshim is lucky. Your family connections kept your brother from the quartering block."

"Now he's just imprisoned."

The arbiter cleared his throat. "He's in a rehabilitation and protection facility for those with dangerous pathology."

And how long before Zoshim's "rehabilitation and protection facility" was hit with a death sweep? She'd heard the stories, even while locked away. There were purges now. Not just raids to put Physiopaths in camps, but to murder them wholesale. No slow wasting away out of sight of the public's prying eyes. They weren't just cordoning them off and denying them resources anymore, no.

"I know it's difficult for someone of your age to understand," the arbiter said, tone patronizing and cloying. "But you didn't live through the Terror, and Friend Uphrasia is taking good care of the Physiopaths, protecting them from themselves."

"Thanks be to her," Hailwic mumbled automatically, the phrase tasting like ash in her mouth.

"Thanks be to her," the arbiter echoed. "There are worse things one can do than murder a man," he said. "But that's exactly what your brother did, to someone who was just doing his duty, executing orders. That man had no qualms with Zoshim, and yet your brother extinguished his light." He reached across the desk, putting one hand over Hailwic's, a sickening kind of *understanding* and *pity* in his eyes. "It can be difficult, acknowledging that our loved ones can hurt others. That they are a danger to themselves and society. Physiopathy is a fundamental evil. Hopefully one day Uphrasia will figure out how to save him, and he will be freed."

It was in Hailwic's nature to argue, to defy. To question. But questioning the munificence of Friend Uphrasia—even hinting at a doubt—would likely have the arbiter declaring her unfit to rejoin society. So her tongue automatically formed the words once more, "Thanks be to her."

The arbiter, somewhat surprisingly, signed off on her release. She walked toward the front doors of the juvenile detention center free of enchanted cuffs for the first time in years. She wanted to blame this place for stealing the last of her childhood—to place all the culpability on its water-stained ceiling tiles and its scuffed rubber floors and its chipped two-way mirrors and its sneering, creeping, *predatory* detention officers.

But her childhood had been stolen the moment her parents wrote *Kairopath* on both her *and* Zoshim's baptismal certificates—there was nothing untoward about twin time wielders, after all.

No—really, it had been stolen before that. The arc of her life, the inability for her and her brother to keep any of their innocence for long, had been ordained before birth. Physiopathy was shameful long before it was illegal. The idea that one could choose to re-form a body, to change, to become—the power to shift and evolve from day to day if one so wished—the *fear* of such malleability, that was what had stolen her childhood.

Zoshim had always made himself small, diminished himself, knowing that fear could lay behind anyone's bright smile and warm eyes and firm handshake. She'd watched him shrink as he grew older, waste away in spirit—and she couldn't stand it. So she'd taken up space for the both of them. Been the defiant one, the loud one.

She'd told him to run.

She'd kept him from the camps, but ensured he was thrown in prison.

An officer from the front desk handed her a clear plastic tarp with her personal items wadded up inside, its seams taped closed by someone who'd never used tape before, it seemed, what with the way it bulged and folded back on itself. There was nothing inside except the clothes she'd come in with, which she wasn't even allowed to put on before leaving. Instead, she wore a citizen's smock—would have to wear one for a year—marking herself as a newly rehabilitated criminal for all the world to see.

It was a formless sack, utilitarian down to the stitching. It wasn't gray and it wasn't white and it wasn't tan, but some sort of in-betweenness that made it look both dirty and overly washed at the same time. It came down below her knees, hitting her calves in an awkward spot, revealing her plain white tennis shoes.

She could not wear jewelry, or makeup, or anything in her hair flashier than a tie to keep it pinned back. She would be issued a thick coat and boots to put over the top of the smock in winter. That was all.

Outside, at the base of the steps, her parents' car sat parked but running, the matte-gray vehicle just as sad and uninspired as she remembered. Bland. Safe.

The outside of the center was parklike, with a well-manicured lawn and beautiful shade trees. If it wasn't for the guard towers set up with gun barrels pointing haphazardly around the place, it could almost be called pleasant.

The door to the backseat of the car opened. Her parents did not get out to greet her.

She wanted to blame it on the guard towers—on a rational fear of the guns ready to go off at the hint of conflict.

But she knew better.

With a heavy sigh, she descended the steps and slipped into the backseat. She was surprised by how much it smelled like home. "I want to see Shim," she said as soon as the car door slammed shut.

In all the times her parents had come to visit her—a handful, really—she'd never mentioned Zoshim. One did not acknowledge the existence of Physiopaths anywhere near cameras, let alone while under the direct observation of Friend Uphrasia's enforcers.

Now that it was just them, her own twin was finally a safe subject again.

Her father glanced nervously at her via the rearview mirror. His dark hair had begun to gray at the temples while she'd been away. "You can write to him," he said carefully.

"They don't allow visitors at . . . at those kinds of places," her mother explained, looking out the passenger-side window, gaze and voice distant. Her hair was as blond and wavy as Hailwic's, her nose the same shape, her lips as plump and her front teeth as endearingly prominent. Hailwic used to love how much she looked like a smaller version of her mother, but not anymore.

"You haven't seen him, then?" she asked, sitting forward, sliding up to the front-to-backseat barrier between them. They both jumped, and her gut went sour, but she chose not to acknowledge it. "How do you know he's okay?"

"He writes to us," her father said, swallowing thickly, eyes darting like a rodent's as he pulled away from the building, driving toward the detention center's barbed-wire-topped front gates.

"He says he's fine. He's learning to knit," her mother said, tone overly bright even as her gaze remained vacant.

"Has he asked about me?" It just figured, she wasn't allowed mail and he wasn't allowed visitors. How convenient.

"We've told him you're fine," her mother said, avoiding the real question.

Frowning—pouting, really, letting her displeasure make itself at home on her face—she sat back and crossed her arms, stewing.

She said nothing as they drove through the city, and her eyes saw little though she kept her chin pointed firmly out the window. She hadn't seen the skyscrapers or the floating billboards or the light bridges and portal jump stations for three years, and yet she took no joy beholding them again.

They passed a hospital, and all she could think about were the Physiopaths that had been barred from medical work—never mind that their magic and medicine were practically made for each other. They stopped at a crosswalk to let a classroom's worth of young children walk by—herded by a harried-looking pair of teachers—and she wondered how many of the little ones were secret Physiopaths, or if their classmates had already faced a cleansing.

Past the city limits they were met with the sprawl of suburbia, and then the heights. Her own neighborhood—with lavish homes and perfectly trimmed yards and gates (so many gates)—now felt anything but neighborly.

As much as the car's interior had smelled like home, somehow their house—as lavish, sprawling, and unimaginative as the next—smelled foreign. It smelled . . . blank. The odor held her at a distance, made her clutch at her own shoulders, fighting off a chill that came from within rather than without.

"Your room is just as you left it," her mother reassured her.

With the hole in the door from the battering ram and all? she wanted to ask, but restrained herself.

And, no, of course not. The door had been replaced—both hers and Zoshim's across the hall—and she remained in the hall as she took in the restaged vision of her old room. Her things had been set back in their proper place from where the cleansing squad had thrown and trampled them. Her prized plush iguana, which she'd had since she was five, and whose head had been torn off in the raid, had, at some point, been inexpertly sewn back together, giving it a curious lopsided tilt.

The blinds over her window were new. She remembered the edges of each piece of flimsy plastic digging into her palm as she tore the old ones down, bending them, breaking them—in a panic—as she clawed through them to get to the window, to get the sash open, to hurry Zoshim through. They'd dropped two stories to the lawn below, then scrambled across the backyard, hopped the fence into their neighbor's yard, crushing petunias or tulips or whatever those flowers had been—Zoshim would know—before stumbling down the driveway and into the opposite street.

If it hadn't been for the trees surrounding their house, shielding the yard, the squad would have seen. The twins would have been caught then and there.

Maybe that would have been better.

She tossed the taped plastic bundle into the corner and shut the door again.

Dinner was remarkably quiet. The company and the food equally cold. Eventually, the clattering of silverware against dinnerware wore Hailwic's patience thin.

"Just tell me," she said, dropping her utensils and sitting back, tone heavy with how weary she was in both heart and body. "Was it you? Did you turn Zoshim in to the cleansing squad?"

Both of her parents remained silent for a long moment, avoiding her gaze, seemingly enamored with the globs of mashed potatoes and bricked meat on their plates.

It was her father, sitting across from her, who spoke first. "My position comes with certain privileges, and certain obligations."

She held her tongue, simply glared, waiting for him to continue, but he fell silent, as though that simple statement explained everything.

Her mother reached out, covering her hand. The gesture was just an echo of comfort; her mother's grasp was stiff. "Honey, we saw what he *did* to you," she said firmly, as though commiserating.

Hailwic yanked her hand back, secreting it away in her lap while her skin crawled at the contact. "What he *did* to me? He never did anything to me. Zoshim would never—"

"The wings," her father said sharply, disappointment making the lines in his face all the deeper, making him look all the older. "We saw the wings."

"We were just having fun. Like when we were little!" The two of them used to fly when they were small—fly as chickens flew. Little hops across the yard with their baby wings. Before that fateful afternoon, Shim hadn't grown wings for her in years. And she'd missed it. She'd missed their faux flights. The freedom, the giddiness, the wonder.

Every now and again she'd seen him change a small part of himself—three fingers one day instead of five. A wider jaw, more feminine lips, a new hair color, a whip of a tail. Nothing dramatic, just different. Whenever he'd catch her eyeing him, he'd change himself back, but that day—that day they'd had *wings* and been *free*.

Now, her father's fist came down hard on the dinner table, making the dishes and cutlery jump. "You aren't a child anymore! I don't believe you were this naïve three years ago, and I don't believe it now. We told Zoshim to never, ever use his magic. Ever. For his own good. We trusted him to do that, and he betrayed that trust, and whether we like it or not, in this world that comes with very specific consequences."

Consequences like a cleansing squad breaking down their front door in the middle of the night.

"I think you were just embarrassed cowards," Hailwic said quietly, not meeting her parents' eyes, swirling her instant mashed potatoes into a goopy mess on her plate. "Embarrassed to have a Physiopath for a son, and afraid for your own hides."

"If we'd covered it up and been found out—if he'd been discovered by someone else, *we all* would have been sent to the camps," he hissed. "Or worse. The Friend—*thanks be to her*—might have just as easily made a public example out of all of us. You think it didn't kill your mother and me to choose each other—to choose *you*—over him? Our safety relies on our trustworthiness, our loyalty, and Zoshim proved this family can't count on him."

She looked up then, lip curling in disgust. *They* failed *him*, how dare they—

She threw her napkin down on her plate like a duelist's glove thrown in challenge, pushing away from the table, her chair legs screeching across the floor. Before she could even pick herself up out of her seat her father barked, "Sit down, Hailwic."

She stood. "I can't even look at the two of you. I'm going to my roo—"

"Sit. Down."

She didn't move.

"You have been remanded into our custody. If you don't sit down right this instant, we can put you right back where we found you."

She blinked at him, taken aback. "You wouldn't."

"It's within our prerogative," he said coldly. "We are to observe your behavior, make sure you've been properly reformed. If we ever question that, we are to alert the authorities."

Hailwic was at a loss—thrown entirely off-kilter.

They were threatening to turn her in. It shouldn't surprise her. If they'd abandon one child for the sake of their own skins, why wouldn't they abandon another?

Her parents had always been strict, straitlaced. Firm-handed and short. But she'd never truly feared them, until now.

"You are in a very privileged position," he went on, "and I hope you start appreciating what it took to get you here. All we've had to sacrifice."

Her mother grabbed for her hand again, encouraging her to sit. In a daze, she did.

"It'll be easy, darling, really," her mother cooed. "You need to demonstrate reform. Put your head down, see to your studies, and we'll reintroduce you to society when the time comes. Maybe you'll get to meet the Friend herself!"

"*Thanks be to her,*" they collectively mumbled.

Hailwic felt like she might vomit. She couldn't hide the nausea, the hopelessness, the shock of what was effectively a slap to the face from the people who were supposed to protect her.

"We've already lost one child," her mother said softly, *lovingly*. "Don't make us lose another."

AVELLINO

It was all Avellino could do to keep Krona from attempting to jump directly into the hourglass. "If you go in, you will not get out," he said, grabbing hold of her, trying to push her back from the edge.

His arms strained—not with the effort of redirecting her, but because it felt so unnatural to touch someone of authority, especially with command. Just as it still felt strange to receive physical affection from Juliet. However, his fear for Krona's safety overrode the fear of touch so baked into his bones. He may never be able to shake the lessons of borders and control instilled in him by Gerome, and if that was the case, then he was determined to *use* that inbred fear to his advantage.

"It was designed to hold Time herself," he said. "We know where she is—this is the closest we've come to any of the living gods. Let it be enough for now. Until we are ready to wake her and know we can get you back again."

He let go suddenly, realizing she'd put up no resistance, that she'd allowed him to move her bodily.

Krona's face was soft, not angry. She understood, even appreciated his vigilance, his insight. She put a hand on his shoulder, and he clutched at his alexandrite pendant for comfort. "If only I hadn't lost the knuckledusters Thibaut gave me when we were fleeing the Savior's keep; they broke enchanted glass. You're right. We'll be patient," she agreed, though he could see her mind working, looking eagerly ahead to Time's day of waking. "We came here for the varger."

"Seems we're snakes in a henhouse," Thibaut said proudly. "Time to ever so discreetly rob the nest."

Procuring the varger was not Avellino's area of concern, and so, he wandered. He circled the pit holding Time, curiously eyeing the embroiled nesting of ducts and pipes around the hourglass. He traced one, from a valve atop a vat to the junction of the hourglass itself. One fed into the other.

Did the varger bolster Time's containment, or was it the other way around?

He continued his slinking, pondering the mechanisms, occasionally kneeling down to run his fingertips through the deep divots of the carved runes, letting cryptopathy surge through his fingerprints, trying to lift the secrets of the patterns up from the pores in the stone.

One thing he'd learned over the years was that an abundance of magic had a scent to it. Just as air carried the scents of where it had been, so did pneuma. Here, despite the differences—the heat and the strange zing of energy in the air—it smelled just like the keep. The background aroma he'd been saturated in his whole life, something he'd been incapable of noticing until he'd been away from it for some time, filled his nose and made him maddeningly *nostalgic*. The keep had been a home as much as it had been a prison and a torture chamber. As much as he'd grown, as much as he understood, now, about the inherent manipulations of the place, he knew he'd never be able to entirely cast off his fondness for it.

Magic also had a feel to it. Personality. Magic was innate in people, came from something in their very being, and the effects of it could not be entirely separated from their person. When he pulled up the ethereal film of cryptopathy from the deep grooves and a familiarity washed over him, his chest constricted.

He could feel *Hintosep* in these markings. They were imbued with *her* power. He wouldn't have been able to sense it so distinctly if he wasn't just like these stones—carved out to fit her secrets inside.

She'd helped build this cage for Time. He might have deduced that; she likely had a hand in all of the temples' designs. After all, she had been the Savior's most trusted once.

She'd been a Guardian, had watched over the Valley's rim, helped many Thalo ascend to their ultimate reward: helping to maintain the god-barrier.

She'd been here from near the beginning, been with the Savior the longest. Of course she'd helped him trap the gods.

Avellino still wasn't sure what had led to her deep disillusionment and betrayal. Why, exactly, after centuries of propping up the Savior's acts with full knowledge of their breadth and ugliness, she'd had an abrupt change of heart. She hadn't gifted Avellino that secret.

He wished she had.

After a few hours, the hunting party determined they'd need additional tools to breach the vats' containment, and Krona made it clear they'd be making many trips back to the hoard to procure the exact bottle-barkers they needed.

They retraced their steps through the carved pillars and past the physiopathically locked door, Krona carefully making lenses to determine if she could jump past the tricks and barriers straight into the heart of the hoard next time.

Avellino dutifully led them back through the darkness and the illusions, warier, even, than he'd been on approach.

Nature's temple had been impossible to breach. Knowledge's had tried to fling them to their deaths, spitting them back out again and again. The presence of so many varger—hundreds of thousands, perhaps *millions*—was terrifying, but not a deterrent all on its own. Not for the likes of anyone keen enough to make it that far into the mine.

They'd missed something. He couldn't shake the feeling that they'd run headlong into new danger they couldn't yet comprehend.

A trap had already sprung, he was sure—he just couldn't see it.

Crack.

Avellino froze as the sharp sound—whip-quick—resonated down the tunnel, its origins somewhere near the mine's entrance.

"Gunfire," Krona said, sprinting ahead.

There shouldn't have been any gunfire if their line of Kairopaths still held.

The quintbarrel wielders raced past. Just as Avellino regathered himself—all thoughts of one worry dashed upon the rocks of another—a firm hand landed on his shoulder. "Don't lose sight of them, but keep back," Thibaut said. "The two of us will only be in the way."

Together, they moved forward with the joint finesse of two mice concerned not with mousetraps but the warring bites and harsh steps of fighting dogs; they were unlikely targets, but easily caught by the jaws of crossfire all the same.

When they came to the maw of the pit, just inside the entrance, Krona—already on the other side—spared them a sideways glance as she spoke with their stationed sentry, but did not make to jump them over.

Thibaut, apparently affronted by her desire to trap him on what was—debatably—the safe side of the sinkhole, immediately scanned the expanse, trying to determine if he could skirt his way around.

The edges were narrow, crumbling, but that didn't stop him from bracing a hand against the stone wall and testing a step with his boot.

Outside the narrow rift that led into the mine, flashes, shouts, and the whip-crack of more guns reverberated. Avellino didn't want to venture outside, but he didn't want to get left behind—saddled with whatever it was that he couldn't place a finger on in the mine: that sense of wrongness wrapped up in anticipation.

Twisting with a terrible combination of reluctance and resolution, he followed Thibaut, throwing his shoulders hard against the bowing wall, willing the edges of the pit to hold fast beneath his feet.

At the entrance, Krona crouched with the sentry. Several of the quintbarrel wielders had run out into the fray already, but she held the majority back.

"What happened?" she demanded.

"Messenger running the lines must have spotted the unnatural stillness. Must have run back to the reserve trench, brought reinforcements," said the scout. "Some of our people have jumped the wounded back to Mirthhouse, but there's a contingent trying to hold on." They swallowed harshly, gazes drooping. "Renee and Cletus . . . both took a bullet to the back of the neck before we knew what was happening."

Krona swore under her breath, trying to get a lay of the land beyond as flashes of gunpowder cut through the haze beyond.

There was far more smoke in the air than when they entered. A miasma, acrid in the nose and eyes, settled all around. The wind had died, the air had compressed, and now they huddled in the mine where the air was cleaner, trying to gauge what they could do—if anything—for those in the trenches beyond.

Krona glanced back at Thibaut. Their eyes locked for a moment. Determination filled Krona's face, her brows knitting together and her full lips pressing thin.

"No," Thibaut said, as though watching a mistake he could not stop. "No, no, *nononono*, Krona—"

She darted away, disappearing into the gray vapors of the fading day.

Thibaut echoed Krona's previous curses, shuffling along the thin ledge of stone all the quicker as Avellino did his best to keep his footing and not tumble into the laughing darkness at the toes of his boots.

More of their people rushed out in the wake of Krona's boldness. Only the scout and a handful of others realized they had not been given orders and remained at the mine.

Thibaut poked his head out of the crack in the stone crag, ducking low while trying to decipher where Krona had gone.

Avellino shuffled up beside him, dazed by the murk of a haze that had settled so low, lending a darkness to the swell of the land while the sun shone high, cutting through the smog like the beacon of a gaslight on a cold, lonely street.

Overhead, a dim whistling started far off—preceded by a strange *boom*—and as the sound sharpened, Avellino's heart kicked in his chest, as though it understood what was happening when his mind did not.

Thibaut shoved him to the ground. The mine's entrance exploded—slammed into by something heavy. Shards of rock sprayed outward.

Facedown, Avellino sucked in a breath, dragging dirt and dust into his lungs, choking on nothing and everything as he tried to blink his eyes clear and shake the ringing from his ears.

Shouts sounded from far away.

Or up close—the ringing made it difficult to tell.

"Avellino!" someone called, their voice muffled. "Avellino, take my hand!"

He reached up, unsure of where the hand was.

Fingers entwined with his.

A tug ripped at his stomach.

He was tossed through a lens—taken on a Kairopath's jump.

He landed facedown in winter-browned grass.

Rolling over, coughing, he caught the silhouette of Mirthhouse a few hundred yards off, rising up out of a spring-promised fog.

Most of Winsrouen's soldiers were conscripts, Avellino had been told. Forced into service without a choice, under penalty of death if they did not comply. Avellino understood such a system. He'd been a soldier all his life, conscripted into the Order of the Thalo from birth, and only now, as a soldier by Krona's side, did he have the words and the tools to attempt to pick apart such a life—examine it from the outside. Until his sister had come to rescue him, he'd never known there was any other path, that there was any other way to be. That there was *choice*.

Five of their friends had been lost in the trenches, but at least they'd had a choice.

The sky was bright while they burned three of the bodies. It started to darken when they tilled the land to bury the fourth. The fifth was taken, in the cover of night, out into the woods for the wolves to find.

Each was handled in the traditions of their home city-state, of their people.

The next day, Krona held a joint ceremony for their fallen few. All of Mirthhouse's residents joined her, far afield of the winter gardens and the old sheep yards. She stood on the crest of a hill, where the mansion could be seen, as well as the silver of the thin river below its cliff.

She did not make trite declarations about sacrifice or greater purpose. Her eulogy was soft and specific, speaking to the hopes and dreams and personalities of each lost comrade.

Avellino stood in contemplative silence between Juliet and Thibaut, trying to stay attentive but ultimately drawn into himself.

Death was new for him. These were not the first of the resistance who'd died at Mirthhouse, but Thalo traditions were far different from others in the Valley. The people of Arkensyre ended. He'd been taught the Thalo went on.

Avellino had known few Thalo who'd died—those that were killed in the field, their bodies sunk to the bottom of Lake Konets. Harvesters and Orchestrators who'd become old or had run afoul of accidents beyond the keep. They existed, but were rare. Most Thalo did not die—they Ascended.

Watched over by Guardians, they were laid—still alive—in rimward salt pits, protected day and night until the salt bloomed over their skin, encasing them entirely, much like Emotion was encased in a very different kind of crystal. As the Thalo forms turned to pillars, their energy resonated with the border, strengthening it, until one day the pillar simply disappeared, dissolving back into grains for the pit, the Thalo within gone. Waiting to be reborn.

Or so he'd been told.

A few hours after the funeral ceremonies, Avellino felt extra disquieted by his nostalgia for the keep. The idea that he could *miss* such a place—feel anything but disgust for its walls and his rituals . . .

Not to mention its people.

With Abby at his side, he sought out Juliet, thinking she could smooth over the strangeness he'd felt in the mine, the hoard. If anyone knew how to analyze emotion and set his fretfulness to rights, it was his performer of a sister.

He found her out near the stream where those in Mirthhouse did their washing. A little creek that eventually fell into a thin, misty waterfall over the cliff to the narrow waterway below. Mandip sat by her side, his curls falling into his eyes as he bent over a torn shirt in his grasp, the tip of his tongue held between his teeth as he carefully pulled the tear closed with needle and thread—his darning directed by Juliet's soft encouragement.

Her hands were busy with their own project, each covered in purple dye up to her wrists as she scrubbed the color deep into a swath of leather.

Avellino was used to seeing them both with swords in their hands. He nearly turned away, thinking now was not the time to unleash his half-thought-out sentiments—not wanting to be a bother—when Juliet caught sight of him and waved a purple hand.

Purple like Emotion's hands. Purple like dark amethyst.

"No, not like that, look at the way the thread is knotting," she said to Mandip as Avellino and Abby drew closer. She reached out a purple finger, and Mandip jerked his project away.

"Don't you dare," he said, the back-and-forth of a familiar tease light on his lips.

"Thibaut could use a humbling stain or two on his shirts," Juliet said.

"He's letting me practice darning with his clothes. I think we both know what kind of a fit he'd throw if I returned them more disheveled than before."

"And we both know that would be a hilarity worth witnessing."

"You, madame, are trouble."

"And you wouldn't have it any other way." She winked at him, then turned to Avellino as he sat down a little way away from her dyeing pale. Abby immediately began rolling around in the grass with a lack of concern for decorum Avellino had never been allowed to possess at zhur age. "Dear brother, how are you?"

Somewhere he possessed the words to describe this strange mixture of nausea and longing that hit him when he thought about the past, but he couldn't find them just yet. "What are you doing?" he asked instead.

She displayed the leather for him—a pauldron. He noticed its mate and a chest piece hanging from a thin tree branch that dangled over the stream not far off. It was another one of Hintosep's abandoned armor sets—less grand than the one lost to Knowledge's treehouse, but sturdy.

"Krona is done with the black of the Regulators, and trying to fill Hintosep's shoes has her feeling . . . let's say *a way* these days. And blue *really isn't* her color, let's be honest—I wasn't joking about that. So, I thought I'd make her a gift. Give her something that feels more like *her*. Royal purple seems to fit the bill to me. With"—she gestured to another bucket of dye—"yellow ties. She'll look smashing." She turned to Mandip again. "Which is why I think you should just let me dye Thibaut's shirt as well. You can't tell me he wouldn't feel a bit of pride matching his *mistress*"—she exaggerated the nickname, gave it a sickening-sweet emphasis that even had Avellino smiling at the cognizance of the joke—"in her leathers."

Mandip smirked, then his face fell suddenly. "I saw him again, the other night. Out of bed, in with Emotion. I took him back to their room. Krona is worried."

For a moment Juliet looked like she wanted to say something breezy to blow away any talk of seriousness, and Avellino could understand her impulse. Mourning ceremonies like the one earlier were all too common these days. Cities were burning, farms were being plowed under. The Valley's people and the city-states were being ripped open by a push from the Thalo and it had them all teetering on the edge of debilitating worry all the time.

One clung to lightness where they could find it.

But she didn't want to dismiss concerns about Thibaut. "We're all worried," she said instead.

Just then, Abby went dashing by, taking a little flying leap into the stream, screeching in utter joy. Clear, steady, and shallow, it was a perfect play spot. The pebbles were smooth, but not slippery, cradling zhur feet without threatening to topple zhim.

Zhe batted a handful of water at the adults, and Mandip raised the shirt to shield himself while Juliet let out a shriek, half-indignant, half-delighted.

Avellino let his unease rest for the time being. Pushing it out of the hollow of his chest to curl in wait at the base of his spine, he swept himself into the water beside his charge, picking zhim up by the armpits and twirling zhim around as zhe giggled.

And then, for a moment, everything else melted away and there was just Avellino and the people he loved on a warm day, safe.

Krona went soft when Juliet presented her with the newly dyed armor. Her stoic strength smoothed over for a moment, and though she was the sort to keep her emotions close and quiet in the presence of others, Avellino could tell she was moved. The gentle *thank-you* she bestowed upon Juliet might have seemed curt to those who didn't know her. Even so, he doubted anyone could miss how readily Krona took to the gift, immediately putting it on, keeping it on.

Juliet had gone so far as to embroider little yellow flowers and leaping varger on the pauldrons and up the spine of the brigandine. There was a regalness to it that made Krona that much more of a striking figure, with her bone wings and long braids and sharp gaze.

She wore it the next time she jumped him, Thibaut, Mandip, Juliet, and Jan into the varger hoard, the party landing in among the ancient pillars that predated their understanding of the Valley's civilization.

It was the fourth time they'd returned over ten days. Each trip to the hoard emboldened them—their confidence bourgeoning as much as their collection of varger.

Krona had another merger to supervise—a joining made possible by the pervious time they'd stolen here under the Order's nose. She jumped away quickly, leaving them to it.

Avellino was here to examine Time again—to decipher how to reach her—while the others siphoned away specific varger with a strange contraption that looked like a chemistry set. Thibaut, Juliet, and Melanie had devised it together, explaining its function with terms like *acid-based extraction, relative turgidity, pneumatic attraction*, and *humor migration*—which Avellino personally hadn't grasped. Somehow it separated specific varger out from one another so they could be independently bottled.

Jan, one of their best hunters, kept guard—at the ready in case something should go awry and a varg be set free—while Mandip assisted Juliet with tapping a vat's lid and attaching the contraption, and Thibaut used his teliomancy to pinpoint the creature they'd come for.

Avellino left them behind, losing sight of them behind the vats as he traced a path toward the goddess.

Time hadn't moved since last he'd seen her. Still stoic as a buried statue, the same swell of a hip and hint of a wing protruding from the sand. Not a single grain had shifted. By his estimate, she matched Emotion's height—twice that of a grown man. He could hardly imagine what that meant for her wingspan, how far they must stretch. She could envelop him fully in one, hide him away like a child hiding in the folds of a Possessor's robes.

Filling his chest with a focusing breath, he paced around the pit's edge, tracing the through line of the imbedded cryptopathy. Knowing Hintosep had enchanted the runes might mean nothing, or it could mean everything. Having wisps of her life imprinted on his person just as the runes were imprinted on the stone could mean that he'd be able to better sense cracks in the warding. Loose threads in the weaving.

And yet, hoping to sense mistakes made by Hintosep was like hoping to sense mistakes made by the rising and setting of the sun. She had been precise, steady. A force unto herself, paling in power only to the Savior.

An ominous clang stopped him in his tracks. It rattled in a way the chemistry set distinctly had not. Fearing they'd broken something vital, Avellino turned back to call out, wondering if they needed help, only to be met with a wall of darkness. It wasn't the darkness of the lights going out. It was a thick curtain of a thing. The cryptopathic creation that turned a lack of light into a blanketing miasma.

And it was rolling toward him.

Avellino stiffened, forgetting his task, fear gripping his lungs and squeezing the air from them.

Out of the approaching dark, Mandip came running, reaching out for Avellino who caught him just before he pitched into the hole beyond. "What is this?" he gasped.

"Someone's here," Avellino hissed back.

A Thalo someone.

The dark descended, capturing the pair of them, making it impossible to see each other though they stood shoulder to shoulder.

It was worse for Mandip, he knew. Avellino could at least sense his way through it, could at least see Mandip's hand as Avellino placed it on his own shoulder. "Don't let go," he instructed. "And keep close. We'll find the others."

He told himself to keep calm. They needed him to have a steady head, to be their light and their guide.

He didn't let himself think too far ahead, to when he'd found them all. Because what then? There was no way to get a message to Krona or any other Kairopaths. No way to signal their distress.

Mandip squeezed his shoulder, and together they took halting steps through the dark. *Mandip is armed*, Avellino reminded himself. *So are Jan and Juliet. Thibaut has his magic. You can confront a member of the Order. You can. You are no longer a Nameless child, and you are not alone.*

An odd sensation suddenly rippled through him, and he paused mid-step, a new jolt of fear shooting through his limbs. It was the knowledge of another shroud—the realization that his ears seemed stopped up. He strained his hearing, searching for sounds, and yes—*oh no*—there.

Voices.

He focused, trying to decipher who they belonged to.

They were yelling. Screaming.

Begging.

The new shroud in his mind was strong. If he hadn't already been working hard to pull back the thick layers of cryptopathy, he never would have noticed it.

The voices seemed far off. *Seemed.* Perhaps they were coming from beyond the hoard. Some echo from the battlefield.

Perhaps not.

Perhaps they were coming from behind him.

Perhaps they were—

Where Avellino had been calm and sure of himself moments before, panic now surged in his sternum, and his heart beat itself against his ribs like a bat that had lost its ability to guide by sound. He felt like he'd missed a step on a familiar staircase, his stomach swooping into his throat.

He put his hand on Mandip's hand, assuring himself the grip was real and solid, then he turned to warn his companion—

Avellino's head turned before his body did. He looked at where he gripped Mandip, and instead of the rich brown of his companion's skin, he saw a sickly pale.

A sickly pale, with familiar blue swirls and sharp, manicured nails.

That hand belonged to someone he knew well.

Someone he'd hoped was *dead*.

Avellino screamed, whirled, tried to struggle away. Maybe it was just an illusion. A new safeguard—a mechanism meant to horrify him into abandoning the hoard and his friends.

But there was an arm attached to that hand. And a body—tall, thin, terrifying.

Had it been Gerome's hand on him the whole time?

"Hello, little spy," Gerome said softly, the filigree-tipped fingers of his other hand lashing out to take hold of Avellino around the biceps. "It's been some time, hasn't it, Child mine? Look how you've grown."

Suddenly, Avellino was eleven again. He was eleven, and Nameless, and ashamed before his Possessor.

Instinctually, he tried to disappear, to become invisible—to hide himself from Gerome's mind.

His Possessor simply laughed. "You've been training, I see. Even without a Possessor to guide you. Ah, but little one, you could have been so much *stronger*."

Gerome gave him a shove, grinned in wicked delight behind his curtain of beads as Thalo Child—*no, Avellino, my name is Avellino*—stumbled, tripping over his own feet to fall heavily on the corrugated metal, landing hard in an undignified sprawl.

He tried to crawl backward—to use his elbows to drag himself away—but Gerome kneeled on his robes.

Robes? He'd lost his robes. He was wearing trousers and a simple shirt, he wasn't—

He was. He looked down to find himself dressed as he had been on the journey to Knowledge's temple. Gerome's hand struck out, raking his fingers over Avellino's face. When he pulled them back, their pale tips were smeared with the blue of false tattoos.

"You didn't earn these," Gerome hissed.

Despair racked Avellino. He *needed* this to be an illusion. He willed himself to see through his Possessor, to find a haze where his body was, an untruth in his own terror. "You're not real," he said, willing the words to wipe Gerome away.

The patronizing smile—full of pity—that split Gerome's face dashed such hopes. "Wherever you've found yourself these past years," he said softly, "*that's* what's not real. That's not your world." Slowly, he stood, held out his hand, palm up. "But you can still come back. You know I am nothing if not magnanimous. So is the Savior. Your cohort misses you. We can all forgive."

The unnerving nostalgia from before came closing back over him, curling up his chest and filling his nose, his lungs, making his head feel hazy.

In many ways, *that* world had been simple. Avellino had been given instructions, was asked to follow them, but never to think. He could think when he was older. He could question when he was older. But now, all he'd have to do was please Gerome and be content, and then everything else would be taken care of. He wouldn't have to worry about war or gods. About rebellions or tragedies or wrongs or rights.

Bits of hopes, fears, ideas, plans flickered through Avellino's mind. Where were the others? Had they been screaming? What had . . . what had Gerome done to them?

And these robes, this paint on his face—did that mean Gerome knew? How long had the Thalo—the Savior—known they'd nearly breached Knowledge's inner sanctum?

Moving carefully, with deliberate slowness, Avellino took Gerome's hand, let his Possessor help him to his feet. The warm smile Gerome gave him sent a chill down Avellino's spine, ultimately filling it with steel.

Simplicity and freedom from responsibility were *Gerome's* vices—which was why he thought his offer attractive. Why he thought his Thalo Child would obviously choose to come back home. All it proved was that no matter how many times Gerome probed Avellino's mind, he'd never bothered to *understand* him.

Avellino cared too much—about Abby, about Juliet, about the *truth*—to ever be seduced by that kind of selfishness.

He wanted to spit in Gerome's face. He wanted to stomp on his feet or punch him in the gut or claw at his eyes.

Except none of those things were who he was either.

So, he ran.

Viciously taking hold of Gerome's lapse in judgment—in his sense of superiority—Thalo Child (*Avellino, Avellino—I will not let him drag me back*) darted past him, away from the hoard's entrance, hoping upon hope that he was leading his Possessor away from the others, that Gerome thought them inconsequential enough to abandon. Krona would not be back to retrieve them for hours still. It was up to him to keep them safe until then; he had no other recourse.

He was seventeen going on thirty-seven any day of the week, Melanie often said. But now—with tears starting to stream down his face as he tried to put as much distance between his tormenter and himself as he could—he was a small child all over again.

He was the only one who could immerse himself among the Thalo, the only one who could infiltrate their spaces. But he was also the only one Gerome could tear down. Could core out. The only one who could be pulled back into the nightmare and *utilized*.

Weaving through the vats, he brushed up against the scorching glass, hissing as it seared his skin.

His robes—suddenly too big for him, or he was too small—wound around his ankles like a noose, tangling his legs and toppling him. His stomach jolted when, instead of hitting the walkway, he kept falling. He must have come full circle, running back toward the pit without realizing. He expected to slam into the hourglass, and thrust his arms out to guard his face.

A surge of water overtook him instead.

Confusion had him gasping, sputtering. Sucking in algae-filled brininess.

He could barely swim. Sebastian had been teaching him, but those gentle lessons hadn't prepared him for the force of a waterfall pushing him down, down—beating him from above as the churning sucked him farther into the depths.

Avellino twirled and tumbled. He fought for the surface, clawing for every inch while everything on his person worked against him. His robes twisted around his limbs, heavy with water, catching around his arms and legs like spiderwebbing sticking to a hapless insect, covering his face like a sucking, waterlogged shroud.

With a surge, he broke back through the surface, coughing—coughing, coughing, coughing until his throat felt raw. Bright sunlight met him instead of the false darkness as he wrestled the clinging fabric off his face.

He realized then that he was in the pool outside Knowledge's temple, where he and Juliet and Krona had taken time to reset after their harrowing experience with the treehouse.

Except, he couldn't be. Not really.

Gerome was real. Gerome was here—here in the varger hoard—tormenting Avellino with flashes of his betrayal. *Little spy*, he'd called him.

Little traitor.

Avellino worked his way to the pool's edge, hauled himself out, still coughing, unable to draw a proper breath even though he knew the water and the robes were all part of a pinpointed falseness. An unreality Gerome had created especially to scrape at him.

But he had to keep running. He might be a rat in Gerome's maze, but he couldn't give up and stop moving.

Droplets of blue fell off his eyelashes as he tore into the jungle, and he could feel the false tattoos running down his cheeks even though they weren't real. He wiped the back of one sodden hand over his eyes, but that only added dirt and pond slime to the mix.

With his lungs burning, his robes clinging, sagging—threatening to trip him again—his paint running, the path lost, and Krona a world away, a bubble of hopelessness swelled beneath his ribs.

Don't cry, don't cry, don't cry, he chanted to himself as he made his feet fly forward.

Thalo Child came the sudden reverberation in his head.

A tremor of fear shot up Avellino's spine, and he nearly cried out in shock. Gerome's voice sounded like it was right in his ear. The Possessor didn't have to be next to him to project his voice into Avellino's mind, and yet, with his powers—his ability to cloak himself from Avellino's sight—he *could* be.

Avellino stumbled—his sodden robes curling around his ankles and tripping him up. With a full-throated sob, he pushed himself back up and kept running.

He ran like varger were at his heels, though it was something much worse chasing him.

He ran.

He ran in a straight line for what felt like hours.

He hit no more vats, no walls. The illusion was solid.

He tripped over a bulging tree root and realized—only once he'd left it behind—that it could have been Juliet or any of the others. Someone in need of his help, and yet the claws in his mind had made him incapable of seeing his own comrades.

Nausea threatened to overtake him. As did despair. As long as Gerome could keep generating such a strong illusion, he was lost.

They were all lost.

He fisted the alexandrite at his throat, trying to see a way to freedom, trying to fight back against Gerome's influence.

You are mine, Child. There is no escape, Gerome assured him.

Avellino ran smack-dab into an invisible wall. A wall that was warm, and living. A wall with arms like iron bars that snaked around his person and held him tight. A wall that hissed directly into his ear—breathy, hot, and smug:

"There, there, now. I've got you. I've got you."

He tried to struggle, to kick and snarl and even bite against the enemy he could not see but knew all too well.

"I've got you," Gerome mumbled again. "I'm going to bring you home."

9

KRONA

Krona wiped the viscera of another successful merger off her hands, nodding to Melanie as she helped their newest Emotiopath to their quarters to rest, before jumping back to retrieve those she'd left at the hoard.

This love-eater had come from there—been ethereal—which meant it had had to be breathed in—flooding its host's throat and lungs and stomach, writhing like worms inside them before Krona had thrust the katar deep into their belly, *twisting* as they'd choked on their own bile and disembodied magic.

It was never easy—slicing into someone, thrusting the weapon as though gutting them rather than curing them. It wasn't easy, but she'd found a rhythm to it, and the remnants of blood on her hands no longer made her queasy.

When she touched down among the ancient pillars, she immediately sensed something was wrong. The remnants of fresh cryptopathy—something she never would have been able to detect before reuniting with Ninebark—crackled through the air, like the tang of ozone left after a lightning strike.

She might have attributed it to Avellino, except the hoard was so, so quiet. The general hum of the place still hung in the air, but there was no idle chatter from Thibaut or Juliet. No bottles rattling. No metal tinkling.

Krona raced into the vat room, on the verge of calling out, when her gaze caught on a slumped form.

Jan—propped up against a vat, head lolled forward. Krona rushed to her, but it was clear from the bottle-barkers' lack of interest that she was dead. The monsters regarded her as just another piece of the scenery, not someone they could claw their way into and make a nest in. She wasn't fit for eating, not anymore.

Her chest was riddled through with quintbarrel needles. She hadn't been shot—someone or something had broken her neck. The needles had been stabbed into her for show.

Just as the pendant around her neck had been left for show. It glimmered and shifted hues as Krona, despite the evidence, checked for her pulse, felt her forehead. Jan was as hot as the vat behind her, and her heart lay still.

Clenching her teeth, seething beneath her purple leathers, Krona gently lifted the alexandrite pendant from around Jan's neck. Avellino never left his chicken-bone gift behind, never loaned it out. There was no reason to think he'd given it to Jan before she'd been attacked.

It had been hung here, on a dead woman, to taunt her.

Which meant the Savior knew she'd been here. Knew they'd been breaching the hoard repeatedly and that she'd be back.

What *else* did he know?

Who else . . . who else was dead?

"Saints and *fucking* swill," she cursed.

Krona darted through the maze of vats, scouring every bare bit of corrugation, every corner, every vent, looking for bodies while she kept her mind blank. It would be so easy to spiral, so easy to start imagining corpses—so easy to paralyze herself with sudden mourning before she'd even found anyone else to mourn.

She circled her way inward, until she'd examined every inch of the giant borehole save Time's resting place.

No one but the goddess resided in the pit.

Which meant the others had been taken. The Savior had kidnapped those who'd been with her at the keep, and killed the one who hadn't.

He wanted her to come for Avellino again—for her friends, for her lover—only this time, on *his* terms.

None of them should have had to step foot in that fortress ever again. Avellino least of all. She shouldn't have put him and the others in danger like this. It was hasty to thrust Thibaut into the field so soon after regaining his magic. Negligent not to have provided Jan and Mandip with better weapons, better protections.

She should have sent another Kairopath. She should have sent a *team* of Kairopaths. She should have—

*Should have*s didn't matter now.

She clutched the alexandrite pendant to her chest, gritting her teeth. Her vision turned red—not the red of a despairstone, but the red of a resolvestone. Red like the red garnet in her old bracers.

No more careful planning. No more halting steps forward. No more biding their time as they tracked varger and slowly built their forces.

The Savior's rule had to end *now*.

Swallowing down a scream of frustration, she created another lens.

Her vision turned bloody. Rage filled her, forced her to jump on instinct. Inside her chest, Ninebark screamed discordantly, the music of her magic turning sour, its tune wretched.

She jumped from the depths of the hoard into dead air, high above the snow-covered mountains of the Severnyy Ice Field, where the sky held the faint purple sheen of the magical border. The Savior's keep clung to the crags directly beneath her, a stone fist with a tight hold not just on the Valley's rim, but all of Arkensyre.

Her wings were just for show. Unable to catch the wind—which whipped harshly at her face, bits of ice in it scraping her cheeks—she fell, plummeting toward the ragged, icy stone of the keep's walls below. She screeched as she descended—a sound of madness, of boiling ferocity. She plunged with a purpose, determined to strike like a descending bird of prey. She'd tear the castle apart brick by brick, stone by stone, to get them all *back*. The Savior had taken her family, taken Thibaut, taken her body and torn it apart, and now she would do the same to *him*.

Dissatisfied with freefall, she turned herself into a spear tip, thrusting herself toward the rushing ground, speeding up her descent while creating a time shield at her fore. She intended to hit the walls like a cannonball—a meteor—pummeling the fortifications, bursting the rock into chunks and dust. She'd sift through rubble until she found the Savior and could pummel his head just the same.

Only feet from impact, a flare of cold blue threw itself up in front of her. She struck it with her shield, and the force of the blow sent her glancing off, sheering to the side, away from the cliff face and into the abyss that lay beyond.

Tumbling, she jumped again, transporting herself high once more. Unthinking, acting in pure, hot-blooded vengeance, she tried again to use herself as a living projectile, hurling herself at the walls.

Once again, the keep repelled her.

She knew the keep had been warded against her—magic shields added after the Savior discovered what Hintosep had done with Krona, what they together had restored.

But she was too enraged to care.

She flung herself into the magical shielding again and again, until she was exhausted. Until one final time, when she went careening away and simply let gravity have its say.

Krona curled into herself. Falling. Falling in despair, shaking with sadness and anger and adrenaline.

A sharp peak of broken stone pointed upward at her falling form, ready to receive her, to slide inside her back, between her ribs, and hold her there forever. At the last moment, she denied it, jumping herself into her own bedroom at Mirthhouse instead, landing in a heavy ball directly onto her bed, which creaked and protested—one leg cracking, echoing the way her heart was cracking.

Krona still had her resolve, was still more determined than ever to see the Savior fall, but here, alone, she allowed the frustration and stress and worry escape from the little prisons she'd built inside herself for years. There was no one here to see her cry, so she let it out. Let the anger and sadness curl her lip and tighten her jaw. She let it force her hands into fists in the bedding, twisting the fabric into tight swirls, like whirlpools.

She had to stay strong for the others, but here, she could indulge.

How had Hintosep managed this? How had she kept herself together while people she supposedly cared for were thrust—by her hand—straight into the Thalo maw?

That was it, though, wasn't it? That *supposedly*. Hintosep's true intentions, goals, fears, and loves had been her own, privy to no one else. It had not escaped

Krona that Hintosep's insistent stories and Krona's own observations had never quite lined up.

Take Abby, for instance. Not a Cryptomancer, and yet Hintosep had insisted that Thalo Harvesters had taken zhim. Perhaps it had been an honest mistake—pulling a Physiopath into their ranks—but Krona suspected otherwise. Krona suspected Hintosep had had no qualms putting Melanie and Sebastian through hells worrying about their child, unnecessarily.

But that wasn't who Krona was. She couldn't use people and toss them aside. She couldn't manipulate others for some greater purpose. Avellino, Juliet, Mandip, and Thibaut were gone—facing some unknown trial—Jan was *dead*, one more body for the hoard, and the guilt was already eating her down to the bone.

She wrenched the blankets against her face, taking comfort in the familiar fragrance of Thibaut. How many nights had they shared this bed now? How long had they been paired, side by side, only for her to fail him when—

Krona's ragged thoughts paused. A strange, unburdened calm came over her as a small set of wheels in her mind—like those in one of Thibaut's clockworks—fell into place and started to smoothly turn.

How many nights had Thibaut been out of bed since becoming a Teliopath? And where had he been found each time?

At Emotion's side.

Krona sat up, blinked her eyes clear.

Of course. The clues were all there—the realization so close to unfolding in the light.

A flutter of hope kicked in her chest.

There was work to do, and now she needed to move more urgently than ever.

Gulping air, she pushed herself up, discarding the bonelessness that came with guilt and despair, turning her movements deliberately harsh and sharp. Creating a new lens, she held her breath and dove through to the one place she'd kept secret from everyone—even Avellino, their protector of secrets.

Immediately, Krona was plunged into icy darkness. Water swamped into her ears, muffling all sound. It washed away her tears, took the salt of them and replaced it with its own particular flavor of brine. She was soaked through instantly, but that was the price she had to pay for this particular hiding place.

The current seemed stronger than usual, and she lashed out to either side, searching for the rocks she knew were there in order to steady herself. On instinct, she flared her wings as well, and the bones fanned out, scrabbling at the algae-covered stone, drawing deep gashes in the centuries' worth of single-celled lake life that clung to the boulders.

Something thick, and long, and slimy slithered past her ear. Heavy, too, by the press of it against her cheek. The giant eels here were territorial. And predatory.

She could not remain at the bottom of Deep Waters for long.

Using her wings to steady herself, she crouched down and began pawing blindly through the silt of the lake bed.

Something nipped at her shoulder in the murky water, and she jerked away, but kept digging.

It didn't take long to hit the small, water-tight chest she was looking for.

Another nip. This time sharp.

The piranhas had found her.

She needed to get the chest just free enough to yank it through a lens. Her fingertips scrabbled through the muck even as a small set of unseen teeth set into her wrist.

An involuntary shout left her, letting the lake rush in, letting the silty water coat her teeth, though she kept it from her lungs.

Two more bites came in rapid succession. There was blood in the water now. The frenzy would start soon.

Cursing at herself, she yanked hard on the chest, throwing her weight backward—stunted bone wings scraping—to lift it out of its hollow. She created a lens beneath her, pulled her wings in tight, and let herself drift back into it, just as another piranha latched on.

With a spluttering *oof,* Krona landed on her back in the middle of Mirthhouse's vegetable garden.

The small terror of a fish that had followed her through detached and flopped awkwardly on the ground among the carrot tops. She picked it up by its tail, and secured the chest beneath one arm, before stomping up to the kitchen door. She tapped on it gently, presenting the fish to Mastrex Tanna, the cook.

"Oh, but they're so bony," fey said with a frown. "And so small, what am I supposed to do with this?"

Krona simply dropped the flopping thing in feir open hands before creating a small time distortion to snap her clothes dry—that parlor trick Juliet had wanted.

Stomping into the great room, she called for Melanie, Sebastian, and Tray—aware her call was tinged with anger and demand. They were at her side in an instant, watching with raised eyebrows as she yanked the katar from its place of honor over the mantel before striding—each step forceful, hulking—into the war room. Every inch she traveled felt like a mile, felt like a huge step over unwelcoming, tiring ground.

The others followed.

"Krona?" Melanie asked, shutting the door behind them. "What is it, why—?"

Without a word Krona strode to the dais displaying Emotion's body, set the box to the side, and raised the katar.

She brought it down with a vengeance, hacking at the center of the crystal form.

The thick casing cracked. Flakes flew. The smash of metal through mineral was immensely satisfying.

To Krona, at least.

The others flew at her, their cries of dismay hollow in her ears as she continued bringing the katar's edge down, again and again, even as they tried to haul her back.

"Krona," Sebastain pleaded. "Krona!"

Tray looped his arms around her middle, dodging the flare of her bone wings as he pulled her away, struggling with her like she was a guard dog determined to fight. "What in the Valley is wrong with you?" he hissed in her ear.

She stopped hacking, but only long enough to make sure she wouldn't injure him when she twisted to the side, out of his grip. "I know why Thibaut kept coming in here," she panted, raising the weapon again, surging at the god once more. "*Emotion's not dead.*"

PART TWO

Plight of the Gods

HAILWIC

In a Time and Place Unknown

Hailwic quickly learned that rebellion didn't mean being constantly *rebellious.* Brashness would get her bullied, being contrary would keep her confined.

She vowed to be the subtler sort. To watch, listen, and wait.

She bore her year of shame with grace, knowing that if she played the repentant daughter, her parents would relax into her new persona. They *wanted* to think her reformed, after all.

They kept her chaperoned at all times, barely let her out of the house, didn't even grant her leave to find a job. But that was fine. All fine. She accepted their rules with a smile, pretended to recognize their overbearing presence as protection rather than intimidation. She said *thanks be* at least a dozen times a day and maintained the family's little living room shrine to the Friend with meticulous attention. Such daily indignities were bearable, but she still knew she was biding her time in a perpetual standoff, and it made day-to-day life a tense production of not just walking on eggshells, but tapdancing on them.

None of them talked about Zoshim. Not in the context of where he was now, not in the context of their happy past. Her parents seemed pleased to pretend they'd never had a son; even the pictures of him had disappeared from the walls. They'd scrubbed his presence, his memory—from their home and their lives—with disturbing ease. It made Hailwic feel like she was going mad, but she couldn't say a word about it, not if she wanted to stay on the outside of the prison system.

She could find help for Zoshim if she was free. Back in a cell, she could do nothing.

At the end of the year she had to do a *restorative interview* in which she confessed to her crimes, renounced Zoshim, verified her love for the country, and praised Uphrasia. She got through it all with a straight face, but promptly threw up in the bathroom after.

Once that was done—once her parents and the law accepted that she had truly seen the error of her ways—she applied for university. School would get her the hells out of the house, and as long as her grades were good and she studied something acceptable, she was sure her parents would loosen her leash.

She hoped there, of all places, she might find people who really saw what was happening under Uphrasia, people who didn't look away, people who didn't make excuses. She'd underestimated the rigidity of her parents' backbones, but she knew there were others out there like her.

To make the transition easier, she applied to her father's alma mater, Helena Academia, and intended to follow in his footsteps and study magichanical engineering. In a different life she might have chosen sociology or history, maybe even art, but *what* she studied was just one more opportunity to either please or disappoint. She needed to please, to ease one more knot from her parents' brows.

Besides, she was a legacy. And with her newly minted government label of *reformed* and the specifics of her record expunged, it was no wonder she found herself enrolling just a few short months later.

However, the "freedom" she found beyond her home's walls was simply a parody thereof. She had freedom of movement, theoretically, except that university students were restricted to traveling between the campus and their place of residence—in her case, the dormitories—during the weekdays and had a strict perimeter of town streets they were allowed to wander on their off days. This was all painted as being for their safety, of course. Helena Academia was situated extremely close to the miles and miles long bright white limestone wall separating Radix from Remotus to the west. Every few weeks Hailwic could look up to see missiles whistling overhead, shot from the nearby military base, aiming to take out some new infrastructure the Remaining Followers of Fistus—the RFF—had installed on the far side of the wall.

It should bother her, she realized. The constant barrage, possible retaliation from Remotus. But for every dozen military engagements initiated by Radix, there was only the occasional homemade bomb from Remotus, and she was numb to that sort of danger at this point. She could not remember a time when the Friend had *not* been pushing back the RFF, the remnants of the former dictator's regime.

When she was little, she hadn't questioned it—the need to reannex the seceding lands, to stomp out the vestiges of the terrible time before. Even now, she did not doubt that Fistus's rule had been dark and bloody and terrible. She'd never met her mother's parents because they'd died when a mob whipped up by Fistus's fervor had attacked a grocer, claiming he was hiding a secret smuggling ring in his store's nonexistent basement. Fistus had blamed the famine on those "controlling" the food. He'd blamed his own sputtering incompetency first on the distributors, then on the farmers, then he'd turned his mania on Cryptopaths themselves.

It had been hells to get through, she did not doubt that.

What she doubted was the Friend's shiny new world, bought at the expense of yet another scapegoat: those who shared their pathy with Fistus.

She'd heard the RFF was gaining strength. That they might have a real army soon.

Hailwic's hope of easily locating like-minded people who'd be willing to share their doubts with her dissipated just as quickly as her rosy idea of new freedom. Her engineering classmates never spoke of politics unless it was to parrot back the usual state talking points, and she soon grew tired of that vapid repetition. She branched out, found herself in bars filled with smoke, booze, and yet more cheap philosophies. The house parties were filled with near the same, except there was always some asshole who'd let his high loosen his lips enough that he'd yell something filled with bravado, but ultimately benign (*Fuck Uphrasia!, Tear down the wall!,* and *Free Remotus!* were all common favorites) which would get him a visit from the Wellness agents—the Friend's public discourse enforcers.

Only one student had been so brave (or so naïve) as to blatantly state, "No one follows Fistus anymore. That's not who they're fighting for in Remotus," and when the Wellness agents had come for her, she'd never returned to class.

Given that, it wasn't exactly a wonder Hailwic couldn't find anyone whose tongue would wag when their head was clear. All of her little prodding hints with new classmates got her worse than nowhere. Instead of making friends and securing allies, she found herself in an ever-widening circle of loose acquaintances that eventually stopped inviting her to things altogether.

By her second year, she learned to keep her tongue sheathed and her ears open. Sometimes it was better to let the proverbial fish swim into a net rather than constantly dangling a suspicious lure in front of its nose.

Poli Sci 2232, Current Events and Diplomatic Relations, was the kind of class that made her long for a different major. She had to take a handful of social science classes to round out her requirements, and while most of the classes she'd chosen had ended up being more pro-state marketing than basic fact, Professor Solric seemed to be skilled at speaking out of both sides of feir mouth, which made Hailwic perk up and really pay attention.

It wasn't simply about what fey said, but the way fey said it. The RFF was never *the RFF,* instead they were *the insurgents known as the RFF.* The party line was never presented as fact without some kind of qualifier. Never, *The insurgent's goal is to wipe out all Cryptopaths and instate a successor to Fistus,* but *According to Uphrasia, the insurgent's goal . . .* The usual adjectives slapped on the foreign countries who'd originally sanctioned Radix over its treatment of Cryptopaths and continued to do so into the present day were conspicuously absent. Fey didn't describe those nations as *havens for moral degradation* or as *greedy countries attempting to suppress Radix's glory.* The sanctions against their economic powerhouse of a nation were still presented as self-interested punishments, but fey said it was about *pushing back on conflict they found ethically at odds with their own systems.*

When it came time to write her first essay for the class, Hailwic applied the same slightly altered rhetoric and was both terrified and thrilled when, a week after she'd turned it in, the professor asked to see her during feir office hours.

Feir office was a well-lit, if cramped, octagonal room on the third floor of the social sciences' main building, with a perfect view of the library out its small window. Inside sat an oversize wooden desk—the kind Hailwic had seen in the warden's office during her detention—stacked high with papers and tablets. In each of the octagon's corners stood a sturdy post that was decorated in some way, mostly with military accoutrements—old weapons, flags of dead nations.

In one was a map of Radix—the version she was accustomed to seeing all her life—with the country whole, the region to the west that was Remotus unacknowledged, save for the clear line of the wall cutting from north to south. To the north was the cold tundra desert and the Capuchin Crater, to the east many smaller countries, and then, depicted to the south, just a sliver of Nosbeq, the largest nation on the continent.

The office carried the faint aroma of sandalwood and gunpowder tea.

There, she found the professor bent over a printout of her essay. Fey were shorter than Hailwic, with slicked-back brown hair and a neatly shorn circle beard that had begun to gray in the dimple below feir lip. Feir skin was a rich brown, and fey wore round spectacles that usually sat low on feir nose. Hailwic had yet to have more than a few words with fem in passing, so her heart was hammering when she entered—sure this was a fork in her road, but unsure where the path was leading.

"Hailwic Sinclare?" Fey greeted her.

She looked around for a chair to sit herself in, found none. "Yes," she said, awkwardly standing just inside the doorway.

"Daughter of Ferdinand Sinclare, who developed the hypodermic metal theory of magiopathic suppression?"

"Yes."

"And you're pursuing a degree in that same field?"

"Yes."

Fey nodded, as if that confirmed something. "I called you in to discuss your paper. Specifically, this line"—Fey underlined the sentence as fey went on—"'During the tenth year of the Friend's reign, thanks be to her, the organization we call the RFF (though that's not what they call themselves) declared independence.'" There fey stopped and looked at her over the rim of feir glasses with one eyebrow raised. "What do they call themselves, then?"

Hailwic let a beat pass as she dared herself to be brave. "I was hoping you could tell me."

Instead of doing so, fey slowly slid the essay across the desk to within her reach. "I've underlined similar various problematic wording in your essay. Revise and resubmit with the corrections made so that I can put that version in your file."

"My file?"

"All students who have been legally reprimanded have their schoolwork submitted for government review at the end of their studies. You will not be issued a degree until said review has been completed and approved."

Hailwic felt all the blood drain from her face. "No one ever said—"

"I know. Legally, we don't have to. So, revise, resubmit." Fey nodded at the paper. "And might I suggest using that copy for kindling?"

She snatched it up, held it so tightly to her chest she crumpled the crisp pages. "Yes. Of course. Thank you. I . . . I'm sorry." She turned to leave—to flee, really—but fey stopped her.

"I watched your restorative interview."

With all the blood rushing in her ears, she barely heard fem. "Oh?" she asked, trying to sound casual, suddenly terrified there was something in that video that gave her away, that everyone could see.

"It was very good. Textbook."

"Th-thank you?"

"That's the eye I want you to give to your essays from now on. Textbook. If you have any questions as to what that means, don't hesitate to come to me." Feir voice was gentle, reassuring. "Understand?"

"I think so."

"Good. You have a sharp mind and a good ear, Hailwic. I mean that."

She spent that entire evening waiting for the Wellness agents to show up at her dorm, but none came. Frantically, she revised the essay and destroyed all copies of the original, running back to the professor's locked office first thing in the morning to slip it under feir door.

For the rest of the semester, she was far more careful with her paper trail, indeed taking the professor up on feir kind offer to help her rephrase when she was unsure.

When finals came, Hailwic spent most of her waking hours holed up in the library, sitting at a study table on the second floor, next to the big picture windows. From there, she could see much of the campus, and the winding walkway that led to the library's main entrance. She was unsurprised to spot Professor Solric on said path, headed toward the door, but startled when fey unceremoniously set down a small stack of books beside her naught but a few minutes later.

"You might find these particularly interesting," fey said, tapping the pile once with a pointed fingertip before shoving feir hands in feir pockets and strolling off.

Hailwic shuffled through the titles, giving them each a cursory glance. *International Relations for the Active Populist*, *Fistus's Fall: The Beginning; Volume I*, *The Friend's Philosophies for Harmony and Function*, *A True Leader: Claiming Security Back from the Mob*, and—

She raised an eyebrow.

Outdated Mathematics: Failed Formulas and Useless Algorithms.

Opening the plain, jacketless cover, she noted the book had never been checked out. A brief flip through its pages revealed it was indeed exactly as it pronounced itself to be, a list of mathematic failures with small anecdotes as to their inventor's intent and pursuits laid out in the driest of prose.

Snapping the cover shut, she picked it up. "Professor?" she asked, turning, hoping to catch fem before fey left to ask about the point of this read. Maybe it had simply been a mistaken pull. Of course, Hailwic was too slow. Fey had already gone, or at least disappeared in among the shelves.

She could simply leave it to be reshelved. That was the logical thing to do. Any typical student likely would have. But Hailwic was not a typical student.

Maybe she was seeing signs where there were none—drawing lines between nonexistent dots. Her ears were constantly perked, and her eyes on the lookout for allies. Maybe this was nothing.

But maybe it was *something*.

Hunkering down in her seat, she laid the book out before her and bent over it, flipping through the pages once again, but more slowly, looking for annotations or underlines—anything handwritten.

Nothing. One hundred and sixty-seven plain pages of mathematical nonsense.

She looked at the cover itself. The spine. Nothing appeared out of place.

She turned back to the only modification to the book besides the sticker dictating where it should be shelved: the blank checkout card. Slipping it from its pocket, she immediately turned it over. There, in a bit of chicken-scratch handwriting, was a different book's call number.

With all thoughts of her studies abandoned, she gathered up her things and immediately went on the hunt. She dared not use an access terminal to look up the book itself, and instead decided to fumble through the shelves to find it all on her own. Would the number lead her to a book slated for banning that had yet to be removed? A bit of subversive propaganda, or anti-Uphrasia writing?

Or was she reading too much into an honest mistake?

She reasoned she could stand to send herself on a wild goose chase, if that's what it turned out to be. She *couldn't* stand to miss an opportunity if one presented itself.

After half an hour wasted just trying to figure out which floor contained the proper collection, she eventually found it in a darkened corner of the library's basement floor. Municipal minutes. Records of local town hall meetings. Right boring stuff—unless, perhaps, one was looking for clues as to how to join a rebellion.

The basement was dank. Far too damp for books. Clearly these copies were all deemed of little use, unworthy of proper care. Motion-sensing lights flickered on overhead one by one as she crept through the stunted shelves, much shorter than the ones on the other floors, all forced stout due to the hefty oppressiveness of the low ceiling. Hailwic felt like even she had to duck down and hunch her shoulders, lest she hit her head.

As she reached the corner she was aiming for, the last light flickered on, then immediately went out again. She had to crouch low and squint to find the volume of minutes she was after.

The binding was large, flat, and wide—more reminiscent of a file or ledger than a book.

Squatting, she laid the minutes across her knees, and, having learned her lesson with the math book, checked the loan card before looking at anything else.

Jackpot.

Behind the checkout card, someone had tucked a flat piece of paper. It said simply:

Once-a-week communiqué. I ask. You answer. Will cease if shared, followed, threatened.

It could be a trap. She knew that. If she couldn't trust her own parents, she certainly couldn't trust a professor she'd known for less than a semester.

She didn't care. She'd been cautious, she'd paid attention. Instinct told her she'd never find a better opportunity. Hope made her reach for a pen.

It didn't explicitly ask for a reply, but she could read between the lines. She wrote *Understood* beneath the message, doing her best to disguise her handwriting. Snapping the ledger shut, she slipped it back in place, feeling for the first time in years like she wasn't crazy. She wasn't the only one who could see the hellscape beneath the utopia.

It was an intricate game of cat and mouse. Only, both parties clearly thought they were the cat. She was trying to catch the rebellion, and, hopefully, the rebellion was trying to catch her.

The professor would leave her a question, and she'd answer honestly and briefly without overthinking. Writing what she thought fey'd want to hear was just as likely to come off as a dangerous front on her part, so even when the truth made her cringe, she stuck to it.

She explained about Zoshim. About her parents. About her loyalties—to the people, not the politics.

Every line written was a risk. Every word damning.

It was all the risk the professor asked of her, but she would have taken so much more.

The academic year ended, began anew, and still Hailwic stuck to the schedule, never asking questions of her own. She'd tried, at first. But all her inquiries had gone unanswered.

Finally, after a year of clandestine messages between her and the professor, she received what she'd been pursuing. An invitation.

Time, date, address.

They were about to speak on the topic of rebellion face-to-face.

When the appointed evening arrived, she hurried to the designated jump point closest to her dormitory, using her kairopathy to step through the giant jump ring from one side of the city to the other.

There wasn't an urban place in the whole country one could go without meeting the glossy eye of a surveillance drone, so she was careful to keep her strides easy and her posture relaxed. Instead of heading straight for the indicated apartment complex, she stopped at a dingy hole-in-the wall tea and sandwich shop and spent an hour with a paper cup full of weak, bitter chamomile, watching through the barred front windows to see if anyone seemed to be following her.

Feeling secure, she abandoned the cup and headed on, finding herself on a stoop without a doorman and without the ability to call for one. Instead, there was a series of buttons meant to ring an individual door.

The one for apartment 32A had no name beside it, but perhaps that wasn't strange. Either close to half the apartments were empty, or half the residents didn't want their name plastered at street level.

She looked around before eventually pressing the button. The neighborhood didn't seem *that* run-down, but then again . . .

"Yes?" came the clipped reply.

"We, uh, we have an appointment?" She meant it to be a statement, but it definitely came out as a question.

A buzz and a click let her know the front door was open, but the resident in 32A said no more.

Inside she passed a row of brass mailboxes and a single elevator with an OUT OF ORDER sign taped to it—surprise, surprise. A manic kind of din met her in the stairwell, growing louder and louder as she conquered each flight, until it was an in-your-face roar once she arrived at the designated door. Constant drums, growling vocals, screeching strings. At least it seemed to be coming from 32B, rather than her destination.

"Hello?" she called, trying to raise her voice above the music as she knocked on 32A's nondescript door.

"It's open!" came the call from inside.

Cautiously, she pushed the door open, revealing a bare entryway that opened straight into a mostly bare kitchen.

Leaning over the sink, silhouetted by the evening sunlight coming through the murky over-sink window, was someone who looked like a proper soldier. All squared shoulders and firm stance, with a weapon of some kind slung over their shoulder—energy rather than projectile, by the look of it.

There was only one thing for certain she knew about the silhouette: it did *not* belong to Professor Solric.

This was a setup.

She immediately shrank back into the hall, and the person's gaze snapped in her direction. Sharp-jawed and hard-eyed, they came at her. "Hey! Hey, wait!"

Hailwic heard a firm *clunk* over the musical ruckus, but didn't stop to figure out what had caused it. She was back in the stairwell inside a minute, trying to calculate if it was safe to make an illegal jump straight back to her dorm, or if that would only land her in more danger.

In her haste to get away, she tripped over the edge of the stair runner, went pitching headfirst off the landing.

She prepared to jump on instinct to save herself from a broken neck, but a hand shot out and caught her wrist, yanking her back toward the stairwell door. Her footing was still wrong, and as she pivoted to fight, her ankle gave an agonizing pop, sharp pain radiating up her calf.

A whimpering sort of half cry left her throat, and all the fight went out of her. Instead of pushing her attacker away, she leaned in, forcing all her weight on them as she favored her poor left ankle.

"Hey, you're okay," insisted a voice in her ear, and she pulled back to note for certain that she was in the arms of the waiting soldier. Their gun was gone; the firm clunk had been its dropping. "I'm sorry I scared you," they said, expression kind, voice calm. There was no reason a Wellness agent or a member of the Contentment Squad would feel the need to lull her into a false sense of security if she was already caught.

"I—" Hailwic tried to put weight on her foot, to distance herself, but immediately hissed and thought better of it.

"I've got a friend who can look at that."

"No, I'll . . . I'll jump myself to the campus infirmary."

"Professor Solric will have my ass if you do. Come on, there's not much inside, but we can get that elevated until Glensen arrives. Fey're an excellent medic."

It turned out the apartment wasn't completely barren. There was a threadbare couch that looked like it had been pulled from the dump. The soldier—Punabi, zhe'd introduced zhimself—found a plastic bucket with a questionable film on the inside and used it to prop up her ankle, contacted zhur medic friend, then headed back to the kitchen.

"Coffee? Tea? I promise you, the water's clean."

"Tea, thanks," Hailwic said, tracing Punabi's every move, just in case this *was* some sort of a sting operation. Zhe was expressive, and beautiful, with brown skin, toned muscles, and a clean-shaven head. Zhur curved, black eyebrows sat above light hazel eyes that had a honeyed glow to them. Zhe carried zhurself in a manner that reminded Hailwic of people she'd seen on the tele, every movement perfect and precise.

Zhe had an easy draw to zhim. An undeniable pull. Instant charisma Hailwic could never hope to possess.

"I know you were expecting Solric. Sorry to disappoint. While a professor meeting with a student in a secret apartment can be explained in . . . *other* ways, Professor Solric would still prefer feir reputation remain unsullied either way."

Zhe returned with a brew of black tea, unsweetened, in a chipped mug that looked like it wouldn't hold water for much longer, given the long, obvious crack radiating down its side. "So, I'll be your liaison."

Hailwic nodded, but kept her lips pressed firmly together, not letting a sip of tea in and not letting a single syllable out, afraid to further incriminate herself.

"Sorry not sorry about the noise," Punabi went on. "It's why we chose this flat. Can count on 32B's band practice like clockwork. Great masking, in case of bugs. But don't worry, I always do a sweep as soon as I get in."

Hailwic was only half listening. Her eyes kept drifting to the gun once again nestled over zhur shoulder.

Another knock at the door drew Punabi away, and only then did Hailwic realize she'd been holding her breath.

In came a petite individual with a heart-shaped face and wavy hair that curled around prominent ears, feir hair and skin both deep black. "You had to maim the new recruit right out of the gate?" fey asked Punabi, dropping a medical bag down beside Hailwic's elevated leg. "No worries, love, we'll get you squared away. Think of something pleasant while I wrap this up—something calming, like being a tree. No worries, just swaying in the wind."

Glensen turned out to be soft-spoken, with a gentle bedside manner that untangled the disquiet in Hailwic's belly. "Not too bad," fey said when they were done tending to her. "A little twist. You're usually gentler with your dance partners." Fey shot that last bit at Punabi.

"I thought zhe was with the Contentment Squad or something. You look enlisted," Hailwic explained. "Were you? Where did you serve before—" She made a vague gesture above her head, still afraid to state exactly what all this was out loud.

Punabi laughed lightly. "I wasn't a soldier before—" Zhe made the same weak motion.

"Oh?"

"I was a dancer. In the national ballet. *Now* I'm a soldier."

"Ah, so that explains the poise."

A warm expression quirked zhur lips.

"So, what happens now?" Hailwic asked.

"That depends on you," Punabi said. "Baby steps. The Friend's got her tests, and we've got ours."

"Whatever you need me to do, I'll do it." Anything to get the tools to save Zoshim—to set him free.

Punabi grinned. "That's what we like to hear."

11

KRONA

Beyond the closed doors of the war room, life in Mirthhouse chattered on. Inside, the air became burdened with unspoken questions as Melanie, Sebastian, and Tray hung—tense and stunned—at Krona's shoulder, watching her hack away at the encased god.

Breathless, allowing herself to crack just a little more, Krona told them in shaken tones what had happened—who was gone. *Where* they'd gone. How they'd been *stolen*. Every frank statement punctuated by the further tinkling smash of crystal beneath the swiftly blunting edge of the katar.

"Thibaut's teliomancy knew something his conscious mind hadn't yet grasped. He was drawn to zhim because Emotion is still alive. Zhe has to be, that must—zhe has to be," she insisted. "We just have to free zhim, get zhim to zhur temple, and we can wake our first god. Emotion will help us get to the Savior and *kill him* so that we can get our people *back* and end the Thalo reign."

Behind her eyes she saw Thibaut smiling at her, felt his warm hand in hers, his breath in her ear.

She imagined him whispering, *Go on. Harder. Smash it. Smash it to bits.*

And she obeyed, muscles clenched, teeth clenched, everything clenched as she hacked her way toward his salvation.

She knew she must look wild, manic—a stunning opposite of her usual self. Pausing, she spun on the others, took in the trepidation in their gazes, but could hardly bring herself to care.

She'd tried to be calculated. Tried to line up all the dominos just so, so that when they took the final steps to wake the gods they'd have an army of magic wielders and tamed fenri to offer them.

What she'd thought of as careful planning had turned out to be an ineffective trudge. A slow plod toward loss.

"*Help me*," she hissed at them, chest and shoulders heaving with feral breaths.

Tray was the first to move, the stunned look on his face shifting to determination as he turned to the shelves and searched briefly among Hintosep's things for something heavy. He came away with a fist-sized paperweight, made of iron and heavy as a hammer.

Unlike Krona, he aimed for Emotion's head.

The sharp sound of metal hitting stone made them all jump. Beneath the tool, fractures sprang through the crystal, like cracks on a spring-warmed frozen lake.

Surprised by the level of his own success, Tray drew back as the fissures continued to fan out, like wild fingers of lightning, cleaving through the entire top half of the casing, not just across the god's form, but directly down to it. The crackling spread of the fissures was stopped only by the deep grooves Krona had already created around Emotion's waist.

A large chunk over the top of Emotion's right eye came free, sliding from the body, from the plinth, to clunk heavily to the floor, leaving the skull exposed, the eye socket—with its crystals—free to the air.

The hair rose on the back of Krona's neck.

All four of them moved away, holding their collective breath.

The Mindless, according to Avellino, were not inert. They simply lacked will. They became tools of the Savior, beholden to his orders. Will-less, but not free of action, or feeling.

What if Emotion was not zhimself?

What if a newly awoken Mindless god came back to consciousness in a rage?

They, this room, this house, this mountain could all be razed to the ground in an instant.

More bits of the crystal fell away, leaving others cleaved and clinging at strange angles. Tense, Krona looked for signs of movement within. She had half a mind to throw herself on Emotion and jump to the mountaintop high above Clavaburn. She might not be able to save herself, but at least she could save Mirthhouse.

As the moments ticked on and the last of the dislodged chunks and flecks settled, nothing moved. No one stirred, least of all Emotion.

Krona had thought the thick crystal was like an Asgar-Skanian coffin. Something to house a body, perhaps to stave off decay—if a god's body could even be touched by decay. But now she considered it to be something more akin to the hourglass they'd found Time in. An enchanted prison that preserved—putting the god in stasis, like a frog in winter.

Cracking it didn't seem to have any effect on its ability to keep Emotion under.

Tentatively, Krona shifted back toward the body, daring to dig her fingertips into one of the fissures and pull another mass of crystal free. When the god still didn't stir, her excavation became hurried, frantic. She tore bits away, flinging them behind her.

The others surged forward without needing to be asked, at her side in an instant.

They scrambled to dig Emotion out of zhur glittering shell.

It took hours. Once the largest chunks were removed, there were still more bits that needed a hammer's attention, still shards and sharp flecks, and clinging dust. It stuck fast to Emotion's body and clothes alike. A thin pale purple shift covered the god, nothing more, and Krona wasn't sure if zhe belonged in something more regal, or simply nothing at all.

The closer they got to revealing Emotion's skin to the air, the more everyone's hands shook, the more the excitement and anticipation in the room took on a heftiness.

There was an unmistakable, preternatural heat coming off Emotion's form, making the crystal clinging directly to zhim difficult to handle. It *seared*, like the vats in the hoard. The air grew humid—thick, sticky.

Somber questions rose in Krona's mind, ones that made her body buzz and her skin prickle, and though she didn't voice them, she wondered if the others were feeling the same unease.

Could one touch a god, skin to skin? Or was their power too great? Would such contact char the flesh from one's bones—annihilate them on the spot?

Or were these just fears of the reverent? Surely humanity wasn't so fragile as to be destroyed by the very presence of their makers.

They had the majority of the crystal removed, and still there were no signs that Krona was correct—that zhe was alive. Emotion remained as inert as anything dead. Perhaps the crystal's influence was not in its thickness. Perhaps every last flake of it needed to be washed away in order for the god to be revived.

"We'll need something to wash zhim properly," Krona said. "I don't know if it's best to simply strip the rest away without making sure we can scrub zhim of the remnants."

"Blessed water," Melanie said quickly. "I can't imagine simple water straight from the stream would suffice."

"I can jump to a coterie," Krona said, "get us some."

"I'll go with you," Tray offered.

She shook her head. "I'll be quicker on my own."

What she didn't say was that she needed a moment. A chance to recenter herself. Her manic energy had drained away in the preceding hours, and now a hollow doubt threatened to fill the vacated space.

Emotion wasn't moving.

She'd been so confident that Emotion yet lived, that Thibaut's sleepwalking had to mean he'd sensed that truth teliopathically.

But had that been the sudden grief talking? Her inability to accept the Savior's upper hand?

The lows and highs and lows again were threatening to puncture her willpower. Part of her wanted to stop trying, to stop moving, to let the doubts have their way and lead her into a state of unending stillness.

If she continued to stand here, chipping away with nothing else to occupy her mind, that stagnating uncertainty would get a chance to root. She couldn't let it.

Tray and Sebastian gathered up a bowl covered in gold leaf, and various dried blooms—lavender, violets, pansies, anything to reflect the amethyst of Emotion's form—from around the dais while Krona went to her room to dress in simple worship skirts with a shawl to hide her bone wings. On the way, she dodged questions from curious Mirthhouse residents, who'd clearly heard the smashing but had feared coming to investigate. All she could do was give them platitudes: "Everything's all right. Don't worry. I'll explain soon."

With bowl in hand, she created a lens and whisked herself away.

It had been a bitter long while since Krona had visited Lutador City proper. It was a place that had both loved and hated her. She'd made a home here, lost a home here. She'd served its people as a Regulator, and the people thought she'd betrayed them by assassinating a Grand Marquis. She had missed its awe-inspiring architecture—the organic forms set in stone, the stained glass that caught sunlight and turned it into rainbows of art that reflected into homes and businesses and onto the streets themselves. The gutters always stank and any gap between the pavers sported perpetual mud, but the street venders bullied out the bouquet of filth with their beautifully spiced foods, and the sidewalks were well swept.

It was a city of contradictions for her. She wondered if it was a city of contradictions for all of its inhabitants.

The first thing she noticed, touching down behind a small grove of trees inside the high limed walls of a familiar coterie, was smoke. Smoke billowing out of a building just on the other side of the street. The air was choked with it, and screams assailed her from outside the courtyard. The priests—who normally would have all been inside each god's cloister—were gathered together in the center of the coterie's garden, leaning back, shielding their eyes, frantically chatting among themselves about whether or not they should evacuate.

Krona's hackles went up as she assessed the area for immediate threats, dropping into crisis mode faster than most people would even be able to comprehend the existence of a threat. It was second nature—the tension, the readiness.

Pulling the bowl to her chest, she drew back, shielding herself in a cluster of ornamental bushes, the blessed water temporarily forgotten.

More cries, more screams. She caught the word *bomb* as a supplicant ran past. Reaching out from her hiding place, she snatched them mid-stride, pulling them down beside her.

"There might be more," they sobbed. "Going off around the city."

"Winsrouen?" she asked breathlessly. How had their army gotten this far north?

The supplicant shook their head—not a no, but a bewildered uncertainty. "Sympathizers, maybe," they said. "Terrorists."

Krona's knuckles went tight around the bowl's edge. The violence all stemmed from the Savior's machinations. This horror, like so many others, could be traced back to the night Hintosep had killed the Grand Marquis and cut Krona off from this city and her former life.

She hated seeing her city like this. She hated her city suffering like this.

Krona's lips parted to offer the supplicant a rescue—a way out of the city.

Before she could speak, they were throwing off her hand and scraping their way out of the bushes. "I have to find the children," they explained.

Krona let them go.

She couldn't save Lutador by jumping each citizen to safety one by one. She had to think on a grander scale. She'd come here for a purpose, and she needed to hurry.

Determined, she scurried to one of the reflecting pools along the courtyard's walkway, kneeling down to gently flood the bowl and rehydrate the flowers. She crushed the drenched petals again and again to make the water fragrant—lamenting that it would also smell of smoke after this. Gathering her skirts and pulling her shawl taut, she then hurried to Emotion's priest where zhe huddled—identifiable by the number of cascading jewels that dangled from zhur cincture.

"You should not be here, child," zhe gasped, startling at Krona's gentle touch to zhur shoulder. With a haunted look in zhur eye, zhe quickly led Krona away from the others, trying to usher her toward the coterie's exit. "We sent all worshipers away—"

"Please, it's important," Krona said, allowing the priest to lead her while presenting the bowl. "This water must be blessed."

Priests, like Regulators, were ever aware of their duties. Instead of arguing, zhe stopped, thinned zhur lips, and nodded. "For the fires?"

"No. It's . . . it's for washing. A renewal. For someone thought as good as dead but who's survived."

"For a transition, then?" Zhe gestured over to zhur colleagues. "Nature's representative would be much more appropriate for—"

"Please, can you do it? Emotion is . . . is the recipient's family patron."

They needed to scrub away every last bit of crystal, but the blessing was really more for the hands that would wash Emotion than Emotion zhurself. To protect and bind them all in the ritual of it—for bathing a god could be nothing but a holy ritual. They could not see to Emotion as they would anyone else bedridden by ailment. Their hands weren't . . . *She* wasn't . . .

Zhe was celestial, and Krona and the others were merely mortal.

The priest gazed past Krona's shoulder for a moment, as though something had caught zhur attention, but after a moment, zhe nodded, holding zhur palms around the bowl before reciting the appropriate portion of the scrolls. After, for good measure, zhe yanked a small bead of a stone from those hanging freely at zhur hip and added it to the water.

"Enchanted amber," zhe explained. "Hope."

"Thank you," Krona said, sincerely moved by the additional gesture. "Thank you."

The priest nodded, and was able to offer a smile, despite the flames and smoke—despite the world crumbling all around.

Krona made to leave—to pretend to exit through the coterie's doors—but only moments after she'd taken a few steps, the priest gasped and called, "Are you . . ." Zhur voice shook. "Are you the omen they speak of? The . . . ?"

The Demon of the Passes.

She realized the shawl must not have disguised the bulge of her wings as well as she'd hoped. She half turned back around, not sure until she parted her lips to speak if she would play ignorant, simply deny, or confess. "I'm no demon," she found herself saying. "No omen, or portent. I go where there's pain," she explained, "and these days, pain is everywhere."

"And why do you take the shape of a human?"

At that, Krona let the shawl sag, let the bones free, let them flare out and flex.

The priest's eyes widened; zhe fell to zhur knees.

Krona found herself echoing what Hintosep had said to her what felt like a lifetime ago: "I'm as human as you are. No more than that, and certainly no less."

"And you worship the gods?" zhe asked in awe.

Krona swallowed thickly. The tenor of the priest's voice, the cataclysm of fear and exaltation warring in zhur eyes, made Krona feel equal parts small and powerful. Guilty and unworthy, but at the same time prideful and ascendant.

"I give of myself to the gods just as the gods gave of themselves for the Valley," she said, purposefully cryptic, unable to express to this single priest all that the gods were to her and she to them in so brief a time.

But zhe seemed to accept this, nodding once more.

As the other priests were still focused on the billowing smoke, oblivious to the exchange, Krona ignored the doors, deciding to lead with honesty. If they were to remake the Valley, then the realities of human power should not be hidden. Without guile, she created a lens back to Mirthhouse and, letting the priest observe every move, stepped carefully back through.

As she feared, a strong essence of smoke and a wafting of ash still clung to her, but it was no more offensive than the smoke from a bundle of incense.

Tray was there in an instant to take the bowl from her, and Melanie rose from Emotion's side, concern in her eyes. "What happened?" she asked. "You look shaken."

"Lutador is burning."

She was glad many of their loved ones were nowhere near the city proper. Her mother, Melanie's mother, Sebastian's aunt. The latter two had gone to the countryside to bring aid to the war's refugees. But that didn't mean they were safe.

Nowhere in Arkensyre was safe.

The late-afternoon light refracted through Emotion's crystal eyes, sending slashes of lavender across the wall opposite the windows. They'd managed to pluck the last of the shards and chips away, leaving only the finest flakes still clinging. No one seemed scorched, and nothing was burnt, but now, with the sun's rays angled through the windows as they were, Krona could clearly see that the god had begun to glow ever so faintly.

Moving with deliberation, Krona set to work. She willed the tremors out of her hands as she took the kerchief and began to wash zhur body. Sebastian went to the kitchen to retrieve washcloths for the others, and together they silently went about ridding Emotion of the last of zhur prison.

Krona began at Emotion's crown, gently dabbing the crystal dust away, oh so extra careful around the cascade of purple grain fronds and spires of verbena, salvia, and wild indigo that were woven together in one thick plait in place of hair. Moving down zhur neck to zhur torso and arms, together they detailed around each surprise marking—shimmering raised symbols, like scars, that matched the engravings on zhur skull-like face. They wiped firmly at each fold of the simple periwinkle shift, gently traced between zhur fingers, and gingerly swiped at zhur hips and thighs.

Krona tried to focus on simply doing a thorough job, trying to remain detached—trying to ignore *who* lay out before her. It wasn't until she reached zhur feet—the skin an ombre of purples just like zhur hands—that her eyes began to grow hot, her vision blurring.

Emotion was well over twelve feet tall, yet laid out on the floor like this, still and defenseless beneath their ministrations, zhe seemed delicate. This was a god, and zhe had been robbed. Robbed of consciousness, of respect, of personhood—*godhood*—by the Savior.

If a being of such power could be reduced to *this* by such a man—

Knocking her misgivings away, she finished her portion of the washing. As the others did the same, they all took a step back.

"Now what?" Sebastian breathed.

Krona went to the chest she'd retrieved from the bottom of Deep Waters and gently opened the lid so the others could see the treasure that lay inside.

Four cubes sealed in red wax sat nestled in velvet within.

She'd kept the gods' minds hidden for years now. Krona had chosen to follow the Savior's example in this instance alone; the leader of the Thalo had put the minds somewhere nearly impossible to reach, so she'd done the same.

"Emotion's is the upper right," she said as Sebastian tentatively reached forward. She'd pressed symbols into each so she could easily tell them apart. A simple four-sided diamond denoted Emotion's. Two triangles formed a rudimentary hourglass on Time's. Nature's was marked by an arrow, and Knowledge's sported the suggestion of a tree.

As Sebastian plucked the cube from its nesting, she noticed the blessed water had left flakes of crystal scattered over his skin, across his hands and forearms. She lifted her own palm to the light and noted the same. Perhaps it was fitting that they shine in the presence of Emotion.

With a letter opener taken from Krona's desk, Sebastian cracked the wax, unmolding it from the sides of the glass box that held the enchanted halite and Emotion's mind. The manifestation of the mind shimmered within, like a golden lightning bolt frozen in place.

"Not here," Tray said, putting his hand over Sebastian's as he attempted to continue with the unboxing.

"Not here," Krona agreed. "We always expected to wake the other three inside their temples. That was Avellino's plan, and I don't see why this should change anything. It'll be safer—for everyone. The rest of Mirthhouse doesn't know what we've done here, and whether we succeed or fail to wake Emotion, it could have dire consequences. There's no way to know what to expect."

Avellino had been positive minds could not be destroyed. Which made them akin to varger and fenri. One could trap a varg, starve it and bottle it, but not kill it. It was ephemeral, something beyond concepts as base as mortality. And yet, Avellino had never been quite sure what a mind would do once released from halite. Without the guidance of the Savior, it was possible the mind would simply float away once released from the salt. An uncatchable wisp, lost to the breeze.

The temples had been built to contain the gods—and they assumed that included the remnants of their minds as well.

And if they *were* successful—well, there was no telling how a newly awakened god might react. She could not unleash zhim on Mirthhouse.

"Make arrangements for Abby's care," Krona said. "Then we'll jump to Xyopar."

12

AVELLINO

Gerome hissed in Avellino's ear as he guided him by one wrenched arm through a series of the keep's passages, promising punishments aplenty. But it wasn't until he said, smugly, "How thoughtful of you, Child, to bring sacrifices for the Savior," that fear shot through his core.

He'd hoped the others had gotten away, but he should have known better. Should have realized it was childish to think they could escape Gerome when he could not.

Gritting his teeth, Avellino swallowed down threats and pleas alike. Gerome wanted a reaction out of him, wanted to know that once again he'd easily rooted out the boy's worst fears. So, he would not keep them secret, he simply wouldn't give them voice.

"You had such potential when you left me," Gerome continued. "Or, I should say, were stolen away. You were weak, were seduced by the sweet promises of those who would use you. It's not your fault."

He couldn't be sure if Gerome believed what he was saying. He spoke as he always had to Avellino—with assurance, authority. There was warmth there, but with a biting edge. Bitterness and arrogance wrapped up in the guise of care and love.

They stopped in front of a sturdy door flanked by torches and riveted with iron. "I'm a Grand Orchestrator now, and in truth, I should hand you over to a Possessor, but I can't have you confusing the other children, worrying them with lies. You'll be staying here until such time as I can turn all of my attention to your reeducation."

The door swung inward on squeaking hinges, revealing a dark space—bare, but not empty.

This is a cell, he realized.

They were in the keep's dungeon.

And he would not be imprisoned alone.

Avellino nearly wept with relief when he saw who sat inside. Hintosep. Hintosep, who he'd feared was dead. Who could have been tortured then sacrificed but instead was here, locked away. Only a small part of him clocked the Cage, secured around her head, and no part of him noticed how still she was, unmoved by them barging in.

He tried to go to her, rushing into the cell—into his own confinement—of his own accord. But Gerome pulled him up short before he could reach her, whirling Avellino around to face him. He grabbed the boy by the chin, bony fingers pressing strangle-tight against his jaw, sharp nails digging half-moons into his cheeks. He *yanked*—made Avellino look up, made him rise high on his tiptoes just to keep himself from dangling by the neck.

"I finally have you back where you belong," Gerome sneered into his face before looking pointedly over his shoulder at Hintosep. "I have almost *all* of you *back where you belong.*"

With that, he kissed Avellino's forehead. His clammy lips were tender. The gesture would have been familial coming from nearly anyone else, but Avellino knew both he and Hintosep took it for the threat it was. Any kiss from Gerome was a demonstration of power, of ownership.

The Possessor bared his teeth at Avellino once more before whipping him to the ground, tossing him aside.

Avellino twisted in his fall, catching himself on his hands, but landing hard on his hip. He knew better than to rise right away. Defiance would do him no good, not yet.

Apparently satisfied, Gerome excused himself from their presence, shutting the cell door lightly. His wooden sandals *clap, clap, clapp*ed evenly away into the distance.

Only when he could no longer hear the echo did Avellino lift his head, balling his hands into fists against the cold, dirty cobbles of the floor. He met Hintosep's eyes. "He means Abby, doesn't he?"

He thinks we cheated him, Hintosep tried to say. Tried, despite knowing her lips would not heed her. *If the three of us, wayward as we are, come back, he can pretend he never failed. He won't simply have* won *in his mind, he'll pretend there was never a struggle to begin with.*

He was always especially gifted at self-delusion. Even as a child.

Carefully crawling forward, staying low on his hands and knees, as though simply standing might summon his Possessor back, Avellino slithered toward Hintosep, setting himself at her feet.

Only then, watching the way her eyes failed to find him, the way she failed to twitch or whimper, did he truly understand that the Cage had her. She was in a prison within a prison. She could not acknowledge him, and he wasn't even sure whether or not it kept her from realizing he was there.

"He wouldn't have put me in here with you if he was worried I could free you," he mused aloud. It felt right to talk to her, even if she couldn't speak back. "But that doesn't mean we shouldn't try."

Hintosep's breath came as steady as ever, her heart never skipped a beat, but internally she frantically shook her head and shouted at him to keep away. *No. No, child. Don't try it. You'll only hurt us both. Don't—*

But there was no way to warn him. The Cage tamped down on even the simplest of her magical abilities. There was no sharing her secrets or feeding him clandestine communication. It all had to come from him, and she had no concept of how his powers might have grown or withered these past years.

He considered her from the floor for a time, studying the way the Cage clung to her, the places where it bore into her. The wounds from its burrowing had long since healed to accommodate the contraption. Like Gerome, she would wear its scars after.

He frowned to himself, tossed off that thought. No. She would not have to bear its markings if she didn't want to. Abby could erase them, if she wished it.

He stood slowly, keeping his distance at first. He was wary of the Cage, of what it could do. He had no idea if it could be commanded to leap from one victim to another—to attack like the metal creature it very much resembled. Like Hintosep, it made no move as he hovered around it, peering at its joints from different angles, taking in the workmanship and detail.

Tentatively, he stretched his fingers toward one leg.

He jumped when he received a mild shock for his efforts.

"Just static," he said under his breath, and he wasn't sure who, exactly, the reassurance was meant for. He touched it again, felt nothing but the coolness of its baser materials. He could not sense the magic imbued in the enchantment, though there was no denying its presence. It seemed a sturdy sort of crown, but not indestructible. Perhaps if he could simply loosen it—pry it a hair's breadth away from her face—she would be free of its influence.

He ran his hands up and down the sides of it, as if it were a string instrument he could strum or pluck, each leg releasing its own special note. Flexing his fingers, readying himself, he took hold of the pair digging into her temples.

One.

Two.

Three.

He *pulled,* arms straining, muscles taut as he gritted his teeth. The legs looked so thin; he had to be stronger than the metal. He had to be.

Avellino closed his eyes, filled his lungs, and channeled all of his remaining strength into trying to tear the Cage in two.

Hintosep could not scream. Despite the tearing and the grinding and the *pain,* she could not scream.

He would not succeed. The Cage could not be removed except by command—not without slicing through its host, perhaps killing her in the process.

As he tore at a set of the upper legs, all of the lower legs dug in, like ticks asserting their bite. They drilled deeper as the Cage *tightened,* refusing to let go. The cursed enchantment had only one purpose, one function, and it would automatically see to its duty without care or thought or deviance.

After only a few moments of struggle, rivulets of blood began to stream, hot and horrible, down her cheeks. They caught on the tip of her chin, hanging heavily for an instant, like a promise, until a dribble of it splashed down onto her lap.

⊳⊣⊲⊳-○-⊲⊳⊢⊲

When he heard a small, steady pattering, Avellino's eyes flew open and he looked down—took in what he had done.

His hands flew away like he'd been shocked again.

Oh gods.

Avellino stared at her in horror, stumbling back.

Tears and blood left varying tracks down her face, but she stared placidly. Still she held herself perfectly rigid. She could do nothing else, no matter her suffering.

"I'm sorry," he said hurriedly, lifting his already ruined hem, dabbing at the flow, so frantic in his ministrations that he smeared it over her clean skin, leaving rusty smudges.

⊳⊣⊲⊳-○-⊲⊳⊢⊲

Thibaut felt like he should have *known*.

He'd only been a Teliopath for a short time, but *still.* Knowing had been his business in Lutador. Knowing was his *essence* now.

He should have known someone was waiting for them. That it wasn't safe.

He was used to failing other people. He wasn't used to failing Krona.

He collapsed against the far wall of the cell, sliding down it to land hard on his bum with his knees pulled up in front of him. He settled his arms atop them, clasping his hands together, worrying them—acutely aware of his missing fingers in a way he hadn't been before.

When his varg had bitten through them—had *eaten* them—the whole event seemed hazy, like a dream. He would have expected losing pieces of himself to be a visceral experience, but the adrenaline coursing through him had made it feel distant, less urgent than focusing on all the other things he'd had to do in the moment to simply *stay alive*.

These past days—weeks—he'd been too focused on other things to spend real time with a Physiopath for proper regrowth. He'd never liked his hands—scarred from sewer scavenging as they were. But he'd kept his scars from the Dregs these past years, and he'd thought he'd wear these new, more dramatic ones, for a while, because he'd *earned them*.

Besides, he could have them grown back anytime.

But now the absence of his fingers was less a temporary badge of bravery and more of an acute loss. He zeroed in on the phantom sense that they were still there, on the odd fact that he had no pain. The injury was relatively fresh, it should still throb, or something. Except Melanie and Krona had worked together to accelerate the healing. It was as though his body had come to terms with the injury before his mind had even caught on to the fact that they were truly missing—that a part of him was never coming back without magical intervention.

"I'm sorry," he said flatly.

From the other side of the narrow cell, Juliet and Mandip's attention shot to him.

Honestly, he'd been surprised Gerome had shoved the three of them in together, and without excess bindings. No chains, no collars, no torturous illusions to break them down and leave them sobbing. The surprise had been brief though when he'd realized why: they were unimportant. Unthreatening. As inconsequential as cattle, simply corralled away until they could be led to the auction block or chopping block or—gods forbid—left to rot without ever seeing another meal or living soul ever again.

"I should have—"

"Oh, stop it," Juliet said, keeping her voice light, though there was an undeniable strain beneath it all. Both she and Mandip seemed to be searching for weaknesses in their cell—cracks or chips or nails to exploit. "Do not expect me to simper or wail. I *do not* play the part of damsel in distress well. Or at all, if I can help it. Plus, we've got someone's arse to save besides our own." She gave him a wry smile and a wink, clearly trying to raise his spirits, but he couldn't manage the same reassurance in return.

With a heavy sigh, she sauntered over to him, lifting the hem of her skirt daintily, sliding some of the rat droppings on the floor out of the way with the toe of her boot. She lowered herself down gracefully at his right, curling up beside him, threading one arm around his. After a beat, she gently lay her temple against his shoulder. "Do not for a moment think this is your fault," she whispered.

Mandip ceased his search, coming to stand toe-to-toe with Thibaut, who looked up at him imploringly.

"We three have been in tight places before," Mandip reminded him. "We managed then. We'll manage now."

Thibaut bit his tongue. He wanted to point out that it seemed like Krona had always been the one to bail them out, and she'd sworn never to return to the keep until all the gods were at her side.

But that fact did them no good in the moment, so he simply stretched out his left hand for Mandip, who took it and let himself be led down to the floor at Thibaut's other side.

Once the young noble was properly sat, Thibaut let his hand go in favor of flinging his arm around Mandip's shoulders, pulling him close.

Both Mandip and Juliet shuffled nearer, and Thibaut closed his eyes, knocking his head back against the uneven bricks of the wall.

There had to be a way out of this. He was a Dreg—he'd once prided himself on his ability to slip in and out of anywhere. Any social situation, any building, any bed. They couldn't wait for Krona; they would have to save themselves.

13

HAILWIC

In a Time and Place Unknown

It didn't take long for Hailwic to realize the professor's—and thus, the rebellion's—interest in her wasn't solely because of her ideals.

Her family had status, connections. *Credibility.*

Hailwic herself was an inroad to some of Uphrasia's closest allies, and, eventually, Uphrasia herself.

After years of work, both secret and public, Hailwic graduated publicly with an advanced degree in engineering, and privately in her branch of the Remotus Fortification Ranks (the RFR). She'd known for a while that the rebellion ultimately wanted to place her in a highly sensitive position, but was still surprised when the assignment came in.

"Command Corp?"

"They, along with Stymex Industries, are working on a new means of magichanical pathological suppression," Punabi said. Zhe too had graduated, from a grunt to a coordinator. Zhe was like a general, giving orders and arranging ranks.

They still met in that same apartment, under the cover of that same homebrew band. But Hailwic could tell that was all about to change.

"We've set up an interview with our Command Corp lead, Dr. Kinwold Theesius," zhe went on, handing Hailwic a thick folder. "The project represents a unique opportunity, because Uphrasia has been keeping a close personal eye on their development. Which means you'll have a chance to get close to her."

"To what end?"

Punabi cocked zhur shaved head and raised a poignant eyebrow. Despite their sense of security, there were still things better not uttered aloud on this side of the border wall.

"Oh."

Oh.

"Look over everything in that folder, then be sure to burn it." Punabi gave her a lingering hug, then left her to digest her new assignment.

Hailwic plopped herself down heavily on the musty couch, whose underbelly had long ago given out and now sagged on the dusty floor. With a deep breath, she let the file unfold in her lap like the welcoming jaws of a carnivorous plant.

The professor had made sure she'd been trained in a number of armaments and close-combat techniques. She'd understood from early on that the rebellion had been training her for violent ends, she just hadn't realized *whose* violent end:

Uphrasia's.

She was supposed to assassinate the Friend. The most well-protected woman in the world.

Breathing deeply, feeling awkward in her clean-pressed, sharp-lined office clothes, Hailwic hurried down the block from her rebellion-secured housing to the nearest designated jump point and stepped herself through to Command Corp.

The building was unassuming. Just another glass-plated skyscraper to match the other glass-plated skyscrapers around it. Each corner on its block was occupied by a busy jump point, with licensed city Kairopaths helping people of other pathies to and from the city center. Everything looked so . . . orderly. Everyone dressed just so. Everyone moving just so.

Stiff.

Everything was stiff, just like her jacket.

It was the opposite of the constant change that Physiopaths could produce. The constant ebb and flow of growth and evolution. It felt as though the immovable order had been imposed specifically to spit in the eye of such magic.

Inside the building, the cookie-cutter mundanity continued. Ignoring it, trying to shake off the feeling that everyone's eyes were tracking her—that they could see through her adoption of their rigidity to the malleable soul beneath—she hurried to an unoccupied jump shaft, asked for a display of the seventeenth floor, and jumped herself up once she had a fix.

Once she introduced herself at the front desk, she found herself rushed through a flurry of corporate introductions. Paperwork was shoved in front of her, a name badge was clipped to her jacket, a coffee station was waved to, cubicles were pointed at. In what felt like no time at all she was led into a private office—which was only private because it had a door, not because the walls were any more opaque than the windows—and placed firmly into a stiff-backed chair in front of a desk. The nameplate adorning the desk read DR. KINWOLD THEESIUS.

But it wasn't Dr. Theesius who greeted her.

A man, pale of complexion, with brown hair that swooped over his fashionable thick-rimmed glasses rather roguishly—given the uniformity of most other styling she'd seen—stood next to the desk. He'd had his back to the door, turning when the secretary opened it, giving Hailwic a stellar smile and extending a warm hand toward that aforementioned seat.

"You must be the person who's come to steal my job," he said jovially. "I'm Lonny."

Hailwic led with a fake laugh that ate at her soul just a little bit before introducing herself and taking his hand to shake it firmly.

"I've been Kinwold's assistant for five years," he said.

"And now he's moving on up in the world," came a new voice. She glanced over her shoulder and caught the name on their badge. *This* was who she'd come here to partner with.

Dr. Theesius was a tall, pale, lengthy individual with a sophisticated drawl, clean-shaven head, and short-shorn gray beard that had once been pitch-black. "Hailwic, so good to have you."

Her series of interviews had all been for show, of course, as was this onboarding, but she went through the motions with dedication and sincerity. The professor had taught her well: if there was even a chance Uphrasia's loyalists were watching, you did not drop your mask for an instant. Survival surpassed truth. That was how the spineless passed their days in this world, and that was how rebels had to function as well.

Assassination was a long game. Hailwic knew it would take years, maybe even a decade, to get close enough to Uphrasia to end her.

In that time, the RFR had a coup to plan, positions to fill. They already had people in key levels of security—Cryptopaths who could proclaim Hailwic guileless during monthly loyalty checks—but the rebellion would need even more Cryptopaths in high places to ensure Hailwic's true goals were never discovered.

Beyond that, there were lines of succession to secure; once Uphrasia's most loyal were dealt with, they had to be replaced with RFR sympathizers. The Friend's reign might end with a single blow, but it would take many coordinated attacks to be sure the system ended with her.

There were many plodding days of regular office work ahead of Hailwic, and the sooner she accepted them as important to her RFR work, the better.

She learned quickly that Dr. Theesius tended to have two facial expressions: absolute delight and utter disgust. Hailwic liked them right away. They were enthusiastic, upbeat, and *exuberant* about this infant field of enchantment engineering, in love with the science and frustrated with any aspect of bureaucracy that got in its way.

Or, if it was an act, it was one they never dropped.

Lonny was good-natured and inventive, if a little inflexible in the way he went about things, which, in turn, meant the way Hailwic went about things. He prepared her to be his replacement with dedication that was commendable, if ultimately unremarkable.

Hailwic thought he was ultimately just another worker, another drone in Uphrasia's army, until Punabi brought him up during one of zhur check-ins.

"What do you think of Lonny? You never mention him."

"You know him?" Hailwic asked. The two of them were sitting cross-legged on the floor of the loud-as-all-hells apartment, slurping spiced noodles out of to-go containers. She shrugged. "I didn't think he was worth mentioning."

A cheap chandelier overhead was their only lighting. Hailwic wasn't sure which operative had been cheeky enough to install it, but it was a nice addition. It gave their space directly under it a warm glow, making the room feel intimate—like they were the only two people in the whole complex, despite the noise.

"Well, he's sure mentioned you a bunch in his outgoing reports," Punabi said, waggling zhur eyebrows.

Hailwic brushed the implications of that waggling away. "Why wasn't I briefed on his involvement in the mission?"

"Oh, 'cause he's not," Punabi said, setting down zhur food, shifting into serious mode. "Right now it just looks like he's getting promoted. Really, he's about to get spectacularly fired. Then we'll have him lay low until his noncompete clause runs out, and get him installed at Command Corp's competitor, Stymex."

"If I'm just taking over his position, why wasn't he tasked with . . . *my* task?"

"Lonny doesn't have the background you have. Can't build the rapport with Uphrasia you can. Plus, we need a saboteur at Stymex ASAP. Their group is rocketing ahead and we can't let that happen."

Hailwic learned exactly why stopping the new method of magical suppression was so vital just a few weeks into her hire, briefed over a private dinner by Dr. Theesius and, to her surprise, Lonny as well.

She arrived at the doctor's town house with a bottle of wine and frayed nerves. The work-focused weeks had been about lulling any potential threats in her new environment into a false sense of security, but they'd lulled *her* as well. Now it was time to get down to business.

Dr. Theesius welcomed her in, took her coat. The tang of spiced tomatoes and cheese hit her nose immediately, and she was suddenly transported back to when she was little. Back to when her old house had been a place of safety, security, and love.

As soon as they were through the door, a little girl—no more than four years old—in a frilly blue top came barreling down the stairs from where Hailwic guessed the bedrooms lay, sliding her hand across the flowered wallpaper as she ran. Her black hair was straight as a string, and her eyes were the deepest midnight blue.

"This," Dr. Theesius said, scooping up the small child and pecking her on the cheek, "is my little Toe Bean."

"Hello, Toe Bean," Hailwic said with a smile.

"That's not my real name," the girl giggled.

"I'm sure it's not."

"Come on, Lonny's already sat," Theesius said with a jerk of their head toward the interior. "I don't know what that young man feeds himself at home, but I'm not sure he knows how to turn on the stove."

Dr. Theesius's wife, Arrallia, soon joined them, taking the child and ushering them all into a small dining room with a table just big enough for four and a half place settings.

Lonny smiled overly brightly at Hailwic, and stood to pull out the chair next to his for her. It was simply a polite gesture, but she couldn't shake what Punabi had implied about his interest. Ignoring her slight unease, she thanked him and sat, turning her attention to the décor instead.

Hailwic had expected the house to feel . . . academic. Perhaps plush in a pompous sort of way. But it was simple, homey. The chairs they sat in were a little rickety, with the finishing rubbed clear off the bare seats and scratches due to constant use scraped deep into the wood. But they weren't broken down so much as *well loved*. Everything in the house seemed well loved.

Dinner was delicious, the company was pleasant, and the conversation light. Toe Bean was as much an active host as her parents, constantly asking Hailwic if she was having a good time.

Once their plates were cleared, Arrallia and her spouse shared a knowing nod.

"Come on, little Toe," Arrallia said. "Come with mommy. Babbi needs to talk to their new friend."

The child ran up to where Dr. Theesius was still sat and kissed their cheek. "Night, Babbi."

"Night, Toe. Lonny, would you be so kind as to help Arrallia for a moment?"

"Of course," he said graciously, and the little girl took him eagerly by the hand, excited to show her Uncle Lonny a new book she'd been gifted.

"I brought him in myself," Dr. Theesius started off, still staring in the direction of the door, as though their former assistant was still standing there. "Lonny. I should have done it sooner, really. He's got a fighting spirit under all that formality and prescriptivism. But I just couldn't bring myself to trust him fully. He's a Cryptopath, after all." They hollowed their cheek as soon as they said it. "As am I," they acknowledged with a self-deprecating laugh. "I hate it. I absolutely hate that this is where we are. Suspecting people based on their pathology. Making assumptions purely based on what kind of magic someone is born with."

"But . . . she grooms Cryptopaths."

They nodded—both of them knew who *she* was. "She grooms Cryptopaths," they echoed. "Deep down, I knew he wasn't working for the secret police, that he questioned the segregation, the camps, but I had to be certain.

"Shall we break out that wine you brought?"

"That would be lovely, yes, thanks."

They retrieved the bottle, but didn't bother to let it breathe before pouring them each a glass. "Since we'll be working together for a long time, I'd like to tell you why I'm here. How I ended up in this position.

"I was on the team that discovered the stable-extraction methods," Dr. Theesius said, staring into their wine as though looking into the past. "We *bottled* magic. We took this ethereal energy—this thing that is part will, part sense, part force—and turned it into a resource.

"I was so young then." They chuckled lightly to themself, speaking as though no one else was there—as though retelling themself the story instead of Hailwic.

"Most people today can't even remember what it was like before enchantments. We have seen more advancements in the last fifty years than we had in the past *five hundred*.

"I wanted—*we* wanted, the team—to bring aspects of magic to communities that just couldn't find . . ." They looked up, as though just remembering Hailwic was there. They set their wine aside and leaned forward. "So many aspects of magic used to be purely cooperative. Individually, we can each apply our magic to people. Magic comes from people and very easily interacts with humans.

"But taking a Physiopath's abilities and applying them to crops is much more difficult. If a farming community wanted to ensure they wouldn't lose a year's worth of work to weather, or, or *pestilence*, what have you, they needed Physiopaths and Teliopaths and Kairopaths working in tandem, full-time, on just one farm. And in rural communities with small populations, you couldn't guarantee you'd have the right people with the right skills just *born* into it. Some towns went bankrupt trying to attract talent and stay afloat.

"So, we thought, if you could take a little magic out of some people, and put it into objects, what then? Every magical talent suddenly becomes accessible to *everyone*. Emotion therapies could come to the people, instead of the people having to track down Emotiopaths. Instead of having to visit a healer *every day* for depression, you could have an object at home to help you—an emotionstone. We wanted to make the world a better place."

"You did," she assured them, wanting to reach out and put a hand on theirs in comradery. Only the memory of her mother doing the same stopped her. "Enchantments have made so many lives better."

An ethereal curtain drew over Kinwold's eyes, their gaze growing haunted. "Until the mutation war. Until the rise and fall of Fistus. Until Uphrasia." They cleared their throat. "Uphrasia has bastardized my research. She is turning scientific achievements meant to benefit everyone into a means to execute her personal vendetta against Physiopaths."

"How?"

"We're working on a way to extract not just small bits of magic, but *all* of it. Every last drop. Total extraction."

Hailwic gasped. "Why?" she asked, though she knew why. It was obvious.

"To rid the world of Physiopaths," came Lonny's voice from the dining room entry. He slid back into his seat at the table with ease. "To neutralize them. Not just suppress them, but divorce them from their magical ability entirely."

As it stood, people could be paid to have a few grams extracted over their lifetime. The people who participated were usually those who had no interest in developing their magical skills. A professional mancer of any kind would never dream of handing over any of their power to be made into enchantments, but on average very few people had the time, energy, or desire to do more with their magic than what they'd learned to do in primary school. Why not get paid a little extra on the side for something you never use anyway?

But to take *all* of it? What would . . . what would that even do to a person?

Even a child as young as Kinwold's daughter had the capacity to do some form of magic.

And the amount of free-wielding magic such mass extraction would create . . .

"What would—what would happen to all that physio magic?" Hailwic asked.

Dr. Theesius caught her stare, held it, their jaw tight. "That's our ultimate concern. I don't for a moment believe Uphrasia just wants bury it somewhere. She'll use it."

"To do what?"

"Radix has been cut from most of the major international trade agreements. Some countries are calling a spade a spade: Uphrasia is perpetrating genocide. Once it comes out that we've developed a way to entirely deprive someone of their magic, there will be out-and-out war, unless she finds a way to deter the international community from attacking."

"Deter? You mean, with the extracted magic?" Hailwic asked.

"Yes."

"She'll weaponize it," Lonny said. "*That's* the threat that must be eliminated. What we've got to put a stop to."

"*Fuck,*" Hailwic spat.

With a shaking hand, Kinwold scooped up their wineglass. The ounce or so of red left in the bottom sloshed dangerously as they brought it to their lips. "Yes, *fuck,*" they agreed frankly before downing the wine in one fell swoop.

Fuck Uphrasia. Weaponized physiopathy was *exactly* what she claimed to be fighting—what she'd said was *the height of evil.* Why Physiopaths themselves were evil.

As Kinwold lowered their glass, the three of them drifted into contemplative silence. After a moment, the doctor moved their glass aside and hid their face in their hands, digging their palms into their eyes.

"It's predictable, really," Kinwold said eventually. "Every tyrant ends up functioning the same way; everything's about what they fear, and what they envy. You're both too young to remember personally, but Fistus's whole schtick was based on segregation, right? The idea you should only relate to those with your pathy, should only marry and work with those who have your same magics. Well, what did he, a Physiopath, do? Used Emotiopaths to whip up crowds into a frenzy, used cryptopathic security—just like Uphrasia. On and on, the hypocrisy was—and still is—endless.

"The Friend fears physiopathic power, so she can't help but want it. If she gets control over transformation incarnate and weaponizes it, well . . . I wanted my daughter to inherit a better world than I did. With things headed the way they are, I'm afraid there won't be a world for her to inherit at all."

"We won't let it get to that point," Lonny said brashly.

"How close are the total extraction teams to achieving it?" Hailwic asked carefully.

"Neither company's been able to extract more than twenty-one grams yet," Kinwold said. "But that's not just down to our stalling and sabotage. It's about the subjects. They've all . . . expired."

Hailwic suddenly felt queasy. "They've all *died*?"

"The older they are the more difficult the extraction becomes. Our youngest . . . thirty. He was the only one our team pulled that much from. Uphrasia wants . . ."

"Younger," Lonny spat.

Kinwold nodded and stared into their empty wineglass as though it might manifest more if they glared hard enough.

An inkling of an idea started to scratch at the back of Hailwic's mind. "Where do you get your subjects from?"

"They *volunteer.*" Kinwold sighed. "For various reasons. To protect family, to avoid the worst of the camps, to receive pardons—"

"So prisoners are eligible?" she asked—too eagerly, by the look on Kinwold's face.

This might be her angle. Her way in.

And Zoshim's way out.

Hailwic was not the first person the rebellion had tried to insert into Uphrasia's personal circle. As such, the files she'd originally studied contained a wealth of information on what methods of assassination were likely to fail given the Friend's vigilant security measures.

It was impossible to get close to Uphrasia with any kind of traditional weapon. She never had fewer than two cryptopathic guards flanking her at any given time, so anything Hailwic might attempt to secret on her person would be found instantly. A former operative hadn't even been able to treat a spare tampon as clandestine without it being immediately whipped into the light, which meant guns and knives and garrotes were off the table.

Poison was out as well. Uphrasia was particularly paranoid about it. All of her food was prepared by personal chefs, and then vetted by a Cryptopath whose sole job it was to act as bite tester and cupbearer. She would accept no lotions or topical ointments that hadn't been prescreened, and disallowed perfumes and anything distributed via atomizer in her presence.

Thousands of gifts arrived at her offices each day, and a thousand gifts were incinerated.

Lonny had previously mentioned he'd attempted to give her a small token early on—a worthless brooch—and the box had never touched Uphrasia's fingers, instantly intercepted by a guard. Neither Lonny nor Dr. Theesius ever saw it again.

The Friend—open and giving and *of the people* as she claimed to be—was ultimately distrustful of everyone and disdainful of anything common and accessible.

So trust would have to be Hailwic's true weapon of choice. She was familiar with winning back trust—from her parents, from the courts. She'd participated in enough propaganda videos as a rehabilitated offender that she knew she could be held up as a beacon of reform. That, along with her family connections and the fact that she shared her kairopathic abilities with Uphrasia was plenty enough to initially endear her to the Friend.

But Hailwic knew she needed more than simple endearment. She needed to prove herself as a true loyalist as quickly as possible. She needed to impress Uphrasia with her commitment, and she'd learned how to achieve exactly that from none other than her parents.

In order to win over Uphrasia, she had to throw Zoshim to the wolves.

"Have someone you'd like to see die a painful death, do you?" Dr. Theesius asked.

"The opposite, actually," she said, leaning in, "and it just might help me win Uphrasia's favor."

KRONA

The sun in Xyopar felt like a different sun altogether. It beat down, fierce and demanding, sapping the air of all its water, making the skin and nose feel dry and vulnerable. But there was no denying the beauty of the sand dunes. Glorious ripples of tan and white and red flowed together in undulating bands across the great heaps. Sandstorms would whip the different types of silica into one, and then slowly, time would see them separate as they resettled, until the next storm mixed them together again.

The dunes were framed by tall plateaus in the distance, and those in turn were framed by the jagged peaks of the rim.

Emotion's temple lay here, in what to everyone, save the world-weary and well-traveled—seemed a desolate space.

The magic guarding the temple oasis distorted the perimeter enough that Krona could not pinpoint the temple itself in a jump. Instead, she jumped them to the nearest definitive landmark—a sandstone outcropping, unadorned, seemingly insignificant, but it was all the marker she needed. From there, she, Tray, Melanie, and Sebastian—carrying Emotion on a long litter they'd hastily constructed at Mirthhouse—began to trek eastwardly, toward the telltale shimmer of the oasis *mirage*.

They were miles and miles from the nearest city. Though traveling caravans were common in Xyopar, the desert was vast, and Krona did not fear an encounter.

Traversing the dunes themselves was slow going. Krona and Tray took up the lead and supported Emotion's head, while Sebastian and Melanie followed at the god's feet. They stepped on the occasional solid rock, but more often than not the ground shifted beneath their boots. They did their best to hold Emotion—supine with zhur hands crossed over zhur chest—steady and level between them, despite the constant uneven footing.

Emotion was disturbingly light for zhur size, as though zhur bones were hollow, just like a bird's. They'd covered zhim in a layer of linen to shield zhim from the direct sun, even though none of them could say if a god needed protection from something so piddling as that. After all, it was the gods' creations who were ill-wrought and fragile, not the gods themselves.

The humans, for their part, had all wrapped scarves around their heads to protect against the sunlight and the heat and the grit. Each of them had strapped extra canteens to their belts, and had given up heavy cloaks needed as

Mirthhouse was just thawing from its winter, in exchange for breathable fabrics suitable for Xyopar's monoseason.

Krona caught sight of the oasis only an hour into their trek. Though they drew ever closer for hours after that, the faintly rippling waters and ethereal desert palms did not fully resolve, shimmering on the edges, disappearing and reappearing from the sands. The image never grew, never shrank. It held itself distant, seemingly untouchable until they suddenly crossed the cryptopathic threshold and were thrust into blinding light.

They all stumbled, losing their footing as though they'd missed a stair in the dark, or, worse, stepped themselves off a cliff.

They fell to their hands, their knees. The litter teetered and fell as they did, half dumping Emotion in the sand.

The blinding flash was there, then gone. Whiting out their vision, stealing their breath, but nothing more.

It was an intense sunbeam, refracted from the glass dome sitting on an island, surrounded by a gentle pool of still water hardly big enough to be called a pond. All around, desert plants thrived, blossomed. Pink flowers adorned succulents like feathers or fascinators, offsetting their ruddy green. Mastic trees surrounded the edge of the enchanted space, and small palms butted up to the water's edge.

The scent of water was cool in Krona's lungs. Crisp. Refreshing.

Alluring in a way that warned her not to drink the water.

The four of them took a moment to catch their breath, each staying where they'd stumbled. Krona recovered first, crawling over to Emotion's side, pulling zhur giant head into her lap so that it would not settle too deep in the sand. Her instincts were protective, despite Emotion's unquestionable power and resilience, and Krona understood herself well enough to know it was how she handled her own terror. She'd tied so many of her own hopes to waking the gods—so many of the Valley's hopes.

In truth, she had no plan for failure.

If not one god could be awoken, they had nothing.

Nothing.

"Come on, we're nearly there," she urged the others. Tray helped her settle Emotion back on the litter, and Krona put a reassuring hand on her satchel of halite-encrusted minds before the four of them lifted the god on their shoulders once more.

"The water looks deep, but isn't," she assured them, seeing through the mild cryptopathic haze that covered it. "Do not trust your eyes or your hands. Trust what I tell you."

"Always," Melanie assured her, making a strange mix of warmth and guilt flood Krona's chest.

They sloshed through the pool, hurrying to the island structure: a dome made of many panes of dichroic glass, all opaque and opalescent, each with a raised swirl to it. It was small, compared to the other temples. A single story tall, with a footprint no bigger than the old barn on Tray's family farm.

It appeared solid, without a means of entry, but Krona knew better. She could not directly see through as many of the cryptopathic shields as Avellino could, but her resistance to Thalo magic meant she could sense the seams of them. Could tell where a falsehood was pushing at her perception. All she had to do when she felt that push was push *back*.

She searched now where the ingress had been before, with an echo of Avellino's voice gently reminding her that things were always shifting. The door may not be as she remembered.

They circled the structure, and Krona did her best to concentrate on the pressure around her, on the ever-shifting air. Until, yes, there—

A draft. A subtle shift. And a sense of unreality, like trying to catch a lost thought that had been at the forefront of her mind only a moment ago.

Her awareness *rippled*—as the mirage had rippled. Like a heat shimmer. It created a thin veil over one large pane of glass, not dissimilar to the way she used to see Thalo when they attempted to hide themselves from her sight, before she'd reintegrated Ninebark.

She focused on that veil, and through sheer force of her concentration, the illusion collapsed before her. The pane disappeared, leaving an open archway and nothing to stop her from striding right into the sanctuary.

Well, nothing except her companion's hesitancy. They did not have her resistance to cryptomancy. Even Sebastian, remerged just as she was, did not share her immunities. On the contrary—he was especially *vulnerable* to secret magic; it was an Emotiomancer's weakness.

As Krona stepped forward, tugging the others after her, they all held their breath, as though expecting to be plunged into deep water.

Inside, a brilliant rainbow of colored light painted the plain flooring. And contained within—almost nothing. The grandeur of the dome itself had nothing to contend with—no exquisite meal under its glittering cloche. Or, so it seemed. The pale polished stone of the floor cradled a simple rock. A geode small enough to place in the palm of one's hand. The stone was whole—the crystals within could be seen via the smallest peephole, no bigger in circumference than the tip of Krona's pinkie finger.

"Here?" Melanie asked, making to lower the stretcher.

"Not yet," Krona said quickly. "In these temples, space is not what it seems." Similar size and distance tricks were at play here as they were in Knowledge's grotto. "We need to be inside the inner sanctum." She nodded to the small stone.

"Inside . . . inside that rock?" Tray asked, incredulous.

Krona began to lower herself to her knees, and the others did the same, careful to keep Emotion balanced. "Just . . . follow me when I crawl inside," she instructed.

Ignoring Tray's sudden gasp, as though he meant to protest, Krona—still supporting Emotion on her left, reached out with her right hand and turned the geode's small window toward her.

She looked deep into its multicolored depths. The stone was clearly unnatural; the crystals within were many and diverse. Krona was no gemologist or emotioteur, but she knew different gems formed under very different circumstances.

The peephole seemed barely large enough for a probing finger, let alone her entire self. But *seemed* was the key word. She stared at it and stared at it, staring until her eyes watered, and she willed it larger while willing herself smaller. She ignored everything logic and sense told her, and insisted to herself that she *could* enter, and she *would* enter.

It swelled in her vision and Krona pitched forward, reaching out, taking hold of one sharp crystal growth, seeing it so small, and yet her hand took hold of it like it was a sturdy pillar. Unbreakable and huge, she could barely grasp it. Heart leaping into her throat, she pulled herself forward, yanking the others with her, demanding the split in the geode make space for them—all of them.

She tumbled forward, over the threshold, scraping her hand and knees on the carpeting of pinpointed stones that met her.

Suddenly the whole space was expansive, bulging into a vast cave as though it had the malleability of a soap bubble.

And then, there it was: an empty throne.

More of a chaise than a straight-backed chair, it boasted gilded edgings and cream-colored cushions. Three waist-high altars, each with a dish of covenant atop, stood nearby, within reach of the throne. Emotion must have actually sat there once. But how long ago? When had the Savior moved zhim, and why?

Unlike the treehouse, the geode saw no point in spitting the invaders back out again. Its prisoner had been removed long ago, and though the key cryptomantic protections remained, the guard-dog tactics of the inner sanctum lay dormant.

Once the others had recovered from the shock of stepping into what they'd been sure was a thimble's worth of space, they collectively hurried to place Emotion.

Gathering up the god in reverent hands, boosting zhur beneath the arms and cradling zhur sagging head, they lay zhur down as though simply lounging. As though Emotion had been overtaken by the softness of a midday nap instead of this sickening eternal stillness.

Bathed in a spotlight from the geode's opening, a small smattering of color glistened across zhur form here and there from where a crystal caught the beam and spun it out again. Zhe looked like a painting; the shadows put all the more emphasis on the depth of zhur eyes, the etchings in zhur skull.

This place had been built to evoke awe, and with the god seated in zhur place of honor, it did not fail in its task.

Hands suddenly shaking, Krona went to one of the altars where a shallow gold dish lay upturned and waiting, like an expectant palm. Krona retrieved Emotion's mind from her satchel, as well as the blessed water, which she dribbled sparingly into the dish. Carefully, she plucked the gold-colored mind from its nesting and held the crystal above the small pool, but for some reason she could not make her fingers uncurl.

"What are you waiting for?" Sebastian asked, and it was barely a whisper.

She was waiting for some reassurance from the universe that this was the right thing to do: to release the mind from the salt here, now. She'd hoped that in this moment a feeling of certainty might hit her, that her uncertainty would be washed away.

But there was nothing. No sign, no herald, no proof.

The uncertainty sat thick in her chest and on her tongue, making her throat tight.

If she was wrong, and the halite dissolved and the mind fled, what then?

Her fingertips asserted and reasserted themselves on the crystal, twisting it nervously in her grasp. There was weight to this moment, and it deserved ceremony, but all she had to offer was heavy doubt, hesitation, and held breath.

Gritting her teeth, she dropped the mind into the water.

The dish *sizzled*. The zing of salt filled the air as the crystal dissolved alarmingly quickly, leaving the mind free-floating, resting on the water's surface, like a slick of golden oil, curling and twisting with the slightest of sloshing.

It did not disappear. It did not dissolve or float away.

She made her lungs work again, releasing that tight breath, and with it, a weight from her bones.

Curious, Krona lightly touched the mind with the tip her middle finger, meaning to swirl it around and watch it roil all molten-like.

Instead, it lurched out of the water—reaching up like a creature, attempting to crawl up her hand.

She shouted in surprise, reeling back, cradling her fingers as though they'd been burned or bitten. Melanie was at her side in an instant, checking her over for marks or wounds, but she was all right. "Startled me, is all."

"It reached for you," Tray said, stunned.

"Like it's looking for a host?" Sebastian suggested.

Fenri, minds—shorn-off bits of people always wanted to return home.

Vibrating from the sudden shock, she carefully brought the bowl over to Emotion's body, knelt down, and prayed she was doing the right thing.

She dumped the blessed water out, right onto Emotion's chest, soaking zhur shift and leaving a splatter of golden mind to sit heavy against zhur sternum. For a moment, the mind simply squirmed—like a tentacled lake creature—with little tendrils sneaking out before snapping back into the globule of the whole.

Slowly, it thinned, plastering itself close to Emotion's chest, becoming so flat and clinging so close that the god's upper body looked gilded. It traveled upward, finding the cracks in the bird skull, filling in the etched portions on the beak before slithering farther into the gaps proper—into zhur mouth and around the amethyst in zhur eye sockets and into the nostrils of zhur skull.

Emotion *convulsed*—zhur body rolling in one long wave. Zhur hands flexed, turning into rigid claws at zhur sides, digging into the cushions, scratching gouges into the fabric. A bellow left zhur beak as zhe threw zhur head back, bill to the ceiling, zhur spine arching.

As a soft glow began to emanate from the god's skin, growing subtly brighter, Krona shuffled backward, holding out an arm, encouraging the others to move away.

The luminosity increased, becoming more and more dazzling until it threatened to white out Krona's vision just as the blinding glint from the dome had done upon arrival.

She turned away from it, bowed her head, bending all the way to the geode's floor in supplication, clamping her eyes shut against the oncoming brilliance.

Not just brilliance, but *heat*. The temperature in the cavern soared as waves of warmth rippled outward from Emotion. Sweat sprang up across Krona's back and around her throat as the air became thick, difficult to draw.

She could hear the others struggling, and reached out, searching. Someone took her hand, and she grasped theirs tightly.

For a moment she feared they'd made a grave error.

Perhaps a fragile human couldn't so much as stand in the presence of a mindful god. Perhaps, once whole, the gods would be unreachable by mortal means—dangerous to look at, maddening to speak to, impossible to touch.

Perhaps she'd just condemned them all to a sad, sudden death. Isolated, secreted away, with no one to know even that they were dead and by what means.

But as quickly as the sweat sizzled on her skin and the light became so bright she could see the flare of it despite her eyelids, both began to recede.

Before she dared open her eyes, the stone beneath her shook with a mighty stomping. The air shifted as Emotion heaved zhimself up, then *stumbled*.

It was surprise and ingrained readiness that had Krona's eyes snapping open and her rising to her feet the instant she realized Emotion had fallen from zhur throne.

The god was half-slumped over the chaise, knees on the crystal-spiked floor, lungs newly heaving, great, muscled arms straining as zhe clenched zhur entire body tight. There was immense power in zhur form—strength and durability. Power enough to kill any one of them with nothing but the strength of zhur hands alone.

And, terrifyingly, there was *panic* written across the line of zhur shoulders and the rigidity of zhur limbs.

Krona had seen enough of the same on the likes of fleeing criminals to know that panic was often a precursor to violence.

Tray—who'd been the one to take Krona's hand—tried to rise next to her. "Stay down," she hissed at all of them. "Don't move."

All it would take was one fear-rattled fist to put any one of them down for good.

There was no way of knowing what Emotion last remembered. No way of knowing what the circumstances surrounding being made Mindless entailed.

"We're here to serve you," Krona said lightly, hands held out placatingly. Her insides withered the instant Emotion's amethyst gaze snapped to her.

Emotion *bristled*. Zhur long bouquet of flora-like hair ruffled and puffed like feathers. Zhe scrambled upright, onto the throne, then over it, knocking it back, making them all jump with the *smash-crack* of it hitting the floor.

The throne was down, but Emotion flared back up, trilling deep in zhur throat. It was a horrid sound of distress—hollow and high and forlorn. Zhe swatted at zhur own beak, as though trying to claw zhur own face away.

Melanie cried out, and she and Sebastian clung to each other.

Krona, gulping down her own panic, pulled Tray over to the couple. The four of them formed a tight knot, cowering, twisting their crouched forms in the opposite direction of the clamoring god.

Emotion turned to the geode's curved walls, striking at them for a moment before flailing out, knocking over one of the altars in an attempt to move to a different section, apparently unable, in zhur panic, to pinpoint the way out.

Once, back in Krona's Regulator days, a finch had flown through the open door and gotten itself trapped inside the den. The poor thing had battered itself against every seam and seal. Emotion's energy was the same—frantic, directionless. But zhe was no trapped songbird.

Keeping the others behind her, Krona stood, took a daring step in Emotion's direction. "You're all right," she tried to soothe, voice pitched higher than she liked. "Please, you're all right. We're here to help you."

Emotion paused, breathing heavily, attention once more caught by Krona. But Krona couldn't tell if Emotion was pausing to consider her words, or pausing because the human had made a sound.

She couldn't even tell if zhe *understood* her words.

Zhur beak opened, then snapped shut again, clicking together like wooden slats before opening wide once more. A strange series of bellows—something like the tangled cords of a deep roar and the high-pitched chirps of birdsong—left zhur mouth.

The strange sounds took Krona's breath away, but not nearly so much as the subsequent sight of Emotion zhimself reeling back from them. Zhe clutched at zhur beak—snapping it opened and closed again, testing its hinges and its bite as zhe suddenly tossed zhur head from side to side like an agitated horse. The respite in zhur panic was over, and the hectic, scrambling flutter was back.

"We should try to guide zhim outside," Tray suggested, yelling as though over a tempest.

"And once zhe's free, then what?" Sebastain countered. "We don't know what zhe'll d—"

Sebastian hissed, clutched at his chest, though Krona barely noticed through her own sudden surge of terrified outrage. Her lungs refused to draw full breaths, her legs felt heavy, her head light. She was lost, angry, head swimming with a deluge of directionless confusion and guilt and regret.

Emotion had taken hold of their feelings—whether by accident or with intent, it hardly mattered.

Krona couldn't think straight, couldn't see straight. Her joints buckled, her heartbeat pounded in her ears. The insidious emotions immediately turned into a monster eating its own tail. The projected panic only served to increase the humans' own terror, which in turn was reflected back to Emotion and bolstered zhur own in a terrible, ugly ouroboros.

The temperature rose again. Invisible fire slung its way across Krona's skin, rolling out from Emotion in waves.

They would all roast alive in this furnace if someone didn't *do* something. "*Sebastian*," she gasped, barely able to get the syllables out over the projected dread blocking up her throat.

He had control over the realm of emotion. But who knew if that meant anything next to the force of a rampaging god.

Whether he'd heard her or had grasped the idea on his own, she couldn't say, but he pushed past her, holding one arm out as though fending off high winds. Sweat visibly poured down from his temples as he struggled forward, and even though Emotion let him come, the god still vibrated with terror and anguish.

The crystals around them all began to rattle—to vibrate with a terrible song that matched Emotion's toil. It was a buzzing and a chittering and a high-pitched tinkling. A cacophony of dismay and discordant fright.

An eerie shift took over Emotion's countenance as Sebastian lashed out with his emotiopathy, reaching with his hands at the same time, as though projecting his will down his arms and out the tips of his fingers.

The god shifted zhur awareness solely to Sebastian, like a predator zeroing in on its prey.

The air was still too thick, too heavy, as Krona tried to shout out a warning, and her cry died in her throat even as it came too late.

Emotion vaulted over the disarray of furnishings to wrap the thumb and forefinger of one giant hand around Sebastian's throat.

The instant Emotion's long, beautiful fingers fell on the dark column of his neck, Sebastian's fen burst forth to defend him.

Twisting light and scattered fog barreled out of his body—a writhing, living cloud, coalescing into a tall creature that scraped the geode's ceiling and kicked Sebastian back, out of Emotion's grip.

His was one of the more whimsical fenri Krona had beheld. A giraffe, its spots a shifting palate of subtle sunset hues, with many butterfly wings instead of a mane and tuft on its tail. The creature always had incredible presence—wasn't prone to shrinking himself like Ninebark. Instead, he sprang from Sebastian's core in full glory, towering above Emotion, standing solid and strong between the divine and his host.

Surprised, Emotion's hands flew up in warding, and zhe cowered back.

Sebastian scrabbled away, letting his fen, Kemba, circle in front of him defensively. The fen ducked its long neck, holding Emotion in his sights, ready to do what it must.

Melanie went to her husband, pulling him away, as Krona watched Emotion. Zhe seemed stunned—fascinated, even, with the ethereal form in front of zhim, head tilted thoughtfully to the side, beak lightly clacking in a sort of chittering.

The panic and anger and attack fled from Emotion as wonderment took over, and thus, the terrible feelings fled from the humans as well.

Krona felt drained. The imposed emotion was gone, but her body was still physically reeling from the rush of humors.

Awestruck, Emotion stretched zhur fingers in the fen's direction.

Krona held her breath as Kemba stilled, letting Emotion's hand come. She glanced to Sebastian, who clutched one hand over his battered throat as Melanie held him about the shoulders, his heart still clearly hammering in his chest.

When a fen was separated from its host, its host had no control over its actions. It shared intent, but could not be expected to always take direction or follow commands, and though Krona knew Sebastian would never attack Emotion outright, he was a fighter when backed against a wall.

Kemba could lash out.

And Emotion would undoubtedly retaliate.

As the god inched closer, hand extended, Kemba ducked his nose. There was a brief pause where both of them stopped, regarding each other in a way Krona, human as she was, could not read. But then, slowly, Kemba closed the distance, nuzzling into Emotion's palm.

Like recognized like. Sebastian's magic came from Emotion, and it, in its corporeal form, must have sensed its origins—sensed *home*.

And yet, Emotion continued to move with undo fascination, reaching out to stroke gently through the wings on the creature's neck, making them flutter.

Did the gods know about fenri? Krona reasoned they must; they'd created humanity from scratch, stitching every muscle, manifesting every humor, pouring in every drop of magic.

But even healthy fenri were a malformation. Humans were never meant to be severed from their magic, never meant to have pneuma torn from their being, never meant to have a cleft in their spirit.

Varger and fenri were unnatural, created by the Savior's meddling, not the gods themselves.

Regardless, Kemba's presence was clearly *calming*. So, Krona took a risk.

She quietly called Ninebark up from the depths, disentangling her from her nerves, her bones, her veins. The fen came forth gently, amassing from a wispy state before trotting over for the god's inspection.

Emotion welcomed the fen eagerly, with a beckoning hand, laying a palm gently on her snout. A burst of fondness swept through Ninebark, directly into

Krona's chest. Specifically, the kind of fondness one might feel for a small animal skittering through a park, or a songbird twittering overhead.

Krona wondered if it was what Emotion felt for humanity.

The idea was both a relief and a worry.

After all, one often did not pay the fate of small animals much mind.

But it was a starting point.

Emotion began to glow again, but this light was soothing rather than cutting. Warm instead of burning. It refracted through the geode's crystals like fairy glitter, making everything sparkle.

The tension eased from Krona, from the others, slowly seeping away like rain into thirsty ground.

Which made it all the more jarring when Krona felt a sudden *yank* from Ninebark.

It was an uneasy, off-kilter sensation. Disentangling the part of herself that was Ninebark and giving the fen free reign was always a struggle—whether it was brought on suddenly by desperation or slowly through intention. It was never effortless to force the creation of two distinct beings out of one. Rejoining with her fen, on the other hand, was always easy as breathing.

This was neither. The yank was something else entirely. Something orchestrated from the outside.

Something *Emotion* was guiding. A dictation through desire.

Fearful, Krona resisted—resisted the pull to rejoin with Ninebark, resisted as she never had before. But it was a physical thing, solid like a rope, like a chain. She tried to plant her boots, but they skidded across the bottom of the geode, shattering the crystal spikes.

Tray dove to her aid, grabbing her by the shoulders as she struggled to stay upright.

Sebastian and Melanie fought just the same, rejecting the foreign urges, the desperate *demand* of it.

But in the end, there was no denying a god.

Both Krona and Sebastian were pulled bodily to Emotion, snapped back into their fenri with a force great enough to punch the air from their lungs and haul their companions right along with them.

The god welcomed them with arms spread wide and head raised high, the clusters of amethyst in zhur eye sockets blazing with light, as though zhe meant not just for the humans to reabsorb their fenri, but to absorb the humans themselves—to fold these piddling, sad little creatures into zhimself.

There were screams. A force—a push and pull and a *twisting*. A flash of light. A yawing darkness.

Krona felt her boots leave the ground.

She became light. Weightless. Like floating in the water, yet floating in nothing.

She and Ninebark were joined again. She and Sebastian were connected, somehow.

Through Emotion?

Through Emotion's thoughts and feelings and direction?

Krona was pushed—from behind and all around. She felt it in her bones, but more important, she felt it in her magic.

If she was dying, Krona's last wish was to see Thibaut again. Just for a moment. Long enough to tell him she loved him. Long enough to know he was safe.

Her body whirled. Her mind tumbled.

And at the last moment, Tray's grip faltered, and she was alone.

15

KRONA

Dry to wet. Hot to chilled. The strange, sharp shine of the inside of a geode had become the hollow darkness of a cave.

The foreign stranglehold on Krona's magic released, making her gasp—like the crushing grip had been on her windpipe instead of deep in her pneuma.

She found herself on her hands and knees, looking at her own darkened, distorted reflection staring back from barely an inch of water strung out over algae-slicked stone. The temperature of the water was familiar, the smell of it—she'd been here not all that long ago.

From her left, a tattered cough—roughened, like he'd had that same phantom noose pulling tight on his throat—drew her attention to Sebastian, on his back, full-body tensing with every unfortunate hack.

Tray's hand was in Krona's face—dangling to help her up—before she'd even realized he was there. Melanie splashed into view, going to her knees next to Sebastian as Krona rose from hers.

Knowledge's grotto seemed no different from before. The great wooden house with a tree at its center still bent its neck against the cave's dank ceiling—its precarious nature and unwieldy posture no trick of magic.

Between Krona and the house, Emotion radiated. Not just light, which perked up the bioluminescent fungus on the walls, shining all the livelier as little blue glowworms came out from hiding to bask in the god's brightness. Emotion radiated more of that stunned-bird energy. Only instead of a small, flighty thing, zhe projected the power of a great eagle or a firebird—stance wide, arms not hanging from zhur shoulders but curving in powerful arcs, at the ready. Though zhe lacked wings, it was as if any moment zhe could take flight—could charge or heave or pounce.

Zhe stared up at the house with determination, clearly knowing who lay inside, ready to claw the siding off the house—or tear it down to its bare trunk of a foundation—to get in.

It made sense that Emotion would seek out Knowledge. Knowledge had been the first god, made by the creator—the Thalo, from which the Savior's order took its name—as a companion for itself when all of its other beasts had been things of making and unmaking, without thought or feeling or solid existence.

Knowledge had asked for a companion of feir own—had bade the Thalo create Emotion, who then birthed Time and Nature.

Knowledge was the oldest, and the embodiment of information and wisdom.

Emotion had regained zhur mind in a world of wrongness—zhe wasn't able to speak, didn't know who these humans were. It was possible zhe didn't remember how zhe'd been captured by the Savior and made Mindless. If anyone could make sense of it all, surely it was Knowledge femself.

After heaving herself up, Krona let Tray's hand fall with a grateful pat to his shoulder, then stiffly approached the god from behind, hoping not to startle zhim, but needing to make one thing clear: she'd yet to lay eyes on Knowledge.

She fished in her satchel, locating the proper box and peeling away its waxy ring. "I tried to reach fem," she said, still unsure if Emotion could understand her. "But the way is shrouded."

Cryptopathy created false ways, but surely it had been physiopathy that had spit her, Juliet, and Avellino out again and again.

Emotion didn't look down at her, still fixated on the house, thinly shrouded chest seething as zhe cocked zhur head, calculating something that was surely innumerable in Krona's own mind.

"If we can get to fem," she said, holding up the freed halite crystal. "We can wake fem, just as we woke you."

An ombre hand, tipped with dark nails, came down to pluck the salt from Krona's fingers. Her stomach swooped as Knowledge's mind left her palms—lifted out of her reach by strangely steady fingers.

Emotion's beak clacked as zhe turned zhur head from side to side, examining the translucent thing clutched delicately between thumb and forefinger.

Inside the salt, the mind shifted.

Krona's insides swooped again, but in a whole new way. Now her butterflies weren't the sudden queasiness of separation, but the giddiness of new excitement.

None of the minds had moved before—not while still encased.

Little bubbles boiled up at the edges, and a shimmer wriggled, the tarnished nickel's surface billowing and condensing, like a woodworm in its burrow.

The mind was reacting to Emotion—to having another god awake and near and whole. Though all it could do was squirm, that writhing was a demand for communion.

Moving with a precision just now mustered, Emotion held steady as zhe lowered the halite back into Krona's upturned palms.

Knowledge's mind continued to move. To pulse with awareness. Even through the solidness of the crystal, Krona could feel that awareness reaching out to her, but also reaching *away* from her—toward the treehouse.

"This way," she called over her shoulder to the others, legs already moving, boots already splashing as she followed that thread of awareness to the house's rickety porch, up its stairs, and to its once mocking door.

Now the door was still. No creaking invitation—a dare or otherwise—from its hinges. It waited. Anticipated.

Emotion—zhur feet bare, footsteps heavy—slipped past Krona to turn the latch, test the swing, and duck inside when no resistance was offered.

The four humans solemnly followed.

The interior was just the same—that smell of bergamot tea, wafting out of nowhere, just the same. Yet with Emotion filling the space, the entire atmosphere was different. The staircase—with its stiff corners that turned and turned and turned in an ever upward spiral—seemed more manageable and more fragile at the same time. Emotion's head nearly rose to the height of the second-story banister, and Krona feared zhur weight would be too much for the questionable craftsmanship of the steps.

Zhe turned to Krona, clearly expecting her to lead the way.

Before, with Avellino heading each charge as they traversed the house again and again, Krona had slowly grown more accustomed to the feel of each illusion, as if via her kairopathy she was learning to see through more and more. Yet she hadn't ever considered attempting the house all on her own, sure she would fail long before reaching the physiopathic carpet at its peak.

Now there was no Avellino to guide her. No extra shoulder to lean on. Emotiopaths were weak to cryptomancy, and if Emotion zhurself had fallen to the Savior's magic, then Krona couldn't count on the god to get them through.

As she mounted the steps, the mind in her hands pulsed. Grew warm. Curious, Krona backtracked and swayed toward the kitchen. It went frigid. She alighted on the stairs again, and the toastiness returned.

Perhaps she'd been granted some help after all.

There was a connection between mind and body just as there was a connection between human and varg. The two pieces longed to be united, and if she could follow the tug of one to the other—allowing the polarized ends of the two magnets to connect—then a new equilibrium could be achieved.

She traced the path upward with a new eye to her surroundings. The others trailed, and she called out warnings. Emotion did make the steps sag and the banisters protest, but nothing was so rickety or so rotted as to drop out from beneath zhur weight.

Floor after floor passed beneath them, behind them, as Krona skillfully avoided the gossamer-thin slats and sidestepped the illusionary walls (which she now realized smelled faintly of tears—all dampness and salt). Still, her body was tense—the presence of a god at her back perceived more as a constant looming judgment rather than a protective comfort.

When they reached the floor with the red carpet, Krona finally hesitated in full. She had resistances to cryptopathy, but physiopathy would forever be her bane. It didn't matter how many secrets she overcame in the lower levels of the house if she could not bypass the flinging red tongue.

Knowledge's mind sensed her uncertainty—or perhaps sensed the physiopathy itself. It warmed further—not hot enough to burn, but enough to make her palms dangerously sweaty against the soluble salt.

"Knowledge beats nature," she whispered under her breath, echoing what Thibaut had said when bypassing the physiopathically locked door.

Tentatively, she slid one boot into the shag. The dangling light in the center of the hallway swayed—conjuring up images of a uvula at the back of a monster's throat as the carpet-tongue rippled at the far end. Krona held the mind aloft as she inched forward, brandishing it more like she might a light vial than her saber.

The tongue began to curl as it had before, rolling toward her, ready to lap her up as easily as a cat laps milk from a saucer. But as it rolled on past the swinging light it slowed, then *recoiled.* She thrust the mind forward and it rolled back as though afraid. If a carpet could cower, it was cowering.

Encouraged, she quickened her steps, running for the pull ring dangling from the trapdoor, just in case the shaggy thing suddenly changed its mind and lunged for her anyway.

"Hurry!" she called to the others, waving them onward while she loomed over the physiopathic threads, holding the mind as menacingly as she could.

Taking hold of the pull ring, Tray yanked, and a ladder slid down from above, its top disappearing into darkness. He climbed it just as surely as they'd all climbed the stairs. Melanie and Sebastian followed. Emotion reached past the ladder entirely, pulling zhurself up into the patch of pure shadow, squeezing through the opening with the grace of the divine.

Krona didn't trust the carpet not to grab for at her at the last second. She mounted the ladder sideways, climbing it with one hand and keeping the other—in which the mind was clutched—low and in clear view. She had no way of knowing what mechanism kept the carpet in check or what teliopathic influence might be flowing from the halite, but she wasn't going to lose the advantage by dropping her guard.

The rungs creaked with each fall of her boot, but that was nothing compared to the way the attic slats protested when she reached the top—yanking the trapdoor closed behind her. Each board clacked as though not nailed down, and Krona trod more carefully than she had with illusions threatening to drop her at every turn.

Here, the only light came from Emotion and the stained-glass window. Both lights were dim, unmoored, leaving most of the attic in reticent shadow.

Unlike every other attic Krona had ever invaded—and she'd invaded many during her time as a Regulator—this one was barren. No overstuffed boxes had been piled high into pseudo-walls. No discarded toys cluttered the floor waiting to be stepped on. No stacks of old papers were there to bear the water stains of a leaky roof or the cobwebs of hopeful spiders.

Likewise, there were no offerings or daises. Nothing that spoke of temples or coteries or shrines.

The naked structure of the high-pitched roof and walls seemed nearly skeletal, the slats gray and flat and empty, save for the thick layer of dust. The five of them kicked motes into the air, which went swirling through the single shaft of light streaking into the room at an angle, yellowed by the stained glass.

A lone chair sat before the window, facing outward, cutting a dark shadow through the light. The bulk of something that could have been a pile of clothes, or a mannequin, but was in fact Knowledge, slumped atop it, as still and eerily ambiguous as any heirloom ever found in the dark and forgotten recesses of a house.

In Krona's hand, the mind purred.

Emotion approached first, moving delicately despite zhur size. The high point of the roof meant zhe only had to hunch ever so slightly, making zhur slink forward look cautious and curious.

Reaching out for the very human-sized throne, Emotion dragged zhur long fingers across the top of the straight, stiff back, making more dust dance as zhe rounded to the front to crouch before Knowledge. Fey wore a deep brown hooded cloak. With a touch delicate enough for butterfly wings, Emotion pushed the hood back from feir brow, revealing feir face.

Chirping quietly, zhe cradled feir bent head, nudging it up into the light.

A soft sadness settled over all of them, emanating from Emotion, spurred by loss and separation and fondly tinged memory.

The moment felt private, and yet Krona had to intrude.

She stepped forward with the flask free and the mind in hand, inching her way to stand behind Emotion, who did not acknowledge her.

Knowledge was so small. Even smaller than the average human. Feir dark, weary head had clearly hung low over feir lap for a long time—century upon century here having placed a physical weight upon feir neck. Feir gnarled fingers curled down over the carved armrests, unnaturally extended, draped and twisted into roots that had burrowed into the floor beneath feir feet, bulging and twisting through the gaps and knots in the boards—as though fey'd become one with the tree and its house.

The mind wriggled in its prison, pressing, looking for seams in the salt. Its body was so near, and it wanted out, *out, out*.

Still wary of Emotion—of interrupting—Krona leaned forward with the halite displayed in offer. "Hold out your hands," she bade, the dimness and the warmth and Emotion's sadness compelling her to keep her voice barely above a whisper.

A beat passed before Emotion moved to accede. Zhe cupped zhur giant hands in Knowledge's lap, spanning the entire breadth of the throne's seat, creating a bowl in which Krona set the mind and spilled more blessed water from the flask, washing over the salt, dissolving it away. The tarnished-nickel-colored mind slithered free of the stone like a snake, coiling over Emotion's fingers, sliding up across Knowledge's chest to squirm beneath the brown cloak.

Stillness followed.

Emotion's waking had been immediate and violent. Unmistakable.

Now, Krona held her breath, eyes raking the withered form, searching for any sign of new life.

A shuddering breath, deep and wheezing, started as the slightest of sounds. Something easily mistakable for the rustle of Melanie's skirts or Sebastian shifting from one foot to the other.

It rose in intensity and pitch over long moments until it echoed out of feir chest and resonated through the walls of the house—making the building breathe and heave just as Knowledge's body heaved.

Feir frail form reared up with an aching slowness—long-unused muscles protesting, having forgotten their function during their lengthy stagnation.

Fey still clung to the wooden throne—still rooted.

With wet hands, Emotion took hold of feir face, beak clacking, wanting fem to focus on zhim first, perhaps hoping to belay the panic that zhe'd felt upon waking.

After a long moment, Knowledge's crusted eyes cracked open, feir papery lips parted, and Krona trembled—unsteady on her feet, knees locked as she leaned in—for want of hearing a god actually *speak*.

"I dreamed . . ." fey said slowly, voice raspy like crumpled tissue paper, creased at the edges and torn in odd places, the tone as withered as feir body with the true weight of years. "I dreamed I was a tree." Slowly, a smile stretched across feir lined lips. "It was a good dream. A dream of ages."

Emotion leaned forward, bringing the crest of feir beaked skull gently against the wrinkles of Knowledge's forehead. Knowledge's eyelids shut again, dropping like it took great effort to keep them lifted.

Together, the gods sat and sighed, breathing each other in—unmoving, silent.

A minute passed. Two.

The gods did not move.

Krona felt even more intrusive than she had before and carefully stepped away, back to Tray's side.

The four humans watched and waited, chests expanded with poised breath, ready to make their entreaties if only the gods would stir.

But the silent communion went on, and on.

Krona began to pace, arms crossed if only to keep her hands gripped to her biceps, to steel the anxious energy that wound tighter and tighter in her spine with each moment of inaction.

She wanted to believe the gods were communicating, though they looked to have fallen into a gentle peace on the edge of slumber. Juxtaposed against hours earlier, when waking Emotion had been a burst of chaos, this startling quiet was *agonizing.*

Anything could be happening to Thibaut and the others while the gods—who'd been dormant for so long—remained sluggish, soaking in each other's presence like nothing had happened to their Valley during their absence.

Her anxiety was well-placed—as logical as it was deeply emotional, which they should both appreciate—but she could not bring herself to affront the divine with immediate entreaties. She could not risk their ire and rejection. She needed them. As painful as it was to wait in such ear-splitting silence—with her heart banging away in her chest while she suppressed the urge to plea and demand—she vowed to bare it so as not to squander the goodwill she *must* have earned through freeing them.

After a while Tray could not take her pacing anymore and grabbed her by the elbow. "Peace," he pleaded.

For his sake, she leadened her feet.

Just then, the gods drew apart, Emotion shaking zhur head, clearly protesting. Krona feared for a moment that she'd offended despite herself, but Emotion's ferocious denials were pointed at Knowledge.

"Seek . . ." Knowledge wheezed. "The siblings."

Emotion squawked a denial.

"Must. Together. Unions done and undone," Knowledge said, voice like a saw on a rotted trunk. "Carvings of thick flesh and thin meat. Slick. Slickness. Wetted with dark things, like blood. Not blood. Vapors. Not the fumes, not to breathe. Brokenness bowing to ego and desperation. Reins, their bits in the mouths of many. If no love, then at least . . . control." Fey slumped farther in feir seat. "Leave me. I must think. I must think."

Emotion rose from zhur crouched position, hackles raised, discontented.

With a creaking, Knowledge turned feir head, addressed the humans. "You have seen her, in glass. One twin, then the other."

It wasn't difficult to understand Knowledge meant for them to seek Time, then find Nature, but fey made no move to stand. Krona wasn't sure if fey could.

"Cannot leave," Knowledge said, clearly reading her mind—if not *all* their minds. "Must think. Go."

They were being dismissed.

If fey could read Krona's mind, then fey *knew* how desperate the situation was. Fey knew what she wanted, why they'd come here, and what had to be done in order to cut the Savior's rule off at the quick.

And yet fey were telling them all to leave fem to feir solitude.

Krona hardened her jaw, afraid of harsh words leaking past her lips, despite how clearly they were roaring in her head.

They had one god who could not speak, and one god who would not move.

Sensing her anger, Emotion knelt next to her, similar to the stance zhe'd taken with Knowledge. This put zhur crystalline eye sockets nearly at level with Krona's.

For whatever reason, Emotion was as unhappy as she was. Zhe did not want to leave Knowledge behind. Nor, it seemed, did zhe want to move on to Time.

Why Emotion would not want to see one of zhur children, Krona could not guess.

Their joint disquiet settled Krona. These circumstances were not ideal for her, and not ideal for the gods.

Emotion, with zhur wide, elegant hands, made a gesture like blooming. Like a bubble expanding or a flower opening. Krona interpreted it as best she could—as encouragement to take them all to Time, while leaving Knowledge to feir musings.

Sliding her relatively small hand into one of Emotion's, she took Tray in the other, and he in turn grasped Sebastian's, and he his wife's.

Focusing, Krona created a lens back into the varger hoard, and left the groaning treehouse behind.

HINTOSEP

"What have you *done,* Child?" Gerome demanded as he opened the cell door and caught sight of Hintosep, a woven basket in hand, waking Avellino from his fitful slumber on the hard stone.

Hintosep herself had failed to sleep. She was typically forced to—the rhythms of her body dictated by the Cage. But either Gerome had forgotten to direct her to sleep, or he desired her painful, groggy wakefulness.

Now, she watched helplessly as the newly appointed Grand Orchestrator rushed into the cell, then past the boy, stepping on his hand in the process. Avellino yelped, scrambled away like a kicked dog, holding his accosted palm to his chest.

Gerome bowled over him to get to Hintosep, to grab her chin and turn her this way and that so that he could examine the new bores.

The wounds weren't Avellino's fault. Not really. He was a good boy. He'd just been trying to help her.

Still, Gerome's eyes blazed. He turned on Avellino as though the child was the villain here, the one with the sadistic streak.

"I wanted you to see her. To understand how even the powerful can be humbled when they go astray. I never considered you would *mutilate*—"

"I tried to free her," he explained from the floor.

"Exactly. You were arrogant and meddled. You thought you could overpower one of the seven artifacts, which shows just how ignorant you are in the ways of the world, and how much those revolting people who stole you away have warped your mind."

Avellino glared, but held his tongue.

Still angry, jaw clenched, Gerome went about the business of feeding them from his basket—tossing first a new set of robes at Avellino and barking at him to put it on before throwing bread and cheese to the boy. In contrast, he delicately tore away chunks of the same to give to Hintosep, making her pluck each bite from his fingertips. She ate grudgingly, as usual, and Avellino kept to his place on the floor, gaze downcast.

Gerome's movements periodically blocked her view, but she watched Avellino as the makeshift meal went on. He pulled the robes on over his other clothes as though being forced to don something slimy. His cheeks flushed as he ate, and his lips pursed tighter and tighter. It was a look of growing resentment. Clearly, there were words of anger and defiance piling up inside his skull, and it remained to be seen if he could keep them trapped for the duration.

As Gerome finished handfeeding Hintosep, wiping his palms together as though to indicate a job well done, whatever dam Avellino had created to keep himself in check broke, and his rebelliousness came spewing out.

"They'll come for me," he said without standing. Without raising his eyes. His voice was hot, low. Cutting. "They came before. I have hope. As long as I have that, I can stand against you." His gaze snapped up, and there was fire in his eyes. "Hope is all I need."

Gerome waved one hand dismissively, clearly unimpressed. "Hope. Come now. You've been stewing this entire time and this is all you have to say to your Possessor? That you have hope? Trite."

"You think me naïve? For hoping?"

"Of course not," Gerome scoffed. Whipping his robes around his ankles, he took two strides toward Avellino and sunk down before him. "I think you naïve for believing hope is anything but a transitory state. It is not a thing in and of itself. You believe you are the only one who can hope? That your enemies are, what, pure despair? They too have hopes. They too can dream. They too see a brighter future for themselves. No, to hope is not naïve. To believe hope discriminates, that it is a power only you hold, *that* is the height of naivety. There is nothing special about hope. We all possess it. It cannot exist without us. It is an ephemeral, liminal thing. We all draw power from it. It is no ultimate, no holy thing. It is nothing without a dreamer, nothing without a goal—aimless and pointless. An untouchable platonic ideal. It is the *will* behind the hope that matters. And yours is no match for mine."

In demonstration, Gerome's hand shot out in Hintosep's direction, his fingers curling through the air as though they were the legs of the Cage themselves.

The Cage squeezed and jerked, channeling Gerome's will, compelling her to her feet.

"My will supersedes that of the great Hintosep, and you would be so arrogant as to think your hopes surer than mine?

"Do you want to know what I hope for?" Gerome asked. "I hope the Savior gives me leave to take these past years from your mind," he said evenly to Avellino, his gaze searching the boy's as he planted his seeds of fear, looking to see if they'd take root. "To put up walls and deny the rest of your psyche the damage. I hope He allows me to care for you properly, to bring you back into the fold under my protection. As it sits, He could choose a thousand different fates for you. But I care for you. He knows that. And so, I hope to rid you of this vile time in your life."

With a flick of his wrist, he commanded Hintosep to sit down again, and he himself rose. "The Savior will be here shortly. Then your fate will be decided."

Avellino turned haunted eyes on Hintosep, but there was nothing she could offer in return. Not comfort, not regret. He was right to be afraid; Gerome could do as he said. He was powerful enough to wall off a few simple years, as life-changing as they must have been.

As if on cue, the familiar, ominous footfalls of Absolon could be heard canting evenly down the hall. When he entered, he was masked and fully shrouded.

Avellino involuntarily shrunk in his presence, clearly still unable to shake the sense of awe and respect that had been instilled in him from near birth.

Hintosep could tell from the tight draw of Absolon's shoulders that he was irritated. Something was amiss. "Quickly," he snapped at Gerome. "Give her the commands. Then I need you to study our other . . . guests. I can sense extra power in one of the men you brought back with you. It's like a greasy film, clinging to everything," he said, rubbing his black-gloved fingertips together, as though he could be rid of said film if he scrubbed hard enough. "He may prove ripe for extraction."

"And . . ." Gerome prompted slowly. "My Child?"

"The boy is your pet project," Absolon said with disdain, as though pestered. Before he could go on, he caught sight of Hintosep's new wounds. He hurried to examine her up close, and she allowed herself to fantasize about biting his fingers off. "You assured me you could keep him under control."

Gerome made no attempt to defend himself, or Avellino's actions.

"Ah, well, it'll all heal in time," Absolon said, then added, "if I let it. Come, now, the commands."

"Follow him," Gerome said, a quiver in his voice as he imposed his will upon the Cage. "His will is my will until you are returned to this room."

Absolon swept from the cell, and Hintosep was compelled after as surely as if she were leashed, with no way of knowing what the boy's fate would be, or even if she'd ever see him again.

She was not wholly unsurprised when Absolon led her once more to the storage space where he'd rent a hole in the keep. There, the Teeth stood out prominently from their lonely position atop their pedestal. A heavy door had been constructed over the torn bit of reality, clearly to protect the keep from outside entry, but also to facilitate further use. He could have forced it to dissipate and disappear, if he'd wanted.

In among the stored gauzy hangings sat spare chairs and a few small tables from elsewhere in the keep, which was clear from their mishmash of stylings. One table was littered with a tinkerer's paraphernalia on a silver tray and opaque, corked vials. A strange automation, a little smaller than Hintosep's fist and made of interlocking metal hexagons, lay nestled in the middle.

"Lessons, lessons, lessons," Absolon muttered. "Seems one is never fully done with their education."

He removed his robes to reveal a journeyman's clothes beneath. His mask came off last, and his gloves remained.

Like this, he looked average. Unremarkable. He didn't even have a Thalo's characteristic tattoos—such adornments were for others, and though she used to think of them as badges of honor, she now saw them for what they truly were: another means of control. Not simply because they were used to trick the young ones into believing that was how they absorbed their power, but because it fundamentally set them apart. It altered them permanently in a way that would always ensure they could not become part of Arkensyre proper. It proclaimed them as other, as separate, as monsters. Even in Xyopar where inking one's self was common, a Thalo's blues would always stand out.

She wondered how often Absolon secretly roamed among the people. She'd thought him reluctant to leave the keep—hadn't seen him do it for hundreds of years before the war that now ravaged the Valley. But he'd been hiding his other magics for who knew how long. He could use kairopathy to jump from his private chambers and back again and no one would be the wiser.

He took up a chair, then sat her down in the one opposite his, regarding her with a frown.

Internally, she frowned right back.

She had no idea what this new *lesson* might be, but it was bound to be infuriating and unpleasant.

"You have been building quite the network behind my back, haven't you?" he asked.

She made no attempt to deny it in her own mind. At this point, she had to assume he'd plucked the secret of Mirthhouse and her other safehouses from either Avellino's mind or one of the others'.

He tutted at her, then taking hold of a fine-tipped pair of industrial tweezers, he tugged one of the vials from the tray and uncorked it with his teeth.

Something inside wriggled. *Scrabbled.*

"Do you remember these? From before?" he asked, slipping the tweezers down inside the tube of glass, pulling whatever it was from the bottom in a gentle grip. "No, I don't suppose you do," he mused. "They were eradicated. Well, nearly."

Slowly, he drew the squirmy thing into the light.

An eyeless pale pink marsupial, no bigger than a fingernail, struggled in the tweezer's grip. It had large ears, a broad snout. Absolon squeezed it lightly—enough to make it uncomfortable—and its tiny jaws opened to display two dozen fishhook-like teeth.

"It doesn't look like much, but this is an apex predator. Nothing eats it, and it eats nearly anything it wants. It burrows, you see. A colony of these will consume, say, a bear in less than an hour. They are venomous *and* poisonous, and a major component in the events that led us"—he sat back and threw his arms wide, still holding the tiny creature aloft—"here."

Hintosep tried to decipher if he was trying to tell her he knew what she remembered, or if this was simple posturing.

Absolon was prone to one-sided conversations, after all. One may discuss things in front of him, but one did not discuss things *with* him. His will was definitive.

He did not have opinions and whims—his decisions were paramount to law, considered divinely inspired and therefore above question let alone rebuke.

So, even before the Cage, she was used to sitting silently in his presence as he detailed plans or philosophized about their place in the grand scheme of human history.

But this was something different. He held a physical threat between them, either as a promise or a warning.

"Powdered vipnika liver was used in the first chemical compounds essential to pneuma extraction, when the technology was still young," he continued. "Before I discovered how to replicate the process magichanically.

"Prior to all that, however, a microdose of a reactive agent found only in vipnika was used for tithing. Vipnika produce a chemical from these glands here." He flipped the small, flailing thing over to point at tiny bulges beneath its forearms. "It's what directs vipnika to swarm. A scout may attach itself to a large prey animal miles from the home burrow, but this secretion, carried on the wind, will call to its fellows."

He leaned forward farther, letting her truly see the strength in the vipnika's snapping jaws, the sharpness of its teeth.

Had he finally decided to kill her, and simply wanted her to anticipate the agony? To fear the inevitable—the many burrowing bites that would make a maze of her body before she succumbed?

But then he sat back, took up the vial, and plopped the animal back inside, securing it away once more. "Tithing is an old-world practice," he said, standing, pacing. "It was an old-world practice even before this world. You know of soullocks, but a tithing is a soul*bond*. It is more intimate than a marriage, makes you closer than family. Tithings can be made up of any number of people, who have any type of relationship, platonic or otherwise. They simply need to consist of people who desire to be interconnected. To be truly tied to one another, forever. They might be parents, children, friends, lovers.

"It lets one feel the others. To sense their shifting through the world. It lets one know if everyone in their tithing is safe, and yes, if one of them has died. Most of the city-states have some bastardized version of this today—something that makes one a slave to someone else's pains. Lutador's Marchonian Guards, for instance. But those could never match the devotion, the gentleness, and true love inherent in a mutual tithe, which, when mixed with the blood of the tithers, only vipnika secretions can create.

"I was part of a special tithing, and I've worked *very* hard to untie myself from them."

Here he stopped his pacing, whirled in Hintosep's direction. He stopped before her, looming for a moment, his eyes wild, before he leaned down, pushing in close to her face, placing all of his weight on the armrests of her chair. "I haven't had to feel their minds working for a *thousand* years," he spat. "And now two of them are *awake*. Including one who should have been out of everyone's reach. One whose location was known by no one but *me*."

He shook the chair, sending a hot course of shock zinging through her veins.

"I have been patient with you. Reeducating where I could have simply killed. Maybe I should have let you Ascend when you asked—when you were tired of your Guardianship—but you've been by my side for too long for me to let you go. I couldn't stand to see you like that; gone from me, encased in crystal.

"I have loved you and been loved by you and as such I thought I could let your darling little rebel cells burn themselves out instead of taking my retribution directly from their hides, but the war is obviously not enough to re-cleanse the lands. Not now that you've brought the *gods* into this.

"You've been wondering why I've used the Teeth to travel, rather than simply jumping myself wherever I please," he said, pulling away. It was not a question, but a stated fact. He could read it in her mind as clearly as any sentence on a page. "The Teeth have helped me create a network of tunnels all over Arkensyre, and now connect a series of very specific places: your safe houses."

He stared at her smugly, letting those last three words hang in the air like three terrible wishes, three tainted promises.

That buzz of shock swamped through her again, and for the first time in a long time, she struggled against the Cage.

"You made these blights. These festering sores in the Valley's hide. And so it falls to you to erase them. I have crafted a very special enchantment. Just for you. Powerful. Potent. One I hope to never recreate. One I may never *be* able to recreate, in truth. It's the reason I've thawed the last of the vipnika from their kairogenic slumber."

Pushing away, he turned back to the tool-littered table and took up the construct of metal hexagons. He twisted the outermost layer of metal, revealing a plethora of moving parts and a hollowness in the middle. "The power of transformation and evolution makes being a lord of secrets look piddling by comparison," he mused to himself, an ages-old bitterness biting through his tone.

Once more he took up the vial with the vipnika and emptied the small creature into the device, sealing the animal inside.

"Things are better as they are now," he said to her, tone ever so reasonable. "You know the world suffered before, but you don't *remember*. I took that from you, and that was a mistake."

She willed him to take down those remaining walls now. The important ones had already weakened, collapsed. She remembered him killing the Unknown—the Fallen, the god of Secrets. She remembered who they were to her, and how all the gods had really come into being. She knew the world was held up by nothing but layers and layers and layers of Absolon's lies. Why shouldn't she now recall how humanity's vast world had been narrowed down to a single, secret-bound valley?

But though she silently screamed at him to show her, he wasn't listening—to her thoughts or otherwise.

He was striding over to the Teeth, lifting them from their place of honor. With the artifact in one hand and his new enchantment in the other, he returned to her side, studying her with an odd expression—like one stares at a choice piece of meat, contemplating where to make the first cut.

"History has shown time and time again that people are willing to use their magic for abuse," he explained. "They cannot be trusted with it. I created a world that removes inborn pathology from the equation. Magic and technology are controlled. Contained. Nothing can get out of hand. It is easy to maintain, reset, and conserve. Higher powers have decided how the people must live, have given them commandments and penalties, and they are protected as long as they adhere to these simple rules." He tucked the Teeth beneath his arm, then curled a finger beneath her chin, lifting her eyes to meet his. "Wanting to give them more is folly. Letting them keep their magic is a cruelty, not a kindness.

"You will eliminate your rebel cells, and then we will deal with your godrousers," he declared, fitting the Teeth over his fist. "Now," he bid gently, "lean back for me."

Her spine bowed, making her soft belly protrude.

She knew exactly what he intended to do with his little vipnika trap.

Despair washed through her. There was no way to fight, to deny, or prevent. Her autonomy had been taken, her will disregarded. She was just a vessel now. Perhaps that was how he'd always seen her—never as someone in her own right. She was just a tool, an extension of his desires. Something fundamentally *lesser.*

And she was the closest thing he had to a friend. To family.

People were just things to control to him. He wrapped his actions in a warm blanket of paternal concern, but he was too far removed from any shred of empathy he might have once possessed to truly feel such a thing.

He wanted the world to be tidy. But humans could never be made tidy. Not without undermining their very humanity.

Absolon pulled the Teeth's levers taut, opening the jaws wide until the smallest set extended outward, threatening and snakelike on its probiscis.

"This will hurt," he warned her, tone awash with sympathy. He waited only a beat more before thrusting his fist forward.

There was no need to remove her clothes or sanitize her skin. The smallest jaws of the Teeth tore into her belly with a magical force, ripping open a cavity for Absolon to plant his creature.

Pain shot through her abdomen. So intense it forced the air from her lungs and locked her jaw, despite the Cage's control. He hadn't even permitted her the ability to scream—an outlet of some kind, a place to put the terrible energy that now coursed through her. Tears leaked out of the corners of her eyes and her muscles shook as he pressed forward slowly, always meticulous in his work.

He parted her muscles and flesh and organs with precision, like a well-practiced surgeon. The Teeth hollowed out the perfect cavity, thrusting everything aside, forcing her body to conform to a new plan, a new shape.

Through it all, her chin remained raised, her gaze stuck fast to Absolon's face—right where he'd put it. It swam before her eyes, his features softened by pain-induced dizziness and the sheer number of tears welling up.

When he was satisfied with his excavation, he hummed to himself, then tucked the enchantment into her torso. It sat like a heavy stone in her middle, hard and foreign. Gently, he pulled the teeth away, making sure the magic sealed her up again perfectly.

Just as their katars could tear through an infant and only remove their pneuma, so too could the Teeth implant an object without leaving so much as a seam. When he withdrew, her clothes were in no more disrepair than they had been before—not a drop of blood graced the fibers. There was nothing on the outside to indicate anything was wrong on the inside, save for the smallest bulging.

"I've sacrificed the pneuma of nearly a thousand Physiopaths for this," he whispered to her. "Don't waste it. We want to make sure we eliminate every single person—every adult and child you've corrupted."

Inside her, the vipnika *wriggled*. She could feel it beating itself against the confines of its prison.

"Now, up!" he bid, snapping his fingers as he removed the Teeth, dropping them onto the side table with little care, letting the artifact *thunk* down among the other tools. "The enchantment is drawing energy from you as we speak. We want you in place when the magic fully engages."

He guided her as she marched, stiff like an automation, toward his rip in reality. The doors opened with a protesting creak, and they stepped through into the hole-riddled world. A few steps in the right direction through a series of rips brought them to the interior of Mirthhouse within a matter of minutes.

Absolon's tear in reality had been concealed by the dilapidated outer portions of the mansion. In a room half-destroyed and half-maintained. The very decay Hintosep had used to shield the safe house had also been used to hide their enemies' access point.

There were no guards standing watch this close to the mansion. Absolon was able to guide her through the illusion, out the room's door and into the great room.

It had been years, and yet the space felt the same. The giant stone hearth was the same—adorned, as usual, with the stolen katar—the smell of the room was the same, its warmth was the same, and its bustle—the people—there were new faces, but it all felt irrevocably the same.

"Hintosep!"

A woman rushed to her side, but Hintosep could not turn her head to see who it was. Beside her, Absolon had cloaked himself, hiding his presence from their detection. "You will watch it all," he told her, even as those around her dithered. His fingers left Hintosep's arm, and he backed away toward his tear. "I will retrieve you later. Once you have sat awhile with the destruction."

Like a puppet with its strings cut, she collapsed onto the floor, eyes wide and staring.

Frantic hands descended on her, pulled her limp form up and onto one of the nearby couches.

Nannette, a familiar old woman, leaned over her, a child on her hip as she tried to one-handedly arrange a pillow behind Hintosep's head.

It took Hintosep a moment to realize she recognized the child. Abby. It was Abby.

"Give her room! Give her room to breathe!" came a voice from somewhere near Hintosep's shoulder, over the back of the settee. "Nannette, fetch her some water from the well, or cider from the kitchen. We'll figure out how to get this contraption off her. Hintosep, can you hear me? Are you all right?"

Nannette set Abby down a few feet from Hintosep, right in her line of sight.

She begged them all to run.

She knew Absolon was already gone. Had already alighted back to the keep and closed those thick, protective doors behind him.

Abby's gaze was strong, piercing. As the small child studied her, zhe clearly became more and more distressed, and clutched zhur blue security blanket tighter to zhur chest. Zhe knew something was wrong. Something the others could not perceive. Perhaps the child could sense the unnatural object lodged in her abdomen. But what did it matter? There was no way for her to communicate, and no time for anyone to investigate.

The enchantment swelled inside her. She could feel its many interlocking sections begin to rotate around one another, pushing against her insides. There was no pain, but the budding pressure and unnatural movement made her queasy. That, and the sickening knowledge that of all the faces here, of all the people she'd recruited in all the houses across Arkensyre, there was nothing she could do to save or warn any of them.

A rough, jerky vibration started in the enchantment's core—the panicked scrabbling of the vipnika inside, no doubt.

Her ears popped, her stomach leapt, and power shot through her core, bursting through her without destroying her, yet sapping her just the same. The force whited out her vision for a terrifying moment, and when it cleared again, every inanimate surface within sight transformed and erupted.

Not into fire, or water, or molten stone, but into soft, pink flesh.

17

HAILWIC

In a Time and Place Unknown

Lonny put on a spectacular show when he was fired. The even-keeled rule follower revealed his unhinged side, cursing out the office at large, knocking over everything in his path, gnashing his teeth at anyone nearby. Hailwic gave him a ready target to aim at, stepping in front of him, making a production of trying to calm him down. He had no qualms telling her exactly what he thought of her engineering skills, her daddy's reputation, and (an odd choice, but all right) her poor choice of wardrobe.

Hopefully the pure venom dripping from Lonny's words would be enough to put any future suspicions to rest. She couldn't imagine anyone suspecting they were still working together after such a visceral severance.

The first day Uphrasia came to personally check on the total extraction project, the atmosphere in the office was palpably different as soon as Hailwic stepped out of the jump shaft. Tension radiated from her coworkers, their shoulders tight, and their eye contact spotty. Jumpy. In contrast, Hailwic tried to project not just cool confidence, but excitement. In the stomach-turning version of herself she now played day-to-day, Uphrasia was an idol.

It helped that the nervous twitch of her fingers could be attributed, then, to giddy nerves and not gently rolling fury.

As she rounded the corner to make for Dr. Theesius's lab, the world shrunk, the air becoming thick and her brain sharpening. The edges of her vision dappled, and all Hailwic could see was the stark silhouette created by the bright purple suit and flowing brown hair at the end of the hall.

Uphrasia.

Friend Uphrasia was *here*.

She'd been planning for this day, this first meeting, for nearly a year now, and here she was, in the flesh.

Hailwic gripped and regripped the familiar pass-card in her hand like it was a weapon—a knife's hilt, a club's handle.

Dr. Theesius greeted Hailwic with an even, steady expression. Nothing betrayed their true mood.

"Ah, there you are," they said. "Friend Uphrasia, I'd like you to meet my assistant. Top of her class at Helena and an absolutely *stunningly* talented Kairopath—so don't go stealing her for your detail," they teased.

The world swam as Uphrasia turned, her motions graceful—not to mention *exaggeratedly slow* in Hailwic's mind. The woman held out her hand, a wide, welcoming smile on her lips. Uphrasia was rumored to be in her eighties, but she didn't look a day past thirty, what with her access to expensive time treatments.

She was beautiful. People tended to trust beauty, to pander to beauty. Didn't matter what was beneath.

"A pleasure," the Friend said.

Moving through molasses, Hailwic slipped her hand into the Friend's.

Internally, she balked at the contact. Here was the woman who'd as soon spit on her brother as look at him. Who'd be just as happy to murder him as to render him powerless.

"Oh, you're Ferdinand's daughter, aren't you?"

"Yes."

"How is he? Haven't seen him in years. I heard your poor family ran into some . . . trouble."

"That's all done with now. Set right," she insisted earnestly.

"Well, I hope so. Good for you, landing here after all that unpleasantness."

"I want to do what I can for Radix. She's been good to my family. I want to give back."

"It is always so good to meet a young person who takes their patriotism so seriously."

The Friend was flanked by bodyguards. Both towered over the pair of women, their black uniforms cutting and precise. They wore helmets with black visors and stood silent, steady. They were simply to be perceived as arms of the state. As extensions of Uphrasia herself, rather than people in their own right.

Hailwic knew her palms had gone cold and clammy, and she prayed it wouldn't give away her desire to *squeeze*—to clench her fist until she felt the fine bones in the other woman's hand grate and *break*.

When Uphrasia reclaimed her hand, she snapped her fingers at one of her guards, and they adroitly produced a handwipe. "Nothing personal," she said, meticulously going over every bit of exposed skin.

"Of course," Hailwic agreed.

"Go ahead, you can ask," Dr. Theesius prompted her.

It took Hailwic a moment to remember her lines. "Oh, no, that's all right," she said quickly.

"Go on," they insisted. "She would really love your autograph," they told Uphrasia.

The woman lit up brighter than the sun. "Oh, well, aren't you just *darling*."

"You wouldn't mind?" Hailwic asked.

"No, of course not. Especially for a friend of Kinwold's."

It was strange how easy it was to twist her murderous desire into an outward display of nervous admiration.

"Did you have something specific you wanted me to sign, or . . . ?"

Hailwic bit her lip and shook her head.

The Friend snapped her fingers again, and a moment later there was a pen and scratch pad in her hand. She signed her name with an exaggerated flourish, then tore off the top scrap of paper and presented it to Hailwic like she was offering a scrap of food to a flighty animal.

Hailwic resisted the urge to tear it out of her grasp and ball it in her fist. She wished she could take it back to her apartment and set it on fire, just to watch the embers consume something of Uphrasia's the way her policies had consumed most of Hailwic's life. But she and Kinwold agreed she'd have it framed, set on her desk, displayed proudly for everyone to see—especially Uphrasia herself, the next time she visited.

It took another year to track down Zoshim's location—his records were sealed, and Hailwic finally understood that her parents had been lying about receiving correspondence from him—but once they'd found him, it wasn't difficult to get Zoshim on the list of test-subject volunteers. That pained Hailwic more than anything. There was no way to alert him that this was really a rescue, that he wasn't penning his life away by signing up to be experimented on.

"Uphrasia will be arriving tomorrow," Kinwold informed her one day, months later, when she came into their office to deliver a stack of reports.

She smiled heartily. They were both sure Dr. Theesius's office was bugged with pin cameras and reverb beads.

"That new shipment of materials we've been waiting on has finally come in, and Uphrasia wants to observe the extraction attempt."

"The new shipment includes the subject I requested?"

"Yes, it does." They smiled at her. "Uphrasia will be highly impressed by your dedication, I have no doubt."

They passed her a folder from the other side of their desk, and she quickly clutched it to her chest, as though the flimsy paper could hide the rapid beat of her heart. She held herself as professionally as she was able, but found she could not speak. A lump occupied her throat, and her voice would crack if she tried to say anything.

Thankfully, the doctor waved her away with a flick of their hand, and she scurried out, eyes unfocused as her feet carried her back to her own desk.

The folder they'd given her for filing was labeled MATERIALS along with the date.

Materials meant Physiopaths.

With shaking hands, she opened the folder.

She never looked at these files when they came to her. Never. She tucked them into the appropriate cabinets—the files kept under enchanted lock and key—but never *looked.*

To look was to know. To understand just how many Physiopaths came into the facility. How many people had "volunteered" to give up their magic for a chance to get some semblance of a life back.

Supposedly they knew what the risks were, but she couldn't bring herself to believe it. No one would sign up for this if they knew no one had yet walked away. That no one had achieved freedom instead of death.

Every Physiopath who entered the labs these days left in a body bag.

Every.

Last.

One.

And yet she'd begged Theesius to bring Zoshim here.

The top page of the file held a profile sheet for an older woman with her booking photograph stapled to it. Hailwic didn't pause to read what her crimes had been—after all, every Physiopath's real crime was *existing.*

One by one, she flipped through the loose pages of each profile, noting young and old alike, people of all genders, races, likely all walks of life. She made herself note their faces.

When she flipped over a sheet and saw Zoshim, she startled. She'd been expecting it—she'd known he was among the volunteers—and yet actually seeing him staring back was a shock. The picture wasn't from his initial booking, back when they'd both been arrested. This one was newer. He looked so . . . old. Unbelievably old for his age, simply because his cheeks were drawn, his eyes empty, brow heavy and furrowed. He wore a scraggly beard and mustache, which changed the shape of his jaw. She'd never seen him with facial hair before. He'd never had an errant hair on his head, let alone his face.

He'd always been clean shaven, she'd never—

For the first time, she realized that had been because of magic.

He'd *never* shaved. He'd simply used physiomancy to appear as he desired.

That realization hit harder than any revelation she'd had recently. That he'd even been denied such a small dignity as choosing whether or not to grow a beard was somehow the thing that opened the floodgates—that broke through her carefully schooled expression and well-held exterior.

She slapped the file shut.

Hailwic told herself she should be used to Uphrasia's presence by now. That her skin shouldn't still crawl, that her heart shouldn't still stutter. But she couldn't even look at the Friend's billboards on the way to work, or keep her tele on when one of her PSAs popped up.

Hailwic couldn't look a facsimile in the eye, and yet she forced herself to meet the woman's gaze here, now.

"Good morning, Miss Sinclare. Don't you look lovely today?"

It was her kindness that was the most chilling. Her niceties.

Some people held that good manners were proof of a civilized world. Hailwic was beginning to suspect they were just varnish to cover up the rot.

And so, like a good little soldier, she returned the Friend's compliments, laid it on with as much sincerity as she could manage, taking in the graceful way Uphrasia politely demurred; she did not stutter or fluster, but brushed aside Hailwic's return sugary sweetness with a gentle, "Oh no, you are too kind," before indicating Hailwic should lead them on to the day's big event.

"Of course. This way," Hailwic said, fumbling with her keycard at the single elevator that led from the offices down into the lab space in the building's subbasements.

The two bodyguards kept close to Uphrasia, blank and unmoving as Hailwic fiddled and flailed, struggling not to crinkle the file folder tucked under her arm.

Hailwic usually only had access to the first three levels of labs—cleanrooms, filled with white-coated or bunny-suited engineers working on various R&D projects with enchanted materials. Today, she'd been granted access to the building's subbasements for the first time. Advanced enchantment technology—the apparatus sprawling across the five floors directly above the subbasements and utilizing more power than ten city blocks—prevented direct jumps in and out of the top-secret areas of the facility, and even now, the elevator the group stepped into would only grant them access to an observation deck.

Uphrasia most certainly had such vast mechanisms protecting her private manor and her government offices.

The lift was slow and cramped, and Hailwic's skin crawled at the shared proximity to the woman she loathed most.

A gentle *ding* welcomed them to the bottom, and the doors slid aside to reveal a wide, dark space. In front of them, the only thing directly illuminated was a gray slab of stone with deep black etching of the company motto: FOR THE FUTURE.

Hailwic felt as though she was stepping onto the surface of a different planet rather than a different level in her own office building.

Instead of stark-white cleanroom walls separated by clear glass and awash in bright light with the space bustling and full of people and machinery, she now found herself surrounded by a vast darkness. An empty, yawing space.

The nearest walls were brutal slabs of dark cement, one of them set at a forty-five-degree angle to the others and ribbed like an old rail line set in stone. She half expected a coal train to come screaming down from the depths of darkness above since there were no lights that illuminated the ceiling, which suggested to the eye that it went on forever. The floor-level lamps only occasionally highlighted the edges of a hanging slab, implying there might be balconies or other floors above. The lamps themselves were set inside planter boxes level with the smooth flooring, which overflowed with ferns, adding incongruously delicate greenery to the otherwise ruthlessly heavy architecture.

Hailwic realized the subbasements were old. Very old. Remnants of something long before Uphrasia. Before Fistus. Before Hannelore and Constansing and Okip. These lab levels were here not just before the office building, but before the city.

Each footstep in this place seemed magnified. Hailwic could make out the individual sound of each shoe, and the clicking of her own pumps against the flooring seemed unnervingly, gratingly loud.

They followed the ferns, on and on. One wall dropped away, leaving nothing but a waist-high railing between the visitors and an even more vast, echoing emptiness. Hailwic couldn't guess what lay below, beyond, and could barely scratch up ideas for what the purpose might be for an area so cavernous and cold. An ancient cistern? Hangar for unknown ships? Eventually they came to a door, asymmetrically cut with a distinct lean, just as the slab of wall leaned. Its lines were clean, sturdy, its lean a show of strength and solidity—a display of pure command over concrete. A single potted ficus added a pop of green, and its modest height only served to highlight the sheer exorbitance of the space.

With another flick of her key card they were through, into a viewing area with a broad glass window, peering out and down ten feet below to the extraction site.

"If you would, please," Hailwic said, gesturing for them to all step forward. "Dr. Theesius will begin shortly. Would you like to review the file on today's subject?" She held out the file folder, surprised to see her own hand so steady.

"Yes, of course." She gestured for Hailwic to go on. "If you please."

"Today we've procured Zoshim Sinclare."

Below, three movable spot lamps, each leashed to long extension cords, came on in turn, illuminating a chair facing the viewing room.

Already strapped into it was Zoshim.

Hailwic froze, her skin suddenly flashing hot, then cold. She struggled not to betray herself. More importantly, not to betray *him*.

He, on the other hand, simply *struggled*.

His ankles, his thighs, his waist, his chest, his elbows, his wrists, his neck, and his head were all lashed to the chair by thick leather belts, and a length of the same had been forced between his teeth. Sweat was already dripping down his temples and his eyes flashed wildly from side to side as he fought against his confinement. The chair itself was bolted to the floor, and—even as he attempted to rock it from side to side—did not sway an inch.

He wasn't alone. Two lab assistants, in uniforms Hailwic had never seen before—black rubber ensembles complete with aprons and gloves and thick black goggles—double-checked his bindings.

And then, from the shadows, came Kinwold.

"Is that . . . your brother?" Uphrasia asked, genuine surprise lightly underscoring her usual tone.

"He was my first encounter with physiopathic violence," Hailwic said coldly.

She'd practiced this in the shower. At breakfast. Alone in front of a mirror, and late at night with Punabi. She could get through it without breaking.

"Is this revenge for you, Miss Sinclare?" Uphrasia asked carefully.

"Oh, no. No, of course not. I love my brother dearly. And this is his chance to be free."

"It is *such* a shame, isn't it?" Uphrasia agreed. "That this young man should be subjected to such vileness. That he should come out of the womb tainted."

Something slimy—with fangs—reared up inside Hailwic, snapping angry wings wide and looming up, up, up to lord high over Uphrasia and slash *down* and—

Hailwic took a gentle breath and put that shadow of her rage back inside its metaphorical cage.

He and I shared that womb. He and I are bound by that womb, she groused. Schooling both her face and her tone, she said sympathetically, "Yes. Such a shame."

"This—you, him—it's why I've made striving to save Physiopaths my life's work," Uphrasia continued, without a hint of sarcasm or mockery—let alone an awareness of the statement's irony. "If we can save them from this awful, corrupting influence by developing therapies that can rid them of this burden and convert them back into healthy citizens—I mean, *that's* the revolution. That's the way forward. Protect them and the rest of society all in one go. After all, it's not their fault, really. Hate the sin, not the sinner, as my father used to say. We all want everyone to be safe, don't we?"

She spoke with such sincerity, such passion. She made herself easy to like through soft words, made her terrible ideas easy to digest via little logic puzzles that made everything she was working toward sound reasonable and right in the moment.

Of course everyone wanted to be fucking safe. But did that man in that fucking chair look safe? Did he feel safe?

Was he safe?

Of course not.

But that didn't matter, because to Uphrasia, he wasn't a real person like her. Not yet. Not until she could neuter his pathy. Sap him of all he was and make him conform to her ideal.

Hailwic knew Uphrasia had used some version of this little speech on almost everyone, somewhere, sometime. There were always hints of it running through her broadcasted orations, snippets of it playing on a loop on the radio. Hailwic even received it occasionally as a PSA via her falsified implants.

The subtle us versus them was one thing—time-honored prejudice, if you will. But on top of that was her savior-bait; the insistence that *she alone* was the one with the solutions. That she was the nation's guiding light, the one who could restore peace and former glory. The one who could wipe out this decade's scourge, which was none other than *your* neighbor, and *your* grocer, *your* cousin, and *that man right there.*

The Friend wove her words well, and Hailwic genuinely could not tell if it was all strategic on Uphrasia's part or if she was just this good at naturally folding atrocities into a shape that appeared *respectable* and *practical* to an absurd number of people.

In a way, it made her the natural heir to Fistus's legacy. Where he had been manic and spluttering, she was even-keeled and firm of tone. He had been a Physiopath railing against Cryptopaths, and Uphrasia's opposition to him had at first seemed to the public like a well-reasoned breath of fresh air.

But it was all reactionary politics on top of reactionary politics. Authoritarianism whose focus had shifted to a different portion of society, but whose goals were still the same: power and control via appealing to prejudice and an unrealistic view of the past. Insist to the present that you've discovered why the glory days are gone, convince them you can restore prosperity, and you'll have them eating out of your palm.

All Uphrasia had to do was present morality as black and white. Clear-cut. Fistus's policies had been undoubtedly evil, and so it was easy to think that anyone opposing him must be undoubtedly good. *She* was that bastion of good, so anyone who opposed her must secretly want to restore the ways of Fistus, the man who'd seen their great nation suffer and fall.

It was a simple story, and people liked simple stories; the ideas were easy to digest, to personally identify with. To integrate into one's sense of self.

And then it was easy for Uphrasia to blur those lines she'd so strongly reinforced herself. Registering Cryptopaths was bad, but instead of destroying the records, she'd simply insisted on leveling the playing field by registering *everyone's* pathies. From there, she'd sowed doubts about the intention of physiopathic doctors—what were they doing, going against nature and mutilating your children?—about Physiopaths altering even themselves. Physiopaths were shunned, pushed to the fringes of society. Barred from being teachers, physicians, lawyers. They could not handle food, they could not be trusted with money.

Then the relocation camps were built. The wall went up, creating Remotus.

Then came the prison camps.

Which had led them . . . here.

Hailwic longed to simply attack. To rip the woman open with her bare hands, if necessary. The more Uphrasia grinned, the more feral heat rose in Hailwic. It went beyond vengeance, beyond blood lust.

Justice required this woman's *end,* and why should justice wait?

Hailwic calmed herself by digging her nails into her palm and reminding herself that justice had to be thorough. Complete. Justice was never successful when ill-timed and half-measured—not when justice was up against this kind of enemy. Not when the stakes were this high.

She needed Uphrasia alone. She needed her close and at ease so that she wouldn't see what was coming. So that not even her guards—her Cryptopaths constantly on the hunt for subterfuge and secrets—could see what was coming.

She needed a new government ready to take the old one's place. This wasn't her plan alone.

If Hailwic tried now, her fingertips wouldn't so much as flick across Uphrasia's neck before the two bodyguards would have her down and beaten. They'd kill her on the spot, no questions asked, and Uphrasia would live to ruin more lives.

"I specifically requested his presence, and he volunteered," Hailwic said, tongue feeling thick, though she articulated clearly. She spoke with carefully tuned passion. "He and I both know this is the right thing to do. Either he is cured or he is a step toward the cure for others. I believe in your mission—it's *our* mission. You see things so clearly, lead us so firmly. Please understand that I will do anything for the cause. We're out to save the world, after all, by ridding it of one Physiopath at a time."

Below, Kinwold prepared a serum while their assistants pulled long, thickly braided electrical cords from the darkness, hauling them around in great coils that slowly unwound before plugging them into the back of Zoshim's chair in ports Hailwic could not see from her vantage.

"In order to extract physiopathic pneuma in these quantities, we have to excite the pneumatic organelles in every cell of the body," Hailwic explained. "This process can be done physically or chemically, but requires that the body essentially be induced into a state of shock. Dr. Theesius has found that electric shock generates the most even and comprehensive reaction, regardless of the cell type."

Uphrasia's eyes never left Zoshim, and though she made the occasional sound of acknowledgment, she was clearly listening as one listens to an explanation they've heard many times before. Still, she did not shush Hailwic or tune her out altogether.

Instead, it was Hailwic who lost track of the words. She remembered her lines, gave a rundown of the intricacies of the process, using technical terms she barely understood but could wield in front of a non-expert. But her own voice became a droning din in her ears. She felt separate from her mouth, her body. Her sense of self was fully focused on her brother, on how close yet far he was. On how scared he looked. On how tightly the leather dug into his skin and how strained his jaw looked around his gag.

She barely noticed Dr. Theesius and the assistants swirling around him, injecting him, sliding two separate IV needles into his arms, attaching those to bell jars filled with naked, whirring machinery.

Could Zoshim see her from his chair? Could he tell it was her? Could he tell it was the Friend who stood next to her?

The last time he'd seen Hailwic, she'd betrayed him. Did he think this the ultimate betrayal—that she would ally with his oppressor, his would-be murderer? Or did he know what Hailwic had gone through to get him here? What she'd promised to do in exchange for his freedom?

She knew the operatives in charge of locating him and getting him to volunteer had been ordered to tell him whatever it took, as long as it wouldn't reveal anything about the rebellion that could be ripped from his mind by Cryptopaths. That left a lot of possibilities.

Hailwic was so engrossed in her own questions that when Zoshim's entire body jolted and locked—bowing away from the chair as far as his restraints would allow—she startled.

Bright light emanated from the machinery inside the bell jars, their gears whirling fast—fast enough that they started to heat, the metal in them taking on a hot orange tinge.

Dr. Theesius rushed in with a heavy-duty syringe, jabbing it into Zoshim's neck before slowly pulling back on the plunger.

The light in the jars grew brighter. A vibration came up through the floor of the viewing platform, subtle at first, then strong enough to make the window rattle and both Hailwic and Uphrasia reach out to steady themselves. The guards seemed to hold strong, but Hailwic could see them struggling not to sway.

Dr. Theesius gritted their teeth, fighting the syringe as they struggled to keep the needle an even depth—to neither lose the grip of Zoshim's skin, nor slam the spike of it in too deep.

Everything bounced and swayed.

The assistants ran to the bell jars, attempting to steady them as everything clattered, but both flew back an instant later, the rubber of their gloves leaving long, melted goopy strands behind on the glass.

The mechanisms within started to smoke.

The bell jars *burst.*

Zoshim went limp.

Dr. Theesius froze, then withdrew the needle and stepped back.

The four of them in the viewing gallery stood stunned, silent.

Below, all was suddenly still.

Zoshim's fine. He's fine.

He'sfinehe'sfinehe'sfine.

Regardless of her desperate internal chant, tears pooled in the bottom of Hailwic's eyes. She allowed them to well up as they would. There was no stopping them anyway. They were real tears—tears of fury. One fell, and she rushed to wipe it away, doing her damnedest to remain poised.

"Miss Sinclare, I'm so sorry," Uphrasia said sympathetically. "Another failure, and . . . and your brother, at that."

"It's better this way," Hailwic said. "He gave his life for Radix instead of rotting for betraying it. I couldn't be more proud."

"You are such a strong young woman. I know we all had high hopes for today, but look at you, so passionate about the project." She took out a clean handkerchief, passed it wordlessly to Hailwic. "We couldn't save him. We'll just have to hope we can save the next. And, if you'd ever like to chat"—she nodded to one of her guards, who pulled a thin card from a narrow billfold and handed it to Hailwic—"that's my private line.

"Now, since the equipment is out of commission, I have to assume the demonstration is done for today? Yes? In that case, why don't you join me for lunch?"

⟫⟫—o—⟪⟪

Zoshim *was* fine. Hailwic wasn't allowed to see him after, given the risks, but RFR operatives smuggled him to the resistance bunker—an ancient series of underground tunnels on the other side of the wall, in Remotus.

Hailwic couldn't go to him, but she could, finally, correspond with him. Punabi brought her pictures, letters, and, once in a while, a personal update when zhe'd seen him in the flesh. And once, not long after they'd rescued him, a phone call.

"Hello?"

The sound of his soft voice broke Hailwic into a sob before she could even greet him properly.

"Hail? Hail, are you—"

"It's just . . ." She took a shaky breath. "Hi, Shim."

She asked after his well-being, his journey to Remotus. She tried to avoid mentions of *that night*.

But it didn't take long for Zoshim himself to begin apologizing all on his own, churning up Hailwic's old guilt.

"I play that moment over and over again in my mind," he said, voice scratchy over the encrypted line. "There were other things I could have done."

"You were defending me."

"In the most brutal way possible. If I hadn't been a minor, if Mom and Dad *weren't Mom and Dad,* I would have been executed. Just one more monster to string up. And they'd have been right to do it."

"No," she said harshly, fists automatically clenching. "That's the trap. That's what they want you to think. They give you no way out, no chance to defend yourself. They wrestled an innocent kid down to the ground and threatened his sister with a gun and then get to be shocked when that kid fights back? I don't think so. If anyone that night had killed either of us, the world would have shrugged and moved on. It was a setup, and no matter what we did, we were the criminals. We were going to be imprisoned for walking down the fucking street, no matter how sweetly we complied. You are not a monster for defending us."

"Maybe no one did the right thing," he said. "I could have just broken his wrist so he'd drop the gun. I could have—"

"You could have been allowed to cross the street and been on your merry way," she countered.

After the call, Hailwic felt no more settled than before. He was safe, but their shared guilt over things larger than they were was still palpable.

Glensen quickly took Zoshim under feir wing, apprenticing him as a field healer.

From then on, he worked on rehousing and treating the displaced on one side of the wall, while Hailwic worked on breaking Uphrasia's personal defenses on the other. He rose through the ranks over the years, taking on more and more responsibility, becoming a leader in his aid work while Hailwic slow-played the Friend, moving from a flustered fan to passionate follower to something like a mentee.

She became someone Uphrasia invited to peruse her secret library where otherwise forbidden books were housed. Someone she confided in about her interest in the outlawed arcane. Someone she could confess genuine curiosity about ancient rituals to, while simultaneously openly condemning them as sick and backward.

Five years. Five years this had been in the works for Hailwic now. A lifetime, it seemed.

Ultimately, Uphrasia was enchanted by the idea that everything she was and wanted was reflected back at her by Hailwic—her primary likes, her dislikes, her vision for the future. Hailwic could mirror those things while maintaining a solid backbone in front of her, and Uphrasia loved having someone around who agreed without groveling. Who deferred to the Friend's expertise and authority without simping.

"Do you know what the most valuable thing in this world is, Hailwic?" Uphrasia asked her one day over lunch.

A conscience? Hailwic's internal monologue offered dryly.

"Loyalty," the Friend said. "Sadly, the world gets divided into winners and losers, and the biggest difference is losers divide and winners stick together. Stick with me and I'll stick with you."

Of course, the fates of those who'd displeased her—who'd been *dis*loyal—were varied and harsh. Rumor and misinformation abounded, but no one doubted Uphrasia's ability to publicly humiliate and privately devastate her opponents. Careers, family, reputation—none of it was safe. To displease Uphrasia was to dishonor yourself, your country, your loved ones, and however she chose to deal with you was considered nothing short of good and right and just.

"I think you could go far in politics," Uphrasia told her. "But I understand if you're married to magichanics."

"I'm dedicated to it, but if there was someplace I could make more of a difference—in a leadership role . . ."

"You'll go where opportunity takes you?"

"I will," she agreed heartily.

"Then have I got an opportunity for you."

Uphrasia had invited her on a thopter tour of the capital. Just the two of them. Well, the two of them and the pilot. But no guards. No extra security. Nothing between Hailwic and her target. The Rebels had a week to get their house in order, because the time to strike was now. Hailwic knew she'd never get a cleaner shot.

She still had to devise exactly how she was going to do it, though. She'd need to incapacitate Uphrasia so that she couldn't use her kairopathy to jump to safety. And a way to take out the witness.

Really, bringing down the whole thopter was probably her best option.

"I don't like it," Dr. Theesius said when she divulged her plan over dinner.

"It doesn't matter if you like it. Professor Solric already gave me the go-ahead. Fey've got a way to secure her cabinet members and take down General Gyrus on the same day, so it's all set."

"And if something goes wrong?" they asked. "What are your chances of escape?"

She let out a derisive little laugh. "What are my chances regardless? Let's face it, I was never meant to escape. You really think I can assassinate the most powerful person in our hemisphere and *survive*? Even if we can take out her cabinet and natural successor, I'll have a target on my back for the rest of my life. Her supporters won't disappear overnight."

She'd had a lot of time to think about it. A lot of sleepless nights staring at the speckled ceiling of her bedroom trying to work out what her life was supposed to be like *after*. There was no going home for her and Zoshim. And she wasn't naïve enough to think that taking out Uphrasia would mean the system the Friend had created would immediately unravel—that Physiopaths would instantly be allowed to walk the streets and be welcomed back into the fold with open arms.

Uphrasia wasn't just the leader of their society, she was a symptom of it. Tyrants were never tyrants alone.

Which was why whenever Hailwic tried to imagine her future, she found she *couldn't*.

There would be no rest for her after this. She would be hunted. Even if there was a regime change, there was no guarantee of clemency.

The best she could hope for was that Zoshim would continue to have a better life than he would have had otherwise.

"Let's be real, Kinwold, shall we? In the long run, either I officially get taken out or I'll have to take myself out before they can get to me. Success or failure, I've backed myself into a corner. There aren't a lot of bright outcomes for me, personally, post-assassination. So I'm not that worried about . . . about going down with her. If I have to."

"*No*," they insisted. "No, I won't allow it."

"You don't get to *not allow it*. If you think there's a reason this version of the plan will fail, tell me that. I know what I'm doing. You have to trust me to execute the mission, or what's the point?"

They breathed deeply, sighed. "You're right. I'm sorry."

Toe, now not so little, came in to clear their plates; she was helping her mother with the dishes, well accustomed to letting her babbi and Hailwic have their private time.

The two of them buttoned their lips immediately, and Hailwic passed her bare dinner plate off to the girl with a soft "Thank you."

After that, she and Dr. Theesius sat in silence for a while longer, a metaphorical morose cloud now casting a shadow on the bright day.

"It's not like I want . . . it's not like I want it to go that way," Hailwic said eventually, after turning the sentiment over and over in her mind. "I've just come to accept that it's inevitable. This leads to my end. Which is fine. I'll go out having made a difference. Not everybody gets to die trying to save the world."

Kinwold said something under their breath. Something Hailwic couldn't quite catch, but it sounded like *Nobody should have to.*

The night before Hailwic was scheduled to take her fateful flight, Punabi came to her apartment with supplies. "All right, I've got all the shit you asked for. Though I don't really understand how Snikums snack cakes fit into the whole scenario."

"Those are for me," Hailwic said, smacking Punabi's shoulder with the back of her hand in playful comradery.

Costumer's liquid latex, protective gloves, a fresh tube of pale pink lip gloss, the box of snack cakes, and a small vial of yellowish liquid were all dumped from Punabi's satchel straight onto the kitchen counter.

Hailwic dropped down to her knees before the small pile, resting just the pads of her fingers and the tip of her nose on the countertop to stare at the items. Punabi regarded her with a frown, then leaned down on zhur own elbows, inspecting the supplies as though there might be something wrong with them.

When zhe found nothing, zhe asked softly, "What are we looking at?"

"The culmination of my life," Hailwic said nonchalantly. Or, at least, she attempted nonchalance. Aimed for pragmatism. But what came out carried a strangled little waver that betrayed her worry and exhaustion. "Everything comes down to this handful of common shit just sitting here on the laminate."

Punabi snorted. "Yeah, well, the drugs ain't so common."

Hailwic gave a little shrug. "Eh. Same topical muscle relaxer you can get over the counter, just stronger."

"Stuff's *potent,*" Punabi reassured her. "It will absolutely be enough to fuck with her kairopathy. Which is why you have to be extra careful with it. If it can stop her from jumping, it can stop you just the same."

"I know," Hailwic said with a melancholy sigh.

Punabi seemed at a loss for what to do about Hailwic's mood. Zhe always got wound up before a mission; Hailwic had witnessed it on plenty of raids. Excitable, nervous energy just bursting out of zhur at every seam. Zhe was locked and ready and just needed to be pointed at the problem so all of that pent-up power had a direction.

Hailwic had felt like that sometimes. But this was different. This wasn't a supply raid.

This was likely the end.

"Hey—" Punabi slapped what was supposed to be a comforting hand on

Hailwic's shoulder, only to stop mid-thought and squeeze roughly. "Shit, you're wound tight."

"Yeah, well, I kinda gotta kill someone tomorrow, so . . ."

"So."

"Yeah."

Zhe took Hailwic by the elbow and gently urged her to her feet, then leaned back against the counter to observe her, lips pressed tightly together in a contemplative line.

She stood awkwardly for inspection, feeling like a poor foot soldier. It all came down to this. What if she couldn't do it? What if it went sideways? What if—

"Well, she'll see you coming a mile away like this," Punabi said, gesturing up and down Hailwic's tense form. "You *look* like you're about to kill someone. You need to relax. Throw back a shot of something."

"Can't. I need to stay sharp. Need to be alert tomorrow."

"Okay, no drinking," Punabi agreed. "But you need *something.* No empathic highs, either, I'd say—I could help you there, obvs, but it can still give you a hell of hangover. How about just good old serotonin from frenetic movement?"

Hailwic raised an eyebrow at zhur.

"Dancing," Punabi clarified, standing straight, offering Hailwic a hand. "Come on, I know a club."

Hailwic took the opportunity to rid herself of her office clothes for the evening, happy to be free of oppressive pencil skirts and dull slacks. Instead, she dug out a short, pleated skirt Hailwic the Professional wouldn't be caught dead in, a pair of heavy combat boots, and borrowed one of Punabi's tank tops. Glancing at her scant jewelry collection before exiting her room, she impulsively decided to put on every last necklace and ring she had.

Last chance and all that.

She threw a peach-colored chunky sweater over the lot of it to keep her warm on the walk there, then left hand in hand with Punabi.

Since the club was the illegal backroom type, they couldn't jump straight to their destination from an approved point, and it was fully dark by the time they'd trekked the distance from the apartment.

A password and a false wall at the back of a deli got them into a dimly lit stairwell that shook with a heavy bass beat. Teal paint peeled from the close walls, and curled bits of it bounced against the corrugated steps as they descended toward the basement level.

A bouncer met them at the bottom—the last line of defense against a raid—along with a thick metal door that opened directly onto the dance floor.

Where the stairwell had been dim, the club was dark, the deep blackness of its shadows cut through by swerving lights in electric colors that did nothing to illuminate details of the space but kept Hailwic's eyes from ever truly adjusting.

Writhing, jumping bodies were streaks of solid black, only revealed when one of the lights cut across the crowd with a sharpness like a knife.

"Come on!" Punabi shouted excitedly. Hailwic could barely hear zhim over the music, which sent a little flood of disappointment through her, but perhaps the volume was a good thing. It was so loud she could barely hear herself thinking.

No room for doubts. Just music.

The basement had once been a parking level, as far as she could tell, with cement columns holding up the shops above. Hailwic tried to encourage Punabi toward one to the side, but zhe seemed determined to occupy the center of the dance floor. There, zhe dropped Hailwic's hand, took a step away from her, and began to move.

On the way over, Hailwic had thought about mentioning that she felt self-conscious dancing in front of zhur. Punabi was a professional, after all. A trained artist. Hailwic was just someone who managed keep time—and that was only because her pathy guaranteed her internal metronome kept on point.

But now, in the middle of pure motion, watching Punabi truly in zhur element for the first time, Hailwic wasn't self-conscious.

She was enwrapped.

The current song had a solid beat, the notes were sharp and dark, and there was a lushness to the arrangement. It felt to Hailwic like her heart was trying to sync with it as Punabi first shuffled back, then danced toward her, zhur movements strong, heavy. Hailwic was used to good dancers looking light on their feet, but Punabi looked like zhur feet and the floor were polarized—drawn to each other, inescapably pulled together. Magnetic. Every time zhur toes left the floor, every time zhur shoulders rose, zhur muscles flexed and strained with a ferocious tension. Every move toward the ceiling was taut, and every move toward the floor was a release.

The precision of each of zhur movements was mesmerizing, but what Hailwic couldn't escape was the *heat* in zhur eyes. Their gazes locked, even in the darkness—full glimpses only caught when the flashing lights swirled their way for an instant, painting them each in fractured, neon rainbows.

Punabi came closer and closer, zhur stare never straying, though Hailwic felt hers wavering under the intensity of the attention. Hailwic rarely felt *shy*. She typically shrank in front of *no one*. But this was different.

Hailwic had tentatively started dancing when Punabi did, her movements hesitant. Now, her own swaying hips faltered, still keeping with the rhythm, though her movements became smaller and smaller until she was barely swaying when she and Punabi were finally toe-to-toe.

Smiling warmly, Punabi stilled, then gently slid a hand onto Hailwic's waist before leaning in to yell above the din directly into her ear.

Zhur breath was warm. Teasing. "Wanna dance? With *me*?"

Hailwic nodded, embarrassed at how overeager she was.

The hand on her waist slid farther around, to the small of her back before tightening, so that their pelvises were flush.

A little gasp left Hailwic, and she smiled through her bashfulness.

Punabi's matching grin was so cheeky, so *pleased*, that Hailwic's heart skipped a beat.

And then they were moving together, Punabi leading, guiding Hailwic through those heavy movements that had so mesmerized her moments ago. She threw her arms around Punabi's neck, laughing at herself as she tried to match zhur footwork, looking down, trying to find her feet, but seeing no daylight between their bodies.

Together, they found the rhythm, swaying, feeling the music and each other intimately. Hailwic still had her neck bent, and when Punabi's forehead came to rest against her own, her gaze flashed up, and she was caught again.

Punabi's eyes were beautiful, and focused. For a moment, Hailwic felt like the center of the universe.

She wanted to kiss zhim—the impulse nearly overwhelming—but she didn't want to break the rhythm, the way they were flowing. Every beat, every sway and stomp, sent a thrill through Hailwic, and she was determined to experience it all to the fullest. To be patient.

The kiss would come, she had no doubt, and would be all the sweeter because she'd let herself anticipate it.

The music flowed seamlessly into new song after new song, the lyrics about rebellion, about defiance, about having one's magic cursed and controlled. Most of it was old, before Friend Uphrasia's time—a reminder that this era was just a new incarnation of the same bullshit. Same energy, same fears, same threats. Different look, new targets.

There was a reason all these songs were banned. It was dangerous to remind people of how they got here, after all. That history was a through line. That the sins of the past and the sins of the present were kin.

But it was also a reminder to keep fighting. Keep defying. Until they could reach the lifetime where everyone was free.

Punabi grinned wide when a particular song zhe liked began to play. Hailwic had never heard it before, but it was clearly a club staple. Every chorus, the crowd paused, clapped, and stomped in time with the rhythm.

Punabi spun Hailwic away with a small laugh, untangling the two of them so they could join in. Hailwic spun herself back, her skirt whirling up around her thighs. When Punabi raised zhur arms above zhur head to join in the clapping, Hailwic leaned forward—going up on her toes and cupping zhur chin with just her fingertips—and landed a light, tugging kiss against zhur lips.

It was Punabi's turn to look stunned. As Hailwic landed back on her heels, she wasn't quite sure what to expect. Perhaps a frenzied second kiss in return.

Instead, Punabi's face turned thoughtful. Zhur cockiness softened, and zhur hands lightly landed on Hailwic's cheeks.

It was as though the entire club melted away. The shadowed forms of the other dancers blurred into the background. The lyrics dissolved into a nonsense din in Hailwic's head. She reached up to gently grab hold of one of Punabi's wrists, to rub her thumb against the back of zhur hand encouragingly.

Their next kiss was deep. Heady. Hailwic whimpered into it, then flushed further, hoping Punabi hadn't noticed.

Zhe smirked against her lips.

"Done dancing?" zhe asked when they pulled apart.

Hailwic bit her lip to suppress a wide grin, nodding.

They ran back up the stairs, through the hidden door, and out into the building's adjoining alley hand in hand, laughing.

They kissed again, Punabi cradling Hailwic's cheek and backing her into the nearest wall. Hailwic's eyes fluttered closed as she gave herself over to sensation—to Punabi's comforting weight against her. They were both breathing heavily when the kiss ended.

"I know another way to get a high," zhe said suggestively, fingers trailing down the front of Hailwic's torso. "Another way to unwind."

"Yes," Hailwic said eagerly—desperately—pressing her shoulders into the bricking, unabashedly pushing her pelvis forward. "*Yes.*"

Punabi bit zhur lip and groaned hungrily, but then zhur expression shifted from seductive to unsure. To vulnerable. "One thing, though. I can't do casual. Not . . . not with you."

"Me neither," Hailwic said earnestly, voice breathy. "Not with you."

She nearly said more. Nearly pointed out that she might not be here tomorrow, anyway. Even if she was successful, she might not get away. Uphrasia's goons could kill her on the spot. Or the secret police could take her away to kill at their leisure.

More likely than not, this was her last night of freedom.

Could be her last night, period.

But Hailwic swallowed all that down when Punabi smiled. Zhur grin lit up the entire alley, made Hailwic feel so cared for and so seen.

Zhe kissed Hailwic firmly one more time—kissed her dizzy—before falling to zhur knees and pushing up beneath Hailwic's skirt, letting it flutter down to cover zhur head and shoulders.

Hailwic gasped—throwing her head back, ignoring the way it thumped against the alley wall—as Punabi's fingers pulled her panties aside and zhur tongue eagerly went to work.

18

KRONA

The varger hoard was as Krona had left it only half a day earlier. Half a day and a lifetime. The bottle-barkers scrambled and licked at the walls of their vats, their eyes and fangs prominent even in their ethereal forms. The strange cloud of steam still hung, unnatural, in the giant shaft, and the atmosphere hummed with a crackling energy.

When they landed, Krona shuddered, training her gaze on the corrugated floor, letting it trail toward the center of the borehole where the sideways hourglass lay imbedded in its pit, ductwork bursting over the edges like some mad amalgamation of pipe organ and Deep Waters cephalopod.

Time's naked human hip was just as she remembered: ashen pale, rising above the sand in one bulb of the hourglass, while the bridge of one black wing mirrored it in the other.

Krona stiffened as a hand found her shoulder. Melanie pulled her down to ask, "Jan?"

"Still here." She pointed listlessly in the direction of the body—hidden by the layers of vats.

Emotion took a mighty single step down into the hourglass's pit, leaning over the top bulb, pressing zhur ombré hands against the curvature of it to peer intently. Perhaps zhe could see more with zhur amethyst clusters than one could with human eyes—perhaps zhe could look past the grains of white sand to the face of zhur buried offspring beneath.

Zhe hadn't wanted to come here. Krona turned that fact over and over in her mind; it was like trying to discern the shape of a weapon—a dagger—in the dark, to determine which way the blade was pointed, what kind of danger it presented.

Gemstone nails scraped against the glass with an ear-searing screech, leaving straight-edged gouges in the bulb, though the bitterness of the clawing didn't seem directed at the glass itself, but the figure within.

Krona's heartbeat fluttered in her pulse point when Emotion turned to her expectantly. The etched bird's skull gave Krona no more clues to zhur hesitancy than it had before. There was no additional light to shine on the sharp object at her fingertips, and she would not be given time to make sure she was picking up the dagger by the grip and not the blade. She was expected to arm herself now.

Avellino had warned her not to jump directly into the hourglass, and she believed his fears grounded. Kneeling down to the stones encompassing the pit, she touched the cryptopathic runes, testing the breadth and depth of their enchantment.

They immediately pushed back against her invasive probing, their wards resisting. The secrets and salts weren't confined to the stones she could see—tracing the bulk of the enchantment, she followed the heft of it down into the rock below the hourglass, below the pit. She sensed pillars of enchanted salt pounded into the earth like the iron pins that would have been used to keep Arkensyre's ill-fated trans–city-state train tracks pinned in place.

Avellino had sensed Hintosep's hand in the work, but hundreds of Cryptopaths had to have been involved in the creation of the masking enchantments—those that kept the hoard hidden and Time's temple shrouded.

Though the cryptopathic footprint was vast, she was more concerned with physiopathic traps. A temple meant to trap Time would not be complete without the ability to suppress her reach, to override her kairopathy—which rolled off the hourglass in droves.

And yet, Krona sensed nothing.

Even if the secret magic itself had been put in place to hide nature magic, she would have been able to feel the shape of it pulsing under the cryptopathy.

Slipping down into the pit next to Emotion, she too laid her palms on the arc of the glass.

Krona tried to shake the image of the dagger—the question of the weapon—tried to reshape it into something warm and hopeful in the dark instead of something threatening.

Instead of nails digging in sharply like Emotion's, she softened her touch to a caress, letting the heat and roundness take the edged worry from her mind. The temperature made the smoothness of the glass more like the smoothness of skin pulled taut, heavy with potential. Like a pregnant belly. Krona searched for the pulse of life within, kairopathy to kairopathy.

She closed her eyes, and let herself fall forward, slipping through a lens, landing softly on her forearms and belly atop the duned sand, a reach away from that bow of a black wing. Her bones flexed in sympathy, throwing off phantom grains, feeling a reverberation of that suffocating confinement.

The air inside the hourglass was thick. She'd nearly expected to be struck with the thinness of it—not enough of it. Instead it was heavy in her lungs, lining them, demanding more of each breath. The grains were smooth, supple. The kind of sand she would have been happy to roll around in on a lakeside.

Beneath, compacted, was the body of her goddess.

Krona looked to Emotion one last time. If there were reasons not to do this, she needed them now.

That same expectant blankness stared back.

Flopping onto her side, mindful of the arc of the glass not far overhead, she wrestled her satchel open. Wax crumbled under her blunted nails as she clawed her way into the box containing the silver mind. Quickly, she dumped the remaining water (she'd have to retrieve more to wake Nature) from her flask into the mind's box—a bit of it sloshing over the side in her haste—letting the halite dissolve.

Once freed, Emotion's mind had remained passive until prodded. Knowledge's had slithered away. Time's was different. Before the salt crystal had completely dissolved, the oily bit of silver struggled, forcing itself out. It pushed the two remaining halves of crystal away before launching itself upward to cling to the bulb above Krona. She reeled away from it—remembering how Emotion's had reached for her—worried this mind might be less measured about looking for its correct host.

It didn't go after her. Instead, it oozed its way toward the neck of the hourglass, crawling like a predator stalking prey—deliberate and measured, yet flighty and jerky in its advance. It bypassed the rough mound of molting wing rising above the sand, inching toward where Time's face was buried.

Hovering for a moment, eventually it let itself drip—a long, viscous line dangling a bead of itself over the surface of the dune, like a fisherman testing river water with a shiny lure.

Apparently satisfied by whatever it sensed, the bulk of its body flowed down the line, burgeoning at the bottom until it plopped down, releasing the glass, only to burrow into the sand like a creature pouncing on fleeing food.

The slick silver disappeared between the grains without a trace, leaving an awful stillness in its wake.

Krona held her breath.

In response, there was a great gasp. The limited air in the hourglass rushed away from Krona, sucked into the sand, before it burst outward again, blowing grit into her face.

A silent song played somewhere. Time's body bent and bowed with it in tortured sensuality as she struggled out of the sand. It was not a struggle for breath above a crushing force, it was a dance of life, of coming back into bodily form. Her arms and wings strained, all trapped in one bulb while the hourglass cinched at her waist and trapped her legs and hips on the other side. She shook the white grains from her feathers, but her six wings could not stretch to their full potential. Flexing feathers slid against the curvature of the glass as though painting the inside of the bulb with black oil.

Krona pushed herself away from the rhythm of Time's waking, plastering herself to the inside of the glass to escape the sharp points of the goddess's reaching fingertips.

Outside the hourglass, Emotion leaned in, head tilting sideways to examine the pair of them like any curious bird.

A great head rose up, sideways, from the grains. Yellow hair clung like damp weeds to her face. Time's eyes were sunken and distant—caked with sand and bloodshot. The goddess's gaze rolled back when she realized she was clamped tight around the waist—stuck in the joinder's manacle grip—and when her glassy stare caught sight of Krona she bared her teeth and screeched high in her throat, like a manic bird of prey.

Krona bowed her forehead to the sand and threw her arms out in front of her, grasping for *worshipful* but landing somewhere between *meek* and *deflated.*

The goddess flailed, her many arms and many wings rising in a sharp whirlwind, beating and scraping at the glass, flinging grit around as violently as any sandstorm. Krona covered her head and flared her own wings before thrusting the ends of her bones into the sand, creating a protective cage around her body.

Dull thudding from the opposite side of the glass was met with a sudden stillness within, though Krona dared not raise her head to see what Emotion was doing. Muffled voices followed, and more scraping—from both inside and out.

A long, sudden hiss.

Clanging.

Shouting.

A blast of freezing air hit Krona, and while she only tensed her shoulders up in shock, Time *screamed.*

A familiar sucking sensation took hold in Krona's abdomen. A jump.

One second, she was half-buried.

The next she was in free fall, sand tumbling all around her like sharp, heavy snow.

Krona toppled, unable to orient herself. Dimness encircled her, a glow seemed to emanate from below, obscured by a haze. Large globes of light—the vats. She was high above them, but closing in fast. She tried to make a lens, but a smack of kairopathy hit her from the left, flinging her sideways into the rounded wall of the hoard's cavern—pinning her there.

The impact forced the air from her lungs, but instead of coughing or gasping, she couldn't draw a breath. She told her lungs to expand, told her fingers to clutch at the wall, told her legs to kick and wings to scrape but her body would not heed her.

Time, for Krona's physical self, had stopped.

But her mind kept churning.

The goddess had jumped them free of the hourglass in a panic, and now had Krona pinned to the wall with her magic alone, like a butterfly pinned in a collection—high above the punishing floor. The goddess herself was nowhere to be seen. Krona wanted to look for her—needed her gaze on who—*what*—she'd released—but Time wouldn't even allow her a small twitch of the eye.

Below, more clangs. Muted shouts. Something was making the haze thicker—spewing steam or something just as white. She was too far away to make anything out, but there was a swirling sort of echo to the way the noise rose from beneath.

Directly in front of Krona, a form descended on the wall, slipping down into her sight line from above, still yards away from her, but crawling closer.

Krona still had no control over her eyes—no ability to track Time as the goddess approached. Time crawled like a six-legged tree frog, dragging her belly, long limbs akimbo, her movements eerie, wings plastered in a long black line down her back. Her sweat-soaked hair resembled drooping tentacles, sticking to her forehead, her cheeks—half covering her eyes. Eyes set in a human face. Her head jerked back and forth on her neck in an involuntarily, spasmodic twitch.

As she drew closer, she climbed out of Krona's purview, moving silently.

Krona could not feel her own heart. She could not draw a breath. She could not swallow. Or scream. But her mind had been allowed to keep moving. How long could the two parts of her exist at odds?

A dark shadow swirled around Krona, crawling overhead. The pitter-patter of four hands and two feet created a scrabbling that put her in mind of many creatures rather than one. Finally, a figure rose in the corner of her eye. Hot breath rolled over her cheek.

"Who," Time began, her voice airy with a raspy click of dryness, "are you?"

Words flooded Krona's mind, her mouth, but had no means of escape.

Time flicked a set of fingers in front of Krona's face, dispelling the time stop in much of her body, though she remained plastered to the stone. Blood and air and other humors began rushing again—her lungs and heart pumped. Spots danced before her eyes, the world swirled and threatened to slip sideways. As Krona's head drooped with the sudden rush of functionality, Time hissed and thrust a giant finger beneath her chin, making her look the goddess in the eye.

"De-Krona," she croaked.

Time's shoulders flexed, and her six wings flared behind her—shimmering and raven.

From below, Emotion called. A tight cawing that snared Time's attention, her face snapping in the other god's direction.

Taking hold of Krona's head in one massive hand, Time pulled her from the wall and wrapped one set of arms around her, clutching the human to her chest as she plummeted to the hoard's floor.

Krona twisted her fists in Time's light shift—a shift very much like Emotion's. Having wondered, only hours before, if she could touch a god and live, it was a new kind of wonder to be held against Time's warmth like a coveted doll.

The goddess stretched her wings before they hit the bottom, swooping them upward before bringing them to a gentle stop, creating a great rush in Krona's chest that left her dizzy.

When Time released her, she was brushed aside, lost her footing, and fell. Sebastian was there in an instant, and Krona flipped her braids out of her eyes to see Melanie and Tray on the opposite side of Emotion, cowering back. All around them, pipes had cracked and steam billowed.

Inside their vats, the varger writhed, excited.

The buzz in the air slackened. The ever constant crackle of power diminished.

The tops of many vats lit up with small yellow blinking lights that seemed to flash out *warning, warning, warning.*

The gods paid their surroundings no mind. They only had eyes for each other.

Time looked stricken—sad and grateful and furious all in one. "I've missed you," she said, rushing up to Emotion, taking zhim by the face. Krona wondered how long they'd each been isolated—how long it had been since they'd seen each other, been able to hold each other. "By the heavens, *I have missed you*."

Emotion let out a clack and chirp in return, but turned away when Time tried to bring their foreheads together.

A momentary flash of haughtiness darkened Time's beautiful human face, but was suppressed nearly as quickly as she took in Emotion's shape, all four oversized human hands now hovering over Emotion's skull as zhe tilted zhur head from side to side. "Who did this to you?"

Emotion touched zhur throat, and let out a small squawk before zhe began to shake zhur head, but Time petted down zhur bill to still zhim. "No, it's all right. I know. It was *him*."

Where Emotion's energy had been flighty and panicked, and Knowledge had been subdued and sleepy, Time exuded a dangerous readiness. If she saw the need to exact vengeance, she would. Swiftly, and without a second thought.

Her violent eyes turned on the humans. "Are they his servants?"

Melanie tugged Tray down to his knees, and they both clasped their hands together, bowing their heads. "No, we are *yours*," she said.

Krona urged Sebastian to follow his wife's lead and keep a knee bended.

This was what Krona had half imagined waking a god would be like. Emotion's panic and Knowledge's indifference had both felt ungodlike, but Time exuded a pointed righteousness. Terrifying and beautiful, beastly yet radiant—all contrasting parts equal in their rawness.

Krona spoke slowly, with reverence and deference. This wasn't just an entreaty, it was a prayer. "The man who trapped you, he calls himself the Savior. We—your people—have sought you out, awoken you, because he is destroying your Valley and our lives."

"*The Savior,*" Time scoffed. "Sounds like a title he'd choose for himself."

"We need you," Krona implored. "We need you to be rid of him."

"Rid of him?"

The darkness in her tone made Krona hesitate.

"Kill him," she clarified.

Time turned away from Emotion, focusing fully on Krona. The goddess swept aside the curtain of her own wings like they were the drape of a magnificent cape before stalking over to her, lowering herself gracefully just far enough to lift Krona by the chin with a single curled finger.

"I am free from that contraption and his mind games for the first time in innumerable years, and the first thing I am asked to do in this new world is *kill* Absolon?"

Krona swallowed harshly, her throat bobbing against what might as well have been an iron bar instead of an elegant knuckle. The harshness of the goddess's eyes made Krona feel smaller than even her height had accomplished. She reached for an apology—what she was sure that harshness demanded—but instead what stuttered out was a question. "Ab-Absolon?"

"He continues with his terrors," Time gritted out, "and assassination becomes the conclusion. Round and round we go."

"*Absolon?*" Krona asked more bluntly, paralyzed by the realization. "Absolon Raoul Trémaux?"

The man who'd written their holy scrolls, who'd lead the Introdus, who'd appealed to the gods for safety from their Thalo creator. That very same man was the Savior. Manipulator, underminer, deceiver.

The very avatar of the Thalo's wickedness in the Valley.

Still alive, all these millennia. Just like Hintosep.

Hintosep who must have known. She must have known Absolon and the Savior were one and the same.

She could have *said*—

"Hmm," Time hummed thoughtfully, then let Krona go, sweeping away toward Emotion once more. "Quickly, do any among you practice physiomancy? This is not a form zhe chose. We must set zhim right."

She asked for it like an easy favor. A talent not unexpected in a sampling of so few.

Krona shared a look with Sebastian.

Time didn't know about their stolen magic.

Then perhaps none of the gods knew.

"We don't . . ." Krona wasn't sure where to begin. "Absolon has taken that from us too."

Time's gaze narrowed. "Explain."

Explain.

One little word that demanded so many in return.

How long had the gods been trapped? How little did they know?

The four humans spun the modern history of the Valley as best they could, highlighting the Savior's lies, his infiltration and manipulations. They told the gods of the time tax and their lost magics. Of the varger—displayed all around—and what they'd had to do in order to reclaim what little power they could.

Krona relied especially heavily on all Hintosep had told them—realizing in the process how many holes her own understanding still contained. They'd lost so much when they'd lost her. And yet, if she hadn't even deigned to tell them that *the* Savior was in fact *that* Savior—the man who'd led the Introdus—

"After everything we went through," Time said to Emotion. "That bastard still did it."

"And he's become incredibly powerful," Krona said. "He has not just cryptomancy, but all five magics at his behest. He must have done this to Emotion—manipulated zhur form, taken zhur voice—all on his own."

"Abomination," Time snapped, spitting on the ground by her feet.

"How can a man have such power?" Krona asked.

Time pursed her lips, prechewed her words. "He was always prideful, covetous," the goddess said. "And I fed into it. He had some misguided ideas, but I never thought he'd . . ." She took a deep, steadying breath. "My brother can undo this," she announced, nodding to Emotion, choosing not to further answer Krona's question. "Can put zhim back in zhur proper body. Lead me to him, and then I assure you, we *will* deal with Absolon, traitor that he is."

19

HINTOSEP

Where there had been a chair a moment before, now there was a chair-shaped pile of vipnika. Not just the furniture, but the rugs, and the walls, and the great stone hearth itself all transformed simultaneously into swarms upon swarms of the small, deadly creatures.

The mansion practically melted, heaps of the little animals becoming unbalanced and toppling over within moments. The very settee she'd been draped over for comfort burst into a wriggling mass that could not support her.

Even her clothes. Oh gods—her *clothes*. The soft weave against her skin turned into the prickle of hundreds of tiny clawed feet, gripping into her flesh for only a moment before leaping away to join the others that were all hungry and on the hunt.

The ground boiled with small bodies. The roof and the walls disappeared, disintegrating and leaving the residents to scream into the open air.

One by one, the people were overrun. Their own garments had grown teeth, the furniture had turned against them. The floor didn't simply writhe with vipnika, it *was* vipnika.

The newly transmuted creatures were an all-consuming mass, nearly indistinguishable from one another. Hintosep couldn't turn her head to take in any one attack, to see whose blood splatter was whose. The sounds of chewing and skittering and agony were everywhere.

Hopelessly, she tried to block it out. To keep strong, keep her sanity, by distancing herself from the carnage. But she couldn't block out the small pile of vipnika directly before her—the child-sized heap. Abby had been swarmed so quickly—in mere seconds—and there was nothing to see past the wriggling vipnika.

That alone broke her spirit.

Which was the point.

Absolon had killed all these people in the most horrific way possible simply to make a *point*.

He could have sent his agents to wall off their minds, to secret away the memory of their rebellious time. But that would take time, invite risk, and he was clearly done humoring the idea that he was balanced and careful and precise. He was impatient and exacting, and if murdering thousands at a time got the job done more quickly and thoroughly, then so be it.

He wanted Hintosep humbled and her network destroyed. Never mind the lives involved.

Never mind mere babies, like Abby, getting in the way.

Absolon had constructed his lesson well. No matter how many clawed their way over her and around her, none bit her. She could play witness to the massacre without becoming part of it.

That is, until the vipnika inside her *died*.

She felt it expire like it was one of her own organs, stilling, shriveling, and calcifying into a hard clot in the bottom of its prison.

The instant it was gone, a single vipnika decided she was indeed just as edible as the people around her—perhaps drawn by the blood of her open wounds. Noting a tender spot, it began to burrow into one of the gashes Avellino had unintentionally created, right at her jaw, eating around where the Cage's leg pierced her flesh. It tore into her cheek, wriggling into her mouth, and already one of its fellows was burrowing in behind.

More little feet, little claws. Little *teeth*—all of them chewing at her face, called by blood to release yet more blood.

The creatures swarmed up her side and over her face, crawling over her eye and blotting out the light on her left, blanketing her skin with their many bodies even as they gnawed it away, creating a mask for her unlike any ever sold in a telioteur's shop.

Never before had an unreleased scream burned so hotly—like acid—in her chest. Every tear, every tug and rip, was acute, each its own snip, its own plunge, distinguishable even in a deluge of bites.

The Cage squeezed at her skull as the nesting for its feet was carved away. It clamped down, determined to do its job—keep her immobile while the vipnika ate her alive.

The left side of her face shredded like so much paper as the creatures stripped her jaw down to the bone, peeling away her lips to get at her gums. The meat of her cheek was gone, the bone bared there as well. Blood flowed in her mouth, and a small body squirmed on her tongue, headed toward the back of her throat, making her gag.

When one started in on the soft bottom of her eye socket, she knew it was a matter of moments before it pierced her eyeball and squirmed into her brain.

A deranged urge to laugh battled against the need to scream. She knew Absolon hadn't meant to kill her, but she was going to die after all. He'd miscalculated, and she'd always see his loss as her win, no matter the twisted nonsense of it. He hadn't meant to lose her, but she would slip from his grasp just the same, via his own mistake.

Never again could he puppet her. Never again could he wall off her inconvenient memories and reshape her reality. The one person who knew him best—the one person he thought he loved best—would know him no more. And it was all his fault.

On her way to the grave, she'd take what solace she could.

The carnage seemed to go on and on. And then, there was only one sound left. An unhinged wail. A scream of horror and resistance, unadulterated by words or enunciations.

Hintosep was surprised when she realized the wail was her own.

She was free.

The artifact had tried to pinch itself tighter—as it had when Avellino struggled with it—but the vipnika had torn away her flesh, left nothing for several of the legs to reach. Without full contact, the enchantment could not hold.

The creatures crawling on her seized up, held still. The one on her tongue turned hard and rigid, as did the one behind her eye.

She sat up, frantically spitting, coughing uncontrollably even as she dug trembling fingers into her face wound to fish out the thing imbedded in her eye socket. Tears and blood and spit ran down her mutilated face as she tried to process having domain over her own limbs. The wonder of it seemed to override the searing pain.

As quickly as it started, everything stopped. No matter where they were, each vipnika let out a harsh, strangled squeak and froze in its tracks, transforming back into the materials from which they'd been birthed.

There were porcelain vipnika, wood vipnika, wool vipnika.

The one she'd spat from her mouth had clearly been transfigured from one of the settee's brass feet.

Now that she could speak again—and weep, and rage—she did. She screamed. She screamed herself raw, gazing about the remains of her former home.

Corpses littered with holes—their forms misshapen, sunken, twisted—were draped all through the unnatural rubble. Nannette, Mavis, Malek—people she'd rescued from Absolon's plots had survived only a few years to die in the most horrible way Hintosep could imagine.

She grieved for everyone she could see, and everyone she couldn't.

Krona, Sebastian, *Melanie*—

At least Avellino was at the keep.

She let out a tragic, gurgling half laugh at that. At least the boy was in Absolon's clutches, and not here, where it was supposed to be safe.

The massacre's staging ground now looked like a manic artist's studio—or, more precisely, a sculptor's discard pit, with harmless figurines everywhere, indistinguishable from something crafted by a master, save that they were covered in blood.

The vipnika that had torn through her people weren't real. They'd never been real. Just facsimiles. Nature's power was transformative, but could not create life. They were terrible, perfect mimics of the real thing inside her, blazing with energy, powered by Absolon's magic and her own life-force. She'd never seen an enchantment like it, had never seen one that could create even one suitable copy of an animal, let alone the thousands that had just devastated the mansion.

Not just the mansion, she reminded herself. Mirthhouse was gone, and so were all her other safe houses. So were all the people in them. Those on away missions—far from the tears created by the Teeth—surely had been spared, but their friends, their allies, their families, and their homes were all gone.

She knew what Absolon wanted her to feel. Regret. Despair. And she did. But he also wanted her to feel responsible for this atrocity, and she refused. She would not blame herself for something *he'd* done. Never.

Never.

She shouted it to the clouds. To the sky. To the river below. If she shouted it enough, maybe she could make it true.

Suddenly, the small pile where Abby had been began to move. She jumped, shuffled back through the vipnika statues made of furniture tacks and stuffing and upholstery, terrified the ravagings weren't over—that some of the terrible creatures still had life in them.

But it wasn't a remaining clutch of animated vipnika. Those now made of her central Marrakevian rug slid off a heaving, cracking dome of gray stone. The stone shifted, losing its stiffness and seams, seemingly melting over the back of the small form beneath.

The material was regaining its original form: a security blanket, soft and supple.

Their little Physiopath had fought fire with fire.

Using zhur own abilities, zhe'd created a shield, enchanting the blanket wrapped around zhim, making it impenetrable to the small, needle-like teeth.

The five-year-old popped zhur head up, and Hintosep immediately feared for zhur eyes. Zhe'd already heard the screams, felt the danger—zhe shouldn't have to take in the aftermath.

Of course, the only alternative was to draw zhur attention to Hintosep's own face. A face that was only half a face. Bare, nicked bone and bloody flaps of skin were all that remained on her left side. Her exposed teeth gave her the manic grin of a half-dead monster. And the Cage must look like a wicked crown.

"Absolon!" she shouted at zhim, using zhur full name in a way she was loathe to do. The word came out garbled as saliva and blood flowed over her clumsy tongue.

Melanie and Sebastian had thought they were giving their child an honorable name. They'd thought they were naming zhim after the Valley's greatest hero, rather than the Valley's greatest villain.

Abby whipped zhur head in Hintosep's direction, and clearly recognized her despite the years and her raw face.

She didn't want to scare the child further. She held a hand over the left side of her face, trying to obscure as much of the carnage as she could, while stretching out her other arm wide, hoping she looked welcoming and not terrifying. "Don't look around. Come to me. Come."

Abby toddled upright, but did not keep zhur eyes on Hintosep. Zhe took in what was left of Mirthhouse with wide, clear eyes, before slowly approaching Hintosep, blanket in hand. The child's gaze caught on the Cage, and Hintosep feared it might keep zhim away—might be the thing that made zhim run.

But Abby seemed fixated instead. Once close enough, zhe absently dropped zhur blanket in Hintosep's bare lap and gently took hold of the Cage's legs in both hands.

"Careful," Hintosep warned zhim, her hands flying up quickly—but landing softly—on zhur small wrists.

"Careful like with 'Rona," Abby agreed.

Hintosep didn't know what that meant, but the child had an earnestness in zhur expression that should have been well beyond zhur years. Zhe seemed completely unfazed by Hintosep's ghastly appearance.

One by one, Abby peeled open the Cage's legs.

Slicing away the very flesh it required had been its undoing, even as it might still be hers. She was still not convinced she would survive. Perhaps her death had simply been prolonged and she'd soon succumb to her injuries.

As Abby worked, each remaining set of pinchers attempted to hold on, pulling at Hintosep's wounds, but they did not burrow deeper—the greater influence of the enchantment now distorted, broken. The Cage had indeed lost its hold on her. The mutilation wrought by the vipnika had seen to that.

Blood poured profusely down her face as she allowed Abby to work the Cage away. She could have done it herself, but she knew if she tried, she'd simply yank it off, taking none of the care Abby did now. So, she let her hands rest in her lap. She stayed still, let the child do what zhe would. Was absent in the process of her own escape.

She'd had plenty of practice letting things simply happen to her, after all.

At last, Abby pushed the Cage off with a disgusted twist of zhur little lips, like zhe was tossing away a putrid, vile thing.

With the weight of it gone from around her head, Hintosep finally felt like she was truly present in her body, like her skin—what was left of it—was hers. And yet, still, she found it difficult to trust her own limbs. They had not heeded her for so long, it was hard to imagine they would now.

Overwhelmed by sadness and relief—a poisonous mixture—tears streamed down her face to join the blood. "Thank you," she gurgled to the child as she cautiously put her arms around zhim, intending to hug zhim tight.

She was surprised when Abby's fingers came back to her face, pressing into her wounds.

"Don't—" she said automatically, jerking her head back, but the little fingers followed.

"I can fix my own owies," zhe said proudly. "Fixed Daddy when he cut his finger. Fixed 'Rona's wings."

Hintosep stopped resisting and let Abby probe where zhe would. The smallest wounds on her face closed over—including the one under her eye—the blood clotting and caking and hardening in seconds.

Of course Melanie's child would be a budding healer. Of course.

The rawness of her jaw suddenly felt slathered in a numbing agent. Skin knit over the bare bone—nerveless, without the usual support of muscle. New lips crawled up over her teeth, hiding them away.

"This one's hard," Abby apologized, prodding at the slowly closing gape in her cheek. "Mommy would do better."

When the child was done, Hintosep skimmed her fingers over the left side of her face, feeling how unnaturally sunken and knotted it was. Most of the flesh itself was numb and immobile, but it was no longer open and flayed.

She would live. She knew now, she would live.

"Your mommy . . . your mommy wasn't here, was she? Where is she?" Hintosep asked, her words slurred. She dreaded the answer, anticipating something like *upstairs* or *in the kitchen*.

"Mommy and Daddy are with 'Rona."

Hintosep finally caught on. "*K*-rona? And they're not here?"

Abby shook zhur head.

She did pull zhim close then. "Thank the skies."

After a moment, Abby pulled back and gestured around. "I could try to fix—"

"Oh, sweet babe," Hintosep said, picking zhim up. "They are beyond your aid, I'm so sorry. But your mommy and daddy are out there somewhere, and we must find them and the other survivors. We cannot let your namesake win."

As she stepped through the rubble, she noticed something metallic and distinctly non–vipnika shaped protruding from a granite heap. Using her bare foot, she kicked aside the stone vipnika to reveal her katar. It had survived the transmutation bomb. Perhaps other enchantments had as well. That was how Abby had survived, after all, by hiding under a shield zhe'd enchanted zhurself.

She let the weapon lie. There was only one enchantment she wished to keep close—keep out of other's hands. Any hands.

Revolting at the touch, she scooped up the Cage. She could not leave it, no matter how much she loathed it.

With a child on her hip and the artifact in hand—naked as the day she was born, white hair whipping about her in the wind—Hintosep stepped out from the ruins of her old home, her taste for vengeance renewed.

20

HAILWIC

In a Time and Place Unknown

Hailwic applied her lip gloss meticulously, careful to stay within the boundaries of the liquid latex that covered her delicate skin.

The restroom attached to the office just off the thopter pad was surprisingly dingy for the number of Uphrasia's officials who came through. The Friend was the type to dismiss a person from her presence if she caught them with a snag in their stockings or a bit of sweat on their collar. Clearly Uphrasia had never chanced peeking past the door to take in the peeling linoleum and chipped porcelain. Even the mirror Hailwic was using had been scratched repeatedly—with a safety pin or some other fine-tipped implement. The bare yellow bulb hanging from the ceiling swayed slightly, and just as she replaced the cap on the gloss she realized the scratches formed letter. Words.

She tilted her head to try to catch them at a readable angle.

Thanks be. Bullshit.

Hailwic smirked at the crudely etched statement. A small defiance, right out in the open, where theoretically the Friend could walk right in and see it—and she'd shut the whole operation down if she ever did. For Hailwic, it was a reminder that there were people already trying to claw back the inches that had been taken from them, they just needed a clear shot at scraping back a mile.

She took one more moment to lock eyes with herself in the mirror, to give her reflection a reassuring nod as she steeled her spine for what was to come.

Out on the tarmac, near the private airfield's designated jump point, she waited with a steward for the Friend to arrive as other thopters took off and landed. And arrive she did, right on time, her guards and a jump assistant right beside her. Uphrasia rarely ever publicly expended her own energy on magic, even something as mundane as travel.

The Friend raised her hands in greeting as soon as she caught sight of Hailwic, a fond smile gracing her lips. Hailwic met her in kind. The two of them exchanged cheek kisses, and Hailwic was sure to land hers flush with a solid press.

An act of affection, coopted.

She'd kissed Uphrasia this way a dozen times, making it her go-to greeting ever since she'd devised her final plan.

The tacky gloss smudged just so against the Friend's skin.

"Oop, heavy-handed with that today, my dear," Uphrasia said pleasantly, though there was an underlying cringe. She snapped her fingers at her guards, and one produced a handkerchief for her, which she used to dab daintily at her cheeks before handing it back.

The initial dose would be enough to make her drowsy regardless. Hailwic wished she'd found a way to make her wear her kisses for longer, but it would do for now.

"Come along," the Friend bade.

As they walked away, the guards stayed put. Hailwic knew it was coming—the thopter was big enough for two passengers and the pilot alone, that was why she'd chosen this as her venue—and yet it still felt unnatural to see Uphrasia unflanked. There were plenty of other bodies milling about—stewards, pilots—and yet the Friend seemed naked and vulnerable for the handful of steps it took to reach their designated thopter.

Their pilot was already in the fish-eye cockpit. The steward helped them get their headsets on, double-checked their seatbelts and harnesses, then bid them a safe flight.

The pilot could give them instructions over the headsets, but he assured Uphrasia that he had both of their microphones muted, just as she'd requested.

"So that it's just the two of us," Uphrasia said to Hailwic with a wink. They sat side by side on a well-padded, forward-facing bench. "We can talk about whatever we like, and it's all private as can be."

Hailwic's stomach swooped as the thopter took off, its three thin wings beating through the air in perfect synchronization, their flexible iridescence reminding her of dragonfly wings.

Up, up they went, first in a low pass over the city, then climbing ever higher.

The capital was undeniably beautiful. There were towers that twisted into the sky, artful spires that carried implant signals and delivered power to everything from lights to air conditioners to stoves and more.

Jumping could never provide such a view.

Wings, on the other hand . . .

As they circled higher, she strained her eyes looking to the edge of the city, sure she could see her old neighborhood from here—perhaps even her parents' house, if the thopter dove that way. Instead, something else caught her eye. A swath of land blocked from the city proper by a wall. The wall was old, from centuries past, and not nearly as high or as fortified as the one separating Remotus from Radix. It was a historical monument many people were familiar with—one Hailwic had passed once or twice when she'd had an errand for Dr. Theesius in the northern quarter. The roads and tunnels leading under it had been under refurbishment for the last several years—there were always construction vehicles milling about and detour signs aplenty.

What struck Hailwic lay just beyond. Fencing she hadn't known was there littered the landscape. It was difficult to resolve at this distance, but it looked like barbed wire and anti-tank barricades had been set up. Beyond that, what had once been a thriving suburb was dilapidated. Shanties and oversized lean-tos surrounded the remnants of what had once been perfectly adequate cookie-cutter houses.

She didn't ask about it. She pretended not to see. A good follower and a true believer would pretend not to see.

If everything went according to plan, she wouldn't have to stomach such a farce much longer.

"It's just so perfect, isn't it?" Uphrasia asked, unexpectedly patting Hailwic's knee companionably.

"It is," she agreed, taking the opportunity to both flatter and disarm. "All thanks to you." Gently, she lifted Uphrasia's hand from her knee to her lips, kissing the back of it as if in gratitude, dosing her once more.

"I asked you up here because I thought it would be the ideal place to offer you a junior position on my cabinet," Uphrasia said.

"Really?"

"Of course. My Minister of Physiopathic Wellness needs new, knowledgeable staffers to interface with both the Physiopath relocation centers as well as the media to make sure our messaging is accurate and the total extraction process streamlined. Once it's fully developed, of course. The sooner we can move every last one of those spine-twisters through the system, the sooner we can get to allocating them preapproved jobs."

"I don't know what to say," Hailwic fluttered (in reality, she could think of a few choice words).

She was about to overenthusiastically exclaim her acceptance when Uphrasia added, "I do have one request, though, before I make the offer officially."

"Oh?"

Uphrasia reclaimed her hand, reaching down into a pocket on the side of her seat to pull out a crisp file folder. "I would love to release a little video, me and you . . ." She flipped it open, revealing a set of surveillance photographs from the university campus. "Outing your old poli-sci professor as the traitor fey are."

Hailwic carefully kept her expression blank and her breathing even as Uphrasia passed her the folder. She flipped slowly through each page, letting her eyes catch details without lingering for too long. Every time she turned one over to reveal the next, it felt like dragging the photograph through molasses.

The pictures weren't just of Dr. Solric, but of other people she knew as well. Mirc, Valarex, *Glensen*. To the untrained eye, there was nothing explicitly unusual about a professor talking to these people. In one, fey were clearly receiving a package in handoff. Perfectly ordinary, unless one had a way of knowing what stolen supplies lay inside. In another, a blink-of-an-eye moment was frozen forever—a slip of folded paper was passed covertly between hands.

Though she could control her face and her breathing, Hailwic could do little about her pulse.

If Uphrasia had these, what else might she have?

Hailwic's gaze flickered upward to the Friend as her mind spiraled, searching for a readiness in the lines of Uphrasia's body.

Was the excursion a setup? Had Uphrasia found out about her?

A tingling flush spread across her limbs. Her toes and lips went numb, her vision threatened to tunnel.

No, no, she reassured herself, wrestling back control of both her mind and body. Uphrasia wouldn't confront her alone. If she'd caught even a whiff of Hailwic's insincerity she'd never have left herself open like this.

When Hailwic said nothing, Uphrasia's brow furrowed. "You *did* take a class from fem, didn't you?"

"Just one," Hailwic said evenly.

"We've just gotten wind over the last few years that some of the major radical upheavals seemed to be flowing from your alma mater, and we've tracked it all down to Professor Solric's activity. The universities have always been a hotbed for traitorous thought—dubious indoctrination—but I thought we were keeping a relatively tight lid on it. Apparently, not so. Heads will roll over that, believe me."

Hailwic made herself nod firmly. Made herself agree.

"We've even uncovered a plot to kidnap General Gyrus. This is one corrupt professor, and I'm so sorry you had to ever be in a room with fem, *but,* I thought that together, you—a new junior member of my cabinet—and I could expose fem. It would be inspirational for other youngsters to see that getting a good education doesn't have to mean losing yourself. Their patriotism can remain sound, because we are dedicated to removing bad actors and groomers from places that should be considered hallowed ground. So, what do you think? Shall we schedule a shoot?"

Uphrasia's easy posture and casual air confirmed she didn't suspect Hailwic herself was tied to the rebellion. It was her tenuous connection to the professor that would add weight to the Friend's next propaganda video. Hailwic would play the poor student whose thinking could have been warped by this devious individual. She could have been a victim, but instead her conviction held strong, her faith in her beliefs had kept her from falling prey to the dangerous remnants of Fistus's forces—that would be the spin.

But Uphrasia wouldn't make such a spectacle without an arrest.

Agents might be on their way to Solric at this very moment. To the university, maybe even 32A.

Hailwic's gaze darted to the cockpit. She'd been waiting for Uphrasia to get heavy-lidded and leaden-limbed before trying to bring the thopter to the ground. It was supposed to be a clean crash—she'd thought of a way to bring the metal bird down without suspicion. There wouldn't be any signs of tampering, and she'd hoped that even the black box would record nothing of interest.

General Gyrus was safe—unfortunately—but the cabinet . . . Uphrasia hadn't mentioned anything about the cabinet members being targeted.

Hailwic's mission was still a go.

She had to put this new information out of her mind and finish it. That was the right thing to do.

It was what she should have done.

But she couldn't shake the image of Glensen right there with the professor. Uphrasia couldn't know Zoshim was still alive and involved, but what about Punabi? They were all in danger—the entire rebellion was at risk.

A good little soldier would carry on. A good little soldier was what the RFR had trained her to be. A good little soldier would focus on her mission to the exclusion of all else—putting aside fears for friends and family and rebellion and country to see the job through without a hitch.

In that moment, she realized *a good little soldier* was something she would never become.

She didn't care if she died today. She was still willing to make that sacrifice. But she couldn't leave this world knowing she could have warned the others and done nothing.

Using her implants, she brought up her contacts, flicking through the list that appeared in the bottom left of her vision at will. She pulled up Glensen's number—fey were already compromised—watching three little dots appear then disappear over and over as the network waited for fem to answer.

"Hailwic?" Glensen asked hesitantly, feir confusion heartbreaking in the moment, making Hailwic's breath catch in her chest.

Glensen knew what she was doing right now. Hailwic was the last person fey expected to hear from—likely ever again.

She tripped over her words, syllables running together as she tried to get a coherent warning out before Uphrasia could react. "You've got to evacuate everyone. Right now. She's IDed the professor. They're coming. She kno—"

Surprisingly strong hands wrapped around Hailwic's throat, cutting her off. Delicate fingers with perfectly manicured nails pressed tightly into her windpipe, thumbs pressing into her jugular, making her gasp and cough and feel light-headed all at once.

"Oh, I can't wait to peruse your call records and see who that is," Uphrasia hissed in her ear.

Hailwic cut the call short—Glensen's uncertain voice dying in an instant—as she threw her weight to the side, headbutting Uphrasia with as much force as she could muster.

The hands were ripped from Hailwic's neck, at least one of them flying up to staunch the blood suddenly spurting from Uphrasia's nose. The Friend reeled back, blinking rapidly. At first, her wooziness looked like it came from the blow, but even as she reared up again it was clear something else was at work.

The drugs were finally taking their toll.

Uphrasia's eyes went wide. "*You—*" she slurred.

The pilot was not oblivious to the fight. He shouted directions at them—surely telling them to stop, but it was nothing but white noise and garbled nonsense to Hailwic's ears. She was too focused on the task at hand. Her throat hurt when she swallowed, and her breath came unnaturally fast while her heart hammered at a bruising pace. It wasn't until he contacted the thopter pad to request an emergency landing that any of the words made sense, and they shot an extra surge of adrenaline through her veins.

It was now or never.

Time to bring it all down.

Kinwold had gone over basic three-seater thopter schematics with her time and time again, and they'd used previous recon to gauge what kind of security measures might be aboard one ferrying the Friend herself. Hailwic knew the cockpit's bulbous windshield and the partition separating the pilot from the passengers was likely bulletproof, the chassis and the electronics were likely crypto-shielded and time-locked in order to protect against tampering. She couldn't get a hand on the pilot, which meant her magical influence on him would be limited, even without protective enchantments in the way.

The wings were guarded, the instruments were guarded. The craft itself was a paragon of safety, practically immune to interference.

But the air it relied on was not.

As Uphrasia tried to claw her way up from the corner she'd slumped against, Hailwic unfastened her harness and thrust one foot out, catching Uphrasia under the chin with her pump, holding the woman at bay with a locked knee.

Reaching through the air, following the flow of it out and around the craft, she created a bubble around the entire thopter, speeding up the air within, slowing down the air without, pushing and pulling at the relative time guiding all the molecules until—in an instant—she'd formed a perfect sphere of near vacuum.

The breath left her lungs.

Her ears popped.

Then a strange, ringing silence, before the thopter dropped like a stone.

She hadn't anticipated the way it would tilt as it dove. The thopter pitched to the side, tossing Hailwic into Uphrasia despite the way she tried to keep her knee locked. Something in her leg popped, and for a moment she lost the vacuum. As pain wrenched through her bones her concentration popped just as firmly out of place.

The thopter caught air as suddenly as it had lost it, the abrupt lift hitting the passengers like a sledgehammer. It was a punch to the gut and a blow to the head, and Hailwic lost all sense of up and down for a sickening few seconds as she tumbled.

Uphrasia clawed at Hailwic's arms, her face, while Hailwic herself clawed at the air, trying to create the vacuum again and *maintain it*.

The bottom dropped out of her stomach as they sank again, tumbling once more. The thopter was like a glass jar, the bugs within being cruelly shaken over and over by a vindictive child. Only, Hailwic was both bug and boy, shaking and being shaken.

She sensed a lens being drawn—not by the pilot, who'd been knocked unconscious—but by Uphrasia. It was wonky, weak, but could be just clear enough to be life-saving.

Hailwic couldn't have that.

She had to split her attention again. They had to be close to crashing—the rooftops hadn't been very far away the entire tour. It felt like they should be dead already. Never in a million years would she have guessed falling to her doom could take this long.

But even as she struggled to get at Uphrasia's hands, to pin them and stop her from finishing her lens, they were still aloft, still alive. Another jolt as the air swamped back in—though it didn't matter now that the thopter was in a nose dive—and her sweaty palms slipped on Uphrasia's wrists.

Uphrasia drew her lens behind herself without looking. She tipped backward, trying to fall into it, to escape to whatever familiar haven she could.

So Hailwic drew her own lens. Beneath the pair of them.

She didn't jump them far.

Where they'd been in a falling mass of metal an instant before, now they were just falling. The pair of them helpless, flightless creatures plummeting to their doom.

Or so she thought.

The lens had changed their trajectory, their speed. When they hit a rooftop, it wasn't at terminal velocity. But it was enough to break bones. It was enough that Uphrasia's face tore open as she skidded atop a row of anti-bird spikes. Yet it wasn't enough to kill either of them outright.

The roof they hit was pitched, and they half skid, half rolled down it until they came to an edge, both dangling precariously over the side to a sheer drop ten stories above the street, side by side.

Less than a block away, an explosive reverberation rocked the city. Hailwic tried to lift her head to see—though she knew it had to be the thopter crashing—and realized her right eye was no longer fully in its socket.

Her arms were broken. One leg was broken. Her back might be broken, she couldn't be sure.

Beside her, Uphrasia groaned.

Still. Not. Fucking. Dead.

The Friend moved, just barely. Haltingly. Trying to draw a lens. Again.

Sick to her stomach, close to blacking out, Hailwic drew from her last reserves to bring her good leg up and *kick*.

Uphrasia shrieked, trying to hold on to the unfeeling edge, adrenaline and the sedatives and her busted body making it impossible.

She tumbled over. Down.

Away.

Hailwic held her breath, waited until she heard an undeniable *crack* of a body hitting cement.

"Thanks be, bitch," she whispered.

Needing to see, she rolled ever so slightly to peer over the edge. The body lay still in the street. People stared in horror. Maybe they screamed, but she couldn't hear.

She wanted to pass out then. Wanted it to just end. But she was, maddeningly, still conscious. Still breathing. She'd thought she'd given everything she had.

Maybe she had just a little more.

Drooling blood, shaking from shock, she drew one last lens. It was a long jump. That in and of itself could be enough to kill her. But that was fine. Whatever happened now, Uphrasia was dead, so it was fine.

"Zo-Zoshim," she pleaded. Not just because she wanted to see him. Not just because she had to warn him.

He was the only one who could save her.

"P-please. Zoshim."

She wasn't sure where she was.

Or who she was.

Or what she was.

A distant ringing buzz inside her own head slowly rose in pitch, bringing Hailwic out of the dark, cool nothingness of unconsciousness back to the hot, throbbing pain of awareness. It wasn't as sharp and total—the pain—as she'd last recalled. *That* had cut off her air and stolen her capacity to think—to see beyond the edges of the pain to anything else. *This* pain had a quiet sincerity to it. Rather than the harsh stab of wounds inflicted moments ago, it was a dull ache that sharpened when she tried to move, as if her body had been in one position for an unnatural amount of time.

Her eyelids cracked open before she wanted them to. She slammed them shut again before she could catch more than color: earthen red.

Her lungs and nose and throat were raw, scraped. She parted her lips and found them tacky and cracked, her mouth overdry.

"Hailwic?"

She tried her eyes again. Sleep grit had them feeling like sandpaper. The dim light in the room felt like the direct assault of a spotlight. She struggled through it, forcing them open with an effort she'd never had to expend before. That same earthen red of an axe-carved ceiling stared back at her, begging to be placed. To be understood. To be situated. But her groggy mind had hardly caught on enough to realize she was prone and not upright, and could not place her in time and space.

A face encircled by a golden halo leaned over her, blurry as her eyes adjusted. "Hailwic?" he prompted again.

Zoshim.

A flash of memory struck her.

Impending danger. Pictures. Pictures in Uphrasia's hands.

Hailwic's heart shot into her throat.

The professor. Glensen. She had to warn them—

She tried to drive herself upright, to reach for Zoshim, only to find her wrists bound by soft cuffs to the edges of her cot. A harsh panic took hold of her, forcing her to thrash even while another part of her screamed for calm.

Her brother's hands pressed against her shoulders, and his mouth babbled half-concerned, half-soothing nonsense that she could not extricate from the fog of still-muddled senses.

"She—she *knows,*" Hailwic croaked out, the words sounding as sandy and dry as they felt leaving her tongue. "We have to evacuate everyone to Remotus. The professor, Glensen—"

Another face appeared from her other side, angelic and dark. Glensen. Fey put a hand on one of her bound wrists, and she stopped thrashing.

"You warned us," fey said, words slow and syrupy to Hailwic's ears. "I'm here. Lie still. Zoshim and my staff stabilized you when you arrived—put you in an induced coma. He and I have been able to repair many of your injuries, but you may still have internal bruising."

"I did my best, Hail," he said earnestly. "I can transform, but fixing's a whole different—"

Glensen put a hand on his shoulder. "You did fine."

Hailwic tried to bring her hand up to cover her eyes, needing a moment in the dark, but her wrists were still trapped. "We didn't want you to hurt yourself when you came to," Glensen explained. "Especially given how you got here."

Here. The bunker. Now that her vision had cleared properly, she understood. She was in the ancient tunnels the RFR used as their base of operations—above her, a long, uneven crack in the ceiling spoke to centuries of shifting ground piled atop it.

She'd jumped here because this was where the professor had sent Zoshim.

Zoshim. She looked to him again, only now realizing this was the first time she'd seen him since the false attempt at total extraction that had killed him in the eyes of the state. This was the first time she'd spoken to him in person since they were teenagers, caught out on the street in the dead of night by Uphrasia's enforcers.

He looked a decade older, as she must.

His jaw had grown more solid, his cheeks were less round. He was clean-shaven, and his eyes today were a defiant, unnatural emerald green.

She reached for him as best she could, fingers straining against the cuff's pull. He understood immediately, took her hand, his other plucking questioningly at her bindings as his gaze rose to Glensen's.

"We're going to untie you," Glensen said. "But I need you to move with care, all right?"

"Yes," she agreed, easing into her pillows as the two of them worked the bindings.

She realized then that the three of them were alone. She could only hear one set of medical monitors. There was no curtain around her cot to separate her from the next patient, and a furtive glance confirmed there were no other patients. No other waiting beds.

They'd isolated her.

Because of the extent of her injuries, or because of her mission?

"Th-the professor—"

Fey didn't look her in the eye, gaze and fingers now fixed on the buckles of the cuffs. "It's been chaos this last week. Lots of comms channels have gone dark. Scouts are doing their best—we get new reports every day, new evacuees to the bunker every day. Several RFR cells working on the Radix side of the wall were already under siege before you got on that thopter—"

"A *week*?" Hailwic asked, the surprise of it making her throat tight.

She'd been out a week.

More quick-snap images and sensations of that day came to her, each flitting before her eyes before being snatched away again and replaced by yet another. The loud yawing of the thopter. The meanness in Uphrasia's eyes. The feel of her cold, strong fingers. Rooftops screaming up to meet them. The crunch of bones.

It made her skin feel clammy in the now, made her want to shout and claw and fight, though her limbs felt weak and uncoordinated.

Hailwic shook it all from her head.

Glensen didn't know where the professor was.

Chaos, fey said. Chaos could mean anything. Chaos could mean open warfare in the streets. Chaos could mean that, with Uphrasia gone, one of their neighboring countries had finally come to their aid and sent troops. Chaos could mean martial law. Chaos could mean a decimated RFR and a still-roaring Uphrasian regime. Chaos could mean the rest of Radix had finally had enough and had formed their own rebel forces.

Chaos simply meant the opposite of order. It told her nothing.

Glensen continued to avoid her gaze, moving to a chart posted beside her bed. A sizzle of apprehension crackled between Zoshim and Glensen across the narrow expanse of Hailwic's cot, making her wonder what they'd spoken about just prior to her waking.

"What are they saying . . . about Uphrasia's death?"

"Maddeningly little," Zoshim said, picking up her hand now that he'd released it, rubbing her wrist.

"We aren't authorized to talk to you about this," Glensen warned. "We weren't assigned to do your debriefing, just to your care."

Hailwic pushed herself into a sitting position, that all-over ache in her body making itself known again. A previously unnoticed IV line tugged at her arm. "Everyone thought I was going to die," she pointed out. "Including me. *No one* was assigned my debriefing." She clutched Zoshim's hand all the tighter. "Tell me what's happening."

He gave a pleading, deferring look to Glensen, worry etched between his brows.

"Or bring Punabi in and zhe'll tell me," she added.

"Punabi's on assignment," Glensen said, reluctance making feir tone heavy. "Zhe volunteered to go back into Radix once it had been confirmed that the professor had gone dark."

Worry welled up inside Hailwic as though from a burst pipe, flooding her insides and her chest until she was gasping for air as she fell back against the pillows once more.

The two of them had a second chance. Except . . . Except . . .

She pawed at her throat. "I'll get you some water," Zoshim said quickly, disappearing from sight.

Glensen turned away, guilt or something like it making feir shoulders hunch. "I'm sorry. I . . . I know you two have grown close. Zhe's still in communication with us. I can't make promises on zhur behalf, but zhe knows you're alive. Zhe's doing what zhe can. We're all just doing what we can."

Zoshim appeared once more with a small paper cup, holding it out in shaking fingers as though to tip it for her and help her drink. Hailwic sat up again and snatched it away, tossing back the meager shot of water in one gulp.

She looked at the thin, wax-covered paper for a moment. It was the fragile, flimsy kind that wound in on itself in a single sheet, coming to a point at the bottom. The kind that was no good once it had been wetted, that couldn't be used for anything too hot or too cold. The kind she couldn't even grip with the usual level of force one gripped a glass cup, or else it would fold and crumple.

The RFR was like the cup. A makeshift semblance of a fighting force, an army. Ultimately, a facsimile of the real thing. Something that needed extra care to maintain.

Someone had come along and cut a hole in it.

She understood now what Glensen had meant by chaos.

With the professor gone dark, the RFR itself was pure disorder and confusion.

Glensen wasn't sure who to defer to in matters relating to Hailwic and her mission.

So Hailwic decided to be in charge of herself.

Kinwold had been her superior in the field. Kinwold would be her superior still.

"Where is Dr. Theesius? I'll send my official statement to them."

"They're here." Glensen's statement was simple, complete, but the full stop felt more like a grand pause. "I . . . I advised them to leave. Them and their family."

"Were they discovered? Like the professor?"

"Not that we're aware of," Glensen admitted. "But given your survival . . ."

"Ah."

Her missing body was a loose end. If she'd died in the crash like she was supposed to, there might not be suspicion cast on those around her. But there were only two bodies where there should have been three. Even if all that was left of the pilot were a few teeth and burnt-out bones . . .

And—

She went cold.

She hadn't thought about it in the moment.

There had to have been a black box aboard. If the assassination had gone to plan, there never would have been any sign that it was more than an accident.

But she and Uphrasia had fought. Hailwic had made a call—

Hailwic crumpled the paper cup in her fist.

If Glensen hadn't been so prescient . . .

"They're all right," Glensen assured her.

"Bring them to me," she ordered. "I need to speak with them, now."

"You need to rest first," Glensen said. "And eat. I'll have someone track them down, but as your doctor I can't advise—"

"I've been resting long enough." The thin gown they'd put her in and the firmly tucked sheets across her legs suddenly all felt scratchy and stifling. She needed to get on her feet. To get up and *do* something—to help.

Someone had to get eyes on the professor. She specifically needed to speak to Punabi, and someone—anyone—had to tell her what in *hells* was happening with the government.

Hailwic kicked free of the sheets, determined to defy doctor's orders.

Zoshim grabbed hold of both her shoulders, squeezing—his touch insistent and steadying. "Unless you've suddenly remembered something world-shattering, a few more hours won't make a difference. Stay with me. Eat with me. Glensen will find Dr. Theesius."

Share a peaceful moment with me, his eyes pleaded. *A quiet like we've not been able to have in ages.*

It would be a false peace, she knew. Beyond this little room that they'd done up like a hospital suite, everyone was on high alert, running triage not just for the wounded and the fleeing, but for their entire rebellion. It had to be *all hands on deck* out there, yet her hands were *idle*.

Then again, perhaps any peace—even false—was a gift.

She hadn't expected to be here. Hadn't expected to see Zoshim again.

She didn't see how she could deny him this request, even if it was more for her benefit than his.

"Okay," she agreed, letting the nervous, call-to-action energy drain from her body. "Yeah. Okay."

"Good," Glensen affirmed, a warm smile gracing feir elfin lips. "Two commissary specials, coming up."

"Don't forget the gelatin cups," Zoshim teased. "They grew on me in lockup."

Hailwic snorted her distaste, even as fondness rose in her chest. "Speak for yourself."

"I'll take hers," he said in a faux whisper, an easy familiarity between him and the older medic on full display.

Before disappearing out the door—a low wooden slab fixed in what must have before been a bare archway, perhaps covered with a cloth and nothing more—Glensen beckoned Zoshim close for a moment. "Maybe you could share some of your new philosophies with her?" fey suggested.

Zoshim pursed his lips and reddened slightly. "Not sure how well that'll . . ."

"Maybe better than you think."

"What was that?" Hailwic asked once Glensen had gone, absently continuing to crush the cup in her hands, liking the way the compacted paper fit into the creases of her palm.

He gave her an awkward huff of a laugh, matched by a smile just as awkward. She used to know exactly what kind of nonsense such a mask concealed, but the awkwardness of the man was so different from the awkwardness of the boy. "Nothing," he said. "I've just been reading."

"Ah yes, reading," she said wistfully, putting him on, trying to find her playful, prodding tone from their childhood. "I remember it well. Tell me, how are books these days? Still lots of words? Pages?"

"I've been reading the Holderdottir Treatises."

She'd read them in part while at Helena—the highlights really. Whatever she'd been expecting him to say, that wasn't it. It made sense, though; he'd been denied his full education, seemed he was correcting that.

"Wow. That's some . . . heavy lifting," she said.

"Those, and Adapa's work on the same subject. And Hi-Hisaru's."

She felt her brow pinch and her hackles raise before she'd even fully registered the meaning. He hadn't been reading the works of just *any* philosophers and social pioneers. "So, you've been studying passivity during wartime?" Even she could hear the defensiveness in her lilt, the insincerity as she tried to reclassify it as, "*Neutrality? Inaction?*"

The very opposite of her own call to arms.

"Nonviolence," he corrected. "Achieving goals in the face of war without aggression."

"Uh-huh."

There was nothing judgmental in his eyes or his tone, though she couldn't say the same about her own. It was likely his initial hesitancy that had put her teeth on edge.

Why would Glensen want them to talk about this, specifically? Hailwic wasn't sure if she should take it as a slight, or a not-so-subtle hint, or simply as a less-than-finessed conversation starter.

She dropped her gaze, fiddling with the wad of paper like it was an intricate piece of folded art she wanted to reverse engineer.

"Hey." He stilled her hands with his. "I just . . . I want to help, to heal. I think

Glensen thought . . . I mean, now that you're finished—now that you've completed your mission—maybe you . . ."

He wasn't condemning her. He'd discovered pacifism, and imagined that she too might see hope in laying down her proverbial spear.

He wanted this faux peace to be theirs, always.

She wanted to treasure his naivety, but it put a bitterness in her throat and a sourness on her stomach.

Zoshim gently pulled the crumpled cup from between her fingers and she let it go. Rubbing it between his palms for a moment, he refashioned it with his physiopathy before dropping it back into her open hand.

He hadn't changed its makeup, just its shape.

Now it was a paper bird. A crane.

She held it up by the tail, letting a twitching sort of smile grace her lips, one that hid much and said much. There was hope in it, and loss, and nostalgia, and regret. "What a pair we make," she said, finally meeting his eyes again. "The pacifist and the assassin. A case study for the philosophers of the future."

When Glensen brought their meals back, they spoke of lighter things, trying to scare away the tension with forced laughter. Their world might be crumbling around them, but if Zoshim wanted to pretend nothing was wrong for a time, Hailwic would humor him—no matter how her ears perked when the door opened, looking for snatches of conversation, or how her hands gripped her flimsy cutlery like weapons without her consent.

She hated how relieved she was when the forced levity was over. She hadn't seen Zoshim in years, yet she couldn't allow herself to ignore the larger goings-on and enjoy their reunion.

On the hour, Glensen and Zoshim took the trays away, bowing aside for Kinwold to enter. Glensen gave them some parting instructions at a whisper—no doubt insisting they avoid overexciting her.

Kinwold nodded, face stoic as the two of them left, eyes brightening and face breaking into an over-wide grin when he approached her bed. "Oh, Hailwic, thank the stars—"

She held up a hand. "Don't. I just suffered through enough coddling to last me a lifetime."

Their smile fell, not in disappointment, but relief. "Glensen wouldn't let me in to see you while you were under," they said, stopping short of her cot, absently flicking the edges of the manila folder they had with them. "Doesn't want me to hug you now."

She lifted her arms regardless. "Just be gentle."

It was good to see them alive, good to feel them solid—if a little thin. Kinwold only squeezed her lightly, but it was enough to feel the bruises hiding behind her ribs and beneath her sternum, though she didn't let on.

Kinwold found a metal stool on the opposite side of the small room and pulled it over. Crossing one long leg over the other, they set the open file in their lap and clicked on a pen, setting in for a serious conversation.

She gave her accounting of the mission, of Uphrasia's surprise proposal. She named everyone she'd recognized in the photographs, and, unprompted, defended her decision to contact Glensen.

Hailwic resented her own guilt. She'd gone off script, and in the process may have exposed as many people as she'd saved. If she hadn't revealed herself to Uphrasia—to that damn black box—then the Theesius family might not have needed to flee their home.

The professor's fate undoubtedly would have been the same, but she'd warned Glensen, made sure fey were safe.

And she'd done her job, in the end. She'd completed her mission and alerted the RFR to their head's discovery.

Kinwold watched her wrestle with herself, quietly making notes, until she once again asked what the official story was from the government's side.

"The official channels have all been strangely mum on the matter," they said with a discontented sigh. "They've acknowledged the thopter accident, but not that Uphrasia was on board. Possibly they're scrambling—the cabinet might be trying to close up the power vacuum before anyone even knows there is one. As far as the world is concerned, Uphrasia is as Uphrasia has always been."

"How have they managed . . ." she trailed off, answering her own question. There were witnesses. She remembered people in the street, gathered near the body.

A visit from the Contentment Squad would be enough to silence those bystanders. To forcibly make them forget.

"What are our next steps?" she asked instead.

"Since Professor Solric was exposed, we've been scrambling to identify the status of all the infiltrating operatives. Support's being sent to the scrimmage lines, and evacuees are being resettled in and around the bunker."

She tried not to worry about Punabi in the field, tried not to imagine a perfectly aimed bullet catching zhim right in the eye, though her mind insisted on feeding her the image over and over and over again.

"Where can I help?" If her hands were busy, her mind would follow.

"I think you've given enough."

"Thank you," she said, sincerely appreciative. "But that's for me to decide. I'll rest when I'm dead."

"That's just it," they said, standing. "You're supposed to be."

The little aches and twinges grew more noticeable once she left her hospital cot. Every bend or sudden move sent shooting pains through parts of her body she'd never had occasion to notice before, and they were only matched in suddenness and intensity by every reminder that Punabi was in the field, unreachable.

Hailwic could see zhim in her mind's eye, inching zhur way through the streets with zhur rifle at the ready, trading hand signals with the members of zhur unit as they wound in perfect synchronicity through the once-bustling city blocks, unsure if around the next corner they'd find hostile soldiers or cowering civilians.

There'd be sweat on zhur brow, and a clench to zhur teeth. A determination in zhur eye like no other. Anyone at the end of zhur rifle barrel would feel a sharp thrill—a twisted kin to what Hailwic had felt when the two of them had gone dancing. Being pinned by Punabi's passions—seductive or violent—could only be heady and pointed.

In contrast, Hailwic's assigned tasks purposefully lacked grit and passion. There were no firearms drills, or knife training, or even heavy lifting for her. Glensen disallowed her any overly physical labor, and until they knew more about the aftermath of the crash, she was confined to the bunker.

She spent her time with their record keepers and archivists, sorting through smuggled documents and illegally procured correspondence. Piles of printouts and hastily jotted notes lay like snow drifts around the aluminum shelving in the archives, many creased and crumpled, as they'd been hastily shoved in boxes or jacket pockets as an undercover operative fled their post.

Now, Hailwic sat cross-legged on the stone floor, the rock smoothed over from many ancient feet. People had trodden these cold halls long before Radix existed as a nation. Long before it rose to an international economic power. Long before it fell into authoritarianism. This specific stretch of stone didn't see nearly as many feet as it used to. What had perhaps been a living area once—a place for a small family to gather, or a close unit of troops, depending on the century—was now a room at the back of one of the bunker's best guarded and least frequented storage areas.

The head archivist had offered her a desk, but she'd chosen to go to the stacks instead of forcing them to come to her.

Drawing another paper-clipped set of leaflets into her lap, she began sorting and prioritizing. She heard the grinding of the stone door in its tract and barely looked up as a record keeper came in to retrieve her already-sorted work for review, switching the piles out for yet another cardboard box's worth of documents.

After they'd left, the door opened again only a few minutes later. She thought nothing of it, running the pad of her finger absently over the edges of the paper, inviting a cut that never came. She'd already let her mind sink into the tabulations, into classifying the data.

When she caught someone out of the corner of her eye, she was only slightly surprised when she glanced up and found Kinwold standing there. She swiftly set her papers aside, using the nearest shelf to drag herself to her feet. It swayed precariously, unused to having to bear more than the downward press of documents and hefty folders.

"Punabi?" she asked breathlessly. They'd promised to bring her any news.

They shook their head sadly.

In that small movement, Hailwic read the worst. Her body went cold, her lips instantly numb and clumsy as they parted in bitter shock.

Luckily Kinwold caught the devastation on her face and quickly corrected her. "No. It's not about Punabi. There's going to be an official Government Address in an hour. Live. On all channels."

Hailwic's instant relief was bullied aside by anticipation and dread.

This was it, then. The announcement.

New propaganda videos had still been forthcoming every few days. Hailwic wasn't sure how far in advance Uphrasia had produced them—how long it would take for the well to run dry. Perhaps it had happened, and the state couldn't deny her absence any longer.

"We're setting up teles in both commissaries and the commons. Everyone will be watching," Kinwold said. "You're free to keep working." They raised a serious eyebrow, a gesture that spoke to delicacy as much as it did to decency. "Or not."

She gave a hollow nod, settling herself back down on the floor, using the shelving as a crutch once more, making it sway in equal protest.

They left stiffly, hands shoved in their pockets, clearly feeling a conflicted way about it themself.

Hailwic gazed around at the drifts of paper, unsure how she could be expected to focus on anything else with *this* on the horizon.

The hour whittled away slowly, the shavings of it landing on the curls of paper, sinking into them, blurring the type and the scribbles alike, leaving a meaninglessness in their wake.

When she finally allowed herself to leave the archive room, her vision was tunneled. She saw next to nothing as she put one foot in front of the other on the way to the general commissary, despite the halls being full of people moving that same way.

The walls of the commissary curved—a circular embrace for the dozen tables set about. Only one table, on the far side of the room, had been moved to make way for the tele on its rolling trolly. Many cables and wires draped away from the bulky box of it—the model decades out of date—snaking out the door and up the levels of tunnel to ensure the broadcast would come through clearly, despite the viewers being huddled underground. All the chairs had been stolen from their tables, set closely together, twisted toward the tele, each already occupied. At their rear, several people had climbed onto a table to see over the others, and at their feet, the stragglers all sat in eager anticipation.

The telescreen was still dark. One person stood beside it, hand on the top corner, eyes stuck to an old analog watch on their wrist.

The pyramid of bodies was oddly artfully composed, and for a moment Hailwic, foolishly, did not want to ruin the composition by inserting herself into the crowd.

As though sensing her hesitation, Zoshim's golden crown popped up from the far side of the group. He beckoned her over, and all thoughts of backtracking left her.

She needed support for this, and was grateful when he took her hand as she settled beside his chair on the floor.

A few people she knew gave nods to her presence, and she absently acknowledged them back, palm already sweating in Zoshim's grip.

Many people knew she'd arrived bloody and broken to the bunker, but most didn't know *why*.

There would be no ticker-tape parade for the woman who'd killed Uphrasia. Which was fine. Her role was the price she'd paid for Zoshim's freedom. If the assassin's name was lost to the history books, so much the better.

When the telescreen clicked on, she jumped.

The state's seal—the Friend's seal—splashed across the monitor, bold and imposing, telling viewers to stand by for the beginning of the live broadcast. The emblem sported a pair of cupped hands in metallic relief, cradling a hawk with a striped military banner in its beak. In a wreath around the hands, four ancient symbols for the four *approved* magics repeated over and over, all atop a curved proclamation of *One Realm, One Protector.*

Hailwic bit her thumbnail on her free hand, one leg bouncing nervously.

The image flickered, revealing a dais and microphones flanked by two of Uphrasia's black-clad Cryptopaths, their faces blank and half-hidden by the glazed visors of their helmets. Behind them, Radix's capital buildings, sprawling and grand. Modern. Fistus had been the last to inhabit the old mansions, now bulldozed and buried.

Who would it be, Hailwic wondered. Who would make the announcement—to the wails and shocked cries of the crowd gathered before the podium?

All the blood drained from Hailwic's face—from her neck and chest and heart—when the first hint of long, dark hair appeared from off screen.

A pale face turned toward the camera, and Hailwic's grip on Zoshim's hand turned crushing. Wordless denials screamed themselves ragged in her head, while outwardly all she could do was stare slack-jawed at the screen.

A double.

An imposter.

She'd watched Uphrasia fall. Seen her body smashed against the pavement like a cracked egg.

There was no way.

But there she was. Uphrasia. The Friend. Flawlessly pressed in a mauve suit, looking healthy and as put-together as ever, save for one thing; evidence of her encounter with the bird spikes still ran across her face, from the right side of her chin angling up to her left temple. A dramatic slash, yet it did nothing to mar her beauty. It had healed near perfectly.

Too perfectly.

The scar was a purposeful work of art, rather than a gnarled badge of resilience.

Of course.

Hailwic drew a shuddering breath and yanked her hand from Zoshim's, hiding her face behind her palms, covering over her grimace and swallowing down her scream.

Hailwic couldn't have survived without physiopathic aid.

And neither could Uphrasia.

Her own personal doctors must have been Physiopaths. The very people she persecuted were the reason she was still alive.

She hadn't even needed to keep the scar. There was only one reason to.

Martyrdom.

Hailwic understood the narrative Uphrasia was prepared to weave even before she spoke: she'd been the victim of a physiopathic attack. She'd borne the violence—made it out the other side. This would be just another page for the propaganda handbook. More pulp to grind into anti-Physiopath fodder.

Hailwic's assassination attempt had done nothing but feed the hate machine.

Only then did it hit her: she'd *failed.*

Since waking she'd been laboring in a fog of worry for Professor Solric, for Punabi, but never once had she doubted her mission was complete.

The first words out of Uphrasia's mouth were sobering in their evenness, her tone stately and practical, only slightly edged with a sigh that didn't reveal fear or weakness, but instead spoke to a *disappointment*—like a schoolteacher who'd expected better of her class.

She detailed her version of the crash, fulfilling Hailwic's expectations, creating a phantom terrorist group of Physiopaths, no longer invoking the spectrum of Fistus, instead fabricating a villainous organization wholesale.

"Rest assured," she told the people, "the ringleader in the attempt on my life has already been apprehended, tried, and eliminated."

The whole commissary let out a collective gasp when Professor Solric's faculty picture appeared—large and unmistakable—in the top left corner of the screen. A giant red *X* cut feir face into quadrants.

"As have many of feir criminal associates," Uphrasia added.

More faces appeared, some gazing out of formal pictures taken for employee badges, others smiling broadly in cropped family photos. Hailwic recognized some from the file Uphrasia had shown her in the thopter.

Each received a bloody red *X* like Solric's, and a shared quaking went through the people gathered around the tele, lungs stuttering and out of sync, strangling sobs and exclamations alike.

This new group had radicalized a young woman, Uphrasia went on, making Hailwic feel faint, her vision dappling at the edges. A young woman that the Friend had graciously—*personally*—given a second chance. These people had corrupted her from the root.

Hailwic blinked, and there was her face.

The whole room stilled, shocked rigid. Then, like something out of a horrid nightmare, heads swiveled on stiff necks, one by one, toward Hailwic.

She didn't look back at them, her gaze caught on her own eyes staring back, the fishhook sharpness of Uphrasia's voice preventing her from squirming away.

She waited.

She hoped.

She wanted to see a red *X* slash across her own features.

She willed Uphrasia to lie. Surely her ego couldn't stand it: that the assassin had got away. Surely it was more important to assure the people that the would-be killer had been dealt with, rather than admit she still ran free.

Hailwic willed this, not for her own sake, but for the others in the pictures. For Professor Solric. If Uphrasia had lied about her own elimination, that meant there was a chance others had escaped as well.

No such reprieve came.

"Unfortunately, the manipulated assassin herself is still at large," Uphrasia said. "I am committed to bringing her to justice, just as I am committed to bringing these other known terrorists to justice."

More pictures. Without *X*s. Those the government had yet to find. Glensen's picture was among them.

"Memorize these faces. Know that anyone who gives succor to these enemies of the state will be treated as accomplices in kind. They may be your coworkers, your acquaintances. Your neighbors. Even your family. But they are not your friends. *I* am your friend. *I* am your protector. They know this, and they tried to take me from you. They do not deserve your sympathy or your shelter. You cannot be for them and for me. To be for them is to be against Radix.

"I have already dealt with those who tried to hide information about the assassin from my agents."

Uphrasia's face, her address, was interrupted by body-cam footage from a nighttime raid. Shaky and occasionally unfocused, it panned across the stoop of a well-to-do yet unimaginative house. One similar to all its neighbors, up and down the street.

A stoop Hailwic knew well, even in the blurred dark. She'd spent many spring afternoons tromping up and down it in bare feet, and many winter evenings stomping snow off her boots at its base. It was one she would have recognized anywhere, in an instant, even if the two terrified figures with their hands up hadn't come stumbling out of the front door.

Beside her, Zoshim made an animalistic cry—sudden and sharp, bursting from his chest with all the force and speed of a snake's strike. His hands went to his mouth, his eyes widened and glazed.

The figures were screamed at by the Wellness agents, forced to get down on their knees, facing their house, facing their own front door, with their hands behind their heads. They both did as they were told, perfectly compliant, expecting to be cuffed.

Instead, they were each shot once in the back of the head.

Their bodies pitched forward and Zoshim pitched with them, tipping over his chair as he fell roughly, a reedy wail—inhuman—drowning out all else in Hailwic's ears.

Suddenly, her body was made of ice, and her mind could not stay there, lest it freeze. So, it fled. She lifted outside herself, suddenly feeling very far away from the room, from Zoshim, from the screen.

She saw herself rise to her feet, saw herself turn. Saw herself slowly walk away from the broadcast, as though distance would change its contents.

From far away, she heard Uphrasia's voice again, her usually calm and frank tone becoming more and more heated, more forceful. More *deranged*.

More like Fistus, as if his ghost were welling up inside her.

The words *total extraction* left her lips. The first time in a public address.

Uphrasia had simply been waiting for an excuse. She'd been looking for a reason to announce to the world that she was ready not just to imprison the Physiopaths, but to exterminate them, and would do it as soon as *total extraction* could be achieved.

Hailwic did not turn back to the monitor. She continued walking unadroitly away, focused on reaching the door and leaving the room and nothing else.

She'd nearly made it when a body appeared from outside to block her escape. She didn't even recognize zhim for a moment. She had no capacity to recognize anything.

There was a flush to Punabi's dark skin, and zhe still wore a traveling cloak wrapped tightly over zhur jacket and uniform, lungs working as though zhe'd run through the tunnels to get here.

"Hailwic," zhe said breathlessly, "you're alive."

Her name snapped her back into her body as surely as a physical slap, sending her reeling, making her feel too much of everything all at once. Bile thrust its way up her throat and she twisted over, vomiting all over poor Punabi's boots.

KRONA

Before Krona agreed to lead the pair of gods away, to Nature's temple, she begged one favor of them—the first of many she intended to plead for.

Jan's body still remained slumped against a vat, right where Krona had found her—and left her—in a rage.

They now stood before the body in a half circle, as Melanie lay it down softly, crossing Jan's hands over her chest and whispering soft prayers of apology that befitted a Healer who could not save a life.

"I will commit her to sand," Time agreed. "Now, look away."

Krona put an arm around Melanie, pulled her away and turned her softly, with Sebastian at her side. None of them were strangers to death or rotting—were not babes whose sensibilities were peach-soft and so easily bruised—but, as they'd been ordered by a god, none of them saw fit to argue.

Tray, however, did not obey.

He did bow his head when Time turned a sharp eye on him. "I've turned away too many times," he said. "Please, permit me—"

"As you wish," the goddess conceded, as if it mattered not.

Krona knew what would follow, what he'd see. Jan, who he'd fought and supped and planned beside, disintegrating into sand, becoming first a desiccated corpse—bloating, rotting, shrinking—before her skin and organs crumpled into nothing, leaving her a bare skeleton before even her bones became dust. Dust that fell between the metal loops of the corrugated floor, clumping and scattering like the finest fall of snow.

Melanie continued her quiet prayers as the air around them tightened and Time thrust the body forward through its natural march to nothingness, allowing Jan to rest properly in the tradition of her people.

Tray stood stoically, an obligate witness, while Krona's hearing snagged on every breathy word from Melanie's lips. Praying to a goddess when she was an arm's length away created a strange storm cloud in Krona's belly—a front of absurdity clashing with a front of necessity. Death required the reverence, Melanie's tongue could not be denied the ritual. And yet, no pleas for a gentle rest were necessary.

Jan had already been blessed, given a gift richer than any emperor or eze could hope for.

One of the Five had returned her to the sand from which she'd been created. The divine that had built her was the divine that had scattered her.

"Now," Time said grandly when she was done, "to my brother."

Winsrouen always felt wrong to Krona. Her skin crawled whenever she strode down the sidewalks of the city proper or visited an outpost in the country. It was true before the war, and it was true now, but for different reasons.

The city-state was hyper-regimented. In dress, in building, in behavior. There were intricate rituals for everything—taking a meal, greeting someone new, getting rid of a broken item—which could have been beautiful. Many *were* beautiful. Krona had been especially enamored of the ceremony required to dispose of a cooking pot—it put even a Lutadorian funeral to shame.

But to deviate from those rituals even slightly was to risk expulsion from society. Reciting a line incorrectly, using an ink of the wrong color, or fumbling a hand gesture carried punishments just short of the gods' penalties themselves.

Their Dregs didn't live in tunnels underground. Instead, they were pushed into the hills, into hermitages, prevented from even forming their own connections with one another.

And that was during peaceful times. Before war came.

A people who could not fathom a single ritual being disrupted fell into utter chaos when no ritual could go undisturbed. The careful control the citizens were expected to exact over every aspect of their lives had been revealed as no more than self-diluting illusion, and the populace had fractured into two main camps: those who clamped on to their traditions with violent, iron grips, and those who sewed their own chaos in light of their newfound freedom, like children finally escaping the watchful eyes of their overprotective parents.

The result was a mess of authority and anarchy.

The plateau lifting Nature's shrine high above the Valley's basin was usually barren—subjected to striking winds that kept stray seeds from taking hold in the cracks between the stones and putting down roots. No birds nested here, there were no small creatures for mountain cats to hunt here. It was lifeless ground—a slight to Nature himself.

Except, on this occasion, it was brimming with activity.

The people of Winsrouen had sought refuge here, running from bombardment and conscription—building shelters that barely withstood the gusts, the flaps of their linen and hide tents snapping violently.

The camp had been built tightly around the single jut of rock that stood tall and wide near the edge of the scoured plateau, easily identifiable from miles away. To the average eye, there was nothing special about it; it was a near pyramid of natural stone, a quirk of geology protruding from the smooth highland.

But it was no such thing. In reality, it was Nature's temple, obscured and disguised.

They arrived in a flutter of wings, glittering amethyst, and stuttering steps, right in the middle of the camp. A fevered pitch went up among the refugees—their reactions varied, from awe to fright to anguish—and though Krona could not blame them and did not want to hide from them, she wished there was a way to soften the shock of it.

Krona was used to her bones being met with cringing hesitation—caution and fear. But her wings were a simple curiosity compared to the two humanoid giants. Their sheer presence was demanding, overwhelming.

Emotion the people did not recognize. They reeled back from zhur presence with wide yet curious eyes. But Time? She was unmistakable.

Their goddess walked among them. Which meant she *wasn't* protecting them on the rim, where they believed she'd been stationed their entire lives. Which could only mean something catastrophic was happening.

There was a moment of stillness, then terror, then stillness again, before a rush of bodies pressed forward, hands seeking, fingertips reaching.

The looks on the faces in the crowd were like nothing Krona had ever seen in a coterie. This wasn't rapture. It was veneration, yes, but filled with dread. War-deadened eyes were alight with questions and a dark certainty—like they were finally staring down the end. The end of everything.

"This was never supposed to happen," Time said, walking from person to person, meeting every outstretched hand, graciously avoiding everyone who cowered in fright. Some people fainted at her touch, others fell to their knees before her and begged her for blessings—for a missing loved one to be all right, for a wound to heal, for a home to return to.

Most of all, they begged her to turn back the clock. She was Time. She made the nights follow the days. She made sure one was young before they were old. She was the one who put the hours in order, so couldn't she—just this once—make them run in reverse?

She did not acknowledge these requests, nor did she speak to anyone directly, but she looked stricken.

Stricken and *unsure.*

There came a giddy shout from the cliffside, and Krona turned just as a woman threw herself from the plateau, tearing at her hair and clothes—rending herself in a mixture of existential dread and spiritual ecstasy.

The bottom dropped out of Krona's stomach even as she jumped, rushing to do what she could—to save the woman.

She'd never attempted to *intercept* anything with a jump before, let alone catch someone mid-fall, and a hideous *thump-crack* was the first thing to meet her on the other side of her lens.

Krona could do nothing but stare at the still form of the woman facedown in shards of shale, perfectly still, with dust billowing up—the curls of it far too delicate for the heavy horror of what had just happened.

Krona stood stunned for a long moment before approaching the body, laying a delicate hand on the woman's back as though attempting to rouse her from sleep. The breath was gone from her, the thrumming of her heart was no more.

An instant in a god's presence and she'd gone mad.

Was this a portent of what was to come?

She lifted the limp form, the woman's weight a solid warmth. Still so alive, yet not living.

Another jump and she was back among the refugees, laying the woman down, backing away as an older woman screamed and threw herself across the body.

Time didn't even look their way.

The goddess could refuse to wipe away these years of war. She could decline to interfere with the forward march of minutes. There was a sanctity in denying to undo what had already been done.

But this? She could have saved this woman.

She could save her *now*.

Even as Emotion subtly dampened the grief in the older woman—shushing her with a wave of cool calm that even Krona could feel—Time marched on, ever focused on reaching Nature.

As she approached the jutting stone, the humans fell back, and Time wiped away the concealing illusion like wiping condensation from a window. One pass of her hand through the air and the rock was gone, replaced by glimmering copper. Nature's temple was rigid and sharp-looking. Tented metal shards—severe, imposing—leaned together precariously. It was a structure whose design had no equal in all of Arkensyre. It felt both like an artifact from a time before memory and a misplaced object from the future.

It had more characteristics of a sculpture than a building. The seams between the shards were tight, flush. At first, they'd seemed bonded, but each piece of metal could be forced to slide, shifting along its brethren. It was a giant puzzle box. Juliet had run the calculations on how many pieces there were and how many possible combinations they could make and had come to the conclusion that, without knowing the set solution, it would take them a century to work out how to open it.

And anything could lay inside. There could be a shaft straight to the center of the planet for all they'd been able to discern.

I should have sent Thibaut here, Krona thought. *Maybe he could have simply read the solution*. A knot of guilt made her throat go dry. If she'd thought to send Thibaut here instead of forcing him to focus on the hoard, he would still be at Mirthhouse—or even here, now.

Avellino and Juliet and Mandip would still be in the Savior's grasp, but at least . . .

No. No *at least*.

They'd retrieve Nature, they'd kill Absolon, and then they'd get them back. All of them, safe and sound.

Time tore down the refugee-built adjacent lean-tos with startling efficiency, wings flapping angrily, kicking up dust as she removed all obstacles from her path. She put two hands on one of the copper panels and slid it to the left, then right, then up, then gave it a twist until it clicked, revealing yet more copper beneath.

"It's a puzzle," Melanie explained, shoulders hunched, trying to be meek and deferent, yet helpful. "And it—"

The goddess held up a hand for silence, gaze roving manically over the temple. "And it will take time. Stand back," she ordered.

Emotion caught her shoulder as she advanced, shaking zhur head. Time looked at the construction once more, seemed to be calculating something. "I have enough," she told zhim in a reassuring tone. One large hand went to her chest, over her heart. She bent her golden head, closed her eyes, looking deep within herself. "I have lifetimes."

For a moment, it looked like Emotion would try to argue, despite their lack of common tongue, but nodded and took a step back, waving zhur arms, ushering any stray humans aside.

Time's fingers lay lightly on the next plate, two of her hands thrusting it into a new position unnaturally fast even as the other two reached for the next. The subsequent piece found a home in a flash, and soon her four hands were moving too fast for the eye to catch as she warped time around herself, creating a space to work beyond human perception. Her body was a blur, her wings nothing but a smear of black and the pieces little more than bright glints as they caught the sunlight on rotation and threw it back. Krona thought she glimpsed the telltale signs of a jump now and again, but she couldn't be sure.

As the goddess worked, the refugee camp fell silent. Slowly, those still standing fell to their knees, and Krona had to fight the urge to join them. Not out of awe, or wonder, but an overwhelming *understanding.*

Krona had thought she herself possessed power. Intellectually, she knew she was nothing compared to one of the gods, but to see such a difference laid bare plucked a chord in her soul that had never sounded before.

Nature's temple bloomed before them. Time's relative speed had the puzzle box opening like a flower, its pieces finally twisting enough to form the proper shape. The pyramid became a concave vessel instead, open to the sky—almost like hands creating the sign of the Valley.

From her vantage, Krona couldn't see what was cupped inside.

Time abruptly rejoined them on the same chronological plane, looking, of course, no different than she had when she began. She did not extend a hand to Emotion, or wait for any of the humans to interject a thought or a protest, she simply rose into the air on her powerful wings, gazing on to either the next challenge or the uncovered throne.

After a few breathless minutes in the air, Time dove into the center of the temple, wings slicked back. Krona lost her form over the edge, and could only imagine the last-minute flip she must have executed to land with grace.

The silence that had fallen over the plateau was suddenly shattered by an unearthly shriek. Something shot up from the center of Nature's temple, rocketing into the sky before falling—rigid and inert—back down.

Emotion shoved Melanie and Sebastian out of the way as a great gilded object smacked into the ground right where they'd been standing, leaving a jagged crack in the earth.

It was a throne.

The throne was empty.

The ornate golden branches that made up the arms and legs were studded through with bits of silver and nickel and iron and copper. Instead of cushion, the seat had been laid with pins—sharp needles at odd angles, clearly creating a brutal bench for anyone who dared claim it.

The points were bloodless, stainless. If Nature had ever been forced to sit there, he hadn't in a long, long time.

More objects came hurtling out of the puzzle box, the people dodging them left and right like ants panicking in a sudden rain. Votive offerings, ceremonial boxes, sashes—bits and bobs that had been set at the god's feet for Absolon's own purposes now joined Nature's vacant throne in a haphazard blast pattern across the camp.

More screeching heralded Time's reappearance, not in the sky, but at the temple's rim, where she hauled herself up and clung like an angry hawk, her six raven's wings flaring out behind her. "*Where is he?*" she screamed.

"I-I—we don't know," Melanie said, stooping, whirling to Emotion, begging for compassion. "Tell her we don't *know*."

Krona's throat went sour as she watched Melanie cower and Time seethe. "Absolon must have taken him somewhere," Krona said quickly, going to Melanie, putting a protective arm around her as she continued to implore Emotion—only with her spine straight and her head held high. "Like with you. You weren't in your temple. You were in his keep."

Time flung herself out of the bowl of the puzzle box, swooping down on top of the upturned throne, batting aside a red sash that had landed atop it as though the map to Nature's true location might be hidden beneath. With her black wings angrily outstretched, her tall body looked like a pale, vengeful ghost set against the night, teeth bared and claws at the ready.

Emotion rushed to her side, zhur hands petting over her arms, her crouched thighs, as zhe made reassuring little chirps.

Time calmed significantly, but the feral fire still raged in her eyes.

Krona took careful steps forward, approaching with her hands out, palms open, not wanting to enrage the goddess any further. "Come back with us to our safe house. We have scrolls' and scrolls' worth of reconnaissance—notes on the movement of Absolon's agents, maps of his sacred places. We can piece together where Nature might have gone, but you need to trust us and give us time."

Emotion nodded zhur agreement, gemstone eyes boring into Time's gaze the whole time.

"Fine," the goddess conceded from her perch. "Lead on."

Tantrums and turbulence were not the way of the divine. Not as Krona had ever understood it.

An uncomfortable, chittering doubt wormed its way beneath her skin.

Tray slid up to Krona's side, pitching his voice low. "What about these people?" he whispered. "Will the gods do nothing for them?"

She spared a glance over her shoulder at the refugees. None had been shaken out of their rapture yet—no one moved save to reach their arms to the heavens or to touch their forehead to the ground. Silent prayers stained nearly every lip.

Then she looked to the gods again—the two of them, lost in their own little world, cooing at each other.

Krona both knew and feared the answer to Tray's question:

No, the gods would do nothing.

22

THIBAUT

Thibaut never claimed to be an honest man. Or a brave man. Or even a loyal man. But he had always fancied himself a *smart* man, which surely made him arrogant at the worst times and overconfident when prudence would have been more useful. He'd always known these things about himself, with the same certainty he now knew, without even touching it, that the mortar around the topmost bricks in the right corner of the cell's rear wall was disintegrating.

He stared at it intently while Juliet and Mandip slept fitfully at his sides, tucked beneath his arms. He hoped that if he stared at the stones long enough he might be able to discern what lay beyond. At the moment, attempting to punch through the weak point might simply see them right into another cell for all he could read with his infantile magic.

It was strange—even though he'd watched Krona come into her kairopathy from the beginning, had seen her falter and fail on her earliest attempts to use it, she'd still seemed so capable, so *powerful*, right from the start. If Krona had been a blaze after her remerger, he felt like a single match point: nearly impotent against the dark, useless against a chill.

Magic was like the rest of the world, he supposed. Seemingly straightforward, its rules clean, yet more and more chaotic the more one actually learned and experienced. And he'd always known information was power. The more one gathered, the more one could do, could be.

And the more trouble one could get into, for certain.

The world now pulsed with things for him to know, little tidbits for him to gather like a squirrel foraging for its stores. Where an animal followed pheromones, he followed vibrations, seeking out the knowledge that was calling to him, resonating with his power.

Now that he'd calmed a bit, his initial guilt and worry settling, he was able to better assess those tidbits he'd gathered on their way here.

Though he and the others had been magically mind-controlled to follow Gerome into this cell—like rats running after a piece of particularly ripe-smelling cheese—Thibaut had not been so lost to himself as to fail to notice Gerome gave off a particular sort of vibration. Information about him was just *there*, swimming in the air for Thibaut to pluck and add to his personal repository of insight. That understanding lingered long after he'd been free of Gerome's manipulation, like a trail of perfume that still remained once its wearer had gone.

The man, cold as he seemed, was desperate for intimacy and approval. This was not a secret of his, or else Thibaut would have no hands with which to grasp at it. Instead, it seemed Gerome did not care who knew—he refused to hide it or stoop so low as to consider it a point of shame.

Thibaut wasn't sure yet how to use this snippet of information to his advantage, but he turned it over and over in his mind.

Needing to stretch, he carefully extracted himself from between the others, letting Juliet and Mandip settle against each other, which they both took to with the ease of the unconscious.

Thibaut tried to remember what he could of the maps of the keep, attempting to situate the dungeon in the diagrams he knew, and therefore how close they might be to freedom. He'd hoped his new teliopathy would improve his recall, as it had for Rodrigo, but, alas, his memory seemed both sharp and dull in all the usual places.

He went to each wall, placing his gloved hands against the bricks, trying to sense small vibrations of knowledge there for the taking. There were a few faint ripples—beacons he could follow, little trails to available information, were he free to follow them—but there was nothing at the ready he could pluck.

Hmm. With nothing to be had and no knowledge he needed to give, he tried looking inward—though self-reflection was not his favorite pastime, to be sure—searching the firmament between his cells for the fen he knew was there, but had yet to meet in its healthy form.

His varg had been a gnarled thing—bigger than most, as was typical for pack leaders—with a torn, raggedy ear and a missing eye. Cautious and cunning, it had known it was being stalked, and Thibaut had almost given up the pursuit since the scouts had been following its footprints for days without a single quill in sight.

When old Nannette had initially performed the conjuration to identify its location, he'd hoped it was bottled. Lucky bastards—everyone who'd already had the Borderswatch catch their varg for them. Stealing a bottle was a simple matter of Krona popping in and out of a vault with a jump. No hunting, no struggling, the blasted creature already set for remerging. It was still dangerous, still brutal—and a mistake with a bottle-barker was much more likely to be lethal than a mistake with a fully manifested varg—but despite that, Thibaut would have preferred the readiness of the vapors to the wild gnashing of teeth.

He rubbed absently at the stubs of his fingers through his glove as he tried to identify bits of himself that were more . . . himself, he supposed. Most fen had been called forth in a pinch, when emotions were high and a situation was dire.

Surely being trapped in the Savior's keep without means of escape was dire, though, right?

He willed his magic to disentangle, to manifest outside his body.

It did not listen, of course. *Why would it?* he scoffed at himself.

Perhaps he just had to will it a bit harder.

Clapping his hands lightly together, and widening his stance as though bracing for pushback, he tried again.

He was so focused, straining so hard, that he did not hear footsteps approaching and startled when the cell door shrieked on its hinges.

On the floor, Juliet and Mandip startled as well, but did not get up from where they huddled together, watching, waiting.

That same pale man—eyes shrouded, hair like a waterfall of ink—strode in, followed close behind by Avellino.

The boy's eyes were downcast, watery.

Well, we can't have that, now, can we? Thibaut thought, a peeve peaking in his chest. To imprison them all was one thing. Making Avellino cry was quite another.

Thibaut reached back into his old bag of tricks, sorting through his carefully crafted personas to settle on the type of performance he thought might put Gerome on the wrong foot.

Thumbing thoughtfully at his own chin, Thibaut looked Gerome up and down, then cocked a hip and strode forward with a coy smile on his lips. "I thought I requested a feather bed and a cozy fireplace, instead you give us torture-chamber chic. I ask you, good sir, exactly what kind of an establishment is this?"

Gerome glowered at him. "You'd be wise to keep your tongue still," he said flatly, unamused.

Luckily, *unamused* and *impossible to amuse* weren't the same thing.

Thibaut guessed charm was sorely lacking here among the cultists of the keep, so he put on a smile he'd been told was quite captivating, and turned his body fluid and flirtatious.

"Look," he said, voice sly yet welcoming, "it seems as though we've all misplaced our purses, but if getting an upgrade is a matter of quid pro quo, I'm sure we could come to some kind of . . . arrangement." He quirked an eyebrow—*suggestively.*

Avellino openly balked, and Thibaut nearly laughed. He imagined the very thought of Gerome being susceptible to something so commonplace as seduction was untenable for Avellino. And then, on top of that, imagining his Possessor engaging in intimacies was likely akin to the disquiet of finding one's parents kissing; there were just certain things no one wanted to know about the authority figures in their life.

Gerome held steady as Thibaut approached, his face doing the slightest bit of waltzing through expressions before he schooled himself. The two-step of confusion was Thibaut's favorite bit; the way his brows knit together ever so subtly under the beaded curtain dangling before his eyes.

Thibaut didn't have to use his magic to understand that Gerome was unaccustomed to his prisoners attempting to beguile their way to freedom. He imagined most arrived to the keep either in a pleasant, secret-induced stupor, or they came into this strange place with confusion weighing on their brow and dogging their steps, certain of one thing and one thing only: that this pale man before them held power over their every waking moment.

To be propositioned like some common citizen on a street corner was surely an experience outside of his repertoire.

Thibaut wasn't the only one who'd noted Gerome's confusion—the crack in the smooth plaster of his demeanor. Avellino's eyes widened in a whole new way. That little jolt of surprise on his Possessor's face—however quick, however temporary—was clearly satisfying to behold.

Good, let the boy feel in his heart what his head already knew: Gerome was just a man.

Thibaut got close enough to trail a finger down the front of Gerome's robes. The slick softness of the fabric was surprising. As was its thinness. "It's awfully cold in this drafty old keep, isn't it? I've been known to heat up a room or two."

He reached up to toy with one of the beaded strings dangling from Gerome's headdress, only to have his wrist immediately caught in an iron grip. Without a word, Gerome slowly turned Thibaut's arm away, twisting it at an unnatural angle until he couldn't keep the flirtatious smile on his lips anymore, replacing it with a near-comical grimace. "Ow, ow, okay. Too forward? More of the slow-burn type, perhaps?"

The line of Gerome's lips hardened. He shoved Thibaut toward Avellino with a sneer.

Avellino caught Thibaut around the waist, helped keep him on his feet as he tripped over himself. In return, Thibaut wrapped a reassuring arm around his shoulder, giving a gentle squeeze of reassurance. *We'll get out of here*, he tried to convey. *We're not beat yet.*

"Just not your type?" Thibaut asked, trying to hold Gerome's attention even if he couldn't pique his interest. "Juliet, darling, you know I'd never suggest you lay yourself on the line for the good of the team—"

"Not every gambit need be a seduction, my dear," she piped up.

Thibaut shrugged. "And yet—"

"Enough!" Gerome barked. "That one goes to the lab for crux extraction," he said, pointing at Thibaut. "The other two will have their time taken—"

"No," Avellino blurted.

Disappointment curled Gerome's lip, underneath it a dangerous heat. "Just as the Savior ordered. We will eliminate these distractions, and then you and I will spend a long session eliminating the unnecessary from your mind." With that, he turned his sneer on Thibaut once more. "You, out. Child, take him."

Together, the two of them stepped into the hall with Gerome close behind.

As Gerome turned, Mandip sprang.

But even Thibaut saw it coming.

Mandip did not have the height advantage, though he undoubtedly had better-developed physical fighting skills than the Thalo—not that it mattered. Gerome backhanded him with ease. Like swatting a fly.

The nobleman staggered, and Juliet swooped in to support him.

"You would all do well to remember where you are," Gerome snapped, before slamming the cell door behind him.

When his fearsome gaze turned to Avellino once more, the boy did not have to be told to march.

And then, just like that, a sense of Avellino's thoughts came rushing into Thibaut's mind. He tried not to listen, but he was too unskilled to turn his teliomancy away.

Avellino firmly believed it was his own responsibility to come up with a plan of escape, but at the moment he was at a loss. The four of them were without weapons, without access to guile since Gerome could read their every secret. He couldn't think of a single avenue of action that wasn't likely to have the impending violence dropped on them all the quicker.

Thibaut tried to reassure him without words. He lifted his chin up, and with a slight jerk of the head encouraged the young man to do the same.

We're not beat yet, he echoed to himself. *We're not beat yet.*

Gerome led the way, and Thibaut and Avellino marched behind like good little soldiers. Instead of focusing on the destination—which was likely unpleasant and therefore not worth thinking about—Thibaut took the opportunity to scan the walls and the halls and the occasional passing real human person (though you'd never know it from the devilish vacantness in their stare) for information that might actually help them get the hells out of this mess.

The dungeons were deep in the keep—though not nearly as deep as that varger gallery they'd found themselves in last time. Luckily, his brain seemed to have keyed in to the mouths of several hallways, lining them up swiftly with the maps in his mind, painting him a portrait of several lovely escape routes that were ripe for running, should they all find themselves free to skip about the castle, though he couldn't imagine how his observations were any more useful than Avellino's own intimate knowledge of the keep.

He needed to *learn* something, damn it. Something new.

Only a staircase away Thibaut was surprised to lay eyes on none other than the Savior once again. He nearly pulled up short, but the master of the Thalo was in no way interested in him. The man marched out of a heavy metal door very unlike most other metal doors in the keep, given how new it looked, and Thibaut soon realized that it was through there that they'd been spirited to this cold place. He reached deep into his garbled memory to pull out fits of imagery and sensation. Yes, through there was a room, and another door. A door that led . . . directly to the varger hoard? That seemed highly improbable, but who was he to argue with his own memory?

If that had been their way in, then it was also their most convenient way out.

The Savior pocketed what could have been a key, though Thibaut knew by now that Thalo keys tended to look very different from average keys. What else had been in that room, other than a door to halfway across Arkensyre? A pedestal. Yes, he distinctly recalled a pedestal with a . . . skull atop? A jaw, at the very least. He remembered thinking there was something important about the jaw—something his teliomancy had picked up, but he couldn't quite pin it down.

More twists and turns and towers and ramparts. They passed a flock of small children led by a hooded figure—though *flock* was the wrong word, Thibaut supposed, since it evoked something wild and free and not this adroit set of little in-step automatons no taller than waist high. On and on they strode until, turning a corner, Avellino's steps began to drag. His strides became longer, yet ate up less distance.

Gerome's sharp senses took note sooner rather than later, and he switched places with the boy, smoothly pirouetting to take hold of the prisoner in his stead and stomp at his heels to keep the boy moving.

"These are the halls of the Grand Orchestrators," Avellino protested. "I shouldn't—"

"Your reverence means nothing if it translates to defiance," Gerome hissed at him, quickening the pace.

They passed narrow, heavy doors that pointed into the buttresses of the tall ceiling like fingers directing a gaze toward the heavens. Each sparkled with a crusting of salt, and Avellino shied away from every one, wary of what lay beyond.

"Here," Gerome said eventually, his tone stopping Avellino in his tracks as surely as if he'd come to a dangerous ledge. An enchanted key, plucked from a hidden pocket in Gerome's robes, made the salt dissolve away, leaving nothing but dark iron and the heavy ring of a pull handle.

Despite the trepidation written in every line of his body, Avellino dutifully yanked it open.

Gerome made to propel Thibaut through, but Thibaut resisted.

"Oh, that's all right. I think I'll just dally about a bit in the corridor for a while longer if that's all right with you."

Unwilling to play Thibaut's game, Gerome grabbed him by the collar and hoisted him across the threshold. Thibaut had the sense to fight back—*good* sense or not could be hotly debated. He threw himself gracelessly backward—nearly bashing into Avellino. But Gerome, willowy as he looked, was strong, and did not lose his grip or his poise.

"Close the door," he ordered Avellino as he dragged Thibaut deeper into what at first seemed little more than a storage closet before he waved his hand and the rear wall disappeared, revealing an archway. Beyond was the laboratory he'd spoken of.

Only on rare occasions had Thibaut ever glimpsed an enchanter's lab—usually through a swinging door at the back of a storefront while his wealthy employer bought some enchanted bauble to amuse the two of them in bed (the number of times he'd been gifted a small luststone only to turn around and sell it for something practical like a month's worth of groceries seemed uncountable). Those labs had seemed little different from cobblers' workshops or artists' studios.

This was something else altogether.

A long hall stretched out before them, the walls very unlike the rest of the keep. The Savior's stronghold largely had a sense of heaviness about it; the years weighed on it, the stones, bricks, and mortar lay bare. But here, the walls had been freshly plastered over and painted a soft gray.

Overhead, strange, steady lights—akin to those in the hoard—spotlit workbench after workbench, all lined up on either side of the hall. Test tubes and burners and weights and measures and wires and strings and contraptions Thibaut had no names for met them at every turn, but Gerome stopped at none of them, keeping Thibaut scruffed and pushing him onward.

The lab held an aura of anticipation, like the air on a hilltop before a stormfront: charged. A high-pitched buzzing batted at Thibaut from deep in the walls, and he couldn't guess what generated it, only suspecting it had to be whatever powered the lamps.

No one else occupied the space, and he wondered if this was Gerome's lab alone.

They eventually came to a workstation of Gerome's liking and stopped. The Thalo slowly spun a small nob on the wall and the dim lights became brighter—just like turning up a gas lamp, but without the flicker of flame—revealing a new horror.

The workbench here was much more akin to a dissecting table, large enough for a grown man to splay atop—which one did.

A grown man just Thibaut's size, yet long expired.

The corpse was dried and shriveled, like the mummified bodies of Xyopar, only instead of seated in honor, this one was prone, its back flayed open, the peeled-back, dried skin pinned through with many needles to make it curl and twist like a parody of butterfly wings. Several glass tubes snaked out from its exposed organs and under its ribs, curling away to glass jars where something viscous, like gelatin, had collected in the bottom. It glowed subtly, a pretty aqua blue, like joystones.

At first Thibaut thought the body's arms were curled at its chest, but on closer inspection, its arms were missing—hacked off.

Gerome released Thibaut's collar in order to attend to the remains, first looking to the beakers that had siphoned that strange substance out of the victim before turning to the disposal of the corpse itself.

Thibaut took the opportunity to slowly inch away, gathering his courage, until he suddenly spun on his heel and snagged Avellino by the shoulders, bullying him back the way they'd come. Out of nowhere, a riveted metal barrier clanged down across the width of the lab right in front of them, blocking off any attempted escape, and he jerked the young man in reverse just in time to save him from a lost toe.

Thibaut snapped back around to see Gerome staring at him with the subtlest of smirks. "Do you think me careless?" he asked.

Thibaut searched for a retort—the sort of scathing remark he was usually quick with—but found himself at a loss. He was usually good at masking his genuine fear with flippancy, with charisma, but this time his dread was getting the better of him. The noose was tightening, the corridors narrowing. The walls were closing in, and a last-minute save was looking less and less likely by the moment.

This couldn't . . . couldn't genuinely be *it*, could it? Theadore de Rex, done for at last?

He forced himself to take a breath, even though his lungs had frozen, gone rigid like he was already as stiff as the corpse Gerome had unceremoniously pushed off the table and onto a waiting trolley, and then—

Thibaut felt the edges of his vision dapple and his head go fuzzy as if with drink, and he only had a moment to resist—to try to deny the shifting reality—before he was consumed.

It was an unnervingly familiar feeling. This was his third time directly under a Thalo's thrall, but it was no less disturbing for it. All Gerome had to do to take him over for a handful of minutes was send him into one of his own secrets. Make him relive a moment or play out a private fantasy. The first time, a Thalo had used a memory of Vanessa. When Gerome had brought him here from the hoard, he'd used an old shame; the first time he'd eaten his own game.

It had been in the Dregs, just after his grandfather died. The old man may have worked him to exhaustion dredging glass pieces out of the sewers with his nimble little fingers, but he'd also been the only person guaranteeing young Theo a warm place to sleep and steady meals.

Being a Dreg, perhaps Thibaut should have been more self-reliant as a fourteen-year-old, but facts being what they were, he'd never been good at the basics. So when the old man's cancer finally got him, Theo had lived off the neighbors' charity for as long as he dared, then begged and bartered until he couldn't beg or barter anymore.

And then there had been the rats. The only warm places to sleep where a useless boy wouldn't be shooed away were also the warm places where rats swarmed. He hadn't been able to catch one to save his life, but when a section of old sewer wall had collapsed and brained a handful of them, he'd found himself with fresh meat for the first time in nearly a year.

He didn't know how to clean them. He didn't know how to properly gut them or cook them.

He ate the first one raw and damn near whole.

And had nearly died of some intestinal disease for his overeagerness.

He hadn't attempted to prepare his own kills after that—had gone back to bartering, with his body and otherwise.

Honestly, when Gerome had let him loose from that awful memory, he was half-surprised he hadn't been gnawing on Mandip's ankles while under. That all-consuming hunger had been so present, his belly still ached with it when he came to.

And now? This time . . .

Not a memory. A private fantasy.

A wedding. How could he be at a wedding? They were at war—with the Valley, with the Savior, with themselves . . .

A wedding. Thibaut looked down at himself, at the fine midnight-blue suit he was wearing, at the pearl-sized joystones embroidered around the cuffs.

Not just any wedding. *His* wedding.

The air was sweet, but crisp. Autumn in Lutador had always been his favorite. The changing leaves, the welcoming cocoon of a warm blanket in the morning, ciders and pies and chrysanthemums and pansies. Mirthhouse was aglow down the hill, and garlands had been strung across the low stone walls of the old sheep fields. Instead of a proper marriage tent he stood beneath a silk awning, and there, at the base of the hill, was Krona, striding up to meet him.

Her gown was all ruffles, like an extravagant cake, and he could only assume that was Juliet's doing. Joystones cascaded over her like the many drops of a waterfall, and she seemed dressed far too grandly for such a simple venue.

Then again, she always seemed grand. There was no scene that could properly contain her.

He couldn't look away as she approached. Butterflies invaded his stomach and his heart did warm little somersaults in his chest.

Biting his lip and furrowing his brow, he tried to remember how they'd gotten here—the proposal.

Early on, he'd truly believed he had no interest in marrying again. What was the point, after all, given the way they lived? It would change nothing.

But the more the certainties of the world crumbled, the more he privately fantasized about the joy of it. And still, he hadn't brought it up with Krona because it all seemed so . . . domestic. And she wasn't exactly the type to find comfort or relaxation in domesticity. There wasn't time, anyway. Frivolous things like weddings and parties had gone by the wayside. They'd had one simple handfasting these past three years, and that had taken all of half an hour, which suited the couple just fine. Thibaut longed for something grander for himself and Krona. A real celebration for them. They were mired in war every day; it seemed its own defiance to actively give time over to an acknowledgment of love.

Now, try as he might, he could not remember proposing. Nor Krona proposing to him. And yet it must have happened, how else would they have ended up here?

He blinked and she was already halfway up the hill, dressed in a simple, billowing aqua blouse and black high-waisted riding trousers. He could have sworn that just a moment ago she was wearing a grandiose wedding dress. But no, couldn't be. And this—this was more like her. This felt right.

And just a single joystone adorned her person—a teardrop-shaped aquamarine set in a black velvet choker.

They would exchange promises to each other here privately, beneath their makeshift tent, before the priests and the guests joined them. Her smile was so warm, so lovely, so unconcerned when she reached him, and his heart swelled as he took her hand. When had he ever seen her so happy? *He'd* done that—he'd been able to give her that.

She leaned in close, her breath hot as she whispered sweet vows into his ear. But he found he couldn't quite hear them—couldn't quite make out the words. His brow furrowed and he parted his lips to ask her to say it all again—and then to *beg* her as he felt the world slipping sideways and his mind go foggy.

And then it was as if the wedding and party had come and gone in a blur. It must have. It must have. For now it was late at night and he was slowly removing his fine suit, tossing each piece to drape over the changing screen. He felt tired suddenly. So tired. But he'd be damned if he was going to miss his wedding night.

Finally naked, he flopped down face first onto the bed, folding his arms around his pillow and burrowing his face into its softness to wait.

He heard, rather than saw, Krona enter the room, and he kept his eyes shut for the big reveal, expecting she would have picked something special to wear for tonight. Likewise, he couldn't wait for whichever little delights she brought out to tease him with. Toys for her to use on him, or vice versa.

When he felt fingertips glide down his bare spine, he shivered.

There came a soft intake of breath, and he braced himself for her orders.

"Wake up," someone—most definitely *not* Krona—demanded.

His eyes shot open and he attempted to sit up. He was not in their bed. He wasn't even in Mirthhouse. He and Krona weren't married, and they weren't about to ravish each other within an inch of their lives.

Instead, he was spread out on Gerome's damned dissecting table, face planted in a lumpy head rest, his hands tied under it. Similarly, his ankles were bound, as were his elbows. He could raise his head and wiggle his hips, but had little range of motion beyond that. He wasn't completely naked—thank the gods—but he had partially undressed in his stupor, leaving his back bare to the cold castle air.

Gerome made no snide remarks about what he'd seen in Thibaut's head, more concerned with laying out his implements. Yet Thibaut still found himself blushing, of all things, hot embarrassment ruddying his cheeks. The fantasy was secret, yet it was so tame. Submissive and homey. He fancied himself a cad, but deep down all he truly wanted was domestic bliss.

And gods forbid *Avellino* had heard anything he might have mumbled out loud.

That was neither here nor there in the moment. A pleasant dream had guided him into the predicament, but no pleasant dream would get him out of it.

He read the auras of information vibrating through the table, his restraints, and the jars with little effort. This close, touching the equipment, their purposes were as clear as if Gerome had monologued about it himself.

He knew what the man was about to do to him, and why.

Not all those who dodged the time tax were so lucky as Sebastian, it seemed. Many of them ended up here, on this very table, or one just like it, their pneuma slowly drained from them, coaxed to the surface through blood and pain where it could be siphoned off and distilled into something the Savior could . . . ingest.

That was how he'd come to possess all five magics.

You are what you eat, he thought manically.

Good old-fashioned needles were enough to remove magic and trap it in inert materials, but living things either burned through the foreign energy in the blink of an eye or rejected it outright. You couldn't simply inject a person with a magic not their own—it was like a varg trying to bury itself in the wrong host. Injury was the only outcome.

But if, instead, the pneuma was pulled out and distilled, gentled through the digestive tract, then a bit of it could be harnessed.

A tidy bit of cannibalism. *Just a smidgen of human consumption, who would balk at that?* he thought to himself sarcastically.

And, just as eating once did not stave off hunger forever, so too did the Savior have to partake again and again and again to properly maintain his ill-gotten abilities.

Gerome was akin to a chef, then. Or a butcher. Ready to cut away the best bites for his one and only customer.

Cold sweat broke out along Thibaut's bared spine.

He was here to be *eaten*.

Eaten, just as many people in this position had been before him. He tried to read weakness in the restraints, a way to break them or slip them, but he sensed nothing useful. He sensed no past escapes and, even worse, no swift deaths.

You have something those other little magical snacks didn't, he told himself. A power only those who'd paid the tax and been torn apart and put back together again could possess. And it was about to tear the lid off this whole situation. His fen would burst forth, revealing a new kind of terrible power to Gerome, and he and Avellino would book it the hells out of here.

He waited.

Any minute now.

Come on, he silently urged.

His fen sure was taking its sweet time.

Exactly how close did one need to be to tragedy for fenri to get a clue?

Somewhere beyond his vision, Avellino let out a quiet whimper. Moments later, a blade caressed Thibaut's back. The scalpel's edge was like ice as it flanked his spine, running down the length of it on the left in one fluid motion. He cried out and jerked at the sting, but there was no fierce, searing pain until that scalpel slid sideways, nimbly slicing his epidermis from the musculature beneath.

Gerome meticulously peeled him, pulling up his skin like the rind of an orange.

Thibaut couldn't help but scream.

Gritting his teeth, clamping down on the pain, Thibaut called out to his fen, *begging* it to rise, to surge forth the way Krona's had.

"Look how it just seeps to the surface," Gerome said in awe as he worked, moving to Thibaut's other side, leaving his back raw and open, burning and wet.

He flexed his fingers against the headrest when Gerome shoved the tubing into his open wounds, needing his pained energy to go somewhere—wishing it was flowing out of him in the form of an ethereal creature he had yet to meet.

When the siphoning began, there was a ringing in his ears, his body crying out in alarm, but not nearly loud enough. His head swam, his stomach swam, his vision swam.

"Pay attention," Gerome snapped somewhere behind him, and it took a moment to realize he was talking to Avellino.

Thibaut assumed the process would make him weaker by the minute—both magically and physically. If he couldn't dredge up his fen, he'd end up just another husk like the poor sap who'd preceded him.

And if that was his fate, that was his fate. But he wasn't going to let his magic bleed away without using it first to the fullest.

He called out with his mind, pushing the images he'd seen on his walk from the cells, pushing every little bit of knowledge he'd gathered since alighting in the keep, hoping if he pushed hard enough that the information could squeeze past his companions' ears and settle in their brains. He tried to picture both Juliet and Mandip, tried to envision whispering the knowledge in their ears, envision pointing out the loose brick and the Savior's door and the hidden labs. He squeezed his eyes shut against the pain and fed his thoughts through the air.

Around him, Gerome positioned his tubes and pipets, digging something sharp into one of Thibaut's muscles before letting out a little satisfied hum as a glowing sort of condensation began to gather on the inside of the glass. "There it is," he whispered to himself.

A jagged sort of lurch took hold of Thibaut's body. A swelling sensation roiled under the bits of his still-intact skin. He was expanding, becoming greater than himself. Becoming *outside* himself. Every molecule in his body seemed to be duplicating—or maybe tearing itself in two. There he was, on the table, but there he also was, lifting up, out—like a ghost.

He nearly laughed in triumph. Finally—*finally*. That damned ugly pack leader that had taken his fingers and fused with his form was coming untangled again.

Ugh, he could cry with the relief of it. He could crow, he could shout. He definitely *would* lord it over Gerome—would mock him mercilessly—if there was anything left of the Thalo puppet once his fen had had its way and Thibaut was finally free.

The burgeoning was fast—but Gerome was faster.

Thibaut jolted at the first strange *pricking* sensation. It was like a needle had caught in his flesh instead of fabric, only his "flesh" was inches from his body, hovering away from his form while still connected. It was real pain and an echo of pain all in one. At first, he thought the strange, layered sensation was due to shock—to his open wounds and taut skin. But the pricking became a pushing, a borehole widened in his flesh-that-wasn't. He writhed, tightening his back and shifting his shoulders to try to throw off the sensation, ignoring how close the scalpel might still be to his spine.

"Seems His theory was correct," Gerome mused. "Takes a tad more than quintbarrel needles."

Thunk.

Thunk.

Fire roared through Thibaut's bones like they'd been struck by a brand. He craned his neck, looking over his shoulder to see two massive metal stakes crisscrossed over his spine, struck through two hazy, layered masses rising up out of his body like beetle wings. The masses even moved like a dying insect, jerking and fluttering as the last sparks of life sent mismatched signals through its limbs.

It was his fen. Stuck half in and half out. Formed yet unformed.

"How ghastly," Gerome mumbled, but Thibaut barely heard him.

His ace in the hole, his loaded die—the one thing he was counting on to save him—was still vulnerable to the same metals as it had been in varg form.

Distantly, he heard Avellino choke on a sob.

An uninvited sense of *resignation* washed through Thibaut. For the first time in his life, his imagination failed him. He couldn't envision a way to beg, barter, con, or cut his way out of this one. He didn't know how long it would take to drain him of his pneuma—perhaps he'd become a husk all the faster given that his magic had already partially solidified—but he doubted a rescue could be mounted in time to save him.

He felt Avellino's thoughts suddenly. Ideas he was purposefully trying to push to the fore of his mind with open honesty so that Gerome could not use cryptopathy to detect them. Plans. Plans to fight, escape. Thibaut couldn't tell if the plans were purposefully being shared with him, but each was flawed, pit the young man against his former Possessor in a confrontation he couldn't hope to win.

Gently, Thibaut tried to tell him *no.* He couldn't share his feelings—the resignation—with him, but he tried to encourage him to focus on the others. On Mandip. On Juliet. Just as he now focused, calling out with his teliomancy in the simplest terms: *Brick. Door. Key. Escape.*

23

HAILWIC

In a Time and Place Unknown

The professor's death was the beginning of the end. Fey left the RFR without a leader, and—given the failure of feir primary plan to remove Uphrasia from power—without a clear direction.

The resistance fractured. Splintered. Focus spiraled.

And Uphrasia saw her chance to increase her violence.

She'd already divided out many Physiopaths into detainment ghettos. Now she attacked them openly; if there was even a hint of unrest or protest, she did not hesitate to meet thrown stones with bullets, broken windows with magic-based ballistae. A pipe bomb was answered with a missile. Bikes with tanks.

Neighborhoods near the wall collapsed—on *both* sides, in Remotus and Radix. All resisters were pushed back as Uphrasia's "cleared territories" widened.

Hailwic's university was among the casualties. The campus was now a crater because one person there had dared attack their precious dictator.

Ground had been won and lost in neighboring nations as well. Uphrasia expanded Radix's borders north and south—well past the Capuchin Crater and the mountains, invading the smaller countries there, claiming it was her right since they'd all once been part of the original Giggus Empire.

A handful of Radix's allies poured resources into her military while most of the rest of the world cut her out of their economic circles despite Radix's size and influence. Still, many of the most powerful nations continued to do nothing but dither while Uphrasia mowed down her own citizens and violently blurred the edges of bordering nations.

After two years of floundering, Dr. Theesius came out as the clear leader of the largest chunk of the professor's originals, and maintained control of the tunnels. Zoshim, Punabi, Hailwic, and Glensen had all become high-profile rebels with their own legions, and added their strength to Kinwold's bid for control. Theesius put their trust in them in return, seeking counsel, assigning them each more and more responsibilities.

They rallied, looking to unify.

The professor had fallen, but the group refused to let go of feir hopes, feir vision for a free people.

In those devastating years that followed, they simply focused on reestablishing themselves, on recruitment and aid. They became sandbags against a deluge, beams propping up a skyscraper about to collapse, cotton balls soaking up blood from a severed artery.

Survival mode for people and organizations looks much the same: they worked minute to minute, simply trying to keep everyone breathing and all in one piece.

Smoke filled the air—chemical laced and acrid. Hailwic could barely see as she and Zoshim zigzagged across the sky, surveying the new damage, tagging dangerous, half-collapsed buildings and looking for survivors still in peril.

The front lines, as always, were hostile—though Hailwic hated thinking of this neighborhood, with its corner market and playground and post office, as the *front lines*. Front lines implied incursion or attrition. It implied a border land, where oil and water met. Where unstoppable forces and immovable objects tested their labels. It implied opposites. Contraries. Antitheses.

It felt so wrong because all around her she saw nothing but the same peoples. The lines being drawn were false as anything. A distinction of whim.

Her sentiments—her philosophical musings on the matter—didn't mean anything to the woman crawling out from under the rubble of what had been the bodega. Or the grandfather calling for his grandchild from the ruined apartment building across the street. Or the hundreds of other people—black-and-blue and bloodied—who were still trying to take stock of what had just happened to their ward, its residents already pushed to the fringes before this, and now . . .

Hailwic and Zoshim flew high above the recently mortared street, circling above, each kept aloft by a single pair of wings. They weren't the only ones—the pair headed a small fleet. Teams of two broke off in the four cardinal directions, surveying the damage.

Today, Shim wore a feminine face, but not one that might have mistakenly marked them as sisters. Feline angles and wholly unnatural cat ears framed slitted purple eyes. He had not forgotten the whiskers.

Did the two of them look like angels from below? Or vultures? Perhaps it was arrogant to think these people—with the recent blasts still ringing in their ears—had even noticed the birds-that-weren't eyeing them from above.

That news thopter in the distance had noticed, though. No doubt a haunting image of bird people would make the nightly propaganda reel.

The sounds of crumbling and sobbing met the twins as they swirled lower. Names called to the wind merged and distorted. So many people were looking for loved ones in the chaos that their shouts blended and became unintelligible. The creaking of buildings under pressure—steel ready to buckle, cracked cement ready to powder—underscored the cacophony of tragedies already in progress.

Using mobile communication units strapped to their wrists, the twins relayed their findings to Kinwold and Punabi's teams on the ground, noting all they could: blocked streets, groups of survivors, blazing fires, and burst waterlines.

Here and there, survivors did what they could to save the remains of their lives. A man bleeding from the head used his physiopathy to gently sever his neighbor's smashed leg to free them from the slab of wall trapping them. Elsewhere, a Kairopath stopped the flames from advancing just long enough for a dog to scurry out of an alleyway. A Cryptopath searched for hidden pockets of air in a collapsed elevator shaft, hoping to find her family inside.

People did what they could for others instead of simply fleeing—even knowing it could damn them further. And every time a Physiopath flexed their magic to aid the person next to them they put themselves at special risk.

No one with even a hint of compassion would blame a person for using everything at their disposal to stay alive, but that was part of Uphrasia's game: back people into a corner, then blame them when they have no other choice but to use their forbidden magic.

Everyone who lived here had been displaced from Radix either because they were a Physiopath, or because they loved a Physiopath. They'd been promised years ago that if they just left Radix proper, if they segregated themselves in Remotus, they could be safe and together.

But it was a lie.

Any society willing to push some of its people to the fringe—to the edges—was just as willing to push them *off* the edge in the end.

A small brown hand caught Hailwic's attention, reaching up from a pile of rebar and brick. Dust and blood clung to the little fingers, and a small, weak voice cried out for help.

Even as she noticed the hand, the rubble collapsed further, sending a dust cloud billowing into the already smoke-thick air. The little voice cut off in pain.

Hailwic didn't hesitate. "There," she said, before folding her wings and diving.

Swooping low, she wasn't sure she could land. Her weight alone might shift the rubble's delicate balance and collapse the small pocket of life inside. Even with her kairopathy, she wasn't sure she could hold the collapse at bay long enough to muscle her way into the debris.

Hovering, she grabbed hold of the largest slab, only able to lift one end because it had found itself high centered on a pointed fulcrum. But when she moved it, the gap created enough room for an iron beam to slide. She caught it with her magic, forcing it to pause as Zoshim fluttered to her side, reaching for the child's hand while changing bits of sharp glass to sugar fluff and attempting to move aside a crumbling set of bricks with his free hand.

Between the two of them, it still wasn't enough. What was left of the building rumbled beneath them, the strain of the careful puzzle of broken pieces giving way and threatening to fold further.

"Pull!" Hailwic told Zoshim, but as he yanked on the small arm another chunk of cement slid. "Wait, wait!" she yelled, backpedaling. "I can't catch that. I don't have enough hands!" She strained to control the pieces she'd already lifted.

She startled as invisible fingers prodded beneath her skin and tugged at her ribs, gasping and gritting her teeth as a rib on each side folded outward, not breaking the skin, instead molding it along itself, growing ligaments. If she hadn't been accustomed to the pain and crawling sensations of transformation, she would have screamed. Even as it was, she felt like she wanted to slip out of her skin to get away from her own body.

"What are you—"

Her new limbs split at the ends, grew joints, nails—fingers.

"You're right. We need more. More hands," Zoshim said.

He'd begun transforming himself as well. His new arms mirrored her new arms, and neither sibling stopped to consider their extra limbs, they simply used them. Digging at the rubble was no less tiring, but the ability to manipulate twice as many bricks—to hold and dig and pull and push in four different directions all at the same time—meant they had the hands they needed.

Together, they pulled the child into the light.

But the boy tried to get away. The tears of terror that had made tracks through the ash on his brown cheeks started anew. He'd been terrified during the bombing, terrified while he was trapped, and now he was terrified of the monsters yanking him free.

"Shh, we're here to help. Shh, it's okay." Hailwic tried to calm him.

His screams did not abate and the two of them held him tighter, but it was like trying to control a wriggling fish. He attempted to dive back into the hole—back toward death—and Hailwic did the only thing she could think of and used the last of her energy to put him in a time bubble.

Glensen headed the emergency medical station at the base of a nearby communications tower, and Kinwold themself had come to oversee that the tents and supplies were efficiently set up and distributed. The rebels created a waystation just outside the blast zone, where Punabi and zhur team could lead the pockets of victims they'd found.

Hailwic and Zoshim brought the boy to the medics, and Hailwic tried to ignore the way many of the people—even other Physiopaths—stared apprehensively at the many-limbed rescuers.

Wings were one thing. They were elegant—a fanciful modification many people could imagine having, wanting. Additional arms were too uncanny. They brought to mind insects, spiders. Things that crept and bit and darted into the cold, secret cracks.

Hailwic held her head high and didn't let the stares bother her. Once they'd completed the mission Zoshim would return their bodies to their natural states anyway.

Before taking off again, Hailwic caught Punabi through the haze of bomb smog, zhur skin glowing faintly—a beacon for the wandering—leading a group of the lost, offering emotiopathic intervention to those who needed calming.

⁂

Long after, when the streets had been cleared and evening fell, Kinwold Theesius and his field generals were still at work, cataloging the last of the damage, arranging transport for the displaced who still needed it.

Zoshim flew to the comms tower's pinnacle, perching atop its blinking red light, and their flock of scouts followed, covering the metal structure just as surely as giant birds. Hailwic landed right below Zoshim, clinging with her new limbs. He commended them all, then in turn sent one after the other fluttering to the ground as he reached out to fold their wings back into their bodies—sealing them away, molding them back into the forms they'd woken up in.

Eventually, only the siblings remained.

As the sun began to set, the movement below became more subdued. Generators clanged and sputtered, and several large floodlights clicked on. The shouting had long disappeared, but the sobbing . . . that still reached Hailwic on her high perch.

A chill followed the sunset, and in the fading light so too did the smoke seem to fade. But when the twilight blinked away and the town's lights came on, it was clear where the damage lay: a dozen blocks were blacked out completely. Like a hole in the world.

She waited for Zoshim to suggest they see if Glensen needed additional help, but he remained silent, sitting on his haunches with his wings folded behind him, his two sets of hands rubbing and wringing as his mind turned an unspoken problem over and over.

The tower's thin metal bars were cool under Hailwic's palms, and she leaned her forehead against one, appreciating how it diffused the heat of the day. "Do you remember those really cheap Jaffa cakes Grandma used to bring us?"

"The ones where the flavor of the plastic wrap had somehow infused itself into the jam?"

She huffed a small laugh. "Yeah."

"They make those in Nosbeq," he said. "Can't get them anymore, since they cut off trade with Radix."

"True," she said, reaching into her pocket to pull out a crinkling package. "Except—" She held up the clear wrapper with two cakes inside, sitting unassumingly, if a little smashed, in their paper cups. "The bodega owner was handing out whatever wasn't pinned under the rubble. Guess zhe had an old box of these. Way past their prime, sure, but with all the preservatives I can't imagine they taste that bad two years past their expiration date."

She pulled open the plastic, and the essence of chocolate and orange assaulted her nose—welcome, after the day's burnt-tar smells. Her second set of arms let her pass one of the cakes up with ease.

"The bodega owner lost everything, and still . . ." he said solemnly, contemplating the cake instead of stuffing it immediately between his teeth like he used to when they were kids. "Those who have so little often give so much."

"Because they know what it's like," she said. "To go without."

He nodded, then stared at the treat.

Nostalgia could be many things—a joyful comfort or a barb-tailed whip. Jaffa cakes were from happier times. *Family* times.

The specter of their parents' ultimate fate still hung over them—*would* hang over them forever. They'd both sought emotiopathic help dealing with it, both only trusting Punabi to guide them through it, but had never spoken directly to each other about it.

Hailwic wasn't sure they ever would.

Guilt still flourished in her gut daily, blooming like poisonous algae that she tried to fight with the algicide of righteous anger. *None* of this would have happened if her parents hadn't spooked themselves into turning Zoshim in. The four of them might have been at home, together, during Uphrasia's post–assassination attempt address, all reeling in their own private horror over the implications. Or, better yet, maybe they would have been watching the announcement Hailwic had hoped for: that Uphrasia was dead. That someone—anyone at all—had killed her.

They'd tried to get their son killed, Hailwic told herself. They'd tried to kill her brother and her by extension. They deserved what they got. They'd *earned* it.

She knew Zoshim didn't see it that way. He'd never blamed them. Even after the truth of Hailwic's first accusations had been proven to him, he'd excused them, giving them leeway for their own fears in a harsh system.

Hailwic refused to fight with him about it, but she could never forgive them. They'd done exactly what the system required to perpetuate itself. They'd chosen their own lives—their own comfort, over their child's, and she would never, ever see them as anything but boot-licking cowards.

But she'd never meant for this to happen. She'd decided long ago that they were dead to her, but she'd never wanted this.

Their public execution had been pure revenge on Uphrasia's part. They hadn't known where Hailwic was. They hadn't seen her, or been contacted by her, in years. She'd never let on to Uphrasia that they were estranged, but if they'd been questioned it would have been readily apparent they'd had nothing to do with their daughter's plot.

It was *her* fault.

If she'd killed Uphraisa cleanly—if she'd killed Uphrasia *at all*—they would still be alive.

This chocolate-and-orange reminder of the past could push Zoshim further away, as much as she hoped it would draw him closer.

Did he blame her as she blamed herself?

Or had he given her the same noble absolution he'd given their parents?

She studied him closely, deciding she wouldn't take a bite until he did.

A faint line appeared down the center of his brow as he was drawn into his own memories. She watched it smooth over, then wrinkle again.

"I had a Jaffa cake at my last meal," he said suddenly.

She furrowed her brow. "Your last meal?"

"The one I had before going to your company," he said. "When I thought I was going to die."

Hailwic nearly let the cake fall from her hand. Zoshim never talked about his time in prison—never mentioned anything between leaving home and being absorbed into the rebellion. She almost said, *I'm sorry no one told you it was an escape plan,* or *I'm sorry I got you caught in the first place,* but he spoke before she could.

"I saw a lot of last meals. *Real* last meals." His gaze shifted from the cake out into the night, toward the blackened city blocks. "Lots of people had their last meals today."

He finally slipped the treat between his lips, biting into it with a sort of automatic absence rather than the pleasant nostalgia she'd hoped to invoke. She did the same, letting the tartness and underlying toxic flavor of plastic sharpen her senses for a moment before the chocolate glaze smoothed it all over.

The cakes were gone too soon, and a heavy silence came after.

"I'm sorry I used physiopathy to change you without asking first," he blurted after long minutes. "I didn't think before I . . ." He waved at one set of arms with the other, his skin crimson in the flashing light. "It comes so naturally to me, just morphing in the moment. No wonder that boy wanted to crawl back into the rubble. We look like the stuff of nightmares."

"He's *living* in a nightmare," she countered. "If flying spider people terrify him while they're saving him, so be it. If this is how we work more efficiently, I can tolerate a child's cries. At least it means he's still alive."

"But he wasn't the only one."

There was an expectancy in the statement, like he was probing for something. Hailwic didn't know what he was getting at, and answered with a shrug. "The nightmare is vast."

Months of turmoil in the southeastern part of the country bled into months of turmoil in the northeast. Uphrasia's army barely gave them a moment to breathe.

Soon it wasn't only the twins and their scouts who transformed before missions. Kinwold decided they could all become icons for the new generation.

If Uphrasia was going to use physiopathic transformation as a boogeyman either way, why not lean in? Instead of pandering to the violence that insisted *if you only behaved, we wouldn't hurt you*; *if you act* normal *you'll have no cause to fear,* they'd show everyone that physiopathy could be hopeful and beautiful and plentiful. That there was richness in embracing all five magics, and that true evil lay in spurning one—or even elevating one—over the others.

Punabi knew zhe could be both a better beacon and distraction if zhe could amplify zhur natural glow into something searing. Zhe became a walking crystal, faceted and sublime. The Charging Light.

Kinwold felt they, in many ways, were the rebellion's shield, and chose to reflect that in a form that came to be known as the Colossus. It took many Physiopaths—under the entwined direction of Glensen and Zoshim—to grow Kinwold to new heights. They stretched, up and up, letting all remnants of clothing fall away without shame as their body shifted into a hulk devoid of all signs of sex or even specificity. As they grew, they lost defining feature after defining feature, their skin becoming a dark gray, their face flattening until it was a circular shield of steel—like something a knight of old might have carried—etched with a coat of arms representing a new, reunited Radix.

They grew larger each time they transformed until they were stories high, their shadow stretching far across the staging ground. So big they could swat war thopters out of the sky.

All four of them became symbols of the rebellion—of evolution and progress.

Zoshim offered to alter Glensen as well, but fey chose to remain in feir typical form for feir own reasons.

"I do best with the hands I've already got," fey said to Hailwic once. "But if I *were* ever to become something other than what I already am, it would be a tree. You know why? Because no one expects a tree to do much; give shade, a little fruit. But mostly a tree just gets to *be*. The day I can be a tree is the day I know rest has finally come."

As the rebellion regained its footing—despite the fracturing of the movement—a new era of hope lay on the horizon.

Only in retrospect would Hailwic realize there was a catch.

That was the thing about the horizon: no matter how hard you chased it, technically, it could never be reached.

24

KRONA

Even as she made the lens, Krona knew something was wrong. Jumping to Mirthhouse was second nature at this point—easy and comforting. She could pinpoint it from anywhere, feel the warmth of its hearth and the din of its people as soon as she reached for it with her magic. But it felt different this time. Quiet. Cold. There was a stillness to the lens—usually capturing a moment across time and space was difficult to pin down, like trying to catch a bird; one had to be firm enough to take hold, yet delicate enough not to simply smash through. Instead of trying to catch a moment, it was like looking at a painting. Unchanging. One moment very like the next.

It was unnerving, and yet she experienced it all in the blink of an eye. The sense of wrongness came on fast and strong, but she was already moving, already jumping through.

With Tray's hand in hers, they, Melanie, Sebastian, and the two gods formed a chain, stringing through the lens to land—

Land somewhere Krona didn't recognize.

Her boots landed on a surreal, uneven surface. Thousands of small figurines—all of nearly identical shape and size but made of many different materials—covered a broad swath of chilly highland. There was no clue to their purpose, how they'd gotten here, or who had created such an obscene pile of statuettes.

Everyone took their own exploratory steps outward; various sounds of surprise and confusion were muttered as they went.

The whole area stank like a slaughterhouse.

Krona could not imagine how she'd miscalculated so drastically. She'd had trouble *landing* her jumps in the past, but she'd always had impeccable aim. They were in the lowest part of the Lutadorian mountains, about where Mirthhouse should be, no question.

But there was no house.

She stumbled upon a human leg with no owner. Not far off, a torso—ripped open, gnawed through. The individual parts weren't recognizable, and Krona's mind still refused to put the pieces together—refused to open *this* cursed puzzle box—until she came upon a body that still possessed its head.

Nannette.

No.

Gods.

Tho old woman had always been quick with a smile and so good with children—

Children.

Abby.

Krona went to her knees, slumping like a rag doll, her bone wings flagging, her stomach filled with ratty cotton—gauzy and lifeless. There was so much sudden grief in her it whited out her mind, burnt out nerves, and blurred her sense of self.

She couldn't comprehend what had happened here. She made a backward-looking lens to try to solve the mystery, but her magic was too limited. She couldn't look back far enough. Whatever the cause, death had happened. Tragedy had happened. Their home and their friends and their family were all *gone.*

Her ears must have been stuffed with the same cotton as her stomach, because the horrified calls that followed when her companions came to the same conclusion were distant and echoing. Far off and dulled. Muted by Krona's shock.

She had no idea how much time passed as she sat there staring at what was left of Nannette. Figures moved around her. There were sobs she vaguely identified as Melanie's. Fingers landed on Krona's shoulder, shook her, but she did not respond. Tray's voice accompanied them, but she did not acknowledge him.

It wasn't until giant, shimmering raven's wings dragged across the rubble in front of her that she snapped back into herself.

Time held one of the tiny figurines in the palm of one giant hand, examining it closely. Krona picked one up as well. The depicted creature looked like a mouse, maybe. Or a wingless bat. Its arms were curled in a strange rigor, like a dead spider, but what caught Krona were its rows and rows of bared teeth.

"Vipnika," Time said thoughtfully.

Krona didn't know what that meant, but she couldn't stand the analytical tilt of the goddess's head, the way everything around her seemed a *curiosity* and not a tragedy.

"Fix this!" Krona shouted, flinging the figurine away and rising unsteadily. She threw her arms wide and spread her bone wings. "Undo this!"

Time's gaze snapped in her direction. "I can't," she said flatly, balling her fist, trapping the figurine inside.

Krona didn't try to hide her disgust. "You can't or you won't?" she demanded, flinging each syllable from her tongue like a razor blade, hoping it would cut.

"I can*not*!" Time snapped. Then, more softly, "Truly, I cannot."

"Then what is the point of you?" Krona hissed, turning her back, striding away as best she could through the strange drifts. There were many things she'd imagined the gods to be, yet *cruel*, *indifferent*, and—ultimately—*fallible* hadn't been among them.

She felt the specter of Time's fury billow against her spine before she heard the beating of the goddess's massive wings or her bare feet kicking through the hoard of figurines. Still, Krona did not cower. She did not turn to confront her anger, nor did she stop walking away. She simply waited for whatever punishment, whatever toll, whatever *penalty* Time would make her pay for her insolence.

A beat passed. The goddess landed no blows, magical or otherwise. A squawk and a growl made Krona risk a glance over her shoulder. Emotion stood between her and Time, feet planted firmly in the rubble, zhur forearm slung up against Time's collar bones to bar her advance.

The two of them had a tense, silent conversation through gaze alone, and Krona still expected to be smote when they were through.

The looks Time threw at Emotion were heated in more ways than one, and the way her hands came up to land on Emotion's narrow hips, gripping fiercely before pulling the line of Emotion's body close spoke of an intimacy very different from that of parent and child.

New questions swirled in Krona's stomach, only half-formed.

Emotion chirped once softly at Time before the goddess enfolded the pair of them inside her wings, creating a curtain of feathers to shield them from the human's sight.

And then, in a blink, the two of them were gone.

Vanished. Away. Gone.

The gods were *gone.*

And Krona and the others were left with nothing.

She went to Melanie's side, where she cradled a blue security blanket to her chest. Krona collapsed beside her, dropping down on loose limbs made heavy and useless with grief.

How had this happened?

How was this possible?

Krona's eyes fell to the blanket, its blue blurring as the hollowness and shock were swamped over by a smoldering, angry version of grief. This anger was not like the anger she'd felt after Thibaut and the others had been stolen. This was aimless, free of a vector. She could not strike at anything in particular or scream at anything in particular or blame anything in particular because her mind could not make sense of what had happened.

So the anger turned inward and morphed into shame.

The four of them drifted like ghosts for some time, slumping when they could not stand, wandering the dunes of figurines and body parts when they could not keep still.

Tray began gathering the remains, laying them as respectfully as he could outside the mounds. Eventually Krona joined him in the task, leaving Melanie and Sebastian to cry together, the blanket fisted between them, its threads protesting as they wrenched at it.

When they'd recovered all the largest pieces, only then did Krona let herself try to gauge how many dead there were—trying to guess at how many people had been at the safe house versus abroad. Sebastian's great-aunt Onara and Melanie's mother, Dawn-Lyn, were away. A team of Kairopaths and quintbarrel wielders—those she'd taken with her to investigate the hoard—were away on an extended hunt, she knew that for certain. Though their absence could mean nothing. Not knowing what had happened also meant not knowing how it had happened, and how far the damage extended.

Her stomach squeezed, hard and painful, as she thought of the other safe houses. Creating another lens, she jumped to the nearest one just over the border in Marrakev.

Ruin awaited her there as well.

She jumped again, and again.

Gone, gone, gone.

She jumped back to the remains of Mirthhouse, falling into a drift of figurines, pulling at her hair, clenching her teeth to hold back a scream.

Krona had lived with grief all her life. It was a heavy thing that changed the colors of the world around it, kaleidoscoping and distorting everything more efficiently and permanently than mirrors or crystals. She was familiar with it, accustomed to its presence in the way one is accustomed to quiet neighbors; it was there, and that was fine. The dull background *thud* of it was tolerable.

She'd only ever been able to meet the torn-up rawness of new grief such as this with *action*. If an emotion was to be so sharp, then Krona thought it only right for it to pave the way toward an end goal: a need for revenge, redemption, resurrection.

We have to search for survivors. We have to— Pushing herself upright she tried to take a step, only to trip over the katar, still fully intact.

The enchanted weapon was fine. Nothing but the usual scratches littered its surface.

How had it survived?

How had the blue blanket survived?

Only then did she think of De-Lia. Of the pieces she'd fought so hard to gather.

Frantically, Krona stumbled over to an approximation of where her room had been, clawing through the figurines, despairing when she found ones made of the same metal as the safe. She muttered heated denials, curse words flying from her tongue just as readily, until her fingers fell on something not rodent-shaped. The hourglass. De-Lia's hourglass. Its stand had been transformed and remolded, but the enchanted glass and the ashes within remained. Her heart lifted into her throat, but it wasn't happiness, just relief, and the devastation all around her gave it a sharp, sour edge.

Enchantments were immune to the devastation. Whatever had taken the materials of their home and morphed them into these accursed shapes hadn't been able to touch what was already enchanted.

With desperation driving her limbs, she shoved great piles of metal and wood figurines away until she'd excavated the blood pen and the journal as well. She prayed Monkeyflower was similarly unharmed, locked away in the cliffside below.

That just left the mask.

More excavating, more grunting. She looked for the bright yellow of the jaguar, the green and blue and red of the birds and foliage around it. Knees digging into the corkscrew tails and sharp limbs of the figures, she felt around for the familiar grain, even hoped to smell the tarry creosote that helped preserve the wood after it had been carved.

The other enchantments had been spared from whatever had happened here, there was no reason to fear this one hadn't been protected just the same.

No reason, save her cursed luck.

As her fingers clasped wood and drew the mask into the late-day sun, there was no denying the massive crack down the center. The wood had splintered; its pale, bare grain revealed beneath the paint. Perhaps someone had stepped on it in their haste to escape, the delicate balsa no match for a harried boot. The leather straps that had once held it snuggly against Krona's face were gone, but that didn't stop her from pressing the bowl of it against her brow, openly begging and praying as she did.

"Please. *Please, please, please.*"

Nothing.

No knowledge. No echo.

No De-Lia.

It was the final straw.

Krona's sob was muffled by the mask, and she let the wood continue to eat up the sound as she bent forward over her lap, mask cradled in her hands, head cradled in the mask.

Nearly everyone she'd known and cared for had just died—a thing so ugly and tragic and confusing she hadn't fully comprehended the horror of it yet.

Losing the mask was nothing—trivial in comparison. Or it should have been. Intellectually she knew that. She knew it was wrong to feel the loss of a mere shadow of her sister more acutely than the loss of everything else, but it was the single point of destruction that made the rest *real.*

De-Lia had been Krona's light at the end of the tunnel—the new dawn that made toiling through the darkness all worth it. She'd promised herself De-Lia. She'd promised Tray De-Lia. She'd promised the world De-Lia.

She'd promised De-Lia the world.

But even that world was gone. The loss of the echo reverberated outward, focusing Krona's grief and amplifying it like a tuning fork amplifying a single note.

This obscene place with its twisted forms had been too surreal before. Something out of focus, incomprehensible as the crisp-edged mansion full of life that she'd known just hours before.

But the cracked mask in her hands connected the two, tugging them together into one, making it all resolve into an ugly reality she couldn't reel her mind away from. She wanted to blur it again—make the daze return, or the anger return. She wanted to sink into a state of numbness. She wanted to disassociate from this place, her body.

They were *all* dead. Even Abby. Maybe even—

Gods, what if Thibaut was dead too?

A shadow fell over her. She expected it to be Tray, but when she looked up, Sebastian stood there, red-eyed and trembling-lipped.

She held up the bowl of the mask like she was asking him to fill it. It was empty—*they were all empty*. All the life that had filled them up had drained away. "She's gone," she gasped. "I know it's nothing compared to . . ." She turned her head abortively to indicate everything. "I know she's been gone for years. I *know*—"

Sebastian sniffed, wiped at his nose with his arm, but did not bother swiping at the new tears that fell freely from his eyes. Dropping to his knees beside her, he said, "Maybe she's still in there."

"You've split a mask like this before," she countered. "You know the enchantment dissipates. Your father—"

"I made a clean cut," he countered. "My father's mask cleaved neatly in two. This? It's splintered, but still whole."

The two of them shared a conversation in a glance.

It was still whole compared to their comrades.

"I can't . . . I can't feel her. The echo . . . Even if the enchantment isn't gone, it's too late anyway." As soon as she set it down again it was as likely to rend in two from the sheer force of gravity as not.

"There is something we could try." He lightly touched the center of his forehead, gaze shifting toward his wife.

Krona instantly understood what he was suggesting, and knew the only subsequent word out of her mouth should be *no*. She'd seen the results of failed knowledge extraction. Trying to replicate the process that had given Melanie Master Belladino's lifetime of healing knowledge was as likely to see Krona go mad or end up catatonic as it was to transfer whatever drops of De-Lia's knowledge or wisps of her echo still remained.

Hells, if they got it wrong, the process could kill her.

But losing the mask was paramount to losing Monkeyflower herself. The essences it contained were essential to building De-Lia anew.

To save an echo when they could not save any of these people may have seemed trivial and useless to anyone outside looking in. What did it matter? It was a memento, a tool, nothing more.

But when everything else has been taken, and you have so little left, even rescuing pieces of the dead can be a triumph. One success to push you forward. One win to keep you on your feet instead of collapsing.

Even if Krona wasn't as confident in help from the gods as she once had been, that didn't mean she was willing to relinquish all hope and give up. Not if there was still a chance.

"Our enchanters' needles were in the war room," she said, her own voice sounding distant in her ears.

"I'll check the rubble," he said with the detached tone of a grieving father who needed to move, to do, to be of service, lest he lay down and never get up again.

Moments after he'd gone, a strange boom shattered the relative calm of the countryside. It was a sharp crack, almost like thunder, though the day was clear without a storm cloud in sight. It sounded again, and again, and had Krona craning her neck, looking for its source as she tried to determine if she'd need to abandon the mask and jump everyone away.

Laying De-Lia's mask on the slope of her knees, she shielded her eyes from the sun's glare with one hand, straining to look up at the zenith of the sky.

Miles above, a winged shape rocketed upward, moving at such speeds that she could even see the air being displaced around them as they surged forth.

Another boom, another burst, and then—

The shape stopped.

It stopped as surely as a bird striking clear glass. It hovered there, held back by an invisible barrier, before falling elegantly downward in a spiral. No, not falling. Gliding, then swooping skyward once more.

Up and up it rocketed, driving the air aside with enough force to create that thunder-like crack. And, again, it stopped painfully abruptly. It spent another moment hanging there—pressed against the sky—before it dropped again, but not nearly as far.

It was Time.

The goddess was trying to leave the Valley. To fly away.

And she *couldn't.*

She bashed herself against the unseen blockade, pulling back and knocking bodily against it again and again and again.

Krona gasped.

The gods were trapped inside the Valley. Not on the rim—not in sacred sacrifice—but trapped just as the humans were.

Krona didn't have the wherewithal to comprehend what that meant. She couldn't trust the scrolls, could barely trust her own eyes these days, but one thing was for certain: if Absolon was only a man, he was the Thalo's hand, no question. Their cruel creator had implanted itself in their realm by proxy, and Arkensyre had been doomed from the start.

⊳⊣⊲⊳⊸○⊷⊲⊳⊣⊲

Krona heard someone approaching through the tinkling of figurines, but still startled when a hand fell on her shoulder. "Sebastian is ready," Tray said, nodding at De-Lia's mask in Krona's lap. "Are you?"

She'd be lying if she hadn't been considering this route for some time. Ever since she realized that not just knowledge but also echoes could be transferred from masks, she'd privately wondered if trying to implant De-Lia's remnants in a living mind would be the quickest way to resurrect her.

But she'd dashed those notions whenever they'd bubbled up inside her like gasses from a tar pit. She'd witnessed what those with echoes inside them experienced, and it wasn't a rebirth for the dead, though it *was* most certainly a supplantation of the host's will. She'd never even wondered aloud if anyone might consider hosting De-Lia. And, until now, she'd thought it was nothing but folly to consider hosting De-Lia herself.

She held out the splintering jaguar mask for Tray to take, and he cradled it like a newborn babe. This was no small moment for him, either.

As she rose to her feet, she wondered if she should ask him if he wanted to be the one to do it instead of her, but she discarded the idea before the question could form on her tongue.

It made sense that it should be Krona. She was De-Lia's kin. They were cut from the same cloth, born of the same womb. If there was flesh De-Lia's essence was likely to settle into, it was her sister's.

Together, Krona and Tray strode to where Sebastian had cleared the ground of the surreal rubble. Melanie had laid the blue blanket down in the bare dirt to make it somewhat comfortable. Both husband and wife moved with an emptiness in their gaze that tore at Krona; they were in shock, had just lost their child, and were pushing all that aside to help Krona save what was left of De-Lia if they could.

With a helping hand from Melanie, Krona lay on the blanket. Tray knelt at her head, his knees framing her temples, and Sebastian, syringe at the ready, stood over her, straddling her hips.

Though he was a lanky man—tall, dark, and stately—she'd never given much mind to Sebastian's comportment before. He was typically courteous, quiet. Unimposing. But now, standing over her, she noticed his strength for the first time. He held himself steady, shoulders square—a man of refined movement, and even in his stunned state it did not fail him now.

Which was good. Steady hands were good. He held two lives in those hands—both hers and De-Lia's.

"Have you . . . have you done this since . . . ?" Krona gestured vaguely in Melanie's direction.

Tapping the syringe's barrel against the flat of his hand, he shook his head. "But I've seen it done. Both successfully and unsuccessfully."

"What was the difference? Between the two methods, I mean?"

He didn't answer. And that was answer enough.

No one knew what the difference was.

"Are you ready?" he asked after a moment.

Krona wetted her lips and nodded.

Carefully, Tray positioned the fragile mask over her brow, letting it settle, letting its shadow block out much of the daylight and the occasional glimpse of a goddess who still insisted on beating herself against the sky.

The slight weight of the balsa against her cheekbones and nose were familiar. She'd settled into bed like this, letting De-Lia's echo roam as it would, hundreds of times before coming to Mirthhouse.

Only now, the mask was quiet. There was no trickle of memories or rush of willpower.

Nothing but Krona's own breath reflected back at her from the bowl of the wood.

Sebastian sank down over her, settling on her belly, and Krona was reminded Hintosep had killed a man exactly this way. Not just any man—a Grand Marquis. Krona had seen her stooping over him, straddling him, thrusting the thick needle harshly down, piercing his brain.

People had died this way and been maimed this way, and only the very few were lucky enough to receive a gift of knowledge from it and nothing else.

Unfortunately for Krona, she was specifically hoping to grasp on to all that *something else* and keep it safe and near until such time as De-Lia could be made whole again.

Someone spoke, and Krona found she could not distinguish who. It was as if the wood wrapped all the way around her head, plugging her ears. Suddenly, all she could hear was a high-pitched ringing, and the voice of a victim she'd visited years ago in the asylum chanting, *This face is all wrong.*

This face is all wrong.

Krona might be about to lose herself, not just her chance at getting De-Lia back.

Perhaps this was hasty. Perhaps this was a mistake.

But before she could renege, Sebastian was already moving, the needle already descending.

She felt the needle's prick twofold, as both the usual sharp stab of a pin and as a hot blade slicing down into her as though her flesh were no more firm than warm butter. She cried out, back bowing, wings flexing until they were digging like talons into the threads of the blanket. Tray pressed down on her shoulders to keep her steady beneath Sebastian's weight.

It wasn't the worst pain she'd ever experienced; Hintosep insisted everyone's worst pain was the soul-rending reality of that first slice of an enchanted katar in infancy. Nor was it the most disorienting; that had been her remerger with Ninebark. This was altogether different, like a hole had been excavated in her forehead—raw and real, with her nerves revolting and her body resisting—and through that hole, cool water was being poured. That coolness both soothed and stung, flowing around her brain to slosh inside her skull.

Though the wound felt gaping, Sebastian's hand was steady and the needle remained shallow—deep enough to draw blood, but not enough to scrape bone. Now, he pulled the needle and the plunger up, backing off.

The coolness began to rush out again.

"Wait!" she yelled. Tray pushed down harder, and Sebastian froze. "It's . . . it's leaving," she tried to explain.

She couldn't be certain, but she instinctually felt the coolness was what she wanted—that was the part she *needed*. Which was maddening, because De-Lia had been anything but cool. It was not a sensation she associated with her sister.

But it was the only sensation that wasn't *pain*.

The mask obscured her view of Sebastian's face, but he seemed to understand. He pushed down on the plunger, and the coolness returned.

"Better. Yes," she said breathlessly.

Slowly, he attempted to pull the needle out again. Nothing changed. The sensation remained.

And then the needle was gone, and Tray was lifting the wood from her face. Sebastian stood again, and his weight rising from her belly was like a weight being lifted from her heart.

It was done. Whatever the results, it was done.

Krona had expected something traumatic, or a shift in her sense of being—like when she'd remerged with Ninebark. But she felt exceedingly the same.

She sat up swiftly, hurrying to her feet and turning away from the others. She touched her forehead, expecting to feel a raised enchanter's mark, but all that came away was a small smear of blood. Tension wafted off her companions, their gazes hot and expectant on her back. They were waiting for a verdict.

As was she.

She waited.

And waited.

She flexed her hands and her wings. Curled her toes in her boots.

She didn't feel any more powerful, or knowledgeable, or any less alone. Ninebark wasn't restless beneath her skin. Even the coolness had faded.

She turned, eyes pleading, looking from each familiar face to the next, silently begging them to call attention to a change, any change.

"It took days for mine to appear," Melanie said, meaning the mark.

The enchanter's mark had appeared almost instantly on the dead Grand Marquis. Perhaps the faster the appearance, the more mangled the results.

"Did it take that long for you to grasp the knowledge?" Krona asked.

Melanie looked away. "No," she answered softly.

She didn't have her quintbarrel with her. It was somewhere in the rubble, along with the enchanted needles. Maybe she wouldn't be able to tell if she was a surer shot until it was in her hand. Quickly, she scrabbled to find it, only half noticing Sebastian had walked away, as though he couldn't bear to watch her wrestle with the questions his actions had left her with.

With the gun in her grasp, she still felt no different. She took aim at a tree far off—undisturbed by the chaos that had gone on here—and felt as she always had.

Maybe . . . maybe she needed to hunt a varg to feel it. After all, it was her phobia that had truly tied her hands and stunted her skill. Maybe—maybe—

Frustrated, she tossed the gun aside and stomped up to Tray, snatching the mask from his grasp to look the jaguar in the eye and make demands of it. Her knuckles strained around the curve of the wood, and her jaw tightened as she struggled not to shout out loud the demands ringing between her ears.

Tell me this isn't it. Tell me there's more. Tell me—

Under duress, the wood couldn't hold.

The jaguar snapped in half in her hands.

Krona startled. Everyone around her gasped.

Daylight cut from its forehead between its eyes and down its snout, slicing straight through its open maw.

"It's—it's fine," she insisted. "It's fine." It *wasn't* fine, but what was she to say? Was she to beat her chest and wail for the loss of someone who was already long dead, when these two had just lost their child? When they'd all just lost a house full of friends who'd been whole and warm and breathing just hours ago?

"I just . . . I need a few minutes. I . . ." She dropped both halves of the jaguar mask, letting them fall where they would, not caring where they landed. They were useless now, no longer a part of her sister.

Dazed, she wandered off, roaming through the debris of their former home, seeing but not seeing.

Krona had long suspected getting De-Lia back was a pipe dream, she just hadn't allowed herself to admit it, and now the result of her wild goose chase was this: emptiness. Nothing. It was a handful of useless enchantments in a destroyed mansion. Yes, there was still Monkeyflower and the other bits, but she'd convinced herself it all hinged on the mask, because that was the only enchantment in which she could still recognize De-Lia. And it was gone. She'd pushed so many people aside in her quest to bring back her sister, and now—

Thibaut.

It was as though a haze had lifted from her mind and his name was suddenly at the forefront of her thoughts.

He hadn't been here. Mandip and Juliet and Avellino weren't here. They might already be dead, but there was a chance they were still alive.

There were living people who still needed her.

Krona looked up at the sky, which had gone silent. She could no longer spot Time. The goddess had moved on.

They had no gods. They had no Hintosep. They had no Mirthhouse. They had fewer weapons at their disposal than they'd had last time they'd escaped the Savior.

It would have to be enough—to save the others, to defeat Absolon.

They had nothing else to count on.

"Why this?" Melanie asked. Krona looked down, realized her feet had carried her back to Melanie's side. She was holding the blanket once more. "The only things that survived were enchantments and Abby's blanket. Why?"

Krona swallowed thickly, dryly, before asking, "Have you found zhur body?" Krona had been adrift while she'd helped Tray, her mind not yet ready to put names to all the fragmented corpses, but she was fairly certain she'd touched nothing belonging to a child.

She expected Melanie to point and indicate some grotesque pile of small remains that perhaps she and Sebastian had moved themselves, but instead the woman shook her head. "I couldn't find zhim. I just . . . I thought, since zhe's so small—"

That zhe'd simply been devoured whole.

Krona had her doubts.

No, better than that—now she had *hopes*. "Only enchanted objects survived . . ."

Abby was skilled enough to transmute a blanket.

But even if the child had survived, why wasn't zhe here?

Krona gazed about, looking for some sign—a trail. But they themselves had kicked and shuffled through much of the debris, further confusing an already chaotic scene. If Abby had fled, the chances they could follow—

A glint of metal caught her eye. Hintosep's katar still lay where she'd tripped over it.

"We need to salvage what we can," she said, moving to extract it. "Harvest supplies from the field, the orchard. Perhaps the stores near the cave entrance are still viable. Anything intact comes with us. We'll eat, rest, then plan our next steps."

The other three quietly agreed.

Krona attempted to take the lift in the pantry down to the river-side entrance, but when she scraped away the figurines from the edge of the tunnel, it became clear that the lift itself had suffered the same transmogrification. It would take a long rope and some hefty lifting to get to their supplies stash this way. She didn't want to simply jump for fear of overlooking something vital. She'd have to take the long way around—a climb down the cliff face, or a sweeping hike down the trail. So be it.

As she set off on the trail alone, her heart panged. She longed for Thibaut's chattering voice in her ear, his comforting hand in hers. He would know what to say to help her through this. As it stood, she'd failed De-Lia, and Mirthhouse, and their network, and the longer she stayed away from the keep, the longer she failed Thibaut as well. He was the one who needed her right now, not the other way around.

Krona was so lost in thought she startled when boots crunched in the gravel right behind her on the path. She whirled to find Tray hurrying to catch up with her. They nodded to each other, then continued the trek side by side in contemplative silence for some time.

But the silence was not companionable. To Krona, it felt swollen with their shared loss. She'd promised Tray De-Lia, had used her sister's memory to gain his trust anew. That fact swirled overhead like a buzzard, judgmental and ready to scavenge off the bones of Krona's previous assurances.

"I'm sorry," she blurted. "I made . . . I made my false hope yours."

"You made your *real* hope mine," he countered. "And, perhaps it's because I've only had it for a short time, but I haven't lost it yet."

She gave a sad little laugh at that. "Perhaps it's because the needle was in my forehead that I feel so sure."

"Or perhaps it's because you've always been a pessimist."

"It's difficult not to be pessimistic when—" She gestured back the way they'd come, to the ruined mansion filled with half-eaten friends.

"I know. But hope feeds, and despair starves. We've got to hold on to what we can to move forward."

"Still, I shouldn't have used De-Lia's memory to convince you to come with me."

He stopped in his tracks, took her by the arm and made her stop as well. "Krona, you are my friend," he insisted. "Do not think for a second I needed more motivation than that. I have learned more at your side in the last two years than I had in a lifetime before. We are fighting for a better Arkensyre, and for our friends who are still alive. You are worth following, Krona. Do not entertain otherwise."

Krona drowsily woke in the middle of the night, as she often did when sleeping alone—caught out on a mission without Thibaut's arms around her or a soft mattress to cradle the two of them—that in itself was nothing to be alarmed about. She'd gone to sleep with her cheek pressed into the grass of the hill just beyond Mirthhouse, with Tray's spine against hers and Melanie asleep at her fore.

But now, as she opened her eyes, she found snow beneath her, but it wasn't cold. It wasn't just that she wasn't cold and the air wasn't cold, but the snow itself wasn't cold. She sat up, brushed it from her face and her clothes, and found that it did not melt at the contact. It fell away again like so much fluff—like raw cotton freshly plucked rather than flakes of ice.

"I've stopped time," came a voice in the dark.

Krona rose, braced herself. She was not with the others. Or, more precisely, the others weren't with her. She'd been taken elsewhere—someplace she could not recognize. All around was endless winter and a starry sky. Even the Valley's rim seemed unnaturally distant. She had to be atop one of Arkensyre's glaciers, but she had no way of pinpointing which.

"I've stopped time all around us," came the voice again, and Krona whirled to mark it. The goddess sat upon a great stone, her wings flowing over the back of it like a magnificent cape, resplendent in the light of the twin moons. "Only you and I and our breath and our blood and everything we are continue to move. All else?" She lifted one of her hands, stretched upward for what Krona realized was a clump of snowflakes mid-fall, and let them play over the backs of her knuckles, petting them as they sat suspended in time. "Well, all else, save the moonlight. Not even I can freeze light itself."

Krona fought the urge to hug herself, to protect her body from the cold her mind told her she should feel, even though her skin assured her she did not. She didn't question why Time had brought her here—the scenario was all too familiar. Krona herself had pulled this very trick on Tray.

She wondered if he'd felt like she did now: cornered, prepared for coercion, or, at the very least, a fight.

"Where is Emotion?" she asked.

Time's gaze grew drawn. ". . . Elsewhere," she said. "I have missed zhim, but we still have our differences. Our disagreements. We are still angry with each other for decisions made long ago."

Krona's lips parted to ask after what kinds of disagreements gods had, though Time clearly felt no need to elaborate. "I've been all over this valley," the goddess continued. "Taken in the war-ravaged lands, seen the celebration of a birth despite it, the mourning of many a death because of it. There is music even amongst screams. The world remains ever the same," she scoffed, plucking that same clump of snow from the air and crushing it in her hand, sifting it through like dry sand. "Your rulers are mad with blood lust, or solitary cowards, or fools who shove their fingers in their ears. When a citizen calls for peace, she is as likely to be stoned to death as heeded by a single person. We brought what was left of humanity to this scar in the ground, and for what?"

"This war is Absolon's doing," Krona protested.

"This war is humanity's doing," Time countered sharply. "I've been to Absolon's keep, noted his Grand Orchestrators, as they call themselves. Seen them scheming. One person can set up the pieces, manipulate tempers and motives, but one man does not a war make. It is easy to ascribe a movement to its leader, but this is not true for the push toward justice just as it is not true about the push toward injustice. Many minds have to come together to wish it and work for it."

She looked directly at Krona, her gaze stern. "Killing Absolon will not rid the Valley of its ills."

"Does that mean you won't do it?"

Time leapt from her perch, stalking forward in her hunched, yet unnaturally graceful way, crouching down in front of Krona so that they could look each other in the eye. Krona noticed her pupils were twinned, and her teeth were sharp. Up close like this, she was far more intimidating than when she stretched to her full height. "I'm telling you," the goddess said quietly, as though whispering to a child in a warm bedroom instead of a grown woman in the wilds, "that even if I do, that is the beginning of the work, not the end. Peace, stability—undoing what Absolon has done, teaching again what he has un-taught—will take time. It is lancing the boil, not curing the infection.

"I have read Absolon's writ—his lies about the world," Time went on. "The undoing is needed deep, in every aspect of your lives."

"So help us begin," Krona pleaded. "You are *Time*, the people will listen—"

Time scoffed. "They should not."

Krona didn't know what to say to that.

After a moment of dead silence—deadened by the very stoppage of time—the goddess asked, "What mechanism keeps the Valley sealed, truly?"

If Krona had been suspicious before, watching Time try to escape into the sky, she was certain now. She tilted her chin up defiantly. "A god would know. So you," she said, trembling with the realization, unwilling to keep the accusatory tone out of her voice, "are not a god."

"I never said I was," Time pointed out darkly.

A chill that had nothing to do with the glacier quaked through Krona. What, truly, had they awoken? "Demon, then?" she whispered, her voice shriveling to near nothing as Time held her gaze.

One of Time's large hands came up, and for a moment Krona feared she'd be taken by the throat. Instead, that hand slipped over her shoulder, its fingertips petting lightly over the top curve of one of her bone wings, sending uneasy shivers down her spine. "Are *you* a demon?" Time asked, her condescension heavy. She snorted when Krona did not answer, shook her head, and backed away in a slinking half crawl. "So," Time said, "the answer is you do not know."

"The barrier protects us from the beasts beyond. The rest of our planet is a wasteland, or is that news to you in kind?"

Time shook her head. "No. *That* I know well. I know your climates are unnatural, kept in working order through our magic—those of us in the tithing. I know you believe your Introdus was three thousand years ago. I know you believe an entity called the Thalo created the world. I know your technological capabilities have been thrown back into the dark ages. And I know I and my brethren are no gods and no demons."

"What are you, then?"

Time bit at her fingernails, gaze far off and hollow. "Fools," she spat.

"Aren't we all?" Krona asked cynically.

"Absolon lied about who we are to one another. And who *he* is to us. When you set out to wake us, you thought you were waking saviors," Time said.

"Yes."

"You thought to lay down your sword, then?" she asked with a sneer. "That once we appeared, your work would be over."

"No," Krona said firmly. "I'm not the sort to think the work is ever done. What the people need—what I need—are allies. No matter what you are, you have the means to help us. So help us. Help *me*. Please. You have Emotion back, and I will still help you find Nature, but *my* family is in danger as well. My . . . the man I love has been taken to Absolon's keep."

Time listened attentively as Krona made her case—as she explained about De-Lia's varg and the Charbon concern and the Grand Marquis's assassination, which had all led here. Just as Krona was beginning to think the not-goddess could be reasoned with, the giant perked like a wild animal hearing the nearby call of prey.

"Did you feel that?" Time asked.

"No. Feel what?"

"Absolon. He's been shrouding his location from me, but now . . ." She closed her eyes, breathed deeply, as though she could scent him on the nonexistent wind. "I know where he is."

Time stretched, shook out her wings, and let the world around them snap back into its natural forward flow. Freezing air swamped Krona, stealing her breath with a sharp, icy kiss.

"Wait!" she cried, her ears suddenly filled with the roar of glacial winds. Snowflakes clouded her vision, and the moonlight now seemed to work against her. "If he's been hiding himself, then this"—she waved out into the world—"is deliberate. You shouldn't go. If one thing was made clear to me the last time I encountered Absolon, it was that he should not be allowed to set the stage. You cannot fight him on his chosen ground."

"He was only able to subdue me in the first place because I let my guard down," Time said. "I believed him kin and incapable of such treachery."

"And the others?" Krona asked. "He subdued you *all*."

"He tricked us all."

"So don't let him trick you again," Krona pleaded.

"He is keeping *Nature* from me." She knelt down in front of Krona. "My brother has always been the most powerful of us all. If you are looking for a savior, you can do no better. As I said, I have been up and down this Valley, and have failed to find him myself. Absolon is the answer. Now come."

"Come? No. I need to return to the others, to my—"

Feathers descended all around her—dark and warm, smelling faintly of some musky perfume instead of like a bird. Their raven shimmer latched on to the moonlight briefly, sending ribbons of purples and greens across her vision before they shut out the light altogether. There was a squeeze and a familiar rush as a jump took her. Only she had no control over the destination.

When Time threw her wings out again, the glacial night was gone, the chill of it sucked away by warm desert air and the striking light of a bright midmorning.

Xyopar. She was in Xyopar again.

Krona turned on the spot, blinking through the glare of the sudden sun, trying to divine exactly where in the southernmost city-state they'd landed. She stopped dead when she saw the towering red sandstone steps that led up into the capital: Xyopar proper.

The city of dead kings.

25

TRAY

Morning brought with it an extra chill. Tray shivered, shimmying backward, looking for the bony lines of Krona's back and, thus, her body heat. She eluded him. He kept moving, hugging himself, feeling as though he'd pushed himself a mile across the grass and still, nothing. The shock of suddenly realizing he was very much alone fully roused him in an instant, and he sat up with a start.

The small fire they'd built in the communal cooking pit had long ago gone out, and none of his companions were in sight. The ruins of Mirthhouse, yards away, down the slope of the hill, were still. Nothing but the typical sounds of scurrying fauna and the mellow rushing of water below the cliffside met his ears. The air smelled of ash from the night before, when they'd gathered and burned what large pieces of bodies they could find on a group pyre.

"Krona? Krona!"

"She's gone," said Sebastian.

Tray turned, propped up on his elbows, to see both Sebastian and Melanie appearing over the crest of the hill, striding down toward their makeshift camp from the direction of the former sheep pastures. They both had firewood in hand.

"So is the remaining mind," Melanie added.

Tray swore under his breath. Surely Krona hadn't taken the failure with De-Lia's echo as a sign to set out on her own?

"I've been up since before dawn, and she was already gone. I thought I heard . . ." Melanie shook her head. "I thought I heard Abby, calling to me." She gestured down into the remains of the mansion.

Sebastian set down his wood and pulled Melanie into a hug. She snuggled into it gratefully, and Tray looked away.

He'd only half lied to Krona about still holding out hope for De-Lia's return. He missed her dearly, and had seen so many new things in the last two years that he no longer thought raising the dead an impossible task. And yet, before Krona had swept him away to that mountaintop above Clavaburn, he'd nearly made peace with De-Lia's absence. Hells, he'd made peace with Krona's absence. He'd accepted that his two childhood friends were gone, and then one of them had come blustering back into his life and turned it upside down.

Or right side up, he supposed.

And now she'd gone again.

"We should eat," Sebastian said, "while we wait for her return."

"What makes you so sure she's coming back?" Tray asked, pulling himself up to help with the preparations.

Sebastian frowned as he began rebuilding the fire.

"The Krona I know would leave if she thought she was protecting us," Tray said.

"And the Krona we know would never abandon her team without a word," Sebastian countered. "Surely her time with the Regulators taught her that."

Tray chuckled as he pulled out a wrapped portion of dried meat they'd recovered from storage the day before. "No. That would be her time with you."

"Mama!"

They all stiffened. The cry had unquestionably come from the ruins.

"Did you—?" Melanie asked hopefully.

"We heard it," Tray confirmed.

Just like that, the three of them were off at a sprint, their breakfast forgotten—but not their weapons. Tray had the presence of mind to take up the katar, just in case.

They kicked through piles of figurines and bits of the dead they'd failed to find the day before. Already the flies had found the errant remains, buzzing in small, grotesque swarms. But they ignored the decay, frantically focused on finding the source of the call.

"Abby! Absolon!" they called over and over.

"Shh, wait, wait!" Tray said after a time, calling for silence. He'd heard other voices. Straining to hear, he followed the far-off sounds. They were quiet, like whispers, their volume rising only minutely as he inched closer. The others followed.

The voices, it seemed, were coming from a patch of dead air.

He stopped, circling the spot, unsure where he was in the layout of the mansion. But, sure enough, the voices remained in place, emanating from a single point.

What new magic was this?

It was Melanie who reached out, and her hand vanished. She pulled it back with a yelp, immediately cradling it to her chest. It seemed intact.

"What did you feel?" Tray asked.

"Nothing," she said, flexing her fingers, watching her own hand as though it might drop from her wrist. "I'm fine," she insisted, displaying her palm.

The voices grew louder for a moment before fading again.

Maybe this is where Krona had gone. Maybe she'd followed the call that Melanie had heard in the night.

"Hold on to me," Tray said, rolling up his sleeve and holding his forearm out for Sebastian to grasp. "If I struggle, pull me back."

Not only Sebastian's, but also Melanie's hands came up to lock in place. They both planted their feet, and Tray took a deep breath before plunging his face into the affected air.

It was like a door to many doors. A rippling tunnel through reality that was both stable and real, yet fluctuating and ephemeral, branched out before him, each pathway ending abruptly in a window to another place. Immediately his mind bucked, rejecting the disorienting sight, sending him spiraling on his own two feet, even though nothing had shifted. He fell forward, and, good to their word, Melanie and Sebastian yanked him back.

"If anyone survived this," he said, gasping, bent over and bracing himself on his own knees, "they went through there."

Thinking Krona must already be inside, the three of them quickly packed up their supplies and gathered all the enchantments they'd found before, one by one, crossing the strange, invisible threshold into the unnatural corridor through space and time.

It seemed both long and short. All the window-doors appeared right on top of one another until they approached and then the windows fanned out and stretched away. The rules of known physics did not apply to wherever they were—a rift in reality.

Along the bottom of the pathway, figurines just like those in Mirthhouse had spilled in from many of the windows. As they strode by, voices from beyond filtered in—the chatter Tray had heard.

They peered through one window after another, trying to decipher what they were gazing upon. Scenes from all over Arkensyre seemed to dance before their eyes, and too many of them were alike—piles of rubble, just like Mirthhouse.

And still, there was no sign of Abby, Krona, or any other survivors. They were alone in the rift.

"How do we choose? Which way do we go?"

"This one," Tray said, approaching a window that was barred by a giant metal door. He set his palm against it, finding it cold to the touch. "The others are all open, which means whoever created this tunnel doesn't care who finds them, who goes in or out. But this one . . . this one matters." He pushed to see if there was any give. But no, it was solidly barred.

"Wait, we don't know what we'll find in there," Sebastian said. "Could be whatever destroyed the mansion. Let me look first with Kemba."

The Emotiopath called forth his fen, keeping it a wisp rather than urging it to take its full form. Pinkish in hue, it pressed at the door's seams, like smoke looking for an escape route. Sure enough, it found a gap, siphoning itself through, whisking itself away.

They waited with baited breath. Not even Sebastian, detached from his fen, could be sure what Kemba might find on the other side.

Long moments passed before the wisps returned, seeping back into Sebastian's welcoming palms as easy as breathing. Once it resettled, he furrowed his brow.

"It's just as you describe it," he said to Melanie, reexamining the door with new interest.

"What is?"

"The keep. This leads to the Savior's keep."

26

HAILWIC

In a Time and Place Unknown

When Lonny asked for a meeting—pulling in Theesius's generals from across Radix and Remotus—a knot of anxiety twisted Hailwic's insides.

She hadn't seen him in person in years. His cover was deep. After the attempted assassination, he was the only one who'd been able to maintain his position. More than that, he'd been able to improve his situation, gaining more responsibility and more trust.

If Lonny was risking contact now, it could only be bad news.

The round, stone doors that blocked the axe-carved tunnels' pathways in the deepest portions of the old passages required a winch placed in their central hub in order to move. Each of the generals had their own, and after Hailwic rolled the last door to the side she secured her winch to her belt, but before she could step through, strong fingers pinched at her waist, making her shriek and jerk back.

"Fancy meeting you here," Punabi purred in her ear, slinking up behind Hailwic and throwing zhur arms around her middle.

"You're a menace," Hailwic teased. Every touch from zhim still sent a thrill down Hailwic's spine and made heat coil in her belly. Grinning mischievously, she turned in the circle of Punabi's arms and walked zhim backward into a dug-out crevasse in the old cave.

This part of the underground city was less intricate than the higher levels—no cathedrals or fully carved-out homes. But there were more intricate locks and doors—like the winch wheels—and parts of it curved past the border wall, well out of Remotus and into Radix, right under Uphrasia's nose.

"I'm *your* menace," Punabi said, punctuating the declaration with a kiss to Hailwic's neck.

"Missed you," Hailwic hummed as she pressed against zhim. They'd endured months of separate assignments.

"Same," Punabi reassured her.

Someone cleared their throat—"*Ahem*"—and they reluctantly put daylight between their bodies, though they were in no rush.

It was Lonny, and he looked wholly unimpressed. Irritated, even. "You'd think the gravity of the situation would foster some decorum," he said gruffly.

With one hand still on Hailwic's waist, Punabi waved zhur hand in front of zhur face and dipped into a dancer's bow before throwing an exaggerated lilt into zhur voice. "My dear Absolon Raoul Trémaux, it is an honor to have you with us today, what with the harrowing journey you must have had on your way here from"—zhe paused and mimed pulling an imaginary cue card from zhur pocket—"your cushy job as one of Uphrasia's favorite engineers."

"Oh, fuck you, Punabi."

"Fuck you right back," zhe said joyfully, leaving Hailwic's side to give Lonny a hug, which he returned one-handedly as he cradled a set of leather-bound books against his chest with the other. "You did make it through okay, yeah?" zhe asked him.

"Still standing," he said when they pulled apart, absently patting the strap of the pack he had slung over one shoulder. "Counts for something. I was . . . I was going to have lunch in the Leadership Commissary before our appointment later. Pore over these." He tilted the books up. Hailwic caught half the titles on each spine, all stamped in gold.

She realized she'd seen such a grouping of titles before.

"Are those from Uphrasia's forbidden library?" she asked, reaching forward to thumb the top cover higher in his grip, revealing more of the title.

The smile he gave her was more like a baring of teeth than a real expression. "Some duplicates I was able to smuggle out. Salvaged them from the Whittlehouse Criterion Archive—picked them out of the piles before the bonfires were set."

"She set fire to the WCA?" Punabi gasped. "Why didn't we hear about it?"

"Archives still stand," he assured zhim. "This book burning was a private threat to the heads of the institution, which was why she didn't publicize it like she did when she ordered the Institute of Sexual Studies' collections burned. Uphrasia wanted some very specific historical pieces wiped out. These I rescued to find out *why*."

Hailwic was impressed. Lonny was doing well if Uphrasia had shown him her library of arcane texts and had brought him to a private book burning.

"Would you like company for lunch?" she asked, plucking the top book from his grasp, though he attempted to keep his hold on it.

**Marcus Quint's Eclectic Spells:
Magical Application Via Rhythmic Transmutations**

Hailwic had seen the book in Uphrasia's collection, but not opened it, of course. The Friend showed off her library as a point of personal pride, not to allow such forbidden materials to be read.

"Sure," Lonny said, answering a question Hailwic had already forgotten she'd asked, too enamored with the contraband.

The bunker's Leadership Commissary was not unlike the impersonal employee lunchroom at any corporate building Hailwic had visited during her time as an engineer. Only, instead of the cheaply fabricated tables being surrounded by wide windows like a fish tank, these were hemmed in by stone and darkness. Both were equally as repressive and unwelcoming, yet briskly functional. Meant to hurry along mealtime instead of inviting diners to bask.

The three of them joined the grub line with flimsy trays and even flimsier flatware, accepting bitter-leafed salads and questionably thick servings of cream-heavy pasta without complaint.

Lonny picked a table in the middle of the room. Everyone else scarfing down their food between duties had chosen something at the edge of the dining hall, somehow making what could have been the center of attention the most private seating available. The circular folding table was unsteady; Punabi drained zhur juice box with rapid efficiency in order to crush it down to a thickness that would steady the short leg.

With a little huff, Lonny shoved his pack beneath the table and dropped his small stack of reading material atop its center, giving a halfhearted wave at the copies, permitting the two of them to peruse as desired.

None of the books were first editions. Old, yes—nearly a century out of print. The leather had gone soft at the edges, flaking here and there. The gold leaf on *Marcus Quint's* had only peeled a little, and *Sixteen Steps to One's Best Pathic Capacity*'s was mostly intact, but the lettering on *Taxonomy of Useful Creatures for Conjurations, Vol. 2* and *The Essential Physio Grimoire* was nearly gone, the imprint in the leather legible only from up close.

Punabi's eyes didn't drift to the pile. Instead, zhe focused on Lonny, gaze discerning. Zhe clearly wanted to ask about the impending meeting. He hadn't risked his cover to bring them forbidden texts.

It would be uncouth to prod him about it before he gave his official report, so ultimately zhe let it lie.

Mindlessly picking at her salad, Hailwic opened *Marcus Quint's*, her concern over the meeting pushed aside in favor of the thrill tickling through her insides. Not only was the topic itself fascinating—arcane magic practices not just out of fashion, *outlawed*—but reading even a single sentence was a slight against Uphrasia.

As far as Hailwic's bones were concerned, she still had a singular mission: remove the Friend. It didn't matter that she'd failed already. That the idea of another attempt anytime soon had been scrapped. That failure was always at the forefront of her mind, her guilt writhing across here entire body, just under the surface, like a second skin.

Intellectually she knew it was over.

Her body hadn't received the memo.

The tingling in her fingertips and the flutter in her chest told her this was *right*. This was her assignment, her focus: learn all she could about Uphrasia, and use it to end her.

That's not your job anymore was the truth, but it didn't matter. Time spent here, with Lonny, was easily justified, after all.

He needed all the help he could get.

The juxtaposition of the Friend's bubbling politeness and ruthless proclamations—the terror wrapped in old-fashioned sweetness—was on display for everyone, but the nuances of her personality were saved for the special few.

Hailwic *understood* Uphrasia—her idiosyncrasies.

Her utter disdain for *most* people—not just Physiopaths—that seethed under her self-proclaimed saviorism. The need to micromanage everything in her life, from the exact portions of food she consumed, to the precise minute-to-minute scheduling of pleasure, to the sanitizing of every surface within a ten-foot radius.

She loved the taste of peppermint, hated cinnamon—unless the cinnamon was in coffee. Loved the scent of lavender, hated sandalwood—unless the lavender was in a boardroom where anything that spoke of relaxation was the enemy.

She loved and hated history. Stories of the past were weapons to Uphrasia. They weren't events that had happened to people who had existed—they were fictitious narratives. There was no *truth* to be found in the past, just a way to frame the future. And those framings were constantly at war, which both captivated and distressed her.

Which led to her often secretly preserving the very evidence she publicly destroyed.

Like a copy of *Marcus Quint's.*

Like *Sixteen Steps, Taxonomy of Useful Creatures,* and *The Essential Physio Grimoire.*

Hailwic understood all this and more. It would be a crime not to lend Lonny her expertise.

She scanned the index page with interest. Daily rituals, runic work—*blood rites.*

Blood rites—a chapter someone obsessed with extracting all pneuma from a Physiopath surely would have read.

She thumbed the pages to the appropriate section, immediately drinking in every printed line, ignoring the stains of decades past—coffee rings and splattered ink. Torn edges and dog-eared corners. Each turning of the page sent the flour-and-must scent of old paper wafting up over the aroma of the commissary.

Disappointingly, most of the blood rites involved animal blood rather than human blood. She glanced askance at where Lonny had his finger pressed to the inner folds of *Taxonomy,* wondering if the two volumes had at one point been sold hand in hand.

Punabi, she realized, hadn't picked up a book at all, zhur stare silently glued to the top of Lonny's dipped head. Noticing Hailwic noticing zhim, zhe glanced to the commissary's analog clock pinned high on the wall, then dove into zhur pasta with a grimace.

Hailwic turned the page again, eyes catching on the simple title: *Tithing.*

A binding—of hearts, minds, and magics, for safety, comfort, and synergy.

Curiously, the author's meandering yet factual tone shifted here. Took on a blatant romanticism in their loving and thorough description of the purpose of the rite and the methods of application. They cited famous tithes—between kings and queens and entire families and even a whole village.

Many of the rites she'd read about up to this point had involved common animals, their blood applied for questionable reasons that likely had more to do with tradition than any real magical influence. But tithing involved vipnika, whose essence was a common ingredient in advanced engineering even today.

That gave the rite a weight in her mind. Most arcane practices were arcane for a reason—they relied on superstition and faith more than anything solid and provable.

"Look at this," she said to Lonny, nudging the book his way, scooting her chair closer as well.

He read quickly, silently mouthing the words as he went. After a moment he turned to *Taxonomy*'s index and found *vipnika* quickly, flipping to the appropriate pages. "Fascinating," he agreed. "May be some truth to these old rituals after all."

"Which is why she's afraid of them," Hailwic said eagerly.

Punabi made a derisive, doubtful sound in the back of zhur throat.

Hailwic glared at zhim for a quick moment before shoving one of the unopened tomes in zhur direction. "Why aren't you helping?"

"Because we're not going to find more effective military strategies in there," zhe said frankly. "You know, something actually useful. I don't need to learn the best methodologies for plucking a chicken under the full moons in order to increase my prowess in the bedroom or whatever."

"You sure?" Hailwic sniped, unimpressed by zhur flippancy.

Lonny snorted under his breath.

Punabi stabbed zhur fork into zhur still ample pile of pasta, leaving its handle pointed at the stone ceiling like zhe'd planted a flag. "It's a waste of time and I'd rather be focused on the meat of things—like why you're here, Lonny."

"All in due time," he said, deciding that was the moment to collect his books again, perhaps in case Punabi continued to wield zhur fork so harshly.

"Due time is in ten minutes," zhe informed him. "And you've barely touched your food. Either of you."

Hailwic reluctantly let *Marcus Quint's* slip from her fingers. "What will you do with the books?"

"I'll leave them with Kinwold," Lonny said. "And I'm sure they'll be happy to lend them to anyone who *doesn't* think they're a waste of time." He dug in properly to his lunch, and conversation was sparse after.

When the appointed time came, they disposed of their trash (save Punabi's juice box, which now had steady employment) and headed into the tunnels once again—Lonny with his pack slung over his shoulder and Hailwic with the books held covetously to her chest.

A line of bare light bulbs hanging from a sagging cord staked into the rock ceiling led them to Theesius's closely guarded inner sanctum. Two sentries allowed them inside, and they had to duck under the low archway to enter.

Zoshim and Kinwold were already there, as were Glensen, Kinwold's daughter, and three other operatives Hailwic didn't know very well.

She could hardly believe so much time had passed since she'd seen Toe Bean. The little girl she'd known was now a woman, bright blue eyes blazing under the coal black of her fringe, which was streaked through with white. She had a hard look to her.

"Toe," she acknowledged with a nod.

"I prefer Hintosep," she said smoothly.

Hailwic gave a second nod.

Once everyone was in place, gathered around the central table, Lonny didn't beat around the bush. He spared a glance for Hailwic and Punabi before clearing his throat and announcing, "Total extraction has been achieved."

Punabi nodded morosely, clearly having expected the news. Hailwic's own assumptions had been thrown off-kilter during their meal—she'd still been so enwrapped in the forbidden books her mind hadn't wandered back around to the implications of Lonny's mere presence.

All through lunch, he'd held the news to his chest. Kept the pain of it close—a time bomb waiting for the appropriate moment to devastate.

Realistically, they'd all known the achievement had to have been coming any day now. Hearing it confirmed made it feel like the floor had fallen out from under Hailwic's boots.

They'd done it.

They'd neutered a Physiopath and stolen their magic.

Perhaps by now they'd done it to many Physiopaths. How long before Uphrasia made an official program? A policy to extract every citizen's physiopathy was surely waiting in the wings.

"But neutralizing Physiopaths won't end her war on us," Zoshim said. "Especially not those who defied her."

"She'll still want to see Remotus wiped off the map," Punabi agreed.

"To her, this is just the beginning," Lonny said. "People like you were always her scapegoats," he added with a nod to Zoshim. "Her excuse. Now she can broaden that excuse. Use it to further encroach on border territories under the guise of *cleansing* them of their physiopathic problem, all in the true service of conquest."

"When genocide is more palatable to the populace than accepting the pure greed of their leader . . ." Kinwold shook their head, trailing off.

"On a lighter note," Lonny said before a dire silence could settle, "I come bearing gifts." Digging in his pack for a moment, he pulled out ten shimmering packets, slapping them down in the middle of the broad table. The substance within the packets—something constantly shifting between a solid and a liquid and without a real physical state at all—changed slowly from bright aqua to subtle fuchsia and back again.

"What are these?" Hailwic asked, hardly able to grasp that the whole pile had been shoved under their shared lunch table like something inconsequential.

"They look like time treatments," Punabi said, flipping one over.

"I nicked them from Uphrasia's personal supply."

"You've been to her compound?" Kinwold asked.

Time treatments, forbidden books, trips to her private residence. Hailwic was *doubly* impressed.

"We've become . . . close."

"We couldn't get her to look your way twice when you were my assistant," Kinwold said, not unkindly, simply factually. "She thought your name was Lenny. What changed?"

Lonny's expression grew hard for a moment. "You always underestimate me. I told you and the professor I could do it before you ever brought in . . ." He abortively raised his hand in Hailwic's direction, then stopped, recentered himself. With a deep breath, he said, "We found something to bond over."

It wasn't difficult for Hailwic to discern what that might be.

"Me," Hailwic said flatly. "My *betrayal*."

Lonny was the only other person near Uphrasia who could claim to have *known* Hailwic Sinclare—not just been aware of her, but had a personal relationship with her. Uphrasia would have known she and Lonny went to Dr. Theesius's home for shared dinners prior to Lonny's firing. It would be easy for Lonny to build a narrative suggesting Hailwic had undermined him, used his trust and friendship to push him out.

"Good," she said, looking up, finding Lonny's eyes. He didn't need her approval, but she wanted him to know he had it. "Smart."

"But what are we supposed to do with these?" Zoshim asked, waving at the pile of time treatments.

"I'd think that was obvious," Lonny countered.

"We can't *use* them," said Glensen, clearly horrified by the thought.

"They're consensually sourced," he assured fem. "People were paid for their time. It's not like the way she extracts pneuma from Physiopaths."

"Still," fey objected. "It's not ethical. We shouldn't."

"Uphrasia does. *This* is where Uphrasia's power really comes from," he said, taking up one of the packets and shaking it to make a point. "She is ubiquitous. A constant. While those fighting her grow old and frail and die, she maintains her prime and *keeps going*. Our *parents* were the first to oppose the rise of the *poor little rich girl* who just wanted some *nice, clean, respectable* fascism," he spat disdainfully. "She's taken over every time-treatment facility in the country. No one gets any without her say-so. She's promising ever-lasting youth as a reward to her most loyal. For the first time in history, we're not looking at a dictator who could be in power for decades, but for centuries. Propped up by lackies who live just as long.

"Do we want our grandchildren to have to start again when we grow old? The resistance needs a leg up. We need the same level of consistency in our leadership that she has. Fight fire with fire." He tapped the pile of packets definitively with one finger. "Look, a bunch of people literally gave up part of their lives to make these. To shove them in the back of a stone-carved pantry somewhere isn't just a waste, it's a disrespect."

"How much time are we looking at?" Punabi asked.

"About eighteen months a packet."

One of the operatives Hailwic didn't know—a stern woman from the northern counties—reached out and shoved the entire pile in Kinwold's direction. "Fifteen more years."

They picked up a packet, fingering it lightly, watching the flow and gush of the time inside. "I'll take *one,*" they said, pushing the pile back toward the center of the table. "I'm not Uphrasia. And I'm not the *answer* to Uphrasia. I won't be hoarding resources like this. Nor will I be dictating who gets them and who doesn't. We share."

"Consider me a conscientious objector," Glensen said, clasping feir hands behind feir back and taking a step away from the table. "I don't want it."

"Me either," said Zoshim, always following Glensen's lead.

"Shim . . ." Hailwic said, tilting her head imploringly.

"We shouldn't be doing this," he said. "The rest of you can decide who gets an extra year, I don't want it."

Quietly, Kinwold pushed one toward Hintosep. She shook her head.

With a heavy, irritated sigh, Hailwic grabbed two. "Uphrasia is out there murdering one-fifth of the populace while another three-fifths stand by and watch. We don't have the luxury of being prim about these things. If this is what it takes"—she held up her claimed packets—"then I'll do it."

"Lonny's right," Punabi agreed. "We have to change our tactics if we want to do more than hold the line. And I'm not just talking about time treatments. We can't just keep reacting to her violence. We need to take the fight to her. Fewer aid workers, more soldiers. We need an army—a *real* army."

"We've just about regained the stability we had before the professor died," Kinwold countered. "We don't have the resources to shift to all-out assault."

"And we shouldn't take any away from our aid work," Zoshim said quickly.

"Which is why we should just *try again,*" Lonny said flatly. He looked directly at Hailwic. She was sure he was talking to her more than anyone else. "We should try to assassinate her again."

"That took nearly a decade of planning," Kinwold reminded them. "If you cut off a snake's head, yes, the body dies. But the government isn't a snake. It isn't one body. Even if we get General Gyrus as well, and there's no clear successor, I have no doubt these events she's set in motion could continue on without her. One woman's death will not resolve generations of violence."

Hailwic understood Kinwold's reasoning. She did, truly.

But.

Lonny's eyes remained locked on hers. They both knew a second try was a chance to right a wrong. Rationally, Hailwic knew her failure hadn't caused the professor's death, but if she'd succeeded, at least she would have honored feir plan, done what she'd promised. If she'd succeeded, maybe Radix's engineering focus would have pivoted, and total extraction would still be a fantasy.

"We hold steady," Kinwold continued. "We keep saving who we can until something changes."

"Something *has* changed—"

"Something that gives us the upper hand," Kinwold bit back, raising their voice in a way they rarely did. Only when they realized it had been Hintosep who'd spoken did they soften again.

"We could reach out," Glensen suggested softly. "We've attempted to show the likes of Nosbeq and Yugalheim what we're up against, but we've never attempted to create real diplomatic ties as the RFR."

"Because we're not a government."

"What are we, then?" fey asked. "This isn't *anarchy*."

"It might as well be," came an incredulously muttered half joke from somewhere at the table.

"What would an ambassador actually accomplish? Our neighbors have watched us struggle for decades and done nothing. They've decided we're not their problem."

"But Uphrasia is hell-bent on expanding the borders. We should *try*."

"Who would we send?" Kinwold asked. "Again, I don't think you understand how few resources we've been working with. The professor was a great unifier—fey were fantastic at bringing us all together. I'm not fem. In the intervening years since feir death, I've barely convinced one of the new cells to come back to us. We're working at less than half the capacity of what we were when Hailwic was recruited.

"We hold steady," they reiterated. "We stay the course. We might not be gaining ground, but we're no longer losing any. I don't want to lose what we have left."

"If we don't do something different, we might lose *everything*," Lonny countered.

"We need to fight," Punabi interjected.

"We need more allies," Glensen insisted.

"We need—"

The meeting devolved into shouts.

The room felt humid, the tension high.

A new fracturing had begun.

27

KRONA

Lutadites saw their dead turned into sand. Asgar-Skanians sunk theirs beneath the Great Falls. Marrakevians left bodies out to be scavenged by the animals, and Winsrouenites tilled theirs into their fields to feed the crops.

In Xyopar, death was not a thing to be hidden. Bodies were not burnt or returned to the land or sunk to the bottom of insurmountable currents. Instead, they went on. They were preserved—mummified—and either left in one of the many dead collectives to be visited on holy days, or returned to continue "living" with their families.

And those were just the common folk.

Xyopar's powerful still made themselves heard. Even in death, their orders were heeded.

The city of dead kings was unique among all the city-states' capitals, for though it counted hundreds of thousands of residents—the largest city by body in all of Arkensyre—almost none of them were living. Not in the traditional sense, anyway. Here, the Eze of Xyopar interpreted the continuing wishes of the great ezes of the past, whose collective power governed the city-state. Those former rulers, along with their courts and favorite servants, were enshrined here in houses of their own, were given living servants of their own to bring them food and drink and entertainment and to keep them presentable, and oracles to report their political desires to the current eze.

"What are we doing here?" Krona asked as Time's wings drew away.

"As I said, he is here." Then, to herself, "Thank heavens Emotion is not. Zhe is weak to Absolon's cryptopathy. I would not expose zhim to such a hopeless confrontation."

Confrontation.

Krona instinctively reached for her saber and found none. Likewise, she had no other weapons. She had her side pouch, and the last mind.

"I will *make* Absolon tell me where my brother is," Time growled. "And then you will wake him, as you woke me."

Winds swirled down from the sandstone cliffs, beating against the entrance to the city which was half built, half carved out of the natural rock gorge. Beautiful banners in yellows and purples—much like the colors imbued in Krona's armor—each stories high, hung from the city's massive twin ceilings, which was formed from the gorge's two overhangs. Between the overhangs was pure sky, the line of it snaking across the city just as the river that had eroded the rock had long ago snaked across the land.

The ancient waters had spilled out of the cliffside and into the desert proper, where the two of them now stood, surrounded by dunes. At least a thousand steps led up from the sand into the rockface, and the case spanned the entire entrance to the city—what had once been a delta nearly a mile across. Time was already mounting the steps; she took them two at a time, and yet they looked like they'd been built for her—built for giants.

Everything was quiet. So quiet. Time's naked feet slapped against the polished stone with unusual clarity. Yes, this was a city of the dead, but those dead had hundreds of living servants. There was no errant chatter, no song. Not even the tang of a cooking fire wafted down to Krona's position.

Something was very wrong here.

Instinct told her to jump away. Time . . . Time was *Time*. Divinity or not, she was something beyond what Krona was. A being of millennia, a being of power and magic like the citizens of Arkensyre could hardly imagine. If she chose to meet Absolon head on, despite knowing his tendency for traps and machinations, then so be it.

So be it.

So why was Krona rooted to the spot?

She needed a goddess's help, not the other way around.

Perhaps even knowing what she knew now, she could not shake the imbedded hooks of religion—perhaps they tugged at her devotion, her need to serve calling her to Time's side, regardless. Or maybe it was the false goddess's recklessness that had dredged up an uncanny foreboding and dread inside Krona, filled her with a need to stay.

Of course, it could be simple kinship. They were both creatures born into manipulation, children of kairopathy, and devoted siblings. And that recklessness she'd noted—Krona saw it in herself as well. Especially when it came to De-Lia.

De-Lia was gone. Beyond her reach.

Nature was not.

Gritting her teeth, Krona followed.

The wind died as they stepped under the protective eaves of the gorge. Stonework houses immediately met them on all sides, shaded and protected. Cisterns and drains lined the causeway directly beneath the ceiling's mighty gap, directing and gathering the rain when it came, turning the drought-prone region into what could have been a thriving metropolis, but was instead an oasis for the mighty. Tall, lush plants—the kind that thrived in the shadows—grew in pots of every size, the clay molded, all bulbous and banded.

Some trees grew not in pots at all, but had been allowed to take root at will in the cracks of the stone flooring—even inside houses themselves, which Krona found strange. A few trees blocked doors, making them unusable. Yet others seemed to have sprung up directly in the middle of the roadways, and she supposed the people had just decided, oddly, to walk around them.

Everything smelled earthen. Even though she'd grown up in Lutador, to Krona it was a homey scent. Comfortable, warm.

There should have been sentries to bar their path at the top of the stairs. Stepping foot in this city without an invitation was forbidden—a mortal sin for a Xyoparian citizen and a declaration of war from anyone else during precedented times. But they were already at war, and these times were anything but precedented. The fact that no alarm was raised and no one rushed to evict them from the city only cemented Krona's certainty: the capital was dead in a way it had never been before.

Time continued to venture deeper into the city, and Krona was loathe to lose her, but could not stop herself from running to various windows, pulling back the woven hangings that Xyoparians used in place of shutters or glass, to peer inside. There were bodies, of course, but all ancient and wrapped, set in places of honor. No fresh corpses. No molded food now being devoured by rats or cats. But nor was there evidence of evacuation—open, bare cupboards and stripped beds. Doors were intact. The walls and waterways were pristine. No sign of fire or destruction—no indication war had come to Xyopar City directly. There was no clear evidence as to where the servants of the dead had gone.

There was as of yet no sign of Absolon, either, and she could not imagine the two things were unconnected.

Time only stopped venturing forward whenever she came across a statue of Emotion, and there were many, all carved in the esteemed Amarna style. As ever, zhe was represented as a starburst, but in many of these, zhur head was a disc, like that of the sun, and a sensual human form was suggested beneath the rays. Xyopar was the land of Emotion, truly, embracing color and creativity and the bonds between people that could not be severed, even in death.

These depictions appeared to speak to Time, and though Krona could not read her every expression, she clearly forced herself to move on when there was something about each that made her want to linger.

A mile into the city, Krona startled when a flock of doves burst from a natural nook near the city's ceiling, darting through the sunbeams eking in through the narrow gap in the top of the gorge. Their wings sent oversized, unearthly shadows dancing, made the sunlight strobe. As one of the alarmed birds came right at her, Krona raised a hand to ward it off, and it wasn't until the doves had departed and the way was clear again that she saw it: the Necropalacia.

And Time was headed directly for the palace's dark maw of a doorway, without concern.

Or respect.

"Wait!" Krona hissed, afraid to raise her voice, afraid the echoes of her call might raise the specter of whatever sinister force had left the capital barren. "We can't go in there."

"Why not?"

"Only the living eze may look upon zhur court."

"That is not a reason."

"It is sacrosanct. And we have not been washed or even blessed. We should not even be in the city, we—"

"In whose name would you be blessed now? You just found out your gods are no such thing."

"Does that mean nothing is sacred?"

Krona, faithful as she was, had never been particularly religious. And, truly, she'd spent many a day pursuing blasphemies. But that did not mean she failed to observe and respect certain customs—most especially when it came to the dead. To the dead that people loved, that they'd poured their hearts into protecting.

There was no one left here to speak for the bodies in the Necropalacia, and it seemed unfair to allow traditions that had been kept for centuries to go completely unnoted—to be obliterated by ignorance.

"I know you're out there!" came a rasping shout from within, cutting Krona's protests short. "*I can feel you.*"

Time was off like a shot from a quintbarrel, bolting into the darkness.

Absolon was already inside—had already trespassed. Of course he had. He'd *built* most of Arkensyre's traditions. Traditions to bind, obscure, and suppress. He felt no need to respect what he himself might have invented on a whim, no matter what it had come to mean to an entire city-state's worth of people.

Krona tried to remind herself that sanctity had no place in war. If the life of the average citizen was no longer held as protected, then she could not expect the dead to fare better.

Still, it was difficult to follow Time. Xyopar was her heritage, where her family roots were planted. Walking into the throne room felt like treading on the bodies of her ancestors, and each step sent ill tremors through her bones.

The throne room itself was longer than any room she'd ever entered, grander even than anything in the palace of the Grand Marquises, but it was by no means empty. Great sandy-colored limestone columns rose several stories high all around, supporting a great roof that was surprisingly open to the elements. Every few feet of ceiling sported a grand skylight, devoid of glass or any other covering, which lit the interior floor. There were no other windows, which meant any area the skylights could not illuminate lay in deep shadow.

Not one, but many, *many* thrones occupied the room. They lined the floor and piled up at the back of the great space like their own city. Each was a bespoke construction, their joiners and stone carvers expert craftspeople, and no two were alike. Their backs were peaked at different heights, like spires, and each was commanding in its presence—as imposing as any tall tower. The grouping of thrones started at the rear of the room and seemed to roll forward like a wave, cresting at a single point: the throne of the current eze.

All the thrones were occupied. Dead rulers sat in silent judgment all around, each tied in a crouching position. Some had their skeletal hands over their faces, shielding their eyes from the sight of the dead around them so that they would not realize that they, too, had died. From between their thin fingers, sometimes their blank eye sockets could be seen, or their curled lips and bared teeth—mouths open in a frozen parody of a scream. Many of the corpses retained their hair, and it was set in elaborate styles atop their near-skeletal heads.

Some of the bodies were adorned with well-woven blankets, light and warm—new, their colors still vibrant, not yet faded by the desert's winds. Others had elaborate headdresses flanked with feathers from the flightless birds native to the lower Valley's oases. Each possessed a ceremonial weapon. Maces, swords, axes, and staves littered the room, some so old that age and rust had clearly touched them, despite the attention of servants.

No matter their age or state of decay, the mummies all wore jewels in the finest settings. Krona did not know if the dead wore emotionstones like the living, but the invocation of Emotion and zhur power was clear.

One with glass eyes caught Krona's attention, the spark of light in what should have been an empty eye socket sending a spike of unease through her limbs. The fake eyes were far more disturbing than the dried-out lumps deep-set in many of the other skulls; these followed her, watched her, seemed to judge her trespassing.

But it was the center throne that caught Krona off guard. She'd expected that one to be empty—for the Eze to be gone, to be wherever all the rest of the living Xyoparians had escaped to—but there zhe was.

Krona was moving before she could think, going to the Eze, slumped on zhur throne, looking unnaturally drawn compared to when Krona had seen zhim just a few years earlier, at the palace rotunda in Lutador. That, of course, had been a pair of bone wings and a lifetime ago.

Zhe was breathing, but try as she might, Krona could not wake zhim. And that's when she noticed zhur hands and feet. At first, they seemed tied to the throne, but no. They were *rooted* to the throne. They were *themselves* roots, dug in and twisted. Like Knowledge.

Then it struck her. The trees. The odd placement of so many. In doorways, butting up against tables, standing in the streets.

Like people.

They *were* people. Or had been once.

Perhaps that was something Absolon could do with his stolen physiopathy. Perhaps.

But . . .

As if merely thinking his name had invoked him, the Savior came striding out of the darkened space between the thrones in the back-right corner of the room, trailing a long, thick leash behind him in one hand, a silver javelin in the other. Just as when Krona had seen him before, he wore a plain black mask, hiding his face, but the cut of his silhouette was unmistakable. This was the same man who'd twisted her bones, who'd laughed in the face of her newfound power.

Krona stumbled away from the Eze, as though thrust back—as though Absolon's presence were akin to a mighty gale, forcing her away and off her feet.

"I see you've acquired a pet," he said snidely, clearly addressing Time.

"You arrogant prick," she spat in return.

"Tad touchy after our long sleep, are we?" He took a deep breath then, shoulders rising and falling dramatically. "No, I'm sorry. I never mean to be cattish with you; you deserve better. But somehow, it simply comes out. Perhaps in another life we could have called it banter."

Time curled her lip, openly disgusted. "In another life I might not find you so *vile*, but in this one, *I remember*," she said, beating her chest with one fist, pointing off into the distance with another. "I remember every twisted thing you said to me while I was under your spell—while my mind was captive. I remember what you had us all do, how we pressed and pulled the land, the air currents, the seasons. And I know how you played with "Emotion's" form like putty. Do not think for even an instant that you can tease or bootlick your way back into my good graces."

Crouching low, Krona crab-walked into the forest of thrones, creeping through the gaps between, weaving her way around and back. Absolon's attention was fixed on Time; they were two great powers meeting head on, and she could only hope that meant Absolon had no spare thoughts for her.

She moved slowly from the left of the great room toward the right, calling up Ninebark as she went. The fen seeped slowly from her, a light mist and nothing more.

"I did what was necessary to preserve humanity," Absolon shot back. "The lot of you had decided it was over, but it wasn't. You were content to have them scratch out a living in barren dirt, and I *wasn't.* You could have made this land a paradise and refused, so I did what I had to and gave it to them. Humanity began anew, in innocence."

"In *ignorance,*" Time countered.

"As long as everyone remembered how the world had been, it was going to poison the present—"

"You decided *everything* for them. You didn't stand back and let them just *be.* You constructed their reality. You robbed them of an essential part of their existence and built a new world from the ground up. You stratified their society from the get-go, constructed kingdoms, divided lands. You wrote their holy texts!"

Absolon tensed as she spoke, and he punched out each of his next words with a fury. "I made you *gods.*"

"You made us slaves!"

Time launched herself into the air, breaking up the shafted light just as the doves had, creating a dazzling flurry of flashes. She was a bird of prey, all tearing talons and rigid limbs. Her face was a tortured portrait of righteous vengeance, eyes dark, teeth bared.

Absolon moved as if unconcerned—not to meet her head on in a fight, but to bring his leashed monstrosity into the light.

The creature appeared from behind him, as if out of thin air, squeezing out of nothing into something, slipping through an invisible seam in time and space.

Twice as tall as Absolon, despite its heavy hunch, it had six limbs, all with too many joints, two upon which it stood, bowlegged, and four of which dragged against the floor. Its hands looked broken and useless, as though they'd been smashed again and again and had been badly set on purpose. It had the body of an overly skeletal man, its bare chest and stomach sunken as if from hunger, its pale skin stretched taut over thin ribs. Sharp hip bones protruded from a dirty loincloth that barely graced the tops of its thighs, and its feet were bare and dry, cracking and gnarled.

The sad creature had the ears of a bat and six veined, leathery wings to match. Hair may have once graced its head, just as eyes may have once peered out from beneath its brow, but now the top of its head was a smooth, doll-like cap of skin, devoid of ridges or definition. Its lips were chapped and puffy—blood visible between the cracking—and they were spread in a wide, vacant smile.

Absolon's leash trailed down from a collar lashed tightly around its neck.

Though the thing did not attempt to pinpoint Time, she stopped short, her fierce descent halting in midair as she processed what she was seeing.

Nature. Krona had no doubt, this sorry-looking thing was Nature.

Time dropped like a stone, landing heavily on her feet. Her gaze saw nothing but her brother, all else had melted away for her. She reached out her hands—all of them, rushing forward for him as if Absolon wasn't even there between them. "Shim?" she asked, her voice sad and pitched high, like a small child's.

Absolon tugged on the leash and Nature *hissed,* bared his fangs, raised one set of dragging hands, and displayed his claws.

Time reeled back, flapping her wings to get away all the quicker from his gnashing.

Krona's hand instinctually went to her side pouch, where Nature's mind still rested.

"You twisted him, just like you twisted Punabi!" Time shouted.

"Oh no," Absolon said, shaking his head. "He did this to himself."

"How? You removed his will."

"And yet there are forces within us governed by other things. The changes came slowly, to be sure. I believe this form better reflects how he truly feels about himself. How he sees himself. As a monster."

"Zoshim wouldn't—" Time's gaze narrowed. "*What did you make him do?*"

Krona saw her chance. Absolon shifted, Nature's wings flared. The Savior was on the offensive. He saw Time's moment of weakness, of openness, and intended to exploit it. Krona would do the same.

She forced out the remainder of her magic, giving Ninebark her full, solid form. The fen charged at Absolon, and Krona held her breath.

Absolon's head snapped in her direction. "As if I hadn't planned for you," he scoffed, raising the javelin with an expert hand, his arm strong and his aim true.

Ninebark leapt and the javelin, thrown in a strong arc, struck, spearing her through, sending her barreling back to the floor in among the thrones, several of them scattering as the fen's form crashed into them. Ninebark shrieked in a discordant tone Krona had never heard before, the usually brilliant tinkling and thrum of her chiming twisting into the cry of a wounded animal. The javelin's end dug into the stone of the floor—like it was a giant collector's pin and Ninebark was a dead butterfly. It immobilized her as surely as quintbarrel needles immobilized a varg, keeping her stuck fast to the spot, her body impaled.

Ninebark was trapped, and Krona's magic was trapped with her.

Krona watched her fen's fall in horror, and when she looked back to Absolon, his satisfaction was clear in the line of his shoulders. She dared not go to Ninebark's side, knowing all it would take was a flick of Absolon's wrist for him to have control of her bones again—the memory of that first twisting sending an ache through her spine and shoulders.

"Be reasonable," Absolon said to Time, attention once again leaving Krona like she was no more of note than an errant bit of dirt he'd had to brush from his robes. "You cannot say this world is worse now than when we came into it. You cannot really look around at these city-states and tell me you'd prefer the Valley as we found it. Now, beyond—*beyond* my Valley, *that* is what happens when human power is left unchecked.

"I leveled the playing field. I ensured that each person comes into this world the same."

"You dictate how they come into this world. You infringe on their rights to their own bodies from nearly the moment they are born. You steal their magic—"

"Magic isn't gone. It's simply controlled. You and I lived through the same apocalypse, *how* can you not *see*—"

"All I see is a wretched man who always yearned for praise and importance. And instead of escaping our former lives, you learned all the wrong lessons and took power for yourself."

"And what about you? You were always a stubborn, selfish *brat* who couldn't see her tasks through."

They were hitting at the heart of each other. These were not the jabs of great political powers—not the insults of emperors or ezes or grand marquises thrown at each other. No, these slights were *petty*.

Personal.

"What do you expect from me, *Lonny*?" Time demanded. "You know I would move the heavens for Zoshim and lay my body between you and Punabi every time, so what are you expecting I'll do now? You think I'll suddenly come around to your way of thinking? That your millennia's worth of manipulation can be discarded so easily? I am awake, and I am willing to rend you limb from limb. Give me Zoshim, and I might yet let you live."

Absolon was silent for a long moment. There was a blankness about his whole person, made all the more unreadable by his mask. Then, definitively, his hackles raised, he stood taller, and though only the smallest of changes had taken place, his entire being looked meaner, callousness oozing from every pore. "What's one less god to a godless world?"

He snapped his fingers.

The Necropalacia shook, grit falling from the ceiling.

Nature's wings and arms rose together, straining toward the ceiling, toward the heavens. His face was a mask of someone else's emotions—puppeted as he was by the Savior's will. His hands cupped, fingers curling skyward as though he could grasp the air and rip through it—as though hefting a great weight upward before tearing it all down. All his sets of wings and arms twisted, ramming downward as his entire body shook with a fury and a tormented cry wrenched itself raggedly through his throat, wordless and awful.

The phantom of remembrance made Krona twist with his arms, anticipating her bones rending and her body tearing itself apart from the inside out, but no such violent deformation came.

Instead, a great creaking rose up around the throne room—like fragile branches breaking in a high wind. And then a great flurry of dust—a small cloud of it rose around each mummy. A haze of centuries' worth of motes and mites fluttered into the air, and everything in the room seemed to slip sideways, as though gravity had shifted. All the corpses lurched forward, thrown from their dignified perches, tossed onto the ivory-and-pearl tiled floor.

And each desiccated pair of hands *caught their own fall.*

The ancient bodies shuddered, shivered, snapped their bindings. Some gasped—their calcified lungs heaving, suddenly pliable, as they pushed against their bonds, the old ropes unraveling in moments. Ligaments snapped and barely there skin sluffed off like so much powder, but none of that stopped the corpses from lurching to their feet. Nature was Absolon's puppet, and these ancient rulers, in turn, were his; his was the power of evolution, change. He could take hold of organic matter in any state and warp it to his liking.

The mummy closest to Krona lifted its face toward her as though she were the sun and it was seeking light. Its dried lips had shrunken tight over its teeth, and its eyes were nothing more than dark pits. The skin of its cheeks was so tight it could barely move its jaw, though it tried—the hard lump of its tongue rolling like a glass marble behind the prison bars of its teeth. A weak whimper rattled out of its chest, like a plea, and Krona tuned away, bile rising in her throat.

She had to believe the mummy's apparent agony was nothing but a by-product of Nature's manipulation—that its skull was empty, and its heart gone, and its nerve endings still shriveled and lifeless.

The scraping of weapons across throne and floor roused Krona from her shock. She grabbed the nearest one she could get her hands on—a nine-ringed broadsword, curved, its rings rusted—before gnarled fingers could grasp it first, and set herself before the living Eze, ready to defend zhim.

The dead rushed at Time. With a shout, she turned half a dozen of them to dust—forcing time to ravage them the way it had yet to naturally—before Absolon forced Nature to throw up wards to prevent her kairopathy from subsuming their forms. As yet more bodies swarmed her, Time went for the snake's head, turning her devastating magic on Absolon himself—whether to stop time in his vital organs or force him to wither from instant thirst or hunger, Krona could not say.

But he was prepared. Nature took him by the shoulder with one bent hand, fortifying him against her attacks. Absolon was weak to Time's magic, but Time was weak to Nature's.

Krona had little time to wonder what that meant for the balance of the fight. Reanimated corpses descended on her as well, their cudgels and blades raised by tendon-less arms just as readily as they'd been wielded in life.

Krona swung the broadsword with precision. Though her weapon was old and dulled her arms were strong, and where the blade could not cut, the force of her swing ripped and tore. She severed limbs, slashed through ribs, and decapitated more than one ancient eze.

As it turned out, the respect she had for the dead only went so far. But it didn't matter how many bits she carved away, the dead did not stop.

Time was forced to turn her attention away from assailing Absolon directly. The bodies were relentless, clawing even after they'd lost their sword arms, biting after they had no more hands to grasp with.

Jewels pinged across the stones. Chains rattled and molted feathers burst. Time wrenched a mace and an axe from the horde, pulling arms away with them, still grasping like the heads of dead carpenter ants at the tangs.

Together, she and Krona pulverized the masses just to keep upright and keep breathing. Behind Krona, the Eze was still safe. Behind zhim, Ninebark frantically chimed but could not move. All around, body parts writhed without their owners, ever unyielding.

These ancient rulers had been intact for centuries. Respected. Cared for. Now they were bone meal. Worse than worm food—dust and chips to be ground into nothing.

Krona was ankle-deep in desiccated flesh, and still, more mummies came—those from beyond the Necropalacia, in Xyopar City. Absolon had seemingly endless fodder to throw at them.

And Krona realized this was how he saw the people of Arkensyre—the living as well the dead. Hintosep had said as much, but now Krona truly understood. To one such as him, everlasting, one person was much like the next, here in a blink, then gone. Just a piece in the ever-revolving puzzle. Part of a picture, but worthless in and of themselves. He spoke of leveling the playing field as if he were only a servant to a noble endeavor, but the truth was all he saw *was the field*—not the players. The schema, not the parts.

The system, not its people.

Dust and dried blood filled the air. Krona sucked it into her lungs and blinked it from her eyes. Though she felled many, there were those who still landed blows. Her arms bore a tapestry of cuts, bruises littered her torso, and a set of teeth had imbedded themselves in her thigh. Sweat dripped down her brow, and she wasn't sure how long she could stay on her feet as the bodies piled higher. Soon she'd drown in them.

Time fared better, batting through the mummies with nary a scratch on all but her wings—mummies leapt onto her feathers, tearing at them, clinging, weighing them down. She bucked them off like a horse biting at flies, but they were only replaced by more and more. She could not stem the flow—nor could she find a spare moment to assail Absolon's defenses, look for weak points. Her cries of frustration rose as round and round they went, too evenly matched.

"Enough!" she screamed, pouring power into that word, vaporizing everything within arm's reach for the briefest respite, before the horde pushed to her side once more. She flew upward, up to one of the skylights, clinging to its edge upside down, and Krona braced herself for an influx of kairopathy.

But Time had other ideas. "I will tear your new world down to its foundations!" she screeched.

Then, in a bluster, she was gone.

Black pin feathers, pulled loose in the onslaught, fluttered down around Krona. She'd been abandoned by Time. Again.

She had no magic, no allies, and no chance of staunching the bleed of Xyopar's dead.

PART THREE

Plight of the Godless

28

HAILWIC

In a Time and Place Before

From out of the pitch-black came a flame. A single, flickering point on the end of a match, held extended by a shrouded arm. It touched down on one wick, seeming to leap through the darkness to another, then another, until the uneven candle stubs—which rose like a black-and-gold miniature city from the center of the table—were all alight. Beneath the little faux, waxy buildings, radiating out from the center, stretched the engravings of a chemical and magichanical engineering slate—so familiar to Hailwic, yet from a different life altogether. The carved concentric circles bore radial markings—hashes, brackets, and guillemets—all plated in various types of metal, which glinted in the firelight.

A tingle of anticipation glided through Hailwic's lips and fingertips, and she was grateful for every face sat around the oval of the slate.

Ever since Lonny had delivered the forbidden books into the RFR's safekeeping, Hailwic had found the occult colonizing her mind. She'd read each book cover to cover. Once. Twice. Three times, at least. Each time, she'd been drawn back to the idea of a tithe. Not just its romanticism, but its practicality. A tithing gave those bound together an edge of awareness; the ability to sense one another's location and general well-being.

Privately, she'd imagined how things might have gone differently if she'd been tithed to Professor Solric. She wouldn't have needed Uphrasia to surprise her with a dossier of surveillance photos to know fey were in trouble. And if she'd known sooner—if she'd been able to call for help *sooner*—perhaps fey would still be alive.

At her behest, those with her now had donned black hooded robes for the ceremony. The shrouds blended with the muted darkness all around, leaving their faces to hover and their eyes to gleam.

Hailwic suspected the robes were dyed recently; the smell of the chemicals from the dye bath still clung. She was thankful Kinwold had gone through the trouble; they could have just as easily thought the ancient trappings unnecessary at best, silly at worst, but had taken Hailwic's plan seriously as soon as she'd proposed it.

Uphrasia coveted what she feared: her use of physiopathic doctors and her desire to harness the power of transformation in physiobombs not only spoke of that covetousness, but screamed it. Uphrasia's twin *fear and fascination* with these books and their ancient magical knowledge loomed large in Hailwic's mind, like it was the lynchpin to the Friend's stability and rule. Hailwic envisioned pulling on that pin, watching everything Uphrasia was tumble—collapse—like so many unmoored building blocks.

If Uphrasia feared the arcane, then she thought she could harness it. And if she could harness it, so could the rebels. So could Hailwic, and Kinwold, and their most trusted allies.

Hailwic glanced at Lonny, who sat directly across from her, rigidly quiet, the fringe of his mousy brown hair hiding his eyes. He'd been the most eager to participate, the most in line with Hailwic. Their unique understanding of Uphrasia bound them together already, like links in a chain, and they were of the same mind when it came to how best to undermine her.

Kinwold flicked their wrist, extinguishing the match. The candle flames threw wavering shadows over their furrowed brow and sharp nose. It seemed to deepen their frown and add decades to their features.

Directly before them, clamped to the slate, stood a cylindrical device, the etchings in its copper-colored exterior lined up to perfectly match the etchings on the marble. Such chemical diffusers were as familiar to Hailwic as the slate itself—both modern, and yet perfectly effective stand-ins for the sacrificial stone and smoldering cauldron the texts had called for.

Kinwold twisted the top of the cylinder, and the body of it shifted shape, the walls becoming hexagonal instead of smooth. The top opened, the lid of it lifting in triangled sections—hinged at the new corners—and folding back.

A faint red glow came from within, and the scent of smoke—far more smoke than could be created by the candles' little flames—filled the room.

Glensen stirred between Lonny and Kinwold, feir dark, elfin face hardened with determination. Fey had insisted on doing a full medical review of the ceremony and its ingredients before consenting—not just to feir own participation, but to anyone's participation. It was clear fey still weren't sure the tithing would even work, but at the very least, fey'd been confident the six of them weren't going to accidently poison themselves.

"That's my cue," fey said, eyes reflecting the red light like embers.

On Hailwic's left, Zoshim searched for her hand in the dark, finding it quickly and entangling their fingers, giving her grip a strong squeeze.

Hailwic unwaveringly squeezed back.

While she'd mused and turned over many *what-ifs* related to tithing and Professor Solric, Hailwic hadn't allowed herself to blatantly imagine *other* tithings. Namely, what might have been salvaged if she'd been tithed to her family.

It hurt too much and the guilt was too great to let herself wonder how many things in her life might have improved if she, Zoshim, and their parents had been able to feel one another's distresses. Would her parents have chosen to better protect Zoshim? Would the four of them still be together, as a family? Would her mother and father, at the very least, still be alive?

As Glensen stood, Zoshim turned to offer Hailwic a small, reassuring smile, which came from unfamiliar lips. He no longer looked as he had when they'd first traversed through the inhabited portion of the tunnels down into this cordoned-off section (made off-limits under the professor's tenure due to structural instability). Now, he was old. Elderly. Hair white and wiry, with a beard curling down to his collarbone and bushy eyebrows that drooped over his lids. But he hadn't simply aged himself. This was another man's face entirely. Stronger nose, stronger cheekbones. Skin paler, and papery.

She realized the skin of his hand *felt* papery too. The bones thin, the ligaments fragile.

It unnerved her for a moment—his abrupt change from strong young man into someone so frail. Looking for strength, she reached out to her right, fumbling for Punabi's hand under the slate, but couldn't find it. For a moment she brushed what she thought was skin, but Punabi suddenly crossed zhur arms, pulling away.

Hailwic tried not to feel rebuffed.

Zhe didn't want to be here. At all. Where Glensen had merely been skeptical, Punabi was resistant and resentful. Hailwic's deep dive into the unknown had stolen hours of her attention and concerned Punabi. It wasn't in zhim to be petty, or jealous of focus turned elsewhere; instead, it seemed to be Hailwic's sudden fervor for concepts on the fringe that raised zhur hackles and put a defensive box around their every conversation.

In the end, zhe'd agreed to participate, and Hailwic was under no illusions that zhe'd given in to Hailwic's entreaties out of love and nothing more.

Zhe had no faith in the process itself. It wasn't even that zhe thought a tithing hokum and expected it not to work; zhe had no qualms making it clear zhe simply thought it *useless*. A wasted effort, whose time and resources were better spent elsewhere—despite Hailwic trying to educate zhim on the benefits.

Glensen scurried into the shadows, to the edge of the room, pulling several tall medical poles into view. Fey set one next to each of their six chairs. Clean, clear tubing coiled down from the hooks on these poles, which Glensen plugged into ports on the open diffuser.

"Arms, please," Glensen directed.

They all bared a forearm, pulling up their robes and laying it out on the slate top, limp and loose. In the candlelight, each limb looked severed. Lifeless.

Sacrificial.

A rattling medical cart made its appearance from the gloom, propelled by Glensen's busy, professional hands. A black-cloth-covered box and several different types of needles lay neatly atop it, looking strangely out of place in their sanitary packaging. "These are cannulas," fey explained, holding one of the packages up. "To help facilitate both the extraction and infusion."

"Awfully modern for this *ancient rite,*" Punabi scoffed under zhur breath.

"Some people used to use their teeth to tear open each other's veins for the ritual," Lonny said flatly from zhur other side. "We could try that."

Hailwic smirked despite herself, wishing she could squeeze *Lonny's* hand in thanks.

His solidarity was unwavering.

"I'll stick with the needles, thanks," Punabi grumbled.

Beneath the black cloth, something chittered.

Kinwold's eyes went wide. "You brought a live one?"

"It has to be fresh," Hailwic said, grinding down the defensive edge in her tone. Kinwold had been gracious to give her this. They took fewer and fewer suggestions these days, preferring to travel in tried and true steps—to be hemmed in by the ruts and tracks created by their predecessor—than forge new paths and risk losing it all. When Hailwic had broached the possibility of a tithing, she'd expected a kind rebuff, and was pleasantly surprised when Kinwold—after serious consideration—agreed.

"We used freeze-dried glands in the lab," they said.

"There's even a synthetic option now," Lonny added, shifting in his chair, his previous liquid smugness turning to brittle discomfort.

"It won't work for the tithing," Hailwic explained, keeping her voice even. "It has to be straight from the source."

Punabi leaned toward Lonny. "*What* does?"

"Vipnika pheromones."

Glensen whisked back the black cloth, revealing a hypodermically sealed enclosure with clear sides—the whole thing no bigger than a shoe—with a small, curled nub of fleshy pink inside, set atop a nest of lichen. After a moment in the candlelight, the vipnika uncurled, stretching and yawning, flashing its sharp little teeth. It looked docile. Adorable, even, to the right set of ignorant eyes. With another high-pitched chitter, it rolled over, still clinging to sleep.

It could kill all on its own. Joined with its brethren, it could strip a living person down to bone in minutes, but a lone vipnika could be just as deadly. All it had to do was launch itself at the right spot, burrowing into an artery or directly into the heart.

It would have been safer for Hailwic to bring a bear into their midst. At least they could keep track of a bear should it escape.

Glensen pushed the tray around the slate, taking up the needles and inserting one end of the dangling intravenous tubing into everyone's arms. Hailwic curled her fist and looked away as it slid into her vein, heavy and tugging, but not painful. Around and around the medic went, checking and rechecking the IVs before bringing the tray back around to feir own chair and breaking the seal on the enclosure.

The seams hissed as they disengaged, translucent vapors wafting into the candlelight for a moment before dissipating. Vipnika enclosures were designed to feed the creatures sedative-laced air, and it would only take a few minutes out in the open for the effects to wear off.

"Hey there, little guy," Glensen cooed, reaching in with a pair of tweezers while the others held their breath. Fey gripped the animal gently, and in response, the vipnika whined—its voice crying out at an ear-piercing register—and gnashed its fishhook teeth. "I know, I know, it's no fun. We'll get you back to the colony soon."

Fey pinned the wriggling thumbnail of a creature to the slate top with the tweezers, then, with the smallest needle Hailwic had ever seen—so thin, it nearly disappeared in the dark—fey carefully pierced each of the vipnika's two glands beneath its little arms, extracting perhaps a microgram of the scent agent. The animal was not happy—curling its legs and tossing its head, calling out for its brethren to come burrow into these humans and eat their fill.

But there were no other vipnika to hear. Their numbers had been dropping in the wild for a long time, and they were eradicated within cities. Scientific collection meant most of their population were housed in labs, farmed for their reactive agents.

Glensen continued to titter at it until fey had it placed safely back in its containment cage. Fey handed the needle with its drop of precious pheromones to Kinwold before going back to feir seat and inserting feir own IV line.

"Are we ready?" Kinwold prompted.

Punabi tensed. Hailwic willed zhim not to protest, not to delay. The vipnika was already breathing clean air. Already its little lungs were pumping sobering oxygen into its bloodstream, clearing its mind and sharpening its senses.

The group had already chosen this path. To waver now—to be divided now—would only increase the danger.

"This feels more like mysticism than magic," zhe said under zhur breath, barely loud enough for Hailwic to hear. "Not very . . . scientific."

"It is scientific," Hailwic whispered back, skin prickling into goose flesh. "The reactive agent in the vipnika will bind with the pneuma in our blood and create a resonance within each of us."

Punabi turned toward her, voice full-bodied. "And the candles? The cloaks? The chanting?"

Kinwold smiled softly, ever patient. "Everything is a circle," they said. "We pretend like physics, chemistry, magic, memory, and spirituality are each their own division of reality. But they are all connected. Just because you do not see the logic behind the effect doesn't mean an effect isn't produced."

"And what effect am I looking for?" zhe pressed.

"A centering," Hailwic said. "A focus. When we hear a repeated rhythm and stare at narrow points of light, we bring our true selves to the surface. A fluttering of pneuma that is entirely subconscious."

"Or so the ancient texts say." Punabi did not hide just how dubious zhe thought said texts.

"Or so the ancient texts say," Hailwic echoed with a firmness.

Softly, Hailwic began the chant. She let the primal syllables escape from deep in her throat: *E ii mai, nomé tu e. Fera no stom. Ii ot. Ii ot. Ii ot.*

Around her, the others joined in, one by one. First Zoshim, and lastly Punabi. Their six entwined tones and rhythms were disparate at first, then slowly synchronized to become one firm incantation—voices entwined, just as they'd soon be entwined body and soul.

E ii mai, nomé tu e.

Fera no stom.

Ii ot.

Ii ot.

Ii ot.

Hailwic had found no direct translation. They could be nonsense words—the sounds more important than any meaning—or they could be a prayer. An entreaty.

It could be an invitation for an ancient deity to rise.

It could be a promise.

Or a curse.

Hailwic couldn't help but assume its potential was their potential. Whatever the chant meant to them, it would mean. Whatever it meant, they would become.

She nearly missed Kinwold moving—inserting the syringe tip with the vipnika hormones into a port on the side of the diffuser. While their lips continued to move in time with the chant, they bent their face over the red glow, watching with eager eyes as the preprepared chemical bath inside shifted to pink, then purple, then soft blue.

With a nod, they told Zoshim it was time.

Beside Hailwic, the old man she knew but did not know held out his hand, fingers splayed wide. The blood began to flow. It rushed from six arms, six veins, through the clear tubing, looking black as tar as it barreled through the loops that lay in shadow.

Nothing pulled, nothing hurt. Hailwic continued with her chanting alongside the others, only vaguely aware that as their blood reached the diffuser, their tempo increased. It had a frantic edge to it, born of uncertainty.

In its cage, the vipnika *screamed.*

Glensen's head whipped in the creature's direction. Kinwold's hand came down heavily on feirs. "Don't stop. Keep the chant going," they ordered.

E ii mai, nomé tu e.

Fera no stom.

Ii ot.

Ii ot.

Ii ot.

Whirring to life, the diffuser vibrated as it performed its duty, mixing their collective essence with the vipnika's, blending it all into a bloody mass before turning it over to centrifugal forces.

Kinwold pressed several switches on the diffuser and a new essence—not blood, not red, not blue, now clear and viscous—oozed its way out of the device's base and into the cervices of the slate. It crawled along the plated divots like they were miniature canals and it was some wretched chemical spill, filling in every divot it could find. It spread slowly but evenly through the etchings, curving through the layers and the symbols, filling them in and encompassing the candles.

Kinwold snapped their fingers and the ooze retreated like a thing afraid—a thing *alive*—back into the diffuser.

The taps were reversed, and what had once been an outlet for blood now became an ingress for the newly manipulated solution. Hailwic watched it coil through the tubing, heart fluttering and lips still moving as the clear fluid snaked toward her.

"*E ii mai, nomé tu e,*" she breathed, voice failing her even as the others' grew.

Fera no stom.

Ii ot.

Ii ot.

Ii ot!

The liquid hit her with a chill. A stream of ice ran through her narrow vein, pushing the warmth of her blood aside, demanding entry with an aching pressure that she'd never felt from a saline infusion.

Pushing. Pushing. Past her elbow, her biceps to clutch at her shoulder and give it a grinding throb. Under her collar, across that delicate bone to seep beneath her ribs and collide with her heart.

A single *thu-thump* of the muscle grabbed hold of that cold and flung it through her body. The chambers of her heart became like frosted snow, crushing and crunching under its own pressure, then expanded and blown about like a flurry through her lungs. She sucked in bits of herself when she tried to breathe, and that breath was frozen. Chilled to a sharp shout of sensation. When she breathed it out, she breathed herself out, and fluttered through the air, misted—atomized—to be sucked in by the stuttering gasps of Punabi and Zoshim and Lonny and Glensen and Kinwold.

Likewise, the bits of herself that had been expelled were hastily replaced with flakes of the others, melding together, reforming inside her body.

She shut her eyes against the sensation of frigid melting. Resculpting.

When she no longer felt like she was fracturing and reforming, she opened her eyes.

Five other gazes sat interposed atop hers.

Five other sets of limbs thrummed with varying pulses beside hers.

Five other stomachs were also queasy.

Five other heads also spun.

Someone swallowed and the spasm hit them all simultaneously, causing most of them to cough, but someone gagged which sent the sensation bouncing through all of them, building and squeezing as they all tried to breathe/swallow/cough/choke at the same time.

Glensen shot to feir feet, reeling backward, and the others reeled with fem. Panic rippled around the slate and everyone started to shout.

"Calm!" Kinwold said, yet Hailwic could feel the words forming in her own mouth. "Stay calm, it'll subside!"

Lonny was on his feet as well, listing to the side as he tried to grab at Glensen across the slate even though fey were out of reach.

The medic spun, falling into the medical cart, catching the vipnika enclosure with a wild arm and flinging it to the floor. The corner caught feir elbow—which meant it caught all their elbows—and they collectively hissed at the contusion.

The creature shrieked in triumph as its cage hit the stone floor and popped open, setting it free.

Hailwic shot to her feet, meaning to contain it—to inflict a small time stop. But rising to her own feet set the world spinning as she saw it and felt it from a half a dozen different angles. She felt drunker than she'd ever managed to get on her own, more in her body and out of her body than should have been possible. She aimed and missed, losing the tiny animal in the dark.

"Stop it!" came a collective reverberation of voices.

Lonny vaulted atop the slate, then over it again, moving faster than she'd ever seen him move, lurching with the sensation of it. He bounded through the darkness like a bloodhound, using his cryptopathy to unhide the hidden.

She felt what it was like to be a Cryptopath, to sense secrets. In a lot of ways it was like kairopathy—expansive. Secrets were everywhere, as time was everywhere. There was a tickling urge to *hide, hide, hide*—a feeling, not words—that Lonny zeroed in on. That a tiny mind like a vipnika's could have secrets seemed both wonderous and absurd.

Lonny zeroed in on that proto-secret, like finding a hot spot in an otherwise cold expanse of room. He lunged, his bare hands curling around his prey. He swung around, desperately trying to reorient himself to the cage as the vipnika began gnawing at his left palm.

The pain was shared pain. The little marsupial wasn't just eating through Lonny, it was eating through all of them. The frantic gnawing gave Hailwic a way to pinpoint her focus—to ignore the drunken duplicity of her mind and apply her kairopathy.

She clamped down on the animal, willing it to pause with its jaws open, head buried between the bones of Lonny's palm. A sense of wonder followed—Lonny's, as he marveled at her pathy in the same way she'd wondered at his.

Glensen scooped up the fallen enclosure, helping Lonny rid himself of the thing.

As the initial chaos of shared sensation began to die, Zoshim disengaged himself from his tubing and went to help heal Lonny's palm. At the same time, Punabi attempted to radiate calm, even though the shock of it all had rattled zhur bones thoroughly.

Hailwic nearly giggled, sensing everyone's pathies at once. She even mourned when the absurd level of sense-sharing waned, evaporated. Soon it reached a steady plane, where she could no longer see through their eyes or feel every small motion.

She could sense them as a force of presence. Their feelings—physical and emotional—were no longer hers, but if they were separated by continents, she knew she'd be able to find them. Could pinpoint them half a world away.

Her heart soared. It worked. She *had* them. They were hers and she was theirs.

They were all tied. Tithed.

Bonded, unbreakably.

29

AVELLINO

"Do not look away."

Gerome's bloodstained fingers snatched hold of Avellino's chin, digging in as the Grand Orchestrator forced him to stare at Thibaut's prone form.

The pale skin of his back peeled outward, leaving a glaring red swath of muscle and blood, over which little fingers of cyan haze petted as if to soothe. The bulk of the fen had tried to rear out of Thibaut's body, but Gerome had captured it—pinned it—with two short javelins of pure nickel thrust through the billowing mass and imbedded in the tabletop, their tips crisscrossing over Thibaut's form.

Gerome went to one of the many pipes curling out of Thibaut's back and jostled a bit of thickened pneuma loose so that it flowed freely. The sharp twist of it made Thibaut hiss through his teeth, and the ethereal fingers whipped upward and tried to lash at Gerome—not like fingers at all, more like many thin tails.

The nickel had the fen pinned fast, just as surely as quintbarrel needles pinned fully fleshed varger. Gerome paid the tendrils no mind.

He took up the scalpel again, extending the edges of the peel a little farther, and Avellino was suddenly assaulted by what he knew of his father's killings—how Louis Charbon had used a scalpel, much like this one, to inflict suffering, trying to bring evidence of magic to the surface.

"Pain can focus and pain can distort," Gerome mused, catching Avellino staring at the instrument. "And pain is always revealing.

"I will have to wall this away when I wall off these past years," Gerome said with a conversational sigh, moving to check and double-check the siphoning process. "The Savior has not permitted me to share this with you." He moved a glass beaker so it was better centered on a copper plate, whose wires ran over the table edge and into the wall. "For now, though, let this man's pain humble you. He would not *be here* if it weren't for you."

A million different ways to attack Gerome bled through Avellino's imagination. In each scenario, he hurtled himself at his former Possessor, gnashing as he'd seen Hintosep gnash at him. He could leap at his ankles, his belly, his throat, his ears. He envisioned ripping off his curtain of beads and gouging out his eyes with his thumbs.

But it was all hotheaded folly, and Avellino was a weak-spined coward when it came to Gerome.

Even so, there was a gentle push at his mind, like someone knocking to get in rather than shoving in the way Gerome often did. Avellino opened his mental door a crack, and a breathy *no, wait, be patient*, whispered through.

Avellino's cheeks grew hot. He was impotent next to Gerome while Thibaut was suffering right before him, and still Thibaut urged temperance.

"Sebastian remembers having his time taken," Mandip said to Juliet, hugging her close. "He came out okay."

Their dungeon cell was cold, the stones frigid to the touch in many places. The two of them huddled together, waiting for their captor's return. Mandip burrowed his nose into Juliet's hair, letting her soft, perfumed curls soothe him, and she nuzzled farther into his chest, though there was a stiffness about it.

"Darling," she said, voice pragmatic, "when the man who brainwashed my little brother says he's going to take our time, what makes you think he means to leave us with any of it?"

He tensed. "Oh."

"Yes. Oh."

Gerome meant to drain them. Which meant that these next few quiet minutes in this cell with Juliet were probably their last.

There were so many things left unsaid between them. Or, perhaps not unsaid, just . . . unconfirmed. Juliet was the type to spread her love widely, and though the two of them had come close on some occasions, they'd never discussed their feelings for each other with any earnestness.

To be earnest was to be vulnerable, and neither of them were very good at vulnerability.

They'd played into the running joke that they were engaged for years now. It was just a bit of fun at first, but the longer they played at it, the more it felt like a promise. *One day*, he'd thought. *One day*.

That one day would never come.

"Aren't you going to say it?" she asked suddenly, the arm she'd slung around his waist tightening.

He crawled quickly out of his own thoughts, instinctually squeezing her back. "Say what?" he asked.

After a moment, she sat up, her gaze intense but warm. She blinked at him slowly, like an affectionate cat. "Silly man. Isn't this the part where you say, *If this is our last night in this world, then I have to confess: I love you.*"

He huffed at her audacity. Leave it to Juliet to take the words right out of his mouth. "You are too impatient, my dear. I was trying to find the right words."

"Luckily I already had them at the ready for you." She leaned in, resting her forehead against his. "Will you say it? Please?"

"I love you."

She smiled softly. "Again?"

"I love you."

Her smile widened to a bright grin. "Again," she purred.

"*I love you.*"

"I knew it," she said triumphantly.

He pouted playfully, trying to stay spirited, but if this was just another tease, it would hurt, no question.

"Took you long enough," she said, jostling him good-naturedly.

"And . . . you?"

Her cheeks took on a bright blush. "And I . . . this is the part where I admit you've teased me so long, I wasn't sure if you truly—"

"*I've* teased *you*?"

"Dear one, I've waited for you to declare one way or another for years now."

He raised a cheeky eyebrow at her. "Waited?"

"Yes, *waited.* Not in utter chastity, no, but I've never claimed to be a monk. And I shan't be one after. As an artist, historically on the move from venue to venue, I don't tend toward long courtships. And, you'll recall, I've been married before—I'm not some blushing maiden that needs a subtle touch. Seize the day and all that. So, seize it now. Seize *me* now. Come on, you don't want to die a virgin, do you?"

"I'm not a virgin!" he gasped.

The quirk of a smile she gave him said she was well aware, and yet it did not stop her from continuing to tease him just the same. "Pity. I enjoy being people's firsts. Means they don't have any bad habits I have to break."

"I'll have you know," he said with faux indignity, "I have never had any complaints. Quite the opposite. I am very skilled at bringing my partner to—"

She cut him off with a kiss.

It was not a shy kiss. Why would it be? Juliet didn't know the meaning of the word. Her lips were firm and her tongue was insistent, and his heart hurt a little because her desperation was obvious. This was their only chance—their last chance. Better to go out seizing more pleasures than holding on to more regrets.

She pushed him hard against the wall and he went, allowing her to crawl into his lap and straddle his hips. Everything about her was soft and luscious. He no longer felt the cold of the stone, just the heat of her body.

Perhaps he should have melted into it. But the more insistent she became, the more he gentled his own hunger. This couldn't be it. This couldn't be all they'd get.

She was perfect. The time and place were not.

"Ju-Juliet," he tried, pulling back, but she wouldn't let him speak. He turned his face away from her adamant mouth and she immediately lowered her lips to the column of his throat. "Wait."

"There's no time to wait," she said, voice husky.

"If we're going to do this—"

"It's now or never."

"No, we—"

Suddenly there were words in his mind, foreign and unbidden.

We're not beat yet. We're not beat yet.

"We're not beat yet," he echoed. Mandip stood abruptly, and Juliet slid from his lap. She let out a little squeak as she lost the support and slumped to the floor. "There's a brick," he gasped.

With a little frustrated huff, Juliet flipped away the strands of hair that had fallen over her eyes and said sarcastically, "Well spotted. There's another there. And there. Weren't we about to—"

"No, no. I mean, a loose brick."

Her cheeks were still flushed, her lips kiss-swollen, but the dazed look of lust immediately left her gaze, replaced by clear-eyed calculation. "How can you tell?"

He walked toward the rear of the cell, stare fixed on the intriguing brick. "I can't, I just . . . know."

She leapt up to join him. "As in . . . the way Thibaut knows?"

"I think so."

He reached for the brick, pushing at it, then trying to rock it, to wiggle it. The mortar around its edges fell away, disintegrating in an instant. He twisted and pressed, realizing that once one had come free, more mortar was happy to crumble.

"We're not beat yet," he said, frantically pulling what he could of the wall down. "We're not beat yet."

Avellino hung his head and dragged his feet as he followed Gerome back to the cells. He'd done nothing for Thibaut, and now could think of nothing to do for his sister and Mandip. They would not become sacrifices—they would not. If nothing else, he knew Juliet would rather risk a leap from the keep's tallest tower—and would jump with a *wink*—rather than submit. But he was running out of time to figure out how to save them.

He was one boy. Some days he fooled himself into thinking he was a man, but a man wouldn't have cowered in the face of his former Possessor, wouldn't have simply stood there, inert, as his friend was cut open and his magic sucked from his marrow. Avellino wasn't big, wasn't powerful, wasn't anything special. Not *here*, not in the keep.

Gerome spoke to him in soft, berating tones as they went, detailing all the ways he was going to humiliate Avellino in the future, even after his memory was altered, but Avellino heard none of it. They were droning promises, a white noise of cutting insults. The smugness sat thick in his ears, gauzy and deafening like cotton. It didn't matter if he paid attention to Gerome's threats or not—either they would come to pass or they wouldn't, there was nothing to be done about it.

Once they were back in the dungeon, Gerome pulled free his keys and casually unlocked the cell door, in no hurry himself. After all, to make haste would make waste—one didn't come across such an opportunity for pure torment often, of course a man such as he would savor it.

But as soon as the groaning of the hinges fell silent, the air of arrogant satisfaction left Gerome, snapped away as if by a cold wind.

Avellino looked up when Gerome gasped.

The cell was empty.

Mandip and Juliet were gone.

Gerome rushed inside, stomping immediately over to a massive gap in the bricking, which led directly into Hintosep's now-empty cell. And that door, as far as Avellino was aware, hadn't been secured again. After all, why go through the trouble of buttoning up an empty room?

Avellino strode forward to examine the hole himself, marveling at the way the mortar simply crumbled at the lightest tough. The cells were old, rarely used these days. The Thalo didn't take prisoners, just *sacrifices*, and the Savior had much more effective ways of punishing those within the Order. When was the last time these rooms had been properly maintained? When was the last time anyone had really tested the walls or the doors or the floors? Hintosep's cell leaked, was full of rats. Was it really any wonder the walls were ready to topple?

It wasn't as if Gerome hadn't known the dungeon's upkeep wasn't what it should be, and yet he turned on Avellino just the same, nose flaring, eyes flashing, teeth bared. "*You*," he seethed. "You did this."

"I-I didn't," Avellino insisted. Surely that was obvious?

Since returning to the keep, Avellino had watched the foundations of Gerome's carefully maintained poise begin to crack. First with Hintosep, then with Thibaut's flirting, and now Gerome's tenuous hold on his composure slipped and fell away. He was all unbridled fury and weaponized disappointment. Avellino had never seen him like this before: truly incensed, out of control. He'd snapped, just as Hintosep had snapped. And when she'd reached her limit, she'd pounced on Gerome like a wild animal, ripping at his throat.

Gerome, in contrast, went for Avellino's hair, fisting it tightly, yanking him back and making his spine bow. He roared in the young man's face—spittle flying, his own snarl so close the beads from his headdress slithered across Avellino's cheek. "You have been my problem for too many years. A thorn, a splinter. Even when you were little, you were disobedient and disrespectful. Prideful and unworthy of even your first tattoos. You should have been thrown out with the rest of the unworthy and been made a Mindful from the beginning."

It was all untrue—Avellino had been a follower his whole life. Quiet, eager to please. And yet coming from his former Possessor, the accusations still stung. He felt the weight of those supposed failures, fabricated as they were.

It took effort to reject it. To heave that undeserved shame *away*.

He'd bent to this man nearly his entire life, and he'd had *enough*.

Avellino wasn't six anymore. He wasn't twelve, or fifteen. He wasn't a boy who could be pushed around and intimidated and destroyed just to patch up the cracks in Gerome's fragile ego.

He did not hide his intent as he gritted his teeth and slammed his heel down on the inside of Gerome's foot, nor did he make secret of why he twisted in his grip and tossed his head wildly, trying to shake the man loose.

Gerome seemed more caught off guard by the spirit of the fight than the struggle itself. He wasn't used to being resisted.

They tussled, like ruffians in the street, twisting in each other's robes, clawing for hair and eyes. Avellino caught something in one of Gerome's pockets—the enchanted lab key—twisted it out of its hiding place, then without hesitation bucked his head up, into Gerome's face. There came a sickening crack as the man's nose gave to make room for the crown of Avellino's skull.

As Gerome's vicious hands retreated to attend to his injury, Avellino sprinted from the cell without looking back, heart hammering in his chest, desperate to get as far away as he could, knowing the consequences would be dire once Gerome caught him again.

Thibaut wasn't sure how long he laid on the table. Avellino and Gerome had gone, leaving him alone with his half-expressed fen and the tubes slowly draining and coagulating his magic. Instead of giving him more freedom, more control, recovering his lost teliopathy had simply made him a target. Course, that was the whole point, he supposed. The Savior had decided to neuter *all of humanity* for a reason, after all.

How could a man with so much power be so afraid? Thibaut wondered.

Perhaps the answer was inherent in the question. Once one gained the pinnacle of power, what was there to fear but having that power challenged?

To stand at the top was to worry about falling.

Falling. Falling, falling, falling . . .

Thibaut himself tumbled into a daze, half in and half out of consciousness. The pain was reduced to a misty gauze all over his body, aching but distant. And yet, not gone.

A soft noise somewhere in the recesses of the lab made his awareness prickle at some point, and still he tried to remain in his twilight of cognizance.

Gentle hands on his sides—away from his wounds—roused him. "I'm here," Avellino said hurriedly. "I'm here, but he's coming."

In his state, Thibaut couldn't determine who *he* was meant to be, but definitely no one he wanted to see, by the hasty pace of Avellino's tone and the labor of his breathing. Thibaut tried to lift his head and found his neck stiff. His shoulders protested, but he just managed to catch a glimpse of Avellino taking hold of one of the metal rods pinning him and his fen to the dissection table.

The young man yanked and Thibaut hissed. The metal wasn't set in his bones or flesh but it was still *in him*.

Avellino tried to leverage the thing out from where he stood, but found it difficult. He retreated to find a step stool of some fashion, then scrambled back, bunching his robes around his knees as he stepped upward. Determined, he began twisting the pin, trying to loosen it in place.

The slicing sort of fire that had been gauzed over in Thibaut's half slumber came back, but he clamped his jaw tight and held his tongue, knowing that Avellino would try to be gentler if he heard squeals of pain. But they didn't have time for gentle—Gerome was coming.

Gerome. Shit.

Thibaut's senses sharpened fully as he realized what it must have taken for Avellino to avail himself of Gerome's absence.

Turning his attention to his hands, Thibaut struggled with the bindings once again. The straps felt like leather, and though they were sturdy, with determination he was sure they would stretch and loosen. Only that would take time, which was clearly in short supply.

Avellino truly had the right idea of it: free the fen first.

Thibaut felt an upward tug in his being, and realized Avellino had pulled the javelin's tip from the table. The boy allowed himself a shout of triumph, and Thibaut glanced over his shoulder again just as he flung the thick pin aside.

He should have held on to it.

A moment later—too fast for Thibaut to warn him—a pale hand came out of the shadows behind Avellino and leveled a firm blow at his head. The young man went flying in the same direction as the pin, thrown from his stool without even a chance to brace himself. He went like a tossed doll, limp and ragged. Thibaut heard him hit the floor but could not see where he fell.

Gerome's face flashed before Thibaut's eyes a moment before it was gone again, turning to where Avellino had fallen and diving out of sight. His nose was already bleeding, his beaded half helm cocked at an odd angle, his long, stringy hair gone wild and tangled. The look in his eye was murderous, and Thibaut knew Avellino wouldn't last without aid.

He pushed at his fen, willing it to leave his body, but the remaining pin still held it down. The tendrils that had been freed writhed and flapped, pulling upward only to be yanked back down like an insect caught in the sticky sap of a tree, waiting to be subsumed.

Still, a part of it could move, and it was still attached to him, and thus beholden to his direct will. He forced the tendrils—fingers? Tails?—to bend and reach, trying to use their dexterity to *grasp*.

He forced them to reach for his wrists, and as they did, they thickened, became denser, and for the first time he beheld part of his fen's true form. And the first thing he felt was *disgust*.

Rattails and sucker-laden tentacles slapped at his restraints, probing and pulling. He shivered, feeling slightly slimy even though his fen hadn't manifested any slime. As he struggled, the wide, flat head of a dung beetle burst through the waving appendages, and he looked himself in the eye.

Perhaps, rather pathetically, he'd thought his fen would take the shape of something graceful or noble. Or at least poetically fitting, like a peacock. Leave it to the cosmos to reveal his insides as *lowly*, reflected in the forms of things that slipped through gutters and crawled through grime.

Shut up, he chided himself, though the voice inside his head sounded much more like Krona's than his own. *They are creatures of dexterity and resilience, cunning and resourcefulness.*

Yes, they came from refuse, lived in the silt, and moved through the underbelly. But why should a scarab be ashamed? Why should a cuttlefish be ashamed?

The tip of one tentacle slipped under the leather, curled around it, pulled—made it *snap*.

"Oh, you beautiful, beautiful thing," he sighed, wriggling his hands free and twisting on the spot to take hold of the remaining pin, forgetting about the glass piping in his back.

As he twisted, they shattered.

Shards struck through him, pinioning his muscles, and sliding in deep. At least one pierced his lung and he gasped at the sudden painful collapse that had his entire body seizing up and stilling, as though caught in the rigor of a lightning strike.

Around him beakers jostled and glass rattled. In the next instant he was trying to gasp, his wheezing underpinning the sounds of a scuffle on the floor. He tried to ignore it all, focusing on the strength of his arms, his fingers. All that mattered right now was getting his fen free and letting it do what it could to save them.

Avellino hadn't heard Gerome approaching, let alone seen the blow coming. The sudden bash to his head left his vision swimming and his ears ringing. Cold stone rushed up from nowhere and his temple made contact before he realized why the world was tilting. He must have lost consciousness, because next he knew he was blinking awake and there were hands descending on him in a fury, pulling, yanking at his dead weight while someone snarled in frustration.

In the distance there was a strange rumble and the floor vibrated beneath his scraped hands, but he paid it little mind, instead trying to make his eyes focus so he could find a weapon—so that he could find that blasted javelin he'd so carelessly discarded.

He didn't have to see Gerome to know it was his former Possessor snarling on top of him. The way he twisted the fabric of Avellino's robes, the gravel of his voice—even his scent—was woven through nearly every memory Avellino had forged since he was six. The weight of him as he pushed and pulled, his towering height, and the extent of his reach were all things Avellino had contended with on a daily basis. They were the building blocks of his existence; noting them had been essential to his day-to-day survival in the keep and that familiarity was now essential to his survival second to second.

He did his best to throw himself away from Gerome's wrenching, spotting the matte sheen of nickel not far off. The javelin wasn't imposing, but it was sharp—could puncture a belly just as well as Krona's saber.

The moment his fingers landed on it—already sweaty from the struggle in the cell and the run here—the keep shook and his teeth rattled.

An earthquake. Avellino remembered the keep rumbling like this once in his childhood, when the volcano that heated the hot springs had groaned and heaved like an old man popping his aching joints. Now, neither he nor Gerome acknowledged it, too caught up in each other, in battling for survival. Its initial rolling boom petered out, but an aftershock quickly followed.

The Grand Orchestrator finally found purchase and hauled Avellino upward, as though he wasn't the one to have knocked him down in the first place. Though his grip was slippery with sweat, Avellino kept hold of the javelin as he was whirled and kept off-balance, stumbling this way and that as Gerome pushed him.

Flung, he suddenly found his spine cracking, his body twisting against the edge of the dissecting table, upon which Thibaut still valiantly struggled to escape, yanking at the second spear of nickel. He didn't have time to help free him—Gerome was already barreling down again.

Instead of brandishing the javelin in his hand, Avellino ducked as Gerome lunged, barely avoiding a clawing swipe at his cheek. Insults that were part word, part snarl dripped from Gerome's lips, and though Avellino tried to ignore them, many found their target: his insecurities, his sense of helplessness, of inadequacy.

"Pathetic," Gerome growled.

Useless. Ungrateful. Wretched. Worthless.

Avellino attempted to dodge each word as he dodged each blow, hoping it would all stop on its own, all come to an end. But as another earthquake tossed the floor beneath his feet, tripped him up, and let Gerome come within scraping distance, he realized such hopes were folly. Gerome would never cease. Gerome would pursue him until the end.

Gritting his teeth, Avellino stopped and whirled, finally brandishing the javelin's sharp tip. To Gerome's credit, he paused. Unfortunately, he stood between Avellino and Thibaut.

Avellino's chest heaved as he tried to catch his breath. In contrast, despite his disheveled state, Gerome was suddenly exceedingly composed. Barely a flush graced his cheeks, and his chest did not heave.

Slowly, the man's hand came up and crawled forward, like some stalking beast, and though Avellino shook the instrument to convey how ready he was to use it, Gerome seemed unconvinced. Those long fingers bypassed the weapon and nested in the front of Avellino's robes, curling tightly, firmly. With the same deliberate firmness, Gerome tugged insistently, urging Avellino closer.

He tried to resist, to use his weight to counterbalance the tug, but ended up stuttering forward until the javelin's raised point was dangerously close to Gerome's jugular. The former Possessor didn't seem to care. "I could have made you great," he said, voice low. "I could have made you a Possessor, and in time left you my position of Grand Orchestrator. I could have molded you into one of the most powerful Thalo this Valley has ever seen. Even with your weaknesses, I could have done it. You were mine to shape. My clay to sculpt."

"*I was your* child," Avellino countered, pushing the pin under Gerome's chin—not pressing, not even touching—its presence more of a warning than a dare. "All I ever wanted was to make you proud. To earn your approval. I thought *that* was the pinnacle of existence: earning a name via *your approval*. Not your *love*, gods forbid it. I didn't even know what love was, not really, until Hintosep brought me Abby. Until my sister came to save me. Until they"—he pointed harshly in Thibaut's direction with his free hand—"made me a part of their family. I have an adoring older sister who can't stand the thought of me succumbing to the least bit of harm! *That* is family. I thought the Order was my family, that *you* were my family, but you cannot build a family out of kidnappers and the kidnapped. You are the opposite of my sister in every way. One who steals children can never love them."

"You are *still* One who Belongs to the Eye!" Gerome insisted, hissing through his teeth.

"People choose to belong to one another," Avellino spat. "An enchantment could never own me. And neither do you. Not anymore."

Another earthquake shook the keep. Then came a *crack,* sharp and shocking, like standing next to a lightning strike. In the next instant the far wall of the lab burst open. Avellino and Gerome both jolted in surprise, but had no time to react.

A strange smear bolted through the gap a half breath later—a shimmer. A blur, a flash. So fast it caused a great, blasting gust as it shot past Gerome.

Shot past Gerome and *struck*.

One moment Avellino was staring at Gerome—at his curled lips and bared teeth and wild eyes that promised suffering like he'd only ever suffered under the Eye—and the next he was staring at nothing.

Nothing.

A hot splatter against his face made him jerk back and flutter his eyes, but Gerome's hand was still caught fast in the front of his robes, holding him firmly.

And yet, Avellino was looking at *nothing.*

Another great booming reverberation shook the keep, and a matching hole punched out through another part of the lab.

As the grip on his clothes slackened, Avellino blinked rapidly, his mind refusing to understand what it was seeing.

When Gerome's pale fingers finally fell away, Avellino screamed, though it sounded like a distant yawing to his own ears, what with the way his vision tunneled and a strange, shocked revulsion rolled from his belly up his throat and down to his toes.

Gerome still stood. But he was headless—*headless*. The blur had ripped it from his shoulders, and his body remained upright only by some morbid post-death rigidity, as if the last signal it had received was to *remain, remain, remain*.

Never yield. Remain.

30

KRONA

Krona was alone. Alone with Absolon and mindless Nature. Alone, and without her magic.

Protect the Eze, she chanted to herself as her limbs began to numb, as each time she lifted the broadsword her arm jolted in protest. She was only human, and lesser without her fen.

Then, from somewhere over her left shoulder, a *chuckle*.

Instantly, the mummies fell. All of them. As quickly as they'd been puppeted back to life, they'd been robbed of it again. Metal clanged as weaponry of all sorts fell to the floor. Krona's breath came heavy and loud in the sudden silence that followed.

"She'll return soon," the Savior said, and it took her a moment to realize he was speaking to her—that he'd thought her worthy of notice. "Your goddess is prone to tantrums, to flights of impulse. Emotion was a bad influence in that way."

He began to stalk toward her, and she held her ground, put herself between him and the Eze. He seemed taken aback by this. By all accounts, he'd given her a chance to flee, but still she did not stand down.

She simply couldn't. It wasn't who she was.

"Yes, I see why Hintosep likes you," he said. "She's just the same. Determined. Even in the face of certain failure." He regarded her thoughtfully for a moment, and she could feel him probing her emotions, her thoughts. Using his ill-gotten powers to find . . . something. "Ah. You've faced many failures recently, haven't you? Lost friends, lost children, lost loves, lost . . . family. You realize I have the power to give you everything you want, don't you? You needn't fight me. You needn't even fear me. I can be reasonable when others are reasonable. Our dear Hintosep is in the process of relearning just how terrible I can be to my enemies, but you . . . you are primed to learn another lesson."

He came closer as he spoke, and Krona retreated until she could go no farther—until backing up would set her upon the Eze's lap in zhur throne. She firmed her spine and held up the rusty blade, leveling it at his neck, keeping him at bay, hating how her arm tremored with exhaustion.

Absolon leaned into it, unconcerned. "There's a worm inside you," he whispered. "Can't you feel it? Something not quite settled. Shall we let it out? I'll let it out, if you ask nicely."

Krona tried to school her face, her feelings. His words sent an uneasy combination of hope and fear shooting through her. "You don't mean a worm," she said, and it came out a breathy sort of begging.

"Don't I? Perhaps not. A nymph? A larval something, for certain. Not fully grown, not fully whole."

He was toying with her. That was all. He'd seen her hopes for the echo, for De-Lia's mask, and now he was toying with her.

"It needs a home of its own, don't you think?" he asked. "A little place to call its own. I can give that to you. To *her*. All you have to say is *please*."

And what'll it cost me? she snapped inside her own mind.

"Oh, nothing more than you're willing to pay," he assured her aloud.

She should have thrown denials at him—should have slashed her blade across his throat when she had the chance. Instead, her hesitancy was her answer.

He knew. He knew what she longed for, what her weakness was. The one thing that could make her stumble here, now, when the whole Valley was on the line.

She half gasped, holding her chest—each breath accompanied by a painful strain in her ribs—ready a moment too late with a rejection on her lips.

Absolon held up a finger, tutting at her. "Say *please*."

The word punched from her lungs—so desperate and needy she wasn't sure if she'd formed it of her own accord or if he'd simply manipulated her tongue. "Please. *Please*."

Just like he'd pulled the bone spurs through her back, now he took hold of her left arm, yanking her up by it, though it was purely his magic and not his fingers that wound around her flesh and jerked her high to stand, straining, on her toes. Her shoulder tensed, popped, as he took the joints and *twisted*. It made her whole body spin, made her turn away from him. She tried to lash out with the sword, but he was already out of reach.

"I see someone's been playing with my work," he said. "Have Physiopaths of your own, do you? Ah, but not the man you sent me, no. He was a Teliopath. Stitched together just like you, like a thing that's had its arms cut off and reattached."

A cold shower of tingles radiated from her crown to pool in her belly. She bowed her back and craned her neck, trying to look him in the eye. "Was?"

"Oh, important to you, was he? Shame. Yes, he's been *processed*. I suspect he's nothing but a shriveled husk and a blob of pneumoplasm by now. A tasty little morsel just waiting for me to swallow down."

Fury blossomed anew in Krona's chest, and she refused to believe him. She would have said as much, but he chose that moment to force her biting comments into a scream as he yanked new bone spurs through her muscle and skin—this time all up and down her twisted left arm.

"Let's make the larva a fitting house. A little pen for your pet."

Flailing, she threw the sword at him, and he deflected it with ease, sent it spinning off behind him.

The bone spurs wove together, growing back into one another, creating a latticelike cage of calcium and marrow around her shoulder, her biceps. She lost all feeling from her elbow down as it morphed into something else—*birthed* something else. Her skin bulged with a new form underneath, something pressing up, flowing under her forearm like her skin was nothing but a layer of satin. Her flesh boiled, bubbled, burst like tar. Something ghastly and bulbous engulfed her wrist—a brow, a claylike face, and her fingers dangled out of its newly opened maw as if they were its teeth. She couldn't feel them, but she willed her fingers to move and they twitched like spider legs beneath the swell of the thing's lips.

Eyes. Three eyes flowed out from under her skin and over the brow of the new head, open and *seeing*. They rolled frantically as they sunk into sockets that formed beneath them. Eyelids stitched themselves on top. Her palm hollowed into some kind of proto-throat that wheezed with air that did not flow from her lungs.

There was nothing human about the form. Its features were otherworldly, and only the fact that it was covered in her own skin suggested it was anything resembling mammalian.

The transformation felt like it went on forever. It could have taken hours or *weeks* as far as Krona could tell.

And then, there—a wriggling in the back of her mind, very much like a worm, as he'd said. It came curling out of the depths, where it had been small and dormant, now forced into the light of consciousness by Absolon's vicious hand. Krona felt it corkscrew through her gray matter, buzzing from the hind of her brain to the fore, curling against her frontal lobe before being pulled down the left side of her face like a physical thing, though it could be none other than De-Lia's echo.

As it went—as the echo was forced into this grotesque pseudo-body—Krona felt hot lines rising first on her forehead, starting where Sebastian had pricked her with the needle. They rose like angry scratches in the echo's wake, down her neck, shoulder, arm. It wasn't until the echo was seated in what was left of her hand—stuck behind a tri-set of eyes—that she could see a pattern in the rising welts.

An enchanter's mark—stretched out and distorted, running from her forehead down through the barreled body of this monstrosity.

The throat in her palm screamed, and it was not De-Lia's voice.

"There," Absolon said evenly—warmly, in a way that made bile rise in Krona's throat. "Together again, at last."

With that, he tossed her—*them*—aside.

Krona skidded through a pile of hacked limbs and lost teeth, feeling stretched like taffy and chipped like a broken dish.

The thing that wasn't her sister and wasn't her arm *writhed*.

"I'm so sorry," she whispered to it, voice wet around the edges.

With her good arm, Krona pushed herself up just in time to see Absolon flick his fingers in the Eze's direction. Slack-jawed, Nature finished his work. In an instant—compared to Absolon's drawn-out agonies—the Eze's body stretched high, morphing into a beautiful tree, leaves bright emerald, roots planted right on top of the throne and trailing into the cracks in the pearl-covered stone floor.

Leash in hand, Absolon looked like he was about to disappear back into the blank nothing from which he'd emerged, but then a far-off cry made him pause. It was the great, pitch-shifting screech of something moving at great speeds, and his chin shot up toward the skylights in anticipation.

"I hadn't expected her to return so soon," he mused.

Time dropped down through the same gap she'd crawled out of, a black mass of feathers landing heavily on the floor. When she stood upright, revealing her pale limbs, she held each hand aloft, displaying her gruesome bounty.

Heads.

In her four bare hands, Time held seven severed heads, each covered in blue tattoos and dripping fresh blood.

Absolon froze and looked, for the first time, truly taken aback.

Without a glance toward Krona, Time threw the heads at Absolon's feet and he jumped back, narrowly avoiding the slack-jawed mouths that would have kissed his boots.

Shaking, he knelt, holding out a hand toward one head, then another. He seemed to have no words.

"I razed your keep," Time spat at him. "Your center of power lies in ruins, and your Grand Orchestrators are *here*."

The smug amusement that had seeped from him like a wellspring while he'd toyed with Krona evaporated. "You *baseborn*"—he ripped his mask away, baring his teeth, and Krona was surprised to see such a simple, forgettable face beneath—"pigheaded *blight* of a woman." He threw the mask forcefully, yet ultimately impotently, at Time and she diverted it with the merest touch. "How *dare you*—"

"How dare *I*?" she cried in return. "I am not the one who betrayed everyone in our tithing. I am not the one who failed to—"

"You want to talk of *failure*?" he roared, turning their shrieking match right back around again. "*You* are the reason it all fell apart. If you had done your job none of us would be here. I wouldn't have had to make the hard choices when the rest of you were content to pretend everything was fine. And, ultimately, who was it? Who rid the world of the tyrant? Me. *I* did it!" Absolon screamed. "I stood over her and wrapped *my* fingers around *her* neck. *I* wasn't the assassin, but I succeeded. I killed her when you could not!"

"And yet the bombs went off just the same. The world *ended* just the same."

"Then we are *all* to blame. At least I turned my attention to preserving what was left. There would be no humanity if you all had had your way."

"Tell me how to leave the Valley. Now."

"You cannot. It is sealed. Permanently."

"I don't believe you! Give me my brother and tell me how to get out!"

"No."

"Then I will throw blue-tatted head after blue-tatted head at your feet until you change your mind!"

He stiffened, then waved broadly at Nature, made the poor thing flare his wings. "I will not see the world I have rebuilt destroyed anew. You leave here again and he's the one who pays."

"You can't kill him," Time countered. "You need him to maintain your Valley."

"I don't have to kill him," Absolon said smugly. "There are so many other *agonies* I could make him endure."

He began manipulating Nature just as he'd manipulated Krona, only this time he forced Nature in on himself—forced the pitiful not-god to use his own powers against himself.

The empty expanses of skin where Nature's eye sockets should have been began to bulge, rounding out as orbs grew beneath. Soon the skin split, but not into lids—two ragged wounds revealed new, blue eyes. Eyes that fell like tears—the orbs rolling out of the sockets, *falling* out of the sockets, on long, stringy pink ligaments until they broke their lines and dropped down to smack wetly against his toes. Then more eyes bulged beneath the skin to replace them, falling once more, and soon Nature was crying a constant stream of eyes, and they littered the ground around his ankles like slopped globs of stiffened jelly.

Nature held out his hands weakly as though he meant to catch them, but could not find them.

Time's lips thinned and her jaw hardened, but her spine was straight—she refused to bow. "Stop it," she said sternly.

"Oh, this is only the beginning," Absolon assured her, waving his hand.

Instantly, gashes appeared in Nature's side and his intestines wiggled out, moving like snakes, curling up his body and leaving slime trails like snails. He jolted in pain, body twisting unnaturally with the force of it. His will was not present, but suffering did not require will.

Time moved to lunge at Absolon, her four hands raised and ready, but just as she coiled, he let out a small, "Ah-ah-ah," and with a flick of his wrist, one long loop of Nature's intestines coiled around his neck.

The coughing choke that followed made Krona sick.

"Stop it," Time commanded again, her voice wavering ever so slightly. "Absolon, so help me—" She abortively jolted forward once more, but Absolon simply tightened Nature's noose.

"Make a move on me again and I will make him tear his own limbs off and have them scuttle around the room!"

Absolon was weak to Time and Time was weak to Nature and Nature was under Absolon's control. It was the same terrible loop all over again. Never-ending.

Or was it?

Absolon had stolen power, but he was still no match for Nature, else he wouldn't need to wield him so—as a weapon, as a shield.

And Krona—she still had the means to wake him.

Her shifting humors and adrenaline spikes made her fingers clumsy, but she managed to wrench the box containing Nature's mind from her pouch, then freed it from its wax. She fumbled the crystal out into the open air, trying to push the fact that they weren't anywhere near Nature's temple from her mind.

She smacked the crystal against the floor, hoping the halite would cleave. Flakes came away, but not enough to give her hope. She had no water, blessed or otherwise. There was nothing in the troughs that caught the overspill from the skylights, and nothing in her canteen. The desert air was dry, sapping the moisture from her nose and tongue, leaving her barely enough spit to wet her lips, and certainly not enough to dissolve the salt block.

But there was fluid running through her veins.

Frantically, she bit at her own wrist, but the pain made her clench and reel and shy away. The skin was broken, ragged, but the bite wasn't nearly as deep as she needed it. The taste of her own blood coating her teeth made her stomach roil, and she feared she'd be sick if she bit down again. She couldn't do it herself. She needed someone else to sever the lines.

And all she had . . . was De-Lia.

She moved her right wrist toward the monstrosity at her left, and the thing jerked away like a wary dog that had been kicked too many times, unsure of her intentions.

"Please," Krona whispered to the echo in its twisted body. "Help me." *Work with me. Work with me as we used to. In tandem. One goal.*

They were still one body. Perhaps the echo could feel her resolve.

The bits that had been her finger and the strange, gaping mouth came forward, tentative at first, then tearing, digging, burrowing into her flesh as best they could.

It was enough.

Her blood began to gush, her heart rapidly pumping it out and away. She held her wrist over the halite, let the waterfall of red cascade across its crystals and cleavage. Slowly, it began eating through to the prize inside.

And still, Absolon held Time hostage with Nature's misery. His intestines had retreated, the eyes had disappeared, but now the not-god hunched down on all fours, and his face broadened, bloated, his skin became hard like an exoskeleton, and his waist and neck thinned, truncated, until he clearly had the thorax and abdomen of some insectoid. What was worse was how Nature vocalized through the transition, clearly in enough agony to make even the hardest hearts beg for it to end.

Time lost her rigidity, her determination. All that was left was a sister watching her brother suffer. "Absolon, stop it!"

"Stand down!" he cried. "Submit to me, *and I might.*"

31

HAILWIC

In a Time and Place Before

The tithe that was supposed to make their bond stronger only served to make it more obvious when they each began to pull away. Even when all were under the same expanse of bunker ceiling, Hailwic's body felt stretched by the distances between them.

Punabi itched for combat while Zoshim sank further into pacifism. Glensen spent days on end drafting communiqués, begging for audiences with officials across the continent. And Kinwold was indeed a colossus—immovable in their resolution to *do the same* and *hold the line.*

There were times where she felt closest to Lonny, even though he was hundreds of miles away. Their focuses were aligned. Though she couldn't hear his thoughts directly or see through his eyes or experience his senses (nothing about the tithing had been as total and acute as during the ceremony) she could tell that his waking thoughts often mirrored hers. There was a resonance between them, silent parallels of intent.

Which was perhaps why she could tell when something changed in him, and none of the others could.

It was an uncomfortable sensation; a covetous burst of awe followed by a throbbing she could only describe as both a melding and a muting at once. Most of the feeling was fleeting, but the unnerving *desire* in it remained.

Initially she'd shrugged it off with a shiver, hoping whatever had made her feel such a distorted shape of him had been a one-off. But it wasn't. It came back. Again and again, the instances growing more frequent and extended.

Something insidious had wormed its way into his blood, into the tithe, and she wished the others could sense it. It made her skin crawl every time it reverberated through—slinking into her from across the landscape, reminding her that something was wrong.

She was surprised it took her so long to realize the first time she'd sensed that same wrongness was during the tithing ceremony. When Lonny had felt her kairopathy flow through him and he'd looked as though he'd seen the divine.

Once total extraction had been achieved, working physiobombs came not long after. Lonny had reported many times that he'd heard tell of underground facilities where small versions of the bombs had been tested with piddling amounts of physiopathy involved. He'd never been able to get his hands on any direct reports, and Hailwic had prayed the whispers were only rumors, though she wasn't naïve. Engineering the enchanted bombs themselves had never been the hard part. Procuring enough physiopathy to power them was the only major stumbling block, and now . . .

Now, within a year of total extraction's success, the weapon's first open-air testing was at hand.

Lonny would be on the ground with Uphrasia, other engineers, and her entourage to observe the test. When Lonny's urgent report came in, Hailwic volunteered to spy from above.

The test was top-secret, its location so clandestine not even Lonny could suss it out ahead of time.

That's where the tithing proved its worth.

Hailwic could track the progress of the entourage moving north by feeling Lonny's presence alone. As the testing date approached and the party moved farther and farther north, it became clear where they were headed: the Capuchin Crater.

The crater was actually a chain of three overlapping impact craters, each roughly the same size, a mile in diameter, easily viewed in all their glory from a nearby ridgeline five miles off. Millenia ago, the three basins had been home to three separate and *rival* monastic orders, each with their own temple complexes sprawling out across a crater floor. In the end, though they all worshiped the same gods, the monks of the three orders had torn each other to bits in what was better characterized as a mob brawl than an actual war. For centuries, the temple ruins had been left undisturbed as a symbol—an almost superstitious warning—of what happened when petty differences were extrapolated into unforgivable evils.

Fistus had flooded the craters. Turned their high, natural walls into a watershed for the surrounding communities. Practical. Useful.

He'd also forbade any diving, swimming, fishing. He'd meant the ruins to fade from memory. And still, in the driest of summers, when the new lakes were lowest, the spire of the tallest temple could be seen, like a sword tip thrust up by an invisible hand.

Years ago now, Uphrasia had evacuated the surrounding towns, claiming the water contaminated, but Hailwic knew it was because many people still made pilgrimages in hopes of catching sight of the spire. Though Fistus had tried to erase the ruin's importance, cultural memory ran deep, and many people still understood their country was barreling down the same dark path.

Given the craters' remoteness, and the fact that the nearest settlements had been forcibly abandoned, it made a perfect testing ground. A way to prove out this new ultimate weapon and simultaneously annihilate the ruins and Fistus's legacy atop them.

⁂

The night before the scheduled test, Hailwic lay awake next to Punabi, listening to zhur soft snores, hoping the rhythm might put her to sleep as well.

From far off, a seething sort of awe hit her—a long distance wonderment with a sharp tin edge that made her sit bolt upright.

Whatever it was that made Lonny feel these insidious feelings, he was doing it again.

Without thinking of the repercussions—of the next day's mission—she jumped, following the tithing's tug, tracing the line straight to Lonny.

She landed in a warm, comfortable room, dimly lit, with the light of a muted tele blinking erratically over a lone figure's features. Lonny, sitting on a leather couch and bent over a coffee table, fiddling with what looked like a clear plastic dish full of small beads.

"What are those?" she asked from the shadows, rubbing at one arm as her skin prickled. Though the space was comfortable, she'd jumped straight from her warm bed, still in her night clothes—an oversize sleep shirt and shorts.

"Son of a—" Lonny startled, swiping at the small dish as though instinct told him to hide the beads or thrust them away. He jumped to his feet, standing between her and the dish. "For the love of heaven, Hail, you shouldn't be here. You can't just—"

"I came because I can *feel it*, Lonny."

"Please, I use my full name now. It's more formal—"

She bowled over his interjection. "—You weren't *you*. You *aren't* you. I pulled myself from the rare chance to share a bed with Punabi and came here just to see this—whatever it is—for myself. So, what am I looking at?"

"What if I hadn't been alone?" he countered, trying to twist her curiosity away, brandishing an accusing tone to clash with her own. "Are you *trying* to ruin everything?"

Th admonishment hit home because it was so flagrantly true. She hadn't been thinking.

"There *isn't* anyone here," he said, his tone a mixture of resigned and reassuring as he caught Hailwic's eyes suddenly darting into the corners. "Uphrasia's not even in the building; she's staying elsewhere in the city, far from any of the engineers. It'll raise fewer eyebrows if she's only seen traveling with her usual entourage."

He was dodging her original question, but given her brashness—her impulsiveness that could have seen them both killed the instant she arrived—she allowed it.

She wasn't sure what she'd been expecting to jump into. She'd imagined whatever gave him—and her, by proxy—these unnatural sensations had to be a private thing. The tinge of secrecy could not be denied. Luckily, she seemed to have, at least, gotten that part correct.

The hotel room was nicer than he could have afforded on his own, so the company must have been paying. Or maybe Uphrasia herself.

The furnishings were clean-cut—boring, but expensive. Brushed metals and crisp whites, with uninspired abstract art taking up an absurd percentage of one wall, and floor-to-ceiling windows half-covered with blackout curtains in a shiny silver fabric. A vase of abstracted black-and-gray silken flowers sat next to the tele, stems made of the same cold steel as the other accents. It was the kind of room that appealed to corporate hierarchs and political jockeys.

Lonny'd never been one to say no to comfort, but he'd never been drawn to the austere.

He turned away, trying to project nonchalance but clearly longing to hide the small dish.

Hailwic thinned her lips, then whipped her words out on a hunch. "She's giving you more than time treatments, isn't she?"

His shoulders dropped. "So what if she is?"

"Show me."

A hitch in his breath betrayed his hesitation, but in the end he didn't wrestle with himself for long. Plucking one of the silk flowers from its vase, he handed it to her like an awkward would-be suitor handing her a rose.

"What's this for?" she asked skeptically.

"You asked for a demonstration."

"I meant—"

He held a finger to his lips, asking for silence. And patience.

With a delicate grasp, he lifted one bead from the dish, and it shone an icy sort of yellow-green in the flashing.

"If you like time treatments, you'll love these," he said slyly, setting it between his teeth, making sure it was on display before he bit down.

A clearly pleasant shiver ran across his shoulders and down his spine, and this close, that expansive feeling of awe hit Hailwic square in the chest. It was a sense of self-wonderment.

Lonny closed his eyes for a moment, slicked back his hair, then approached her with a catlike grin.

Instinctually, she took a step back. She'd never seen Lonny *predatory* before.

But when he reached out, it wasn't for her. He took the false flower from her grasp and held it between them. "Silk today," he said softly, before blowing on the black petals. They quivered, became translucent, like ice—faceted and rainbow-filled, tinkling as he continued to blow until they were completely changed. "Diamonds tomorrow," he finished softly, returning the stem to her baffled fingers.

Her mouth fell open as she swept the pad of her thumb across one petal. It *had* changed, in form, not just appearance. Startled by the trueness of its alteration, she dropped it. Gracefully, Lonny swooped down to pick it up off the floor, and she marveled as the crystal quality began to melt away a moment later, leaving a *fresh* flower in its wake.

Before the last of the stem had transmuted into greenery, though, the change halted, and the flower snapped back into its original silk-and-metal form.

"It only lasts for a few minutes, if it's not your pathy," he said, laying it down on the coffee table. "And if you take too many that don't align with your pathy, you'll get a hell of a hangover in the morning. But if it *is* your pathy?" His head twitched to the side, rolling back and forth on his neck for a moment. "Fucking *power up,*" he whispered.

That ill-fitting awe that had made Hailwic's skin crawl at a distance took hold of her now, not projected from Lonny but arising from her own chest. She felt uneasy in her body, but intrigued, pulled toward the idea. As if to counter it, she took a step back. "How—? This isn't like time treatments."

"No," he agreed. "It's much better. She's got a team working on it," he offered with a little shrug. "Extracting from every pathy, trying to make the stuff last longer and make it more potent, without the side effects. It's only safe to take one type at a time right now, but can you *imagine* . . ." He trailed off.

She swallowed dryly. This was . . . this was terrible. The possibilities for abuse were boundless. "She'll be unstoppable," she gasped.

"No," he said quickly, his air of wonderment tripping into defiance. "We won't give her the chance." He reached into the dish again, proffering a bead, this one cobalt blue. "Try it."

"No."

"C'mon."

"*No.*"

"You are such a bore sometimes," he scoffed. "Zoshim's not here to judge you for it. Here." He took her hand, forced it into her palm. "It's cryptopathy. I'll send a handful back with you. Use them tomorrow, it'll make it easier for you to get past the perimeter. Uphrasia is developing tools, and we can't be so prideful as to discard them."

"It's not pride," she spat. "It's *decency.* Using the tools of the enemy against her is still *using the tools of the enemy.*"

"And how many time packets have you used now?" he asked, turning up his nose. "Your brother and Glensen have the holier-than-thou positions covered, you don't need to join them. Especially when you and I know what has to be done."

Hailwic looked at the bead in her hand. Unobtrusive. Just a little pill. A little point in the universe that spoke to so much possibility and so much pain. A little treasure, a little threat.

How did Lonny, of all people, have these at his disposal?

An unnerving little fishhook caught in Hailwic's mind, tugging her thoughts in an uncomfortable direction.

"Why did she give you these?" she asked slowly.

His silence was potent. As it stretched, Hailwic stretched with it, her niggling misgivings becoming all-out suspicion.

"What is she to you?"

"A target," he insisted, overly harsh. "Even if Kinwold still can't handle that." He picked up the dish, slapped a lid atop it so that the beads jounced around inside like in a baby's rattle. "Take it. Take it all. Hand them out to the others or toss it in a river. Whatever you want."

"Is this some kind of peace offering? What do you want in exchange?"

He had the gall to look hurt, but still held the beads out and cleared his throat. "Kinwold continues to underestimate my potential—*our* potential. They're too timid to lead us, you must realize that now. You and I have to do what we can—we can't let the others hold us back. And we need to be united."

"We're *all* supposed to be united."

"Things change. And it's Kinwold who hasn't noticed."

Her hand moved as though without her input, and the two of them held the dish between them for a moment, like a physical promise. Once she tugged it away, he let himself drop back onto the couch. "See you tomorrow," he said, then, "Or should I say, hope *no one* sees you tomorrow. Remember, cryptopathy doesn't work on tech—like cameras. If you use the beads, you can only secret yourself away from organic minds."

She paused for a moment, wanting to give another denial. To insist that she wouldn't be using them. Instead she said, "Noted."

"Good."

She looked at the beads for a moment, at the little rainbows they made, all mixed up and side by side. A new pit opened wide in her stomach, disquieting and deep—a rift. A rift, like she felt between the tithing. "Good night, Absolon," she whispered before jumping away again.

* * *

Punabi let out a small, sleepy groan when Hailwic jumped back. She stepped through the lens to drop right onto their bed with ease, barely ruffling the sheets, barely letting a flutter of hotel-room air conditioning follow her.

Only the smallest thread of ribbon lighting added a glow to their windowless room in the tunnels, giving off barely enough light to make out the silhouette of Punabi's brow, zhur nose.

Hailwic stared, unblinking, at zhur profile until her eyes began to water. She rolled the container in her hand—noted how light it all felt.

Pneuma extract, turned into tiny little pills for the taking.

Bits of someone's humanity. Bits of self. Ready to be cannibalized.

Dropping lightly off the bed to rummage through her supply pack, she found the small pillbox with emergency pain killers and dumped them out, depositing the beads in their place. All except one.

She pinched the cryptobead between her thumb and forefinger, expecting it to feel a way—oily, or throbbing, or frigid. Instead, it just felt like a little bit of glass. Like something innocent.

Quietly, she stole out of the room with the bead in hand and pillbox pocketed.

This is okay, she told herself. Using these, just a few of them, was fine.

She needed every advantage she could get to ensure her recon mission went well tomorrow. Using everything at her disposal was only logical. Rational. And she needed to make sure she knew how to properly utilize the beads before then.

Swallowing down bile—and guilt, and trepidation, ignoring what Punabi always told her about emotion, that it was the body's understanding, the mark of truisms that the brain couldn't talk itself out of, couldn't fake itself into believing—she popped the pill into her mouth when she heard voices up ahead, and let the stolen cryptopathy flood her veins.

The sky was clear. A perfect day for announcing a new calamity.

Hailwic flew high, scanning the crater complex from a great distance, several of the beads Lonny—*Absolon*—had given her clutched in one of her four fists.

She was surprised to see the craters drained. There were still spots of water—old cisterns and wells left behind by the monks, now havens for the last of the lake's seeded fish. She swallowed a cryptobead, hoping it would help hide her from any magical detection, and swooped lower for a better look. Coldness ran through her veins and her head throbbed, like she'd swallowed ice. Excess power ran through her arms, and in a wild ploy to control it she willed herself invisible—hidden to any seeking minds.

The entire area had a waterlogged odor to it, though most of the ground was dry. The ruins were remarkably well-preserved. Archways still rose sturdy, and statues of the monks' many-headed deities still stood, though most had lost limbs. Even some of the ancient enamel still skirted the foundations in starburst patterns, representing the cosmos and the swirling cradle of creation.

The craters were drained, but not entirely abandoned. People milled about, preparing for the test with a manic sort of enthusiasm.

As she approached the famed tower and its spire, she noticed brand new scaffolding had been set up at its base. Not the kind that supported renovation workers, but the kind that supported various testing equipment. Cameras were positioned all around, ready to capture the moment of detonation.

Swooping upward again, she noted a giant X painted on the overlapping rim between the northern and central craters.

A viewing station had been set up five miles away on the ridge at the base of what had once been a bustling tourist lodge. The station's boxy sides were no doubt well insulated and its wide windows thickly glazed. She could feel Lonny there.

She wondered if Uphrasia was at his side.

A wailing bomb siren went off, and a resonating "Clear the area, clear the area. Physio-bombardment in T-minus . . ." rang out.

Their work finished, people scrambled to leave.

Hailwic caught a current, sent herself soaring miles away.

She waited.

Everything was still. Calm. The countdown was the only sound besides the wind, the announcer's voice high and reedy, the words nearly indistinguishable at her distance.

And then, there it was, sent by a single-use enchanted jump pack: the bomb itself, shot from a stationary platform outside the southern crater rim. Creating a brief time lens next to it, she got a better view, observing it up close for half a second in all its glory, cased in gold, with runes etched around the circumference and long metal tubing braided together to guide the offshoot of energy in a high arc, up and out.

She collapsed the lens.

The countdown ended.

The bomb detonated.

Her vision went white.

The initial flash was blindingly bright. Even at her distance, she had to shield her eyes from the sharp flare. A rolling wave of energy roared out from the blast site, growing redder and redder as it went. The hot, crimson glare of it blasted through her fingers like a sunrise, and as she cringed away from it she realized, fully, that they were too late.

Everything they'd been trying to stop had come to fruition.

She wished she could see through Lonny's eyes—see Uphrasia, bathed in that bloody shine. Hailwic imagined a smile on the Friend's face, her evil glee highlighted, the light distorting her broad grin into something unnatural and inhuman.

A billowing cloud sprouted up from the detonation site, taut and springy like a bubble, except it was an impossible shape for a bubble to be, tall and covered in ulcers, its base spreading like the sizzling fingers of a wildfire. The orange-red hues shifted into yellow-green before deteriorating into electric pink and then a sickly sort of mauve.

Inside the bubble, the land *boiled*. Not with blisters of lava but pustules of impossible matter. A dark, oozing tar reached upward as though alive, with fingers grasping, before it collapsed back and burst into pure white feathers and then molten gold before blowing away like powdery snow. Buildings became puddles of something orange before rebounding upward into trees that couldn't be trees because they were made of metal one instant and bees the next.

The remaining lake creatures that had found refuge in the wells now came bursting forth as though thrust upward by geysers. They grew impossibly large, as big as houses on their own, before being stretched like taffy and unraveled like twine. Some grew legs and landed, scurrying away before being absorbed into the bricking of a building that was in the next moment just a ball of cotton, and then a slab of some silvery ore.

The very air became fire before it became something opaque and dark, and then thickly fogged.

The central spire was the last object to be recognizable as fingers of pale pink and purple crystal cut across the splitting ground toward it. The land opened, making even the lodge quake, and some manifestation of proto-creation crawled forth, a hulking thing, scaly and raw in turns—armored and skinless. It had no head, but had direction, slinking after the path of those growing crystals, scaling the side of the monastery as the mineral wound its way upward, toward the spire, toward that lasting symbol of folly.

Before reaching the top, the abomination of a creature faded back into nonexistence, melting into the rooftop like broken jelly. The crystal consumed it and the spire, staking the sky with a crystalline spike.

Several land fragments escaped the mass, thrown high into the air, taking on varying arcs as they continued to morph. Form fighting form, matter fighting matter, all fighting gravity. A heat blast rippled the air around Hailwic in a terrible, whirling column, throwing the fragments off course and slamming into Hailwic with unnatural speed.

Caught off guard, she lifted one set of hands, used one set of wings to shield her body while the others fought to take her higher. Embers landed on her feathers—manifested from a nonexistent fire—scorching her wings, twisting and curling her feathers.

Where a stunned awe had settled in her chest before, now fear wormed its way in, cracking that awe, liquefying it—forcing it into its own writhing mass of unnerving shifts from terror to anger to piercing sorrow.

She kept aloft, and when the heat blast melted away she found not only had her wings been burnt and bent, but several of the feathers were now crystal. Twisting in on herself, she wrenched the heavy feathers from their follicles.

One of them screamed and bit at her with bloody teeth that emerged from between the barbs. The teeth stuck in her fingertips as she flung the grotesque thing away. Where it went—if it suffered or if it survived—was the furthest thing from her mind.

The little pin-teeth in her fingertips writhed, burrowing like mites, and she scraped at the skin with her other hands, digging at them, tearing her fingers open in a tight panic until her hand was raw and all her arms bloody.

Her flesh crawled like it wasn't her own. Her mind fought at it, chewing the sensation, mutilating it just as she mutilated her own flesh. She kept trying to dig the feeling out, even when the teeth had dissolved and were gone.

Even when the land had settled. When there was nothing but purple crystal in the craters.

Raw in the aftermath, breath heaving when she finally determined the teeth were gone, Hailwic hovered in the air, flapping her wings manically, trying to make sense of what she'd just seen.

Unrestrained physiopathy had eaten and regurgitated everything in its path. The land had come alive and died. Living things had come into existence and winked out just as quickly. And anything already living had been obliterated. There was nothing recognizable left of the Capuchin Crater. The Monks' War had been erased, but so had the scars in the land itself. A geography millions of years old, created through the sheer violence of heavenly bodies colliding, was gone.

If the scars of cosmology couldn't resist Uphrasia's razing, what hope did the people have?

Uphrasia had to be stopped. This all had to *stop*. Now.

No matter the cost.

She'd dropped the rest of the cryptobeads in her struggle with herself, but that didn't matter—she'd forgotten about them.

Wings pulled tight against her body, she made herself a missile, aiming at the heart of the observation station.

That image of Uphrasia in her mind—the sneering caricature, basking in her own capacity for destruction—was all Hailwic could see. A bright, beautiful smile twisted at the edges, rippling with malice. Hailwic would relegate that smile to a bloody, toothless smear. Absolon would take that terrible woman by the throat and hold her steady while Hailwic figured out how to pull the pneuma from the Friend's veins—make her feel as helpless and torn apart as she'd made all the dozens—hundreds, *thousands*—of Physiopaths whose magic it had taken to make this bomb.

The reinforced windows of the observation station reflected the crystal spire, sharp as a dagger through the heart of day, a moment before Hailwic swooped in front of it. A quick slice of sunlight flashed off the panes, and then behind them, Hailwic saw clearly, the Friend in all her glory. Beautiful and terrible as she remembered.

The glee Hailwic had imagined on her face wasn't there, however. Neither was a self-satisfied smirk or a hungry stare, gobbling up the sight of the destruction and gulping down her newfound power.

She looked *soft*. Her eyes doe-like, half-lidded, and aimed not at the destruction beyond but at the man by her side.

Lonny—Absolon.

The Friend's hand cupped his face, her thumb petting at his cheek.

As Hailwic approached, time seemed to slow, but it wasn't her doing—wasn't her magic. It slowed as ice crawled through her veins, as a realization hit and she watched in horror as Absolon and the Friend drew closer.

When their lips touched—gentle as the kiss was—it tore through Hailwic, the sight rattling her down to her foundations.

She pulled up short, reeling back from the scene, slamming into it as harshly as if it were a solid wall. In that same moment, the guards positioned all around Uphrasia and Absolon began to point, shout, though Hailwic couldn't hear much past the pounding of her own heartbeat. Her focus narrowed, and the yelling sounded like a muffled rumble from far off.

Absolon's head whipped in her direction.

Their eyes met.

She could not read his gaze.

It was empty. Calculated.

Something zipped by her, the motion of it fluttering the tip of her flight feathers on one wing. A moment later she heard the crack of the shot.

With a great heave, she pushed at the air with her wings, propelling herself high into the air—high and away to safety, as more shots followed.

Her body soared on autopilot while her mind twisted the puzzle box of what she'd just seen, trying to glean a plethora of answers from that single glimpse.

Seduction was a well-worn infiltration tactic. She'd understood it was a tool Absolon was ready to wield. But to *see* it— To be struck instantly by a sense of wrongness— Of *their* wrongness—

What if it wasn't just a play to get close to Uphrasia? What if he'd betrayed *them*? The RFR, the tithing? This whole time, when they thought he'd been infiltrating the Friend's circle, he could have been infiltrating *theirs.*

No. No, that was ridiculous.

. . . Wasn't it?

Of course it was, she chided herself. This was the play, his plan.

They'd all underestimated what Lonny was capable of. Both the professor and Kinwold had insisted he didn't have the ability to get close to Uphrasia—that was why they'd brought Hailwic in to begin with. And then they'd left him in place, to sabotage, because it seemed convenient, but in reality, when Hailwic thought about it, he'd done a remarkable job of shielding his reputation—of distancing himself from his association with a confirmed assassin.

Now he was this new man—Absolon. A man who'd helped Uphrasia reach total extraction, a key component in the development of physiobombs. Close enough to the Friend to steal time treatments from her personal stash. Close enough to be gifted experimental beads. Close enough to be invited to the weapon's formal tests.

Close enough to lay his lips on hers—and not just in the privacy of the Friend's quarters. He wasn't some seedy secret.

Bland, forgettable little Lonny had done all this.

Hailwic could hardly understand it. They were blood-bound. Tithed. And yet, she clearly didn't know him at all.

In many ways, Lonny had been introduced to her as a walking afterthought, and she'd given him little due beyond that.

Of all the dangers she faced, she'd never thought her own dismissiveness could lead to such a downfall.

32

HINTOSEP

Hintosep and Abby followed the paths torn open by the Teeth like two phantoms, moving in and out of reality to bear witness to a livid level of destruction. She'd never seen such absolute devastation. Not since—

Since Uphrasia's bombs.

When the wall in her mind had first cracked—when the memories Absolon had repressed had first surfaced, she'd thought they were a dream. Well, a nightmare. A vague recollection of some misremembered nighttime terror.

Clouds of fire. Roiling lands. Crystal trees and water that had lungs and used them to *scream*. The natural world hollowed out and its insides regurgitated into something tortured. Animals fused, plants melted. Rocks with eyes and houses with feet.

Nonsense. Horrific nonsense.

But as the wall continued to crumble, those flashes of memory turned into tortured vignettes. She remembered people she'd forgotten. And a whole life before this life.

A family before Absolon.

She'd thought she'd lived all her long years inside this Valley.

She was wrong.

In a way, she'd always known there was something before the beginning. She knew humanity hadn't started here, and that Absolon had led them in. She knew she was among the first. But whenever she looked back that far in her own memory, there'd been nothing, and she'd thought, perhaps, that it just wasn't worth remembering. That it had been so bleak and so long ago that her mind had naturally discarded it.

How had she ever been so naïve?

It wasn't until a portion of that mental wall collapsed into rubble that she remembered it: the ultimate betrayal. She remembered whom Absolon had murdered to ensure he would be the master of this new world. Who he'd thought was expendable for the sake of preserving his own vision. Someone who'd simply wanted to give the people of the brand-new Valley the truth and a *choice*.

Just like everyone in her safe houses had simply wanted truth and choice.

Each house she alighted on was just the same—Absolon had been thorough. Half-eaten bodies surrounded by the transmuted materials that had killed them. A few lucky survivors who'd been away during the massacres had already arrived on the scene, but she did not disturb them. They were grieving just as she was grieving. They would rebuild just as she would rebuild.

Absolon wanted to break her, but he'd only emboldened her.

If anyone saw her and the child, they did not approach. She wasn't surprised, she must have looked like some harbinger of fate—naked, ageless, wounded, with a babe by her side and the Cage in hand. She felt no need to clothe herself—didn't bother trying to seek out scraps of fabric in any of the rubble. She was raw inside, and her bareness felt fitting. She was a thing of the world, an animal molded by it, and when she saw Absolon next she would be the beast he'd forced her to be—dangerous, feral, untamable.

The pair of them moved through the day and into the night. Hintosep would not rest until she'd taken stock of each ruin. She let the little one wander at each stop, allowing zhim to pick berries or scavenge scraps. As they traveled from scene to scene, occasionally Abby would call out for zhur parents, and Hintosep would do her best to soothe zhim. They *would* find zhur parents again, at some point. She had no idea where to start looking, but as long as they hadn't been at Mirthhouse, there was hope.

Hintosep stepped out of the tear and into the streets of Winsrouen City in the murky twilight of predawn, shivering slightly as the cool air shifting between the tightly packed buildings made gooseflesh of her arms. Abby trailed only slightly behind, fingers entwined in hers, zhur focus fixed on the bit of tough bread zhe'd snatched up at their last location.

Here, the devastation was far worse than at her more rural locations. The weaponized physiopathy had roared through blocks and blocks of dwellings—had clearly started fires and sunken half the street into the sewers.

Here in the old town, the fachwerkhaus half-timber architecture with its narrow first floors and widening second and third floors had led to the buildings all tilting over time, and had earned the neighborhood the nickname the Little Gossips because it looked like the buildings were all leaning in to whisper to one another over the narrow streets.

But the sloping eaves of the Little Gossips had allowed the fire to leap from roof to roof, over the roads, consuming the timber frames slowly but ultimately leaving them shells—cored-out carcasses, nothing left but charred bones.

The remnants of smoke still hung on the wind, and ash fluttered up underfoot, like insects fleeing her step. It was unnaturally quiet for the heart of a city—she wondered how many residents had already fled months ago, displaced by the war for one reason or another.

She contemplated what officials might say about this particular bit of structural collapse. She knew what she would have made them say about it, if she'd still been a proper Thalo, covering up Absolon's machinations and twisting hearts and minds to fit his needs.

She'd have convinced them it was rats. That the war had driven rats in unholy numbers to seek shelter under the city streets, and that they'd just so happened to congregate and invade a cheese shop. Yes, that sounded good. A cheese shop. They'd eaten through the flooring and knocked over oil lamps and destroyed everything in their devious little paths. What, figurines you say? No, no, don't you know a petrified rat corpse when you see one? Clearly the high heat mixed with the cheesemaker's rennet had produced—

Hintosep stopped herself. It was so easy to slip into that mindset. To see situations as puzzles and people as pieces to be manipulated within them.

There came a shriek from down a side street as someone noticed her. Nowhere had indecency laws quite as strict as Winsrouen, and Hintosep was sure she was a sight to behold for such sensitive eyes. There were more voices but she paid them little mind, sure she'd be gone before a concerned citizen called the Illustrious Guards to come cover her.

But then one of the voices—it was familiar. As if the fire in her belly had dredged it up, Absolon's voice came singing to her on the wind. The sharp whip-cracks of his *K*s and the kick of his *T*s were unmistakable. She spun, looking for him among the debris, and Abby watched her, wide-eyed, as she scanned the narrow byways.

He was not in Winsrouen. No. His voice was being carried through the wounds he'd made in space. He was very near his Teeth-created tunnel. Somewhere. Out there.

She gently yet firmly tugged Abby back the way they'd come, urging the child to pick up zhur feet.

Absolon was so close she could taste it. Taste it just as readily as she'd tasted Gerome's blood on her tongue.

The two of them slipped sideways through reality once more, Abby trailing her in trust. Hintosep almost left the child in the rift, almost ordered zhur to stay in the disordered limbo just so zhe wouldn't see what came next. Hintosep wasn't sure what she'd find once she made her way to Absolon's side, but she did know that what she intended to do was not fit for a little one's eyes.

But the tunnel had its own dangers. Absolon could get away and find zhur there. Others could wander in. Abby could wander *out*. Best to keep zhim close. And zhe'd already witnessed atrocities, what was one more?

The haziness of the in-between land—the tunnel, the tear, whatever one wanted to call it—was familiar by now. It was a place that was and that wasn't. Liminal and transitory and yet steady and nonexistent. It played with the mind—one's sense of space and time. But Hintosep was used to tricks of the eye and a warping of perception. Others might enter such a place and lose their balance, but not her.

And not Abby.

Hintosep followed Absolon's voice to a slice in reality that smelled of hot stone. Hot stone and . . . old bones. And there, the familiar lilt of a woman—a woman she'd known long ago—tossing angry pleas like she was throwing knives, her words sharp as razor blades.

Hintosep turned to Abby, dropping the child's hand to press a finger to her lips. "Shh," she said slowly.

Abby nodded, holding a finger to zhur own lips. "Shh."

Hintosep ducked her head out of the tear and into Xyopar only to be confronted by figures she hadn't seen in an age.

Time, Hailwic, *awake*. And Zoshim—

Nature was writhing.

"Absolon, stop it!" Hailwic pleaded.

"Stand down!" Absolon cried. "Submit to me, *and I might*."

For a brief instant, the years weighed more heavily on Hintosep than they ever had before. She'd given lifetimes to this man, thought him a protector if rarely ever a friend. She'd believed in him. Trusted him. Done horrible things in his name.

This man, who'd stolen everything from her.

Somehow it made it worse knowing that her love for him had been real once. She'd trusted him without walls in her mind. He was part of the tithing, and though she was not, to her that had always meant he was family.

An image of the Colossus swam before her eyes. The Fallen—god of secrets, and no god at all. She saw them shrink, revealing the very human form beneath the giant. She saw them and Absolon argue. She saw Absolon striking out with overpowered cryptomancy, fed by Uphrasia's cursed beads—

She remembered the instant her real love for Absolon had been carved out and discarded by his own hand.

Now, so caught up in the moment was he, so focused on torturing Hailwic and Zoshim, that he had not a thought for the vulnerability of his back. Hintosep stepped calmly from the rift into the shadows of the Necropalacia, her footfalls light and graceful. Cupped between her hands she held the Cage, its legs splayed wide, ready to welcome its next student home.

Absolon sneered at Hailwic, feigning triumph even if he hadn't fully achieved it yet. He threw back his head, ready to blurt out a mocking laugh, and that was when Hintosep struck.

She lunged, snapping the Cage around Absolon's skull, willing it to drill its little clawed feet into his flesh. The revolting artifact fit like a dream, crating him in just perfectly. He made an aborted half cry of shock as the legs burrowed, reaching out convulsively, clearly trying to get Zoshim to do something to stop her. To *save him*.

Instead, Absolon went limp, fell to his knees. Nature collapsed onto his side.

All was quiet, but it was shock that filled the palace instead of silence.

Ignoring the gods and whoever else lurked in the corners of the Necropalacia, Hintosep knelt down behind Absolon. As the Cage's new Possessor, she could feel him struggling inside it just as she had. The pure panic in his mind, in his eyes, was delicious. He'd lost control, of everything. He could not dredge up his own magic, let alone his stolen magics. He could not will his fingers to twitch, let alone take up a weapon against her. He was powerless, trapped by his own enchantment.

It was a fate he deserved. A fate he'd *earned.*

He'd warped her mind so many times, building walls and rearranging them, making her forget who she was and where she came from. He'd taken everything from her, and now she'd return the favor.

Feeling near sick with triumph and the rushing of adrenaline, she leaned in close, over his shoulder, to whisper in his ear, "I should make you stay in the Cage. I should make you suffer in it, like you made me suffer in it. Like you made me make children—your soldiers—suffer in it. But you've proven too wily. You win again and again. You weasel out of consequences, and there's only one way to put a stop to it."

She reached for one of the ancient swords that littered the tile nearby, pulling it to her across the floor as she stood, dragging its rusted, blunted tip, grinding it against the stones.

She could not hear his thoughts, but she imagined him pleading. Imagined him promising all kinds of riches, favors, powers. He would tell her they could go back, be like they were before. That they could wipe the slate clean. That he would give her anything she wanted, anything at all.

"There's only one thing I want," she told him, raising the sword in both hands, aiming its tip between his shoulder blades. "And all the suffering in all the world can't give it to me."

She plunged the blade down, *in*. When the rusty thing stopped after sinking only a few inches, she leaned on it harder, not caring how cleanly it cut as long as it *ruined*.

As he spluttered, thick blood welling up between his lips that he was unable to staunch, unable to heal using his stolen physiopathy, she let go of the pommel, leaving the sword in his back as she moved in close to sneer in his ear again.

"I want my babbi *back*."

He fell forward, and she watched the life—the blood—seep from him. She waited for the sour-sick feeling to morph into satisfaction, but it did no such thing. A heavy finality settled over her, and she realized that would have to be enough. There was no retribution to be had. Absolon's death was an end, not a renewal. It could be no more, no less.

After a moment, she noticed another shimmer of red. She noticed *Krona,* bleeding out with one torn wrist and a—

Dear gods.

And there, beside her—while Hintosep had been finally—*finally*—enacting her revenge, Abby had snuck past and gone to zhur dear 'Rona's side. The little Physiopath was already trying to see to her injuries. Already zhe was beginning to do what zhe could.

Zhe was zhur mother's child.

Near Krona, there was a spark—or more of a glint. A red crystal in her hand cracked, and something akin to both smoke and oil seeped out of it, darting through the air straight for Zoshim.

His mind.

It seeped across his mutated form like a fog gathering around a warming surface at dawn, swiftly sinking into his carapace. He shivered, then shifted, his body morphing, reconfiguring into something more akin to a man, with one of the handsome faces Hintosep remembered from her youth, though he kept his six limbs and maintained his wings, letting feathers burst across the bared skin.

Time had eyes only for her brother. Absolon's sudden death had seemed to shock her, but he and his assassin were forgotten the moment Zoshim showed signs of real awareness. Hintosep was almost certain Hailwic hadn't even recognized her.

"Shim," Time said softly, helping him to his feet once his transition was over.

"Hail?" He seemed in a daze. He would remember what happened to him while Mindless, but confusion would come first.

"I'm going to take you away from here. I'm going to take you to Punabi," Hailwic assured him.

She moved in close, pulling her wings up and around the pair of them, and then . . . they were gone.

Absolon was dead, and the twins were reunited once more.

33

ADHAR

General Adhar Basu could not be persuaded back into his bunker, landing a boot up on the fire step, leaning hard against the elbow rest at the trench's rim as he brought his spyglass to bear on the activity well beyond the two hundred and fifty yards of barren land south of his position. The supply line attacks deep into Winsrouen territory hadn't gone as well as Adhar had hoped. There were reports of one hundred new cannons leaving the factory in northern Xyopar, and at least forty had made it all the way to the minefield and were being set at this very moment.

Upward of fifteen thousand souls occupied the enemy trenches—body for body matching the north's own gathered forces on the opposite side of this muddy, overchurned land. And yet, sometimes it was so quiet Adhar had been able to imagine the Winsrouen side had given up and all gone home. The peace was inevitably shattered only moments after he'd allowed the thought, a new hail of fire raining down, often falling just short of the trenches themselves, but landing close enough to burst dirt clods and spray soil down around his people.

Those same people now all ducked low behind the edge of the trench, at the ready, rifles clutched to chests, ears open for orders, backs plastered to sandbags and bare dirt alike. Each soldier mentally prepared themselves their own way—with hardened hearts, or surreptitious glances to their fellows left and right, or lips moving in mumbled prayer to their patron god.

The spyglass's eyepiece lay cold against Adhar's overheated skin—made tacky by Asgar-Skan's humidity—as he tracked the progress of one of his mounted agitators.

Each bronzed barrel of an enemy cannon was dragged behind a team of horses, its bespoke ammunitions crate mounted high on the limber. Atop their steeds, Adhar's agitators sniped first at the soldiers driving the limbers, then at the infantry that rushed to unhitch them. The agitators needed to slow the setup—buy Adhar's own batteries time to re-aim at the new threat—and each maneuvered expertly even under a barrage of cover-fire.

Twelve enlisted worked on each unfastened cannon, steering the weapon's massive spoked wheels along slick duck boards meant to keep the artillery from plowing itself into the mud. Whenever a soldier went down—winged or worse—another was right there to take their place in the cannon's entourage.

As the first cannon found its bedding—its chassis stabilized—Adhar barked for an update on their own cannons' repositioning, still keeping his eyes trained to the distance.

He had fewer ordinances currently at his disposal—only twelve guns to their forty. But his were rifle-bore to Winsrouen's and Xyopar's smoothbore. He had fewer cannons, but surer shots.

Once the line was set, the barrage would begin. He knew their aim wasn't to decimate his line directly—these new guns would be filled with grapeshot instead of solid balls or canisters, its primary purpose to trigger the moment-mines. After the field was cleared, a full-on assault would follow, with the southern soldiers rushing the pitch, ready to claim the expanse of barren, muddy land that had so eluded them these past months.

One of his agitators toppled from their horse—the mount going down right after.

Word reached him that his first battery was ready, but that the enemy guns were deemed just on the edge of their reach. An extra advantage of aiming for the moment-mines was the south's ability to be well within the range of their target and out of range of the northern defenses.

But Adhar was still determined to try. He sent word back to fire when set.

Teams of eight managed each of Adhar's cannons—four officers of the artillery matched by four rotating gunners. Because twelve perched around each of the Xyoparian barrels in kind, he could not determine if the extra personnel was due to the unwieldy nature of the bronze cannons compared to his iron ones, or if Winsrouen and Xyopar were more prepared for losses.

Adhar covered his ears as the first shot of their countermeasures was announced, its blast barely muffled by his gloves. The ground rumbled, and he could sense the gun's recoil in his own bones. Another shot was off a minute later—then another and another, until they were rolling in quick succession as each cannon took a turn.

After a five-minute barrage, the cannons took a breath—an assessing pause. Adhar raised the spyglass again, noted new scars in the earth past the foremost enemy trenches, but short of their targets.

He ordered the batteries' positions reassessed as he counted five, six, seven bronze barrels now in place.

Adjust position, fire.

Adjust position, fire.

At the first confirmed hit, a cheer went rippling across the line—but it was a forced thing. A burst of excitement not brought on by the headiness of success but the relief of having mounted a resistance in any meaningful way.

They'd been able to hold the line here for so long because of the mines they'd back-buried when forced out of their originally held position. They had no other such reserves. Once the enemy forces had triggered them all and cleared the area, a forward surge would follow on its heels.

The soldiers here hadn't seen the whites of their opponents' eyes in quite some time. By the end of the day, they might be suddenly face-to-face.

The most experienced among them—those who'd been in and out of tour since the war began—came from the Borderswatch. And though they guarded against smugglers and naves moving from city-state to city-state, their main quarry had never been their fellow man, but the monsters from beyond.

The youngest among them—some watery-eyed, some overly determined—had grown up with the idea of war as a distant thing, a remnant of the past.

Just as Adhar had. This savage spike in Arkensyre's history still felt unnatural to Adhar, though he lived it day in and day out.

The five city-states had been friendly toward one another for the entirety of his youth—the entirety of his life—and yet when that friendliness turned icy, turned cruel, turned violent, the spiral downward, out of control, felt devastatingly inevitable and yet inherently pointless. Witness to diplomatic relations dissolving right before his eyes, Adhar had often wondered at the slide of conflict, the way a small slight could have been waved away but was instead left to fester and grow.

The First Grand Marquis's assassination had not been the first blow, but the culmination of unraveling relations.

Relations everyone could *see* unraveling, and yet even the most powerful people seemed powerless to stop the tragedy of conflict from coming to fruition.

A tragedy that put thirty thousand people—who might otherwise have come together as friends and fellow citizens of the Valley to sing together during a bright welcoming of spring—standing at odds on the field of battle.

The stalemate created by the moment-mines had been its own tense level of hells. Death had met any head daring enough to poke above a trench line more often than not. But holding a reenforced line was different from facing a charge head on.

Thirty thousand souls would clash over this sickened pit of land today, equally as inevitable as war had, to Adhar, originally felt impossible.

Three more of the enemy guns fell. Four.

Around Adhar, morale rose like the duning sand in the bottom of an hourglass.

Until the first burst of grapeshot rang out from the other side.

The size of the shot at such a distance made discerning how many mines were triggered nearly impossible.

The exact number didn't matter. The scatter shot was meant to trigger as many as it could. The more frequent their shots, the wider the spread, the more successful their campaign.

The cannons continued to call back and forth for a long while. Smoke billowed out over the battlefield, drenching it in the pungent bitterness of gunpowder and burnt fibers.

The echoes of the southern guns drew closer, their shots raining down across a new expanse of land. Onward they pushed, encroaching farther and farther.

Adhar readied his troops; when the bronze cannons ceased their onslaught the charge would commence.

A throbbing lull fell on the field.

The southern lines went quiet for too many heartbeats before the distant cry of thousands rose up in a collective, urging shout.

The enemy trenches seemed to roll with breath and *rise*. A wall of bodies heaved their way to the surface, running with rifles in hand, running with the manic assuredness of those confident their boots would find no buried switches and latent traps.

The order to *charge* left Adhar's lips, echoing down the lines on either side. Bodies surged, flanking him before climbing up and out, clambering into the mud, past the wood-and-wire barricades, across the scored land.

Screaming, shouting, firing.

The whipcrack of guns.

The cut-off cries of those unlucky enough to find mines that still remained.

More smoke.

A spider-webby shroud wove over the earth and sun, catching soldiers off guard as they ran up on one another sooner than expected—firing then, in a panic, or forgoing their firearms for bayonets, blades, or their own bare hands.

The organized chaos of battle rumbled uninterrupted across the land. Adhar's cannons still fired, trying to take out their counterparts who still answered. Harried feet found fallen bodies, stumbling over them like rocks or logs and paying them equally as much mind as the tripped soldiers scrambled upright again.

Still at his post, Adhar lost his footing when the trench itself rumbled, quaked. A new kind of quaking, which didn't jar down into the ground from above as a shell found its target, but a shaking that reverberated from below, up into his spine. The ground itself was shaking, heaving, like a great creature protesting the violence upon its back.

The screams from the southern side suddenly shifted. They were no longer battle cries meant to stiffen spines and propel feet forward. Screeching and shocked, they sent shivers of sudden terror down Adhar's back.

The color of the smoke shifted, evolving from gray-white to molded green. A green that grew brighter, sharper, deeper with each added shriek. Adhar brought his spyglass to bear once more, desperate to peer through the smoke and make out whatever new weapon Winsrouen and Xyoper had brought—mind reeling as he tried to figure out why no intelligence on the matter had come his way.

For long, strained moments, he could see nothing new. Neighbors fighting neighbors and nothing more.

Until an acidic-green wisp broke through the background smoke, chasing a soldier who ran for all he was worth—ignoring the whizzing bullets and rumbling bombardments, bent on escaping as if the frenzy of desertion had overtaken him.

The man wasn't one of Adhar's. He wore the black-and-white of Winsrouen—all the better to highlight the unnatural sheen of the pursuing vapors. The man had no hope of outrunning something that moved as the very air, and as Adhar looked on the wisp wrapped itself around the man's head, making his eyes bulge and his mouth hang wide. He struggled against it, falling to his knees as his fingers raked through nothing.

The wisp forced his jaw wider, forced itself *in*—and only then did Adhar understand what he was looking at.

Varger.

Not just one. Not a single ethereal monster but enough to light up the sky. Enough to change the luster of the smoke and the color of the battle.

How many varger would that take? Hundreds? Thousands? Tens of thousands?

How could so many appear so suddenly? It was as though the creatures had burrowed up from the very depths of the battlefield. As though some giant bottle had burst, letting thousands of barkers break free.

This was either the work of a madman, or of the gods themselves—and he could think of no one mad enough or careless enough to weaponize varger.

His soldiers had no hope against them.

No one's soldiers did.

Frantically, he bade his bugler signal for retreat.

They'd turned this expanse of land into minced earth with their mines and their bombardments. They could have been so callous as to salt it and abandon it—leave it truly scorched and sullied in parting. But no army alone could leave land so ruined and unwalkable as these monsters.

The varger would not stop—could not *be* stopped—until every last person on the battlefield had been eaten.

And even then—

He waved a desperate hand as the bugle sounded—knowing the trumpeting would be lost to at least half the ears—hoping his signal would be telling in its unwise agitation.

The dark, hollow barrels of unseen guns turned his way—he could feel them—ready to take out the foolhardy Lutadorian general. He might be cut down by a soldier he would have otherwise saved.

Every instant he thrashed above the trench line was another instant to alert someone to the danger. They had to retreat—*now*. The land was lost, and every last life was sure to follow.

The bugle blared, over and over, cutting sharply across the sky. Bodies still dropped, but soldiers began to fall back—some in answer to his orders, and some in terror as they registered the monsters stalking them in the mists.

Adhar tossed his spyglass aside, holding out a hand for the first person who would take it, then the next and the next. Soldiers wearing uniforms of all colors streamed past—not just the earthen yellows of Lutador, the jungle green of Asgar-Skan, and the speckled blues of Marrakev, but the black-and-white of Winsrouen and the deep purple of Xyopar. He offered his aid to them all, clasping their shaking, outstretched fingers surely, pulling them down into the trench before reaching out his hand again and swiftly pulling in the next.

They were all the same in this. Borders and uniforms did not matter.

Underneath their city-states' colors, they were all fresh meat.

Beyond the barricade, beyond the wall of retreating bodies, Adhar saw a varg burgeon into its fully fleshed form before his eyes. The vapors thickened, darkened, grew heavy. Its paws dropped to the ground like stones before the weight of the rest of it had been realized. As it formed legs, the swirling mass of green became thick, black quills and bulging blisters that burst the moment they were born, oozing down its new hide. Powerful haunches lead to a strong back and tense shoulders; ragged ears and a haughty tail followed. The transformation culminated in vengeful eyes and wicked teeth buried in a long snout.

New blood splattered as it lashed out sideways with massive claws, raking a man across the belly, barring him to the ground and tearing into his face with its teeth.

Adhar cried out, faltering for a moment, his instincts nonsensically pushing him to crawl out of the trench—to rise up and run to the man, though he was surely already dead.

Adhar could not remember how many people a bottle-barker had to eat from the inside out before it could manifest. Could not think straight enough to calculate how many soldiers must have fallen to this one, practically in the blink of an eye.

One of his linemen took him by the shoulders, wrestled him down from the step. They hissed in his ear, though he couldn't make out the words, and then he was being propelled along, guided by a firm hand at his back as he and his commanders were forced to retreat as well, to concede the line and the entire barren field.

Pressed in with many other bodies, he ran the zigzag of the trench line until he reached the communications trench, falling back farther to the reserve trench, and then beyond. As he ran, Adhar prayed with everything he had—his full chest and his full voice, meeting the many prayers and wails of those around him. He prayed to the gods—to Time, Lutador's patron; to Knowledge, his family's patron. Even to the Demon of the Passes, beseeching her to deliver them from the swarm and restore peace to the Valley.

THIBAUT

Thibaut pulled the second javelin free from the dissecting table just as Avellino screamed. Rearing up, he ignored the painful pull at his spine, the tight sucking of his injured lung, and the renewed wetness running into the waistband of his trousers. Thibaut whirled, thinking his fen would throw itself between Avellino and Gerome, only to realize Gerome—

"Gods," Thibaut breathed, staring at the headless corpse.

The upright figure suddenly folded, as though it had just grasped it was dead.

Avellino's face was drawn—*green*. All the blood had drained from his cheeks and he looked like he was either about to lose his lunch or collapse alongside the body.

The rumbling and vibrations that had permeated the keep for the last few minutes continued to worsen. Dust and bits of old stone began to rain down around them until his fen flared out a scarab wing, covering him over like an awning. The suckered tentacles covered the skinless parts of his back, draping against his bared muscles to protect them, pulling at the filleted parts of him like trapdoor spiders pulling their nests closed. Similarly, he felt the rattails slither inside him, finding his lung, forcing out the displaced air and stopping up the puncture.

He couldn't see most of his fen, but he knew then that it would not fully disentangle or fully remerge anytime soon. It was holding the broken bits of his body together until he could find someone to make him whole.

He wondered how much pneuma he'd lost. How much his infant abilities might have been stunted.

Sliding himself from the dissecting table, he limped over to Avellino, calling up a second beetle wing to shield him as well.

The young man's stare was caught on the remains of his Possessor like a fish on a hook. His pupils were wide, his brows bowed in distress, but he clearly could not look away.

"He's gone," Avellino gasped. "He was there, and now he's just—"

"What happened?" Thibaut asked, hoping it didn't sound like an accusation. Like it didn't sound as though he was asking *what did you do?*

"I don't know," Avellino said earnestly—more plea than denial. "*I don't know.*"

Thibaut could line up the holes in the walls with the height of Gerome's shoulders easily enough, though that explained exactly *nothing*. Whatever had punched through the keep had clearly punched through the man, and he didn't fancy waiting around to see if it would return. "This whole place is shaking like it's going to collapse," Thibaut said over the now-constant grumbling din. "We need to find Mandip and Juliet and get out."

He tugged Avellino into motion, and the two of them ran through the laboratory.

Before they reached the exit, Thibaut's eye caught on a bulky bit of silver set on a cushion atop one of the lab station tables. A large piece of armature held a magnifying glass over the top of it, and what looked like jeweler's tools lay to the side.

"Well, I'll be—" he breathed, pulling up short to swipe the object from its cushion. He tucked it swiftly into his trouser pocket.

"What was that?" Avellino asked.

"Something my mistress has been missing," he said as they hurried out of the lab and back into the halls proper.

Some of his fen's tentacles slid out from under the skin flaps at his back and slid along the stones behind them as they ran, limp from overexertion or injury. Both his body and his magic were in a fragile state, torn between insides and outsides. He had the distinct impression he could drop at any moment, and yet he moved as if little was wrong, his legs happy to carry him and his arms happy to jerk Avellino along.

"Not that way," Avellino said, yanking Thibaut to a halt when he realized they were headed back to the dungeon. "They're not there. They've escaped."

"Good for them, rather discombobulating for us," Thibaut mumbled.

"Come. Back the way Gerome brought us here."

Tray and the others had worked the metal door for hours, doing all they could to get it to budge. They'd gone back out of the strange tear to look for tools and only been able to scrape together a lone hand axe and two shovels. At one point, Melanie was sure she'd heard Abby again, but what with the way parts of the tear overlapped and melded, creating something that seemed like a straight path yet actually possessed many bends, she couldn't pinpoint where the child's voice might be coming from. Regardless, they'd all agreed to keep at the metal, sure that behind it lay the answers to their missing companions.

"It'll take us a week at this rate," Tray grumbled, planting the blade of the shovel at his feet while he wiped sweat from his brow.

"And you're sure it's not enchanted?" Melanie asked him through gritted teeth, using the hand axe as a lever to try to pop a stripped bolt head free.

"It doesn't have any of the telltale signs we usually look for in Regulation."

A ripple went through the walls of the tear, an uneasy constriction and then a shudder, like they were standing in a gulping throat.

"That can't be good," Tray intoned. Another gulp, and a steady heave from under their feet. Then the walls seemed to thin, as though they were dissipating. Like whatever had created them—or *whoever* had created them—could no longer maintain the magic. If the tear sewed itself up while they were still inside . . . "Any ideas for how to move this along?"

"There is one thing we haven't tried yet," Sebastian admitted, tossing his shovel aside.

"What's that?"

Sebastian rolled up his sleeves higher, tucking them above his elbow. "Anger," he muttered, popping his neck and rolling his shoulders. "Stand back."

A sigh emanated from all around them, a high, whiny sound. The tunnels pulsed and bent and faded. It was undeniable: the tear was disappearing. Not closing, not sewing itself back together, just *disappearing.* Where would it leave them? Would they disappear as well?

Sebastain's fen, Kemba, roared forth again, imbued with emotiopathic might, a creature bellowing with self-induced rage. He battered his long neck at the door, then reared up, hooves scraping at the bolts and seams. Desperation braided itself into the surge of pure destructive anger as the tunnel contracted and all three humans gave a gasp, stomachs fluttering and dropping, as though they were falling from a great hight.

Turbulent and mighty, the fen rammed the door again and again, buckling it, twisting the metal as it stampeded through, knocking the bent slab to the side.

The three of them dove inside after, thrusting themselves over the threshold just as the sighing and gulping in the tear took on a harsh, forced quality, like the great tension of glacial ice sliding across stone. A hole had been cut into the fabric of the tear already—not like its doorways, but like a leak. The space that had been displaced to create the tunnel was rushing back in.

Together, they stumbled into the keep, collapsing against the floor. When Tray looked back, what had been their entry point was now solid stone, as if no portal had ever existed.

Kemba pranced once, twice around the room before thinning out himself and swooping back into Sebastian. When the fen resettled in its home, Sebastian shivered as if with fever. Tray went to pat him on the back, but Melanie stood between them, staying his hand.

That anger that had toppled the door, that rage, was still there. Still heightened. Still damaging.

Tray backed away, giving him space, turning his attention instead to the keep. The room they'd alighted in wasn't overly large or grand, though the ceiling seemed exceptionally—perhaps deceptively—high. It had the feel of a space that had been gutted, its original purpose discarded, its original contents purged. What occupied it now was a couple of workaday chairs, a small table with a set of surgeon's tools, and a pedestal with whatever was atop it covered by a shimmering, opaque cloth.

His ingrained instinct to investigate had him striding over to the pedestal as if pulled. Taking a corner, he peeked beneath the cloth and nearly jumped back as he revealed a grinning maw of sharp teeth mere inches from his fingertips.

Tray had never seen anything like it, but immediately assumed it was enchanted. Looking closer, he realized it was also a gauntlet, meant for wearing.

A door on the opposite side of the room flew open. "Fancy meeting you here!" came a familiar yet strained voice.

Tray pulled the enchantment from its pedestal and whirled. The Thibaut who met him was not the Thibaut as he last remembered him, what with the monstrosity of tentacles and wings at his back. By his side, Avellino.

"What did they do to you?" Melanie asked, rushing forward, circling Thibaut, horror writ across her face.

"Hopefully nothing you can't patch up," Thibaut said. "Come on, we have to hurry—something's happened and I fear the whole place is about to go." He moved toward the bare patch of wall where the portal had been, only to pinch his brow in confusion.

"We can't go back that way," Tray said.

"Clearly. Don't suppose you've run into Mandip or Juliet recently?"

"We haven't," Sebastian said. "Have you seen Krona?"

Thibaut balked, eyes going wide. "No, why would Krona—please tell me she didn't come alone."

"We can't be sure she came here at all," Melanie said, reassurance writ in her lilt and her gentle touch of Thibaut's arm—though it only served to rile him more.

"Did she leave?" he demanded. "Was she . . . she wasn't taken, was she? What's—"

"There's so much to tell you—"

A deep brontide, like the bellowing call of shifting glacier ice, reverberated beneath their feet. The walls groaned, something beneath the stones slid sideways, and a jagged crack split through the encasement.

"No time now," Avellino said, turning on his heel. "This way."

Avellino still felt the hot splatter of his Possessor's blood on his face, though it had long since crusted over, drawing his skin tight. He still saw him the moment before his decapitation, looming, angry. Still felt that mix of defiance and triumph and the dizzying shock of the moment.

Gerome was *dead*. He hadn't wanted that. To fantasize about it was satisfying, to fight for his own life against his Possessor rational, but to know he was truly gone left him dazed. A conflicting sense of freedom and loss warred inside him.

He wanted to crow.

He wanted to cry.

And was sourly embarrassed by both.

For now, he needed to *run*. He could examine this shamefaced confusion once they were safe.

They couldn't move as fast as Avellino would have liked. Thibaut limped, dragged. Sebastian offered his arm as a crutch, and Thibaut only occasionally accepted, gritting his teeth to put on a brave face. Still Avellino rushed them on, winding toward the nearest means of escape, counting each step as a success.

Watching his former home crumble only added to the harsh tumble of conflicting emotions. He loved and hated the keep as he loved and hated Gerome.

As they fled through its stately halls—oppressive and grand, cold yet familiar—chaos met them around every corner. Thalo barking at one another, some running, some shocked still—even some attempting to hold back bulges in stone walls as though all the keep needed was a few sturdy hands to prop it up. Even the smell of the keep changed, became a swirl of ages-settled dust, sharp sweat, and hot rock.

Avellino and company were all but ignored as the priests shouted among themselves and the Possessors rushed their herds of Thalo Children up and out.

The news of the Grand Orchestrators' deaths spread like jagged lightning from Thalo to Thalo, the shock of it making the air crackle. Even as booming shockwaves of entire rooms collapsing bucked the stones beneath their feet, the news of the Grand Orchestrators' mass beheading caused far more upheaval.

"It's this way," Mandip insisted, tugging Juliet by the hand, their sweaty palms stuck tight, their fingers intertwined.

"No, not that way," she countered, pulling up the hem of her skirts as two Thalo stomped past, ignoring the prisoners. "That's the way to that damned cave and such where we found Emotion. There was no exit, remember? You were half drowned, so perhaps your waterlogged brain couldn't grasp it at the time, but we needed Krona to actually escape. We'll trap ourselves in a dead end if we go out that way."

"You're both wrong," said a voice from around the corner, coming directly at them.

"Avellino!" Juliet shouted, overjoyed despite the circumstances. As soon as she saw Thibaut, her joy dissipated. "Thibaut, oh gods—"

"*What have they done to me?* Yes, I've been hearing that one quite a lot. No time to wail about it now, we need to move."

As he limped past Mandip—who made no secret of his gawping, taking in the long, thick tentacles skimming the ground behind him—one of Thibaut's knees gave out. As he sagged, the tentacles rushed to prop him up, to keep him on his feet. Mandip did the same, catching Thibaut's arm, throwing it over his shoulder.

He was careful not to touch the gory seam from which the tentacles protruded.

"Are you—" he began to ask when Thibaut gritted his teeth and swore under his breath.

"No, I'm not," Thibaut said, words heaving.

He was not all right. None of them were all right.

"We need to keep moving," Thibaut added. "Another step. Then another."

There was no time for Mandip to ask how the others had gotten here, and in the moment it hardly mattered. "Juliet—"

She was there at his call, slinging herself under Thibaut's other arm, echoing how they'd all held one another not just in the cell but hundreds of times before in warmth and support. And yet this was so very different. Thibaut had wings and tails and tentacles—his body held together like taxidermy, but with threads of magic rather than cotton.

"Come on," Thibaut said again, taking a step, thrusting his hips forward like the others were the ones lagging, the ones who needed encouragement. "I refuse to be the reason we die."

"Pride won't help us escape any faster," Juliet faux-scolded him as the group hurried on.

"Ah, but my dear, with these slimy things wriggling at my spine, a show of pride is all I have left."

Leave it to Thibaut's vanity to still make a show of itself. Even when he was standing on death's stoop, if not yet fully knocking on its door.

His fen was a ghastly sort of beautiful, even in its half-formed state. The tentacles nearly looked like a regal cape as they draped along the floor. Mandip squeezed Thibaut's wrist where he held it steady over his shoulder and resolved to spend a day or two purposefully inflating his ego about it if they got out of this.

The wall they were following buckled unexpectedly—a long crack racing past them through the stone—and Avellino was forced to concede they'd need to take a different path, lest the way implode.

Thibaut was a hot line against Mandip's side. Feverish. Though the dexterity of the tentacles assured he kept up a steady pace, the paleness of his cheeks and the clammy sweat on his brow told a grim story.

"Maybe we should rest a moment," Mandip suggested.

"Not unless you want it to be an eternal one," Thibaut countered.

"Thibaut, you're—"

"On the verge of dying? Tosh. On the other hand, do I think if I stop moving for an instant, I'll stop moving forever?" He shrugged. "Perhaps. Yes, my insides are struggling to stay that way, but I can only handle one life-threatening emergency at a time, and I think a keep falling on our heads takes priority." He was clearly trying to keep his tone teasing, chipper, but added, more solemnly, "I just wish . . . Krona . . ."

"You'll see her again," Mandip said quickly. "I know you will."

The group came to a wide staircase and began their ascent only to have a great chunk of the ceiling come barreling down, obliterating the top landing. They scrambled back, diving behind a banister to shield themselves from the debris.

Avellino waited for the dust to settle, hoping the stairs were still viable, cursing his luck when it was clear they were not. Turning on his heel, he led them on, toward more familiar halls that sent a chill of unwanted memory through him.

Suddenly he was a child again, standing awkwardly among his peers as Hintosep handed him an infant.

Abby.

The nursery was this way.

He realized they'd seen Possessors rush by with their charges—schools of children. But no babies.

A sharp cry of help as they rounded a corner had everyone's heads snapping up. No one had called out for their help yet, and no one had offered it.

"Eldest!" Avellino shouted in recognition. The Eldest of the Nameless. "Fey mind the babies," he said, the explanation thrown over his shoulder as he began running forward toward a tall, thin, pale-haired figure.

"We need help!" fey insisted. "*Please.*"

Avellino came skidding to a halt in front of fem, reaching for feir hand, intending to simply pull fem along when he realized fey were standing at the nursery door.

Inside, a plethora of small children, fifty or more, clung to a handful of teenaged Thalo who huddled around a smattering of adults. Every time the keep shook they shrieked and ducked low in unison, as though the collective resonance of their fear could create enough pressure to keep the roof from falling on their delicate heads.

"*Please,*" the Eldest insisted again. "I can't leave them."

35

HAILWIC

In a Time and Place Before

A wild horror overtook Hailwic. In the thin air high above what had been the craters, she seethed, screamed in a wooden, reedy way that made her throat raw and her chest tight.

If she'd only killed the Friend—if she'd only brought her to an end when she was supposed to—

Her intestines coiled, felt like they were sliding through her—as a snake, a python. The rogue physiopathy had boiled itself out, but seeing Absolon kiss Uphrasia had transformed Hailwic far more fundamentally.

She was sick with it. Haunted by it. Made numb and nauseated in turns.

There was more to that kiss than Absolon would ever let on.

She needed to tell the others about it—as urgently as she needed to report on the bomb.

Hailwic flew up, up, where the wind was as violent as her insides, as her emotions, letting it take her wings and her hair in its abusive grip before slapping herself through a jump.

Expecting the silent, warm solace of her room, she jolted when she landed. Instead of the softness of her bed, or even the scratchiness of her rug, cold, unyielding tile bit into her knees and palms. Startled shrieks rose around her like the whistling bursts of firecrackers, and many sets of naked feet stomped all around—throwing water in her face. Water that poured down from above.

The bunker's communal showers. She'd missed her bedroom by a long shot.

Disoriented, she hid from what she thought was rain—overly warm rain—feathers ruffling, her wings drawing in close. They repelled the water, sluicing it away. Curling into a ball, she shied away from the bright lights cutting through the storm—which made no sense, but nothing she'd experienced in the last hour made much sense.

Two sets of bare feet stopped in front of her. Hands gently touched her spine. She reared up just enough to lash out, hissing like a mad animal. Sweet-scented steam filled her lungs, heavy with soaps, oils.

Her head ached, her stomach clenched, and the shrieking voices turned apologetic, kind. No less harried, but less frightened.

"Get help," someone ordered.

Hailwic wrapped her four arms around herself, shaking with something that wasn't sorrow, wasn't adrenaline.

Maybe it was anger. Slick and shiny. Cold and cutting.

Or maybe it was the cryptobeads. She'd swallowed several. Lonny had said they'd give her a hangover. Now that the invasive magic was dissipating, her sanity felt like it was dissipating with it.

Her own feathers felt like little knives against her skin. Not wounding, just dragging. A promise. Sharp and fierce. Whether she'd be covered over in thin slices or caressed with blunted tips depended entirely on how she composed herself—how she broke the news to the others in their tithing.

The communal showers cleared, perhaps minutes later, perhaps hours later. Hailwic's sense of time was disjointed and adrift—something she once would have thought impossible. She kept herself fetal, feeling more like a gangly, unnatural creature than she ever had before. Her cheek pressed against a dirty drain while she tapped at the tiles with twenty fingers, making little splashes and whishing . . . whishing . . .

"Hail? Hailwic?" Punabi's voice was sharp above the hiss of the water. Taps squeaked. The false rain stopped. Boots appeared before her, leaving unfortunate watery mud tracks in their wake.

Zhe kneeled, took her face in both hands, warm palms and steady fingers brushing away the wetness—the water and the tears.

Hailwic still ducked away from the bright lights; they stabbed at her eyes, made her skull throb. She sought refuge in Punabi's chest, half crawling into zhur lap. The gentle palms that carded through her wind-knotted hair were welcome in their familiarity. Disoriented, pained, and tortured, Hailwic clung to the kindness.

Punabi began to hum softly, zhur voice mixing with zhur magic to weave a cradle of ease around Hailwic's chest.

Zhe didn't ask what had happened; Punabi was privy to her mission parameters. A debrief would come all in due time. Right now, zhur only concern was Hailwic's well-being.

Slowly, a solidness returned to Hailwic's sense of self. A still, quiet point inside her latched on to Punabi's soothing, tethering her to reality, to safety, letting her uncurl the protective ball of her body and mind.

Punabi brushed the hair back from her forehead, kissed the bared skin. "Do I need to get you to a medic?" zhe asked.

Hailwic rolled over in zhur lap, keeping zhur pinned to the wet floor, though it hardly mattered anymore—zhur fatigues were just as soaked through as Hailwic's. Her wings stretched, their tips curling upward, creating a dark garden all around them, stark against the pale tile.

"I think it'll pass," she huffed, the twist of her own body still making her stomach spin and spin. "Absolon—Lonny—implied it would pass. The beads. Their aftereffects. He gave me . . . had me swallow . . ."

Punabi stiffened. "What? What did he give you? Did he—did he poison you?"

"No." She shook her head sharply, was rewarded with her brain ricocheting off the inside of her skull. "No . . ." Poison might have been preferable. Though her veins did feel as acidic and sluggish as they did after far too much drinking. "But he—"

Bile rose in her throat. The aftermath of the bomb hadn't made her vomit. The terrible hangover from the cryptobeads hadn't made her vomit. But the memory of her tithe-mate sharing such easy intimacies with *that woman*—

She swallowed hard, choking, but keeping it down.

"Do you think you can stand? Walk?"

"Not yet," she said, voice meek. "Just . . . sit with me a little while longer. Please. Please."

⊱⊸⊰

The news of Hailwic's abrupt arrival spread through the bunker like fingers of fungus, creeping and infecting every ear it reached. The heightened anxiety in the tunnels could not be mistaken, and by the time Hailwic was well and her brother had changed her back to her natural state, the sense of wrongness clinging to everything and everyone in the tunnels had thickened into a bristling preparedness.

She both dreaded and anticipated the debriefing in equal measures.

There were the days before the test, and then there were the days after. The divide was unquestionable. Just as, in her gut, there were the days before Lonny had ever thought to kiss Uphrasia, and the days after he'd crossed, irrevocably, into such cursed territory.

Entering Kinwold's appointed debriefing room, she paused in the doorway, meeting her tithe-mates' eyes—Glensen, then Zoshim, Punabi, and Kinwold themself—before pulling out the small pillbox with the remaining beads and striding over to lay it gravely in the center of the table.

Feeling hollow, she told them everything. Of the beads, the bombs, and Uphrasia's seduction.

None of them had imagined plain Lonny—mild Lonny, *forgettable* Lonny—was capable of such a feat.

⊱⊸⊰

The professor's death had caused a fracturing, and this—Absolon's hard right into Uphrasia's intimacies, the scope of the bomb—took a sledge to those cracks.

Hailwic should have known the tithing was never enough to keep them together. *It takes more than love, more than promises, more than sheer will—more than magic—to keep people together when the world is crumbling apart,* she acknowledged, only to herself. Especially those who think themselves architects—not only of their own destinies, but the future's.

The tithing remaining in Remotus had more petty squabbles, and harsher disagreements on how to apply their troops. Each of them moved more keenly into their own strategizing and more often rejected the others' input.

As for their tithe-mate still in Radix, Hailwic had imagined confronting Absolon many times. Jumping to his side just as she had before the test, demanding an explanation for what she'd seen. For why it had felt so *wrong.*

She knew exactly how the conversation would go. He would reassure her it was an act. A time-honored method of infiltration, just as she'd thought. *Of course I still mean to kill her,* he'd say. *Of course I'm still with you. Of course I'm on your side.*

He would say all that and more. He'd give her more beads to take back, or some other gift meant to appease.

Ultimately, she never went through with the jump because she knew it wouldn't make a difference. He would tell her exactly what she wanted to hear, and that *wrongness* she'd sensed meant she no longer trusted him enough to take him at his word.

She kept waiting for Kinwold to recall him from the field. To send him a summons that would prove his loyalty and help convince Hailwic her unease was unfounded. But they went on as if nothing had changed, their faith in Absolon's commitment as strong as it had always been. As long as the time treatments kept flowing, they reasoned, everything was as it had always been.

The others weren't so sure.

Glensen was the first to leave, though it wasn't framed as such. It was a pilgrimage, one fey were undertaking with Kinwold's spouse, Arrallia. One of Glensen's pleas for a diplomatic audience had finally been answered by Yugalheim.

Hailwic was sure the offer to share a firsthand report of Radix's new superweapon had shaken something loose.

It was important work—to Glensen, it was the most important mission fey'd ever undertaken outside of direct field medicine.

But Zoshim wasn't ready to say good-bye.

After the formal farewell, he and Hailwic escorted Glensen and Arrallia to the bunker's southernmost air hatch. He stopped them just short of leaving, taking Glensen by the arm and crowding fem off to the side while others came and went. Tunnel life continued on, but Zoshim's attention was fiercely focused, a sad sort of disbelief in his eyes.

"You're our best medic," he said, tone pleading. "Arrallia is equipped to do this on her own, why do you have to go?"

Fey had a rugged pack over feir shoulder—anyone not in the know might have thought fey would be back within a day, but Hailwic knew: Glensen was already gone, for good. Fey'd been on this mission in feir mind for a while now, it was just feir body that had yet to follow.

Fey took his face in feir hands. "This is my burden. We have a chance for aid. Real aid. They have to know that Radix poses an existential threat not just to its own people, but all people. Besides, I might not be the best medic anymore." Glensen punched him lightly, playfully in the arm, and Zoshim tried to smile, but failed. "You'll do fine without me."

"I don't want to do fine without you." Hailwic hadn't heard him sound so young in so long. He kept his voice firm, but there was the whimpering of a child behind it. Shim had looked up to Glensen from the first day they'd met. Fey'd been a stable, supportive older figure the likes of which he'd never had before.

"You're a sweet kid," Glensen said. "Don't ever let that change." Fey gave him a warm clap on the side of the neck, then nodded to Arrallia and moved out from the shadow of his form.

"Good-bye," Hailwic bid the pair. "Good luck."

The two of them climbed up the ladder on the left of the hatch while someone else scooted down the right. Fey didn't look back before emerging out into the daylight. Suddenly, indignation made Hailwic hot around the throat, mostly on Zoshim's behalf.

He looked lost, eyes searching now for a purpose that wasn't there.

After Glensen, Zoshim started disappearing little by little.

Most death Hailwic had witnessed in her life was violent, if not sudden. Chests torn open by incendiary devices, limbs mangled by heavy debris, brains scattered across roads like the insides of gourds. The raw savagery of resistance and war meant ends were the stuff of blades, bombs, and poisons. Her parents had died in two quick pops of a distant gun right before her eyes.

Retreats were forced. Partings were *severings*.

She wasn't equipped to imagine a slow burn of a loss. A leaving that simmered and hissed instead of suddenly boiling over. She'd thought if Zoshim ever left her, it would be in a hail of bullets—and she'd be there to absorb half the lead.

Their bond was stronger than anything the world could put in their path, she was sure.

The square shattered husks of bombed-out buildings looked like jagged teeth to Hailwic from where she rode atop the last TriMite in the convoy. She crouched low atop its boxy metal roof, steadying herself with her wings and arms, ready to take flight the moment she eyed a threat.

There was nothing left in the town above a story high. The cement blocks now looked chalky; the stucco had powdered. Rebar thrust up from sheared-off walls, bare, like rusted bones. Piles of debris stood like snowdrifts off the main thoroughfare—the one road that had been cleared to let aid in. Still, the five TriMites had to pick their way around deep potholes and chunks of apartment buildings thrust too deep into the roadway to move. Their six armored legs shifted in and out of tandem, keeping the carriages perfectly level while their magichanical limbs twisted, turned, extended, and withdrew.

TriMites weren't meant for long-distance travel. They were stabilized carriers, jumped to secure locations before being repositioned. These were filled with sacks of rice, barrels of water, and various medical supplies, the distribution overseen by Zoshim and his unit while Hailwic's troops provided security.

Each vehicle in the convoy was topped by six soldiers at the ready, with four more inside the unit to protect the supplies and aid workers, and another up front to cover the bulbous capsule in which the pilot sat working their levers and exciting the kairopathic nodules that powered the TriMite's movement.

Hailwic's team had Cryptopaths who'd shrouded their arrival point to protect it from ambush, and now those same Cryptopaths scanned the wary faces they passed for secrets while Emotiopaths would take the temperature of crowds once amassed, checking for undue stress and adrenaline spikes.

Children followed the slow plod of the convoy, hands outstretched as they ran alongside asking for treats and handfuls of rice—which Zoshim's team was in no position to give until they'd stopped and secured the vehicles.

Hailwic's troops kept their firearms poised, pointed off the sides of the vehicles, aimed at anyone who came too close, no matter their age.

The children themselves didn't seem to mind the guns, having grown used to the sight of them. That in itself would have been a gut punch to a much younger Hailwic.

She heard a commotion toward the front of the convoy and looked over her shoulder to see Zoshim kneeling atop the second TriMite, arguing with several of her people, clearly trying to get them to lower their weapons, making pleas on the children's behalf.

"Orders are orders," one of her soldiers rebuffed loudly, keeping their sights trained on the nearest round little face. "Take it up with Hailwic."

Zoshim's gaze shot to where she was crouched, and she held it.

Today he was in the guise of a tall goat-man. Horns spiraled up from his brow. His comically large eyes held eerie, horizontal pupils, and his face was covered in hair. When he stood, it was clear he wore no boots and instead sported cloven hooves.

With several powerful strides, he bounded from the top of one TriMite to the next until he reached her side.

"They're *kids,*" he said without greeting.

"And this isn't RFR-secured territory," she told him. "The threats here aren't just from Uphrasia. If you want to distribute in this area, then you'll have to accept the heightened security."

"And heightened security means pointing guns at six-year-olds with snotty noses?"

"*Yes,*" she snapped. "The wannabe warlords around here are happy to use little kids as carriers for all kinds of things. Bombs, poison gas. So we need to be ready to move, even against a kid, no matter the optics of it."

"*Optics?* It's not about the *optics,* Hail, it's about the *morality—*"

"Then take it up with the warlords."

He glared at her, but said no more.

The TriMite convoy crab-stepped its way into what had formerly been the town's largest park, now a scorched stretch of grass and stumps that contained at least a hundred tents all huddled together. The pilots guided their vehicles into an easily defendable half-moon, and a coordinated team of both Zoshim and Hailwic's people guided the amassed survivors into lines before the TriMites' rear doors were opened.

The plan was to off-load the rice and water, then distribute the sacks and barrels as quickly as possible before buttoning up the vehicles again and moving them out. Zoshim would remain behind for hours after with a contingency of his medics.

As the slackened faces of exhausted adults and the tear-stained cheeks of infants joined the exuberant children in line, Hailwic soared high to get a better lay of the land. Once she'd verified her soldiers were in position and had all entrances to the park locked down, she went to help Zoshim unpack his supplies.

He'd already set up an awning to shield him from the sun, and was readying a cooler filled with antibiotics and vaccine vials. He greeted her with a thin grimace.

"I didn't mean to sound flippant about your concerns earlier," she apologized. "But we can't afford to be naïve."

"Maybe I can't afford to treat children like rabid dogs ready to bite," he countered.

"Then stick to your role and I'll stick to mine. I'm not handing you the gun. Glensen molded you into a pacifist, I get it."

"Do you?" he asked, voice rigid to mask its incredulity. He set the cooler aside and took her by one arm, ushering her away from the other medics and the refugees already queuing.

"In the detention center," he said in a harsh whisper, "I used to see the man I killed. Not even in my sleep, I'd just see him. Disassociate back to that moment. You stopped me from killing anyone else, and I'll always be grateful for that, but Glensen helped me understand that *that* moment wasn't the pinnacle of who I am. I can never go back. I can never undo it. But I can move forward. Not once was I afraid of myself when Glensen was there with me. Sometimes I could even forget that I'm a murderer at all."

"You were just a scared kid, hounded into a corner—"

"Exactly. Exactly, Hail. I was a kid staring down a barrel, just like *those* kids. I was hunted. I can't be a hunter in return. I can't watch you—any of you—point a gun at innocent people *on the off chance they might be dangerous* and not feel something. Guilt, remorse, hopelessness—the violence and the suspicion feed on each other. Believe me, I've rationalized and de-rationalized my own violence a thousand different ways. I blame the dead man, I blame myself, I blame the squad, I blame Uphrasia. There's plenty of blame to go around. But it all just changes the context. Not the death. The death I have to live with."

Hailwic didn't say, *It's not like you're the only one here who's killed someone*, even though the condescension flashed behind her teeth.

She understood the distinction he was trying to make.

The war itself was formative for many—a shared tragedy.

That night, in the alley—that instance of kill or be killed—belonged to Zoshim alone. And it had changed him in a way he'd never be able to leave behind.

"But that's why I'm so grateful for Glensen. Not just for teaching me how to heal, but about what pacifism really means. How to own it. It's a refusal of violence, not a refusal to fight. You fight things that don't take fists. You fight hunger with food. You fight cold with blankets. Rain with roofs. You realize there are more jobs during wartime than just *soldier*."

"Still . . ." Hailwic said. "There has to be someone who meets violence with violence."

"I know. I do. But that can't be all of us, or else the whole world becomes nothing but bloody. And it can't be me, I can't . . . I can't be around it."

"You're in a war zone, you don't have much choice."

"Then maybe I can't be in the thick of it like this anymore."

A heady shout interrupted their conversation. A knot of refugees swayed back and forth in a tight tussle at the back of the fifth TriMite. A sack of rice lay torn open on the ground, its contents spewed across the grass and already trampled. Three scrawny teenagers pulled at one another's shirts and sent open-palmed strikes lashing out haphazardly. Those around them shied away while trying to remain queued, far more afraid of losing their chance at a meal than getting caught in the scrabbling.

It wasn't uncommon for people to fight over rations or their place in line, but Hailwic's suspicions were perked all the same. She'd been in excitable crowds where each person was as high-strung as the next, prepared to lash out at the slightest provocation. *These* people had dragged their feet, stares distant, and even now they observed the fight with an exhausted detachment.

Security team members were already calling for calm, and while most attention was turned on the scrimmage, Hailwic looked elsewhere.

She reached out with her kairopathy, looking for temporal disturbances.

She felt a shimmer of augmented relativity around the first TriMite. The type of bowing of time and space associated with a lens. She jumped there herself without a word of explanation to her brother.

Landing lightly on the roof of the vehicle among her soldiers, she eyed the surroundings for unusual activity and didn't need to look far. Below, in the cab, the pilot was pushed from their place at the controls, replaced by someone else. Two additional people in knitted masks hefted themselves over the top of the pilot's capsule, crawling in her direction to aim some kind of homemade launcher at the roof guards.

Adrenaline instantly zinged through Hailwic's limbs. "Get down!" she shouted, grabbing the soldier next to her and slamming zhim into the roof just as a smoky projectile burst from the wide mouth of the barrel.

Loud clangs all around her rang out as the rest of the soldiers dove to the deck.

Screams from the crowd followed as the projectile—just a smoke bomb given the particular sting of the acrid smell—arced over its intended target and fell among the people. A fistfight couldn't rile them, but a firefight sure could.

Beneath Hailwic the TriMite rose up on its legs once more, urged into motion by the hijackers. Hailwic rose to her feet as well, trying to discern if there were more than six attackers—the three on the TriMite and the three in the brawl—in order to calculate the overall danger and who, exactly, was attacking. Whoever these people were, they were organized enough to create a distraction, but not organized enough to sport the numbers needed to surround the convoy.

Only one TriMite had been commandeered—the others still sat stationary and under RFR control.

Probably not sent by a warlord, then. Maybe just a local gang.

Reaching out, she created a time stop to encompass all three masked attackers. The two with the homemade launcher stiffened, caught in her bubble. The new pilot kept driving, pushing back, kairopathy to kairopathy. At the same time, they seemed to lose some nuance of control, and the TriMite's chassis dipped awkwardly.

Beside her, two of her men were up with guns at the ready, barrels pointed at the two in the time stop.

"I've got them," Hailwic said.

"Ma'am, they shot at—"

"*I've got them*. We don't shoot prisoners." Her voice wavered in a way it hadn't in a long time—and never while giving orders. Her conversation with Zoshim was distracting her, his voice pinging around in her head. "Someone needs to stop the pilot or stop the—*stop the TriMite*." That was it. "I need a practicing Physiopath."

"Here, ma'am," said the soldier she'd pinned to the roof.

"How good are you with pinpoint dissolution?"

"Um, not very good, ma'am. But I can break something, if that's all you need."

Zoshim would've been able to pinpoint a specific bolt in the TriMite and turn it to dust—and restore it just as easily. But she'd work with what she had. "Take out our suspension."

"Ma'am, one of our snipers on the road ahead has a clear shot of the pilot—"

"Tell them to hold and sever the TriMite's suspension. Now."

She took the gun from the soldier and zhe dropped to zhur belly, pulling zhur gun gloves off and pressing zhur palms flat to the metal.

Long moments passed as Hailwic held the two hijackers and waited impatiently for the TriMite to stop, the vehicle teetering along, ferrying its goods farther and farther from the people who needed them. She gritted her teeth, impatient. Zoshim would have shut it down in an instant; his inherent skill had spoiled her.

"Ma'am, it'd be easier just to take them out—"

With a frustrated rumble in the back of her throat, she tried to halt the TriMite's legs with her kairopathy, hoping it would help the Physiopath, even knowing it was folly. They'd been magichanically engineered to keep going, to be resistant to outside kairopathy. "We can fix the damn machine," she said, feeling Zoshim's words, his fears, his guilt skittering around in the back of her mind. "We can't paste a dead man's skull back together, so *keep trying*."

She could sense the regard of her soldiers shifting. They were used to harsher, more direct combat orders. She knew none of them objected to sparing life where they could, but with so many unknowns, she usually put the safety of her unit first and had them dispatch any threats as soon as they were identified.

She grew more and more irritated with herself as the Physiopath struggled, drawing out the encounter. The field was no place for an internal ideological scuffle. Why hadn't Zoshim waited to infect her with indecision back at the bunker, where she could shake it off before the next mission?

The TriMite began to stagger as though drunk, listing to the side while the pilot struggled for control. Something was breaking in the carrier's bowels—the suspension was going, but it hadn't yet snapped.

A desperate, shaking hand extended from the cab, pointing a handgun at an awkward angle, up and back toward the roof. The pilot knew they were losing the machine, knew they had to scrape off the soldiers while they still had a chance.

The barrel bounced wildly as the TriMite reeled.

Hailwic sensed dozens of possible shots through her kairopathy. Every instant where a harsh jolt of the TriMite forced the clearly inexperienced hand to squeeze the trigger.

But the inevitable came faster than she'd expected.

She was quick, but not quicker than a bullet. By the time the pilot had taken their potshot, it was too late to try to freeze it in midair. She created a shield around herself as rapidly as she could, but couldn't slow the bullet enough to keep it from penetrating her shoulder.

The force of it knocked her off-balance, forced her to release the other two masked attackers, who surged up, trying to scramble atop the roof.

Her soldiers didn't hesitate. A barrage of fire rained past Hailwic.

The sniper on the road ahead took their shot.

The TriMite wheezed to a halt.

⁂

Hailwic sat in a rickety folding chair while Zoshim extracted the bullet from her bone. In the center of the park, the public still queued for their rice and water, despite the wailing of the three cuffed teenagers who knelt over the tarp-covered bodies of their previously masked fathers.

Zoshim kept rubbing at his eyes with the back of his gloved hands while he worked. His fingers shook where they probed her wound.

He didn't look like a goat-man anymore. Any joy he usually got from shifting his form had been stolen today. He simply looked like his regular self. Blue eyes red-rimmed, pale face blotchy from sadness and righteous anger.

Not anger at those who'd attacked the convoy. Not at the group of neighbors who'd banded together to rob their other neighbors of supplies. He'd never be angry at the desperate. He was angry at the world. At the violence. At the circumstances that had driven these people to make such rash, dangerous plays for supplies and control.

Hailwic didn't ask, but she thought he must be angry at her, too, for the men's deaths. For doing her job to protect him and the rest of the people.

She didn't tell him she'd hesitated. Had tried to do it his way, as best she could.

His lip trembled heavily when one of the teenagers began beating his chest and rending at his clothes. He sat back to find something substantial to wipe at his eyes with, slipping away from her—in more ways than one.

He was haunted after that. Walking through life like that grieving, wailing boy was at his back, spitting his grief every waking moment.

He left the bunker permanently only a week later.

"Do you know why I keep shifting bodies?" he asked her before he left, pack slung over the low yolk of a shoulder. His proportions were all exaggerated today, and he gave the impression of being a cross between a man and a praying mantis.

They stood at the same hatch they'd seen Glensen disappear through.

"I thought it was because you enjoy looking like someone new," she said, trying to keep her tone light and her eyes happy, even though she was loath to see him leave.

He sniffed dryly, looked at his boots, shifting uncomfortably. "I always look like me," he informed her. "Or never look like me; I'm not sure which it is. I make us match on a lot of missions because it's simpler that way. The people who need to recognize us do. But that form? With the wings? Or my . . . let's call it *neutral* form—neither are right for me. I keep shifting bodies because I haven't found one that feels right yet."

"Oh," she said flatly. "Why haven't you said so before?"

He shrugged. "Why didn't you ask? You see me shift all the time, you could have asked why."

"I thought you'd get mad at me," she scoffed. "Or you were *testing me*—trying to see how weird you could go before I said anything."

"Weird?" he mocked, holding one elongated hand to his elongated face "I look weird to you?"

"Oh, come on, *this* can't possibly be *the one*."

He smiled over-bright—horrible, long teeth and all. "No, I suppose it isn't. I feel . . . I feel like I should have found *the one* by now, though. It's like I don't have all the pieces to put together a whole picture of *me* yet," he said. "Worse, I don't even know where to look for them. There's a hole"—he waved at his side—"like there's an entire other side of me I haven't even met yet. I know that doesn't make a lot of sense. But the absence has always made me feel adrift. But that's why, when I can, I keep shifting. Keep searching.

"Glensen was a big help in that regard," he added, wistfulness turning his tone airy, like it was a secret he hadn't really meant to let loose. "Grounding. I always felt like I was free to shift so much because fey were so *solid.* Fey took my hands—hands that had murdered a man long before I ever saw war—and showed me how to heal with them instead. Whatever I tried with them was okay, you know? Fey made sure I knew it was okay.

"I might . . . I might not know what's missing, or who I am fully yet, but I do know this about me: I can't be around the violence anymore. I can help elsewhere, but not where me bringing people food also brings people death. I can't heal and hurt at the same time."

"Where will you go?"

He shrugged. "I've written to Glensen. I don't think fey're gonna write back. But it's okay. I'll be needed somewhere."

I need you here, she didn't say. *All those kids you were worried about?* They *can't leave. They can't escape. Stay here. Stay here and do what you can for them.*

But he couldn't help them if he crumbled inside.

For so long she'd rebelled in the name of Zoshim's freedom, and she refused to deny him freedom in this. He wasn't frozen in the moment he killed that squad agent. He wasn't frozen in his body. And he wasn't frozen at her side.

"Stay safe," she bid, kissing his forehead.

And then, in a blink, he was through the bunker hatch and gone.

His absence left her feeling untethered. She awoke awash in sadness every morning, even before she was fully lucid and could remember *why* she was sad. She'd thought they'd remain side by side forever. That they were inseparable. As twinned in their destinies as they were in birth.

At least he was in control of his own life. She consoled herself with pride in that.

Punabi was the third to leave, and it truly caught Hailwic off guard.

". . . wic. Hailwic? Are you listening?"

"Hmm?"

They were in their quarters, the lights low, air warm and smelling of the two of them—their entwined lives. Hailwic had a desk lamp shining on the thin pages of a new book of the arcane she'd acquired through a dealer one of her lieutenants knew. She wasn't sure yet if it was anything of value. The title was unfamiliar: *The Power of Raw Gemstones in Pneumal Experimentation*. It *might* have been a volume in Uphrasia's secret library and she'd simply forgotten about it. Perhaps a close read would spark something in her memory or understanding.

Abruptly, she realized Punabi had been talking to her back for an unknown amount of time, and zhur voice had only now filtered through. "Sorry, what?"

"*Skies above*, it's like talking to a wall," Punabi spat. "Whenever you get your hands on that useless stuff you just go somewhere else entirely."

Hailwic bristled. "It's not useless."

"Found the secret to plucking out Uphrasia's eyes and using her spleen to gain dominion over animals yet?"

"What is with you lately?" Hailwic asked, slamming the cover shut, turning.

"What's with me? What's with *me*?" Punabi stood near the bed, a half-packed duffel within reach and a crumpled shirt in hand. "Ever since Zoshim left, I can't have a proper conversation with you. You're entirely disinterested in anything I have to say unless it's somehow about assassinating Uphrasia."

"That's unfair."

"Is it? Hail, I've been packing for half an hour and you haven't even noticed."

Hailwic took in the evidence—the open drawers of their single dresser. The missing slippers that should have been at the door. The toiletries bag bulging where it lay on the rumpled sheets next to the duffel bag.

"Where's Kinwold sending you?" she asked slowly.

"Nowhere. I'm sending myself. I'm splitting away from the RFR. I'm taking my unit with me."

What?

Hailwic was on her feet before she even realized she was moving. "What are you talking about?"

"I'm leaving," Punabi said, punctuating the heavy words with a heavy sigh. "I can't get anything done here. Kinwold won't authorize even a third of my mission requests. My soldiers are rotting from disuse. All Kinwold ever thinks about is Arrallia gone on her mission, and all you ever think about is your missing half—and that other half *isn't* me. I can't waste away here with the two of you when there is a real fight to be had out there against an actual enemy that wants us all dead. So yeah, I'm serious. I already told Kinwold, and they didn't even try to stop me."

Hailwic's mind tried to latch on to the words, tried to make them make sense. The abruptness made them feel airy, wispy. Insubstantial.

This . . . this couldn't really be happening.

"How can you just spring this on me?"

"You're joking, right?" Punabi asked flatly, unimpressed.

"How, *how* as an Emotiopath can you be this insensitive?"

"Insensitive?" Punabi parroted, voice half an octave too high.

"To just drop this on me out of *nowhere*."

"We've talked about the possibility *many times*—"

"I didn't know you were *serious*," Hailwic snapped. She scanned back over the last months in her mind, trying to pluck out the conversations that had led here. She'd been distracted lately, yes. But had she been *that* distracted? She did remember Punabi talking about going up north, out of RFR territory, to the edge of Uphrasia's reach. She remembered the tone of zhur voice, the thinly veiled disgust whenever Kinwold's name came up. She hadn't imagined it would come to anything. She thought Punabi's dissatisfaction was transient, or inconsequential. She'd thought—

"Then I'll say it again: yes, I'm serious. I'm going."

Hailwic ran after things, people. She'd pursued her brother, pursued the RFR, pursued Punabi. And once she had them, she intended to retain them. She chased, she caught, she kept. They weren't, in turn, supposed to pursue other things.

She knew it was a childish sentiment. But she felt childish, selfish, and she wasn't ashamed of it. With a quick stride, she covered the distance to the bed, taking Punabi's hands—not holding them, but covering them both in hers, grasping them together in a loose shackling before sinking onto the mattress. Hailwic tried to find the words to tell zhur to stay, but took too long to locate them.

"We've all grown apart. As leaders. As rebels. As people," Punabi said sadly. "The further you go down that path," zhe nodded at the book, "the more I can't follow. The entire bunker is stifling right now. We're losing more territory day by day. Kinwold sends out fewer and fewer troops. They're hunkering down, waiting to be overrun. And I can't hunker down with them."

"But you're not . . . you're not asking me to come with you."

"I'm not," Punabi confirmed flatly. "I'll always love you, Hail, but I can't be with you right now. We want different things. I don't even think you want me around right now, not really."

"What are you talking about? I *need* you."

"Radix and Remotus need me. You need me to wait around until you want me again."

A cold snap cut through Hailwic's belly, and that selfish, adolescent resentment came back tenfold.

She didn't just want to keep Punabi; she didn't want anything to change.

Their lives were pure upheaval outside the tunnels. Everything about the bunker sang of stability and home to Hailwic. It was where she could rest and loosen the constant tension in her neck and jaw and chest. Here she *trusted*. Trusted the place and its people.

Hot annoyance replaced the cold, crawling up her spine instead of sitting in her stomach. She couldn't understand why Punabi would need to disrupt that trust and ease and safety. They weren't in danger of being overrun, they weren't in any more danger than they'd ever been. There had to be another reason.

"I'm having a hard time with Zoshim leaving, so you're just going to *abandon* me?"

"I'm not abandoning anyone. I'm *fighting* for you. The world isn't stopping for any of us."

"Kinwold isn't really letting you go?" she tried.

"Of course they are."

Maybe that in itself was proof of Punabi's assessment of Dr. Theesius—of their weak spine.

A real leader would never let their best assets walk out the door.

She thrust Punabi's hands away, standing again. "No. You can't go."

"I'm not asking your permission," Punabi grated out, throwing the shirt still in zhur hand into the duffel bag.

Tears prickled in the corners of Hailwic's eyes, but the thick denialism in her throat stopped everything up, kept the tears back. She didn't want to believe Punabi could so easily leave her behind. "You're not going."

"I have to."

"I can't *lose* you."

"Not everything is about you, Hailwic. Not everything is about *us*. There's a bigger picture—"

"You can't go."

Punabi tossed zhur toiletries in, then zipped up the bag. "Stop being so childish. I'm *sorry*. I'm sorry this hurts. I'm sorry we've been talking past each other for months now. I'm sorry Zoshim left. And I'm sorry you didn't kill Uphrasia, but we've all got to *move the fuck on*."

The sharpness of Punabi's tone felt like a poniard to the back of the skull, and the silence that followed left a ringing in Hailwic's ears. The cold fear that had warmed to hurt and heated to anger now became molten meanness.

Hailwic gripped that imaginary poniard imbedded in her skull and yanked it free, spinning it around to point the bloody tip directly beneath Punabi's chin.

"I tried to give my *life* so that you would all be safe," she bit out. "So don't you *dare* pretend like my guilt is something petty. Something I'm just clinging to for, for what? Pity? Don't accuse me of being distant and hard to talk to when *you're* the one leaving. Not when the tithing is already stretched so thin I feel like bursting out of my skin every day because it's already pulled taut by Zoshim, and taut by Absolon, and taut by Glensen, and now you're going—"

Punabi put zhur head in zhur hands, rubbed at zhur eyes. "The tithing was a mistake," zhe said tiredly behind the cup of zhur palms.

A disorienting tingling swamped over Hailwic, making her cold then hot then cold again from head to toe. "Get out," her tongue snapped before she could even think the words themselves.

She'd said *get out,* but she'd meant *shut up*.

"*Don't leave, get out,* make up your mind." Punabi sighed bitterly, sinking into flippancy while Hailwic grew more and more embattled. "You have to admit, everything we've ever tried as a group has ultimately made things worse."

"You're wrong."

"I'm not. Mistake after mistake, bad call after bad call. Maybe we haven't yet done more harm than good, but I want to try to make it right before we do."

"*Stay* and I'll prove to you that's not true."

Punabi gracefully put zhur hands out, gave a sad shrug before picking up the duffel. "I can't, Hail. I just can't."

Hands bunching, clinging to her own clothes, Hailwic spun on the spot, vision tunneling as she searched inside herself and out for something she could do. Anything to make Punabi stop, just *stop*.

She froze when a slick film of grease coated her spine, making her shiver.

She felt dirty. Oozing.

"What if I stop you?" she heard herself say. It was a dark thought. Slimy.

But oddly gratifying to speak aloud.

"Yeah, sure," Punabi scoffed uncaringly.

"I could *make* you stay," Hailwic said, voice stringent and cold. Stiff like an automaton, she turned to face Punabi. Extending one arm, fingers spread, she held steady, solid. Not a single tremor shook through her. She felt like she was outside her body, watching herself. "One push, and it all stops."

Disbelief flashed in Punabi's eyes before every muscle in zhur face tensed in denial. Zhe cocked zhur head to the side in an abortive shake, unable to believe the threat because it was unthinkable.

That so-steady hand faltered for a moment. Hailwic expected Punabi to call her bluff, to scoff again and give her reason to grit her teeth and close her fist and let out a burst of angry kairopathy.

Instead, zhe waited.

The silence stretched, tense and burdened.

"*I could,*" Hailwic gritted out.

"So you'd, what? Imprison me in a time bubble? Imprison us *both*?"

"I could!"

Her stomach flipped as she recognized the tone coming out of her mouth as her father's. *You have been remanded into our custody. If you don't sit down right this instant, we can put you right back where we found you.*

It had been a decade since she'd even thought about that moment. Now here she was, echoing it. Mirroring it. Embodying it.

"And I could make you feel a hundred different things," Punabi said, devastatingly calm. It wasn't the calm of clarity or reassurance. Zhur voice held a tinny flatness that made Hailwic ache. She needed zhim to scream, to fight back. "I could take away your anger with a snap of my fingers." Zhe raised zhur hand, poised to do just that.

Hailwic's throat went tight and her heart thumped all the faster. She stood up straighter, itching for Punabi to *try*. Her own fingers curled, her kairopathy seeping out, ready to ensnare.

Punabi's hand dropped slowly, fingers unsnapped, emotiopathy untapped. The heat returned to zhur gaze. Where it had previously been the heat of irritation, it was now edged with disgust. "I could, but I would never manipulate you like that," zhe said through bared teeth.

As zhe flitted about the room, gathering the last of whatever zhe needed, Hailwic still stood at the ready, as though she'd already paused time. She couldn't bring herself to move, to step back from the precipice. Everything in her screamed to pull it all to a halt, if only to give her time to think. There had to be something she could say to make zhim stay.

Nothing came to mind. Her thoughts swirled as though down a drain, sank as though into quicksand. She reached for wisps of phrases, pleas, only to have them dissipate before they reached her deadened tongue.

"You've always been self-centered," Punabi bit out when zhe was done, bracing zhurself in the doorway, gaze lowered to the floor. "But there's never been a *meanness* to you before."

It's because Zoshim's gone, Hailwic thought. *It's because Absolon's gone, and Glensen's gone, and you're* going. *You're all leaving me and taking the best bits with you.*

Punabi's eyes snapped up, locked with hers. For a moment, Hailwic hoped—

"You can play ignorant, Hail," zhe said, "but don't play at brutal. It doesn't suit you."

Zhe shook zhur head sadly, and walked out of Hailwic's life.

Hailwic was the last to leave, giving Kinwold no other choice but to be the one ultimately abandoned. Hailwic reasoned they weren't truly alone—they had Hintosep—but that only slightly lessened her guilt.

Without her brother, without her lover, and without a clear path to ending Uphrasia, there was nothing left for Hailwic in the place she'd once loved as a home.

KRONA

The false gods were gone, but there was Hintosep, alive and bared and covered in grime, hair wild, face gnarled, her chest heaving as she staggered back from Absolon's limp body.

The Savior almost looked bent in supplication, ready to receive benediction. The Cage had kept him from expressing his fear or surprise in life, and now it made him look peaceful in death, the curve of his spine over his knees a soft bow rather than a tortured prostration. The rusted sword protruding from his back looked less a weapon and more a favor bestowed.

One he deserved.

Beside Krona, Abby petted over her torn wrist, knitting the ragged skin back together. Zhur little knees were stained red as zhe kneeled in the pool of Krona's blood, but the child didn't seem to mind. Krona wanted to help, to add her kairopathy to Abby's physiopathy to make sure the healing was swift and sure, only to find it missing. Ninebark was still speared through, occasionally kicking out a hoof like a creature in its dying throes.

Krona was not built for so much all at once. The last forty-eight hours had been a lifetime unto itself, with birth and death all intertwined. She'd been on the verge of gaining everything. The gods had been right here, *right here*. But they weren't gods, just as Krona was no longer a rebel leader as there was no rebellion to lead.

The loss of everyone at Mirthhouse finally hit her fully. The dull ache she'd pushed to the side as she and Tray had stacked bodies now thumped beneath her sternum, trying to break through. She let out a sudden sob, shaking her head at poor Abby when the child thought zhe'd hurt her. Krona needed to wipe her eyes, but the little Physiopath had her bleeding arm, and her other could no longer bend enough to touch her face, even if she'd been in control.

All she could do for long moments was weep, until the shuffling of Hintosep's bare feet grew near, and even beyond. Krona couldn't look up. Couldn't make herself meet Hintosep's pale eyes. The people Hintosep had left in Krona's care had met a gruesome end, and it didn't matter if Absolon died his same sudden death over and over—once for each of them—it would never be enough.

When the skin of her wrist was finally sealed, though the wound was still pink and raised, Abby laid a gentle little kiss there, the way Krona had seen Melanie kiss the child's scraped knees before the Physiopath had learned to tend to zhur own little ouches.

"Thank you, sweet one," Krona said, her head still swimming from blood loss, gaze swimming with tears. Abby turned to her other arm, but Krona quickly jerked her whole body away, making the world rock. She braced herself on the floor with her good arm, eyes fixing on the bloodstained floor while she tried to regain her steadiness—tried to banish the dizziness from her mind and the shaky giddiness from her limbs. "You did well. This one's fine," she gasped.

Remembering she still had Avellino's alexandrite chicken bone, she pulled the pendant into the light and slung it around Abby's neck in thanks. "You can gift it to him again when you see him," she said, brushing the child's cheek with her thumb. "He's going to be so proud of you."

"Even when I was young," Hintosep said, "in a time and place before, I never saw a budding Physiopath so talented. Nature himself was by far the most powerful I'd ever encountered, but Abby . . ."

Many questions flickered across Krona's foggy mind: how Hintosep was still alive; how she and Abby had come to be here, now; what Hintosep really knew of the false gods and why she'd kept it a secret. But now that she was nearly cried out, all of her questions were secondary to the urgency rattling around in her chest to *remerge.*

Since first regaining Ninebark, Krona had never felt this vulnerable when the two of them were separated. They'd never been apart this long save the first time the fen had appeared, bursting forth to take down the Thalo in their keep.

The keep.

Time had been to the keep. She'd said—she'd said she'd razed it.

Thibaut. Thibaut and the others. Krona couldn't rest now, she couldn't simply rejoin with Ninebark and retire to regroup and lick her wounds, she had to—

Krona finally sat up, turning to Hintosep, ready to tell her about Juliet's capture and begin barking orders again, but her mouth went dry and her tongue fell heavy when she turned to find dead eyes and a slack jaw only a few inches from her face.

Hintosep held one of the decapitated heads in her hand, the flesh of its scalp pulled taut by the grip she had on its hair.

"Oh, gods," Krona cursed, turning away from the grim sight.

"Gerome. Avellino's Possessor, and my charge," Hintosep said, as if that explained why she'd felt the need to scoop up the head, to carry it. There was satisfaction there, in her tone, but also regret, as if this all could have had a different outcome, if only.

If only.

Cradling her De-Lia arm, Krona pushed herself to her feet and hobbled over to Ninebark. "I need your help again," she told the echo, and the arm's morbid mouth wound around the metal javelin. Together, they yanked hardily, again and again while poor Ninebark let out chiming squeals of discomfort. "I know, girl, I know," Krona tried to soothe her.

When the javelin finally clattered to the floor, Ninebark flowed up Krona's good arm like a small animal seeking refuge from the cold under a sleeve, burrowing in eagerly, filling Krona with warm relief.

That is, until Ninebark tried to seep into Krona's left arm. A stormfront built inside her where Ninebark and the foreign echo clashed. They both hissed and scratched, trying to dominate the other. The fight twisted Krona's joints, made her skin feel too tight. "Stop, stop it," she ordered, mentally yanking on Ninebark like she was a cat caught by the scruff. The fen still clawed, but eventually gave in to Krona's manhandling and filtered back out of the offending arm. Still, it needed somewhere to settle, and as it tried to curl up along itself, to settle multifold in her cells, Krona felt uncomfortable. Bloated.

Carefully, she sifted part of the fen back out again, up her spine and shoulder blades, out across her exposed bones, weaving it between them to span like the thin chitin of butterfly wings. She still could not use her wings to fly, but the shifting pale pinks and purples, turquoises and greens made the bones seem more delicate, more fairy-like. More *complete,* and less like a twisted half idea. As she spread one, observing the way wisps of the fen curled off and coalesced again, she thought she perhaps finally saw the bones as Thibaut had seen them: beautiful, powerful.

Finally the bloated pressure ceased, and she felt comfortable in her skin again.

Settled once more in her own bones, Krona let go of the helplessness she'd felt during the fight, the sadness and frailty that had gripped her after. Silently, she watched Hintosep as the woman roamed the body-covered floor with a still-dripping head in her hands. Krona was suddenly struck by how much Hintosep looked like one of them—the gods—how easily she, as a new deity, could sit beside them in the pantheon. Not a goddess of an elemental magic, but a goddess of vengeance to counter the Thalo. Protective destruction to balance uncaring creation.

Centering herself, Krona went to several of the fallen mummies and carefully pulled the clothes from their tattered corpses. It hardly seemed real that just hours ago she'd feared defiling this place simply by stepping through the door; now she desecrated it with ease and could not hate herself for it.

She offered the clothes to Hintosep who was lost in her own fog now, as though she'd inherited Krona's daze. "Are you with me?" Krona asked gently. When she received no answer, she slung the garments over her shoulder and pried Gerome's hair from Hintosep's fingers, tossing the decapitated head aside with a sickening *thump.* "We have to hurry. Time said she destroyed the keep. We have people there, we need—"

"Hmm? Yes. It's just . . . it's been so long. I've thought about this day for so long, and now he's dead." She turned in a slow circle, bringing Absolon's corpse back into her line of sight. "He made me—" Her face contorted and her knees buckled. Krona hurried to catch her as Hintosep grabbed hold of Krona's shoulders, hands as strong as iron. "He used me as his weapon again and again. Rebuilt me from the ground up whenever I asked too many questions. And now, Mirthhouse."

"Hintosep. Hintosep, we don't have time. We have to go. Dress. *Now.* We have to get as near the keep as we can. Last time I tried it was warded against me."

Hintosep nodded, coming back to herself as she swiftly slipped on the decaying threads, babbling about what had happened, pouring her own guilt and grief into Krona. Krona, who was already overflowing with her own, but stood there and took it because she needed to know. She had to understand how such an awful thing had come to pass. And once she was done raging about the small animal trapped inside her, she went on, detailing what she'd endured in the Cage at Gerome's and Absolon's hands. She explained how she and Abby had come to be here, in Xyopar, because of an artifact called the Teeth.

"And now the Teeth's Possessor has died," she said. "His will kept the portals open. Now they've likely closed. We cannot go back that way."

"And what of his other magics, his wards?" Krona asked, helping Hintosep slip into the garments she'd gathered. "Time got in." She thrust her chin at Gerome's severed head.

The Thalo woman shifted uncomfortably in her borrowed finery, the bright colors—the yellows, oranges, and greens—even faded as they were from exposure, did not fit her. Blue—Krona had only ever seen her dressed in blue. "They might still be up. They might have fallen. Time's power is far beyond yours. They might have failed to keep her out, or she might have destroyed them, I can't say."

"Nothing for it, then, but to try to jump through."

Krona swept them back to what was left of Mirthhouse first, planning to leave Abby with her parents. But the drifts of figurines lay still and silent. She called for them, making small jumps all over the mountainside to search, muscles becoming tighter and tighter, sour worry flooding through her the longer they tarried.

If the keep had collapsed, then Thibaut could be trapped in the rubble. He could be losing time, losing air—

She refused to consider he might already be dead.

"They're gone," she concluded, landing back among the figurines. "I don't know how; we didn't have steeds. They shouldn't have gotten far on foot."

"Perhaps they followed the same paths Abby and I did."

"The paths that are *gone*?" Krona asked. "Then they could be anywhere."

Hintosep pursed her lips and gave her a mournful look, but did not speak to spare the child. Krona understood.

They could also be *nowhere.*

"One thing at a time. The keep won't wait," Krona said, preparing to make a lens. "I'll be back for you."

Hintosep took hold of her elbow as she lurched forward, stopping her. "And what if you aren't? You may never find your way without me. *Abby* knows that keep better than you do."

"I'm not taking a child into that mess."

"I'm not letting you go on your own, and I'm not leaving zhim here. I've ferried five-year-olds through much worse." She paused, lowered her voice. "You know I'm right. Let's not waste time arguing."

Krona leaned into Hintosep's grip. "When they are safe and this is done, I expect you to tell me everything. Not just about the last few years, but the last century, millennia—however long it's been, and who those gods really are and how this happened."

"I will. I'll tell you everything I can remember. I swear it."

THIBAUT

Thibaut's heart stuttered when they came to the nursery door, finding it thrown off its hinges with dozens of children cowering inside. The ceiling was lower here than in the halls, which might have made the space cozier—if indeed any room in this frigid palace could be thought of as cozy—in gentler times. Now it simply meant the heavy stone had that many feet fewer to fall.

The Thalo Avellino called Eldest rushed in, grabbing for a teenager's hand, trying to haul them out of the room. They resisted, and then the other Thalo around them resisted, pulling the teen in the opposite direction.

"We need to convince them to come with us," Avellino said, chest and shoulders heaving with worry.

"They don't look to be in the convincing mood," Thibaut pointed out, unslinging his arms from around Mandip and Juliet.

He'd thought he could support himself, but with his first real step into the nursery, one knee buckled and one ankle twisted, sending him to his hands and knees. The following gasps and whimpers that arose when his fen burgeoned to slide a helpful tentacle or two beneath his kneecaps was not lost on him.

"Come now, children," he said from the floor, waving a dismissive hand. "Some of you must have known Gerome. This isn't the first time you've seen a monster."

Juliet was at his elbow in the next instant. "Maybe you could put the self-deprecation in your back pocket, seeing as how we have a gaggle to save. What would Krona think, to hear you talk this way?"

He allowed her to take his hand, raise him up. "My mistress is hardly a stranger to kneeing me in the proverbial soft bits."

"As a tease, darling. She'd never kick you when you were down. So don't do it to yourself." She passed him off to Mandip, then looped her arm through her brother's, stepping forward. "Right!" she announced, voice raised. "Hello, everyone, we're going to play a game. And that game is called Follow the Leader—"

"—Or Else We're All Going to Die," Thibaut whispered in Mandip's ear. He didn't seem to find it nearly as amusing as Thibaut.

"Your impending collapse has made you giddy," Mandip grumbled to him. "Or maybe the blood loss."

"Better than a myriad of other things it could have made me."

Juliet strode about calmly with Avellino on her arm while Melanie and

Sebastian gathered the smallest Thalo—the babies, the toddlers—handing them to those big enough to carry them. "This is a team game. Together we can all win. If my lovely assistants haven't handed you anyone to hold, then you should find a partner and link arms just like so." She bumped out Avellino's arm with her own. "And then my brother and I will take the lead, and it is your job to follow our movements as exactly as you can. If we duck, you duck. If we run, you run, yes?"

"There aren't enough hands," Thibaut said to Mandip, noticing how many infants there were compared to children large enough to carry them. "You should help."

Mandip looked skeptical.

"I'll be fine," he assured him, then, "Master Amador, why don't you give that delightful contraption to me and make yourself equally useful?" He nodded to the unusual gauntlet-like enchantment in his hands.

Before either Mandip or Tray could move, another heavy quake shocked its way through the nursery, and it was too much for the ceiling to bear. Debris rained down, pelting the terrified children and the adults that dove over them. A large slab above them jolted, one end sagging then dipping and sliding and Thibaut didn't think—

He rushed forward, the lightheadedness pushed aside in sudden panic, his previously jelly-like muscles and uncooperative joints overridden by a primal instinct and a surge of adrenaline. Skidding across the dust-covered floor he slid beneath the edge of the stone as it fell, catching it on the back of his neck, across his shoulders, and with his fen's many appendages.

It could have crushed him as readily as the children. Might have done, if it hadn't been for Kemba bursting from Sebastian's chest to stand alongside him, the giraffe's neck craned beneath the slab, sturdy and strong.

"Get them out of here!" he yelled, arms outflung, the slice of ceiling cold on his skin and stinging in his wounds. His muscles shook and his teeth clenched and he didn't know how long he could take it, but with the weight of it pressing with a devastating firmness, he knew Kemba couldn't hold it alone.

Somebody shouted his name. He thought it was Melanie or Juliet until he realized the timbre was richer.

Krona.

She seemed to appear out of nowhere, like a dream. Like the last wish of a dying brain conjuring comfort for itself.

She swung around in front of him, her hands instantly on his face, his sides, and she felt real. From behind him, near the door, a small child yelled, "Maman!"

Then the others began to mutter. The Thalo chittered, but not with fear, with awe. Someone whispered, "Hintosep."

Krona kissed him. A dire sort of half kiss. Something quick, a need undeniable, but fleeting. Her lips were warm. She tasted real, smelled real.

"Whoever did this to you—"

"Is already dead, love," he assured her. "No time for pleasantries, you can ravish me once we've got everyone safe. And I don't know how long—" he stuttered and shifted his weight, muscling the slab higher on his shoulders, tentacles writhing.

Ninebark began to emerge from her pores, giving her a glow, but he gritted his teeth and told her no. "Don't help me. Help *them*. Get them out into the hall."

"There isn't any more hall!" Tray shouted. "It collapsed when the ceiling collapsed. There's too much rubble; it's all caved in."

"Even better," Thibaut said sardonically. "Krona, you're the only one who can jump them to safety. Then I can let go."

She nodded swiftly, and as she whirled away again he caught sight of her left arm.

It seemed they'd both suffered transformation during their parting.

"Just like I said before," Juliet called out. "Only Krona is the leader now. Follow Krona, she's got you. Everyone link hands. Form a chain."

Sweat began to trickle down Thibaut's body, his brow. His abdomen clenched and his skull hurt and he widened his stance, yet the shaking in his muscles only worsened. Beside him, Kemba tried to take more of the weight, but he was already supporting most of it. There was little else he could do.

Thibaut couldn't focus on the frantic calls and orders of the others anymore. His ears buzzed. All he could do was stand there and not fall apart.

Mere minutes later, though it felt like hours, Krona was back from her jump, raging. Cursing Absolon, cursing the gods.

She'd tried to take everyone at once, but only managed four. The fifth person in the chain had been forced back. "I'm too weak to get them all at once. Either Ninebark is still injured, or the echo arm is interfering. I can only manage a handful."

"Then go, keep going," Hintosep urged.

"Eldest next," Avellino said. "So the little ones have someone on the other side."

Krona wasted no time. Back and forth she went, back and forth.

And still, her rescue wasn't fast enough.

She was only through about a third of the children when the slab sitting atop Thibaut and Kemba snapped. A chunk fell from the mass of mortared stones, slipping past Kemba, striking Sebastian in the temple, knocking him out cold.

"Sebastian!" Melanie cried, diving for her husband.

Kemba immediately dissolved, hurrying back into its host, doing what it could to keep him safe first and foremost—leaving Thibaut with the weight of the entire ceiling on his shoulders.

"I can't hold it!" Thibaut shouted, voice trembling. He could feel the blood leaving his face, nausea rising in his belly as he forced his already broken-down body to give everything it had left. Any moment now, he would fracture under the strain.

Tray ran to his side, wedging himself beneath the stone, doing what he could—one hand bared, one buried in the gauntlet he'd taken.

"The Teeth!" Hintosep said, as though she'd just glimpsed the treasure in Tray's grasp. "Use the Teeth! The Teeth can tear a path out—just let them bite!"

"Stay with me," Krona went to Thibaut, cupping his face as she pushed her own shoulders against the slab. She forced him to look her in the eye, and until that moment he hadn't realized how much his vision had blurred. "Just a little longer."

The gauntlet gave a metal-on-metal screech as Tray worked something inside it. The mouth opened wide, revealing three sets of jaws open and ready to bite. "How do I—?"

Hintosep gasped. "Just don't—"

Whatever she'd meant to warn him against, it was too late—he'd snapped all three jaws shut simultaneously, ripping at the air before him, wrenching open a gaping hole in reality itself.

This hole was nothing like the passive tunnel that had led to the keep. It wasn't a little path that rippled just to the left of normal movement, taking one gently to wherever they desired to go. This was a sucking, demanding *whirlwind* of a thing.

Everyone was instantly pulled off their feet. Thibaut felt the stone leave his back and for a horrible instant expected it to come back down with a vengeance and shear his head clean from his body just as surely as Gerome's had been sheared. Instead, he was pulled away from it. Away from everything. From the floor, from Krona, from the keep—from anything he could recognize.

Hintosep impotently raged at herself. All three sets. The Regulator had torn open reality with *all three sets* in tandem. Which meant he hadn't cut a pathway out into the Valley, he'd created a pocket-world built on his own fantasies and fears alone.

There was no telling what awaited the children there.

The others were gone in a flash, leaving Hintosep and Abby, who stood farthest off, a half second more to gasp and try to deny the yawing tempest that ate everything in its path, sucking up debris and stone and cradles and blankets and all.

It dragged her forward even as she tried to deny it. "Abby!" she shouted at the child, clutching zhim tightly, unsure what she was even telling zhim—or begging zhim—to do.

Abby scrapped zhur palm across the half-standing archway of the door as the portal pulled at them, changing the stone into something else at the lightest touch and holding on fast. Hintosep frantically grabbed for it as well, but her fingers missed by a gulf, leaving her tethered only by her hold on Abby zhurself.

It only took the initial tough yank on the child's small body—wrenching zhur little spine, for Hintosep to make a split-second decision.

She let go.

Hintosep couldn't even call out a word of reassurance before she was gobbled up by the portal, but Abby screeched and reached for her, releasing zhur handhold and following through.

Together, they were spat out into a new world.

38

HAILWIC

In a Time and Place Before

Hailwic roamed—a solitary warrior—for years. If it hurt Uphrasia, that meant it helped someone else, and that was all that mattered.

Before putting the bunker behind her, she'd had a team of Physiopaths put her permanently into her winged form. No one individual could achieve it the way Zoshim could, and they never got it quite right. Her feathers seemed duller, the wings themselves more angular. The hands on her extra set of arms mirrored her originals too perfectly—were just dittoed copies of what she already had instead of carrying individual nuances.

She heard stories. Of the Colossus, Kinwold, and the Charging Light, Punabi, and the Winged Saint, Zoshim. She caught sight of Glensen once, unchanged except for the natural years weighing on feir body. She saw Absolon—the Friend's Consort—on old tele sets and new, his face always lurking in the background of propaganda broadcasts and replays of *Patriotism Hour*. Uphrasia dressed him well, and he stood taller than he ever had before. Hailwic broke more than one screen in rage when she caught sight of him.

She felt them all—each like a hand on her puppet strings, yanking her this way and that. She only hoped her drag was the same: that she was a thread that pulled and snagged, unraveling their sanity.

Her twin was a saint, but what was she? With her wings that mirrored his—when he chose to brandish them—and her yellow hair and sharpened teeth.

Roaming One. Darker Half. Golden Raven.

Madwoman.

More often than not, she snarled at those who asked for help—unless they were children. She never spoke down to children.

When she heard news that Arrallia had been killed in a car bombing outside Yugalheim's parliament, she stifled the urge to jump to Kinwold's side, instead sending a bland letter of condolence with no return address.

She knew she'd grown bitter, but who was left to care?

She saw armies clash and borders bend and nations begin to crumble and fall under Uphrasia's onslaught.

She jumped from conflict point to conflict point—the various fronts pushing ever outward from Radix. She fought, ran ammunitions, spied, scouted, but never remained in one company long enough for anyone to see her as part of their regiment. She rarely took meals with other soldiers—other people—preferring to take any provided rations to secluded places.

She didn't want to be alone, but no longer found herself comfortable in company.

She'd chosen to keep her wings, and they were *her* now. Even totally liberated Physiopaths largely conformed when in the military—shifted themselves back to that state Zoshim had dubbed *neutral.*

Her choices set her apart.

Always an icon.

Never a comrade.

She told herself that suited her just fine.

She'd tied her life to others' before, and that had gotten her nothing but heartache.

So, wandering warrior she remained.

And then, one winter morning, the world . . . ended.

It's strange, what one remembers of tragedy—what particular imagery is seared into the retinas and burned in the synapses when a shock to the system locks a terrible moment in time. For Hailwic, it wasn't the bright burgeoning of a physiocloud—the bubble-like blast she'd seen only once before—that was sharp enough to be the sting that set an image. Or the two additional physiobomb detonations that followed close on its heels. Those she later barely recalled. Their borders were hazy in her mind. Unfocused. Like soap bubbles in her memory: silky, smooth, harmless.

Even when their edges slammed into one another and instead of canceling each other out only amplified their destructive power, the resonating forces growing and the rate of transformation increasing, sweeping the land—churning it up before scraping it clean.

What she remembered most keenly were the birds.

Winter had made her a feral thing of the woods. She hunted for her own food in lean times, in the blast-scorched countryside, on the outskirts of small towns, in the fields and the forests. And she'd grown accustomed to hunting with her claws, just like an animal. Twisting time, she could weave it into a blanket to keep warm or a net to ensnare, and she found other, more modern tools unnecessary.

It was little trouble to spot a snowhair from the sky. Little trouble to descend and hook it with her kairopathy, breaking its neck and gutting it swiftly, sharp talons doing the work of a hunting knife with far more precision. Its blood was hot on her fingers, the scent meaty in her nose. Here, where there was no one to see, she was free to lick her claws clean without judgment.

A tremble through the land made her look away from the entrails as she scattered them—from the rabbit's insides splattered red across the hardpack on the hill—to a wall of black rising in the northern distance. The wall rippled—shrinking and growing at the edges, gathering thickness as it went. New bursts of black silhouettes rose from the ground, the tree lines, the rooftops to join.

Through the chill air, a distant chatter plucked at her hearing, growing into sharp cries and caws just as the wall grew, all of it moving toward her—each part tumbling over itself to flee *something else.*

Tucking the limp, bleeding corpse of the rabbit into the satchel tied to her hip, she launched herself into the air once more—rising a few hundred feet—feeling less the hunter now and more the wary pray.

The wall grew thicker, becoming a wave, then a mountain, as more and more panicked creatures rose into the sky.

Behind them, that unmistakable bulging blast. Hailwic's breath caught in her throat before it died in her chest.

Then, to the east, a bright light and another blast.

Hailwic hovered there—stunned—paralyzed for what was likely moments, but seemed an eternity. That innate sense of time that always plodded through her slipped a cog and the gears stopped.

It wasn't until the birds in the trees directly below her began to stir that her wings moved of their own accord, twisting her in the sky to drag her away.

Immediately, she found herself in a frenzied flock, birds of all kinds rushing to escape, flapping just as frantically as she. The sky grew dark with small bodies, many bashing into her—the clumsy flying human thing who wasn't where she belonged, who was in their way, not the other way around.

Raid sirens howled as the air thickened with feathers, with the musk of birds, and then—new limbs. New limbs—not wings—smacking into her, tangling her, pulling her down before she thrust them away.

Vision blurred by the hoard of wings, she hadn't seen the other person until it was too late and they'd collided. She recovered, but the other mass of human limbs fell.

A Physiopath.

Her terror-filled flight path took her over the nearest town—the rooves slanted, their tiles baked red. Suddenly there were more—more *human* flyers, some experienced, some clearly trying to mold wings, unsuccessfully, for the first time.

Below, people ran. To bikes, horses—vehicles of all kinds, while Kairopaths frantically tried to jump themselves and their families to safety.

But there was no safety to be had.

Another flash, to the south.

Flash—bloom—bubble—burst.

Flash, flash, flash.

Each burning clap of light made silhouettes of the birds in front of her, like thick charcoal drawings or little bodies burnt to a crisp. When the light faded, spots coopted her vision and then she could see only wings and nothing beyond.

So many wings, black and brown and shimmering, and hard beaks, pointed like arrows. A roar of reedy screams from below continuously shot through the onslaught, reaching her even as she was surrounded by the crack of birdcalls snapped directly in her ear.

Hailwic didn't have to risk a glance back to know she could not outfly the blasts.

With an unknown number of physiobombs going off, jumping would do her no good.

The land below rippled, shockwaves radiating through right before the magic itself undulated through matter.

Hailwic turned her face to the sky. She'd never flown more than five hundred feet into the air, but now she had to. She flapped her wings with a frantic force, pulling on the wind, clawing her way higher, teeth bared to the cold air, yellow hair streaking back in twisted knots.

Everything felt thin around her—not just the air, but reality. Time. She boosted herself with kairopathy, but it meant little.

Climbing out of the fray left a black blanket beneath her. Crows. There were birds of all types, but later her memory turned them all to crows. A cawing, scrabbling murder of corvids darkening the sky and slicing through their own animal panic on obsidian-black wings.

Up she went. Flying too high suddenly felt like swimming, like she was struggling for the surface, only she was the wrong way around.

Another flash—just a pinprick on the horizon. Another country speared through.

Uphrasia wasn't holding back. This wasn't a simple test of might. She meant to end all opposition.

She would end far more than that.

Heat on her spine and cold at her fore told Hailwic she wasn't flying fast enough.

Fast didn't even matter when there was nowhere to go.

The sky above her rumbled as the hot and cold fronts smashed into each other. The hair on her arms stood on end, her heart skipped a beat, and a bolt of lightning speared past her, finding its home in some sharp reaching finger of a tower miles away. Still, she spun from its trail in a panic, unable to expel the zing of hot ozone from her nose.

The sun, once blotted out by wings, was now crossed in a haze of clouds, spreading and thickening just as rapidly as the blast zones.

She did not look back. Did not look *down*.

Hailwic drove herself higher still. Small scraps of ice flicked at her cheeks and threatened to accumulate on her wings.

The land was gone. All she had was the sky. All she had was upward.

Little licks of heat shot up her ankles. She tried to keep her eyes upward, but the grip of tiny fingers—not metaphorical, *real* fingers—on her boot drew her gaze down like an anchor. Expecting a child's hands, she gasped in revulsion as dozens of individual, disembodied fingers wriggled up past the top of her boot like bony worms, scaling her like a tower.

She kicked, desperate to dislodge the things, skin prickling with further disgust as a blob of something else—cold, wet, sticky—smeared up her back and attached itself to her spine. She twisted, meaning to hurl it from her body, and instead it slid to her left along her shoulder, up into the soft scapulars at the base of her center wing, climbing its way up the curve of it, morphing into something that left an acidic slime trail, burning away barbs and entire feathers as she scrabbled to find it with her fingers and pull it free.

The acid ate and ate and ate, down to skin, then bone, forcing her to compensate hundreds of feet in the air for a wing on *fire*.

Splattering. *More* splattering—like she'd been caught in the edges of a mud geyser. Or worse, like mud flung at her by a playful hand, unaware of how it hissed and burned. Dollops of it smacked into the back of her head, her neck, and plastered over her left side—her wings, hands, hips.

The fingers crawling up her legs shifted into molten lead, searing through her clothes down to the skin. The new tongues of hot metal branded her—each hot line forcing its own special octave from her throat—and yet refused to fall away once the claim had been made.

Mud turned to breakfast cereal, turned to soap, turned to mucus, turned to tiny pinpoints of terrible starlight, dangerous and heavy, devastating her left arms, her left wings—even eating into the base of her skull and sniping her out of the sky just as surely as a gun blast.

Staying aloft had been a struggle with one wing eaten into. It was impossible now.

Then the stars were gone. Turned into a haze of oxygen or nitrogen, blending with the winds, carried away by their new brethren.

It would have been kinder if the physiopathy had shorn her limbs clean off. Instead, each bone had crumpled—pulled and crushed into unnatural angles by the sheer gravity of the pinpoint stars. Blood poured down her spine from the back of her head and she damned the star there for failing to deliver a killing blow.

The ground would do that now.

She fell looking upward. Wind whistled past her ears, lashing her sodden hair across her face. Her two right arms dragged after the rest of her limp body as she fell, as though reaching for salvation.

The storm roared, the physiopathy boiled.

She anticipated slamming into beaks and claws, but there were no more birds.

There were no more rabbit entrails strewn hot on a snow-covered hill because there was no more snow. No more hill.

No more town.

No more people.

When she struck the ground, she *sank*. The fine film of the land stretched to accommodate her like it was made of rubber, easing her fall, catching her instead of striking her—dispersing the force of her fall gently, syphoning the kinetic energy away, through its unnatural elasticity. It snapped taut again slowly, bringing her up when part of her had hoped to be swallowed.

The land did not bludgeon her.

It did not devour her.

It spared her.

Cruelly.

Her mangled left side twitched and contracted without her consent—the nerves confused, flailing and kicking like the legs of a dying cockroach. Pain radiated outward from the contorted forms, hemorrhaging into her jaw, her neck, shoulders, ribs.

Wetness pooled under her head. Blood, but also tears, running down her temples and past her ears.

She dared not lift her head. Dared not look around. Above, the storm still raged. Maybe, if the fates were merciful, she'd be struck by lightning and be spared the knowledge of what the world around her had become.

Through the pain and the shock, a different kind of agony took her. Fear. For those who'd left her behind.

She clutched at her chest, curling a fist there as though she could physically take hold of the tithe, keep it together, keep the tethers from breaking free.

For long moments, the fear stole her breath, making her gasp and struggle, and every heartbeat had her terrified one invisible strand in her hand would snap.

Everything became those five thin threads. If they held, she could hold as well.

If they lived, she could live.

Long hours she lay there, trembling, lost in herself, staring up at the storm that rolled across the sky but refused to strike her down or spatter her with rain.

Beneath her, the ground felt smooth. Featureless. Stiff. Nothing like the springing softness that had caught her. That in itself kept her down, prone, until the *silence* became too much.

There should have been shouting, sobbing. The cracking of stone or the explosion of transformers, gas lines—something. And yet her ears only rang with the *lack* of sound. There was no echoing aftermath. No chittering animals or splintering trees. No children crying. No yawing of machines.

Still holding her fist to her sternum, centering herself with the firmness of her heartbeat, she sat up.

Purple glass, perfectly smooth, bowed away from her in all directions.

Unable to take the pressure building in her chest—or the frustration behind her eyes, or the bold nothingness in her ears—she unclenched her jaw and screamed, giving voice to the desolation, the emptiness, the absence.

Night came. As did the rain (thank the blasted skies—it still *rained* clean, clear water). And the cold. It was no longer the cold of winter, though. The nip in the air was now sour instead of bright. The quiet not that of animals hunkering down beneath snowpack, but the sheer lack of anything alive for miles.

She expected to see a thopter overhead at any moment, searching for survivors or coming to claim the unusable land for Uphrasia. The stars and the moons remained the only lights in the sky. Even the horizon was unnervingly dim, the glow of cities now lost.

Hailwic had no way of knowing how far the destruction had spread, but she refused to entertain the mental whispers that insisted *everywhere*.

Walking toward the trailing moon, she did her best to guide herself in the direction of the nearest tithe-pull. She still felt all five strings, and if her tithe-mates were still alive, then that had to mean others were as well.

Though she was injured and exhausted, eventually she tried to jump straight to it—using the feeling as a guide as she had with Absolon—but it didn't work. She found herself stumbling face first into yet more smooth glass, unable to tell how far she'd traveled or even if she'd really traveled at all. She wondered if the transformation of the land had ruined the way her kairopathy interacted with it—like she was a bird who could no longer migrate properly because the planet's magnetic field had morphed.

She continued to walk but could no longer be sure she could trust the tugging in her soul.

The next day she saw the first imperfection in the glass—a small hump. She ran for it, latching on to the subtle landmark as though it were an oasis in a desert—as though her hindbrain thought it might *provide*.

When she came upon it, she immediately reeled back.

The hump was a baby, sealed inside the glass, preserved like a fly in amber, its little hands now crab claws. Fungus grew off the side of its head like hair.

Hailwic stumbled away, sure she'd vomit if she stared at it too long.

On she went. On. And on.

Eventually the glass gave way here and there to other pits of matter. A crater of blackened coal. A pile of raw diamonds. A pool of mercury. A puddle of something gooey and sweet-smelling—like applesauce—that she dared not touch, especially since it was already greening at the edges.

All she had to sustain her was the rain and her rabbit. Perhaps the last rabbit she'd ever see—the last rabbit *anyone* would ever see.

On her fifth night in the wasteland, she heard a roar.

The sound came to her from miles away, she was sure, but it rang out strong and forlorn. She stumbled when it died out, falling to her knees to cry, because thank the skies: something out here besides her *lived*. There had to be an end to the surreal desert of gunk and glass—an *edge* she could reach.

The random pits and pools became less homogenous. An actual swamp cut through her path, complete with plants, though she recognized none of them. She had no idea where she was—there had undoubtedly been no swamp here before—but it was better than pure glass.

Her first handful of mangled but breathing people was a shock to the system. Her mind denied her eyes at first, insisting the shapes approaching were trees or outcroppings given false movement by the way the glass reflected and bent the light.

But they were *real,* and terrified, and had no idea what had happened. With the comms towers subsumed, their implants were useless. The Kairopath in the group hadn't been able to jump anywhere of use, just like Hailwic. Their Teliopath could divine nothing from the land, as though all information had been scrambled.

The youngest of the group—a teenager—theorized they were all dead and this was Hel, like in the old-world religions. Hailwic saw no reason to disabuse them of the notion; they had a living beehive where half their rib cage used to be.

It was the same with the others: they'd all been touched by the blast, twisted in some barely survivable way. They all assumed her wings and arms were the same. She didn't disabuse them of that notion, either.

Gathering wanderers became her new focus. Helping those she could. The few Physiopaths she found were nowhere as skilled with their magic as Zoshim, but they did their best to untangle the worst of the ravages. She never asked them to fiddle with her own body, though—strangely covetous of its pains, proud of its burdens like they were something she deserved, and there was only one person whose healing she'd accept.

Beyond the blast epicenters the changes were no less pronounced, but more varied. New forests, new lakes, new mountains had sprouted everywhere. The old biomes were gone, and the new ones . . . she was sure none of them were stable. Cactuses full of maple syrup, birds that became fire-eggs when they died, and spun-sugar flowers would not last.

She'd been nomadic before, but now she had a tribe. They moved, they gathered, they survived.

What they scavenged to eat and drink made them sick more often than not.

Months in, she was surprised to receive a white-haired visitor at her camp.

A woman she *knew*.

A woman whose face was like a sunrise to Hailwic, bringing her a new day with new possibilities.

"Hintosep," she gasped, smiling in a sudden bursting warmth of familiarity. She threw her right arms around the young woman, clutching her close.

Only then did it register that Hintosep was unchanged. Even her clothes were clean, in good shape. Her shoes had no holes.

Her eyes held a light.

"The bombs," Hailwic began. "How did you—?"

"The bunker," she said. "The deepest levels were spared."

"Then your babbi—"

"They're all right. They used the tithing to help me find you. Hail, I've come to bring you home."

⟡

The new scar in the land stretched for hundreds of miles. A valley, overlaid on what remained of the bunker, its top stories gouged out. Only, the valley spanned far beyond the bunker's original boundaries—a rugged green-and-brown gouge in the smooth purple skin of the land.

The massive tear in the glass was far less startling than all the *life* it contained. Most of the vegetation and animals were changed, but less so than in the pockets beyond, like only a whisper of physiopathy had reached them rather than the blasting scream she'd endured.

The deer were a little too fine-boned, the sheep far too large. The fruit was too sweet, the water strangely spiced. There were vines with minds of their own and rabbits—*rabbits!*—with antlers, worms large enough to rival snakes, and lions who only ate honey.

Still, many of these things weren't meant to exist side by side. Nothing here was permanent, no continuation guaranteed. These things lived, but for how long?

Hailwic thought of the people, asking herself the same question.

"Some of the animals wandered in," Hintosep explained as she led the trek down from the rim via a steep path toward a boggy, muddy land below. "Some of them were our livestock. Some were pets, maybe, in Remotus. A lot of them died in the first few days. The vegetation that survived—a lot of it seems overly hardy now. Anything that looks overgrown, keep out; it's probably carnivorous and likes big game.

"A few Physiopaths have tried to mold stuff back into their original forms. Sometimes it works. Sometimes it doesn't stick. Sometimes they mean well but just don't know enough about biology to make it work." She sighed. "Everybody's trying their best."

Hintosep wasn't alone in leading their introdus—surviving members of the RFR met Hailwic and company before they reached the valley floor, bringing fresh water, medical supplies. They brandished weapons too. Heavy guns and shock artillery. More out of habit, Hailwic guessed, than anything else.

Hundreds of small camps huddled in the bowl of the valley. Raised platforms kept people out of the dirt. Thick tarps kept some new strain of biting flies away. Campfire smoke continuously curled into the sky.

"You and yours are welcome to bivouac wherever there's solid ground," Hintosep said.

Hailwic wanted to see Kinwold right away, but Hintosep nudged her efforts toward taking care of her people.

"I have one more journey to make before you can see Babbi," Hintosep said, "but I promise, soon."

"Why?"

"They want you all to meet on equal footing."

You all could only be the tithing.

It had been a long trek from the wastelands to the valley floor, and in truth Hailwic still felt like she was striding through a dream. Pre-bomb and post-bomb were entirely different existences. She saw no reason to rush—had no energy to protest or strike out on her own to find Kinwold.

⊱⊰

The summons came in the dead of night, and she was jumped (by a Kairopath she didn't know) from her modest tent with its sinking stakes and ragged flaps into a circular great hall.

In these past months, she'd seen no true remnants of the cities she knew before. The land was so changed that it was hard to lay its new forms over any mental images of the old.

Here, what was left of the bunker still retained its axe-carved floor and its hand-hewn pillars, though the pillars looked victimized by acid rain, their contours and designs gnawed at, like the soft flesh of an apple gnawed by worms. Above that gnawing, the top-most sections of the pillars had turned—not to the same purple glass that engulfed so much of the countryside—but into a glass of yellow-green. It spread out into a perfectly mirrored ceiling stories and stories above.

Hailwic easily recognized this place. It had once been their largest silo.

Growing up out of its center now was an uneven bulk of stone only vaguely reminiscent of a chair, itself a full story high. Atop it sat Kinwold, large enough to scoop Hailwic up with one hand, their skin silvery and crackling, like swirling molten lead. Instead of a face, a dim orange light globed in the center of their head, radiating warmth.

Her colossus, on a throne. The heavy shadows that surrounded them battled at the halo of light emanating from atop their shoulders, making them look like a fantastical portrait set to canvas by a master painter's hand rather than something she could approach and touch.

*Hello*s were not the first thing to cross her mind. Instead, various apologies vied for purchase on her tongue.

Before she could pick one from the lineup, a creature slithered out from behind the base of the throne, bearing itself forward on a long body like a centipede's, segmented and heavy.

Its form was held aloft by many human hands rather than insectoid feet, each arm long and daisy yellow. Several sets of thick mandibles lined its mouth. Bluish tufts of fur ran down its back and hung shaggy over its brow, where its only other human features—its eyes—stood out stark and bright.

Moving like a silverfish, fluid and sleek, it propelled itself to stand between her and the Colossus, its numerous arms gliding on their extra joints, busy fingers plucking at motes in the air.

Only the tug of the tithe told her she knew this creature.

Without preamble, she surged forward, throwing her two right arms around him, burying her face in his carapace and fur. He smelled musty, like an old carpet, and his exoskeleton was crusted and hard, but she didn't care.

He could have been a sticky slug writhing on the ground and she still would have buried her face in his non-neck.

Zoshim delicately squeezed back.

Behind her, white light flooded the silo, reflecting off the green-yellow glass, giving everything a brilliant chartreuse glow. Hailwic turned without letting go of Zoshim, shielding her eyes until Punabi's form dimmed as the Kairopath that had ferried zhim to the meeting jumped away again.

Hailwic waited for Punabi to run to her. Instead, zhe did not meet her eyes as zhe came to stand before Kinwold.

When Glensen arrived—looking just as old as feir years, with crepe skin, crow's-feet, dark liver spots on feir dark skin, and graying hair, having never partaken of the time treatments—fey went to Zoshim first, but he slithered away, up the side of Kinwold's throne to rest on the bulky back of it. Out of even Hailwic's reach.

The tension between all of them still remained, then.

Hailwic had naïvely hoped the transformation of the land—the erasure of all they'd known—would have wiped their own slates clean as well.

Kinwold did not speak until Hintosep arrived with their last guest.

Old pressures had already strained the reunion, giving it an aura of unease and awkwardness where moments prior Hailwic had been filled with happiness and hope. But Absolon's addition was *poison*.

He'd promised Hailwic he would kill Uphrasia. He was there to halt her hand the moment she tried to use the physiobombs, and *yet*. Yet he'd stood passively, *glibly* by the Friend's side on many televised occasions, looking for all the world like a proud, besotted fool. He'd been within reach of all of Uphrasia's vulnerable bits more times than Hailwic cared to imagine, and yet the woman had still been hale enough, in the end, to destroy everything.

Perhaps he'd never been as committed as Hailwic thought. She'd been ready to give her life to take Uphrasia's. Surely he'd had ample opportunity, if only he'd been willing to make the same sacrifice.

Unless he'd never been willing at all—unless he'd stood by Uphrasia's side for the power and the pleasure of it, and not because he ever intended to put a stop to her violence.

Either by faintheartedness or malice, he'd never completed his task.

Hailwic wasn't sure which was worse: confronting a coward now, or an enemy.

Clearly, she wasn't the only one in the tithing who now doubted his allyship.

Glensen, Punabi, and Hailwic all braced themselves for a fight, instinctually dropping into defensive positions even as Kinwold's voice—in their heads, for they had no mouth—tried to belay their fears.

Wait, wait. My friends, wait.

Friends. The sentiment felt saccharine to Hailwic.

She refused to hide her distaste at Absolon's presence in this otherworldly great hall. She was surprised he dared show his face. After all, most people could be counted on to recognize the Friend's consort, and none of the survivors would have any inkling of his mission. Bitter amazement coated her throat, and she could hardly imagine how he'd been able to make it this far into Kinwold's valley without being torn to shreds—largely because that was the impulse itching at her own fingertips this very moment.

And yet a thrumming in her being finally settled. *All of the tithing is here,* it purred. All of her tithing was here and well and alive and that should have been wonderful.

The last time they'd all been in the same room . . . well, Hailwic found she couldn't remember the last time. If they'd parted explosively, suddenly, perhaps such a monumental moment would be seared into her mind. Alas, they had drifted. Shifted apart like wayward ships, flotsam in a river, or leaves on the breeze.

And now, like ball bearings in a bowl, they swirled around each other, the distances closing, their own weighted history and the gravity of the tithe pulling them closer. It should have been comforting, having them all together, finally. Instead, it was agonizing—a reminder of joint failures, connections lost, and lives wasted.

The *world* a waste.

They gathered not like old comrades, Hailwic realized, but like dignitaries—from different factions, different countries. Maybe most of them could still call one another ally—tenuously—but they could not call one another friend, despite what Kinwold said. They each represented different people, different interests, who were only here, now, because there was nowhere else to be.

Everyone's clothes—those who wore clothes, Zoshim and Kinwold excepted—were tattered and mismatched. Blankets and sheets and tarps had been reworked into robes and tunics. Their boots were overworn, their hair shaggy. They were as clean as one could get in a spiced river, as filthy as one expected of people living off the land.

Hailwic had thought them ragtag back in the day. That was nothing compared to how they looked now.

"I mean you no harm," Absolon said coolly, hands held up and empty, as if all his harm hadn't already been wrought—wasn't already evident all around them.

He stood taller than Hailwic remembered, with a new confidence squaring his shoulders. His face was placid and open, his tone imploring.

"Uphrasia's *favorite,*" Punabi spat. "I should gut you—"

"Where I stand," he finished for zhim, a melodramatic sigh on his lips. "Do you honestly think I have betrayed you?" He glanced around, irritated, bemused. "All of you? We had a goal, and *I* was the only one to follow through."

He's never stopped sending us time treatments, Kinwold assured the others, *or pathic beads.*

"*And* I killed Uphrasia," he added bitterly. "I did what the rest of you only simpered about."

"I don't believe you," Punabi spat.

"And even if you did, what does it matter?" Hailwic added, waving wildly at everything within sight.

It matters, Kinwold boomed. *It matters because we have to pick up the pieces and we cannot begin in a place of distrust. Continued infighting will get us nowhere.*

"And what are you, *king* here?" Punabi asked, whirling on Kinwold. Glensen placed a hand on zhur shoulder, but zhe shrugged it off.

I'm what's left *here,* they countered, leaning forward, looming over the others. *I'm no ruler. No king, no dictator, and no one has elected me.*

"But everyone here looks to you," Zoshim said in a strange, clicking cadence.

On the contrary. A great hand lifted, pointed beyond Hailwic, beyond Absolon, to where Hintosep stood humbly to the side. *They look to her. She searches, she finds, and she settles.*

"We were privileged to have protection from the bombs," Hintosep said. "Almost everyone in the tunnels was—and it would be unthinkable not to open what's left of our sanctuary to an introdus of survivors."

You among them, Kinwold added to the tithing. The subtle nudging to be gracious was not lost on Hailwic.

"Why did you call us together?" she asked.

Is it not enough that I missed you?

"It would have been," she said. "But that's not why we're here."

We need to decide how to proceed. How best to support the survivors Hintosep finds.

Glensen, thoughtful as ever, slowly strode away from Punabi's side toward Absolon, who watched fem with wary eyes. Fey stopped an arm's length away, holding femself stiff and proud. "I want to see for myself," fey said flatly.

Absolon understood, nodded, bent low so fey could touch his temple, but Glensen hesitated. "And I will show them as well," fey said, gesturing at the others, then holding out an expectant hand for anyone who chose to take it.

"You can do that?" Punabi asked.

"Hintosep?" Glensen called. "Would you be so kind as to retrieve us all a hearty helping of teliobeads? The tithing will make the connection easy, but the beads should make the memory transfer vibrant, its details distinct for all of you."

Hintosep disappeared behind Kinwold's colossal throne, while Punabi looked slightly appalled. From his high seat near Kinwold's ear, Zoshim made a distressed clicking.

"You always rejected this stuff before. The treatments, the beads," Punabi said as though Glensen needed reminding.

"I'll make an exception this once," fey said. "We cannot move forward if suspicion and mistrust remain."

When Hintosep returned with a small lockbox, she offered the teliobeads to everyone in turn.

I don't need to see it to believe him, Kinwold said, waving the offer aside. *I know his heart.*

Likewise, Zoshim did not move from his perch, though he shifted. His many legs folded in on themselves and his segmented body shrank, everything pulling into itself before sprouting outward again in two arms, two legs. Until he was simply, clearly human. A portrait of the young man Hailwic had grown up with. He chose to clothe himself in a black-and-green tunic—something distinctly from a different age, and he let one leg swing as he watched the others with pointed interest.

"Fuck that. I want to know," Punabi said, striding forward to swallow a smattering of beads and slap zhur hand into Glensen's proffered one.

Glensen swallowed three, as did Absolon.

Hailwic paused. Could she even trust him to reveal the truth? She'd felt the strength of the cryptobeads herself—she couldn't imagine how enhanced his cyrptopathy might be if he took them regularly. Could he create an illusion of success? So thorough not even a seasoned, enhanced teliopath like Glensen could tell it was a lie?

She decided she'd rather live with his possible falsehoods than his word alone.

Slinking forward, she accepted three beads, swallowed them, before feeding a hand into Punabi's, squeezing in a way she hoped felt friendly and not overly familiar.

Zhe did not squeeze back, but zhe did not pull away.

Absolon's gaze flickered to Hailwic, and she regarded him coldly. A veil of hurt covered his face, but it was thin, and she couldn't gauge if it was genuine.

Hailwic's balance was suddenly upset by the smattering of eager information she sensed yawing through the air. Little whispers of facts, like thrumming strings on an instrument, begging to be plucked.

Beside her, Punabi shifted uncomfortably, experiencing the same.

After another beat Absolon closed his eyes, and let them see.

The tithing made everything stronger than it otherwise might have been—the scents, the sensations, the emotions (bolstered by Punabi)—and yet receiving a memory secondhand made it hazy, even with the beads. A copy of a copy—something imperfect and irregularly fleshed through. Nothing like the broadcast-level clarity Hailwic had first expected.

It took Glensen's interference to keep them all focused on a single scene. Other memories begged for attention—not just Absolon's, but Punabi's and Hailwic's as well. Only Glensen's skilled, guiding magic kept them on track, placing them deep in a moment of Absolon's recollection.

Through Absolon's eyes, Hailwic found herself suddenly in a bunker. A modern one, nothing like the ancient tunnels they still physically occupied.

It smelled like antiseptic cleaner. A thing new, previously unused. Virgin in a sanitized, stringent way. Wall after plain white wall slid past as Absolon jogged along the corridors, with Uprhasia's beautiful, perfectly styled hair bouncing along in front of him, and the Friend's personal guards flanked him on either side.

A rush of confusion and questions swirled in Absolon's mind. He hadn't been told any specifics; Uphrasia had brought him with her as part of her entourage, not as an advisor or a partner—as she might insist on bringing a favorite pet.

He knew nothing of her plans to launch the bombs.

Or, at least, that was what the memory conveyed.

He was distraught, heart pounding, at a loss for how to conduct himself, trailing farther and farther behind as they wound through the facility deep underground. It was cold, stark. The white walls gave way to brushed metal, and eventually they came to a central saferoom where he, Uphrasia, and two of her most trusted cabinet members were unceremoniously locked inside.

Monitors lined one wall—effectively creating a window—a series of couches and chairs formed a seating area around a low coffee table, and five jars, each filled with a different type of pathic beads, sat heavy at its center.

"Are we under attack?" Absolon asked, not for the first time, if the edge in his voice—the harried demand of it—was anything to go by.

The bordering nations had sent several bombing raids in the last few months, but none had propelled Uphrasia underground like this.

The cabinet members ignored him entirely, the pair speaking low yet frantically.

With a flick of Uphrasia's graceful finger against a keypad, one bare wall opened to reveal a recessed kitchenette, amply stocked. She swiftly poured Absolon a glass of golden liquor and shoved it in his hands, as though to pacify him like a whining child. "Sit," she told him bluntly, punctuating the order with a possessive kiss.

Absolon—the Absolon of now, sharing his memories—deadened his emotions, blocking how he'd felt in that moment. Hailwic sensed Punabi trying to squeeze them out, but his cryptopathy easily overrode zhur emotiopathy.

When he dropped himself onto the couch, Uphrasia nodded once, then strode toward the bank of monitors and turned them on with a snap of her fingers, revealing dozens of camera feeds, all broadcasting from different international locations. He saw cities in Nosbeq, West Donmark, the Radical Republic of Central Ioll, Mosenheim, Ki Ki Sai, Xina. Not just enemy states, either. Radix's allies were represented as well.

A tingling dread washed over him, head to toe.

Then the memory hazed further—like Absolon had been holding his breath until his vision dappled at the edges—and instead of experiencing the bombs launching and detonating in real time, everything sped forward in a rush, as though the recollection itself had explosive force. The bright flashes, the strange bulbous, physiopathic frothing across the screens, the erasure of each pocket of civilization and the many living things around it all took place in a blink.

In contrast, Absolon himself seemed to be moving in slow motion. He rose from the couch in quiet shock, mouth hanging open, drink in hand forgotten as he moved forward to get a better look.

The two suited advisors became a blank in his peripheral, and all he could see was Uphrasia, silhouetted against the destruction.

After a blink that was a terrible eternity, Absolon stumbled backward, as though putting distance between himself and the screens could remove some of the horror.

In his retreat, he bumped the end table with the five jars, their beads tinkling softly inside as his untouched drink sloshed over the rim of his glass, spilling onto the thin carpet.

The others paid him no mind, too enamored with Uphrasia's rotten power.

Absolon glanced down out of habit, mind still reeling, but just as he was about to look away again, he saw them.

Really *saw* them.

His world, for a moment, narrowed to those beads.

His gaze slid sideways toward the door, trying to calculate how many strides away it was and how many seconds he had to act before Uphrasia's guards could burst their way through the saferoom door.

Not enough.

Moving quickly, he upended each jar onto the carpet, mixing the beads together in a pile before scooping a fistful up in his dampened glass and shooting them into his mouth, swallowing like a madman in the desert drinking down sand because he couldn't find water.

He'd only ever taken one bead at a time before.

He'd only ever taken one *kind* at a time before.

"Absolon!" Uphrasia gasped, rushing at him, having finally noticed him down on all fours. She used the same tone a pet owner might use when surprised by the disappointing antics of a dog.

A dog. That's really all he was to her.

She crouched down next to him, and he didn't think—time around the two of them slowed, or rather *he sped up his own time.* With a strength he didn't know he possessed, he wrapped both hands around her throat and whipped her down onto her back on top of the scattered beads.

The glee slid from her face, replaced with horror—her docile dog suddenly had its teeth in her neck—and he instantly felt her kairopathy flare to stop him.

But she'd handed him the means of her destruction. She'd introduced him to the beads, bade him take them like they were a recreational party drug and nothing more.

He channeled all of that cold, clear physiopathic energy into his hands, changing them. He felt his nerves blaze with pain, then deaden and die as the flesh and bone of his fists shifted to solid, unrelenting marble clamped tightly around her windpipe.

She choked once during the shift, then went silent, unable to get so much as a squeak out for lack of air. Instead, she kicked, but he turned the bones in his hips and legs to stone as well, made himself too heavy to push away.

Two other voices in the room shouted for help, but they were so, so distant. And the time beyond himself and his hands and Uphrasia moved so, so slowly.

"You have no idea what kind of a world you have just created," he yelled in her face. "You think *this* is awful? My hands now immovable weights against your throat? You have been an immovable weight to humanity for decades. And that out there? That is the end. That is the fucking *end*."

The door burst inward. Her guards flooded the room in slow motion, screaming orders at him, guns poised. They gave him one second to comply.

That was one second longer than he thought he'd get.

He shifted his bones, his skull, built armor plating over his heart. Bit by bit, his body went cold and numb and impenetrable.

But not completely invulnerable.

The first shot took out the skin and hair across the right side of his head. He ducked down, planting his face in the crook of his elbows, high above where his flesh met rock.

For half a moment he expected to feel the crushing push of another Kairopath trying to stop him, but then he remembered.

Uphrasia only employed Cryptopaths.

Cryptopaths. Cryptopaths everywhere. They were her guards, her servants, her advisors—even her fucking lover. Even *him*. She surrounded herself with Cryptopaths because she thought they couldn't hurt her. They were weak to her very presence, and so she thought she could ultimately control them—no matter what.

Ripping, grasping hands now forced his bleeding head upward, pulled him back, tried to pull him off. But his fists now blended into each other, as surely as if a sculptor had carved them from a solid block.

Another guard rushed in front of him, gun holstered. Instead, they wielded a machete.

Lonny reinforced his own throat, thinking they'd go for his head to lop it clean off.

But the blade came down on his forearms, and the blow was strong and the edge sharp.

He shrieked as the dead weight of his hands was severed from his body, the numbness in his arms making the pain dull and distant, but the horror of seeing them fall away, their heaviness forcing Uphrasia's head to twist to one side like a manacle, made him go mad in the moment.

And that abject hysteria was catching.

He didn't know how many emotiopathic beads he'd swallowed, but it was enough to affect the entire room.

His delirious panic swept through the guards. They grabbed at their chests, at their helms, buckling at the knees and bending at the waist as they shared in his panicked derangement.

Beneath him, Uphrasia was still. Her eyes unseeing.

Shaking, screaming, he lifted his arms up before his eyes, tried to force his hands to regrow.

He didn't have the skill nor the true power. He managed to stop the bleeding, but couldn't even make his skin cover over the open wound.

He could feel the stolen physiopathy fading. He'd used it all up, worn it all out.

Which meant it would all fade soon, and he had to—he had to escape.

Stumbling to his feet, he took maladroit steps toward the door, stepping around the writhing guards, still looking at the ends of his arms where his hands should be. He was slack-jawed and dazed, his mind half in and half out of his body. He could hardly believe anything that had happened in the last ten minutes was real, but that didn't matter.

Nightmare or not, real or not, he had to get out.

He looked at the monitors. They were filled with static. The feeds had been cut. All but one. One just outside the bunker. One showing the road their caravan had driven. It now ended in a sheer cliff—the land had been scooped out as easy as cream.

He stared at that new ridge line, the new drop-off, and wished he was at the bottom of it. He willed himself to be at the bottom of it.

Stumbling, he went to the monitor, pressed his forehead against the glass.

The world fell away.

There was a rush, a crunch, a sting, and a mouthful of dirt.

Somehow he got himself upright, to his knees. He pushed at his body, trying to change the numb pieces back—to make the stone bone again. It all itched, felt like festering sores deep in his body. Off in the distance, the sky pulsed with unnatural luminescence.

Barely able to breathe, to form words, he tried to contact someone—anyone—on his implants, but they no longer worked. Either his transformations had morphed them into something unusable, or there was no one to hear.

He was alone.

He wondered if the others could feel him. Feel his pain, his distress. That was what the tithing was for, to connect them, to give them all one last hope if something went wrong.

If they *could* feel him, would they even care? Would they come?

"None of you did."

The memory cut off and Hailwic gasped, coming up for air, coming back into the moment quick and off-kilter. Guilt burgeoned in her chest like acid, and she swallowed it down, corking it with bitter sarcasm. "Apologies. I was too busy fleeing for my life," she snapped, thrusting her left side forward, flexing the ruined mess of her wings and arms.

"Hintosep found me a few days later," Absolon grumbled.

"No doubt on Kinwold's instruction," Punabi said, dropping both Glensen's and Hailwic's hands.

I told her not to go, Kinwold countered sadly.

"Babbi didn't want any of us to risk the surface so soon," Hintosep said. "But they knew you were all alive, knew Absolon was closest. I couldn't just hide."

Glensen kept hold of Absolon, took his other hand as well, examining them. "Zoshim did good work," fey said.

Absolon took back his fingers, clearly uncomfortable with the scrutiny. "Zoshim always does good work," he agreed. "Are you all satisfied now? Uphrasia is dead."

The hollowness the word *satisfied* bored into each of them did not go unacknowledged.

"Why did she do it?" Hailwic asked after a moment. "I mean, why, *really*?"

"Launch everything? Hubris," Absolon said simply. "She thought Radix would be spared. None of us anticipated the resonance. No one had run calculations on what might happen when one blast hit another. She thought she'd be the architect of a new world order, and, well—" He raised a hand in an acerbic display. "Wish granted."

HINTOSEP

Beneath Hintosep's feet, sand like grains of amethysts rolled with each step, pocketed through by whorls of shining, obsidian black. The grains were too large—bigger than what one would find on the shores of the Deep Waters, but too fine to be set like gemstones. There was a wind here—the kind that scrapes along the land itself but somehow won't ruffle even the lightest hairs on someone's head.

The purple sand went on as far as the eye could see in all directions. The only obstruction was the portal the Teeth had made—on one side this vast nothing, on the other the keep had collapsed fully, blocking off the tear, making it impossible to tread back. Whatever force had created the suction had now equalized, but the edges of the tear still slowly bled.

Children cried all around, and most of the other adults—Mandip, Juliet, Tray—did their best to comfort them, though they all shared vacant, bewildered stares, caught off guard by their surroundings. Abby ran straight to Avellino as soon as zhe regained zhur footing, and the young man met zhim with a fierce embrace.

Melanie's lap was occupied by her battered husband, and Krona laid Thibaut down on his front by the healer's feet. Dozens of tentacles and tails writhed up out of his spine. Shaking with adrenaline, Krona carefully swept his fringe out of his eyes.

"You came for me," he said, clearly trying for a tease, but his voice was so weak, it came out like disbelief.

"Of course I came for you," Krona said, obviously trying not to let her new worry show. She was doing her best to keep his wounds clear of the gemstone sand. He was gaunt—far thinner than he'd been last Hintosep had seen him. He was bruised all over, and his back was crusted with dried blood at the edges, while his spine was damp and oozing.

Krona looked to Melanie, who said nothing, but shook her head minutely. Even the master healer wasn't sure what to do for him. "You silly man," Krona said. "I'd come for you even if the world was ending, just to spend our last moments together." She looked to Hintosep, who gave her a nod but said nothing. "Stay still, now. I'll be right back," she promised, kissing his temple.

His hand shot out to fumble for hers before she could move from his side, and she squeezed his fingers in reassurance, ducking down to brush her lips against his ear. "I love you," she said—quiet, weighty, like a promise.

Hintosep turned away. Shading her eyes, she squinted into the distance, begging her gaze to catch on something, anything.

Krona came to stand beside her, back to the group. "Where are we?"

"Ask your Regulator friend," she said, nodding over to Tray, and—more pointedly—to where the Teeth lay half-buried in sparkling purple beside him. "It is whatever his consciousness made it."

Krona called to him and he immediately heeded her, bounding over, leaving a crying babe in Mandip's lap.

"This is your reality," Hintosep said quickly. "We need sustenance, shelter, water. Where would we find it?"

He looked at a loss. "I—I don't—"

He didn't understand. She did her best to explain. "You used the Teeth. When Absolon used them to create a place such as this, there were things he needed there. Monsters to do his bidding, which he could move from his mind into our world. This is a place of your making, deliberate or not. Whatever your subconscious thinks should be here will be here."

He was quiet for a long moment, turning her words over the same way he might turn over an enchantment he suspected was counterfeit. After a moment, he shook his head. "That doesn't . . . that doesn't feel right."

"What do you mean?"

"I didn't make this place. I can't have made this place."

"You did," she corrected.

"I *didn't*." The initial billowing, bewildered look he'd worn now stiffened. He was sure. "Why would this be of my mind? Nothing but amethyst as far as we can see?"

"Perhaps it's because you created the portal without purpose . . ."

"No. If the enchantment works as you say it does, then this is someone else's fantasy land."

"It can't be anyone else's. Right now, you're the Teeth's Possessor. You're the one who wielded them, and as such you've forged a reality that—"

"This can't be my reality!" he insisted, rattled.

Clearly, she'd hit upon some implication about his mind. The way it worked, what he wanted. "How do you know?" she asked carefully.

"Because she's not here!" he yelled, before snapping his mouth shut and turning away, a dark cloud passing before his eyes. "If my mind was going to spin a reality for me to escape into, one where it could make anything it wanted, De-Lia would be there. She's not *here*."

"But she is," Krona said carefully. She raised her mutated arm. "In part. Her echo . . ."

He went pale. "I—I didn't do that, did—?"

"No," Krona assured him quickly. "Absolon. Absolon did it."

He set his jaw. "Then it's not the same. I would have imagined her as . . . as she was. If Absolon could create monsters from thin air with this thing, then I would have brought her back to *life*."

Hintosep's instinct was to keep arguing. It might pain him to think he would have woven a world without De-Lia, but that didn't negate the fact that he *had*. She knew the seven artifacts intimately, even those she'd never wielded herself. Absolon had made sure she understood—

She caught herself.

"Of course," Hintosep breathed. How could she have been so naïve? How could she continue to believe any of his lies even when she had contrary evidence right in front of her? "He said they were from his imagination. The monsters. But that's not how magic works. It can't invent something from nothing. It moves energy, it can't create it. It can't make life. I know that. I *know* that."

She balked at how easily he'd been able to convince her of impossibilities.

"What does that mean?" Krona asked.

Hintosep closed her eyes. She let herself feel the sun's rays and the way her weight shifted the sand. She opened her ears, listening. There, a faint hum. Magichanical. A sound she'd been familiar with in the before times. A sound that had been hidden behind the walls in her mind for centuries.

The last of Absolon's tampering finally fell away.

"It was me," she gasped, pressing the heel of one hand to her temple as the remembrance rolled from the back of her mind to the fore. "Absolon didn't lead the people here . . ."

I did.

She remembered before. *All* of before. And she remembered how many times he'd gone back into her brain to twist and conceal, again and again, until she was who he'd wanted her to be—his most devoted.

"It means I know where we are," she said, opening her eyes. "We're beyond Arkensyre. We're in what's left of a place called Remotus."

The two former Regulators shared a look but took her declaration in stride. That was clearly easier to believe than a land of imagination. "How far away from the Valley are we?" Tray asked.

"I'm not sure, exactly. But it can't be far. Not far at all. I hear machines. Come, everybody up."

She went around to the others, helping them to their feet. Mandip hoisted a young one with a twisted ankle onto his back, and Juliet took the hands of two five-year-olds. Sebastian, thankfully, was awake again. Abby had passed a hand over his face, stitching up the gash above his eye.

Krona helped Thibaut to his feet, made him turn so she could look closely at the gash in his back. "I can try speeding up the healing," she suggested. "Or we can have Abby try?"

"I've already expended so much energy, I'm not sure adding time without first adding sustenance is such a good idea. And I don't want to overextend Abby—this might be a stretch, even for a child with so much talent."

"Nature could do it," Hintosep said. "We'd just need to find him again. His name is Zoshim, for what it's worth."

Thibaut furrowed his brow. "You mean, the literal god?"

Hintosep looked at her shoes—old and stolen from an ancient eze. "Indeed," she said.

"Only not so literal," Krona corrected. Thibaut tilted his head at her, and she waved him off. "We'll get to that. Long story. At least let me make sure all of your bleeding has stopped."

"Hard to say no to such a sweet proposition."

She let her palm hover over his back, smoothing down the air around his body, letting it fill with kairopathy. His fen curled over the backs of her hands, welcoming the aid. "This won't be enough to make your fen retreat."

"I'll be fine, I'm sure." He gave her a warm smile. "As long as you'll still have me with a cosmic horror sprouting from my spine."

"Luckily we make quite a pair," she said.

"Wings are looking better than ever," Thibaut said, nudging Krona playfully with his shoulder.

She smiled lightly at him, humming in agreement. "But the arm . . ."

"I overheard. Hello, De-Lia," he greeted her. The echo did not acknowledge him. "You could ask Abby to have a go there," he said.

"No," she said quickly. "I don't want to risk it."

"Even like this you're afraid of losing her."

She looked down at the arm, apparently so she wouldn't have to look him in the eye. "Yes."

"Hey." With a gentle hand, he traced his fingers down her other arm. "Even like this, you love her," he said. "That's nothing to be ashamed of. Even like this, you love *me*."

"I don't care what form you take, as long as you are you."

"So you would love me if I were a rock? A sloth? A worm?"

"You *are* a worm," she teased.

"And you, my dear," he said sincerely, lifting her chin to gaze into her eyes, "are an angel."

Hintosep cleared her throat. "All right to travel there, Thibaut?"

"Seems I'll have to be."

"The Valley has to be miles away, though," Tray protested as they made ready. "All these children, they'll never make it that far."

"It's a deception," Hintosep reassured him, picking up a child herself while he did his best to herd the others into a line. "We're in the Wastelands, and the border primarily acts as a *shroud*. Just as I can deceive the eye to hide myself from sight, so too does the border protect Arkensyre from unwanted detection. From our current vantage, the Valley is simply invisible."

"Then how do we know which way to go?"

Hintosep waved at the portal, pulled a toddler up and onto her hip, then strode over and picked up the Teeth. "We use that as our signpost. We came from that direction; we go that direction."

The Teeth were heavy in her hand. Weighty and cold. Familiar, yet foreign. Holding the enchantment away from the core of herself—like a dead thing that might weep or bleed—she presented it to Tray once again.

He shook his head, held up his palms in protest, clearly meaning to defer to her expertise in the matter. She shoved the artifact against his bared hands, waited until he curled his fingers over the contours of the Teeth and held fast. "I have no desire to act as Possessor ever again," she said.

When he nodded his acceptance, she addressed the party once more. "Everyone set? All right then. Keep the children between us. That's it. And we're off."

Despite her confidence in the rim's nearness, it was still slowgoing, what with so many little legs struggling across shifting dunes.

She kept alert as she led them, scraping her mind for all the memories of before. There were beasts out here. Dangers. Absolon hadn't lied about that. The physiobombs' destruction and transformation had been unpredictable. In the intervening millennia, many of the creatures born of those explosions may have died out, living a single lifetime as solitary amalgamations incapable of breeding. Yet others may have been able to spawn. New ecosystems would have emerged. What had once been an annexed portion of Radix was now a whole new world, alien, invaded, and terraformed.

Though she kept her eyes open, she saw no new dangers. She caught a glimpse of something dark in the sky, but it was so distant and so brief it might have been a trick of the light refracted off the sparkling desert.

As they marched, the humming grew louder. At least they were on the right track.

Soon a thin black lattice resolved in her vision, draped like a fancy piece of lace across the purple sands ahead, as though the contours of the desert were really the contours of a fine neck and shoulders. Evenly spaced nodes, like beads, dotted the lattice at even intervals.

The closer they strode, the clearer the nodes became, and the slower Hintosep moved forward, acutely aware of the many children in their party.

They were all Thalo Children, of course. Given over to a life of darkness from the moment they were snatched from their cradles. Still, as soon as Hintosep was sure the nodes were not simply human-sized but human-*shaped*, she stopped dead and bade the others keep the children back while she investigated alone.

A few dozen yards separated each form from the next, close enough to impress upon her that there were many thousands woven through the latticework that stretched from horizon to horizon across the heavy curvature of the dunes. Each was a hunched figure, down on all fours, human in all regards save the texture of their skin and the strange uniformity of shape: as though every person had been purposefully stripped of identity, broken down into a nakedness that went beyond their lack of clothes to a lack of personhood.

They had no hair, no accentuated features. The salt crystals that created the skin of their bodies were very unlike stone, the texture laying somewhere between the scales of a fish and leaves of delicate paper. And beneath, all was *gray.* No richness of melanin or vibrancy of pink flush.

Collars leashed to heavy cables circled every neck. Bits, like those for horses, had been jammed into grimacing mouths—the lips peeled back to reveal teeth as black as luststones. Their fingernails were the same: pricks of obsidian straining against the roll of the sands.

Each body's back arched or bowed—stiffened into a rigor of either ecstasy or resistance. Their eyes were so encrusted with salt Hintosep couldn't tell if they were closed or open—if each figure stared out blindly over the expanse of waste, or if they'd been forced to forever look only inward, examining the backs of their own eyelids for some meaning in this madness.

It was impossible to tell if there was still life left in them. They looked like gruesome statues—something wrought by a mad hand—but these had been Thalo once. She knew that for certain. They'd lived and breathed as she did now.

Kneeling, she curled her hand over the nearest one's forehead, trying to sense secrets within. Nothing came directly from the figure. No hidden thoughts, desires, or deeds. Perhaps parts of the body still worked, to keep the pneuma flowing, but she could detect no sense of self inside.

There was only one place so many bodies could have come from. One ritual that could have seen them transported away without her understanding: Ascension.

The means by which Thalo gave up their corporeal forms to the aid of the god-barrier so that they might be reborn and live again.

She'd asked to Ascend herself, long ago. Absolon had even reminded her of it before sending her to Mirthhouse—reminded her how he'd denied her request.

She'd watched over the Ascendants for many centuries as a Guardian on the rim. She'd buried them—still breathing—underneath piles of enchanted salt. She'd done it carefully, lovingly with her bare hands, honored to protect them as the salt crystals hardened and their bodies were encased. Honored to stand watch until inevitably, while she herself slept, their bodies vanished.

She'd never questioned that vanishing. Never asked herself to envision what their energies or their magics or their bodies became after—in what way they'd been transfigured into a spiritual form that could aid in the Valley's concealment.

Clearly, the Ascension was not a transfiguration at all.

They'd been brought here. Been affixed *here.* Had the remainder of their pneuma drained here.

They had ascended to protect the border, just as Absolon had promised.

Like with all his promises, the reward was rot. The price a torment.

Hintosep ran her cupped palm up over the figure's bald head, trailing it down their neck, between their rigid shoulder blades, across their back and down their flank, raking off salt scales as she went, following the line of the thick cabling that attached to the collar and bit like particularly cruel reins.

The cables were the lace, the Ascendent Thalo the beads. If the dunes were the shoulders and the lace itself a collar, what formed the throat around which it draped?

Hintosep asked herself this already knowing the answer, but she followed the lead regardless, first to another body, then another and another.

Each Ascendant let her pass without sight, without movement, without feeling. But not without decay.

For all their uniformity, the bodies clearly were not of a uniform age. Like statues carved from stone a touch too soft, the bodies had begun to melt under the onslaught of weather. The older ones—the innermost ones—had lost their true-to-life angles, becoming more and more like wax imitations the farther she followed the line. Heads and hips and shoulders had weathered away. Their hands were like mitts, faces like molted egg casings.

And as she followed the trace line of time—back, back—the magichanical buzzing became louder. She knew it was shrouded from the others by cryptomancy, just as the source would be shrouded from their sight.

Eventually the melting forms became little more than oddly shaped blobs. Collars and bits lay tumbled by the sands—the necks and mouths they'd once belonged to now dissolved into the landscape. And yet the cables still trailed on, leading to the throat of the matter.

Giant, curving spikes—like the ribs of a gargantuan serpent—sprung out of the sands, the latticework all fanning outward from their bases. Each colossal machine—a giant, towering enchantment in its own right—was as wide at the base as Melanie and Dawn-Lyn's old cottage, narrowing upward into a sharp, arched tip. The towers wound away to her left and right in a long, winding line, outlining the Valley itself, though it appeared that nothing but more dunes lay at the heart of their piercing hold.

Plated copper and iron covered the towers like armored scales—each having gone streaky blue and green and red from ages' and ages' worth of open exposure to the elements.

Hintosep jumped back when a bolt of energy shot out in an arc between two of the enchantments, sizzling through the air.

These towers drew their cryptopathic power—their ability to shroud the Valley—from the Ascendants, whom Absolon must have bent and collared himself. And, over time, as each Ascendant's pneuma ran dry, another had to be added to the mesh to replace them.

Each layer in the net of cables was like a ring in a tree, revealing the age of Arkensyre, and the extent of Absolon's rule.

Now that Absolon was dead, there was no one to replace the Ascendants once they expired, even if they wanted to. If *she* didn't have the knowledge, then no one did. The border would collapse eventually.

Arkensyre's days as a haven from the wastelands were numbered.

She looked back at the throng following her—*trusting* her. They stood atop a dune in the distance, their dark silhouettes no bigger than a thumbnail—no bigger than the vipnika that had torn through her safe houses and the people who'd called them home.

They'd have to tear their way back inside now, but soon, the world would come flooding in all on its own.

"Regulator?" she called. "Master Amador?"

He came sliding away from the group, skidding through the sand with the hurried gait of an eager student called to action by a favored tutor. His eyes only briefly strayed to the bodies as he passed, focused instead on what Hintosep would have him do.

When he stood breathlessly beside her, gauntlet in hand but not over it, she asked, "When you used the Teeth before, what were you thinking?"

"That we had to get out. Just . . . *out*."

"This time, think of somewhere safe. Someplace specific"—she gestured toward the others in the distance—"where so many children might be welcome."

The eagerness fell away from his brow. "The Valley's at war."

"And I trust you to find us a place of peace."

He thought hard, nodded. He forced the Teeth's gauntlet over his fist, and she pointed him past the tower. "Lead the way," she bade.

40

HAILWIC

In a Time and Place Before

Hailwic trudged behind Glensen and Absolon, watching closely even as she kept her distance. A stiff wind blew grit across the shell of the earth—the bowing expanse of glass that went on and on and on *and on*. She drew the thin scarf she wore tighter over her nose and mouth, blinking rapidly, ducking her head to avoid the tiny bits of glass scraping and swirling in the air. A thick haze had formed just above the low wind, churning a gauzy film up over the sun, giving the atmosphere a waxy look.

Hailwic had never jumped a valley search party this far south before, all the way to what had been Mosenheim. This close to the pole, patches of hidden ice made trekking extra hazardous, and at night the cold seeped so deep into the glass it burned to touch it.

She glanced down briefly to step over a strange gouge in their path—like deep scratches from massive claws—and caught the glitter of Punabi's shine dancing through the prismatic purples from behind.

Just as she still prickled in Absolon's presence, so Punabi prickled in hers.

Behind zhim, a handful of other scouts marched, brandishing pickaxes, sledgehammers, and the like. Breaking ground was far more literal these days.

"I think we're nearly there," Glensen called over feir shoulder, pulling down feir cowl to make sure they were heard.

The valley's biggest boon to date might be right under their feet.

Mines, bunkers, vaults—anything set deep enough underground had had half a chance of surviving. While the face of the world was barren, priceless treasures lay buried beneath. Not just the likes of Uphrasia's stock of time treatments and her stores of pathic beads, but tools, archives, *food*. Their means of continuation. Survival—not just for the next month or year, but long enough to rebuild.

The primary challenge wasn't getting to such places, it was finding them.

Over the past year, Hailwic and Zoshim had tried to remap the world from the skies, while Absolon and Glensen (who'd given in to the necessity of it all) binged on crypto- and teliobeads to heighten their ability to perceive the world—the secrets, the knowledge. The hidden and unhidden.

Now, both Glensen and Absolon dropped down suddenly, their gloved hands smoothing over the glass as their enhanced magics sensed what the eyes could not: the remains of the Great International Seed Vault.

"Here!" they called together. "We dig here."

Punabi pushed forward with zhur team, giving Hailwic a wide berth as zhe did so—so obviously wide Hailwic couldn't help but internally scoff.

The physiopathy-created glass was no delicate thing. Punabi took up a sledgehammer and swung, bringing it down with a *crack* that sounded more like the sheering of cement than the brittle, clinking burst of stemware shattering. Thick iron rivets went into the fissure, and the team pounded the pins to a steady rhythm, widening and deepening the wound.

Hailwic gave them aid, speeding up their work, allowing them to cleave through in record time—though not without tremendous effort. And she didn't miss the way Punabi instinctually fought the kairopathy, tensing and resisting, though zhe'd known all along Hailwic would *push*.

They were down two men. Both had gone missing before they'd left the valley, and Absolon had insisted they move out rather than search for new volunteers.

That happened every once in a while—people vanishing. Sometimes they'd been wandering too close to the carnivorous tree line, or met a beast while on patrol. Sometimes they'd left the valley of their own accord, seeing fit to wander—either because they'd given up hope or had had their hope renewed—searching for a more suitable refuge.

Other times, Hailwic wondered if the land reclaimed the missing.

It was a silly notion—that there were somehow pockets of physiopathy lying in wait to burst and claim yet more victims, turning them into smears of oil, or rock outcroppings, or vine-covered deer in an instant. Zoshim and Absolon and Kinwold had all reassured her that wasn't possible, but the imagination flies where it will.

When they cut through the last glass chunks, a dark hole met them. Cold air seeped upward, stinging Hailwic's already wind-bitten cheeks. Still, she did not hesitate to lower herself into the chasm, preparing to freeze any wayward physiopathic abominations in their tracks.

But the vault was silent, nothing moved. Nothing pitter-pattered in the shadows. There was no stench of rot or the foreboding ambience of death. The bombs may have sheared off the top of the mountain—the four hundred and fifty feet of sandstone that once sat atop the seed vault—but the bank itself had remained untouched.

She called the all clear, then jumped Punabi, Absolon, and Glensen to the bottom.

Their only light was Punabi zhurself. Instead of zhur brilliance bouncing off glass cases or metal lockboxes, Hailwic was surprised to be met by rows and rows of rickety metal shelving stacked high with gray plastic tubs.

"Are you sure we're in the right place?" she asked, approaching the nearest tub, noting it was labeled with a longitude and latitude.

"Yes, this is it," Glensen said excitedly, standing on tiptoes, reaching up as high as feir little frame would allow. "This is one of three vaults in the GISV. Look at how well preserved everything is. Not one puncture, not one transformation. Everything is still cold—I'm sure the glass insulated the Mosenheim permafrost. We'll need to make sure we reseal everything when we leave. Ah, this is wonderful!"

Absolon was far less impressed. He put a hand to the cement wall of the vault, testing its temperature, but likely also trying to detect the direction of the other two nearby vault rooms. "I'd have thought the inner workings of someplace so important would have been more advanced," he said, moving away to pop the plastic clasps on a tub, lifting the lid with a skeptical furrow to his brow. "With systems to monitor the exact temperature of each case, digital readouts, electric climate controls. Something modern—more than just a cold, well-sealed hole in the ground. Something to create *order*. This is no more sophisticated than any suburban garage."

"Quite the contrary," Glensen said. "If the systems had been more advanced, these seeds would have lost viability months ago." Fey popped the seal on feir own hefty gray container, retrieving one of the enchanted glass tubes inside, turning it over and over in Punabi's glittering light to reveal a gathering of pale seeds the size of a thumbnail. "The nearest power stations died with the bombs. If they'd been required for preservation, all would be lost. This place was built to survive a cataclysm, and it did.

"Simple and precise are sustainable, while innovation has its place. It's wisdom to know which better serves any given purpose."

"So many different plants," Hailwic mused, going down the rows, skimming over each label. "Too bad we'll have to leave the majority here."

"Why would we do that?" Absolon asked incredulously, two other glass vials in hand.

Hailwic countered with the obvious and a shrug: "We can't grow them."

"Of course we can. The Physiopaths can create whatever soil requirements we need. Whatever water levels, whatever temperatures."

"To what end?" Hailwic asked. "There are fewer than a thousand of us in the valley. That means, what, a couple hundred Physiopaths, maybe? We should order them to create the perfect microclimates to grow everything here, and *then what*? They'd need to put in constant effort to maintain such states. It'd be far more practical to take what's suited for the bog and the floodlands. Maybe in the future, if the environment changes—"

"We could change it right now," Absolon gritted out, as though he thought Hailwic dull-witted. "With all the pathic beads we recovered from Uphrasia's vaults, there's enough additional pneuma to bolster everyone's power for at least a decade. Instead of scraping by in the valley as is we could make it into whatever we wish it to be. We have the tools; we only need the focus."

"*Or* our energy could be better spent adjusting to what remains. What happens when the beads run out? Shouldn't we be conserving them?"

"You want to wallow in the mud forever when we don't have to?"

"That's not what I mean." She found the section bearing Radix's and Remotus's coordinates, then fondly skipped over them, looking for more appropriate materials. "I *mean,* we are barely surviving as it is. No one's in a place to hear grand schemes of a garden paradise. We need basic stability first. Once we can stop worrying about the essentials, we can start to plan for such a future. Ten years of swallowing physiobeads by the dozens will leave us nothing but empty-handed when they're gone." She side-eyed him. "Unless you know how to make them?"

He said nothing, pretending to be preoccupied with a new tub.

She was sure he knew more in that regard than he was letting on, but now was not the time to press.

"Having access to every variety of fruit we can think of is less important than making sure there's enough food to go around," she continued. "We have to be smart and sparing with our resources."

Absolon pocketed several vials, then shoved the lid back on the tub. Before going to another, he strode to her side, turning up his nose and pinching his gaze as he leaned near. "You're starting to sound like Kinwold," he spat.

He meant it as an insult. To his ears, she sounded too timid, too reserved. Unimaginative. Weak. "Good," she shot back. "They're the only reason any of us are still alive."

Their disagreements did not end there. The six of them could not agree on what kind of mass housing to create, what kind of farming structure to implement, what kind of precautions to set in place when venturing beyond the bog, beyond the unnatural forests, beyond the valley. Even with only a small hamlet's worth of people to care for, they could not set aside their egos long enough to *listen.*

So Hintosep set to listening instead.

She had opinions on the tithing. She'd thought Babbi had entered into the covenant too hastily. Yes, they'd known each of their tithe-mates since she was little, many of them she thought of as family. Absolon had held her as a baby and she sometimes still thought of him as Uncle Lonny.

But family and politics were often at odds.

They all argued. Constantly. Without end, it seemed. They'd set to discussing how to proceed—not even in the next year, just for the next week—and one of them would inevitably storm out of the meeting (not Babbi, never Babbi).

She wanted to scream at them that the world was new. It was all new. All the old terms, the old reasonings meant little. Their assumptions were of the past, their methodologies of the past.

Half of them wanted to wall off the valley. The other half wanted to expand their reach. Some of them thought that training the remainders to use their magic more skillfully would help restore a livable world faster. Some of them thought encouraging the people to use their already developed, non-magical talents was more efficient.

Sometimes Punabi contradicted Hailwic and Hailwic contradicted Absolon and Zoshim contradicted Glensen and Absolon contradicted everyone else all just to be contradictory. Just to feel right, superior. Petty personal slights long in the past still hung over them. It divided their attention, soured their perspectives.

Deep down, they all felt they'd failed. Failed one another, failed the world. And that bitterness rankled and festered, poisoning every attempt at reconciliation and reconstruction.

While they debated, Hintosep worked. If a hut builder needed an extra hammer, she hammered. If a family needed help identifying edible plants from inedible, she analyzed. If a calf needed birthing, she was there with clean hands and open ears to follow the cattleman's lead. Every few months she went on a wandering pilgrimage to look for more survivors, finding fewer and fewer as time went on.

She even looked for the missing, and most of the time came up empty-handed. Once in a while she found a body. Some with faces missing—caved in, swirled, like some creature with a giant sucker had molded their face like putty. Others were unscathed, completely unharmed, yet inexplicably dead. She didn't know what to make of it, but returned the corpses to their villages just the same.

She kept a knife in her boot and a waterskin always filled. She wanted to be ready for whatever the world—the wastes or the valley—threw at her.

She had no desire to *lead* and *decide*. She would leave that to the strange, *ineffective* council the tithing had formed.

What she hated most was their talk of what to do *about the people*.

Not *for* the people.

About them.

These were mostly Absolon's musings.

Today she walked the perimeter of the council room slowly, itching to leave, but staying because Babbi had asked. They sat atop their throne (*not a throne*, they always corrected, though never offered another name for the high seat), gazing down with their otherworldly face as Absolon made an even-keeled argument, though his passion was evident in the line of his body, the squareness of his shoulders.

He'd found suits in Uphrasia's bunker tailored to his size though he'd never touched them before. He'd greedily taken every last one, and was the only one in the council room pressed and perfect. The only one whose clothes would not have been out of place in the world before.

"There are so few of us left because we let our magical differences destroy us," Lonny said, tone chanting *this is logical, this is logical, hear me, this is logical.* "What if there were no magical differences?"

"And how would we achieve that?" Punabi asked, arms crossed defensively, each hand a hard fist against zhur biceps. "Swallowing pathic beads that don't align with your own magic makes you sicker than a dog."

"Think the other way around," he said, catty.

You want us all to stop *using our pathies?* Babbi asked. *You could no sooner ask people to stop using their right hand.*

"There're so few people and so little magic left already," Glensen said. "And weren't you the one who suggested we throw everything behind pneuma-based skill development?"

"Listen," Absolon insisted. "Just listen. Hailwic—" He went to her imploringly, holding out a pointed hand. "Just the other day you had to break up a fight between a Cryptopath and a Kairopath. Why?"

She looked irritated to have her anecdote used in illustration. Her wings ruffled. "The Cryptopath accused the Kairopath of sabotaging their garden."

"With?" he prompted.

"With a time stop," she admitted. "Actually, I think he even suggested the other man made his sprouts shrink backward instead of grow, which we all know is *incredibly* difficult and not worth—"

"Thank you," he said dismissively, turning back to the others. "The point is not whether or not the Kairopath *did it*. The point is our various magics create power imbalances amongst individuals. And even perceived imbalances can create conflict. What happens when another Fistus, another Uphrasia, is born tomorrow? We have so little left, we can't afford to lose it."

He paused dramatically, a smirk playing at the corner of his lips. "What if Uphrasia was on the right track, but for all the wrong reasons?"

Absolon clearly expected an uproar, and to everyone's credit, no one gave it to him. They regarded him coldly, refusing to rise to the bait.

Hintosep continued her pacing, taking in each tithe-mate from different angles, watching the way they all privately tried to calculate what he was getting at and how seriously they should take him.

"She gave us the means to level the playing field," he continued.

Total extraction, Babbi intoned.

"You would use total extraction to be *rid* of magic?" Zoshim asked, speaking up for the first time. He was a many-antlered lion today, lounging at Babbi's feet.

"Not be *rid* of it. I don't want to eradicate it. I want to contain it. The whole point of developing enchantments was to make sure everyone had equal access to magic. So why not put it *all* there?"

At this they all went a different kind of quiet. A *thoughtful* kind.

"You might get some volunteers," Glensen said. "But not everyone."

Absolon laughed, quick and humorless. "I don't expect everyone will simply give it up because we asked. If my time with the Friend taught me anything, it's that most people can't be counted on to do the right thing voluntarily."

"So you'd force them?" Punabi said plainly.

"We'd make a law," he said, far too evenly.

"I won't do it," Zoshim said, raising up to his pawed feet, not in a show of intimidation but of defiance. Losing the ability to shape-shift when he'd already had to reclaim the right was paramount to sentencing him to prison once more.

"I wouldn't expect you to," Absolon reassured him. "Any of you," he added, casting his gaze around the room, arms open as if in friendly invitation.

"So when you say all, you don't mean *all,*" Hailwic commented, unimpressed.

"We, the seven of us"—he tipped his hand to acknowledge Hintosep—"have a higher calling. A *responsibility*. We already take the time treatments when others don't. Eh, don't argue, I haven't heard a single one of you suggest we widen the distribution. Yes, yes, Glensen, conscientious objector, you're exempt. But the beads, though, you partake now as well, and none of you have been excited about redistributing those, either. And don't tell me *scarcity* is the only reason.

"We could oversee the fair use of the new enchantments. We could ensure stability, and we could prevent another attempt at empire before it even begins. We're already here, *right now,* discussing the fate of everyone still alive. We have already decided we are in control and we make the decisions."

"Is *that* what we've decided?" Hailwic asked caustically, lip curling.

He turned on her, spine a tense, forward curve. "Go open the doors and invite everyone to council if you're so keen. Keen to throw off the duty you've taken up so readily yet refuse to acknowledge by name. In the land of a thousand, we rule. We *are* ruling. Naïve protests to the contrary won't change the facts."

"You're not just talking about ruling," Punabi said. "You're talking about impugning the autonomy of everyone else. Protecting your body and desecrating theirs."

"All I'm asking is that you think on it," he insisted. "Consider the idea. You'll see that I'm right. It's the safest, most secure way to move forward."

I don't believe we need time to think on it, Babbi said. *This decision I'm happy to make in haste.*

They stood, gave a light nod to Zoshim, and began to stride forward, toward Absolon. As they did, they shrank. What could have been covered in one stride took five in the next instant, then ten. Zoshim pulled them down into their neutral form, swathing them in trousers of blue and a tunic of white.

"We can't take away *choice,*" they said, clasping their hands behind their back. "We can't force people to use their magic, and we certainly can't force people to *give up* their magic. Would you force them to *bear* children? Would you force them to *give up* children? No? You understand how wrong that would be? Good. Then how do you not see how terrible this idea is? The personal sovereignty of the body, the right to use it as you will, to morph it as you will, to adorn it as you will, to move through the world *as you will* . . . it's everything. For many of those people out there, it's all they have left."

Absolon stood perfectly still for a moment before inclining his head ever so slightly in acquiescence. "If that is how you all feel," he said smoothly, tone belying nothing.

Babbi clapped a comforting hand on Absolon's shoulder, ignoring the calm mask that had so easily displaced the barely restrained passion of his oration moments before.

They discussed other strategies and Hintosep continued her circuit, but this time with eyes only for Absolon.

With each passing moment, she trusted Uncle Lonny less and less.

When the council was adjourned, he left swiftly.

Hintosep followed.

She kept her footsteps light, but did not try to disguise her presence.

His shoulders sagged as soon as he was out of sight of the silo, but tension balled his fists and his jaw tightened, making his neck cord-tight. Turning down a silent corridor, he shoved one fist into the pocket of his trousers, pulling out a small silver pillbox.

He stopped abruptly, turning gracefully to prop his back against the tunnel wall as he popped several beads into his mouth. Completely unsurprised and unperturbed by Hintosep's presence, he held out the box as she approached.

"Cryptobead?" he offered.

The council had agreed to use the beads sparingly.

They'd also put Absolon in charge of distribution.

She reached for one, scrutinizing his expression as she did, half expecting him to snap the box shut just short of her fingers as a tease—a wonderful little joke in his own mind. He used to tease her mercilessly when she was a child, knowing she preened under the attention.

Ages had passed since she'd seen him in a joking mood.

Taking one gently, she held it carefully between thumb and forefinger, examining it in the low light, trying to look within to the drop of pneuma.

"You look at everything like you've never seen it before," he said offhandedly. "Even beads you've swallowed dozens of times."

"You know how to make them," she said, raising her eyes to his. It wasn't an accusation, just something she knew with surety.

"Only in theory," he admitted.

"And you still haven't told them."

"They don't want to hear it. They don't want to hear anything I have to say. They tolerate me because we are bound . . ." It was surely not the first time that exact thought had crossed his mind, yet the sudden wideness of his pupils and the furrow of his brow suggested a spark of something new, a realization he'd failed to have before—as though his understanding had needed fermenting.

He shook his head, banishing whatever it was. "Did you need something, Toe Bean?"

To keep an eye on you, she thought. Secrets were writhing beneath his skin—the others couldn't see it, but she could. She wished she was skilled enough to pry them out.

She popped the cryptobead between her lips, split its shell with her back teeth, knowing it wouldn't be enough.

He smiled, and there was something *cracked* about it.

41

KRONA

Trailing children past body after body, Krona felt like she was a Regulator at the Chief Magistrate's jubilee gala all over again, playing docent, explaining the gruesome enchantments—the foulest of art—to guests who only had the vaguest of understanding. The children were fascinated by the bent forms—some drawn in, some wary, all wide-eyed—and trudged by the bodies no more and no less revolted than by the magenta sands or the sickening bow of the sky—so vast and unbridled by the high walls of a valley, as was good and proper. Only the other adults shared Krona's looks of horror.

After the loss of Mirthhouse—indeed, all of Hintosep's safe houses—Tray was at first hard-pressed to divine where he might lead them, until he realized it wasn't so much about *to where* as *to whom*. Melanie's mother, Dawn-Lyn, and Sebastian's great-aunt Onara had been tasked with aiding refugee camps—traveling the countryside dispensing aid while also searching for new recruits among the displaced.

He, quite rightly, could think of no one better to receive them.

Krona was therefore unsurprised when they came into the Valley low on the western rim in Asgar-Skan, not far from the moment-minefield: she'd stationed the two women there herself.

The bivouacs here among the sloping bits of jungle and jutting rock were more well-established than those she'd encountered near Nature's temple. The firepits were deeper, their stones long blackened. There was a kick to the air—the sharpness of said fires mixed with the butteryness of poorly washed skin and the curtness of snapped greenery and the tang of fresh blood. Tarps had been strung between the branches of thick trees not just to keep the rain off but to catch it, funneling it into large wooden barrels whose lips were hooked with all quality of kitchen ladles. People hung the washing on tent lines just as efficiently as they would have in their own backyards—without fear and without flare.

Tired eyes tracked them as their handful of adults and many children emerged from the curtained vines and concealing leaves uphill from the majority of the camp. If anyone looked surprised, it was the surprise of the weary calculating how many more mouths that would be set around the communal gruel pots.

The don whose land had been subsumed by the failed railway and then the minefield had moved his household and his tenant farmers out of harm's way to these foothills months ago, and had endured here ever since. A slow trickle of their neighbors had followed, but now it seemed a deluge had descended. The site teemed with people—and not just those the local dons employed, farmers and trappers and fishers and their families, but soldiers too.

Soldiers bearing all manner of colors. Those of different allegiances mingled freely, propping one another up, ignorant of borders and betrayals, more concerned with broken legs and battered eyes. Winsrouen soldiers leaned on Lutadorian soldiers. Xyoparian and Asgar-Skanian soldiers swapped canteens.

A Marrakevian scout limped by.

None of the long-standing refugees appeared to find this odd. Nor did they accost them and attempt to drive them off, just as they'd been driven off by these selfsame armies.

"What happened here?" Mandip asked of no one, echoing Krona's own silent question.

She gestured for the others to follow as she descended farther down the sharp slope where any little jut and outcropping that hadn't already been colonized by trees was now colonized by tents and firepits. Her boots skid on slick leaves and patches of mud as she wound her way past those slogging uphill and equally struggling with the bearing of the terrain.

Wide eyes swept over her, and it wasn't until people started reeling back that she remembered she could not comport herself among the general population as she did among the resistance.

She was the Demon of the Passes and had no hope of blending in.

The moment that struck her, she felt her spine straightening and her gaze lifting, hardening. She was no longer only looking for Dawn-Lyn or Onara. Grabbing a nearby Lutadorian soldier by the sleeve, she asked, "Who is your commanding officer here?"

"G-General Basu," they said, pointing a shaking hand farther down the embankment, toward a large awning with steam billowing from beneath—likely the grub tent.

The lunchtime soup was far too thin, but it needed to reach more bellies every day—or at least, that was what Dawn-Lyn said in apology when she caught sight of Krona stomping beneath the tarp to scan the long planks—once barn siding—laid out as the camp's communal table. The older woman embraced her daughter, son-in-law, and grandchild before calling for the camp's healer to attend to Thibaut. Mandip eagerly made his way to where Adhar sat huddled over a bowl near the end of the planks—not at the table itself, but set awkwardly atop a nearby stump. The general's spoon shook in his hand.

Krona accepted a moment's rest, even allowing herself a bowl of soup, shrugging off the stares and trying to ignore the bubble of awe many of the refugees instantly swaddled around her. At least in that regard, she wasn't alone.

Thibaut's fen sent people reeling, and Hintosep and the blue-tattooed children hovered on the outskirts, attended no less enthusiastically by Dawn-Lyn and Onara but eyed with a sense of suspicion that Krona suspected had once been reserved for the soldiers who now all huddled together like kin.

The healer brought to bear on Thibaut was a Physiopath abroad from one of the Winsrouen safe houses. They took Thibaut only a few feet away from the soup line to a lean-to, cracking open a light vial and stringing it up in the vault of the makeshift ceiling to create a spotlight by which to work. Thibaut was only given a lumpy bag of laundry to kneel before and bend over so that the Physiopath might have better access to his spine.

Krona began pacing outside the lean-to until Thibaut called her in. He distracted himself from the pain of the healer's press and pull by squeezing Krona's hand as she stood beside him, eventually tugging her down to his level so he could brace both hands on her knees while the healer bent him farther forward still.

She distracted herself from his hissing and grimacing by running her fingers through his mass of hair—combing out the knots—and training her eyes past the healer to a blue-and-gold chrysalis dangling precariously from the underside of a giant leaf just beyond the lean-to's mouth.

What kind of insect emerged from such a cocoon? A moth? A butterfly? Was there anything to glean about the creature's final form from its neat little incubator?

She'd thought she'd known what to expect from the gods. She'd looked down at Time's jut of hip and crook of feathers sticking up from the sand in her glass cocoon and made so many assumptions.

They aren't what we thought, and they don't want to be here.

Just like none of these people wanted to be here. These were families, soldiers, lost children. Rich and poor alike. Noble and common. Farmers, soldiers, bakers, enchanters, scribes, members of the Watch.

The man who'd orchestrated the war—setting up its dominos before tipping them over one by one—was dead. But what did it matter to any of these refugees? The damage was done, his influence perpetual. He didn't have to keep his finger on the first domino to ensure the others continued to topple. This conflict was self-sustaining.

She'd hoped the presence of the gods would shock it all to an end. That they would rise up and shout *stop* and it would just go away.

She'd denied that to Time's face, and yet now, looking around with so much left to do, she realized that was exactly what she'd wished for.

Krona craned her neck to get a look at her people again—to mark them as they ate or helped administer the meal. Juliet was already making herself at home trying to aid whoever she could however she could, and doing it with a flare. Krona caught Melanie and her family out of the corner of her eye, frowning when she saw Melanie's brow furrow as Dawn-Lyn readily explained something, new tension twisting her, making her warily cock her head.

Krona felt a shift in that small tilt of the head, and in the way Sebastian suddenly snapped out his hands, with an *Are you sure?* easily readable on his lips.

A grim shadow fell over Dawn-Lyn's brow. She raised a finger, pointing downslope, the gesture ominous, like a specter's accusatory hand.

Krona's line of sight was suddenly interrupted by Mandip, his face grim as well, bearing a frown so deep, it cut down to his chin.

Dread blossomed in her chest.

Before Mandip could speak, Thibaut flinched harshly.

"Enough. Enough, please," he begged the Physiopath at his spine.

"But you still—" The skin of his spine was knitted, but something beneath was still uneven, displaced.

"Please. I'll live, and that's what matters," he assured them, his fen batting them away with a heavy tentacle. "Someone bring me a chemise."

Krona stood as Thibaut stood, her gaze locking on Mandip's, mirroring his wide-eyed expression. She rushed toward him. The ground felt brittle beneath her feet, the air thin and swimming around them. "What is it?"

He drew a deep breath. "The hoard."

"There," said Adhar, handing Krona his spyglass and pointing to the southeast at a swath of acid-green slashed through dark mud.

He'd brought her and Mandip to a ridgeline where the canopy parted just enough to offer a peek down to the Valley floor. Even with the spyglass, it was impossible to resolve the masses and smudges of color into definitive shapes, though she had no doubts about what she was seeing.

"At first I thought Winsrouen had released varger to counter us," Adhar said. "But those who fled with us deny it, and I'm inclined to believe them. No one would be mad enough to believe they could control the monsters—and there must be thousands."

"Hundreds of thousands," Mandip whispered.

"Maybe millions," Krona said gravely.

"They decimated our forces on both sides within minutes," Adhar said, knuckles gone pale as he gripped at the tall, arching roots of a kapok tree. "The closest villages are already under threat and will be overrun in a day."

"Then the next and the next," Krona said. "The whole Valley is at risk—no one's ever had to face this many varger en masse before." She passed the spyglass to Mandip. "Wait for me. I need to get a closer look."

Krona threw her lens high, dropping through it above the razed land, *falling, falling, falling* until she jumped herself into the sky again.

What had previously been the moment-minefield was now a no-man's-land of monsters.

A thousand full-fledged varger roamed below, bloated with their fresh meals, quills raised, teeth bared at one another, fighting openly, ripping into one another with claws and teeth since gorging on humans did nothing to stop the constant hunger and pain of being cleaved from their hosts.

The trenches were empty, ravaged. Claws had made them wider, scattered weapons and supplies. The cannons Adhar had warned of had been torn from their wooden-wheeled bases and now lay together in hapless piles like flood-thrown logs. Tattered, bloody clothes had been crushed into the mud beneath heavy paws or now blew loose on the breeze.

There were no soldiers. Those who hadn't made it out with Adhar likely hadn't made it out at all.

The stench of so many varger clustered together in the humidity was nauseating, punching Krona in the face even at her height hundreds of feet above.

Most of the mines had likely already been triggered—the varger now wrestling and running over the expanse freely. One lone monster stood suspended on its hind legs, frozen in place as its fellows circled, likely feeling the pulse of the magic.

And still, from the ragged crack that was the mine's entrance, more ethereal varger poured forth, seeping out. Each vat must have failed in turn, creating a cascade of releases, steadily feeding more varger back into the world.

Already, the hoard had spread beyond the confines of the trenches, the brave pack leaders venturing out to find fresh game now that their food source in this battered land had been exhausted.

It wouldn't be long before the others caught on. The hoard's territory would continue to expand. There was no force in all of Arkensyre prepared to deal with this many varger—monsters who could not be killed, would not back down, and never lost their appetites.

This is our fault. My *fault*, she thought. They'd upset the balance of the vats—interfered with the containment system.

She jumped herself back into the foothills, a hundred yards away from Mandip and Adhar, giving herself a moment alone to deal with the sharp guilt and building anxiety.

Though she wasn't *completely* alone. Her echo arm squirmed as though trying to buck away from Krona's self-incrimination, and it shook Krona out of her stupor before she could spiral.

She hadn't gathered so many broken bits of souls into one place. *She* hadn't violently separated them from their hosts. She'd returned what was stolen. She'd rescued tortured beasts and helped make them whole again.

This was just a poisoned parting gift from Absolon.

There had to be a way to contain them again. Many people from the Borderswatch had become soldiers in the past few years. How many still had access to their quintbarrels? It would take more than a single brigade to conquer the beasts—it would require a monumental effort of cooperation. Cooperation between peoples still at war.

They'd need something to rally behind. Or someone.

The five weren't gods, but they were still so much more than Krona was. And now they were scattered. She had no way of tracking Time, Emotion, or Nature.

Yet, Knowledge . . . Knowledge still remained in feir treehouse. Fey'd been burdened with eternity and the maintenance of Absolon's Valley, just like the others, and in truth fey owed its people nothing.

Krona had thought all along to beg a favor of the gods in return for their release. She'd meant it to be De-Lia, restored. Instead, she'd ask the only not-god she could find to help contain Absolon's mess one last time.

But she wasn't sure she could convince fem to leave feir throne. In order to attempt it, she'd need to understand fem—not as a god, but as a person. And only Hintosep could shine light down that path.

Regardless of whether or not Knowledge agreed to help, she knew they—the people of the Valley—could not rely on fem alone. The hoard threatened the whole of Arkensyre, and the whole of Arkensyre would have to come together in its defense.

With a steadying breath, she returned to the brothers, instructions already poised on her lips. "There are still more coming. They'll snuff out each farmhand, eat their way through the villages, and decimate the cities. We are the only people who can rally enough troops to stop them, understood? Follow my lead."

She'd never been one for rousing speeches. As they made their way back to camp, brushing aside fern fronds and stepping over half-rotted logs, she did her best to formulate a call to action. She'd never had to win the hearts and minds of those in Mirthhouse; Hintosep had garnered their faith for her. Similarly, her Regulator captaincy had seen her head a team already familiar and willing to follow her lead. These soldiers, these refugees only knew her as the Demon of the Passes, and she could not be sure if that would help or hinder.

42

HINTOSEP

"They'll spread to every corner of Arkensyre within weeks," Krona declared from atop the long makeshift table, the boards bending under her each time she took a step left or right. Her bone wings flared with emphasis, her good hand first open in entreaty, then fisted tight. The awning above flapped taut in a sudden breeze as though it were as roused by her passion as she hoped the crowd would be.

The soldiers and refugees had all gathered round at her and Adhar's behest. Krona did not spare any time easing them into the facts: hundreds of thousands—*millions*—of varger were about to beset not just the battlefields, but their homes, their coteries, their capitals.

"This camp is not safe. *Nowhere* is safe."

Krona's eyes shone with a renewed fire Hintosep could not match.

Leaning against a rough tree trunk wrapped in uneven vines, Hintosep peered over dozens of heads to watch Krona do what Krona did best: push forward. She was so good at taking the next step, and the next, despite dwindling reserves, dwindling hopes.

Hintosep was the same. Or had been.

The weight of her last walled-off memories had struck her as firmly as a blow to the brow. Her ears rang with it—the truth of who she was, and who Absolon had been.

Her ancient mind was a jumble. She remembered reality, and she remembered Absolon's falsehoods. She remembered what it had been like to scrape by in the bog, and how beautiful the Valley had been right before this war had torn up much of its physiopathically manipulated ground.

She mourned the outer world and her parents all over again.

She mourned the loss of *Hintosep the Grand Orchestrator and Guardian.* She mourned the loss of *Hintosep Theesius, loyal daughter and careful watcher.* She mourned the loss of *Toe Bean* to the inevitable march of time.

She mourned the loss of Uncle Lonny, now sickened by the figure he'd become.

She watched Krona march up and down the boards, envious of the force behind her rallying cries and the clean clack of her teeth as she bared them. She possessed an energy Hintosep could no longer bring herself to muster.

Perhaps that was all right. Krona could bring the fire and Hintosep would bring the mettle. Duty would not let her rest just yet. The duty she'd paid to Absolon she now owed to the Valley in his stead. *Because* of his stead.

"We all want—" A thick hitch in Krona's throat—the click of sudden tightness—stole her momentum. It drew a hush over the camp, their hearts with hers and their ears straining for the next words. "We all want the same things."

Krona's eyes drew over the gathering, landing and lingering here and there. On Melanie. On Juliet. On Tray and Mandip and Avellino and, of course, Thibaut. Krona's gaze even met Hintosep's own. "We want our loved ones safe. Our homes safe. This desire *unites* us, but we've let our leaders wield our want as a wedge to drive us apart.

"No matter what city-state you hail from, we are all citizens of the Valley. I could send you all home to raise your own defenses. To leave each of you to protect your own, to devise your own plans. But no matter how effective those plans, divided we are *weaker*. I ask you to put aside your differences and your allegiances. Your ambitions and your pains. Unite with me, and we will have one plan, one defense. A joint effort, meant for all of us, driven by all of us."

There was no cheer of affirmation or ruckus of optimism. Every face lay grim, with clenched jaws and thinned lips and hard stares all around. A wave of somber determination ran through the camp. Krona's words hit home: to forsake yesterday's enemies in the fight was as good as forsaking oneself. The crisis of the war had been subsumed by a new crisis, an existential threat to the entire Valley.

The first of many, Hintosep thought, thinking of the rim's dissolving defenses.

Krona was already assigning tasks—to see her at work again was a wonder.

They were a handful of people, but as citizens from all over Arkensyre their network ran deep. They needed people with quintbarrel training. As many as they could gather. A majority of these soldiers had been pulled from the Borderswatch and had the skills, but not the proper weaponry.

Questions alighted around Krona like leaves falling from the trees. How were they to gather enough people? Enough quintbarrels? Surely the varger could spread faster than they could possibly account for. Even if they could reach other units in their armies, how would they convince them to stand down? And how were they to contain *so many* monsters? There couldn't be enough enchanted bottles in the whole of the world.

Krona's unchained magic did much of the explaining for her. She called Ninebark from her body, stretched her bones to their full expanse and brandished her transformed arm as solidly as if it were her saber. She bade Tray demonstrate the Teeth—which could take them anywhere they needed, could bring back any number of reinforcements—and asked Thibaut to scrape knowledge from the air.

Not once did she mention the gods, and not once did she draw undo attention to any of the Thalo. She simply needed to convince the camp that what she aimed to achieve was possible, that the means were there if they had the will.

She called for maps, and for paper on which to sketch her own. She divided the soldiers and refugees into units—five that would disperse to their city-states, following the paths that Tray would create to gather quintbarrels and willing hands from Borderswatch stations and Regulator dens. She set Juliet, Mandip,

Adhar, and Adhar's closest commanders to lead the charge. Avellino insisted he remain in the camp to protect the Thalo Children, and lastly, Krona pulled Hintosep and Thibaut aside for a mission all their own.

"They'll stop the spread . . ." she said as she led the two of them away from the meal tent.

"But you still don't have a plan to permanently contain them," Hintosep realized.

"No," she admitted, "but I know who can devise one. You need to tell me a few things first. The hoard—is the containment failing because Absolon is dead?"

"Yes and no," Hintosep said. "It's because Time is free. The vats weren't stable—they required constant additional kairopathy."

"The pipes," Thibaut said. "The wires—"

"The lack of additional physiopathic locks around Time's hourglass," Krona added.

Hintosep nodded tiredly, hoisting herself up on an outcropping, following Thibaut's scramble and suddenly feeling her true years like never before. "She'd needed to work her magic while Mindless, to feed Absolon's varger-trapping machines."

"Bottle-barker jars don't need any extra input," Krona said. "Why would he risk such a failure? He must have known."

"He knew. He knew how to build stable, sustainable. That was never what he wanted—with the vats, with the climates, with the border, with any of it. He wanted his version of paradise. He wanted everything just so. He was the creator, and to leave his creation to its own devices was unthinkable."

The fetter of fungus wafted up as she trod in a rain-soaked hollow. Fungus that could not have grown so readily without Glensen's memory of it or Zoshim's ability to recreate it. What would happen to it now? If the barrier fell, would it spread to the world beyond, or would the entire Valley succumb to the wastes?

"Absolon didn't want a Valley that could go on without him," she went on. "He needed . . ." She drew a deep breath. "He needed to be needed."

Krona drew them far enough away from the refugees to prevent them from being overheard, yet remained close enough to still glimpse the people moving hastily between the trees. Pulling to a halt, she lay a hand on Hintosep's shoulder. "We're going to Knowledge's temple," she said. "But first, Thibaut and I need to know what you know. Tell us about the five, and Absolon. Tell us everything."

"Everything . . ." Hintosep echoed, pulled into herself and the history she'd been denied for so long. "Absolon *took* my everything."

In a Time and Place Before

Hintosep continued to stalk Lonny at every turn, feeling a reticence build in him, watching it spring to the fore on his face and in his stance whenever he thought no one was looking. Every time his suggestions were dismissed, no matter how small, he prickled, and she could see him coiling inward, a spring winding tighter and tighter.

Intricate plans were developing in his ever-working mind—not just the type he wished to share with the council, but machinations of a personal nature. No one else seemed to see it. Or perhaps no one else cared.

After all, it was only Absolon. Only Lonny.

She cared. She cared and she knew something would happen when he could wind himself no tighter and instead was forced to snap.

She couldn't keep tabs on him at all times, and once in a while he disappeared for days at a time, off somewhere she could not find, doing what she could not fathom.

She watched closely, but could never have been ready.

It was a warm, bright day. Most people were outside, taking advantage of the clear weather. Babbi was darning while Hintosep did the washing. Absolon strolled up casual as anything and asked Kinwold to accompany him on a walk through a part of the jungle he'd been tending. Her babbi did not hesitate to agree, setting aside a pair of hole-riddled socks, making ready to leave with him at once.

Hintosep, with her arms deep in suds, pulled the tunic she'd been washing from the basin and pinned the tattered thing haphazardly to the drying line before insinuating herself into the walk as well, begging no permission.

She expected Absolon to admonish her. Or at least balk if he was up to something.

Instead, he eagerly welcomed her along. Everything in his expression said nothing was amiss. They were just three Cryptopaths in their perfectly neutral guises, out for a pleasant walk to Absolon's private garden.

"Watch out for the snapdragons, they bite," Absolon teased once they were hours away from the bog and well into the encroaching, bomb-morphed woods. He pointed at a carnivorous plant with human teeth that looked nothing like a snapdragon and everything like a set of dentures with leaves.

They followed a well-cleared path to an equally well-cleared bubble of a climate. It was warm, wet, all in a way distinct from the surroundings. Like a greenhouse that had no need for walls and a roof.

Several tilled lines with rows of thin, new plants covered the small area. "These I took from the seed vault," he said, crouching down next to the nearest bush with red berries just beginning to show. "Coffee," he explained. "Avocados there. Did you know a lot of tropical plants needed their seeds constantly replenished in the vault? Their viability could only be maintained for weeks at a time, regardless of conditions. Now, lost for good."

He ran his fingers thoughtfully through the dirt as Babbi strode past him to examine the next plant—something spiky. Hintosep stayed near the garden's entrance, arms crossed, stance wide, like a bodyguard.

She didn't trust the pleasantness of the day, or the pleasantness of Absolon's tone.

She waited for Babbi to sense it too—the smugness under the affability. The strange self-assuredness that felt so very unnatural wafting off of Uncle Lonny.

Absolon dusted his hands off, stood. "I've come to a decision," he said definitely. "I reject the council's verdict."

"Which verdict was that?" Babbi asked, still moving down the row of plants, admiring them.

"Your refusal to consider total extraction for everyone."

Kinwold sighed.

Hintosep tensed. She bounced her leg just to feel the weight of her knife in her boot.

Kinwold pinched the bridge of their nose. "We rose up against Uphrasia when she decided to rob the Physiopaths, but now you want to rob everyone? You think these people won't rise up against you as well?"

"Kinwold, if we do this right, if we do this *now*, they'll never even have to know. People used to wall away their trauma. Cryptopathic doctors did it all the time. Given how many cryptobeads we have, between the two of us it should be no trouble at all; we can make *all of them* forget their pathies. We can cut off their memory of Uphrasia. We could wall off *everything* from before. Everyone can start fresh, without the pain, without the indignity, without—"

Hintosep's own mounting horror was nothing compared to Kinwold's—to the way her babbi's eyes grew wide and their mouth became a thin, pale line as they leaned sharply forward right before they snapped out, "These people *trust us*."

The air in the grove seemed to cool, freeze. Hintosep shivered.

"Exactly," Absolon hissed. "We're heroes to them. Icons, just like you wanted. Practically *gods*. For the time being, anyway. Which means we need to act quickly. We need to put an end to access to personal magic *now*. People cannot be trusted with it all on their own."

Kinwold's disgust was open, blatant. They made no attempt to hide their disappointment or keep the contempt from their tone. "Absolon, what have you become?"

"I've simply stopped simpering in your shadow. You were not the leader we needed after Professor Solric, and you aren't the leader we need now. Leaders have to make hard choices, and you'd rather make no choices at all."

Hintosep slowly crouched down, not wanting to draw Absolon's attention. Her fingers slipped into her boot, found the grip of her sheathed dagger. Her magic was no match for Absolon's. But a blade was a blade.

"We can't let this happen again," Absolon said, waving at the wider woods around them—at the wider world. "*I* won't let it happen. I don't care what it costs."

Kinwold's tone was even. "That's easy to say when you won't be the one paying the price."

"You think I haven't already paid the price? Do you have any idea what it's like to be forced to end the woman you *loved*? To choose *the world* over her?"

Babbi scoffed. "You didn't love her."

"I did!" he shouted, moving to stand nearly chest to chest with Kinwold.

"You expect me to believe you were *in love* with a genocidal dictator? You were in love with the woman who would have ground Zoshim, a man you are *tithed* to, into dust beneath her heel?"

"I did!" he insisted, fire in his throat. "Who are you to say I wasn't in love?"

"You didn't love her, Absolon," they said tiredly, every syllable also a heavy sigh. "You know how I know? You can't *assassinate* someone if you love them. No one murders people they love." They turned away, waving dismissively through the air as though every word Absolon spoke was simply nonsense to be batted aside like an irritating fly.

Every muscle in Lonny's body went taut. A strange calmness replaced the exuberance. His voice—previously impassioned and animated—went stony, his next two words landing with a granite-like *thud*. "Watch me."

Hintosep bolted out of her crouch, knife in hand. "Babbi!"

Absolon's hands shot out, grasping Kinwold by the back of the head, pulling hard, making their spine bow. Down he yanked, until Kinwold's head rested on Absolon's shoulder, next to his own face.

Hintosep was two steps away in an instant, blade poised to ram into Absolon's lower lumbar, ready to split his spine if he didn't let her babbi go.

He felt the oncoming rush—knew she wouldn't stand by and watch him batter Kinwold without a fight. Twisting the fingers of one hand cruelly under Babbi's jaw to keep their head flung back, Absolon threw out his other arm behind him, hand splayed wide and directly at Hintosep, as though his palm itself were a weapon.

It was.

The blast of kairopathy was unlike any she'd ever felt before. The natural thrust of a Kairopath's magic had always felt soft, like the body wasn't really aware that it was shifting through time and space any differently. But the time stop Absolon created *crackled* across her chest and stomach and face and legs—a force wielded by an unskilled hand.

Hintosep froze, knife still poised, knee raised in a half step, body leaning unnaturally, precariously forward.

Babbi seemed frozen just the same.

She expected her mind to blank out, or to become so sluggish as to falter. But she perceived everything outside the stop as usual. He'd frozen her bones, kept her in check, but either didn't have the skill or the desire to stop the rest of her.

With both of them trapped, Absolon growled out accusations against the side of Kinwold's face. "You've always been *dismissive*," he snarled. "Now you presume to tell me how to think and what I feel. All of this could have been avoided if you and Solric had let me be the assassin first. I would have killed her years ago and the world would still be whole. I won't let you underestimate me again. I won't let you drag these people through unnecessary pain *again*."

He twisted Kinwold around to face him, pushed them down to their knees and took hold of both sides of their head, squeezing their skull. Kinwold's own hands surged up to push Absolon's away, even as Hintosep still struggled to do so much as blink.

They fought—they fought to rise, to reel out of Absolon's grip, to do more than grit their teeth, but pressure built and built and built on their face, turning it a dire red.

"Hold *still*," Absolon barked. "Hold still and we'll both get through this. Hold still, I said. I can't use the kairopathy, or it won't work. If you don't stop—Kinwold, *stop*!"

Kinwold thrashed. Hintosep willed them to keep struggling, to break free, to run for their life and reveal Absolon for the traitor he was.

"Absol—*rgngh*."

A gurgling sound left Kinwold's throat, and their features went soft. Not soft like serene, soft like *putty*. Their nose caved inward, their lips and eyes and cheekbones following. Hintosep shrieked into the bubble, the sound stoppered in her throat. It was like no transformation she'd ever seen. This was not a Physiopath's power of transmutation, but something else entirely. Something born of cryptopathy.

A wisp of something orange-red—not quite liquid, not quite gas—curled out of their face. Absolon tried to grasp at it, throwing Kinwold to the ground, not as an afterthought but as punishment for some imagined betrayal. The wisp rose up, up, drifting like a dandelion seed, out of his reach. He called to the thing, coaxing, and it came back down, curling around his fingers. But then it thinned, evaporating. "No, no," he muttered, trying to hold what was unholdable. "No, no, no!"

He turned to Kinwold, crumpled backward on the ground, face to the sky. "I told you to stay *still*," he spat at them, flinging himself down on top of her babbi, grabbing at the front of their tunic, shaking them though they'd gone limp. "I would have had it. I would have kept it and you would have been restored one day, you stupid, stubborn—*if you'd just listened to me*!"

Hintosep flushed hot and cold and hot again, struggling to escape the stop, struggling to call out or weep. There was no life in her babbi's limbs. The front of their skull was swirled and caved in—a parody of what Zoshim had created when he helped them transform into the Colossus. Instead of a guiding light, nothing shone forth.

Dead.

Absolon rose to face her, angry, cheeks blotchy. He had tears in his eyes. "You weren't supposed to be here for this," he chided her. "When it happened, I was . . . I was going to . . . I was just going to lock their mind away in halite. I wasn't going to kill them, Toe. I wasn't. *I've practiced.* I've practiced and I was ready, *but*

Kinwold wouldn't listen," he babbled, pointing wretchedly at Kinwold's form, stomping like a boy who was supposed to get his way.

Hintosep vibrated in the time stop, her horror and grief and anger building with nowhere to go.

She'd seen a face, like Babbi's now, before. Several faces. Faces on those who'd gone missing, whose bodies she'd dragged back to their loved ones.

"They were *practice*," Absolon insisted, reading her thoughts, veins clearly coursing with teliopathy as well. "No, it wasn't all me. All the missing. But if someone wants to trek back into those unforgiving glass-lands, why should I let them throw their lives away when they could be *useful*?"

Absolon turned on the spot, wiping his eyes, his brow, muttering to himself. "They'll know. They'll feel it. This wasn't supposed to . . ."

After a while he recomposed himself, faced her again, gaze narrowed and calculating. He inched closer to where she was suspended, searching her eyes for something. He lifted his fingers, ready to snap her free.

She'd make sure her face was the last thing he'd see.

As soon as he broke the skin on the time bubble, she surged at him, the half-dozen cries that had been building in her chest breaking free all at once and tangling together into a call of feral rage and tear-laced denial.

She slid the dagger smoothly into his belly, splitting him deep and clean, the edge sharp and her thrust true.

He met the blade gladly.

He cupped her face and clasped her wrist, keeping her hold on the hilt firm, preventing her from backing away. "I'm going to need that keenness of yours, now more than ever," he said. "I am sorry. It wasn't supposed to go this way."

The familiar coolness of cryptopathy filled her skull, pressing behind her forehead and swamping in behind her ears.

She whipped herself backward, trying to avoid her babbi's fate.

He had so much worse in mind for her.

Absolon gripped harder, twisting her wrist, twisting the knife in his own gut to keep her close.

A heavy weight, like a castle gate clanking down, fell across part of her mind.

"I need you to trust me, Hintosep."

"No!" she yelled, kicking, fighting, but somehow tripping and falling out of her own body, her own sense of where and when.

"I need you to trust me," he repeated, pushing harder with his cryptopathy, bolstered as it was by the beads.

"No!" she shouted again, trying to fling herself around his body—hand slipping off the dagger, now too slick with his blood—needing to get to Kinwold, to their body. "*Babbi!*"

Absolon grappled with her more forcefully. "I need you," he gritted through his teeth, sending icy chains of magic through her gray matter to wrap around the walls and hold them in place while he mortared up the seams, "to *trust* me."

She wrenched herself free—or he let her go, she couldn't say—and she tripped through the dirt, landing on the corpse in front of her.

The corpse with no face.

Just another corpse with no face.

Her hands were wet. She raised them up, looked at the blood, bewildered.

"Who—*what*?"

A figure moved behind her. "I know this is confusing," said Absolon.

She turned to him. He was bleeding. A knife lay on the ground, the blade shining red in the sun. Someone had attacked him.

"What happened?" she breathed, reeling away from the nameless body, shuffling backward, running into a thin line of plants—young bushes. Coffee plants.

Setting his jaw against the pain of his wound, Absolon reached down, offering his hand. "I need you to trust me."

Her fingers slid into his with the familiarity of one who'd taken that same hand time and time again, since she was small. "Of course," she said. "Of course I trust you."

Now

It was an ice pick of a memory, skewering her as surely as she'd skewered Absolon himself, in the end. That rapid loss of the moment, of her surroundings, of her pain and anger and fear and, not just her babbi, but even the image of their face in her mind.

Absolon had waved his hand and taken it all.

The moment his heavy wall inside her mind had finally fractured, she'd vowed to take everything from him in turn.

"He needed to be needed, and he had to *make* people need him," Hintosep said. "Nothing here is built to last. More things will fail now that he's gone and the gods are free. Not just the hoard's systems. All the falsehoods that make the Valley what it is."

"How can we stop it?" Krona asked.

"Maybe we can't."

"I refuse to believe that," Krona said.

"Then maybe we *shouldn't*," Hintosep amended. "Instead, we should prepare for what comes next."

Krona took a step away. "What comes next will have to wait. I'm not letting a varger hoard run amok in Arkensyre. You promised to tell me everything. I need that now. I need to know what happened to these not-gods, and how we might convince them to lend us their strength."

"Each holds a key to another's heart," she said, remembering the heady devotion that had led each of them to agree to the tithing for their own reasons. "They were a circle of trust once, each holding out a hand to the next."

"But?"

"But that trust was betrayed. They had disagreements, made threats, and hurt one another, often without meaning to—like any family. But that hurt warped the circle. Made it brittle."

Like any family—Krona's gaze turned inward when she said it, no doubt recounting the tragedy of her own family, perhaps even Charbon's family. When her eyes cleared again, there wasn't just a desire to know shining behind them, but a desire to understand. To face the hidden history of the gods and the Valley with a focus not on the epic, but on the keen tragedy of commonplace pains—monumental all the more for *being* commonplace—that had driven them here. "Tell me everything."

43

KRONA

Reality molded and unmolded itself as Hintosep spoke; her story played with it like Krona had learned to play with time—warping and twisting. The history of Arkensyre was a stage play, the Valley the theater, the people the unwitting performers and mindlessly clapping audience all in one. The man behind the curtain had soaked in the applause, pulling his levers and directing the scenes with gusto, with Hintosep his stage manager, the holy scrolls the playbill.

The remnants of a dead civilization rotted outside, but the show went on.

Somewhere in the middle of her tale, Thibaut had sat himself down on a partially rotten log, sending centipedes and beetles scurrying for safety. One of his fen's tentacles lay itself over his chest, clutching him tight in comfort.

"Even as he died, I'm sure it satisfied him," Hintosep said, tone bitter like her tongue itself was made of salt. "That it all lasted so long. He truly thought of himself as a savior. In a twisted way, he was. There were many peaceful sunrises. Many bellies filled. Many minds at ease."

"With just enough stratification and inequality to keep us poised at each other's throats," Krona bit out.

"To keep you occupied. Tigers fighting in captivity have no time to contemplate the intricacies of the cage." She shook her head, grimaced. "His walls made me forget, his lies persuaded me, but my actions were my own. Absolon did not create this alone. There is someone out there who likely wishes to plunge a rusty blade into my back in turn—for sealing away memories, killing their loved ones, sculpting their reality." Krona did not deny it, and Hintosep was not fishing for reassurances. "Lutador's Grand Marquis is first in line, I'm sure." Hintosep nodded curtly—she seemed very far away, from her own mind, her own body. "In the end, I may let him."

From the camp there came Adhar's distinct bark of command. His unit was ready to gather their supplies and place themselves on a new front line—between the people and the expanding hoard. A futile task if even Knowledge couldn't devise a way to capture them for good.

Krona hardened her jaw. "You have work to do before then," she said to Hintosep instead of reaching for dissuasive platitudes. "Wrongs you have to right."

Knowledge's temple held even more wonder for Krona now, knowing all that she did about its delicate occupant. A healer, like Melanie. A gentle soul, like Sebastian. Someone to look up to . . .

. . . like De-Lia.

Someone who'd refused to help before, though. Someone rooted and still and tired. Someone who may remain immovable.

If Knowledge refused to rise from feir throne, Krona didn't know what she would do. She had no second plan, no other place to turn.

She jumped the three of them in behind the waterfall—the spray of it somehow catching her off guard, making her blink and suck in a sharp breath as the water flicked against her cheek like little fingers demanding she be alert.

Hintosep unwove the cryptopathy hiding the grotto with firm twists of her wrists, pulling down invisible curtains. They ducked beneath the bone chimes, and entered the cavern with clear eyes. The shallow puddles greeted her just as before, and the occasional sharp drip of water from a stalactite echoed across the cave. It was beautiful, and quiet compared to the hum of insects and caw of birds outside.

A lovely haven from which to ignore the world.

Urgency begged them not to dawdle, and their boots splashed quickly through the water, kicking the humid scent of damp growth into the air.

Thibaut's still-exposed fen began to radiate with the same pulsing light as the glowworms, and his eyes sparkled with understanding. He reached out, as though running his fingers through something ethereal in the air or sensing the welcoming heat from a warm hearth. He rolled the invisible information over the backs of his knuckles and nuzzled against it with his cheek as though there were threads and threads of it—spider silk–thin wisps of knowledge.

His strides grew long and confident as they approached the house, while Hintosep's faltered. When they drew up to the landing she stopped altogether, trailing her fingertips down one of the porch's wooden posts.

"What is it?" Krona asked.

"I designed this temple myself," Hintosep answered, tone distant and sentimental, "and I think . . . I think I based it on a place I knew but had forgotten."

"Where's that?"

"My childhood home," she said, reaching for the front door. "Just one of many things Absolon tried to hide from me but could not erase entirely."

The door whined on its hinges, swinging open at Hintosep's light touch, and she peered inside. "The wallpaper," she whispered. "The kitchen, the dining room. My mother used to . . ." Her voice caught in her throat and she pursed her lips to keep the words down rather than encourage them out. Redness suddenly rimmed her eyes as they turned glassy, but she fought back any tears with a determination.

Krona dipped her head in empathy, touched Hintosep's wrist gently. "Yes," Hintosep said with a forced smile. "Even I had a mother once. A babbi, too."

The Unknown had been only human as well. With a family. With a daughter.

It was all just . . . people. The horror and the pride and the greatness. No gods, no monsters. Just people.

Hintosep pulled her shoulders back, swiping her palms over each other to bring herself back to center. There was magic to be worked.

She went to the staircase, gripped the banister, brushing away the deceptive shape of it like brushing away so much dust, revealing a salt-and-metal pillar, an enchantment, with many dials and knobs that she twisted and rearranged. It was another sort of puzzle box, its secret formations mirrored in the way the house changed itself to keep its secrets. In the way the doors became walls and floors became emptiness and up became down.

A satisfying hiss left the enchantment when she finished, and she slid her fingers up the nearest wooden balusters like they were the strings of a particularly stiff harp.

"If you've been to Glensen's side, you should be able to jump us straight to fem now," she said. "With the illusions dispelled, the house is just a house."

It didn't feel like *just a house* to Krona. With the way Thibaut's eyes trailed up and up the spiral of the stairs, she could tell he sensed it, too. There was breath here. Life. Maybe it came from the tree—but she'd never known a tree to expand and contract with the filling of lungs, or to thump strangely as though it possessed a heart.

"Hold tight to me," she commanded, shutting her eyes—wondering if she was simply imagining that distant thumping. Maybe it was the blood rushing in her own ears. She reached out with her kairopathy, feeling the space and the time it would take to traverse, sensing the solidness of the levels and the certainty of the floor.

She could do it this time. She could make the jump.

Still, she braced herself, counting down silently when they each clung firmly to her shoulders.

Three . . . two . . . one.

Dust billowed up from their shoes, making faint little clouds even as much of it clung to the dampness of their soles.

The attic was as Krona had left it: quiet, dark, still. Knowledge still sat hunched on feir throne, shoulders moving lightly with every papery flutter of breath.

Thibaut reached out to play with another invisible string and this one caught, tugged, lit up like a solid tether before Krona's eyes. It ran from Thibaut's grasp to Knowledge's wrist, whose head tilted as though they'd caught the call of a distant horn.

"There they are," fey rasped. "And I wake to find I must dream again."

The thread pulled taut, began to shrink. Thibaut tried to drop it but it stuck to him like webbing, urging him forward, nearly off his feet.

Krona reached for him, but he gave her a placating "It's okay," before following the pull, the tightness of his jaw the only indication he wasn't fully convinced it was, indeed, okay. She followed him cautiously.

"Let me look at you," fey said, drawing Thibaut before fem. "Let me understand you."

Thibaut's fen wriggled, its legs and tentacles radiating outward to frame him in a spectral halo—the light from the stained-glass window making him shine. "Why don't we try to understand each other, hmm?" he offered, getting down on one knee, covering Knowledge's wizened hand with his.

Thibaut knew Krona had thought to take point in this plea for help. Hintosep had likely thought the same. But playing ambassador to a wretched and regal ancient was well within Thibaut's wheelhouse, even if he'd never tried to charm the likes of anyone quite so regal, quite so wretched, or quite so ancient.

Besides, they were of a pair.

Thibaut wondered how long it had been since Knowledge—Glensen, *Glensen*, fey insisted inside his head—had encountered another Teliopath. The eagerness with which fey stroked through his magic with feir own spoke to a long loneliness. Fey mentally embraced him as though he were an old friend, instantly worthy of trust and intimacy—though not the kinds of intimacy Thibaut usually thought of first. There was an eagerness to know and be known—to be deeply *understood*, just as fey'd said.

Glensen was a quiet sort of social—very much the inverse of Thibaut's chatty boisterousness. Fey were someone who needed people—to simply be near them. To be wrapped in the warmth of humanity and shared experience. The other minds had been dormant in their salt crystals, but not Glensen's. It had slowly absorbed information for centuries, the teliopathy innately reaching for what it could. While Mindless, feir body had sought the closest living thing, the tree, communing instinctively with the wood, looking for whatever social connection it could.

It had been a subliminal torture—the severing, the isolation. And waking after, to a bombardment of newness flooding in from all directions, had been too overwhelming.

Thibaut let Glensen feed that torrent of newness to him so he could understand just how different the Valley was since the last time fey'd been awake.

Absolon had, in the early days, wielded Glensen's body as a tool with which to imbue certain knowledge into the populace—a way to teach them en masse how to handle living in his falsified timeline, at a technology level so rudimentary compared to before the bombs, and seemingly so advanced after.

But that had been many centuries ago, and Glensen had been left to become part of feir own temple, bleeding into the wood just as the wood bled into fem.

And the tree—oh how Glensen loved the tree. To be a tree. To grow and bend and breathe and *be*.

Glensen searched Thibaut's mind for what he knew of the tithing, shuddering when feir mind ran up against the word *gods*. Fey shared many of the things Hintosep had told them, but from a firsthand perspective. He saw the friendship and the fractures, the failures and triumphs.

And then he felt the questions, and it was his turn to share. Knowing the world was different wasn't the same as understanding those differences, and though Thibaut had never fancied himself much of a teacher, he guided Glensen through his own memories and experiences in explanation, lingering urgently on the varger and the fenri.

His still-unnamed fen preened as Thibaut cataloged its features, and gave a happy purr—if a tentacled bug creature could purr—when he shared the memory of Ninebark's first appearance, when she had saved him from certain death.

It recoiled when he unfurled the layout of the varger hoard, laying it out like a gruesome offering in his mind. He shared the few times he'd witnessed varger up close—the times he'd seen them maim and *eat*. He shared his own hunt—the way he'd stalked his varg and been stalked in return, and his fen whimpered, recalling its time as a quilled mass of pain and hunger.

They cannot be destroyed, he emphasized to Glensen when fey reassured him fey could read direct thoughts. *Only contained—ideally, converted and rejoined. And right now, with so many, we don't know how to stop them.*

We need someone far wiser than our own sort to help us muddle through. We need you.

Thibaut's hand had only been on Knowledge's for a moment, and yet Krona could feel with her magic that his sense of time had been distorted. An unnatural amount of information had passed between them in an instant, their shared teliopathy smoothing the way.

Wanting to give them space, she kept to the edge of the attic, drawing parallel with the throne in time to catch Knowledge's sleepy eyes turn sharp and feir lined lips give way to a cracked smile. "You are a quick study," fey said aloud to Thibaut, the air around their joined hands shimmering. "And a charming one," fey added.

"I find it usually helps to be complimentary, rather than demanding, when need is dire," he said.

"And your need is very dire," fey agreed. Feir throne groaned as fey shifted upon it. "Come, all four of you, before me."

Both Hintosep and Krona extricated themselves from the shadows. "There are only three of us," Hintosep pointed out.

"Ah, Toe," Knowledge chuckled lightly. "I could have very well said the six of you, what with the number of split beings I have in my presence. The boy is two, and yet the girl is three."

It had been a long while since anyone had deigned to refer to Krona as a mere girl, but it was endearing coming from one so obviously old. "This is De-Lia," she said, holding out her transformed arm for feir approval.

"Your sister."

"What's left of her."

"Ah, and yet, there is more." Fey shook feir head as though to clear it. "A rumination for another time. Snapping jaws and noxious vapors. A world on the brink now that certain machinations are gone, gone." Fey stared openly at Hintosep. "I can read it all on your face." Feir tone was warm. "In the lines around your eyes, in the crease of your lips, and the ink of your tattoos. You did what had to be done. But what to do now? What to do . . . A great burden. He used us to build, and we must build again. You cannot alone, your people. You need magic. So much magic. That, he fed us. That, we can use.

"I need my tithing. You must bring my tithing to the churning place."

"You sent us to them before," Krona protested. "They were barely any help. You can't dismiss us again—"

Fey shook feir head. "No dismissal. I needed to think, and I have been thinking. Churning field, churning bodies. It will take us all. We must come together, as we failed to do before. I will show you."

The old one rolled feir shoulders, trying to sit up straight, spine popping like warped wood as fey battled for inches of uprightness. Thibaut skittered backward as fey wrenched feir hand out from under his, the bones rolling under feir paper-thin skin as fey yanked and snapped feir finger-roots from their nesting.

"Hold on," fey instructed before using those splinter-like fingers to give a sharp whistle, as though summoning a pet to feir side. "Awake!" fey called. "Time for you to get up."

The whole house gave an ominous creak. A great, strained sound that shuddered through the rafters and down through the studs. Outside, the cave rumbled.

The floor tilted, sending Krona off-balance and a sharp zing of surprise through her chest. She and Hintosep lowered themselves next to Thibaut.

Oh gods, was the house finally coming down?

The floor bucked upward.

Everything lurched.

It lurched to the left.

It lurched to the right.

It lurched forward.

Left, right, left, right.

Forward, forward, forward.

Krona scrambled to her feet and went to the window, pushing at the pane until it swung open.

The house wasn't falling.

It was *walking*.

Below, two sets of thick roots chicken-stepped across the cavern shallows.

"Wood learns," Knowledge said. "Wood remembers."

Krona steadied herself against the window frame, bracing herself inside it with the tips of her bone wings so that each staggered step wouldn't jostle her right out of the attic. "What are you doing?" she demanded.

"Bringing your hoard a vessel," fey said, voice like the creaking of branches in a high wind.

"This house can't contain them," Krona yelled, once again maddened by the decision of a would-be god. "It's barely keeping itself together."

"Not the house alone; not in this state."

The treehouse crossed the cavern in a handful of strides, then bent low to leave the grotto. A great deluge poured over the roof and siding—seeping through the many cracks in the house—as it slid beneath the waterfall and out into the fading light of the setting sun.

Crashing through the jungle, the house forged its own path across the ridges and clearings. The rickety thing took great, bounding strides, angering birds and scattering other wildlife. Wind whipped through the lone window, fluttering hair and clothing alike.

The initial lurching became a roll, a steady back-and-forth, rise and fall. Night would be upon them soon, and it would be so much more difficult for the soldiers to combat varger in the dark.

If not for the direness of the hoard breaking free, Krona might have reveled in the trek. Arkensyre was beautiful from this lumbering vantage, stories high. While still deep in the jungle, there were only vague signs of war, and it was easy to imagine the curls of dark smoke in the distance to be the result of nothing more than bonfires welcoming the freshness of spring. Where the air was clear and crisp she could see for miles—the roll of the land, its abrupt ridges and natural swoop up into mountains was breathtaking.

To think, all this had been forged through the efforts of the unwilling. A scar in the ground converted to such lushness, the grotesqueness of its creation covered over in pretty wrappings, like flowers bursting from a Winsrouen field, feeding on tilled bodies, disguising the rot.

Krona could not bear to lose the beauty, but could not abide the abuse.

Concentrating, Krona reached out with her kairopathy to see if she could create a lens large enough to jump the house to the moment-minefield, stopped when she felt Thibaut's hand on her shoulder. "It's too big," he said knowingly. "And Glensen needs you elsewhere."

"I need my tithing," fey croaked out. "I can show you where to seek them."

"And what if they won't come?" Krona asked.

"They will. They may just need reminding of who they truly are."

44

KRONA

With one last look out at the expanse of Asgar-Skan, Krona turned her back on the foliage falling to the treehouse's long strides and carefully picked her way across the shifting slats to Knowledge's side. Fey stretched out one hand to receive her, feir splinter-tipped fingers unnaturally long and stiff.

"I feel them as I always have," fey said with a sigh, closing feir eyes to concentrate. "You'll find them among trees and death. You've been there before."

Knowledge granted her a sense of their tethering—a clear, pinpointing pull south.

"Go quickly. I will reach the surge by sunrise. I will need them. We will need each other."

Lens made, Krona reached for both Hintosep and Thibaut, but he did not rise from his place at Knowledge's feet. "I'm going to stay. Fey shouldn't have to go it alone."

She took in his brave little smile—meant to be both pleading and reassuring—and couldn't help but rake her eyes down his clothed spine, superimposing his ragged skin and bared muscle from just hours earlier. "I just got you back," she said.

"And you know exactly where to find me," he replied. "I'll be all right. I've got one supposed-god locked in place. I'll leave the other three to you."

She knelt down briefly to give him a heady kiss, then dropped one more on the crown of his head before taking Hintosep by the arm and stepping halfway across the Valley.

The Necropalacia instantly loomed before them.

The wide maw of the overhang at the top of the city's steps was as equal parts awe-inspiring and foreboding as it had been when Krona had been whisked here by Time. Above, the stars had just begun to glitter in the still desert sky.

"Why would they come back here?" Krona asked, pausing for a breath before mounting the giant steps.

"It's quiet. Private," Hintosep suggested. "There are few places that offer such peace."

The pair stepped lightly, unsure what might have changed since the army of mummies had swarmed the Eze's throne room.

All was still silent in the city. The trees that had been people still grew as if they'd spent their entire lives on their chosen spots, roots holding fast, digging deep between the baked bricks and cracked tiles. Oil lamps had been automatically lit throughout the city, their clockwork mechanisms in tune with their duty and oblivious to the transformation of the residents.

Krona checked every doorway, every window, every side street, ears perked for indications of activity, godlike or otherwise.

Hintosep, usually so focused, wandered as if distracted, trailing Krona like a lost pup instead of the woman who'd rid the world of Absolon—the Thalo—the man who thought himself their creator-deity. Eventually, she broke the silence with a whisper. "You told the soldiers that we all want the same things. Our loved ones safe, our homes safe. Is that true? Is that all you want?"

Krona paused in her advance, raising an eyebrow in question.

"Your sister is gone," Hintosep continued, running her hand down an intricate mural painted on the side of a sandy-stoned house. "Your city rejected you. People all over Arkensyre call you *demon* and think you're a bad omen. I know you feel responsible for the hoard, want to see an end to the war, but what then? You don't want power, that's not what drives you. You don't want praise. I don't even think you're concerned with clearing your name in Lutador and making sure the people know you didn't kill the Grand Marquis. What does *safe* mean—what is it, besides a motivating platitude? What *more* do you want?"

It was a question she'd avoided asking herself ever since Sebastian had plunged a needle through the mask and seemingly failed. What then? What *now*?

When De-Lia was alive, she'd wanted nothing more than to match her sister in *something*. In leadership, in confidence, in their maman's eyes.

When De-Lia had died, she wanted recompense. She wanted revenge on the Thalo who'd taken her mind and twisted her to do Gatwood's bidding. That had led to a spiral into conspiracy, into a belief that De-Lia could come back—a belief the very woman at her side had fueled for her own long-awaited revenge.

Now De-Lia was reborn at Krona's side, but it wasn't *right*. She knew the echo was in pain—not like a varg was pained, but the dull ache of the unsettled. She'd thought to ask the gods to bring her back, but they could not. They were just people. Powerful people, but with no more command over the spark of life than anyone else.

Now she wanted De-Lia to be at peace. Whatever that meant.

She wanted them *all* to be at peace.

She wanted to hear Juliet sing with abandon. To see Tray and Mandip spar simply for the fun of it. To know that Sebastian and Melanie could expand their family without worry if they wanted.

She wanted Avellino to have the last of his adolescence to do with as he pleased, and Abby to grow up into someone who could don the name Absolon with pride, claiming it as zhur own, casting off the associations of anything that had come before.

She wanted to give the full force of her attention to Thibaut without the specter of the next threat clouding her mind. To be with him as he tinkered with his clockworks, she herself plucking at some string instrument inexpertly, just for the joy of basking in each other's presence.

If the Valley was doomed for collapse, as Hintosep predicted, then perhaps none of it could ever come to pass.

Still, it was what she wanted.

"I meant what I said. It wasn't a platitude. I want them to be okay. My friends, my family. I want us all to be all right. I've had other ambitions before, but now . . ."

"That is an awfully simple desire for the Demon of the Passes."

Krona shrugged, made no comment as she moved forward. It wasn't simple at all. Mundane, perhaps. Ordinary. But a struggle to bring to fruition; they did not live in a world of quiet, of resting, of peace.

"I ask," Hintosep went on, "because I no longer know what *I* want. I don't know what keeping people safe means to me anymore."

Krona understood. For so long, Hintosep had protected secrets in the name of safety, and nearly everything she'd devoted herself to had made people—those she loved—*less* safe.

"Then perhaps what you want," Krona suggested, "is to find out." Soft moans interspersed with harsh cracking and whimpering tickled Krona's ears, distant. Emanating from the direction of the throne room. "And I can think of a few people who might need to relearn right alongside you."

They stopped their careful, investigative inching in favor of a near sprint toward the Eze's seat of power. This time, Krona stepped over the threshold without hesitation; a sin, once committed, felt like no sin the second time.

Instead of haphazard piles of bodies and mummified limbs, she was surprised to find all the ezes of the past seated once more. They were jumbled and out of place, their postures less like kings and more like rag dolls set as best as a child could set them, but the intent of respect was evident.

The bits that had been powdered were now swept to the side in small drifts, the center floor and its water troughs cleared and clean. Mostly.

The blood remained.

Absolon's body remained.

A lone fly buzzed around the corpse's head.

In the back center of the hall, set before the throne where the tree that was the current eze grew, a long stone bench—hip-high for a being of twelve feet—had been created out of the floor itself, patterned just as the tiles, molded up out of it as though the clay had been fired on the spot.

Before it stood Nature, wings folded neatly at his back, only instead of brown like in the depictions they were golden. Just like his hair. Atop the bench sat Emotion, zhur face now human, mostly, save for zhur left eye that still burst outward with purple crystal. The plantlike cascade of hair remained, and while one hand had been returned to a deep golden brown, the other was still purple-tipped. The beautiful curves of zhur bare torso melted into a deeply runed belly, unnervingly pale violet.

Emotion hissed with every prod of Nature's hands, clenching zhur teeth, clearly trying not to complain. Zhe faced Absolon's corpse, focusing in on the sight of him—bent and dead and ruined—as if it gave zhim the strength to endure Nature's work.

The approaching footsteps did not go unnoticed.

Emotion's human eye caught them first. Krona refused to let herself be pinned by that gaze as she would have only days ago.

When Nature turned, it was with protectiveness flaring out of every joint in his body, his wings spreading to block Emotion from view. "Stay back," he ordered, in a voice much less grand than Krona had expected.

Those strong wings and determined stance faltered, his face opening in recognition a moment later.

"Hintosep?"

Beside Krona, Hintosep sagged, then surged, crossing the rest of the distance as quickly as she could. She'd been quiet and near stunned in Knowledge's presence, but the sight of Nature struck something in her. The woman who was ageless in Krona's eyes melted into someone young—a girl from centuries ago. With each step she took toward Nature she shed decades, until she threw her arms around his middle and was for an instant a child who'd finally found her way home.

She looked it, too, what with him towering over her.

Nature patted her white hair in disbelief, unable to understand in the moment how she could be here. He stroked the left side of her face, where the skin was knotted and sagged, and she nodded to him lightly when he raised an eyebrow in question. He settled a giant palm over the scars, and a moment later the muscles and flesh were full and flush. "How—" he began.

She didn't let him dwell on it. "Later. Why haven't you finished?" she asked, voice heavy with a familiar firmness, her stance taking on the same, which eased a knot in Krona's chest.

"Absolon cut runes into zhim," he said, waving at Emotion in illustration. "Molding anything with physiopathy is about understanding the underlying structure. He . . . obfuscated it."

Emotion dropped a hand to Hintosep's head in greeting as well, and made no attempt to hide the venom zhe harbored. "I've been the bastard's favorite guinea pig. He was trying to figure out how to make himself impervious to transformation—to Zoshim—in case he ever slipped his chains." Zhe spat in Absolon's direction. "All the good it did you, Lonny!"

Krona stayed back, held herself at a distance, on the peripheral, allowing the reunion to breathe even though her palms itched to force them all into action, to race to the minefield.

Despite that, it was Nature who beckoned her over with a curled finger.

Feeling like a child called to speak before the class, she approached.

"You freed me."

"I did."

He'd been will-less at the time, but unlike Emotion or Knowledge at their freeing, he'd been awake, seen and felt everything that led up to that moment. He cautiously reached out for her De-Lia arm, and the arm moved to meet him, the echo resting its malformed head in his upturned palm.

The echo closed its eyes, content, nuzzling into his warmth like an affectionate pet. In turn, something shifted in Nature.

He *blossomed*.

His pupils dilated, his face aglow. A pleased shiver ruffled his feathers, and a literal bed of flowers flourished beneath the echo's head, sprouting up from his skin like a gift.

"Oh," he sighed, barely above a whisper, like he'd had a revelation. "*There you are*."

A corresponding wave of happiness fluttered up the echo arm into Krona's chest, unnerving and unexpected. She stepped away, and Nature's face fell, though he didn't try to explain or reach for her again.

Krona cradled the arm to her chest, an awkward and unrooted sense of *jealousy* hitting her from out of nowhere. Not the jealousy of a covetous lover, but the sort of envy she used to feel toward De-Lia when her older sister had drawn their maman's praises and she had not. Only now, she felt it toward Nature, absurdly resenting the comfort he'd given De-Lia's echo, when residing in Krona's flesh and blood seemed to be nothing but painful.

She *wanted* the echo to be at peace, and chided herself for the selfishness of wanting to be the one to deliver the respite.

But the moment passed, and the Valley's newest need was at hand. "The varger," she reminded Hintosep. "Knowledge."

"Glensen," Hintosep agreed before looking up at Nature. "Glensen sent us."

Convincing them to help was an easier task than Krona had expected. They trusted Hintosep in a way, even now, Krona could not—as though she was a person wholly without guile, who'd never said a false word in their presence. They listened with earnestness, agreed with an earnestness, even at their own expense.

"I'll be fine," Emotion insisted. "I have my voice back, my mind, my magic. The rest of my body can follow later."

"Then, before we leave—" Nature went to the tree growing over the throne, its roots flowing like a wooden waterfall over the dips and rises of the seat. He took two branches as if they were hands, and in the next moment they were. The Eze's form rapidly returned to zhim, dark bark softening back into dark skin. Zhe drew a deep breath when given lungs and a mouth and nose, and blinked as though just awakening when there were once again lids to flutter.

Until she saw it, Krona had doubted that such a thorough transformation could be reversed. She'd thought the Eze and the people of Xyopar as good as dead.

"If it still lives, it still lives," Nature said plainly as they swept back through the city, his hands transforming trees back into human beings at every turn. "The dead cannot stay, and if it was never alive it cannot be, not really. But a tree and a bird, a mouse and a fox—life is life is life."

What was an echo, then? A varg?

Life? Not life?

Both?

She ran her fingers over the bone cage around De-Lia.

By the time they'd reached the massive staircase leading up into the city, the Necropalacia was buzzing with voices.

The people were people again. The dead had their caretakers once more.

"What of Time?" Krona said as they stepped out of the city's overhang. The chill of the desert night hit her full force, and she tried to shrug it off like an unwelcomed hand.

"Yes, where is Hailwic?" Hintosep asked.

"She's there," Nature said, pointing up into the dark sky. After a moment, a black silhouette blotted out star after star, swooping over the city, keeping its distance.

Emotion muttered something and Nature gave zhim a disappointed frown. "Punabi didn't want her near while we worked."

"You still haven't forgiven her?" Hintosep asked.

Zhe crossed zhur arms. "I'm not sure *she's* forgiven *me*. Ask *Zoshim* if he's forgiven Glensen for leaving him behind."

"Of course I have," he answered, too quickly.

"You haven't asked about fem once," Emotion noted.

"I do not wish to rehash old slights," he said. "Not now."

"Then when?" Emotion grumbled.

Krona watched the silhouette come close and perch itself atop the city overhang, just outside the reach of the lamplight. Unseen eyes bore down on them, and the crawl of Time's gaze made Krona shiver harder than the chill had. Nevertheless, she called out, "Knowl—I mean, Glensen—Glensen has asked for you. Your temple where we found you, it's—"

As silently as Time had landed, her departure was equally as noisy. A tight scoff and a ruffle of many feathers retreated swiftly into the night.

The sudden rebuff was more disappointing to Krona than surprising. "I should go to her," she said.

"It won't do any good," Nature countered, shaking his head. "She's already decided this world has nothing to do with her. Not now that she's free." He held out his hand for Krona. "Take us to Glensen. If curiosity gets the best of her, she will follow."

45

HAILWIC

In a Time and Place Before

The remnants of Zoshim's physiopathy coiled through Hailwic's bones, warm and welcome. He'd fixed her wings years ago, but today he'd grown her entire body larger, made her tower so that she could push an ox plow all on her own, tilling up the soil.

The rice patties were growing well, and it was time to see if they had suitable land for wheat grains. Around her, more experienced farmers examined the seeds, and a Physiopath tested the drainage of the soil. She'd been reassured a dozen times this was a good plot of land for a test crop, but everyone still checked and double-checked its viability, unwilling to make a single mistake and lose one seed if they could prevent it.

A sudden discordant twang thrummed in her insides—like a piano string snapping.

She slumped atop the ox plow, gasping, her knees burrowing sharply into the dirt as she half collapsed. A great, gaping *absence* opened inside her—a hollow through which a thin string had previously been threaded now was nothing but a tight, painful gouge. The tether that had been there was simply gone.

The tether that connected her to one of the tithing had dissolved.

Someone was *dead.*

Panic flashed hot and cold through her body as she clutched at her chest, wrapping her mind around the rest of the strings, following each of them to their ends, desperate to sense who was missing.

Kinwold. She couldn't trace Kinwold.

Stumbling away as though drunk, she forgot about the plow. She forgot about the farmers and the field. A small, human-sized hand fell on her giant side and she waved whoever it was off, unable to speak.

She could trace the other lines easily still—they were all exactly where they were supposed to be, miles apart, busy at their own tasks. They must have felt it just as she did—blindsided, unmoored.

Where had she last sensed Kinwold? She tried to think, to recall if she'd been told where they'd be today.

She had to find them. She had to see. The loss of the string was so raw, and still she didn't want to believe the feeling until she could *see.*

Without an explanation, she took off into the sky, fumbling, her flight unsteady as she scanned the ground through tears in her eyes.

She searched for long hours, felt the others circling closer to one another, no doubt drawn together by the loss, just as scared as she was. She half expected Zoshim to join her in the search, but the sky remained clear.

Far afield, in the jungle, she saw them. A body. Limp and faceless but undeniably Kinwold.

She dropped from the air, legs unable to keep her upright once she touched the ground, making her fall forward on her hands, forcing her to crawl forward to Kinwold's corpse. She framed the gape of their skull with straining fingers, unable to touch, unable to pull away. Revolted and terrified, a shuddering sob worked its way up the whole length of her body.

She didn't know what to do, couldn't place how such a thing could have happened, or why they were here and all alone—

A twig snapping had her coiling, half to protect the body, half to protect herself. She gazed across the small clearing—only vaguely noting it was a garden—to see Hintosep sitting there with her back against a thick tree trunk, knees up, hands draped casually atop them as she purposefully snapped pieces off a thin, fallen branch.

"H-Hintosep?" Haiwlic sobbed.

Her face was disturbingly blank. "What's happening, Hailwic?" she asked as though from far away, through a fog. Casual, yet lost. Not sad, not broken, not grieving, just distant.

A bluster of wind brought Zoshim down from the sky. He landed far more gracefully than she had. With him was Absolon, carried in his overlarge arms.

Hailwic stumbled upward, running to them as Zoshim set Absolon down on his feet. She expected to see her shock and confusion mirrored, yet was met with more cold stares. More empty distance, like Hintosep's.

Except, as she grasped at Zoshim's open arms, she realized his distance was different. His eyes were empty. Devoid of anything like real sight. Like Kinwold's death hadn't left him *feeling* hollow, he *was* hollow.

"What's happening?" she asked, echoing Hintosep, but with much more fervor. "How could . . . how could Kinwold . . ." She turned imploringly to Absolon, holding out a trusting hand, though she recoiled as soon as their gazes met.

He wasn't hollow.

There was glee there.

It was a hard, forced look. Like he was *willing* himself to feel it. Like he'd slipped the countenance of satisfaction over a naked pain that matched hers.

It turned her stomach, heightened her confusion.

Suddenly, Zoshim's welcoming embrace turned crushing, though his expression did not change. His physiopathy coiled around her in a way it never had before—demanding and immobilizing. Uncaring, in a way he never was.

She couldn't resist. She was as weak to his physiopathy as Absolon was to her kairopathy.

Just as the thought struck her, Absolon spoke. "You had to be last," he said. "I wasn't sure I'd catch you so quickly, but Zoshim's always made fine bait, hasn't he?"

The blood drained from Hailwic's face.

She couldn't understand what was happening, only that Absolon had done it—killed Kinwold, puppeted Zoshim, put Hintosep in her daze. She tried to demand *why*, and found her lips would not move as he exerted unnatural control over her body.

We trusted you, she shouted in her mind. *I trusted you. I believed in you, we both wanted the same things, we knew what had to be done—*

Zoshim pushed her to her knees, keeping her there so she and Absolon were more of a height.

"No," Absolon snapped at her. "Even before the bombs, you were patronizing. And no matter what you say, none of you have trusted me, even after I took her out. I went along with all of your half-assed schemes and poorly executed plans, knowing the entire time that I had the right of it and I could do it, and all of you did nothing but stymie our chances of success at every turn! So no more discussions. No more diplomacy. No more waiting for you all to come around to my way. I'm taking control, and doing what is needed *now*."

She glared at him, stuck behind her physiopathic gag. *How?* she thought at him. *What's wrong with Zoshim?*

"Nothing," Absolon said. "I've just separated him out a bit. His body is here, under my control, and his mind is . . . elsewhere.

"We are a perfect circle, aren't we?" he went on. "Even though zhe's wary of me, Punabi was so easy to ensnare, given zhur vulnerability to cryptopathy. I've never actually tested my bounds with an Emotiopath on purpose before. It wasn't difficult at all, to pull zhur mind out. Don't worry"—he held up a staying hand—"zhe's fine. Kinwold . . . Kinwold was a mistake. Once I had Punabi the dominos all fell, just as expected. Punabi gave me Glensen, Glensen gave me Zoshim, and now I have you. Honestly, I thought it would take days to get to you all. Weeks if one of you figured it out. If I'd known you would all fall to me in *hours* . . . well."

He spoke cleanly, with no remorse, though a small tremor at the corner of his lips revealed just how unsure he really was.

As if to cover up his quaking, he pulled his pillbox from his pocket, dumping out and swallowing a fistful of cryptobeads. "I don't want to hurt you, Hailwic," he reassured her, lifting his hands to hover around her face, just as hers had hovered over Kinwold's. "I never wanted to hurt any of you. Saving what's left demands sacrifice, and I wish we'd all been able to agree.

"Now, don't struggle, don't resist. Or your face will cave in, just like Kinwold's."

She raged at him internally, screaming obscenities at him. They'd all given him their trust, they'd all tried to mend the cracks in their tithing, in their understanding of one another, and *this* was the result.

She wished she'd stayed away. Wished she'd rejected Hintosep's invitation to the valley. Wished she'd kept her hard, bitter shell, wished she'd trusted her jaded gut and yelled in Kinwold's face when they'd asked them all to work together again.

Trust only led to entrapment. Comradery was for fools.

46

KRONA

Asgar-Skanian nights were always far more humid than those in Xyopar, but the stickiness that hit Krona's skin as she landed the four of them atop the stone outcropping that served as the mine's entrance was disturbingly different. She could smell blood on the wind, taste it in the air. The hot, wet mist that dampened her face contained as much viscera as it did rainwater.

She wished she could be thankful for the night, wished it hid the sight—if not the stench—of all the rotting forms (varger and corpses alike) so close. The loss of the sun simply meant the glow of the freed bottle-barkers shone all the brighter. Ethereal varger swirled at the base of the outcrop, leaching up from the crack in the plinth. Across the field, the misty creatures that had yet to find a suitable meal snaked in long, winding rivers around the heavy, clawed paws of their luckier brethren.

The creatures had spread well beyond the trenches, a plague rolling out across the land. The bodies they'd left in their wake lay twisted and mangled—some with arms reaching at unnatural angles, some with rib cages blown out from within, others missing heads or whole spines.

Krona openly balked, gagging and quaking the moment they touched down. No matter the number of varger she'd exposed herself to over these past years, nothing could quell the paralyzing knot of phobia that threatened to lay her out cold on the spot.

Hintosep put a hand on her shoulder, squeezed.

It was enough to keep her upright.

"Look," Hintosep whispered delicately in her ear, pointing out beyond the mass of monsters into the farmland and the foothills and the budding tree lines.

Fires. Bonfires. Not like those of villages set on fire. More like those that signaled for aid, only these were strung out in clear lines, creating a long border.

She hoped those were Tray's fires. And Adhar's and Mandip's and Juliet's and all the others'. She hoped those were the fires of quintbarrel wielders amassing, of Arkensynians from all over the Valley coming together to protect it.

But there was no sign of Knowledge or feir treehouse.

From out of the green-tinged blackness to her right, a heavy mass suddenly barreled through the air, falling at them as if from nowhere.

Krona automatically pushed Hintosep behind her and threw her kairopathy out like a shield, halting the mass midair, catching it in an abrupt pause.

Teeth. So many teeth, bared and ready to rip into them if she hadn't caught the jumper out of pure instinct.

Trembling, sweating, she held the varg there, now unsure. Beside her, Emotion and Nature inched closer to the creature, both seemingly fascinated. Krona swallowed harshly, panting like a dog. "They can't be killed," she reiterated. "Only contained."

"What about transformed?" Nature asked, reaching out, trying to curl his magic around the jumper.

Nothing happened.

With a mighty effort, Krona flung the jumper as far as she could, speeding it away, praying it wouldn't attack them again.

"Perhaps your kairopathy was interfering," Nature said, though his tone was clearly skeptical, and he struck out instead at a wisp of a varg seeping through the crack below. It bucked in his grip, then wormed its way back out again. It wasn't a physical thing, and therefore immune to his methods.

Undeterred, he flung himself from the rock into the air, soaring farther afield to try with a fully fledged varg, finding he could twist it around, buckling its legs and making its quills rattle and shatter, but change nothing.

He tried with another, and another, his expression becoming harder and harder, his face pinching and reddening, sweat glistening off his bare torso as he struggled to do what he clearly thought should have been *easy*.

He returned to the rock with a heavy landing, pinching up the ground nearby, turning it into another pillared outcropping just like the one on which they stood, as if just to be sure it wasn't his own skills that had faltered.

"When you morph the body, you don't change the soul," Emotion said. "These are beyond you."

"And what about you?" he asked, wiping his brow, chest heaving.

Zhe cocked zhur head, shrugged. "They're angry, aren't they? I can work with that."

Without moving zhur arms, there was a push. Krona felt it flutter past her like a gust of humid wind. The nearest varger billowed away from it, bowing and shaking their heads, avoiding the ripple of emotiopathy—deterred by it.

The two faux-gods shared a look. "We can work with that," Emotion said. "Glensen said we needed to build, right?"

"Yes," Krona confirmed. "Fey said you needed to build, and that we needed magic. The magic Absolon fed you."

"He had us cannibalizing our own kind for centuries," Emotion said, disgust curling zhur lip. "It might have been beads and capsules and serums, but it was cannibalism all the same. Time to put it to good use."

"I'll create a pen," Nature said.

"And I'll be the cattle dog," zhe agreed.

Nature took hold of zhim, and together they launched away, ripples of power and magic undulating from their forms, curving the air, heating it. They were a bright burst of speed and light, more dangerous than any cannonball, turning themselves into the pointed missile Krona had desired to be when she first threw herself at Absolon's keep.

Arching upward, they split apart—two meteors streaking from on high to pummel the ground where they landed, skidding back, rucking up mud and rocks and weeds, leaving long hollows in their wakes.

Now on opposite sides of the minefield, they began their work, moving in tandem like they'd been part of a thousand such missions, attuned to each other's every action even with a quarter mile between them.

Nature pulled up the land, plying it as if it were clay and not bedrock, creating swooping walls that curled upward—a sloshing made solid. The air around Emotion throbbed and pulsed as zhe guided heady emotions into the surrounding varger, urging them this way and that, reaching to close off their means of emotional escape whenever one tore away from the pack.

The surge of creatures rounded Nature's walls, darting for the clefts he'd left open.

Krona clutched at Hintosep as dozens of varger—ethereal and fully formed—lurched into the pen.

"Take me to the fire line," Hintosep said, pointing once again at the flames in the distance. "I'm no help atop this rock."

Uniforms of all colors greeted them, just as in the camp. Krona was struck immediately by the lack of chaos. There was no shouting or infighting or bodies scrambling to strike or flee. Pairs of soldiers crouched behind furniture- and farm equipment–based barricades, the supplies clearly liberated from the nearby ruined homesteads, just like the fuel for the beacons. One in each pair sniped at any large, quilled forms bursting out of the night, while the other swapped the sniper's empty quint for a fully loaded one whenever need be. Behind the staggered pairs, nearest the bonfires, lay a receiving station for new recruits. A handful of soldiers stood at a crack in reality, quintbarrels at the ready to defend the Teeth-created tunnel if push came to shove. From the doorway itself came a steady trickle of new people, directed by none other than Mandip, to head toward a small arming depot where a stockpile of quintbarrels and ammo were handed out by Juliet.

"Darlings!" Juliet greeted them. "Come to check on the operation? How's the whole *permanent containment* situation coming along?"

"We're working on it," Krona said, glancing eastward toward Knowledge's temple. "Emotion and Nature are herding the varger together."

"Oh? The way you spoke of them—and then *didn't* speak of them—earlier, I thought the gods were a lost cause."

"Some more than others, perhaps," Hintosep said, reaching for a quintbarrel herself, examining the cylinder flutes and the firing pin to make sure the weapon was well-maintained before claiming it. "What?" she asked when she caught Krona giving her a look. "What do you think my primary purpose was as guardian? Making sure the defenseless Ascendants didn't get eaten by wild animals. Varger included."

Krona's left shoulder popped as her De-Lia arm moved of its own accord, pawing-slash-mouthing at the grip of one of the laid-out guns.

Her first instinct was to yank the arm back before she realized the echo's draw toward a quintbarrel was only natural. This was what it had been preserved for, why it existed. She let it take the gun, sensing the weight of it but not the control of it. It felt unnatural, but right.

Mandip jogged over, grabbing a quint himself. "That's the last of the recruits for now.

Juliet smiled softly, if a little patronizingly, gripping his chin before kissing him. "As tonight's Master Armorer, I don't think I should issue you one of our prized weapons. When have you ever fired a gun, let alone a quintbarrel?"

"Never," he admitted. "How hard can it be?"

Krona promptly took the needle gun from him, setting it back on the table before Juliet. "I'll try not to be insulted by that."

"Don't pout," Juliet told him, though he was doing nothing of the sort. "I could use your support here, my love."

"You love me?" he asked wryly.

"I love you," she confirmed, kissing him again.

Given her relationship with Thibaut, Krona wasn't one to roll her eyes at awkwardly timed displays of affection. Still, she shook her head fondly, realizing they were reviving some tête-à-tête from another time.

"I want to check the other rallying points," she told Hintosep. "I leave you in their capable care."

"Surely you're leaving us in hers," Juliet countered graciously.

Before she jumped, Krona looked once more for signs of the treehouse in the distance. She saw nothing. Knowledge had said to expect fem at dawn, but Krona had hoped for sooner. Regardless, she squeezed Hintosep's shoulder one last time before leaping away, hoping the other portions of the front were faring just as well.

She jumped and jumped and jumped, pleased with what she found at each encampment along the blazing line. Hours went by, and while the soldiers held a steady perimeter it was Nature and Emotion who filled Krona with the most concern.

The dozens of varger they'd initially gathered in their pen became hundreds, became thousands. The two of them never stopping, never pausing, working the land and the air with wellsprings of power Krona herself hoped never to taste.

They pushed and they pushed and they pushed.

But it wasn't enough.

Cracks formed in Nature's walls, the varger deliberately bashing into them, widening them enough for the bottle-barkers to seep free. Emotion reached to take hold of their rabid feelings while Nature shored up the cracks, only to lose whatever mass zhe'd been guiding in the moment, the group spinning off and scattering like seeds in the wind, needing to be gathered again.

The longer they worked, the more the varger fought back. Nature tried to turn the walls into a dome—a cap to cut them off—but the tallest edges crumbled. All he could do was hold what he had, stuff up the gaps, and steady his grip.

"Come on, come on," Krona chanted to herself, snagging a spyglass to trace the jungle canopy, begging for signs of Knowledge.

Instead, she received a different sort of sign.

Both moons had risen, their faint light adding next to nothing with so many fires to fill the night, though they did highlight a many-winged creature soaring just in front of them, drawing a few murmurs and pointed fingers from the soldiers closest to Krona.

Time had come.

Hope surged in Krona's chest.

Time had *followed* them, even when her brother hadn't been sure she would.

Still, she simply circled. Just watching.

Help us, Krona thought at her. *What are you waiting for? An invitation?*

Maybe so.

Krona scoffed incredulously, but tossed herself through a skyward lens just the same.

KRONA

The air was too thin, Time was too fast, and Krona was falling. She'd jumped herself to Time's location only to miss the circling woman entirely, plummeting past, her clipped call for attention dying on the wind. She tried again, jumping higher, farther in front of Time, thinking maybe Time would deign to catch her and keep her aloft. The not-goddess did no such thing, rolling to the side to avoid a collision and nothing more.

Each of Time's four fists was curled in an anxious hold around the hilt of a rusted scimitar plundered from the Necropalacia. The full force of her attention was turned to the barrier sealing the sky as she rocketed upward like a lone firework, erupting into a starburst of feathers and sparks, trailing the blunted blades over the concealing magic, sending friction-fire coiling down around her, her bellows of frustration as bold as any gunpowder *bang*.

"You know that won't work!" Krona shouted out of pure frustration, fully aware Time couldn't hear her properly. Krona had the perfect bargaining chip—an *actual* means of escape—if only she could get Time to stop her frenzied volley and *listen*.

The more she watched her, the more she came to realize that Time's blows were haphazard. An embittered flailing rather than a calculated assault. She was venting her rage at the sky rather than channeling that energy into aiding her brethren.

Swallowing down the spark of fury that ignited deep in her belly, Krona attempted to hail the mass of feathers and wrath again and again, reaching for Time, who artfully avoided her, apparently never surprised to find her in her path but never caring enough to so much as snarl at her to stop. At least, not until she took a casual swing at Krona's neck with one of the blades, and Krona realized she couldn't hope to win any more attention than a gnat this way—would likewise earn a violent swatting if she continued to pester.

She needed to meet Time on more equal footing if she had any hope of gaining her ear.

Krona jumped herself to Nature's side, boots skidding in the churned-up mud, eyes zeroing in on his golden form to the exclusion of all else—closing her ears to the roars and growls and howls emanating from the other side of his wall.

"Time's power contained them before," she yelled over the gnashing, waving at the figure in the sky. "We need her, and she won't stop to listen to me. Maybe she'll listen to you."

"I can't go to her," he said, straining, jaw tight, knuckles white. "If I let go, this all falls apart."

"Then I need to face her better equipped. I need you to make me *like you*."

It wasn't something she asked lightly or proudly. She'd already had her body twisted too many times for her liking, and had no personal desire to be anything more than what she was. She did not ask to be godlike out of anything more than necessity, and was sure she'd hate every second existing in a body not fully her own.

He eyed her for a moment, exertion already pulling his features tight. "I can do that," he conceded, dipping his head before tossing his sweat-slicked hair from his eyes. "You do already have the bones for it."

With a deep breath he widened his stance, preparing to split his efforts. Keeping three of his hands splayed toward the earthen wall—the tremors making the joints in his fingers buckle—he turned the fourth on her.

He paused as though unsure, and Krona stepped closer, swaying forward until his palm landed across her sternum. "*Do it*," she insisted, bracing against the agony she knew was coming.

His fingers curled against her chest the same way they curled in the direction of the wall, his oversized hands and oversized abilities demanding the shape of things *change*.

The pain wasn't the same as when Absolon distorted her. That had been violence for the sake of violence, painful on purpose—unmitigated and cruel. Though Nature worked quickly, he did what he could to numb the bits that broke and morphed, changing stabbing heat into slithering unease instead. It wasn't pleasant, but it wasn't the *wrenching-slicing-heaving-cracking-clenching* that she'd dreaded.

She curled with his magic, turned and bent as though he were writing a song with her sinew, forcing her to dance and sway to the new tune of her body.

Inside, Ninebark stirred uncomfortably, protesting against his physiopathic intrusion in a way she'd never protested against Abby's. Krona calmed herself, smoothing over her fen's anxieties, giving herself fully to the shifting. To the thrusting burst of newness in her spine.

When Nature finished, the wings at her back had new weight. They sung behind her, swishing lightly with every move. She snapped one outward, taking in its impressive expanse, shocked to find down that wasn't black, or white, or brown, or gold, but *red*.

The feathers he'd given her were scarlet. Like a macaw, like a cardinal.

The color of mourning.

The color of funerals.

The color of plain rubies and despairstones and the little roses on De-Lia's hourglass.

The color of blood.

The blood that surged in her chest and beat through her body. The color of the life-force that meant she could love and fight and *fly*.

Her wings weren't the color of sadness, but of power. The same power everyone held. The power of the living and the breathing.

"And what about her?" Nature asked, nodding at her De-Lia arm, which still clutched its quintbarrel with the ferocity of a child unwilling to let go of their security blanket. "May I?"

"Don't—" Krona said immediately, instinctually pulling a wing in front of De-Lia like a shield.

He understandingly brushed the curtain of feathers aside. "I won't take her away. I can make her more herself."

"She is not really alive," Krona said. "More like an imprint of a life."

"A footprint in the sand. An aftertaste of drink," he agreed with a nod.

"An echo. But she's dear to me."

"I will not harm her, you have my word. But I can make her more comfortable and more useful. Will you trust me?"

If she could trust him with the varger and trust him with her own wings, she should be able to trust him with De-Lia. Pulling back her new feathers, she held the arm out in reluctant offer.

Testing, he prodded at the arm with his magic, petting over her affectionately. "She has the flavor of a Physiopath," he said.

Those large fingers took hold again, probing her De-Lia arm inside and out. The echo writhed, but not in pain. It wriggled as Krona had, slithering around inside the skin to accommodate the changes as Nature reshaped the pitiful horror Absolon had created into something regal and powerful and less and less and less like an arm at all with each passing moment.

The bone cage that twisted down from Krona's shoulder retreated. The unnaturally stretched enchanter's mark did not fade, but was instead covered over as her arm sprouted slick black fur from every pore. Krona reeled from the sight—skin crawling, a protest poised in the back of her throat, then an order to stop clipped tight against her teeth. Before she could beg for a different texture, the revulsion seeped away as he petted over the back of her hand and two soft, rounded ears opened upward like butterfly wings.

The mouth, with its limp, toothlike fingers became elegant feline lips, the fingers retreating to leave proper fangs in their place. The shape of what had been Krona's knuckles changed, became boxy and muscular, the jaws tight and crushing with long whiskers spanning forth to test the air and sense the space around it.

Even as it warped, the arm did not let go of the quintbarrel. Instead of forcing it away, Nature laid his hands on it, too, using its materials in the transformation—liquifying its metals until they seeped into the creature's new skin.

Five beautifully jeweled cat eyes glistened over the snout, each with a glint like a quintbarrel needle.

Krona did not hold back a gasp, though she strangled her sob.

Even Nature had sensed it: Monkeyflower's shape in her glass prison, De-Lia's mask. Her sister's affinity for jaguars that extended beyond a passing fancy and reached deep into her soul.

If ever Monkeyflower had been permitted to become a fen, Krona had no doubt this was the shape she would take.

The black jaguar's spots were just visible in the sunlight, its coat glossy, the lines of its muscles powerful.

It was Krona's arm and yet it was not her arm. The great, morphed cat head swung itself into her chest, and Krona instinctually held it close, petting its soft fur.

A deep purr rumbled from its throat, buzzing in her chest.

"She's a weapon now," Nature said, "for combating these monsters, just as she was always meant to be. Maybe you can even use her to capture Hailwic's attention. Do what you must, but treat both our sisters with care."

"I only want to talk to her," Krona reassured him.

"She'll make you earn it," he said ominously. "Do you have a blade?"

"Will I need one?"

In answer he crouched, drew a line in the dirt with two fingers. A silver trail erupted in their path, and when he stood again he presented her with a straight-edged short sword. She took it carefully, recalling her induction ceremony into the Regulators where her saber had been bestowed.

This too was an initiation.

When she had it firmly in hand, Nature wished her good luck. "I've created plenty of wings before," he said. "Your muscles will know what to do, but even birds bumble out of the nest. Be careful," he warned before turning the full force of his attention back to the barrier.

The blade's balance was nothing like her saber. It was stouter, heavier. Did not have the reach she was used to. But if he thought she'd need it, it was far better than facing Time's scimitars with nothing but her body alone.

Krona stepped aside, giving her new wings room to work. The muscles in her back, neck, and shoulders felt thicker, denser, and as she extended what had been nothing but bone minutes ago, a heavy drag now yanked her tendons taut. She pulled at the air, scooping it under her new feathers, straining skyward.

Krona's feet left the ground and she teetered to the side, swiftly overcompensating, slinging herself upward and sideways. She yawed through the air the way a great tree yaws as it's toppled by the woodsman's axe, falling more than anything. The pitch sent her toward a stampede of varger held together in a cluster by Emotion's magic.

Struggling for altitude, she twisted. Up, up, flapping as hard as she could, fearing she'd barrel into the waiting jaws. With a desperate heave she righted her trajectory, soaring above them at the last second.

De-Lia yanked her left, and Krona dreaded plunging again. She turned with the arm's momentum, snapping her wings out to glide rather than tumble. The arm took aim of its own accord, lips pulling back as it roared and bared its teeth.

With a snap of its short neck it fired, expelling a long golden needle that rammed into the base of a love-eater's skull, sending it stumbling over its front paws to nose-dive into the churned mud.

A surge of wonder and pride sloshed back and forth between Krona and the echo. It had finally achieved its purpose: not just helping anyone hunt varger, helping *Krona* hunt varger.

The arm coiled for another shot, and Krona allowed it to snipe another varg to its knees before circling them higher. "We'll do our part once we've convinced Time to do hers," she assured the echo.

Fledgling though she was, Krona tested the wind, looking for currents, demanding her body listen to her just as she would demand Time listen to her. Up she went, panting with exertion, focusing hard, lest a wrong snap of the wing send her plummeting. It was like sprinting with no ground, climbing with invisible handholds.

Above, Time made flying look effortless. Her shimmering black wings grew and grew as Krona scraped her way closer.

Krona pinpointed the exact moment she finally snagged Time's attention. The ineffectual scraping against the sky paused, and Time hovered, body open, arms wide, swords poised to receive a new threat.

Krona kept her blade down, clutching it near the pommel, hoping she looked like a ready equal but not someone to strike without greeting. For half a moment she wished she'd rejected Nature's sword, but the glint of violence in Time's eyes, even as she held herself steady and did not lunge, was unmistakable.

Flexing the tips of her wings like fingers, Krona brought herself to eye level with Time, doing her best to maintain height even though she was sure the sky would hold its breath at any moment and she'd go tumbling down without the wind to prop her up.

Krona realized she should have asked Nature for Time's height as well. She was a red sparrow next to a raven—a fledgling easily gutted by the cruel corvid, should the corvid so choose.

"I see my brother's been playing," Time sneered.

"Your brother is *struggling*," Krona countered. "As is Emotion. They need your help. The varger—"

"Tens of thousands above ground already," Time observed. "By my count there should eventually be *millions*."

"Then you understand why they need you. They can't contain them on their own. *Help them*."

"The only way to help them is to get them *out*," Time said. "They'll be safe once we leave this place."

"And what about the rest of us? The war ravaged much, but these creatures will devour people until *none* are left. They don't discriminate between soldiers and children. They don't care if they consume every last human and can never eat again after. You saw the refugees, you saw how people had to flee from their homes, but there will be no refuge from this."

"So what?" Time snapped.

Krona drooped. Hostility she'd been ready for. Denials she'd been ready for. The cold, cutting indifferent *so what* struck her all the more violently because she hadn't been prepared for it. "So, *help them*," she pleaded.

"No," she said darkly.

"Why?"

"Because maybe it's better this way."

"You can't mean that." She could tell by Time's tone—the overwrought conviction, the forced bite of her *Ts*—that she didn't.

"I told you how much work it would take to undo all of Absolon's lies. Maybe it's better to let nature take its course and have Absolon's own folly wipe the slate clean. I am done with his playland and just want to be free of it." She raised her swords, shooting upward, slinging them against the barrier, slicing with enough power to split a man in two. More sparks flew, and the border remained unbreached.

The De-Lia arm growled her frustrations, echoing Krona's own. She flew to Time again, who flew farther off, trying to shake Krona with irritation radiating off her in waves.

"There are thousands of innocents out there who know nothing of the truth," Krona tried. "Thousands of hands who would willingly do the work you speak of if given half a chance."

"How very naïve of you to think so. All of this," she shouted above the din of a harsh gust, waving a scimitar erratically, "is the result of so many people sitting on their hands while an ineffectual few struggled against the woman who ended the world. They knew she was a dictator, they knew she was genocidal, they *knew*, and they sat back and protected their own hides—even when their own *children* were thrown to her mercy.

"Every *waking* moment of my life, the world has gotten worse. Worse until it was *gone*. My reality unraveled and then dissolved. Those closest to me left and betrayed me, the earth *heaved* and the water boiled and cracked.

"Do not deign to tell me how many hands make lighter loads, because *many hands* do not *lift a finger*. If they are relatively safe and comfortable, then they do not care if others are thrown to the wolves. They look in on themselves, after themselves, and *that is all they care about*.

"Perhaps it is my turn to be selfish. My turn to save just the ones I care about and let everything else go. This"—she sliced north to south, across the length of the Valley—"is nothing. *You* are nothing. *They* are nothing. This entire place is just a dream—a madness cooked up by Absolon: a man who could not accept the world as we'd ruined it, and who could not envision letting go. So let it sink. Let it be devoured. Why shouldn't the ghosts of old consume the phantoms of today? Let it die. Let it *all* die!"

Krona let her rant. Let her strike out in rage with her words just as she'd struck out with blades at the sky. A sinking futility clung to every syllable. Time was tired. A bone-deep, soul-deep tired. The kind of tired only anger could prop up. Without that anger, she was liable to lay down and give up—stop trying altogether. Stop *living* altogether.

"You don't believe a world scraped free of humanity is preferable to what Absolon has wrought," Krona said hollowly when the rant died down. "You don't. Yes, we spoke of work, and you said killing Absolon was lancing the boil, not curing the infection. You did *not* say you wished to see the body die—to see all of Arkensyre *die*—then. This is not how you feel."

Time lunged forward, bringing her snarling face within inches of Krona's, filling her vision with wild eyes and a manically cruel grin. "Spend a thousand years with an ego-driven madman cooing at you under glass, then tell me how you think I feel."

"Emotion and Nature—"

"Stop—" Hailwic gritted her teeth. "Stop calling them—us, any of us—those terrible titles. Those aren't our names. We aren't your *gods*. We aren't your *anything*!" she shrieked, jerking herself back just far enough to swing her scimitars.

Startled, Krona froze, dropping like a stone the instant she stopped flapping.

That was good enough for Time, who went back to her futile task, looking for seams, trying to cut out the clouds and the stars as Krona struggled to right herself again.

Determined, Krona played the part of the buzzing fly once more, pressing her luck. If Time had wanted to murder her on the spot, she'd have had no trouble. Krona would already be a headless corpse slamming into the ground at speed.

Still, the swords continued to swipe, and as Krona began to better learn the nuances of her new body, she parried back, unwilling to be cowed when the need was so dire. The scimitars were of a usual size, but the arms wielding them were not. Deflecting one of Time's blows was nothing like meeting another Regulator in the sparring ring, or even a murderer on the street. Time was pulling her swings, but when their blades clashed, the force still sent Krona spiraling.

Krona came back, again and again, hoping to wear her down, hoping the repetition might bring clarity to at least one of them.

"You're right. You're right. H-Hailwic, *you're right*. I don't know what a thousand years at his mercy is like. I can't imagine. But now you're free—"

"And I'll do anything to keep it that way!"

"—but you didn't achieve that freedom *alone*. You are free because my people and I worked hard to free you. Look. Please, just look." She waved pointedly down at the bonfires. "Those are people from all over the Valley working together to stop this. They didn't ask for it any more than you did. They too have been Absolon's prisoners. They too want their freedom and are standing up for it."

"I won't go back!" Hailwic shouted. "I don't owe you my continued servitude, and you can't have it."

"I'm not asking for your servitude, just your aid."

"For now. Until you realize it's the only way."

A thousand years under glass rang through Krona's mind. Then she understood. Hailwic wasn't just angry and tired.

She was afraid.

Hailwic knew how to contain the hoard not just for a moment, not just while Punabi and Zoshim manned their makeshift pen, but for always—she'd been doing it for lifetimes.

And feared she'd be made to do it for lifetimes more.

She's just a woman, Krona reminded herself. A bitter woman for whom death should have come long ago. Who'd been abused by a man she'd once trusted, hooked up to his machines and tapped like a tree for its sap.

Now Krona was asking to tap her again. Begging her to willingly return to the job she'd been forced to do for millennia.

That was not work. That was not healing. That was slavery.

Krona could no more expect her to be magnanimous about it than she could expect a kicked dog not to bite.

She wasn't a god. She was only human. With a human's wants and needs and fears and hopes. Desperation had her lashing out. Had her masking a body of pains under a thin sheet of anger.

Be gentle with both our sisters, Zoshim had pleaded.

Krona held up her hand and dropped her sword, jumping it away to stab safely into a deserted hillside miles away. "I don't want to fight you, and I'm not here to force you. I will beg if I have to, but I fought to give you back your autonomy and I will fight for you to keep it.

"You saw my bones before they were proper wings. Before that, they were near-deadly spurs, pulled from me by Absolon. He forced them out of my back—overran my body and twisted it. I could have had them cut off, but instead I reclaimed them. I didn't get to choose what he did to me, but I chose what happened after.

"Once we learned the truth about varger, there were many people who chose not to seek theirs out. If I'd been a different person, I could have forced people to rejoin with their magic—ordered them, no matter how dangerous. But I didn't. Because it was important they get to choose. I'm not perfect, though. I tried to keep the man I love away from his varg because I was scared for him. But just because it was my fear, that didn't mean it was my choice. He rejoined anyway, against my wishes, as was his right. He reclaimed his power, and many others have rejected theirs, and that is their choice.

"All those people down there are in mortal danger—a danger you were forced to guard against for lifetimes. I'm not asking you to endure again what never should have been your burden in the first place. I merely want your help. I'm begging for your help. And when we are done, if you still want to leave the Valley, I will help you leave. I know how to get you out."

Hailwic casually flipped one scimitar into another hand, holding both blades like a pair of slim daggers as she caught Krona's now-empty sword arm, yanking her close instead of sending her away.

"I don't believe you," she said, lip curling. "You had no idea on the mountain, why would that have changed?"

"I can prove it to you."

Hailwic thrust Krona away. "Then do it."

Krona took a shaky breath, felt her lungs and lips quiver. She felt herself nod as if from far away, knowing this was a dangerous gambit. She had to offer Hailwic the choice. And to truly offer choice meant accepting the worst outcome. For herself, for the Valley.

But it took trust to get trust, especially from someone who'd been so burned before.

She'd give Hailwic the means to escape, then pray she'd reconsider.

Krona shot upward before diving down low, plummeting with her wings pulled back until she could snap them open and glide along the bonfire line. She searched the camps for signs of Tray or a glint off the artifact's sharp incisors, heart thrumming nervously.

Her unease and current fear was so unlike the fear she felt from her phobia, or when she'd fought Absolon, or stared down a criminal. This fear was a giddy thing, lined not with desperation or determination but a rare kind of uncertainty. This felt like a gamble in a way few decisions ever did. She wanted to trust Hailwic. She needed her, and that need made her hope. But that hope could be pure folly.

When she found Tray, standing guard by one of his rifts, she found herself tongue-tied. She batted away his amazement at her wings, trying to find an explanation for what was ultimately a simple ask.

"I need the Teeth," she eventually blurted.

Tray, bless him, handed the gauntlet to her immediately.

She felt she owed him an explanation, felt she owed Hintosep foreknowledge of her decision, and perhaps even Zoshim as well. If she gave the Teeth to Hailwic and Hailwic fled with them, their loss would be purely Krona's fault.

But there wasn't time.

"Make sure the tunnels are clear," she told him, unsure if the tears would hold once someone else wielded the artifact. "They may close suddenly. I don't want anyone caught off guard."

He agreed and asked nothing, trusting her completely, moving to evacuate the rifts as she flapped back into the dark sky, the weight of the gauntlet far more unsettling than the weight of any sword.

Krona flew another circuit over the frantic field, taking it in as she gave Tray a moment to work, terrified she was throwing away one of their greatest weapons on a folly. Could they do this without Hailwic? Could they get everyone home without the Teeth? Or would all of their effort be for nothing in the end, allowing the varger to run amok?

Back at Hailwic's side, Krona found the other woman had calmed and was simply hovering in place, neck craned back, observing the sky. "There are so many more stars than in my time."

Her strange greeting caught Krona off guard. "How is that possible?"

Hailwic lowered her chin, gave a sad smile. "Not literally. Our cities used to shine so bright they blotted them out. Light pollution, they called it. Is it strange to miss something dubbed pollution? I guess I only really miss it because it means the cities are gone."

Krona tried to imagine it. Not even the gas lamps in Lutador had ever shone that brightly. She hefted the Teeth up—the jaguar helping to lift the artifact with her head. "This is how you get out," she said. "You don't trust me. I understand. So I'm going to trust you first." She demonstrated the way the gauntlet worked, then held out the Teeth in offering. "You could take this and go right now. You and Zoshim and Punabi and Glensen could leave us behind."

Hailwic plucked the Teeth from her grasp, sliding one finger in to test the mechanisms. "How do you know we won't?"

"I don't," Krona admitted. "That's what trust means."

"It was all so pointless," Hailwic sighed, looking to the stars again, clutching the Teeth to her chest. "You're only setting yourself down a path as pointless as mine, trying to control this—trying to stop it. One woman, one man, one person cannot hold the whole of everything together out of sheer desire. We each tried to be architects of the future. We each thought we knew better and this is where it got us."

"I don't want to be an architect," Krona said. "You don't have to be, either. Don't try to build a castle. Or a wall. Just lay a brick. When people play at making mountains, *that's* when things go wrong."

Time nodded. "Don't be a king. Or a master. Or a *god*."

"Be one small step," Krona said. "Let your brother be a step, and your lover be a step, and I'll be a step with you. You're right, not everyone will become steps along with us, but they don't deserve to be swept aside for living in the world as it was created for them. They *do* deserve the truth. The knowledge of what happened and who they are and where they come from. Give them the chance to learn, and to *choose* to help. Just like I hope you'll choose to help."

Time looked at the gauntlet again, worked her fingers inside the grip, and reached above her to the open sky.

She tore it open in an instant, creating a gouge in the magical barrier, one that dripped and boiled, bits dropping away only to evaporate into nothing. Hailwic pushed one of her other hands through, testing the truth of the gap.

"I could leave now."

"You could."

Hailwic looked down at the battleground, scanning the land, the pen—the pen that now boiled with varger, thousands and thousands, while Punabi pushed more and more inside. "Or I could hold them. *Just for now*," she added quickly. "Not indefinitely. You'll still owe me a real solution."

"Glensen is working on it," Krona reassured her. "Fey have a vessel. Only . . ." She still didn't understand how the treehouse could contain the mass, let alone trap it.

Light was just beginning to peek over the horizon. Dawn was nearly upon them.

"Then we wait for Glensen," Hailwic said, tossing the rusted scimitars through a time lens just as Krona had with her blade. Then she swirled high before diving down low, driving the winds ahead of her instead of riding them.

Krona's heart soared in equal measure. She let herself look to the tear in the sky, let her fingers flutter over the brim of it in wonder and relief. She'd done it—she'd convinced her to stay.

With a crow of triumph echoed by a roar from the jaguar, Krona circled down herself, watching as Hailwic wove together a time bubble larger than any Krona had thought possible, billowing it over the bowl of the land, freezing the roil of vapors and bodies, capping it cleanly. The stones Zoshim had so expertly sculpted bowed and trembled, like the bubble had weight. He moved outward, pulling new fences from the land, channels to better steer those Punabi brought into the fold.

The trio's stamina, their power, their sheer force of will was beyond anything Krona had seen anyone wield.

And it wouldn't last forever.

As Krona circled, the echo shot every stray varg it could see, doing its part just as well as those fully among the living.

And then, in the distance, Krona finally snatched a glimpse of the pitched roof between the ragged leaves. Glensen had arrived at dawn, just as fey'd said.

As Krona bent time, creating a lens that would snap her to Glensen's feet, she tried not to think about what would happen if four faux-gods still proved too few.

KRONA

Krona touched down in a burst of red feathers, eliciting a rather birdlike squawk from Thibaut.

"*By* the *five*—or whoever we're swearing on now," Thibaut gasped, clutching at his chest, sitting heavily on the attic planks not far from Glensen's throne. "I thought you were an entirely new threat to deal with."

"Apologies," she said, widening her stance to brace against the swaying—every step of the house a dramatic rise and fall. "The change was necessary. I'll try not to let the sudden transformations become habit."

"Nonsense, you know I love a good wardrobe change."

"Did you manage . . . ?" Glensen asked slowly, voice creeping up from feir chest like a vine. The deep, questioning furrow between feir brows smoothed into satisfaction a moment later. "You did."

"Your tithing is in place." Krona went to the window once more, staring past the open stained-glass pane to pinpoint Time in the sky. A ray of morning sunshine carved down over the mountaintops to shimmer green and purple off her raven feathers. Even at this distance, Krona could see Hailwic's capping time bubble warping and sagging, threatening to burst. She flew back and forth, shoring up what she could at lightning speed. "They're holding on; I don't know for how long."

We have to hurry.

Only a few more strides would see the house break free of the tree line.

"Not much longer," Glensen declared. "They won't need to for much longer. I will take their burdens. And you . . . should hang on."

The house sprinted forward, forcing Krona to catch herself in the window frame as they barreled toward Nature's pen. She shivered, feeling moments rushing past her too quickly, everything coming to a head too soon.

Thibaut kept himself low to the floor, and Glensen still held fast in feir throne.

Branches slapped at the house's siding, leaves stripped away through brute force fluttering in through the window, catching in Krona's hair and wings. The green smell of the jungle burst like a soap bubble on the tip of her nose—welcome after the death and rot that permeated the moment-minefield.

The careful, rhythmic steps of the house became a bounding as soon as they were clear of the woods, became proper leaps once they trounced down into former farmland and past the fading bonfires and the line of diligent, harried soldiers who had no idea what to make of a walking house.

One, two, three bounds through the now-thin numbers of the free-roaming hoard—many now stuck in place by quintbarrel needles—toward the tall, mashed mud-and-stone-and-mine-and-wire wall of the pen. And then Krona's heart was forced into her throat as the treehouse vaulted upward—the root legs bent and sprang, making Krona's stomach quiver and drop as the house caught the edge of the pen Nature had sculpted, and precariously perched atop it, like a fat chicken fluttering to its roost.

The attic tipped forward over the top of the tree legs, like the open window was a giant eye through which it might survey the mass of varger. Below, thousands and thousands of bodies—slowed via kairopathy, soothed with emotiopathy, trapped by the physiopathically molded wall—tumbled over one another, all stinking, all growling, all looking up at Krona framed in the window like the meal she was.

She scrambled back, away from the window seal, skidding on the tilting floor as the treehouse struggled to keep its balance, bits of the earthen wall clearly crumbling beneath its feet.

"How do you intend to get them in here?" Krona asked.

"It's not that simple," Glensen said. "I need to speak to my tithing, but we cannot leave our posts. We need a conduit. De-Krona, would you gift me three feathers?"

Krona could not fathom what three feathers could do to aid their circumstance.

When she hesitated, Glensen laughed. "Don't worry, the others will be confused as well. Overindulging in teliopathy makes a strange beast, and I doubt anyone else has ever made feathers speak with the wind."

Krona shared a look with Thibaut, whose brow was just as furrowed, before pulling three feathers free and delivering them to Knowledge's hand. There was no time to ask questions and no point in arguing.

Fey curled the three strips of red tightly in feir fist, whispering low and quick into the spurs of them.

"Thibaut, will you deliver the feathers to my fellows?"

Thibaut scrambled to his feet and bowed slightly as he accepted the feathers from feir hand. "How am I meant to reach them?"

"Ninebark?" fey prompted.

Krona was stunned to find her fen seeping forth, solidifying at her side in an instant—large and firm and warm like a natural-born horse, though her features were no such thing. The fen had emerged not as though compelled, simply called. Like an eager pet or small child darting into the next room to meet the owner of a pleasant voice.

Krona felt like she'd been caught in a fairytale. A strange, dire fairytale—the kind that usually featured thorned bushes and cloaked figures and evil Thalo puppets lurking around every corner, ready to pluck out children's eyes. Those always had magics with no logic. Wild, senseless power that twisted at some otherworldly creature's will.

She'd been struck by the other not-gods—their magic as awe-inspiring, towering as they were.

Knowledge was different.

Knowledge was terrifying. At first, so slow. Like the stillness of a tree in winter—leafless, near lifeless to an outside observer. And just like a tree, spring had come. Glensen's flower-petal mind had blossomed. Fey were swift and mercurial, a sprite of a person even in their gnarled state. Now fully awakened, quick to action, quick to understanding—*quickquickquick* in a way that made Krona's head spin.

Thibaut was well acquainted with Ninebark, petting down her nose as she stretched her wings and back like a cat that had just uncurled, her eight legs stamping lightly. "I'm supposed to . . . ?"

"Ride. The substantiveness of your fen, Thibaut . . . Matter and energy in flux. Ninebark is *stable.* But still, the shape is a reflection, not a truity."

"Meaning she's not really a horse and her wings are . . . just for show?" he asked.

"She can flutter with you on her back. Don't try to reach Hailwic. Too high. Make her come to you. Krona, stay. Stay by my side. I need you."

Another whistle from Glensen's cracked lips, and the wall around the window frame *split.* Bits of tree branch pushed it apart, popping nails and severing boards. The stained-glass pane broke at its leaded seams, the pieces falling away into the varger pen. Thibaut ducked behind Ninebark to hide from wayward splinters, and Krona maneuvered her wings to shield her from the same.

The attic's front was now a gaping hole, large enough for an eight-legged, winged horse to trample through unimpeded.

Wind now filtered through the boards, lightly whistling, and making the dead wooden planks and rafters creek worse than the dexterous tree branches.

"Tell them to hold their feather tightly," fey instructed Thibaut, who Krona expected to look bewildered, but instead looked confident in a way she'd never witnessed before. "Their function is similar to their old implants." Fey looked to Krona. "Or your reverb beads."

Ninebark bowed down, kneeling to give Thibaut an easy mount, muscles shifting under her thin coat of unnaturally pink hair, withers flexing as Thibaut lightly laid a hand on her thick neck. He slid onto the fen with no hitching as the tentacles of his own fen gave him an added boost. While the fingers of one hand coiled tight in Ninebark's mane, the others clutched Krona's feathers—their bright red all the starker when set against the pinks and greens of the two fens.

"You take good care of him," Krona said to Ninebark.

"Of course she will," he said, leaning down for a small kiss. "She's you." He straightened up and cleared his throat. "Time to go play the dashing hero," he declared. "Embrace the danger and all that."

"Don't fall off," Krona said sternly.

"Really, Krona, must you attempt to jinx me right befo*ooo-aaahhhrrr—*"

The end of his sentence was lost as Ninebark turned on the spot and leapt from the newly created breach, bounding right onto the time stop. For a moment Ninebark touched down like it was a solid thing and not a displacement of relativity. Then her wings flicked outward and she reared up, catching the wind and sailing off—spiriting away both Krona's magic and her love for a time.

Krona plopped down heavily next to Glensen's throne, bracing herself against the slope of the floor, learning in the moment how to properly fold her wings to keep them out of the way. "Why do you need me?"

"You will see. The communion is through you. They are your feathers." Glensen laid a hand on the crest of one wing. "You've been through much," fey said after a moment of silence. "You and your sister's echo there."

Much seemed such a trite way to put it, but at the moment Krona's senses were awhirl. "Yes," she answered, little more than an afterthought.

"You think it's time to let go."

"No," she said too quickly, defensively, pulling the jaguar in close, clutching it to her chest.

The denial was reflexive.

Glensen was only stating the truth as fey'd read it with feir teliopathy.

Krona petted the bastardized thing, scratching it behind the ears, taking comfort in that rumbling purr once more. "I've disturbed her enough," she admitted.

"The past is the past," Knowledge said. "A place nearly impossible to tread. Even for Kairopaths. There is no one who hasn't wished *something* undone. Not a wrong corrected; a wrong erased. Deletion is preferable to the effort of correction."

The wind changed direction, streaming in harshly through the open wall, blustering in, wafting against Krona with enough force that she bowed into it, raising her hand to block the grit and dust and leaves thrown into the attic.

The breeze carried more than dirt. Voices seemed to drone along it, rattling through her wings, growing stronger and curling up around her until they settled in her feathers.

Glensen's hand on the crest of her wing pressed lightly, encouraging Krona to spread her wing out so it fell up over the throne and across feir lap. Fey stroked the surface of her flight feathers carefully, like one might playfully scatter a reflection on the surface of a pond.

"Can you hear me?" fey asked of the wing, feir teliopathy sliding between the barbs of each feather like silk.

Three stunned voices rose up in unison. Krona didn't hear them so much as feel them, humming through her just as De-Lia's purr hummed. Each vibration was distinct, had its own pulsing aura. Punabi's was bright, poised and precise as a whipcrack. Zoshim's was fluid and sweeping, swelling and shrinking with a rhythm like the beating of a heart. Hailwic's was all cold fire, sharp and stinging.

Glensen's was there too. On feir lips the words were barely a murmur, but they stood out loud and solid and imposing as any forest in Krona's mind.

The four auras collided inside her, meeting but not melding or fighting, instead plaiting together in a gentle braid, the strands all the stronger for being woven together.

Krona felt suspended on that weave, though she was the one holding it together. They were all linked through her, speaking through her.

Soothing words of praise and encouragement seeped from Glensen, and the others were elated at feir arrival.

But their reunion was fated to be short-lived.

Glensen quickly laid out feir plan—a way to raise the remnants of the hoard vats and reseal the monster away.

The elation fizzled.

"A new vault—malleable, living, strong. It will need a consciousness at the heart of it," fey added, letting the words out at a slow drip. "And we need not argue over who is to do it. This is my house, my tree, my plan. It will be my burden."

"It needn't be *anyone*," Nature protested.

"No arguing now, Zoshim. We worked at cross-purposes with Uphrasia and the bombs. If we had set aside our pride and chosen just one path—*any* of our proposed paths—we might not be here today. But we have to join together now—put all of our weight behind one method and one goal. Trust me. Just trust me. Let me do this."

"You've only just awoken," Nature cried. "We've only just gotten you back! I can't even—I can't even *see you* to say good-bye this time."

"That is the price we pay for our disunity before: we cannot bask in togetherness now," fey said regretfully. "But you know better than anyone, this is not good-bye. It is not a death. I'll be right here. Right here, always."

"I should do it," came Hailwic's voice, and a sick feeling curled in Krona's belly. She'd promised her it wouldn't be her burden anymore. "I've been holding them, I should—"

"Let go," Glensen countered. "You never asked for that. I ask for this. You all know this is something I've long desired," fey said with a sharp glint of true humor. "If you all wish to play the noble heroes, play for the people. You are not gods, but the citizens of the Valley believe you are. Don't abandon them. If we live in the world, we have a responsibility to it. That is something no single person can escape, no matter how tired.

"I choose this responsibility. You need each choose yours."

Glensen petted over Krona's wing one last time before plucking an individual feather for femself and releasing her. "The connection is established," fey said. "Your necessity to the communion has ended. Thank you. I ask one more thing."

Krona refolded her wings, placed her hand over Glensen's where it lay on the throne's armrest once more. "Yes?"

"Hold them to it," fey said to her. "Promise me you won't let them forget they're needed."

"They won't thank me for it." Especially not Hailwic.

"Ah, but I will. The Valley will."

A harried series of startled human grunts and a high-pitched horse whinny heralded Thibaut and Ninebark's return. The fen's hooves sounded like a stampede unto themselves as they touched down, and a rather windswept Thibaut stumbled from her back onto shaky legs.

"I don't think a pair of wings are in my future," he said to Krona as he stutter-stepped to her across the inclined floor.

"That's unfortunate," Glensen said.

"Why?" he asked suspiciously.

Glensen remained silent, but Thibaut read what he needed. "Oh. Gods, all right. Krona, time to go. Unless you'd like to put down permanent roots here as well?"

The treehouse lurched again, and Krona didn't need to be told twice. Grabbing Thibaut's hand, she pulled him along as she ran at Ninebark—slamming into the fen as she burst into a haze, reabsorbing her in an instant. "Hold tight to me!" she ordered Thibaut, leaping from the attic as he threw his arms around her neck.

She spread her wings wide, swirling out into the early morning sky as the treehouse staggered forward, taking one last fateful step inside the boundary of mud and rock just as Hailwic released the bulk of the time bubble capping the pen.

The slowed varger inside began to surge once more, clawing at the house's rooty ankles, pawing at them like predators angry their pray was too far out of reach.

Hailwic pushed them still again, screaming as she did, the effort enough to have her wings slipping for a moment, her body dipping. Krona went to her side. Feeling like a child compelled to help lift a weight they could barely touch, she added her kairopathy to Time's, while Thibaut clutched tightly to her front.

The house teetered to the center of the pen, guided by Glensen's sharp whistles. There, the root-feet plowed into the ground, plunging into the dirt like hands plunging into a washbasin. They burrowed down and down and down, searching, Krona knew, for the enchanted glass vats hidden below.

Zoshim pushed the rock-and-earth walls inward, tightening the circle, closing the noose, forcing the hoard to pile up, many bodies on top of one another. Those not quite pinned by Hailwic sought to climb the house's outer walls, and Krona worried they would bring it down before Glensen could excavate feir prize.

Punabi climbed the crest of the pen, pushing a softness forward, driving an ease into the monsters clinging to the house, making them drowsy with it so that they fell back into the pit.

Realizing her own kairopathy meant little, Krona loosed De-Lia instead, letting the great, quint-eyed cat take aim at would-be escapees, pinning them in their tracks.

The crackling of glass rose up through the dirt as thousands of pieces were thrust into the sky around the outskirts of the pen. Glensen's roots had doubled back on themselves, pushing shattered chunks of enchanted glass up through the ground. The wood formed a new fence and began squeezing in just as the stone squeezed inward.

Zoshim changed his tactics. As soon as the roots curled over the top of the stone, he shifted the stone to match. Wood, wood, and more wood, adding to the tree's mass—even stretching the already stretched treehouse higher, pulling it up and thickening its walls, blending it with the trunk at its core, morphing everything—the stone pen, the house, the land, the shattered vats—into a single sighing tree.

The mass of varger were subsumed, the roots tipped with glass curling inward to the trunk's base and smashing down like hammers, thrusting the creatures and the vapors into the wood just as surely as Krona had used the katar to thrust varger into their hosts.

Roaring and writhing, crushed and compacted, the monsters were gradually subsumed into the wood and glass and ground.

Nature's push became a pull, as did Time's. Krona followed the faux-goddess's lead, yanking at the roof of the treehouse with kairopathy, not to pull it away but to hasten its changing.

Branches twisted out of it, bouncing and bowing as they widened outward into a canopy, huge leaves unfurling, each a different glittering shade of jade and just as light-catching as any such stone.

The two women flew higher as the branches continued to stretch, fluttering out of their reach. The tree grew larger and larger, its reach nearly expanding across the whole of the moment-minefield, its base broader than Mirthhouse's foundations.

Inside, Knowledge squirmed. Krona could still feel an echo of connection, sense the way fey thrust and thrashed in tandem with Nature's machinations.

Great, white five-petaled flowers, each as big as an infant's head and just as new, blossomed and burst between the leaves, thousands of them growing stamens and billowing out pollen in an instant before shriveling and fruiting as the seasons ran wild along the branches. The flowers' sweet honeysuckle scent remained on the air, drenching Krona long after the petals were gone.

In their place, teal bubbles of fruit—the same color as the vat glass—began to burgeon in tight clusters, like berries. At first they were small, then grew to fists, then flourished into heavy teardrop cases large enough for someone of Krona's size to curl inside.

The skin of the pods was thin, translucent. The pits inside did not lay still like in normal stone fruit. These rolled, squirmed. Like babies in a womb.

Thousands and thousands of varger drooped from the branches, encased in their own glass pod, shining like jewels in the light sifting down through the grand leaves.

"Ready for the plucking," Krona gasped to herself.

The growth stopped. The pods swayed. The branches creaked. The leaves whispered.

Hailwic let go.

Krona followed, swirling down around the tree to land herself and Thibaut lightly on their feet.

Zoshim dropped to his back, exhausted. Hailwic collapsed with him. Punabi's light flared then fled as zhe strode over, falling on top of the both of them.

A distant hum—a buzz—filtered over the land. It took Krona a long moment to realize it was the sound of distant cheering. Of the soldiers and refugees screaming at the dawn sky in triumph.

"There are still stragglers to catch," Thibaut said to Krona.

Krona flexed her wings, looking across the torn-up land, listening to the heady push and pull of the not-gods' breaths as they lay together on the ground, worn-out. She pet over the ridge of De-Lia's head, felt the great cat purr once more.

"And still so many wounds to heal," she said. "Come on, then," she said to her De-Lia arm. "Time to go a-hunting."

The work had just begun.

EPILOGUE THE FIRST

KRONA

The gods walked among the people, a new Tree of Knowledge grew monstrous fruit, and the god-barrier would fall in the near future, leaving the Valley exposed to the realities of the wastelands. It might have all seen Arkensyre dig deeper into war—deeper into panic, deeper into chaos—but the three roaming gods had not taken Knowledge's last words lightly. They had a responsibility to the people and the land. As hostile as Absolon had been, they couldn't embrace that hostility.

The gods did not have penalties. Absolon had created the five penalties based on his own failures—his own ill touch, his own toil for humanity, his own waste of knowledge, his hoarding of emotion and misuse of secrets.

The gods did not have penalties, but in their place, there were lessons.

Nature taught the virtues of choice. One's body could be molded to their own whims, just as one's environment and community could be molded when the choices of many were brought to the fore.

Knowledge taught that choice without responsibility was no choice at all. One could not decide without education and wisdom on which to base a decision.

Likewise, knowledge could never be separated from feeling. There were no dry facts, and human beings—living things—could never be reduced to numbers. Emotion was just as valuable, just as telling, just as important.

Time's lesson was that years should not be squandered. Life was limited, and it was one's to do with as they pleased, but there were responsibilities. One could not run from emotion, or knowledge, or choice. One was born into a world connected to those around them, and connected they would remain.

And secrets? There was no god of secrets. And yet Hintosep knew what she would have picked: secrets should never be kept out of malice or shame.

Krona kept her promise to Knowledge. The remaining three could not claim to be divine, but they could not deny the focus millennia's worth of mythology had placed on them. The people looked to them, and that burden could not be shoved away so easily. They presented themselves to the city-states, sought audiences with grand marquises and ezes alike. Krona gave in to her title as the Demon of the Passes, accompanying the three whenever she could. They sought communities where they could help educate and rebuild. They saw to diplomacy—the war would not end on their whims alone, but it had to be broached.

Hintosep and Avellino looked after the Thalo, brought them down from the ruined icefield, gave them homes, communities. Reintegrated them and attempted to build trust between the five city-states and the sixth foreign state over which Absolon had reigned.

Baby steps, all of it. Not the grand, swift changes of deities, but the reaching struggles of people simply doing what they could.

⊱⊰

And the world went on. Seasons changed.

Hintosep built anew on the ruins of Mirthhouse.

Juliet proposed to Mandip.

Melanie was once again with child.

Thibaut healed and learned to call his fen, Goliath, at will.

Krona even built up the courage to see her maman again.

Punabi and Hailwic slowly learned to trust each other again.

And Zoshim built a house at the base of Glensen's tree.

For a long time, Krona didn't acknowledge the longing he exuded every time she was near, uncertain as to its origins. Zoshim ached in a way the other two did not. He spent time nestled in the upturned crooks of Glensen's roots, or shifting into birds and lizards and squirrels to climb feir branches with Krona's gifted feather clutched in talons or teeth.

There was a loneliness in him that changed whenever Krona visited. It took her many months to realize it dimmed when he greeted De-Lia's echo. When he petted the jaguar's head or let the cat lick his fingers with her rough tongue.

"She likes you," Krona said one day, unsure how to frame the proposal that had been gliding through the back of her mind for weeks now.

In the form of a plain man—no fits or flares save the green of his lips—he handed her a cup of tea as she sat before his welcoming hearth. His cabin was modest—little more than two rooms, each cozy, private. The path leading up to it was constantly lined with offerings, no matter how often he swept them away.

He chaperoned the brave few who sought to regain their magic, taking up the task of plucking their fruit if it was there and rejoining them to the missing part of themselves.

Now, he made a soft hum in the back of his throat, but offered no comment.

"The first time you saw her," Krona pressed. "You acted as if you recognized her. *Oh, there you are,*" she quoted.

His eyes stuck to the flickering fireplace. "I did. It . . . it doesn't make sense," he said, trying for dismissive, self-deprecating.

"Your mentor is a tree and you talk to fem through feathers you grew for me," she said, coaxing. "Very little could make less sense than all that."

He gave her a sad, appreciative smile, obviously thinking her sweet for humoring him.

He still didn't know her very well, Krona realized. She was not sweet.

"Ever since I can remember," he began, "I have been missing *something.* I used to think the absence was in my shape, that one day I would shift into the right form and feel fully like myself. But I am not me if I'm not constantly in flux. I can no longer imagine taking one form and no other, but the hollow remains."

"A hollowness that lessens whenever De-Lia is near."

"I can't explain it," he said swiftly, apologetically, like she'd uncovered a shameful secret he never meant to lead into the light. "Maybe I've taken up the role of guide here because I can lead others to what I cannot find myself. Just like Glensen is now a vessel, I feel like I too have always been a vessel. A vessel without purpose, without its proper contents."

"And De-Lia . . . she fits just right."

He nodded. "You know, Glensen told me how you did all this—brought us back—not just because you wanted to be rid of Absolon, but because you wanted your sister back. That's how it all started for Hailwic too," he said warmly. "She wanted to save me. Perhaps this Valley wouldn't even exist if it hadn't been for how fiercely my sister loved me."

Krona set her tea aside on a small end table. "How many people have come to you for help with the fruit?"

"A few dozen since I shaped my cabin. Why?"

"There should be more."

"Even those who come find the idea daunting." He gave an introspective frown. "They find *me* daunting, no matter what shape I'm in. I admit I find it difficult to communicate with them on equal footing. I try to set them at ease, but . . . I'm a stranger in an unfamiliar land. Perhaps someone of your"—he searched for the proper descriptor—"*era* would make a better guide than I."

And here was her opening. She shook her head. "They need someone who can speak to Glensen, who understands the nature and depth of the magic they're accepting. But you're right in that they need someone who understands who they are and how they live. Someone who can set them at ease and encourage more people to come. Someone who knows the present in a way you don't, and someone who *also* understands the past. A guide merged of two worlds, into one."

She stroked the jaguar's fur nervously. "If I were to give you everything I have of De-Lia—her blood, her ashes, her varg, her words, m-my arm—would that be enough for you? If you merged with her like we merge with our varger, if you became her vessel more completely than I ever could, would that—?"

He cocked his head, taken aback. "I would not steal her from you."

"I'm offering," Krona countered. "The echo has never felt at home in me. I struggled with it when it occupied her mask; we pained each other when Absolon brought her to the fore, and now—now she's restless. Every waking moment. *Except* when we're with you.

"Maybe it's your dual physiopathy, maybe it's cosmic resonance, or maybe you two were fated to be connected across centuries. Maybe gods *really do* exist out there, somewhere, and this is their handiwork."

He snorted softly.

"It doesn't matter where the connection comes from. I've spent far too long trying to bring De-Lia back, rather than allow what's left of her to move forward. She and I never belonged together like this." She petted the jaguar, and it nuzzled into her hand. "Can it be done?"

"I've never even heard of such a thing being attempted," he said. "But in my time, there was no such thing as an echo or a varg. The fact that the echo resides in you now is the greatest proof that it is possible.

"She wouldn't be the De-Lia you knew, though. You must understand that. Your sister is dead, but parts of her remain. And I wouldn't become some kind of chest of drawers, hiding away each piece. If I were to do this, I would want us to sincerely become one. Intertwined. I'd be giving up much of who I am. I'd be transforming in a way I never have before. We'd be a new person entirely, twin-souled. It wouldn't be *bringing her back,*" he said firmly.

"I know," she admitted sadly. "And I've come to terms with that. I will always love her as she was. And I love her now—the remnants of her. The echo. How could I deny the two of you peace, and the Valley a greater hope, if that's what a merger would achieve?"

⁂

Zoshim spent a long time communing with Glensen on the matter, divining how he might best integrate parts of the dead.

Hailwic had a hard time accepting Zoshim's choice, but did not try to stop him, and instead did what she could to help him. Together, she and Krona spent months developing a ritual conjuration, testing the magic where they could and hoping where they could not. It felt like a long good-bye present to her sister, and Krona slowly grew into a sense of closure she'd thought she would never reach.

Likewise, as they drew closer to readiness, Zoshim's excitement burgeoned, his loneliness abated.

De-Lia's scattered pieces were carefully assembled, sigils practiced and precisely drawn—between the roots of the Knowledge Tree and on its trunk.

It was a beautiful day, with the sun bright but not blazing and a cool breeze that brought no chill. Glensen had made hollows in feir trunk and thickest limbs for toucans to nest in, and they and other tropical birds squawked and whistled throughout the brilliant green canopy, paying the varg-fruit only casual attention.

Zoshim stood between two of Glensen's raised roots, the sigils branching out around him over the wood and dirt and newly grown moss in equal measure. He wore a simple shift, and his godlike form, standing with the trunk at his back. His and De-Lia's loved ones spread out in a half-moon before him—each with a part to play.

Tray, pale and nervous, held his saber at the ready, Abby and Avellino quietly standing at his back. Thibaut—tentacles proudly on display, draping over his shoulders like a grand cape—stood with Acel, holding De-Lia's journal. Hailwic held De-Lia's sand, Punabi the blood pen. Hintosep kept guard over the glass jaguar bottle that housed Monkeyflower, and Krona, of course, carried the echo.

Hailwic gave her brother a mighty hug at the center of the grand sigils, careful not to scuff the lines made of salt and ash and lye. They mirrored each other today—their wings, their height, their arms. Time's twin would be irrevocably changed after this, and she clearly mourned for him, even while welcoming the new person he'd become. Her mourning was different from Krona's, but they both had to learn to let their siblings go.

Punabi strode up behind Hailwic and gently disentangled her, allowing Zoshim to kiss them both on the cheek before retreating away.

On the edge of the sigil Hintosep strode, chanting softly to herself as she sprinkled a chemical concoction to aid in energy transfer around the edges.

When Hintosep was finished Thibaut knelt down, sending a ripple of teliopathy across the drawn lines. Everyone placed their relics at an even pacing inside the half-moon's edge. Krona reached out with her echo arm, and Zoshim took it as though holding a normal hand.

"Ready?" Tray asked, raising his saber.

Punabi clutched at the back of Krona's neck, making her blood rush, flooding her with adrenaline and endorphins. Krona gritted her teeth and nodded.

With a shout, Tray chopped down, slicing the jaguar away, severing it from her body just as cleanly as he'd ever severed a hand while exacting a penalty.

It came away freely, Krona's head roaring, her heart pounding. She stumbled away from the sigils, rushing to Abby, who sealed off the wound as Acel rubbed circles into Krona's spine. Zoshim—or whoever he was after—would grow her a new arm later. Now they needed to act while the severed arm still had life in it.

Zoshim grasped the bloody thing to his chest, hugging it like an infant, a child of his own. Rocking slightly, he began to shift, his torso expanding and softening, making way for the jaguar, accepting the arm into himself.

With tears in her eyes, Hailwic fed him time, siphoning off years from herself to aid in the energy he was expending.

De-Lia's relics rose into the air, swirling around him, moving faster and faster until each in turn shot into the center, drawn into him, into his body. He cried out after each impact, first taking the blood pen, then the sand, the journal.

Last was Monkeyflower. Last was De-Lia's lost magic.

He folded in on himself, body bulging unnaturally as he fit everything under his skin, as he slowly absorbed it. Bits of his form bubbled, skin creeping and shifting. His wings disappeared, collapsing in as though crushed. The dirt beneath his feet shuddered and became fur for a moment as he struggled to keep his own physiopathy under control, focused inward.

Hintosep and Thibaut's hands were both outstretched, monitoring something unseen.

Zoshim made a terrible gargling sound, spitting up blood before wiping it off his chin, absorbing it back through his fingertips.

The longer he struggled, the more Krona began to doubt. The more she wondered if she'd let her hopes guide Zoshim down a far too dangerous path.

Thin roots emerged from the ground around him, reaching up like new flower stalks in spring. They formed a webbed binding around him—lashing over his shoulders and around his waist and legs—before pulling him *down*. His feet sank into the hardened earth as easily as if it were quicksand. Glensen's roots guided him deeper and deeper, subsuming him. He let out a tortured gasp before his golden head was thrust under as well, leaving a shuddering, sudden silence behind.

The ground in which he'd disappeared now looked untouched. Even the sigils had disappeared.

Krona chanced a sidelong glance at Hailwic, saw how red her cheeks were, how wide her eyes.

The moments stretched. The uncertainty lingered.

High above, a sudden shift in the branches disturbed a flock of toucans, sending them fluttering—green, yellow, and black—into the sky. Krona caught a glimpse of something between the emerald foliage, but couldn't quite make it out. Whatever it was dropped from on high, coming toward them, but not at great speed. It took long minutes for Krona to realize it was a new teardrop-shaped fruit gently falling from above, its descent gentled by broad, outstretched leaves working like hands. They cradled it like something fragile, bringing it carefully to the base of the trunk.

Larger than the varger pods, this plump specimen was opaque with a smooth, white, stony skin. Like that of an opal—a griefstone. Little rainbows danced across its surface in the dappled sunlight filtering through the tree.

Everyone stood perfectly still as the fruit came to rest, waiting.

It did not stir. Nothing erupted from within.

"I can't take this," Hailwic said eventually, the sentiment bursting from her chest just as she burst forward, falling to her knees next to the pod before running her four palms over it. Unable to find any seams, she hooked her fingers into its unexpectedly dry, spongy flesh, tearing at the rind, excavating the pit they were all certain lay within. Slowly, she revealed two sets of arms and one set of legs, but no wings—all tucked together like a baby's in a womb—before uncovering a face.

Given air to breathe, the form within gasped and rolled out of the pod. Hailwic retreated, giving them space.

Zoshim no longer looked like his neutral self, but nor did he truly look like De-Lia. His skin was darker than it had been, his brow softer, lips lusher.

Whoever lay before them now was neither Zoshim nor De-Lia, but an amalgamation—a child of them both.

Krona knelt next to her maman and Abby, cradling the stub of her arm. Her body was too light, her shoulder unnaturally free. The weight of De-Lia was gone. The sad, beautiful, dark, familiar cling of her was gone.

Tray rushed in as the figure huddled against the ground, naked and taking great gulps of air, and no one stopped him.

This new person didn't look like De-Lia, but they looked close enough. She was there, and he could not fight the recognition on his face, the hope in his expression.

"Hey," he said gently, brushing back a thick, black curl from their eyes, offering a hand to help them sit up.

"Tray?" they croaked.

"Yeah. Yeah, it's me." His lip trembled. He gave them a watery smile, then tried to pull away, but they held him fast, wonder on their soft face.

"I remember you," they gasped, gaze flickering inward as days long past—yet entirely new—fluttered through their consciousness. "I . . . I am not her," they said, "but I remember *us*."

Tray's eyes were bright with unshed tears. He didn't have De-Lia back. The love of his life was gone.

And yet, that love itself was not gone.

The turmoil on Tray's face was reflected in Krona's own, she was sure.

This was not her sister.

And yet, they shared her sister's history, her past, her understandings. They were just . . . more.

They reached up to touch Tray's face in turn, expression full of warmth, remembrance, and want. "May I kiss you?" they asked.

With a pained little gasp, Tray nodded.

Krona's eyes were too full of tears to watch their gentle embrace.

One Year Later

"Do you miss them?" Krona asked, trailing behind Hailwic, who pushed an ox plow, leaving the dirt around Glensen's roots well-turned.

"Who?" Not-De-Lia asked. This new person had yet to decide what to call themself other than the Shepherd.

One by one, they buried bottle-barkers from the city-states' vaults in the soil. The Shepherd dropped each like a seed, and Krona quickly covered them over—with two hands whole and hale—leaving the rest to Glensen. The tree would take them up and sprout them out again, renewed and ready for harvesting.

"The children we once were," Krona said, fingers deep in soft dirt, burying the angry haze that gnashed at her.

"Were we ever children?" The Shepherd laughed. "Seems unlikely."

"And yet . . ."

They continued on, dropping the next bottle, and the next.

A line of pilgrims waited at the Shepherd's cottage. They came from all over Arkensyre every day via wagons, on horseback, by handcart, and on foot, looking to be restored—to eat of the great tree and have their eyes opened to a new life.

"The wedding starts in a few hours. Are you sure you and Hailwic won't come?" Krona asked eventually.

If the Shepherd didn't come, this might be the last time Krona would ever see them.

The Shepherd shook their head. "I'm needed here." They waved in the direction of the cabin. "There are many, many pilgrims today. And I don't think Hailwic can be convinced to leave my side."

When they were finished, Krona wiped off her hands and hugged the Shepherd close, inhaling deeply, trying to memorize their warmth, their strength, their smell. "I will miss you dearly."

"It's all right to still miss *her,* too," they assured her. "To still want her with you, me with you. Even if we have to forge our own paths."

Hailwic joined them, towering high, but shrinking slowly back down to size at the Shepherd's slightest flick. Krona stepped aside and Hailwic took her place in the Shepherd's arms.

"They do need you here," Hailwic said, though she sounded like she was trying to convince herself.

The Shepherd nodded. "And the Valley needs *you* to go out into the world. To figure out our place in it. To bring back news." They put a hand on both women's faces. "Though, with the memories I have of you two, it does feel like madness to let you go."

"What is love if not a type of madness?" Krona asked with a half laugh. "A thing that makes us capable of so much, of doing what we never would otherwise? I'm mad, Hailwic is mad. The skies know Thibaut and Tray are both mad. We've all gone mad. Oh, and Juliet and Mandip—they have for sure completely lost it."

"And Hintosep? Has she decided what she'll do? Stay or go?"

"She says she'll decide after the wedding," Krona supposed. "Though she said she'd decide after Abby's birthday, then Avellino's, and that's all come and gone."

"She hasn't got much time, we're off tomorrow," Hailwic said.

"Sometimes it's difficult to make grand decisions," the Shepherd said, looking to Glensen. "And sometimes it's the easiest thing in the world."

The babe in Sebastian's arms screeched happily all through the wedding ceremony, counterpointed by Abby's attempts at helpful shushing. No one seemed to mind.

The new version of Mirthhouse was stunning on its cliffside, and made the perfect backdrop to the outdoor after-vows party. Long wooden tables had been set with many candles interwoven with candied fruits and pastries for the guests' enjoyment. Wine flowed freely as did song. Given it was the wedding of La

Maupin, it wasn't simply family and close friends at the gathering, but all manner of show people, artists, and eccentrics from across Arkensyre.

Krona and Thibaut stood shoulder to shoulder on the outskirts of the merriment, picking at fruit tarts and trying not to let the inevitable melancholy of leaving sour the mirth of the occasion.

They watched as the bride, Juliet, shamelessly flirted with nearly every guest, much to the alternating delight and chagrin of her groom.

"Perhaps they will take a third into wedded bliss," Thibaut commented, amused to see Juliet shift from flirting with the woman on her right to the person on her left. "Or a fourth, or a fifth," he added with a fond shrug. "They certainly deserve as many happy spouses as they can get their hands on."

"The three of you made quite the trio," Krona said, recalling the way Thibaut would often light up in the midst of bantering with the couple—usually when he and Juliet ganged up on a flustered Mandip. "In another life you would have made a fine husband for the pair of them."

"Mandip could not have survived Juliet and me both," he chuckled, snaking his fingers into hers. "Besides, that other life you speak of could only happen in a world bereft of you." He brought their clasped hands to his lips, left a lingering kiss on her knuckles. "Having known this world, I could never be truly happy in that one."

"Will you be happy, though?" she asked. "Out there?" She nodded to the rim, and they both knew what she meant.

"My dear, you are my home. As long as we're together, I am content. In fact—" He cleared his throat and dug into his jacket pocket with one hand, pulling forth a rectangular jewelry box. "Let me prove my sincerity with a gift."

Raising an eyebrow, she temporarily exchanged her tart plate for the box, then carefully worked the small hinges open.

Her eyes widened in surprise, and Thibaut grinned from ear to ear.

Her missing knuckledusters. The ones he'd gifted her years before, which she'd lost in the keep. "How did you—?"

"The Thalo keep taketh and the Thalo keep giveth, or something like that," he said with a wink. "Fleeing for my life I still stopped to pick up something shiny for you."

She punched him lightly in the arm, then leaned in for a kiss.

Eventually, Mandip noticed Krona and Thibaut hovering on the edge of the festivities. He gave a warm peck to his new wife's cheek, then headed in their direction with two dainty glasses of gin.

"Your bride is breaking additional hearts already," said Thibaut, raising his glass in Juliet's direction before tossing back his drink in one go.

Mandip smiled sheepishly, clearly more affected by the acknowledgment that Juliet was indeed his bride than by the implication she may be found snogging one of the wedding guests before the day was through. "That's Juliet for you," he said warmly, besotted with every aspect of her personality.

Thibaut's eyes took on a fondness as he looked at Mandip. There was a sense of longing in it that Krona understood. She felt that same tug as she looked out across the revelries. Leaving the Valley behind meant leaving everything they'd ever known. *Everyone* they'd ever known. Their friends here, their family. They would not be here to witness all of Melanie's baby's firsts. They would not see Avellino come fully into his adulthood. They would not see the growing pains of a world coming to terms with its new, inborn magic.

This was their last chance to make sure they showed their friends what they meant to them.

She gave Thibaut a little nudge with her elbow, making her thoughts easily readable. He arched a questioning eyebrow at her and she nodded encouragingly.

Thibaut cleared his throat. "Perhaps I could be permitted to kiss the groom?" he asked Mandip. "One last time?"

Mandip was wide-eyed for a moment, then nodded silently. Thibaut handed Krona his glass and his empty tart plate before taking Mandip's face between his palms. The press of their lips was chaste, but full of meaning. There were years of love and friendship behind it, and wishes for the future.

A future they would not share. Not for a long while, at least, depending on what lay beyond in the wastelands.

"You're really going, then?" Mandip asked as they broke apart.

"We have to," said Krona. She tried to catch a glimpse of Hintosep in the crowd, but got the distinct feeling the older woman was trying to avoid her. Perhaps she still hadn't made up her mind about which world was for her. "With the barrier failing, we need to know what's out there—what the Valley will be up against when the time comes."

EPILOGUE THE SECOND

KRONA

Krona bent her face to the sky, testing the sun. Its warmth seemed the same. The wind seemed the same. There was very little difference between standing on the edge of the Valley rim on the inside, and stepping through the wound in the barrier out into the amethyst desert. With her walking stick in hand, she turned, looking back across the border between Arkensyre and the wasteland—the vast, unknown beyond—and into the Valley basin. They could even see Glensen from here, the tree a bright spot of pure, luscious green. Larger than any tree naturally grown, a monument of magic and landscape.

Thibaut took her arm, and she leaned into him.

"It's beautiful," he whispered against the crown of her head.

"The tree, or—?"

"All of it. No one's ever seen the Valley from this angle before. It's beautiful."

"It is," she agreed. "The others will take good care of it while we're gone."

"Course they will."

"Don't patronize me," she teased.

"Never," he mumbled.

"I still don't see anything," Punabi said. "Past the dunes. It's just sand. Purple sand, on and on."

"There was a world out here once," Hailwic said. She and Punabi were both of a more usual size, with two arms and two legs, though Punabi still kept the one crystalline-cluster eye, and Hailwic had refused to give up her wings.

Just like Krona.

"There's a world out here still," she said.

They'd brought horses with them. Krona now hopped up on Allium, recovered from the Iyendars' estate.

"How long will the horses last if we can't find water?" Punabi asked, mounting a steed of zhur own.

"We'll find it," Hailwic said. "Have faith."

Nickering to the horses, the four of them began a new journey.

It'd been three days.

Out here, the sun constantly beat down on the land. That low-slung wind was ever present, and they had nothing but the sky to navigate by.

The open yawing of the dunes took some getting used to. Even when one stood on the valley floor at the widest point of Arkensyre, there were always walls to be seen. Here, nothing hemmed them in. There were no touchstones. Just dunes and dunes and more dunes, shimmering and shifting.

The air smelled of baked rock. Of hot crystal and dust. They still had plenty of supplies, but if they didn't find water eventually, they'd have to start bloodletting the horses. Their expedition was one of discovery. They needed to know what the Valley would encounter when the border finally fell. They needed to know if there were dangers, supplies, allies.

So far, there was nothing.

Krona refused to turn around. The waste wasn't all there was—it wasn't, she was sure. Even Hailwic and Punabi were sure, which left the practicalities and skepticism for Thibaut.

Krona heard a strange shout, and turned Allium in a circle, looking for its origin. Something shimmered on the horizon. Not water, but a figure. Everyone braced. It could be anyone, anything.

It was another rider, headed their way at speed.

Krona put a hand on her sword hilt, readying for confrontation, and she could feel Hailwic and Punabi tense in turn.

But as the rider came closer, their shimmering resolved.

Hintosep.

"Are you mad? Coming after us all by yourself?" Krona chided.

"I need to see it. I need to know. For Babbi," she said simply.

"What of the Thalo?"

"I have faith in Avellino. He's come into his own. The order needs a new face to look to. Mine carries too much history. Baggage."

They welcomed her into the party, and though Krona grumbled again about her late addition, she was happy to have her.

Then, finally, not half a day later, water. Thank the go—thank—thank goodness. Water.

They rushed for it, urging their mounts on at a breakneck pace. Suddenly the dunes sprouted around them—the pure purple sands giving way to orange and then soft brown before grass pushed up through the grains as they approached the shimmer. More and more vegetation greeted them the closer they came to what appeared to be a simple stream.

There was *life*. They'd yet to encounter an animal, but the plants could not survive without insects. There were no creatures, beasts, let alone monsters, that they'd seen, but the sharp tufts of desert grass were enough to make Krona's heart soar. There was existence beyond the Valley. The stories of total devastation were just as untrue as the stories of constant death and blood.

The horses were as eager to stray right into the stream as the humans, plunging their noses into the cool, clear running water. The group laughed as they dismounted, taking not a care for their clothes as they hurried over the bank and into the brook. They all splashed and yipped with joy. It was the first real sign that they were right—that there was more beyond.

Could there be people out here? Villages, towns, nations? A planet was a big place.

Thibaut and Krona yelled at the others to keep their distance while they wandered downstream to find a place to make love. They were jeered as they sloshed away, wading through the middle of the waters, but they didn't care. Hand in hand they gladly went, both pointing out any new scrap of foliage they spotted.

And then, a bird. An honest-to-real-life *bird*. It was an odd thing, with five eyes and fur and a pouch on its beak, but a bird nonetheless. It squawked when it saw them, revealing a razor-lined throat, but took off rather than attack. They were both so stunned they froze in their tracks, watching it disappear into the sky, becoming no more than a speck within minutes.

"A bird," Krona said in awe.

"A bird," Thibaut echoed.

They both turned to each other. "A fucking *bird,*" Krona announced, yanking Thibaut near to kiss him for all she was worth.

"We're really here," he said breathlessly once they broke apart. "We really made it."

Later, the group followed the stream in the direction of its flow, certain it would have to lead to a lake. It widened into a proper river, and Krona found herself fantasizing about something as magnificent as the Deep Waters—something big enough to sail on.

The land swelled upward, and they had to mount a hill to keep following the river, even as it widened, became something like a delta. The air changed, carried a sharp brine, more intense than that of Lake Konts, and then—

Krona pulled Allium to a halt at the crest of the hill. Below, the river flowed out into another desert. A desert not of sand, but of water. Water that touched the sky in all directions. Enough water to flood the Valley many times over and drown everyone and everything inside. Water without end.

Beside her, Thibaut was just as speechless. Just as stunned.

But the gods, oh—

"The ocean!" Hailwic shouted.

"The what?" Krona asked.

"The sea," Hintosep said wistfully, breathing deeply of the salty air. "I never thought I'd see it again. Never thought—"

The water, calmly lapping at the sand not moments before, suddenly bubbled. The tide went out—all in a rush, in a way Krona had never seen in Deep Waters. It swirled and swelled and crashed back at the shoreline in a violent rhythm as something rose up out of the depths.

A creature. Tall as a mountain, glossy and wet and pale as the underbelly of a fish. But it was no fish. It had tentacles like Thibaut's fen, each large enough to flatten an entire block in Lutador with a single strike. Two arms, long and slick and exaggerated, but undoubtedly *human*like, rose up out of the jumbled mass as the creature turned, catching them in its sights. Clusters of dark eyes littered a wide, flat skull, and when the thing opened its jaws, it bellowed deeply, wordlessly.

And then it began wading toward them.

"Shit," Punabi gasped.

Hailwic was already moving, already reaching out. "Hold on. We are getting the *hells* out of here."

Still astride Allium, Krona grasped firmly at Thibaut and Hintosep on either side of her, and just as the monster raised a tentacle to swipe them from their hill, Hailwic jumped them all.

Jumped them across time and space. Into the unknown.

ACKNOWLEDGMENTS

Big thanks to everyone who helped make *The Teeth of Dawn* a reality, including but not limited to my agent DongWon Song, my editor Will Hinton, cover artist Reiko Murakami, mapmaker Jennifer Hanover, Devi Pillai, Oliver Dougherty, Steve Wagner, Alexis Saarela, Khadija Lokhandwala, and Sara Thwaite, as well as everyone in the production, design, audio, marketing, and publicity departments.

Special thanks to my Patreon supporters, especially Andrew Weldon, Sara Benham, Dave Otto, Mary Richards, and Madison Tinsley.

I'd also like to thank the members of my writing group (the MFBS), my family, and last but not least my husband, Alex, for supporting me with kind words, big hugs, and honest critiques (not to mention drawing up my Periodic Circle of Elements).

In the Five Penalties series, though the struggle continues, the war ended. Alas, in our world war seems a constant. It ravages bodies, minds, and souls, and leaves people bereft of the basic necessities: shelter, food, and water. The World Central Kitchen helps feed refugees from both war and natural disaster in places like Haiti, Gaza, and Ukraine. You can learn about their work and donate to help their emergency relief programs at wck.org. Likewise, there are people in every community struggling with food insecurity, and local food banks are on the front lines of the fight. I'd like to thank my local food bank, the Northwest Arkansas Food Bank, for their work in Northwest Arkansas. You can learn about the organization and donate at nwafoodbank.org.

ABOUT THE AUTHOR

MARINA LOSTETTER is the author of the Noumenon series and *Activation Degradation*. *The Helm of Midnight* was her first foray into fantasy. Originally from Oregon, she now resides in Arkansas with her husband, Alex.